GEPT

全民英檢中級單字100%攻略
左腦式聽力學習×紅膠片高效練習！

英檢指定＋名師嚴選
一切就從精準的單字選擇開始出發！

考試和一般學習的差別在於它有「時間壓力」，在有限的準備過程中，走「越少冤枉路」的考生，就能「越快抵達終點」。因此本書收錄的單字皆選自英檢官方指定的範圍，並輔以名師多次應考所特選的單字，避免你浪費時間在艱澀、少考的單字上，只針對出題頻率高、或者容易混淆的重點單字作加強，完全命中真正會考的單字！

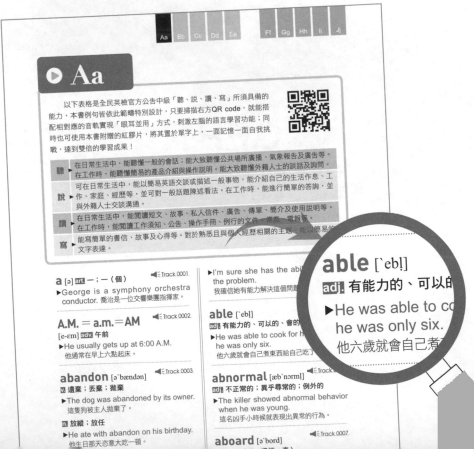

以下表格是全民英檢官方公告中級「聽、說、讀、寫」所須具備的能力，本書例句皆依此範疇特別設計，只要掃描右方QR code，就能搭配相對應的音軌實現「眼耳並用」方式，刺激左腦的語言學習功能；同時也可使用本書附贈的紅膠片，將其置於單字上，一面記憶一面自我挑戰，達到雙倍的學習成果！

聽	在在日常生活中，能聽懂一般的會話；能大致聽懂公共場所廣播、氣象報告及廣告等。在工作時，能聽懂簡易的產品介紹與操作說明。能大致聽懂外籍人士的談話及詢問。
說	可在日常生活中，能以簡易英語交談或描述一般事物，並可對一般話題陳述看法。在工作時，能進行簡單的答詢，並與外籍人士交談溝通。
讀	在日常生活中，能閱讀短文、故事、私人信件、廣告、傳單、簡介及使用說明等。在工作時，能閱讀工作須知、公告、操作手冊、例行的文件、傳真、電報等。
寫	能寫簡單的書信、故事及心得等。對於熟悉且與個人經歷相關的主題，能以簡易文字表達。

a [ə] **art** 一；一（個） ◀ Track 0001
▶George is a symphony orchestra conductor. 喬治是一位交響樂團指揮家。

A.M.＝a.m.＝AM ◀ Track 0002
[e-ɛm] **adv** 午前
▶He usually gets up at 6:00 A.M.
他通常在早上六點起床。

abandon [ə`bændən] ◀ Track 0003
v 遺棄；丟棄；拋棄
▶The dog was abandoned by its owner.
這隻狗被主人拋棄了。

n 放縱；放任
▶He ate with abandon on his birthday.
他生日那天恣意大吃一頓。

I'm sure she has the abi[...]
the problem.
我確信她有能力解決這個問[...]

able [`ebl] ◀ Track [...]
adj 有能力的、可以的、會的
▶He was able to cook for h[...]
he was only six.
他六歲就會自己煮東西給自己吃了[...]

abnormal [æb`nɔrml] ◀ Track [...]
adj 不正常的；異於尋常的；例外的
▶The killer showed abnormal behavior when he was young.
這名凶手小時候就表現出異常的行為。

aboard [ə`bord] ◀ Track 0007

able [`ebl]
adj 有能力的、可以的
▶He was able to co[...]
he was only six.
他六歲就會自己煮[...]

▶Welcome aboard Easy Jet Flight 240!
歡迎搭乘易捷航空240號班機！

aboriginal
◀ Track 0008

[ˌæbəˋrɪdʒɪnḷ]

adj. 土著的；原始的；原有的；原住民的

▶The Australian government is committed
to preserving their aboriginal cultures
and languages.
澳洲政府致力保存當地原住民文化和語言。

aborigine
◀ Track 0009

[ˌæbəˋrɪdʒɪni] n. 土著居民；原住民

▶The aborigines have lived in this area
for hundreds of years.
這些原住民已在這個區域住了上百年。

about
◀ Track 0010

[əˋbaʊt]

prep. 關於；在……附近；大約

adv. 到處；在附近；大約

▶There are about 50 students in the
playground.
操場上大約有五十名學生。

above
◀ Track 0011

[əˋbʌv]

prep. 在……之上；超過；勝過

adv. 在上面；高於、大於；以上

▶He's a selfish guy. He puts his own
interests above anyone else's.
他是個自私的人，將個人利益凌駕於他人之
上。

adj. 以上的；前述的

▶We hope the above book list will be
helpful for you.
我們希望上列書單能夠對你有幫助。

adv. 在國外；到國外

▶He went abroad for advanced studies.
他到國外深造。

abrupt
[əˋbrʌpt]
◀ Track 0013

adj. 突然的；意外的；唐突的；魯莽的

▶The meeting came to an abrupt end
when an ex-employee burst into the
office. 公司前員工衝進辦公室時，會議突然
就中止了。

absence [ˋæbsns]
◀ Track 0014

n. 不在；缺席

▶The absence of her mother left an
empty hole in her heart. 她的母親在她
的生命中缺席，造成她的內心留下了空虛。

absent [ˋæbsnt]
◀ Track 0015

adj. 缺席的，不在場的

▶She has been absent from school for
three days. 她缺課了三天。

absolute [ˋæbsəˌlut]
◀ Track 0016

adj. 絕對的；完全的

▶Absolute power
絕對的權力

ab

absence [ˋæbsns]
◀ Track 0

n. 不在；缺席

▶The absence of her mother left an
empty hole in her heart. 她的母親在她
的生命中缺席，造成她的內心留下了空虛。

absent [ˋæbsnt]
◀ Track 0015

adj. 缺席的，不在場的

▶She has been absent from school fo
three days. 她缺課了三天。

lute [ˋæbsəˌlut]

依官方公告範圍撰寫例句
在最適中的難度裡逐步攻城掠地！

「例句」是單字學習中不可或缺的好幫手，因此合適的例句，對於單字的
記憶會有大大加分的效果。本書例句皆依英檢官方公告的中級程度範疇，
量身設計撰寫，不會出現「例句單字太難看不懂」或「例句太簡單了學起
來沒挑戰性」的狀況，讓你在讀例句的時候，不僅可以複習單字意義，同
時也在練習語感，提升聽說讀寫的全面英語力！

單字例句全錄音

左腦式聽力學習法，是一次過關的滿分兵法！

「聽」是人類最原始、最快速、也最直覺的學習管道，即便是不識字的小嬰兒，也能透過聽力來學習語言，所以本書除單字外，特別也為所有的例句全都錄製音檔，讓你能以「視覺＋聽覺」雙重刺激的方式來達到雙倍的記憶效果，只要拿手機一掃書上的QR code，就能立刻聽到完整的例句錄音，且接近真正口語的語速更能訓練你在考場上臨危不亂的能力！

Bb

以下表格是全民英檢官方公告中級「聽、說、讀、寫」所須具備的能力，本書例句皆依此範疇特別設計，只要掃描右方QR code，就能搭配相對應的音軌實現「眼耳並用」方式，刺激左腦的語言學習功能；同時也可使用本書附贈的紅膠片，將其置於單字上，一面記憶一面自我挑戰，達到雙倍的學習成果！

聽	在日常生活中，能聽懂一般的會話，能大致聽懂公共場所廣播、氣象報告及廣告等。在工作時，能聽懂簡易的產品介紹與操作說明。能大致聽懂外籍人士的談話及詢問。
說	可在日常生活中，以以簡易英語交談或描述一般事物，能介紹自己的生活作息、工作、家庭、經歷等，並可對一般話題陳述看法。在工作時，能進行簡單的答詢，並與外籍人士交談溝通。
讀	在日常生活中，能閱讀短文、故事、私人信件、廣告、傳單、簡介及使用說明等。在工作時，能閱讀工作通知、公告、操作手冊、例行的文件、傳真、電報等。
寫	能寫簡單的書信、故事及心得等。對於熟悉且與個人經歷相關的主題，能以簡易的文字表達。

★因各家手機系統不同，若無法直接掃描，仍可以電腦連結https://goo.gl/WAU2Ce 雲端下載收聽

B.C. [bi-si] ◀ Track 0370
=Be·fore Christ abbr 西元前
▶The battle took place in 20 B.C.
這場戰爭於西元前20年爆發。

baby [`bebɪ] n 嬰兒 ◀ Track 0371
▶The baby has rosy cheeks. 寶寶有玫瑰色的臉頰。

babysit [`bebɪsɪt] ◀ Track 0372
=ba·by·sit v 當臨時保姆
▶She babysat her sister's children after school. 她放學後幫姊姊照顧小孩。

babysitter [`bebɪsɪtə] ◀ Track 0373
=ba·by·sit·ter n 臨時保姆
▶She was a babysitter before being a kindergarten teacher. 她當幼稚園老師以前是位臨時保姆。

bachelor [`bætʃələ] ◀ Track 0374
n 單身男子；學士
▶He had a bachelor's degree in accounting. 他有會計學的學士學位。

相關片語 **bachelor party**（結婚典禮前為新郎辦的）單身漢派對
▶They held a bachelor party for Jason before he got married. 傑森結婚前，他們幫他辦了一場單身漢派對。

back [bæk] ◀ Track 0375
adv 向後；以前；原處；回覆
▶He put the scissors back into the drawer. 他把剪刀放回抽屜裡。

n 背部；後面
▶There is a swimming pool in the back of the house. 屋後有個游泳池。

v 後退；支持；做...後面的
▶He backed his car into the garage. 他倒車進入車庫中。

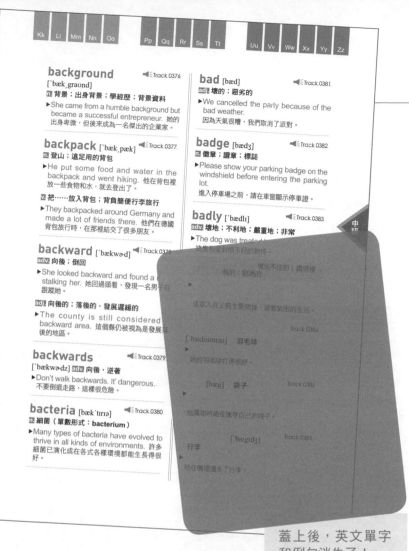

background

[`bæk,graʊnd`]

n. 背景；出身背景；學經歷；背景資料

▶ She came from a humble background but became a successful entrepreneur. 她的出身卑微，但後來成為一名傑出的企業家。

◀ Track 0376

backpack [`bæk,pæk`]

n. 登山、遠足用的背包

▶ He put some food and water in the backpack and went hiking. 他在背包裡放一些食物和水，就去登山了。

v. 把……放入背包；背負簡便行李旅行

▶ They backpacked around Germany and made a lot of friends there. 他們在德國背包旅行時，在那裡結交了很多朋友。

◀ Track 0377

backward [`bækwəd`]

adv. 向後；倒回

▶ She looked backward and found a m stalking her. 她回過頭看，發現一名男子在跟蹤她。

adj. 向後的；落後的、發展遲緩的

▶ The county is still considered backward area. 這個縣仍被視為是發展落後的地區。

◀ Track 0378

backwards

[`bækwə-dz`] adv. 向後，逆著

▶ Don't walk backwards. It' dangerous. 不要倒退走路，這樣很危險。

◀ Track 0379

bacteria [bæk`tɪrɪə`]

n. 細菌（單數形式：bacterium）

▶ Many types of bacteria have evolved to thrive in all kinds of environments. 許多細菌已演化成在各式各樣環境都能生長得很好。

◀ Track 0380

bad [bæd]

adj. 壞的；惡劣的

▶ We cancelled the party because of the bad weather. 因為天氣很糟，我們取消了派對。

◀ Track 0381

badge [bædʒ]

n. 徽章；證章；標誌

▶ Please show your parking badge on the windshield before entering the parking lot. 進入停車場之前，請在車窗顯示停車證。

◀ Track 0382

badly [`bædlɪ`]

adv. 壞地；不利地；嚴重地；非常

▶ The dog was treated 這隻狗受到很不好的對待。

◀ Track 0383

中級

境況不佳的；窮困的

糊的；窮困的

這家人在父親生重病後，過著窮困的生活。

[`bædmɪntən`]　羽毛球

Track 0384

她的羽毛球打得很好。

[bæg]　袋子

Track 0385

他購物時總是攜帶自己的袋子。

[`bægɪdʒ`]

Track 0386

行李

她在機場遺失了行李。

蓋上後，英文單字和例句消失了！

4 隨書附贈一張高效紅膠片
成為你的英檢考試不敗武器！

身為考生的你一定知道「考試前一定要做過練習才行」，但往往在背完一堆單字以後，整個人就筋疲力盡了，哪有心思再做額外的複習？為了避免你虎頭蛇尾，本書附贈的高效紅膠片，幫助你能在記單字的同時就一面做自我挑戰，遮住單字，看看自己到底還記不記得它的意思，如此的練習方式省時又省力，也讓英檢中級考試高分離你更接近！

Preface 作者序

　　全民英檢（GEPT）是台灣最常見、最常考、也最常被學校和企業做為英語能力評估的測驗之一。雖然與托福、雅思這類考試的難度無法比擬，但其仍舊有許多考高分的「眉角」存在。本書就是針對英檢單字部分，以最具經驗的角度，將應考的高分訣竅分享給各位考生為目的而撰寫設計。

　　全民英檢考生常遇到的難題有以下四種：

1. 經驗值不足

　　即便準備得再多，還是有可能因為不熟悉正式考試的題型與內容，在實際踏上考場時感到緊張，表現失常錯失分數。本書考慮到這點，因此每個單字的例句均依據英檢官方公佈之常見出題範圍（如：聽力的出題範圍多為「價格」、「時間」、「地點」；寫作的出題範圍多為「便條」、「賀卡」「填表格」等），而非一般隨興地自由發揮造句，造一些內容與實際考試完全扯不上邊的句子。相信考生在閱讀本書例句時，同時便可以熟悉考試中常出現的內容範圍，正式上考場時就不致驚慌丟分。

2. 字庫量不足

　　單字量不夠，在正式考試時題目看得霧煞煞先不說，口說與寫作測驗時更是腦筋一片空白，遲遲一個字都生不出。事實上，英檢不但考的是你是否認得單字，更考你是否會活用，光是死板地背下每個單字的中文意思是不夠的。幸好，官方公佈了英檢初級、中級所需的所有單字，本書將「英檢中級」所需的單字全數收錄，並加入教育部公佈之必備字彙及名師嚴選試題最常出現重點單字作統合，如此完整又精準的內容選擇，相信考生只要熟悉本書中的單字，在考試時的作題能力與臨場的快速反應肯定大幅精進。

3. 練習量不足

　　以為單字已經倒背如流了，但真正上考場時卻一個都記不起來，為什麼呢？因為你沒有做好「複習」與「練習」的動作。本書附贈的紅膠片，就是為了讓考生們能更有效率地複習、練習所因應而生，將紅膠片覆蓋在單字上，就可以快速測試自己是否有真正深刻記憶每個單字，不會讓辛苦記來的單字「左耳進、右耳出」，同時節省下更多時間，有餘裕在腦中補進更多單字。

4. 準備時間不足

　　學生有課業、打工的壓力；上班族有工作的壓力，事實上，並不是每個人都有充裕且完整的時間來準備一次英檢考試，但記憶單字這件事，只用零碎的時間學習，效率往往不高，因此本書才會特別構想，若能透過手機線上聽MP3，就能在通車、睡前等時間裡，好好利用，毫不浪費地準備考試。只要掃描QR code，就能線上聽到MP3音檔，沒有時間與空間的限制，也就沒有考不好的理由了。

　　最後，希望本書的單字選擇、編排設計，線上MP3等等的規劃，可以幫助你用更輕鬆的方式獲得高分，當然也要你自己發揮100%的用心和努力才行，所以一起加油吧！朝著英檢高分的路一步步邁進吧！

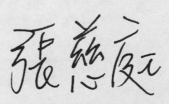

全民英檢大解密！

什麼是全民英檢？

　　全民英檢（GEPT）是「全民英語能力分級檢定測驗（General English Proficiency Test）」的簡稱，為台灣最常見的英文檢定考試之一。此測驗從2000年開始，試題內容分別由「聽、說、讀、寫」四大項目組成，其程度由簡至難共分五等級——1.初級（Elementary）、2.中級（Intermediate）、3.中高級（High- Intermediate）、4.高級（Advanced）、5.優級（Superior），用以評量考生的英語能力，並作為台灣學校、公家機關與民營企業了解考生（受試者）英語程度之參考。

想通過英檢中級，你得具備哪些英語能力？

　　全民英檢中級的檢測對象為一般社會人士及國中以上學生，目的是檢視考生能否理解、使用淺易日常英文用語。其又分為「初試」與「複試」兩次考試，內含聽、讀、寫、說四類測驗，所需具備之能力如下：

聽	在日常生活中，能聽懂一般的會話；能大致聽懂公共場所廣播、氣象報告及廣告等。在工作時，能聽懂簡易的產品介紹與操作說明。能大致聽懂外籍人士的談話及詢問。
讀	可在日常生活中，能以簡易英語交談或描述一般事物，能介紹自己的生活作息、工作、家庭、經歷等，並可對一般話題陳述看法。在工作時，能進行簡單的答詢，並與外籍人士交談溝通。
寫	在日常生活中，能閱讀短文、故事、私人信件、廣告、傳單、簡介及使用說明等。在工作時，能閱讀工作須知、公告、操作手冊、例行的文件、傳真、電報等。
說	能寫簡單的書信、故事及心得等。對於熟悉且與個人經歷相關的主題，能以簡易的文字表達。

英檢中級初試的考試內容有什麼？

測驗項目	初試	
測驗項目	聽力	閱讀
總題數	45題	40題
總作答時間	約30分鐘	45分鐘
滿分分數	120分	120分
測驗內容	看圖辨義 問答 簡短對話	詞彙和結構 段落填空 閱讀理解
總測驗時間 （含試前、試後說明）	兩項合計約2小時	
通過標準	兩項成績總和達160分，且其中任一項成績不低於72分。	

英檢中級複試的考試內容有什麼？

測驗項目	複試	
測驗項目	寫作	口說
總題數	2題	13-14題
總作答時間	40分鐘	約15分鐘
滿分分數	100分	100分
測驗內容	中譯英（40%） 英文作文（60%）	朗讀短文 回答問題 看圖敘述
總測驗時間 （含試前、試後說明）	約1小時	約1小時
通過標準	80分	80分

　　全民英檢中級的考試目的旨在檢視考生的基本英語使用能力，因此內容偏向生活化、不艱澀，只要掌握考試要訣並擁有基本的單字概念，想拿到高分並不困難。其他英檢相關資訊（如報名費用、考試時間、採納英檢成績之學校／民營單位／公家機關名單等等），則以英檢官方網站不定期公告的內容為準。

Content 目錄

左腦式聽力學習法，
針對A～Z開頭單字例句錄音QR code線上MP3

在書中，你可能會看到以下代號。原來，它們是這個意思……

n. 名詞　　　　　　**adv.** 副詞　　　　　**aux.** 助動詞
v. 動詞　　　　　　**prep.** 介系詞　　　　**det.** 限定詞
adj. 形容詞　　　　**pron.** 代名詞　　　　**interj.** 感嘆詞
art. 冠詞　　　　　**abbr.** 縮寫　　　　　**conj.** 連接詞

a b c d

e f g h

i j k l

m n o p

q r s t

u v w x

y z

▶ Aa

以下表格是全民英檢官方公告中級「聽、説、讀、寫」所須具備的能力，本書例句皆依此範疇特別設計，只要掃描右方QR code，就能搭配相對應的音軌實現「眼耳並用」方式，刺激左腦的語言學習功能；同時也可使用本書附贈的紅膠片，將其置於單字上，一面記憶一面自我挑戰，達到雙倍的學習成果！

聽 ▶	在日常生活中，能聽懂一般的會話；能大致聽懂公共場所廣播、氣象報告及廣告等。在工作時，能聽懂簡易的產品介紹與操作説明。能大致聽懂外籍人士的談話及詢問。
説 ▶	可在日常生活中，能以簡易英語交談或描述一般事物，能介紹自己的生活作息、工作、家庭、經歷等，並可對一般話題陳述看法。在工作時，能進行簡單的答詢，並與外籍人士交談溝通。
讀 ▶	在日常生活中，能閱讀短文、故事、私人信件、廣告、傳單、簡介及使用説明等。在工作時，能閱讀工作須知、公告、操作手冊、例行的文件、傳真、電報等。
寫 ▶	能寫簡單的書信、故事及心得等。對於熟悉且與個人經歷相關的主題，能以簡易的文字表達。

a [ə] art. 一；一（個） ◀ Track 0001

▶George is a symphony orchestra conductor. 喬治是一位交響樂團指揮家。

A.M. = a.m. = AM ◀ Track 0002

[e-ɛm] adv. 午前

▶He usually gets up at 6:00 A.M.
他通常在早上六點起床。

abandon [ə`bændən] ◀ Track 0003

v. 遺棄；丟棄；拋棄

▶The dog was abandoned by its owner.
這隻狗被主人拋棄了。

n. 放縱；放任

▶He ate with abandon on his birthday.
他生日那天恣意大吃一頓。

ability [ə`bɪlətɪ] ◀ Track 0004

n. 能力；能耐

▶I'm sure she has the ability to solve the problem.
我確信她有能力解決這個問題。

able [`ebl] ◀ Track 0005

adj. 有能力的、可以的、會的

▶He was able to cook for himself when he was only six.
他六歲就會自己煮東西給自己吃了。

abnormal [æb`nɔrml] ◀ Track 0006

adj. 不正常的；異乎尋常的；例外的

▶The killer showed abnormal behavior when he was young.
這名兇手小時候就表現出異常的行為。

aboard [ə`bord] ◀ Track 0007

prep. 上（船、飛機、車）

▶He got aboard the train at Manchester Station. 他在曼徹斯特站上火車。

補充片語 meet with acceptance
被接受；受歡迎

accepted [əkˋsɛptɪd]
◀ Track 0027

adj. 公認的；被視為

▶Academic liberty is an accepted trait of this school.
學術自由是這間學校的公認特點。

access [ˋæksɛs]
◀ Track 0028

n. 接近；接近的機會；
進入的權利；通道、門路

▶The FBI agents were allowed access to the supermax state prison to investigate a crime.
美國聯邦調查局探員獲得許可進入這間最高戒備的州監獄來調查一件刑案。

v. 使用；接近；取出（資料）

▶This card allows you to access the confidential files of the company.
這張卡可以讓你獲得公司的機密文件。

accessory [ækˋsɛsərɪ]
◀ Track 0029

n. 附件；配件；飾品；同謀、幫兇

▶She designs accessories and jewelries for a famous fashion house.
她幫一家時尚公司設計飾品和珠寶。

adj. 附加的；附屬的；同謀的、幫兇的

▶Because he helped his friends avoid arrest after the robbery, he was charged with being accessory to the crime. 他因為協助朋友搶劫後躲避追捕，而遭起訴為共犯。

accident
◀ Track 0030

[ˋæksədənt] **n.** 意外

▶He was paralyzed from the waist down after the accident.
他在意外發生後，腰部以下癱瘓。

accidental
◀ Track 0031

[͵æksəˋdɛntl] **adj.** 偶然的；意外的

▶The scientist made an accidental discovery that led to the invention of penicillin. 這名科學家的意外發現促成了盤尼西林的發明。

相關片語 accidental death 意外死亡

▶The actor's accidental death shocked the world.
這名男演員的意外死亡震驚了全世界。

accommodate
◀ Track 0032

[əˋkɑməˌdet]

v. 能容納；能提供……膳宿；可承載

▶The lecture hall can accommodate about 600 people.
這座大講堂可容納約600個人。

accommodation
◀ Track 0033

[əˌkɑməˋdeʃən] **n.** 適應；調節；住處；膳宿

▶The school provides accommodation with amenities such as free Wi-Fi and a flat-screen TV, etc. 這間學校提供住宿及Wi-Fi和平面電視等設備。

補充片語 flat-screen TV 平面電視

accompany
◀ Track 0034

[əˋkʌmpənɪ] **v.** 陪伴；伴隨

▶She enjoys being accompanied by friends rather than family.
她喜歡被朋友陪伴而不是家人。

accomplish
◀ Track 0035

[əˋkɑmplɪʃ] **v.** 完成；實現

▶She finally accomplished her dream as a flight attendant.
她終於實現當空姐的夢想。

中級

accomplishment ◀€Track 0036
[ə`kɑmplɪʃmənt]

n. 成就;成績;完成;實現

▶His extraordinary accomplishments have won worldwide respect.
他的傑出成就已贏得世人的敬重。

accord [ə`kɔrd] ◀€Track 0037

v. 與……一致;符合;使一致、調解

▶His testimony did not accord with your story. 他的證詞與你的說法不一致。

n. 一致;符合

▶We have provided a copy of the document in accord with your request. 我們已依照你的請求,提供了一份文件的影本。

補充片語 in accord with 與……一致

according [ə`kɔrdɪŋ] ◀€Track 0038
prep. 根據;按照

▶We installed the software according to the instructions of the manual.
我們依據手冊的指示安裝這套軟體。

accordingly ◀€Track 0039
[ə`kɔrdɪŋlɪ] **adv.** 相應地;因此;於是

▶Please tell me what color and decorations you want in your room and I'll do it accordingly. 請告訴我你想要房間將漆成什麼顏色和放哪些裝飾,我會照做。

account [ə`kaʊnt] ◀€Track 0040

n. 帳戶;帳目;描述;解釋

▶I have an account in this bank.
我在這家銀行有個帳戶。

v. 報帳;解釋、說明;
對……負責;將……視為

▶He is accounted a maestro of classical music.
他被視為是古典音樂界的大師級人物。

相關片語 take sth. into account
一併考慮;考慮進去

▶The teacher took into account her students' ability before setting her expectations . 老師在預設期望前,有將她的學生程度納入考量。

accountant ◀€Track 0041
[ə`kaʊntənt] **n.** 會計師

▶My father is a certified accountant.
我爸爸是一位有合格證書的會計師。

accounting ◀€Track 0042
[ə`kaʊntɪŋ] **n.** 會計;會計學

▶She teaches accounting in a college.
她在大專院校教會計學。

accuracy [`ækjərəsɪ] ◀€Track 0043

n. 正確(性);準確(性)

▶The child played the notes with accuracy. 小孩正確無誤地彈奏這首曲目。

accurate [`ækjərɪt] ◀€Track 0044

adj. 準確的;精確的

▶They gave an accurate description of what happened.
他們精確描述了事發的狀況。

accusation ◀€Track 0045
[͵ækjə`zeʃən] **n.** 控告;指責;罪名

▶The CEO immediately denied the accusation that he took the company's money for his personal trip. 執行長立即否認他挪用公司的錢用在私人旅遊的這項指控。

accuse [əˋkjuz]
◀🔊 Track 0046

v. 控告；指控

▶The civil servant was accused of embezzlement. 這名公務員被指控貪污。

accustomed [əˋkʌstəmd]
◀🔊 Track 0047

adj. 通常的；習慣的；適應了的

▶She has become accustomed to her life in Canada. 她已經習慣了在加拿大的生活。

ace [es]
◀🔊 Track 0048

n. （骰子的）一點；發球得分；能手、佼佼者

▶She is an ace at networking. 她善於經營人脈。

adj. 第一流的

▶He's an ace makeup artist in the fashion industry. 他是時尚界第一流的化妝師。

v. 得分；在……做得好

▶He aced the TEOIC. 他的托益考得很好。

ache [ek]
◀🔊 Track 0049

n. （持續的）疼痛

▶He has a dull ache in his stomach. 他的胃隱隱作痛。

v. （持續性）疼痛

▶My tooth is aching. I need to see a dentist. 我的牙齒在痛，我需要看牙醫。

achieve [əˋtʃiv]
◀🔊 Track 0050

v. 完成、實現；達到

▶Many people went to the United States to achieve their American dreams. 許多人為了圓他們的美國夢而去美國。

achievement
◀🔊 Track 0051

[əˋtʃivmənt] **n.** 達成；成就、成績

▶Besides his medical achievements, he's a great philanthropist. 他除了卓越的醫學成就，還是位偉大的慈善家。

acid [ˋæsɪd]
◀🔊 Track 0052

n. （化）酸；有酸味的東西；尖酸刻薄

▶Some chemicals can cause acid rain. 有些化學物質會造成酸雨。

adj. 酸的；有酸味的；（化）酸性的；尖酸 刻薄的

▶She always speaks with an acid tone. 她講話總是尖酸刻薄的。

acne [ˋæknɪ]
◀🔊 Track 0053

n. 痤瘡；粉刺；面皰；青春痘

▶If you eat properly and sleep well, your acne will clear up. 你如果飲食適當、睡眠良好，痤瘡就會消失了。

acquaint [əˋkwent]
◀🔊 Track 0054

v. 使認識；使了解；使熟悉

▶After moving to the US, she quickly acquainted herself with the country's customs and law. 她移居到美國後，很快就讓自己熟悉該國的習俗和法律。

補充片語 acquaint oneself with 使自己熟悉

acquaintance
◀🔊 Track 0055

[əˋkwentəns] **n.** （與人）相識；相識的人

▶I don't know much about her. We are only nodding acquaintances. 我和她不太熟，我們只是點頭之交。

補充片語 nodding acquaintance 點頭之交

中級

相關片語 **make the acquaintance of sb.** 結識某人

▶He made the acquaintance of a young woman from New York. 他認識一位來自紐約的年輕女士。

acquire [ə`kwaɪr] ◀ Track 0056
v. 取得；獲得；學到

▶He acquired the company and made it a family business. 他收購這家公司並把它經營成家族事業。

acre [`ekɚ] **n.** 英畝 ◀ Track 0057

▶The man inherited a 200-acre mansion from his parents. 男人從雙親繼承了一戶200英畝的豪宅。

across [ə`krɔs] ◀ Track 0058
prep. 橫越、穿過

▶There's a fast food restaurant across the street. 對街有一間速食餐廳。

adv. 橫過；在對面

▶I ran across, and noticed that there were many people swimming under the bridge. 我跑了過去，然後發現有很多人在橋下游泳。

act [ækt] ◀ Track 0059
n. 行為、行動；表現

▶An act of violence is not an act of courage. 暴力的行為並不是勇敢的行為。

v. 行動；做出……舉止；表演

▶She acted on her doctor's advice and quit smoking. 她聽從醫師的勸告戒菸了。

補充片語 **act on one's advice** 聽從某人的勸告

action [`ækʃən] ◀ Track 0060
n. 行動，行為

▶We need to take action to address global warming. 我們應採取行動，解決全球暖化的問題。

active [`æktɪv] ◀ Track 0061
adj. 活躍的；積極的；主動的

▶My grandfather is still very active in the community. 我祖父在這個社區仍很活躍。

activity [æk`tɪvətɪ] ◀ Track 0062
n. 活動

▶The school provides a variety of extracurricular activities. 這所學校提供很豐富的課外活動。

actor [`æktɚ] **n.** 男演員 ◀ Track 0063

▶Hugh Jackman is a brilliant actor. 休傑克曼是一名優秀的演員。

actress [`æktrɪs] ◀ Track 0064
n. 女演員

▶The British actress won the Golden Globe Award in 2018. 英國女演員贏得2018年的金球獎。

actual [`æktʃʊəl] ◀ Track 0065
adj. 實際的；事實上的

▶The actual cost of the advertisement was less expensive than we expected. 這則廣告的實際成本不像我們預期得那麼貴。

actually [`æktʃʊəlɪ] ◀ Track 0066
adv. 實際上、真的

▶He's actually quite good at singing. 他實際上很會唱歌。

adapt [əˋdæpt] ◀ Track 0067

v. 適應；使適應

▶ She adapted herself to the new school very quickly. 她很快就適應新學校了。

補充片語 **adapt oneself to** 使自己適應

adaptation ◀ Track 0068

[ˌædæpˋteʃən] **n.** 適應；適合；改編；改寫

▶ This film is an adaptation of a best-selling novel. 這部電影是由一本暢銷小説改編而成的。

add [æd] ◀ Track 0069

v. 加、添加、增加

▶ You can add some cheese and raisins to add flavors in your salad. 你可以加一些起司和葡萄乾在沙拉裡添加風味。

addict [ˋædɪkt] ◀ Track 0070

n. 上癮的人

▶ The singer was a heroin addict. 這名歌手是個吸食海洛因成癮的人。

v. 使入迷；使沉溺；使成癮

▶ She admitted that she used to be addicted to marijuana. 她坦承曾經沉迷於吸食大麻。

相關片語 **selfie addict** 自拍狂

▶ The Internet celebrity is such a selfie addict. 這名網紅真是個自拍狂。

addiction [əˋdɪkʃən] ◀ Track 0071

n. 成癮；沉溺；入迷

▶ Her son suffers from an addiction to online games. 她的兒子有網路遊戲成癮症。

addition [əˋdɪʃən] ◀ Track 0072

n. 加；增加的部分；加法

▶ The students are learning how to solve addition and subtraction from their teacher. 學生正在跟老師學如何解加減法的問題。

相關片語 **in addition** 此外

▶ He's a singer. In addition, he's a music composer. 他是一位歌手，此外，他也是一位音樂編曲人。

additional [əˋdɪʃənl] ◀ Track 0073

adj. 添加的；額外的

▶ We need additional information to make a better judgment. 我們需要額外的資訊以做出較好的判斷。

address [əˋdrɛs] ◀ Track 0074

n. 地址

▶ We need your address to mail you our catalogue. 我們需要你的地址，以便寄送目錄。

adequate [ˋædəkwɪt] ◀ Track 0075

adj. 足夠的；適當的；可勝任的

▶ The zoo was shabby, and the food was not adequate for the animals. 這家動物園很殘破，而且沒有足夠的食物給動物吃。

adjective=adj. ◀ Track 0076

[ˋædʒɪktɪv] **n.** 形容詞

▶ "Beautiful", "kind", and "generous" are all adjectives. 「美麗的」、「仁慈的」和「慷慨的」都是形容詞。

adjust [əˋdʒʌst] ◀ Track 0077

v. 調整；改變……以適應

▶ He adjusted his tie before seeing his boss. 他去找上司之前，整理了一下領帶。

中級

administration
Track 0078

[əd͵mɪnə`streʃən] **n.** 管理；經營

▶He is studying for an executive master of business administration. 他在管理碩士在職專班（EMBA）就讀。

admirable
Track 0079

[`ædmərəbl]

adj. 值得讚揚的；令人欽佩的；極好的

▶He did an admirable job in taking control of the crisis. 他在處理危機事件的表現令人欽佩。

admiration
Track 0080

[͵ædmə`reʃən]

n. 欽佩；仰慕；讚美；引人讚美的人或事物

▶She looked at her son with pride and admiration. 她看著兒子時，感到驕傲與敬佩。

admire [əd`maɪr]
Track 0081

v. 欣賞；稱讚

▶He admires his father, who is always supportive of him. 他很敬愛他爸爸，因為他爸爸總是很支持他。

admission [əd`mɪʃən]
Track 0082

n. （學校、會場、俱樂部等的）進入許可

▶He got the admission letter from Penn State University. 他收到賓州大學的入學許可信。

admit [əd`mɪt] **v.** 承認
Track 0083

▶She admitted that she made the wrong judgement. 她承認做了錯誤的判斷。

adolescent
Track 0084

[͵ædḷ`ɛsnt] **n.** 青少年

▶When he was an adolescent, he was rebellious. 他青少年時很叛逆。

adj. 青春期的；青少年的；不成熟的

▶The research studied the impact of television violence on adolescent boys. 這份研究調查電視暴力對青春期男孩的影響。

adopt [ə`dɑpt]
Track 0085

v. 採取；收養

▶The couple adopted a child from Cambodia. 這對夫妻在柬埔寨領養一名小孩。

adorable [ə`dorəbl]
Track 0086

adj. 值得敬重的；可愛的

▶She's such an adorable girl. 她是如此可愛的女孩。

adore [ə`dor]
Track 0087

v. 崇敬；愛慕；極喜歡

▶He became a father when he was 45, and he absolutely adored his son. 他四十五歲才當爸爸，非常疼愛他的兒子。

adult [ə`dʌlt] **n.** 成年人
Track 0088

▶Three adult tickets and one student ticket, please. 我們要買三張成人票和一張學生票。

adulthood
Track 0089

[ə`dʌlthʊd] **n.** 成年；成年期

▶Some experts say that adulthood begins at the age of 24 since many young people are still studying in college and delaying parenthood. 有些專家說，成年的年齡應從24歲起算，因為許多年輕人仍因就讀大學，而延遲成家立業。

advance [əd`væns] ◀Track 0090

n. 前進；發展 **v.** 前進；發展；將……提前

▶He took an advanced English class at the community college.
他在社區大學的英文進修班就讀。

advanced [əd`vænst] ◀Track 0091

adj. 在前面的；先進的；高級的；年邁的

▶He completed the advanced management program at the Wharton School of the University of Pennsylvania. 他在賓州大學華頓商學院讀完進階管理課程。

advantage ◀Track 0092

[əd`væntɪdʒ] **n.** 有利條件；優勢

▶Beauty is one of the singer's advantages.
這名歌手的優勢之一是美貌。

adventure [əd`vɛntʃɚ] ◀Track 0093

n. 冒險；冒險活動；激勵人心的經歷

▶He had some interesting adventures in the forest.
他在森林裡經歷了一些很有趣的冒險。

相關片語 adventure novel 冒險小說

▶Her adventure novels were top-sellers in many countries.
她寫的冒險小說在多國暢銷。

advertise
=ad·ver·tize [`ædvɚ͵taɪz] ◀Track 0094

v. 做廣告；為……做宣傳

▶They bought a web banner to advertise their new product.
他們買了一個網頁廣告來宣傳新產品。

advertisement ◀Track 0095

[͵ædvɚ`taɪzmənt] **n.** 廣告；宣傳；公告

▶The advertisement was offensive due to its content. 這廣告因為內容不妥，令人感到不快。

advertiser ◀Track 0096

[`ædvɚ͵taɪzɚ] **n.** 刊登廣告者；廣告商

▶The advertiser was an official sponsor for the Olympics. 這家廣告商是奧林匹克的官方贊助商。

advice [əd`vaɪs] ◀Track 0097

n. 勸告，忠告；建議

▶He gave me a very good piece of advice. 他給我一個很好的忠告。

advise [əd`vaɪz] ◀Track 0098

v. 勸告，忠告；建議

▶She advised her clients on how to make the smartest investment decisions.
她建議客戶如何做出最明智的投資決策。

adviser=advisor ◀Track 0099

[əd`vaɪzɚ] **n.** 顧問

▶He hired a foreign advisor to write news releases for his company. 他聘用外籍顧問幫他的公司寫新聞稿。

affair [ə`fɛr] ◀Track 0100

n. 事情，事件

▶As a diplomat, he is very concerned about foreign affairs. 身為外交官，他非常關心國際事務。

affect [ə`fɛkt] **v.** 影響 ◀Track 0101

▶She helped people affected with AIDS, mental illnesses, and cancer. 她幫助受到愛滋病、心理疾病和癌症影響的病人。

中級

affection [ə`fɛkʃən] ◀ Track 0102

n. 影響；感染；感情；鍾愛；愛慕之情

▶He has difficulties showing affection to his children. 他有無法向子女表達關愛的障礙。

affectionate ◀ Track 0103

[ə`fɛkʃənɪt] **adj.** 充滿深情的；有愛心的

▶Bobo is a very affectionate and playful dog. 波波是隻很有感情、好玩耍的小狗。

afford [ə`ford] ◀ Track 0104

v. 提供；給予

▶He couldn't afford to go to college due to his family's circumstances. 他因為家境的關係而無法上大學。

afraid [ə`fred] ◀ Track 0105

adj. 害怕的；擔心的

▶The child is afraid of large dogs. 這個小孩很怕大狗。

after [`æftɚ] ◀ Track 0106

prep. 在……之後

▶They went to the movie theater after school. 他們放學後去看電影。

conj. 在……之後

▶She was inconsolable after her son died. 兒子死後，她傷心欲絕。

afternoon [`æftɚ`nun] ◀ Track 0107

n. 下午，午後

▶We played hockey in the afternoon. 我們下午打曲棍球。

afterwards ◀ Track 0108

[`æftɚwɚdz] **adv.** 之後；後來

▶We went swimming at the beach, and afterwards we had a barbecue. 我們去海灘游泳，後來我們烤肉。

again [ə`gɛn] **adv.** 再次地 ◀ Track 0109

▶He made the same mistake again. 他又犯了同樣的錯誤。

against [ə`gɛnst] ◀ Track 0110

prep. 反對；逆著

▶Some people are against euthanasia. 有些人反對安樂死。

age [edʒ] **n.** 年紀；年齡 ◀ Track 0111

▶She became a movie star at the age of 14. 她十四歲時成為電影明星。

v. 變老

▶After the death of his daughter, he aged a lot. 他的女兒過世之後，他蒼老很多。

aged [`edʒɪd] ◀ Track 0112

adj. 年老的；……歲的

▶Gemma, aged 16, is one of the supermodels in the fashion industry. 十六歲的潔瑪是時尚界的超模之一。

agency [`edʒənsɪ] ◀ Track 0113

n. 專業行政機構；代辦處；仲介

▶She was signed by a modeling agency when she was only 14. 她十四歲就被模特兒經紀公司簽下。

相關片語 **travel agency** 旅行社

▶The group trip was organized by a travel agency. 這次的觀光團旅遊是由旅行社安排的。

agent [`edʒənt] ◀ Track 0114

n. 代理人；代理商；仲介

▶She is a real estate agent.
她是房地產仲介。

aggressive [ə`grɛsɪv] ◀ Track 0115

adj. 侵略的；挑釁的；有進取精神的；
有企圖心的

▶She is aggressive and at times
overbearing. 她個性很挑釁，有時傲慢。

ago [ə`go] **adv.** 在……之前 ◀ Track 0116

▶He was here two hours ago. 他兩個小時
前還在這裡。

agree [ə`gri] ◀ Track 0117

v. 贊成，同意

▶I don't agree with you, but I respect your
opinion. 我不認同你，但我尊重你的意見。

agreeable [ə`griəbl] ◀ Track 0118

adj. 令人愉快的；欣然贊同的；一致的

▶Both countries found a mutually
agreeable solution. 兩國都找到了雙方能
接受的解決之道。

agreement ◀ Track 0119

[ə`grimənt] **n.** 協議；同意

▶They signed a prenuptial agreement
before their marriage. 他們結婚前簽了婚
前協議書。

補充片語 prenuptial agreement
婚前協議書

agriculture ◀ Track 0120

[`æɡrɪˌkʌltʃɚ] **n.** 農業

▶Most villagers here practice subsistence
agriculture.
這裡的村民大部分以務農為生。

ahead [ə`hɛd] ◀ Track 0121

adv. 在前；事前

▶They walked ahead of us.
他們走在我們的前面。

aid [ed] **n.** 幫助；救援 ◀ Track 0122

v. 幫助；救援

▶The teacher used audio-visual aids to
help his students learn English.
老師用視聽輔助教具幫助學生學習英文。

AIDS [edz] ◀ Track 0123

n. 愛滋病（後天性免疫不全症候群）

▶Princess Diana changed people's
perspective on AIDS when she visited
an AIDS clinic and shook hands with
patients.
黛妃訪視愛滋病診所並與病患握手，改變了
人們對愛滋病的觀感。

aim [em] ◀ Track 0124

v. 針對；瞄準；以……為目標

▶She aims to be an interpreter.
她立志要做口譯員。

n. 瞄準的方向；目的、目標

▶His aim in life is to be a medical expert.
他的人生目標是做一個好的醫學專家。

air [ɛr] **n.** 空氣 ◀ Track 0125

▶He went outside to get some fresh air.
他到室外呼吸一些新鮮的空氣。

air-conditioned ◀ Track 0126

[`ɛr-kənˌdɪʃənd] **adj.** 裝有空氣調節設備的

▶We worked at an air-conditioned office.
我們在裝有空調的辦公室工作。

中級

air conditioner ◀Track 0127

[`ɛr-kən͵dɪʃənə] n. 冷氣；空氣調節裝置

▶The air conditioner isn't working.
這冷氣故障了。

aircraft [`ɛr͵kræft] ◀Track 0128
n. 飛機

▶Many military aircrafts have cutting edge technology. 許多軍機配備尖端科技。

airline [`ɛr͵laɪn] ◀Track 0129
n. 航線；航空公司

▶The airline has the best safety record in the world. 這家航空公司擁有全球最佳的飛安紀錄。

airmail [`ɛr͵mel] ◀Track 0130
n. 航空郵件；航空郵政

▶The company sent me the goods by airmail. 公司用航空郵件寄商品給我。

airplane [`ɛr͵plen] ◀Track 0131
=plane n. 飛機

▶He is the pilot of the airplane.
他是飛機的領航員。

airport [`ɛr͵port] ◀Track 0132
n. 機場

▶Heathrow Airport is a major international airport in the UK. 希斯羅機場是英國重要的國際機場。

airway [`ɛr͵we] ◀Track 0133
n. （礦井的）風道；航空公司；航空路線

▶Qatar Airways is a world-class airline. 卡達航空是世界級的航空公司。

aisle [aɪl] n. 走道；通道 ◀Track 0134

▶She walked down the aisle with her father. 她在父親的伴隨下步上結婚紅毯。

alarm [ə`lɑrm] ◀Track 0135
n. 警報；警報器；鬧鐘

▶My alarm clock didn't go off this morning. 我的鬧鐘今天早上沒響。

album [`ælbəm] ◀Track 0136
n. 相簿；集郵簿；唱片

▶The singer's latest album is critically-acclaimed. 這名歌手的新專輯廣受好評。

alcohol [`ælkə͵hɔl] ◀Track 0137
n. 酒精

▶The punch contains alcohol. 水果酒含有酒精。

alcoholic [͵ælkə`hɔlɪk] ◀Track 0138
n. 酒精中毒者；酗酒的人

▶He used to be an alcoholic. 他曾是個酗酒的人。

adj. 含酒精的；酗酒的

▶I'd like to have something non-alcoholic, like grape juice. 我想喝非酒精飲料，例如葡萄汁。

alert [ə`lɝt] ◀Track 0139
v. 使警覺；使注意；向……報警

▶The traffic signs on the highway alerted drivers who go home late to be careful. 高速公路上的交通號誌警示著夜歸駕駛人注意安全。

adj. 警覺的

▶She was alert when a stranger suddenly approached her. 當有個陌生人突然靠近她時，她提高了警覺了。

n. 警戒；警戒狀態

▶He is always on the alert of any change around him. 他對週遭發生的變化總是保持警戒。

algebra [`ældʒəbrə] ◀€Track 0140
n. 代數；代數學

▶He teaches algebra at high school. 他在高中教代數。

alien [`elɪən] ◀€Track 0141
adj. 外國的；外國人的；性質不同的；不相容的

▶When I first came to this place, it all felt very alien to me. 我第一次來這個地方時，覺得一切都非常陌生。

n. 外國人；外僑；外星人

▶Thousands of aliens were put in the shelters when the war broke out. 戰爭爆發時，數以千計的外國人被安置在避難所。

alike [ə`laɪk] ◀€Track 0142
adv. 一樣地；相似地

▶She dressed her children alike for church every Sunday. 她每星期天都讓孩子穿著一樣去教堂。

adj. 相同的；相像的

▶He and his brother look very much alike. 他和弟弟長得非常相像。

alive [ə`laɪv] **adj.** 活著的 ◀€Track 0143

▶She was alive, but she was in a deep coma. 她仍活著，但陷入嚴重的昏迷。

all [ɔl] **adj.** 全部的；所有的 ◀€Track 0144

▶I have all the information you need. 我擁有你所需要的全部資訊。

pron. 全部，一切

▶All of the students in her class passed the math exam. 她班上的所有同學數學考試都及格了。

adv. 完全地，全然的

▶He was all right after his girlfriend broke up with him. 他的女友與他分手後，他還好。

allergic [ə`lɝdʒɪk] ◀€Track 0145
adj. 過敏的；過敏性的；對……過敏的

▶He is allergic to pollen. 他對花粉過敏。

allergy [`ælədʒɪ] ◀€Track 0146
n. 過敏症；反感

▶She was diagnosed with a wheat allergy. 她被診斷出對麵粉過敏。

alley [`ælɪ] **n.** 小巷，胡同 ◀€Track 0147

▶She lives down an alley in Kensington market. 她住在肯辛頓市場裡的巷子。

相關片語 **blind alley** 死胡同；沒有前途的職業

▶The policy led the country into a blind alley. 這個政策把國家帶到一條死胡同裡。

alligator [`ælə,getə] ◀€Track 0148
n. 短吻鱷

▶The baby alligator poked its head out of the egg. 短吻鱷寶寶從蛋殼中探出頭來。

allow [ə`laʊ] **v.** 允許 ◀€Track 0149

▶Parking is not allowed in areas restricted by signs. 標有限制區的地方不准停車。

allowance [ə`laʊəns] ◀€Track 0150
=pocket money **n.** 津貼；零用錢

▶His father gives him a weekly allowance of twenty dollars. 他爸爸每星期給他二十元零用錢。

中級

almond [`ɑmənd]
🔊 Track 0151
n. 杏仁；杏樹；杏仁色
adj. 杏仁色的；杏仁味的
▶ I brought an almond cake to the party.
我帶了一個杏仁蛋糕去派對。

almost [`ɔl,most]
🔊 Track 0152
adv. 幾乎，差不多
▶ My son is almost as high as my husband. 我兒子和先生幾乎一樣高了。

alone [ə`lon] **adv.** 獨自地
🔊 Track 0153
▶ He went to see a movie alone.
他獨自去看電影。

adj. 單獨的；只有、僅
▶ When I am alone, I listen to the music.
我一個人時會聽音樂。

along [ə`lɔŋ]
🔊 Track 0154
prep. 沿著……
▶ He rode his bike along the riverbank.
他沿著河岸騎單車。

adv. 向前；一起
▶ Do you want to come along with us?
你要跟我們一道去嗎？

alongside [ə`lɔŋ`saɪd]
🔊 Track 0155
prep. 在……旁邊；沿著……的邊；
與…… 並排
▶ During World War II, the US fought alongside its allies. 第二次世界大戰期間，美國與同盟國並肩作戰。

adv. 在旁邊；沿著；並排地
▶ The prince waved to the crowd with his girlfriend standing alongside. 王子和群眾揮手，他的女朋友就站在旁邊。

aloud [ə`laʊd]
🔊 Track 0156
adv. 大聲地；出聲地
▶ He read the poem aloud to the class.
他大聲朗讀這首詩給全班聽。

alphabet [`ælfə,bɛt]
🔊 Track 0157
n. 字母系統；全套字母
▶ My three-year-old son can sing the alphabet song. 我三歲的兒子能唱字母歌。

already [ɔl`rɛdɪ]
🔊 Track 0158
adv. 已經
▶ He's already finished his homework. 他已經寫完作業了。

also [`ɔlso] **adv.** 也，還
🔊 Track 0159
▶ She is not only beautiful but also compassionate. 她不但美麗，而且很有同情心。

alternative
🔊 Track 0160
[ɔl`tɝnətɪv] **n.** 供選擇的事物；選擇的餘地；選擇；二擇一
▶ Do we have any other alternatives to meet our client's requirement? 我們還有任何選擇來達到客戶的需求嗎？

adj. 替代的；供選擇的；二擇一的
▶ Alternative energy has been the subject of intense interest. 替代能源是最近很夯的話題。

補充片語 alternative energy 替代能源

although [ɔl`ðo]
🔊 Track 0161
conj. 雖然；儘管
▶ Although Princess Diana has passed away, her legacies remained. 黛妃雖已過世，她的遺澤仍存在至今。

altitude [`æltə͵tjud］　🔊 Track 0162
n. 高度；海拔；（等級、地位）高處

▶High altitude can be a problem for people with cardiopulmonary disease. 高海拔的地方對有心肺疾病的人來說可能會造成困擾。

altogether　🔊 Track 0163
[͵ɔltə`gɛðɚ] **adv.** 完全，全然；全部

▶He liked the proposal, but convincing his business partner would be altogether more difficult. 他喜歡這個提案，但要說服他的商業合夥人就難多了。

always [`ɔlwez]　🔊 Track 0164
adv. 總是；一直、永遠

▶He has always taught his children the importance of empathy. 他總是教導孩子同理心的重要性。

am [æm]　🔊 Track 0165
v. 是（用在第一人稱單數現在式）

▶I am a babysitter. 我是保姆。

amateur [`æmə͵tʃʊr]　🔊 Track 0166
adj. 業餘的

▶He is an amateur painter.
他是業餘畫家。

n. 業餘從事者

▶The competition is open to both amateurs and professionals.
這個比賽開放給業餘和職業選手參加。

amaze [ə`mez]　🔊 Track 0167
v. 使驚奇；使驚愕

▶Her talent for music amazed the audience. 她的音樂天賦讓觀眾驚奇不已。

amazed [ə`mezd]　🔊 Track 0168
adj. 吃驚的；驚詫不已的

▶We were amazed at how quickly he responded to the incident. 當我們對於他如此快速處理這件事，感到非常驚訝。

amazement　🔊 Track 0169
[ə`mezmənt] **n.** 驚奇；詫異

▶To our amazement, the monkey can use sign language to communicate with people. 讓我們感到驚奇的是，這隻猴子會用手語和人溝通。

amazing [ə`mezɪŋ]　🔊 Track 0170
adj. 驚人的；令人驚奇的

▶It was amazing that the teenage boy could solve the math problem. 這名青少年能解開這道數學難題，真是令人驚奇。

ambassador　🔊 Track 0171
[æm`bæsədɚ] **n.** 大使；使節

▶She used to be an ambassador of Japan to England. 她曾是日本派駐英國的大使。

ambition [æm`bɪʃən]　🔊 Track 0172
n. 雄心；抱負；追求的目標

▶The young king's ambition was to conquer the world. 這名年輕國王的抱負是征服全世界。

ambitious [æm`bɪʃəs]　🔊 Track 0173
adj. 有野心的；顯示雄心的；野心勃勃的

▶She is an ambitious gymnast. 她是個很有抱負的體操選手。

ambulance　🔊 Track 0174
[`æmbjələns] **n.** 救護車

中級

▶The ambulance rushed the injured man to the hospital. 救護車把受傷的男子趕忙送到醫院。

America [əˈmɛrɪkə] ◀Track 0175
n. 美國；美洲

▶Canada is a country situated in Northern America. 加拿大是位在北美洲的一個國家。

American [əˈmɛrɪkən] ◀Track 0176
adj. 美國的；美洲的 n. 美國人；美洲人

▶Julia Roberts is an American actress. 茱莉亞·羅勃茲是一位美國女演員。

amid [əˈmɪd] ◀Track 0177
prep. 在……之間；在……之中；
被……包圍

▶The mayor unexpectedly resigned amid speculation that he will run the president. 市長無預警地辭職，留下他將競選總統的疑雲。

among [əˈmʌŋ] ◀Track 0178
prep. 在……之中，在……之間

▶I'm the oldest among my siblings. 我在手足之中是年紀最大的。

amount [əˈmaʊnt] ◀Track 0179
n. 總數，總額；數量

▶The amount of the budget is about one million dollars. 預算的總額大約是一百萬元。

amuse [əˈmjuz] ◀Track 0180
v. 使歡樂；逗……高興；為……提供娛樂

▶The comedy is meant to amuse its audience. 喜劇片的目的就是提供觀眾歡樂。

amusement ◀Track 0181
[əˈmjuzmənt]
n. 樂趣；趣味；娛樂；消遣活動

▶He looked at his young son with amusement. 他看著小兒子，不禁覺得很逗趣。

相關片語 **amusement park** 遊樂園

▶We went to an amusement park today. 我們今天到遊樂園玩。

amusing [əˈmjuzɪŋ] ◀Track 0182
adj. 有趣的；好玩的

▶The story is rather amusing. 這個故事很有趣。

an [æn] ◀Track 0183
art. 一個、一（用於以母音開頭的名詞之前）

▶She is an open-minded person. 她是心胸開闊的人。

analysis [əˈnæləsɪs] ◀Track 0184
n. 分析；解析

▶The data analysis is very useful. 這個數據分析很有用。

analyst [ˈænl̩ɪst] ◀Track 0185
n. 分析師

▶He is a stock analyst. 他是股票分析師。

analyze [ˈænlˌaɪz] ◀Track 0186
=an·a·lyse （英式英文） v. 分析

▶He analyzed issues of securities fraud. 他分析有關證券欺詐的問題。

ancestor [ˈænsɛstɚ] ◀Track 0187
n. 祖宗，祖先

▶His family had noble ancestors and connections with the Swedish royal family. 他的家族出身名門並與瑞典皇室有密切關係。

anchor [ˋæŋkɚ]　◀ Track 0188

n. 新聞節目主播；靠山；錨

▶She is the lead anchor for BBC World News America. 她是英國廣播公司的美國世界新聞主播。

v. 主持（廣播節目）；拋錨泊船；固定

▶He anchored CNN's evening newscast. 他主持美國有線電視新聞網的晚間新聞。

ancient [ˋenʃənt]　◀ Track 0189

adj. 古老的；古代的

▶The ancient building is well-known for its courtyard. 這座古老的建築以它的庭院聞名。

and [ænd]　◀ Track 0190

conj. 和、及；然後

▶My family and I went to Scotland last summer. 我和我的家人去年夏天去蘇格蘭。

angel [ˋendʒl]　◀ Track 0191

n. 天使；天使般的人

▶She has a face of an angel. 她有天使般的臉孔。

anger [ˋæŋgɚ] **n.** 怒氣　◀ Track 0192

▶He yelled at me in anger. 他生氣地對我大喊大叫。

補充片語 yell at 喊叫

angle [ˋæŋgl] **n.** 角度　◀ Track 0193

▶He looked at the issue from a different angle. 他用不同的角度看待這個議題。

angry [ˋæŋgrɪ]　◀ Track 0194

adj. 生氣的

▶His wife gets angry about everything. 他的妻子對任何事都發脾氣。

animal [ˋænəml]　◀ Track 0195

n. 動物

▶Owls are nocturnal animals. 貓頭鷹是夜行動物。

ankle [ˋæŋkl] **n.** 足踝　◀ Track 0196

▶He fell down from the stairs and sprained his ankle. 他從樓梯摔下來並扭傷了腳踝。

anniversary　◀ Track 0197

[ˌænəˋvɚsərɪ] **n.** 週年紀念日；結婚紀念日

▶Tomorrow is the 60th anniversary of the founding of the company. 明天是公司成立的六十週年紀念日。

相關片語 wedding anniversary 結婚紀念日

▶They are going to hold a party to celebrate their wedding anniversary. 他們要舉行派對慶祝他們的結婚紀念日。

announce [əˋnaʊns]　◀ Track 0198

v. 發佈；宣布

▶The company announced that its profits increased in the second quarter. 公司宣布第二季營利增加。

announcement　◀ Track 0199

[əˋnaʊnsmənt] **n.** 通告；佈告

中級

▶The prime minister made an important announcement this morning. 總理今早發表一項重要的聲明。

announcer
Track 0200

[ə`naʊnsɚ] **n.** 宣布者；廣播員；播音員

▶He was an announcer for the Oscars. 他是奧斯卡獎的播音員。

annoy [ə`nɔɪ]
Track 0201

v. 惹惱；使生氣；使不快；打擾

▶The boy's rude behavior annoyed his teacher. 男孩無禮的行為惹怒了老師。

annoyance [ə`nɔɪəns]
Track 0202

n. 惱怒；使人討厭的事物；煩惱

▶To our annoyance, the train was delayed for two hours. 讓我們很惱怒的是火車誤點兩個小時。

annoyed [ə`nɔɪd]
Track 0203

adj. 惱怒的；氣惱的

▶She was annoyed to discover that her friend revealed her secret. 她發現朋友揭露了她秘密，讓她感到很火。

annoying [ə`nɔɪɪŋ]
Track 0204

adj. 令人不快的；令人氣惱的

▶There's an annoying hum coming from the refrigerator. 冰箱一直發出令人不快的噪音。

annual [`ænjʊəl]
Track 0205

adj. 一年的；一年一次的；每年的

▶We spent our annual holidays in Spain. 我們休年假去西班牙。

n. 年刊；一年生植物

▶Are tomatoes annuals? 番茄是一年生植物嗎？

anonymous
Track 0206

[ə`nɑnəməs] **adj.** 匿名的；無名氏的；來源不明的

▶He received an anonymous love letter. 他收到一封匿名情書。

another [ə`nʌðɚ]
Track 0207

pron. 另一個；再一個

▶The cupcake is so delicious. Can I have another? 杯子蛋糕真好吃，我能再來一份嗎？

adj. 另一的；另外的

▶She drank another glass of orange juice. 她又喝了一杯柳橙汁。

answer [`ænsɚ] **n.** 答案
Track 0208

▶She gave the correct answer to the teacher's question. 她針對老師的問題，給了正確的答案。

v. 回答

▶She answered the reporter's question appropriately. 她很妥當地回應記者的問題。

ant [ænt] **n.** 螞蟻
Track 0209

▶Why are there so many ants in the living room? 客廳怎麼有這麼多隻螞蟻？

Antarctic [æn`tɑrktɪk]
Track 0210

n. 南極地區

▶Antarctic region is situated in the Southern Hemisphere. 南極位在南半球。

adj. 南極的

▶Antarctic animals include whales, seabirds, fish, and penguins. 南極動物包括鯨魚、海鳥、魚和企鵝。

antenna [æn`tɛnə]
Track 0211

n. 天線；觸角

▶Butterflies and moths have two antennae.
蝴蝶和蛾都有兩根觸角。

anthem [`ænθəm] ◀ Track 0212
n. 聖歌；讚美詩；校歌；國歌

▶The Star Spangled Banner is the national anthem of the United States. 《星條旗》是美國的國歌。

antique [æn`tik] ◀ Track 0213
adj. 古代的；年代久遠的；古董的；古風的

▶The antique furniture was made in 1881.
這個古董傢俱是在一八八一年所製做的。

n. 古董；古物

▶The kitchen cabinet is a valuable antique.
這個廚櫃是珍貴的古董。

anxiety [æŋ`zaɪətɪ] ◀ Track 0214
n. 焦慮；掛念；令人焦慮的事

▶The mother felt anxiety at her son's behavior. 媽媽對於兒子的行為感到焦慮。

anxious [`æŋkʃəs] ◀ Track 0215
adj. 焦慮的；令人焦慮的；掛念的；渴望的

▶He is anxious about tomorrow's exam. 他對於明天的考試感到很焦慮。

any [`ɛnɪ] ◀ Track 0216
pron. 任何一人；任何一點

▶He has two brothers, I don't have any.
他有兩個哥哥，我一個都沒有。

adv. 少許；稍微

▶I can't walk any further. I need to take a rest. 我走不動了，我需要休息一下。

adj. 任一；絲毫；所有的

▶If you have any question, please feel free to let me know. 你若有任何問題，請不要客氣讓我知道。

anybody [`ɛnɪˌbɑdɪ] ◀ Track 0217
pron. 任何人

▶She didn't know anybody in the town.
她不認識鎮上的任何人。

anyhow [`ɛnɪˌhaʊ] ◀ Track 0218
adv. 無論如何；總之

▶The doctor couldn't save her anyhow.
醫生無論如何都救不了她。

anyone [`ɛnɪˌwʌn] ◀ Track 0219
pron. 任何人

▶Did anyone answer the phone?
有人接電話嗎？

anyplace [`ɛnɪˌples] ◀ Track 0220
adv. 任何地方

▶You can go anyplace you want.
你可以去任何想去的地方。

anything [`ɛnɪˌθɪŋ] ◀ Track 0221
pron. 任何事

▶Do you have anything you want to talk about? 你有任何想說的事情嗎？

anytime [`ɛnɪˌtaɪm] ◀ Track 0222
adv. 在任何時候；總是

▶He eats anytime he feels upset or unhappy. 他生氣或不快樂時就開始吃東西。

anyway [`ɛnɪˌwe] ◀ Track 0223
adv. 無論如何，反正

▶It wasn't her forte, anyway.
反正那也不是她的強項。

anywhere [`ɛnɪˌhwɛr] ◀ Track 0224
adv. 任何地方；無論何處

中級

▶Did he go anywhere last night?
他昨夜有去什麼地方嗎？

apart [ə`pɑrt] ◀Track 0225

adv. 分開地；相隔地

▶The houses were built 20 meters apart. 這些房子每戶相隔二十米。

adj. 分開的；單獨的

▶When Gina and her husband were apart, they talked to each other online. 吉娜和先生分居兩地時，他們用網路交談。

相關片語 **apart from** 除了

▶Apart from the soup, I liked the meal and salad. 那頓飯除了湯以外，主食和沙拉我都喜歡。

apartment ◀Track 0226

[ə`pɑrtmənt] **n.** 公寓

▶She lives in an apartment near her office. 她住在離辦公室很近的公寓。

ape [ep] ◀Track 0227

n. 猿黑猩猩，大猩猩；模仿他人者

▶To protect apes, we should also protect the forests in which they live. 為了保護大猩猩，我們也應保護牠們棲息的森林。

v. 模仿；學⋯⋯的樣

▶The child aped his father in whatever he does. 小孩模仿父親的一舉一動。

apologize ◀Track 0228

[ə`pɑlə͵dʒaɪz] **v.** 道歉；致歉

▶We apologize for any inconvenience caused by the delay of the train. 我們對於火車誤點造成的不便致歉。

apology [ə`pɑlədʒɪ] ◀Track 0229

n. 道歉

▶Please accept my sincere apology.
請接受我由衷的歉意。

apparent [ə`pærənt] ◀Track 0230

adj. 表面的；明顯的；顯而易見的

▶The apparent cause of her mental illness was her husband's infidelity. 她情緒失調的明顯原因是丈夫的不忠。

apparently ◀Track 0231

[ə`pærəntlɪ] **adv.** 顯然地；顯而易見地

▶Apparently, he didn't like Jenny.
他顯然不喜歡珍妮。

appeal [ə`pil] **n.** 懇求 ◀Track 0232

▶He made an appeal to his wife to forgive him. 他懇求妻子饒恕他。

v. 請求

▶She appealed to her friends for help.
她向朋友求援。

appear [ə`pɪr] ◀Track 0233

v. 出現；看來好像

▶She appeared in court without a lawyer. 她在沒有律師的陪同下出庭。

appearance ◀Track 0234

[ə`pɪrəns] **n.** 出現，顯露；外表，外貌

▶She made her first public appearance two months ago. 她兩個月前首度在公眾前亮相。

appetite [`æpə͵taɪt] ◀Track 0235

n. 食慾；胃口

▶He didn't have any appetite because he had a stomachache. 他因為胃痛沒有食慾。

applaud [ə`plɔd] ◀Track 0236

v. 鼓掌；向⋯⋯喝彩；讚許

▶The president applauded him for his courageous deeds. 總統讚許他英勇的事蹟。

applause [ə`plɔz]
Track 0237

n. 鼓掌歡迎；喝彩；嘉許

▶Let's have a round of applause for the talented violinist who is going to perform for us. 讓我們鼓掌歡迎才華洋溢的小提琴家，他將帶給我們精彩的表演。

apple [`æpl] n. 蘋果
Track 0238

▶An apple a day keeps the doctor away. 一日一蘋果，醫生不登門。

appliance [ə`plaɪəns]
Track 0239

n. 器具；用具；裝置；設備

▶The kitchen of the restaurant is equipped with modern appliances. 這間餐廳的廚房配有現代化的設備。

applicant [`æpləkənt]
Track 0240

n. 申請人

▶We are looking for applicants who have a wide range of knowledge. 我們正在尋找學識淵博的申請人。

application
Track 0241

[͵æplə`keʃən] **n.** 應用、運用；申請、申請書

▶He enclosed a resume together with a letter of application. 他附上履歷表和求職信。

補充片語 a letter of application 求職信

apply [ə`plaɪ]
Track 0242

v. 塗，敷；申請

▶She applied for a job with Carrefour. 她向家樂福應徵工作。

appoint [ə`pɔɪnt] v. 指派
Track 0243

▶The detective was appointed to investigate the crime. 警探被指派調查這件刑案。

appointment
Track 0244

[ə`pɔɪntmənt] **n.** 約定；約會

▶I have an appointment with Dr. Lee tomorrow morning. 我明天早上與李博士約好要見面。

appreciate [ə`priʃɪ͵et]
Track 0245

v. 欣賞；感謝

▶We appreciate your continued support. 我們感謝你持續的支持。

appreciation
Track 0246

[ə͵priʃɪ`eʃən] **n.** 欣賞；感謝

▶The cake is a token of our appreciation for your timely help. 你及時幫助我們，我們謹以這個蛋糕來表達對你的感謝。

approach [ə`protʃ]
Track 0247

n. 接近、靠近；通道、入口

▶His approach to the problem is very practical. 他解決問題的方式很務實。

v. 接近；與……商量、聯繫；著手處理

▶Dragon Boat Festival is approaching. 端午節就要到了。

appropriate
Track 0248

[ə`proprɪ͵et] **adj.** 適當的

▶He is appropriate for the job. 他是這份工作的適當人選。

approval [ə`pruvl]
Track 0249

n. 批准

中級

▶The plan had the approval of the government. 這個計畫獲得政府的認可。

approve [ə`pruv]
Track 0250

v 贊同；批准；認可

▶I don't approve of binge drinking. 我反對過量飲酒。

補充片語 binge drinking 暴飲（酒）

approximate
Track 0251

[ə`prɑksəmɪt] **adj.** 接近的；近似的；大約的

▶The approximate cost of the project is $10,000. 這項計畫的成本大約是一萬元。

v 接近；近似；大致估計

▶The cost of the production will approximate $1 million. 製造成本大致估計為一百萬元。

April [`eprəl] **n.** 四月
Track 0252

▶The CEO announced that he will resigned on April 1, but it turned out to be an April Fool Day's joke. 執行長在四月一日宣布要辭職，結果這一切只是愚人節的玩笑話。

apron [`eprən]
Track 0253

n. 圍裙；工作裙

▶She tied on her apron and started cooking. 她繫上圍裙並開始煮飯。

aquarium [ə`kwɛrɪəm]
Track 0254

n. 魚缸；水族館

▶Cleaning an aquarium can be a tough job. 清理魚缸可能是件麻煩的事。

arch [ɑrtʃ] **n.** 拱門；拱狀物
Track 0255

▶My son has very high arches. 我兒子的足弓很高。

v 使成弧形；拱起；使成弓形

▶The trees arch over the river from both banks. 兩岸的樹木在河面上交織成拱形。

architect [`ɑrkə,tɛkt]
Track 0256

n. 建築師

▶My sister is an architect. 我妹妹是建築師。

architecture
Track 0257

[`ɑrkə,tɛktʃə] **n.** 建築學；建築風格；建築物

▶This is one of the most splendid architecture I have ever seen. 這是我見過最雄偉的建築之一。

Arctic [`ɑrktɪk]
Track 0258

n. 北極地帶；北極圈

▶The Arctic is one of the most pristine and beautiful places on Earth. 北極是地球最純淨天麗的地方之一。

adj. 北極的；極寒的

▶Due to global warming, the Arctic region is warmer than it used to be. 由於全球暖化，北極地區氣候比以往溫暖。

are [ɑr]
Track 0259

v 是（第二人稱或第三人稱複數使用）

▶Are you sure your cyber friend is a general in the US army? 你確定你的網友是美國陸軍的將軍？

補充片語 cyber friend 網友

area [`ɛrɪə] **n.** 地區
Track 0260

▶She lived in a remote area in Arkansas. 她住在阿肯色州的郊區。

arena [ə`rinə]
Track 0261

n. 競技場；（有觀眾席的）比賽場；圓形運動場

▶He is very powerful in the political arena. 他在政界很有影響力。

aren't [ɑrnt] abbr. 不是
◀Track 0262

▶They aren't going to the movie with us. 他們不和我們去看電影。

argue [`ɑrgjʊ]
◀Track 0263

v. 爭執；爭論

▶I don't want to argue with you. 我不想和你爭論。

argument
◀Track 0264

[`ɑrgjəmənt] n. 爭執；論點

▶They had an argument about money. 他們為了錢而爭吵。

arise [ə`raɪz]
◀Track 0265

v. 升起；產生；出現

▶Should the opportunity arise, I'd love to be an exchange student. 要是有機會的話，我很想當交換學生。

arithmetic
◀Track 0266

[ə`rɪθmətɪk] n. 算術

▶He has been very good at arithmetic. 他的算術向來很厲害。

adj. 算術的

▶Our teacher gave us a horribly tedious arithmetic problem. 我們老師今天出了一道很冗長的算術題。

相關片語 mental arithmetic 心算

▶She did a quick mental arithmetic and decided not to join the membership. 她快速心算後決定不參加會員。

arm [ɑrm] n. 手臂
◀Track 0267

▶He has a tattoo on his left arm. 他的左手臂有一個刺青。

armchair [`ɑrm͵tʃɛr]
◀Track 0268

n. 扶手椅

▶My grandmother likes to sit in this armchair. 我祖母喜歡坐在這個扶手椅裡。

armed [ɑrmd]
◀Track 0269

adj. 武裝的

▶Armed police surrounded a gunman in the city center. 警方武裝包圍在市中心持槍的一名男子。

armour [`ɑrmɚ]
◀Track 0270

n. 盔甲；裝甲

▶The police body armour provides stab and ballistic protection. 警察的防彈衣能防護銳器穿刺和子彈。

arms [ɑrmz]
◀Track 0271

n. 武器；戰爭

▶The supply of arms to the country will only compound the situation. 提供武器給這個國家只會使情勢變得更複雜。

相關片語 brothers in arms 戰友

▶They were brothers in arms and went everywhere together. 他們是戰友，一起出生入死。

army [`ɑrmɪ] n. 軍隊
◀Track 0272

▶He enlisted in the army when he was 19. 他十九歲時加入軍隊。

around [ə`raʊnd]
◀Track 0273

prep. 在……附近；環繞

▶We sat around the camp fire. 我們圍坐在營火周圍。

adv. 到處、四處；周圍、附近；大約

▶I turned around and saw my dog playing with a cat. 我轉身看到我的狗和一隻貓在玩耍。

中級

arouse [əˋraʊz]
🔊 Track 0274

v 喚起；叫醒

▶The subject aroused my interest. 這個主題引起了我的興趣。

arrange [əˋrendʒ]
🔊 Track 0275

v 安排；整理

▶We arranged to have brunch together. 我們安排一起共進早午餐。

arrangement
🔊 Track 0276

[əˋrendʒmənt] **n** 安排；準備工作

▶Our tour guide made travel arrangements for us. 我們的導遊幫我們安排旅遊行程。

arrest [əˋrɛst]
🔊 Track 0277

v 逮捕；拘留 **n** 逮捕；拘留

▶He was arrested for driving under the influence. 他因酒駕而被逮捕。

補充片語 driving under the influence 酒駕

arrival [əˋraɪvl]
🔊 Track 0278

n 到來；到達；到達的人或物；新生兒

▶Hundreds of fans waited for the pop star's arrival at the airport. 數百名歌迷在機場等候流行歌手的抵達。

arrive [əˋraɪv] **v** 抵達
🔊 Track 0279

▶The planed arrived at the Frankfurt Airport at 6:00 A.M. 飛機在清晨六點抵達法蘭克福機場。

arrogant [ˋærəgənt]
🔊 Track 0280

adj 傲慢自大的；自負的

▶She was arrogant and demanding. 她很傲慢又苛刻。

arrow [ˋæro] **n** 箭
🔊 Track 0281

▶The athlete aimed the arrow at the target. 運動員將箭瞄準箭靶。

art [ɑrt] **n** 藝術；美術
🔊 Track 0282

▶Her sculptures are simply works of art. 她的雕刻作品簡直就是藝術品。

article [ˋɑrtɪkl] **n** 文章
🔊 Track 0283

▶His article on foreign affairs drew nationwide attention and comments. 他談論外交事務的文章引起全國關注及評論。

artifact [ˋɑrtɪˌfækt]
🔊 Track 0284

n 手工藝品；加工品

▶She collects Taiwanese aboriginal artifacts. 她收集台灣原住民的手工藝品。

artificial [ˌɑrtəˋfɪʃəl]
🔊 Track 0285

adj 人工的；人造的；矯揉造作的

▶Instant noodles contain artificial flavors and preservatives. 速食麵包含人工調味料和防腐劑。

相關片語 artificial intelligence 人工智慧

▶According to Stephen Hawking, the development of full artificial intelligence could spell the end of the human race. 根據史蒂芬・霍金，人工智慧發展到極致將終結人類的生存。

artist [ˋɑrtɪst] **n** 藝術家
🔊 Track 0286

▶Gauguin was a French post-Impressionist artist. 高更是法國後印象派藝術家。

artistic [ɑrˋtɪstɪk]
🔊 Track 0287

adj 藝術的

▶Few people were conscious of the artistic value of Vincent van Gogh's paintings when he was alive. 梵谷在世時很少人知道他畫作的藝術價值。

as [æz] ◀Track 0288

conj. 像……一樣；當……時

▶She is not that strong as you think. 她不像你想像中的堅強。

prep. 像，如同；作為

▶He worked as a real estate agent in that company. 他在那家公司擔任房地產仲介。

adv. 一樣地，同樣地

▶I am as tall as my father.
我和爸爸一樣高。

ascend [ə`sɛnd] ◀Track 0289

v. 登高；上升；登上

▶We sat on the grass watching the hot air balloons ascend to the sky. 我們坐在草地上看熱氣球升空。

ascending [ə`sɛndɪŋ] ◀Track 0290

adj. 上升的；向上傾斜的

▶Queen Elizabeth ascended the throne when she was only 25. 伊麗莎白女皇年僅二十五歲即登上王位。

ash [æʃ] ◀Track 0291

n. 灰燼；骨灰；廢墟

▶Ashes to ashes, dust to dust. 塵歸塵，土歸土。

相關片語 rise from the ashes 東山再起；浴火重生

▶She finally rose from the ashes when she met a wonderful man and started a family with him. 她遇到一個好男人並與他結婚生子後，終於浴火重生了。

ashamed [ə`ʃemd] ◀Track 0292

adj. 羞愧的；恥於……的

▶He was ashamed of working in that company. 他因為在那家公司工作而感到羞恥。

Asia [`eʃə] n. 亞洲 ◀Track 0293

▶Taiwan is considered a beacon of democracy in Asia. 台灣被視為亞洲的民主燈塔。

Asian [`eʃən] ◀Track 0294

adj. 亞洲的；亞洲人的

▶She works at the Asian Development Bank. 她在亞洲開發銀行上班。

n. 亞洲人

▶Many Asians work in the Silicon Valley to pursue their American dreams. 許多亞洲人在矽谷工作追尋美國夢。

aside [ə`saɪd] ◀Track 0295

adv. 在旁邊；到旁邊；離開、撇開

▶I took him aside and told him the good news. 我把他拉到一邊告訴他這個好消息。

補充片語 take sb. aside 把某人拉到一邊

ask [æsk] v. 問；要求 ◀Track 0296

▶She asked me to give her a ride after school. 她要求我下課後讓她搭便車。

asleep [ə`slip] ◀Track 0297

adj. 睡著的

▶He fell asleep while watching TV. 他看電視睡著了。

aspect [`æspɛkt] ◀Track 0298

n. 方面；觀點；外觀

中級

▶Have you considered every aspect of the project? 你有從各方面考慮過這個計畫嗎?

aspirin [ˋæspərɪn] ◀€Track 0299
n. 阿斯匹靈

▶He used aspirin to relieve his headache. 他服用阿斯匹靈緩解頭痛。

assassinate ◀€Track 0300
[əˋsæsɪnˌet] **v.** 刺殺

▶Martin Luther King was assassinated in 1968. 馬丁‧路德‧金恩於一九六八年遭到刺殺身亡。

assemble [əˋsɛmbl] ◀€Track 0301
v. 集合;召集;聚集

▶More than three thousand people assembled in the plaza. 超過三千人在廣場集合。

assembly [əˋsɛmblɪ] ◀€Track 0302
n. 與會者;集會

▶They had a rehearsal in the assembly hall. 他們學校集會禮堂彩排。

補充片語 **assembly hall** 會館;禮堂

asset [ˋæsɛt] ◀€Track 0303
n. 財產;資產

▶My children are my greatest assets. 我的孩子是我最大的資產。

assign [əˋsaɪn] ◀€Track 0304
v. 分配;分派

▶She was assigned to investigate a terrorist. 她被指派調查一名恐怖份子。

assist [əˋsɪst] ◀€Track 0305
v. 支援;協助

▶The charity assisted in providing refugees with meals and shelters. 慈善單位協助提供難民食物和庇護所。

assistance ◀€Track 0306
[əˋsɪstəns] **n.** 援助

▶We thank you for your assistance in arranging our trip. 我們感謝你協助安排我們的旅程。

assistant [əˋsɪstənt] ◀€Track 0307
n. 助手

▶She worked as an assistant to the editor-in-chief of a fashion magazine. 她是時尚雜誌總編的助理。

adj. 助理的;有幫助的

▶He is an assistant professor. 他是助理教授。

associate [əˋsoʃɪt] ◀€Track 0308
v. 聯想;使有聯繫;結交

▶Most people associate Japanese food with sushi. 許多人會把日本食物和壽司聯想在一起。

n. 夥伴;同事;合夥人

▶Mark is my business associate. 馬克是我的生意夥伴。

association ◀€Track 0309
[əˌsosɪˋeʃən]

n. 協會;聯盟;公會;聯想;結交

▶I have learned immeasurably from my association with Janice. 我從與珍妮絲的交往中學習到很多。

assume [əˋsjum] ◀€Track 0310
v. 以為;假定為;認為

▶I assumed that you had walked the dog. 我以為你已經遛完狗了。

assurance [əˋʃʊrəns] ◀Track 0311

n. 保證；保險

▶The company gave us its assurance that it would cooperate with us. 公司向我們保證將與我們合作。

assure [əˋʃʊr] ◀Track 0312

v. 向……保證；使放心、使確信

▶The mechanic assured me that my scooter will be ready by Wednesday. 修理工向我保證我的機車星期三可以修好。

asthma [ˋæzmə] ◀Track 0313

n. 氣喘；哮喘

▶My classmate had an asthma attack this morning. 我的同學早上氣喘病發作。

astonish [əˋstɑnɪʃ] ◀Track 0314

v. 使震驚；使驚訝

▶I was astonished by his bold attempt. 他大膽的舉動讓我感到詫異。

astonished [əˋstɑnɪʃt] ◀Track 0315

adj. 感震驚的；大為驚奇的

▶We were astonished to discover that her father was a billionaire. 我們很吃驚地發現她的爸爸是億萬富翁。

astonishing [əˋstɑnɪʃɪŋ] **adj.** 驚人的；令人驚訝的 ◀Track 0316

▶The little boy showed astonishing courage during the hijacking. 小男孩在劫機事件中展現令人驚訝的勇氣。

astronaut [ˋæstrəˏnɔt] ◀Track 0317

n. 太空人

▶Anne McClain is a NASA astronaut. 安妮・麥克萊是美國國家航空暨太空總署的太空人。

astronomy ◀Track 0318

[əsˋtrɑnəmɪ] **n.** 天文學

▶He's an expert in astronomy, relativity, and cosmology. 他是天文學、相對論和宇宙學的專家。

asylum [əˋsaɪləm] ◀Track 0319

n. 避難；政治庇護；收容所

▶Many orphans were put into an asylum after the war. 戰後有許多孤兒被送到收容所。

相關片語 **political asylum** 政治庇護

▶Edward Snowden was seeking political asylum. 愛德華・史諾登在尋求政治庇護。

at [æt] **prep.** 在（某地點）；在（某時刻）；對著向 ◀Track 0320

▶He was at breakfast when I phoned him. 我打電話給他時，他正在吃早餐。

athlete [ˋæθlit] ◀Track 0321

n. 運動員

▶The athlete is very popular because of his good looks. 這名運動員因為長相英俊而受到歡迎。

相關片語 **athlete's foot** 香港腳

▶Athlete's foot is a kind of fungal skin infection.
香港腳是皮膚霉菌傳染的一種。

athletic [æθˋlɛtɪk] ◀Track 0322

adj. 運動的

▶He has an athletic built.
他有運動員的體型。

atmosphere ◀Track 0323

[ˋætməsˏfɪr]

n. 大氣；（某地區的）空氣；氣氛

中級

▶The meeting was conducted in a friendly atmosphere. 會議是在友善的氣氛中進行的。

atom [`ætəm]
◀ᴱTrack 0324

n. 原子；微量、微粒

▶Atoms are the basic units of matter. 原子是物質的基本單位。

atomic [ə`tɑmɪk]
◀ᴱTrack 0325

adj. 原子的

▶The full development of AI can be far more dangerous than an atomic bomb. 人工智慧發展到極緻可能會比原子彈還危險。

attach [ə`tætʃ]
◀ᴱTrack 0326

v. 貼上；使附屬；附加

▶I attached a PDF file in the e-mail. 我把一個PDF檔案附在電郵裡。

attack [ə`tæk] **n.** 攻擊
◀ᴱTrack 0327

▶He had a heart attack and nearly died. 他心臟病發，差點死亡。

v. 攻擊

▶The president was attacked by media commentators for failing to improve the country's economy. 總統因未能改善國家經濟而遭到媒體評論者攻擊。

attempt [ə`tɛmpt]
◀ᴱTrack 0328

n. 企圖；嘗試

▶He made a few attempts to maintain friendly contact with a girl he was romantically interested in. 他嘗試過和他心儀的女孩保持友好關係。

v. 企圖；嘗試做⋯⋯

▶The athlete attempted to break the world record. 運動員嘗試打破世界紀錄。

attend [ə`tɛnd]
◀ᴱTrack 0329

v. 參加；出席

▶We invited him to attend the meeting. 我們邀請他出席會議。

attendance
◀ᴱTrack 0330
[ə`tɛndəns]

n. 到場；出席；出席人數；伺候

▶Due to the difficulty of the lecture, the attendance was low. 由於講座難度高，出席數很低。

相關片語 **take attendance** 點名

▶The class sat down before the teacher started taking attendance. 全班坐下後，老師開始點名。

attention [ə`tɛnʃən]
◀ᴱTrack 0331

n. 注意；注意力

▶May I have your attention, please? 可以請各位注意聽嗎?

attic [`ætɪk] **n.** 頂樓；閣樓
◀ᴱTrack 0332

▶We set a mouse trap in the attic. 我們在閣樓擺放了一個捕鼠器。

attitude [`ætətjud]
◀ᴱTrack 0333

n. 態度

▶We don't like his attitude. 我們不喜歡他的態度。

相關片語 **give attitude** 耍脾氣

▶She gave attitude to her teacher today. 她今天跟老師耍脾氣。

attract [ə`trækt] v 吸引　◀ Track 0334

▶His magic shows attracted a large audience. 他的魔術秀吸引了很多的觀眾。

attraction [ə`trækʃən] ◀ Track 0335

n 吸引力；受人喜歡的事物

▶Neuschwanstein Castle is one of the most popular tourist attractions in Germany. 新天鵝堡是德國最受歡迎的觀光景點。

attractive [ə`træktɪv] ◀ Track 0336

adj. 有吸引力的；引人注意的；動人的

▶She is a very attractive young lady. 她是個吸引人的年輕淑女。

auction [`ɔkʃən] n 拍賣 ◀ Track 0337

▶The antique will be sold at auction tomorrow. 這個古董在明天將會被拍賣。

v 拍賣

▶They will auction this painting next week. 他們下週將拍賣這幅畫。

audience [`ɔdɪəns] ◀ Track 0338

n 觀眾；聽眾；讀者

▶The audience was clearly impressed by her performance. 觀眾明顯地對她的表演印象深刻。

audio [`ɔdɪˌo] ◀ Track 0339

adj. 聽覺的；聲音的

▶She learned how to edit an audio file. 她學習如何剪輯音檔。

auditorium

[ˌɔdə`torɪəm] n 觀眾席；會堂；禮堂

▶The auditorium has 300 seats. 禮堂有三百個座位。

August [`ɔgəst] =Aug. n 八月 ◀ Track 0341

▶We went to England last August. 我們去年八月去英格蘭。

aunt [ænt] =auntie=aunty n 阿姨；姑姑；嬸嬸；舅媽 ◀ Track 0342

▶My aunt is very good at cooking sweet sour pork. 我嬸嬸很會料理糖醋肉。

Australia [ɔ`streljə] ◀ Track 0343

n 澳洲

▶He went to Australia to further his study. 他去澳洲進修。

中級

Australian [ɔ`streljən] ◀ Track 0344

adj. 澳洲的；澳洲人的

▶She obtained Australian citizenship when she was a child. 她小時候就取得澳洲公民的身分。

n 澳洲人

▶My sister married an Australian when she studied in Perth. 我妹妹在柏斯唸書時嫁給澳洲人。

authentic [ɔ`θɛntɪk] ◀ Track 0345

adj. 可信的；真正的；非假冒的

▶This signature is authentic. 這個簽名是真跡。

author [`ɔθɚ] n 作者 ◀ Track 0346

▶Mark Twain is one of my favorite authors. 馬克・吐溫是我最喜歡的作者之一。

authority [ə`θɔrətɪ] ◄Track 0347
n. 權；權力

▶Only the president has the authority to make this decision. 只有總統有權力做這個決定。

autobiography ◄Track 0348
[ˌɔtəbaɪ`ɑgrəfɪ] **n.** 自傳

▶I enjoy reading Benjamin Franklin's autobiography. 我喜歡讀班傑明‧富蘭克林的自傳。

autograph [`ɔtə͵græf] ◄Track 0349
n. 親筆簽名；親筆稿

▶The movie star gave autographs to her fans when she walked on the red carpet. 這名影星在走紅毯持給粉絲親筆簽名。

v. 親筆簽名於

▶The author autographed books for us. 作者幫我們在書上簽名。

automatic ◄Track 0350
[ˌɔtə`mætɪk] **adj.** 自動的

▶She bought an automatic camera. 她買了一部自動相機。

automobile ◄Track 0351
[`ɔtəmə͵bɪl]
=auto n. 汽車

▶He passed away in an automobile accident. 他在一場車禍喪生。

autumn [`ɔtəm] **n.** 秋天 ◄Track 0352
▶Autumn is my favorite season. 秋天是我最喜歡的季節。

auxiliary [ɔg`zɪljərɪ] ◄Track 0353
=aux.
n. 輔助者；輔助物；附屬組織；助動詞

▶The researcher hired three auxiliaries to work under him. 研究員雇用三名助手他工作。

adj. 輔助的；附屬的

▶She has been active in a regional medical auxiliary organization. 她在區域醫療組織很活躍。

available [ə`veləbl] ◄Track 0354
adj. 可用的；可取得的；有空的；有效的

▶Are you available this Saturday? 你星期六有空嗎?

avenue [`ævə͵nju] ◄Track 0355
n. 大道、林蔭大道；途徑、方法

▶The struggling brand closed its Fifth Avenue store in New York. 這個搖搖欲墜的品牌關閉了位於第五大道的實體店面。

average [`ævərɪdʒ] ◄Track 0356
adj. 一般的；平均的；中等的

▶The average age of the team is 25. 這支隊伍的平均年齡為二十五歲。

n. 平均；平均數

▶Her academic performance was above average. 她的學業表現高於平均數。

v. 算出平均數；平均

▶Interns in this company averaged $20,000 per month. 這間公司的實習生平均薪資是二萬元。

avoid [ə`vɔɪd] **v.** 避免 ◄Track 0357
▶I avoided her as possibly as I can. 我盡可能地避開她。

await [ə`wet]
◀ Track 0358

v. 等候；等待

▶She anxiously awaited the result of the exam. 她焦急地等候考試結果。

awake [ə`wek]
◀ Track 0359

adj. 醒著的

▶They stayed awake all night. 他們整晚保持清醒。

v. 喚醒；使覺醒；醒來；覺醒；意識到

▶The patient awoke from a deep coma. 病人從重度昏迷中醒了過來。

awaken [ə`wekən]
◀ Track 0360

v. 醒；覺醒；喚醒；喚起；意識到

▶My dog seemed to awaken from a nightmare. 我的狗似乎從一場惡夢中醒來。

award [ə`wɔrd]
◀ Track 0361

n. 獎品；獎狀

▶She won the award for best supporting actress. 她贏得最佳女配角獎。

v. 給予；授予

▶He was awarded a medal for his heroic deeds. 他因為英勇的事蹟而獲頒獎章。

aware [ə`wɛr]
◀ Track 0362

adj. 知道的；察覺的

▶He wasn't aware that he was good-looking. 他沒意識到自己長得很好看。

away [ə`we]
◀ Track 0363

adv. 離開；不在；離……多遠；消失

▶You'd better stay away from those drug addicts. 你最好遠離那群吸毒成癮的人。

awe [ɔ] **n.** 敬畏
◀ Track 0364

▶We gazed at the pope in awe. 我們敬畏地看著教宗。

awesome [`ɔsəm]
◀ Track 0365

adj. 可怕的；有威嚴的；使人驚歎的

▶She looked awesome in the evening gown. 她穿這件晚禮服真是美到令人驚歎。

awful [`ɔfʊl]
◀ Track 0366

adj. 可怕的；嚇人的；糟糕的

▶The service of the company is awful. 這家公司的服務很糟糕。

awhile [ə`hwaɪl]
◀ Track 0367

adv. 片刻；一會兒

▶He sat awhile pondering this case. 他坐了一會兒一邊想著這個案子。

awkward [`ɔkwɚd]
◀ Track 0368

adj. 笨拙的；棘手的；尷尬的

▶The journalist asked the mayor an awkward question. 記者問了市長一個很尷尬的問題。

ax [æks]
◀ Track 0369

=axe （英式英文）

n. 斧頭；解僱、退學

▶My grandfather used an ax to chop down some of the branches of the tree. 我祖父用斧頭把樹木的部分樹枝砍掉了。

v. 用斧劈；解僱；撤銷、削減

▶He was axed for taking drugs. 他因吸毒而被解僱。

中級

▶ Bb

　　以下表格是全民英檢官方公告中級「聽、說、讀、寫」所須具備的能力，本書例句皆依此範疇特別設計，只要掃描右方QR code，就能搭配相對應的音軌實現「眼耳並用」方式，刺激左腦的語言學習功能；同時也可使用本書附贈的紅膠片，將其置於單字上，一面記憶一面自我挑戰，達到雙倍的學習成果！

聽 ▶	在日常生活中，能聽懂一般的會話；能大致聽懂公共場所廣播、氣象報告及廣告等。在工作時，能聽懂簡易的產品介紹與操作說明。能大致聽懂外籍人士的談話及詢問。
說 ▶	可在日常生活中，能以簡易英語交談或描述一般事物，能介紹自己的生活作息、工作、家庭、經歷等，並可對一般話題陳述看法。在工作時，能進行簡單的答詢，並與外籍人士交談溝通。
讀 ▶	在日常生活中，能閱讀短文、故事、私人信件、廣告、傳單、簡介及使用說明等。在工作時，能閱讀工作須知、公告、操作手冊、例行的文件、傳真、電報等。
寫 ▶	能寫簡單的書信、故事及心得等。對於熟悉且與個人經歷相關的主題，能以簡易的文字表達。

B.C. [bi-si] =Be·fore Christ `abbr.` 西元前
🔊 Track 0370

▶ The battle took place in 20 B.C.
這場戰爭於西元前20年爆發。

baby [`bebɪ] n. 嬰兒
🔊 Track 0371

▶ The baby has rosy cheeks. 寶寶有玫瑰色的臉頰。

babysit [`bebɪsɪt] =ba·by·sit v. 當臨時保姆
🔊 Track 0372

▶ She babysat her sister's children after school. 她放學後幫姊姊照顧小孩。

babysitter [`bebɪsɪtɚ] =ba·by·sit·ter n. 臨時保姆
🔊 Track 0373

▶ She was a babysitter before being a kindergarten teacher. 她當幼稚園老師以前是位臨時保姆。

bachelor [`bætʃələ] n. 單身男子；學士
🔊 Track 0374

▶ He had a bachelor's degree in accounting. 他有會計學的學士學位。

相關片語 **bachelor party** （結婚典禮前為新郎辦的）單身漢派對

▶ They held a bachelor party for Jason before he got married. 傑森結婚前，他們幫他辦了一場單身漢派對。

back [bæk]
🔊 Track 0375

adv. 向後；以前；原處；回覆

▶ He put the scissors back into the drawer. 他把剪刀放回抽屜裡。

n. 背部；後面

▶ There is a swimming pool in the back of the house. 屋後有個游泳池。

v. 後退；支持 adj. 後面的

▶ He backed his car into the garage. 他倒車進入車庫中。

background
[`bæk͵graʊnd]

n. 背景；出身背景；學經歷；背景資料

▶She came from a humble background but became a successful entrepreneur. 她的出身卑微，但後來成為一名傑出的企業家。

Track 0376

backpack [`bæk͵pæk]
Track 0377

n. 登山；遠足用的背包

▶He put some food and water in the backpack and went hiking. 他在背包裡放一些食物和水，就去登出了。

v. 把……放入背包；背負簡便行李旅行

▶They backpacked around Germany and made a lot of friends there. 他們在德國背包旅行時，在那裡結交了很多朋友。

backward [`bækwɚd]
Track 0378

adv. 向後；倒回

▶She looked backward and found a man stalking her. 她回過頭看，發現一名男子在跟蹤她。

adj. 向後的；落後的、發展遲緩的

▶The county is still considered a backward area. 這個縣仍被視為是發展落後的地區。

backwards
Track 0379

[`bækwɚdz] **adv.** 向後，逆著

▶Don't walk backwards. It' dangerous. 不要倒退走路，這樣很危險。

bacteria [bæk`tɪrɪə]
Track 0380

n. 細菌（單數形式：**bacterium**）

▶Many types of bacteria have evolved to thrive in all kinds of environments. 許多細菌已演化成在各式各樣環境都能生長得很好。

bad [bæd]
Track 0381

adj. 壞的；惡劣的

▶We cancelled the party because of the bad weather. 因為天氣很糟，我們取消了派對。

badge [bædʒ]
Track 0382

n. 徽章；證章；標誌

▶Please show your parking badge on the windshield before entering the parking lot. 進入停車場之前，請在車窗顯示停車證。

badly [`bædlɪ]
Track 0383

adv. 壞地；不利地；嚴重地；非常

▶The dog was treated badly. 這隻狗受到很不好的對待。

相關片語 **badly off** 境況不佳的；處境糟糕的；窮困的

▶The family was badly off after the father got seriously ill. 這家人在父親生重病後，過著窮困的生活。

badminton
Track 0384

[`bædmɪntən] **n.** 羽毛球

▶She can play badminton well. 她的羽毛球打得很好。

bag [bæg] **n.** 袋子
Track 0385

▶He always brings his own bags when shopping. 他購物時總是攜帶自己的袋子。

baggage [`bægɪdʒ]
Track 0386

n. 行李

▶She lost her baggage in the airport. 她在機場遺失了行李。

中級

baggy [`bægɪ]　◀︎Track 0387
adj. 袋狀的；寬鬆下垂的

▶She wears a baggy pajama when she's at home. 她在家裡都穿著寬鬆的睡衣。

bait [bet] **n.** 餌；引誘物　◀︎Track 0388

▶They put down some bait to catch a polar bear. 為了抓一隻北極熊，他們放了一些餌。

v. 置餌於……；引誘

▶He said something provocative to bait her. 他說了一些挑釁的話，故意刺激她。

bake [bek] **v.** 烘焙；烘烤　◀︎Track 0389

▶I baked an almond cake. 我烤了一個杏仁蛋糕。

bakery [`bekərɪ]　◀︎Track 0390
n. 烘焙坊；麵包店

▶He bought a loaf of bread from the famous bakery. 他在這家有名的麵包店買了一塊麵包。

balance [`bæləns]　◀︎Track 0391
n. 平衡；均衡；和諧

▶The gymnast lost his balance on the pommel. 體操選手在鞍馬上失去平衡。

v. 使平衡；保持平衡；使相稱

▶She managed to balance work and family pretty well. 她很巧妙地保持工作和家庭的平衡。

balcony [`bælkənɪ]　◀︎Track 0392
n. 陽台

▶There's a balcony in the master bedroom.
主臥室有一個陽台。

bald [bɔld]　◀︎Track 0393
adj. 禿頭的；無毛的；露骨的

▶He became bald because of too much stress. 他因為壓力過大，變成禿頭了。

ball [bɔl]　◀︎Track 0394
n. 球；球狀物

▶He gave a yellow smiley ball to his little son. 他給小兒子一個黃色的微笑球。

ballet [`bæle]　◀︎Track 0395
n. 芭蕾舞；芭蕾舞音樂

▶She learned ballet when she was a child. 她孩提時期學過芭蕾。

balloon [bə`lun]　◀︎Track 0396
n. 氣球

▶Be careful. The balloon is going to burst. 小心，這顆氣球快要爆掉了。

ballot [`bælət]　◀︎Track 0397
n. 選票；投票權；（不記名）投票

▶About 50% of young people cast a ballot in this election. 大約有百分之五十的年輕人在這場選舉中出來投票。

v. 以不記名投票表決；投票選舉

▶The school decided to ballot whether their students are required to wear school uniforms or not.
學校決定投票表決是否規定學生要穿校服。

bamboo [bæm`bu]　◀︎Track 0398
n. 竹子

▶There's plenty of bamboo for the pandas in the zoo.
動物園有充裕的竹子給貓熊吃。

ban [bæn] v 禁止；取締　◀ Track 0399

▶The movie was banned because it was way too violent. 這部電影被禁，因為內容太過暴力。

n 禁止；禁令

▶The government puts a ban on this advertisement for its attack on certain religions. 政府禁播這則攻擊特定宗教的廣告。

banana [bə`nænə]　◀ Track 0400

n 香蕉

▶He baked a banana cake for us. 他幫我們烤了一個香蕉蛋糕。

band [bænd]　◀ Track 0401

n 帶；細繩；橡皮圈

▶She used a lot of rubber bands to make a jump rope. 她用很多條橡皮圈做了一條跳繩。

bandage [`bændɪdʒ]　◀ Track 0402

n 繃帶

▶The athlete put a bandage on his knee. 運動員在膝蓋包上繃帶。

v 用繃帶包紮

▶The veterinarian bandaged the wound on the puppy's paw. 獸醫將小狗腳上的傷口用繃帶包紮好。

band-aid [`bænd͵ed]　◀ Track 0403

n 護創膠布；OK繃

▶She put a band-aid on her scraped arm. 她在擦傷的手臂上貼了一塊OK繃。

bandit [`bændɪt]　◀ Track 0404

n 強盜；土匪；惡棍

▶The bandits were arrested by the police. 土匪被警方逮捕了。

bang [bæŋ]　◀ Track 0405

n 猛擊；砰砰的聲音

▶He got a bang on the forehead. 他的額頭撞到東西了。

v 猛擊；砰砰作響

▶He banged his fists angrily on the wall. 他氣憤地用拳頭打牆壁。

bank [bæŋk] n 銀行　◀ Track 0406

▶I just opened an account in the bank. 我剛在銀行開了一個帳戶。

banker [`bæŋkɚ]　◀ Track 0407

n 銀行家

▶My father is a banker. 我爸爸是銀行家。

bankrupt [`bæŋkrʌpt]　◀ Track 0408

adj 破產的；完全失敗的

▶He announced that his company went bankrupt. 他宣布他的公司破產了。

v 使破產；使赤貧

▶Their risky move to the market bankrupted the company. 他們太過大膽前進市場，導致公司破產了。

n 破產者；（在某方面）完全喪失者

▶She was declared a bankrupt last year. 她去年被宣告破產。

banner [`bænɚ]　◀ Track 0409

n 旗幟；橫幅

▶He bought a web banner to advertise his new product. 他買了一幅網頁橫幅廣告來宣傳新產品。

banquet [`bæŋkwɪt]　◀ Track 0410

n 宴會；盛宴

▶He was invited to attend the state banquet. 他受邀參加國宴。

中級

v. 設宴款待

▶The president banqueted the Secretary of State after meeting with her. 總統接見美國國務卿之後，設宴款待她。

bar [bɑr] **n.** 酒吧；條狀物 ◀Track 0411

▶He went into the hotel bar and looked depressed. 他進入飯店的酒吧，看起來很沮喪。

barbecue [`bɑrbɪkju] ◀Track 0412
=Bar-B-Q **n.** 烤肉；烤肉餐館

▶My family will have a barbecue tonight. 我家今晚要烤肉。

v. （在戶外）烤肉

▶After playing volleyball, they barbecued in the garden. 他們打完排球後在庭院烤肉。

barber [`bɑrbɚ] ◀Track 0413
n. 理髮師

▶She used to be a barber. Now she is a pet groomer. 她以前是理髮師，現在是寵物美容師。

barbershop ◀Track 0414
[`bɑrbɚ ʃɑp] **n.** 理髮店

▶My father always has a haircut cut at this barbershop. 我爸爸總是去這家理髮店剪頭髮。

bare [bɛr] ◀Track 0415
adj. 裸的；空的；無陳設的；勉強的

▶She walked around at home in bare feet. 她打赤腳在家到處走。

v. 使赤裸；露出；揭露

▶She bared her ankle to show us a tattoo she just got. 她露出腳踝，讓我們看她剛剛完成的刺青。

barefoot [`bɛr fʊt] ◀Track 0416
adj. 赤腳的

▶When the child was found, he was barefoot and homeless. 小孩被發現時，是赤腳而且無家可歸的。

adv. 赤腳地

▶They walked barefoot along the beach. 他們赤著腳沿著沙灘走路。

相關片語 **go barefoot** 打赤腳

▶People with diabetes should not go barefoot. 糖尿病患者不宜打赤腳走路。

barely [`bɛrlɪ] ◀Track 0417
adv. 僅僅；勉強；幾乎沒有

▶He had barely enough to eat. 他幾乎沒有足夠的食物吃飽。

bargain [`bɑrgɪn] ◀Track 0418
n. 協議；買賣、交易；特價商品

▶The online shopping mall offered last-minute sales at bargain prices. 網路商城提供最後時刻的廉價特銷。

v. 討價還價；達成協議

▶They bargained the price with the gondolier. 他們跟船夫討價還價。

bark [bɑrk] ◀Track 0419
v. （狗等）吠叫

▶I don't know why the dog is barking at me. 我不知道為何那隻狗一直對我吠叫。

n. 吠叫聲

▶The little dog has a surprisingly loud bark. 這隻小狗的吠叫聲很驚人。

barn [bɑrn] ◀Track 0420
n. 穀倉；牛欄、馬舍

▶The barn was converted into a lovely house. 這個穀倉被改建成很漂亮的房子。

barrel [`bærəl]　◀ Track 0421
n. 大桶；一桶的量

▶It costs the company US$3 to produce a barrel of oil. 製造一桶汽油要花公司三美元的成本。

相關片語 **a barrel of laughs** 開心果

▶Leo is a barrel of laughs. 里歐是個開心果。

barrier [`bærɪr]　◀ Track 0422
n. 障礙物；路障；柵欄；剪票口

▶Language is not a barrier for him to make friends. 對他來說，語言不是構成交友的障礙。

base [bes]　◀ Track 0423
v. 以……為基礎；將……建立在某種基礎上

▶The jury based their conclusion on the testimony given by the witnesses. 陪審團根據證人的證詞做出他們的結論。

n. 基礎；基本部分

▶You can use this moisturizer as a base for your makeup. 你可以用這罐保濕霜在妝前打底。

baseball [`bes,bɔl]　◀ Track 0424
n. 棒球

▶Children are playing baseball in the stadium. 孩子們正在體育館裡打棒球。

based [best]　◀ Track 0425
adj. 有根基的；有基地的

▶The Discovery Channel documentary is based on the FBI agent's memoir. 探索頻道的紀錄片是根據美國聯邦調查局探員的回憶錄所拍成的。

basement [`besmənt]　◀ Track 0426
n. 地下室

▶The supermarket is located in the basement of the building. 超市在這棟大樓的地下室。

basic [`besɪk] adj. 基本的　◀ Track 0427

▶His basic salary is US$1 million per annum. 他的基本年薪是一百萬美元。

basin [`besn]　◀ Track 0428
n. 盆；洗滌槽；盆地

▶There is a shelf above the basin. 臉盆上面有一個架子。

相關片語 **hand basin** 面盆

▶There is a white porcelain hand basin in the bathroom. 浴室有一座白色陶瓷的面盆。

basis [`besɪs]　◀ Track 0429
n. 基礎；根據

▶The paper has no scientific basis. 這篇論文沒有科學基礎。

basket [`bæskɪt] n. 籃子　◀ Track 0430

▶He put all his office stationery in a basket and moved to another cubicle. 他把所有辦公文具用品放入一個籃子裡，然後搬到另一個辦公室小隔間。

basketball　◀ Track 0431
[`bæskɪt,bɔl] **n. 籃球**

▶Jeremy Lin is an NBA basketball player. 林書豪是美國職籃的球員。

bass [`bes]　◀ Track 0432
n. 男低音；男低音歌手；低音樂器

中級

▶He is a leading bass in Austria. 他在奧地利是頭號男低音。

adj. （聲音）低沉的；男低音的；（樂器）低音的

▶The judges of the singing competition were all impressed by his lovely bass voice. 歌唱比賽的評審都對他迷人的低音感到印象深刻。

bat [bæt] **n.** 球棒；蝙蝠　◀̲ Track 0433

▶He bought a baseball bat online at Amazon. 他在亞馬遜網站上買了一支球棒。

batch [bætʃ] **n.** 一批　◀̲ Track 0434

▶She brought a fresh batch of homemade egg tarts to the party. 她帶了一整批剛出爐的自製蛋塔參加派對。

bath [bæθ] **n.** 沐浴　◀̲ Track 0435

▶I take a bath before going to bed. 我睡前都會洗澡。

bathe [beð]　◀̲ Track 0436

v. 浸洗；給……洗澡；使沈浸其中

▶He bathed his dog yesterday afternoon. 他昨天下午幫小狗洗澡。

bathroom [`bæθˌrum]　◀̲ Track 0437

n. 浴室；洗手間

▶There are two bathrooms and three bedrooms in the house. 房子裡有兩間洗手間和三間臥室。

battery [`bætərɪ] **n.** 電池　◀̲ Track 0438

▶The electric car uses batteries instead of gasoline. 電動車用電池而不是汽油。

相關片語 **recharge one's batteries** 使重新充電；使休息而重新得到活力

▶He needed a power nap to recharge his batteries.
他需要好好睡一覺，讓自己充個電。

battle [`bætl̩]　◀̲ Track 0439

n. 戰鬥；戰役 **v.** 與……作戰；與……鬥爭

▶He lost his battle against cancer and passed away last night. 他抗癌失敗，昨夜過世了。

bay [be] **n.** （海或湖泊的）灣　◀̲ Track 0440

▶They bought a mansion in the bay area. 他們在海灣地區買了一棟豪宅。

bazaar [bə`zɑr]　◀̲ Track 0441

n. 市場；商店街；市集；義賣市場

▶They are going to have a Christmas bazaar to help the needed. 他們將辦一場聖誕義賣幫助貧困的人。

be [bi]　◀̲ Track 0442

v. 是；成為；正在（與現在分詞連用）；被（與過去分詞連用）

▶He used to be a prodigal son. 他曾經是個敗家子。

beach [bitʃ] **n.** 海邊；海灘　◀̲ Track 0443

▶We went to the beach last weekend. 我們上週末去海灘玩。

bead [bid]　◀̲ Track 0444

n. 有孔小珠；一串珠（念珠、淚珠、露珠、汗珠）

▶She wore a bracelet made of wooden beads. 她戴著用一串木珠串成的手鏈。

v. 使成串珠狀、形成珠狀

▶The pearls were beaded into a necklace. 珍珠被串成項鍊。

beak [bik] ◀Track 0445
n. 鳥嘴；喙狀嘴

▶Humming birds have long beaks. 蜂鳥有很長的喙嘴。

beam [bim] ◀Track 0446
n. 笑容、喜色、光束

▶We managed to find our way out of the forest in the weak beam of the flashlight. 我們在手電筒微弱的光束下，找到走出森林的路徑。

v. 堆滿笑容、眉開眼笑

▶His father beamed with delight when he received an award from the mayor. 他從市長手中領到獎時，爸爸高興得眉開眼笑。

bean [bin] n. 豆子 ◀Track 0447

▶*Mr. Bean* is a famous comedy. 《豆豆先生》是知名的喜劇片。

bear [bɛr] n. 熊 ◀Track 0448

▶The polar bear cub attracted tens of thousands of visitors to see him. 小北極熊吸引了上萬名遊客去看牠。

v. 忍受；承擔；生（孩子）

▶She couldn't bear to see her son tortured by the unknown disease. 她無法承受看著兒子被不明的疾病折磨。

beard [bɪrd] ◀Track 0449
n. 山羊鬍；下巴上的鬍鬚

▶My father shaves off his beard everyday. 我爸爸每天都會把鬍子刮乾淨。

beast [bist] ◀Track 0450
n. 野獸；粗暴的人；畜生；獸性

▶Alcohol brought out the beast in him. 酒精激發出了他心中的野獸。

補充片語 bring out the beast in sb. 激怒某人；激發某人的獸性

beat [bit] **v.** 打；跳動 ◀Track 0451

▶He was beaten by a schoolyard bully. 他被校園霸凌者毆打。

n. 敲打；心跳聲；拍子、節奏

▶His heart skipped a beat the first time he saw Mia. 他第一次看到米亞時，激動得心跳停了一下。

beautiful [`bjutəfəl] ◀Track 0452
adj. 美麗的；完美的

▶The princess is beautiful and kind. 公主美麗又仁慈。

beauty [`bjutɪ] ◀Track 0453
n. 美；美人；美好的事物；優點

▶She was a campus beauty when she was young. 她年輕時是學校的校花。

補充片語 campus beauty 校花

because [bɪ`kɔz] ◀Track 0454
conj. 因為

▶He was given a promotion because of his hard work. 他因勤奮工作而獲得升遷。

become [bɪ`kʌm] ◀Track 0455
v. 成為；變得

▶After his near death experience, he became more generous and compassionate. 他經歷了瀕死邊緣後，變得更慷慨、有同情心。

bed [bɛd] n. 床 ◀Track 0456

▶I went to be early last night. 我昨晚很早就上床睡覺了。

中級

bedroom [ˋbɛdˏrʊm]
◀ミ Track 0457

n. 臥室

▶There are three bedrooms and two restrooms in this house. 這棟房子有三間臥室和兩間衛浴室。

bedtime [ˋbɛdˏtaɪm]
◀ミ Track 0458

n. 就寢時間

▶His usual bedtime is 11:00 P.M. 他通常晚上十一點鐘就寢。

adj. 睡前的

▶She reads bedtime stories to her children every night. 她每晚都對小孩説床 故事。

bee [bi] **n.** 蜜蜂
◀ミ Track 0459

▶She was stung by a bee. 她被蜜蜂螫了一下。

beef [bif] **n.** 牛肉
◀ミ Track 0460

▶He doesn't eat beef or pork. 他不吃牛肉或豬肉。

beep [bip]
◀ミ Track 0461

v. 吹警笛；發出嗶嗶聲

▶The doctor was beeped to the emergency room. 這名醫師被呼叫到急診室。

n. 嗶聲

▶I left a message after the beep on the answering machine. 我在電話錄音的嗶聲後留了一個訊息。

beer [bɪr] **n.** 啤酒
◀ミ Track 0462

▶This ginger beer is alcohol-free. 這薑汁啤酒不含酒精。

beetle [ˋbitl] **n.** 甲蟲
◀ミ Track 0463

▶He spotted a black beetle walking on the leaves. 他看見一隻黑甲蟲在樹葉上行走。

before [bɪˋfor]
◀ミ Track 0464

prep. 在……之前

▶In this painting, we can see that the valley is before the mountain. 在這幅畫中，我們可以看見山谷是在山的前面。

conj. 在……之前

▶Finish your homework before you watch cartoons. 看卡通前，先把功課做完。

adv. 以前

▶Have we met before? You look familiar. 我們曾見過面嗎？你看起來很面熟。

beg [bɛg] **v.** 乞求
◀ミ Track 0465

▶I beg your pardon, please? 請你再説一遍，麻煩了。

beggar [ˋbɛgɚ] **n.** 乞丐
◀ミ Track 0466

▶Beggars can't be choosers. 要飯的哪能挑肥揀瘦。（別無選擇。）

begin [bɪˋgɪn]
◀ミ Track 0467

v. 開始；著手

▶The new semester will begin in September. 新學期在九月開始。

beginner [bɪˋgɪnɚ]
◀ミ Track 0468

n. 初學者；新手

▶The class is for English beginners. 這門課是給英文初學者上的。

beginning [bɪˋgɪnɪŋ]
◀ミ Track 0469

n. 開始起點

▶In the beginning, he seemed cold. But later, I found he was quite nice. 他一開始看起來很冷淡，後來我發現他為人其實還不錯。

behave [bɪˋhev]
◀ミ Track 0470

v. 做出……舉止，表現；行為舉止

▶Stop arguing. You behave like a six-year old. 別再爭辯了，你表現得像個六歲小孩。

behavior [bɪ`hevjɚ]
◀ᴇTrack 0471
=behaviour（英式英文）
n. 行為；態度；舉止

▶He is notorious for his violent behavior. 他因行為暴力而惡名昭彰。

behind [bɪ`haɪnd]
◀ᴇTrack 0472
prep. 在⋯⋯之後

▶He hung his jacket behind the door. 他把夾克掛在門後。

adv. 在背後；（留）在原處、在後；遲

▶No child should be left behind in our education system. 在我們的教育體制中，我們不應放棄任何一位小孩。

being [`biɪŋ]
◀ᴇTrack 0473
n. 生物；人；存在；生命

▶Apollo 11 was the first successful mission to land human beings on the moon. 阿波羅十一號完成首次成功將人類送上月球的任務。

belief [bɪ`lif]
◀ᴇTrack 0474
n. 信任；相信；信仰

▶Do you have any religious belief? 你有任何的宗教信仰嗎？

believable [bɪ`livəbl]
◀ᴇTrack 0475
adj. 可信的

▶What he said was not believable. 他的話並不可信。

believe [bɪ`liv] **v.** 相信
◀ᴇTrack 0476
▶He believed that people were inherently selfish. 他相信人類天生是自私的。

bell [bɛl] **n.** 鈴；鐘
◀ᴇTrack 0477

▶My dog expects food when the bell rings. 我的狗一聽到鈴聲就知道會有食物。

belly [`bɛlɪ]
◀ᴇTrack 0478
n. 肚子；腹部；胃；食慾

▶Her eyes are always bigger than her belly when she goes to all-you-can-eat buffets. 她每次去吃到飽的自助餐廳都胃口不大。

補充片語 eyes bigger than belly
眼大肚子小（胃口很小）

belong [bə`lɔŋ]
◀ᴇTrack 0479
v. 應被放置某處；屬於；適合

▶The suitcase belongs to me. 這個行李箱是我的。

belongings
◀ᴇTrack 0480
[bə`lɔŋɪŋz] **n.** 財物；攜帶物品

▶He put his personal belongings in the backpack and left the hotel. 他把個人物品放進背包並離開旅館了。

beloved [bɪ`lʌvɪd]
◀ᴇTrack 0481
adj. 心愛的；受鍾愛的

▶She went to England to see her beloved boyfriend. 她去英格蘭探視心愛的男友。

n. （指丈夫、妻子或男女朋友等）心愛的人

▶He sent a box of chocolate to his beloved.
他送了一盒巧克力給心上人。

below [bə`lo]
◀ᴇTrack 0482
adv. 在下面；以下

▶She hit me below the belt several times and was never punished for that. 她多次暗箭傷我卻從未因此受罰。

中級

補充片語 hit below the belt. 暗箭傷人

prep. 在……下面；在……以下；低於
▶She always wears skirts below the knee. 她總是穿過膝裙。

belt [bɛlt] **n.** 帶狀物；腰帶　◀ Track 0483
▶The belt was studded with crystals. 這條皮帶鑲了一些水晶飾品。

bench [bɛntʃ]　◀ Track 0484
n. 長凳；長椅
▶Be careful. The paint on the bench is still wet. 小心，這張長椅上的油漆還沒乾。

bend [bɛnd]　◀ Track 0485
v. 彎曲；使彎曲；使屈服；使致力於
▶She bent down and kissed her daughter. 她彎下身子親了女兒一下。
n. 彎；轉彎處
▶There is a sharp bend in the road that you cannot see from here. 這段路上有一處急轉彎，在這裡還看不到。

beneath [bɪ`niθ]　◀ Track 0486
prep. 在……之下；向……下面；低於
▶She hid her pocket money beneath the mattress. 她把零用錢藏在床墊下。

beneficial [ˌbɛnə`fɪʃəl]　◀ Track 0487
adj. 有益的；有幫助的
▶Fresh fruit and vegetables contain high levels of antioxidants that are beneficial to our body. 新鮮蔬果含有高量的抗自由基物質，對人體有益。

benefit [`bɛnəfɪt]　◀ Track 0488
n. 益處
▶The new museum will be a great benefit to this community. 這座新的博物館將為社區帶來很大的益處。
v. 對……有益；有益於
▶People will benefit from the new health care system. 人們將從新的健保制度受益。

berry [`bɛrɪ] **n.** 莓果　◀ Track 0489
▶I had a bowl of cereal and berries for breakfast. 我早餐吃了一碗穀片和一些莓果。

beside [bɪ`saɪd]　◀ Track 0490
prep. 在……旁邊
▶My dog sat beside me in the park. 我在公園時，我的狗坐在我旁邊。

besides [bɪ`saɪdz]　◀ Track 0491
prep. 在……之外；除……之外
▶He can play the piano besides violin. 他除了能拉小提琴，還會彈鋼琴。
adv. 此外；而且
▶You don't need to be so harsh on yourself. Besides, it's not your fault. 你不需對自己這麼嚴苛，何況這並不是你的錯。

best [bɛst]　◀ Track 0492
adv. 最好地；最適當地；最
▶She was listed as one of the twenty best-looking women in the world. 她被列為全球前二十名最美的女人之一。
adj. 最好的；最適當的
▶He is the best candidate for the job. 他是這個工作的最佳人選。

bet [bɛt] **n.** 打賭；猜測　◀ Track 0493
▶My bet is that she will win the best supporting actress award. 我猜測她會贏得最佳女配角獎。

v. 打賭；敢斷言

▶I bet the president won't get re-elected.
我敢斷言總統不會連任成功。

betray [bɪ`tre]　◀◎ Track 0494
v. 背叛；出賣；洩漏

▶The double agent betrayed his home country. 這個雙面間諜出賣了母國。

better [`bɛtɚ]　◀◎ Track 0495
adv. 更好地；更適當地；更

▶I think she likes you better than I do.
我覺得她比我更喜歡你。

adj. 更好的；更適當的

▶He is looking for a job with a better pay.
他在尋覓待遇更好的工作。

between [bɪ`twin]　◀◎ Track 0496
prep. 在……之間

▶The relations between the two countries are friendly and fruitful. 兩國關係友好並具成效。

beverage [`bɛvərɪdʒ]　◀◎ Track 0497
n. 飲料

▶She only drinks beverages that are alcohol-free. 她只喝不含酒精的飲料。

beware [bɪ`wɛr]　◀◎ Track 0498
v. 當心；小心；提防

▶Beware of the boss. She's crabby today.
小心老闆，她今天很易怒。

補充片語 beware of 注意；小心

beyond [bɪ`jɑnd]　◀◎ Track 0499
prep. 在……另一邊；超出

▶The theory of relativity is beyond my comprehension. 相對論超出我的理解範圍。

adv. 更遠處；此外

▶From the top of the mountain, we can see the entire city and the woods beyond. 站在這個山頂，我們能看到整座城市和遠處的森林。

bias [`baɪəs]　◀◎ Track 0500
n. 偏心；偏見；偏愛

▶Some people have bias against homosexuals.
社會上有些人對同性戀有偏見。

Bible [`baɪb̩l] **n.** 聖經　◀◎ Track 0501

▶To understand the true meanings behind the Bible is a lifelong work. 了解聖經背後的真正涵義是一件畢生的功課。

bicycle [`baɪsɪk̩l]　◀◎ Track 0502
n. =bike 自行車、單車、腳踏車

▶He goes to school by bicycle. 他騎腳踏車上學。

bid [bɪd]　◀◎ Track 0503
n. 出價（投標）；喊價

▶The company won the bid for the governmental procurement project. 這家公司成功競標到這項政府採購計畫。

v. 命令；吩咐；喊價（投標）

▶She bid $500 for the gramophone record. 她出價五百元買下這個黑膠唱片。

big [bɪg]　◀◎ Track 0504
adj. 大的；年齡較長的

▶The big dog is actually very timid.
這隻大狗其實很膽小。

中級

bike [baɪk] n. 腳踏車　◀ Track 0505

▶She went to the grocery store by bike.
她騎腳踏車去雜貨店。

bill [bɪl] n. 帳單　◀ Track 0506

▶As the bread winner of the family, he has a lot of bills to pay. 他是家中的經濟支柱，有很多帳單要繳。

billion [`bɪljən]　◀ Track 0507
n. 十億；大量；無數

▶There are billions of stars in the outer space. 外太空中有無數的星星。

bin [bɪn]　◀ Track 0508
n. 貯藏箱；（貯藏用的）容器

▶He emptied a bag of sugar into the bin. 他把一袋糖倒入貯藏箱裡。

相關片語 trash bin 垃圾箱

▶He throw the flyer into the trash bin.
他把廣告傳單丟到垃圾箱裡去。

bind [baɪnd]　◀ Track 0509
v. 綑；綁；紮；裝訂；黏合

▶She bound the old newspapers with strings. 她用繩子把舊報紙綑起來。

bingo [`bɪŋgo]　◀ Track 0510
n. 賓果遊戲

▶He won a car the first time he played bingo. 他第一次玩賓果就中了一台汽車。

binoculars　◀ Track 0511
[bɪ`nakjələs] n. 雙筒望遠鏡

▶We used binoculars to watch birds on the lake. 我們用雙筒望遠鏡觀看湖上的鳥。

biography [baɪ`agrəfɪ]　◀ Track 0512
n. 傳記

▶He was reading Elon Musk's biography.
他在讀馬斯克的傳記。

biological　◀ Track 0513
[ˌbaɪə`ladʒɪkl] adj. 生物學的；生物的

▶She didn't intend to look for her biological parents because her foster parents treated her like their own child. 她無意尋找親生父母，因為她的養父母對她視如己出。

補充片語 biological parents 親生父母

biology [baɪ`alədʒɪ]　◀ Track 0514
n. 生物；生物學

▶She is a biology professor in Cornell University. 她是康乃爾大學的生物學教授。

bird [bɝd] n. 鳥　◀ Track 0515

▶The bird is a raven. 這隻鳥是大烏鴉。

birth [bɝθ]　◀ Track 0516
n. 出生；分娩；誕生

▶My sister just gave birth to a beautiful baby. 我妹妹剛生了一個漂亮的寶寶。

birthday [`bɝθˌde]　◀ Track 0517
n. 生日

▶We celebrated his birthday at a karaoke pub. 我們在KTV酒吧慶祝他的生日。

biscuit [`bɪskɪt]　◀ Track 0518
n. 小麵包；軟餅；（英）餅乾

▶She brought ginger biscuits and a vanilla cake to the party. 她帶了一些薑餅和一個香草蛋糕到派對。

bit [bɪt]
◀€Track 0519

n. 小片；小塊；一點點

▶He did a bit of exercise this morning.
他早上做了一點運動。

bite [baɪt] **v** 咬
◀€Track 0520

n. 咬一口；（口）便餐

▶She bites her fingernails when she feels nervous. 她一緊張就咬指甲。

bitter [`bɪtɚ] **adj.** 苦的
◀€Track 0521

▶The pill is bitter to swallow.
這個藥丸苦到很難下嚥。

bizarre [bɪ`zɑr]
◀€Track 0522

adj. 古怪的；異乎尋常的

▶Her behavior was rather bizarre.
她的行為非常怪異。

black [blæk]
◀€Track 0523

adj. 黑色的；黑人的

▶I'd like a cup of black coffee. 我要一杯不加牛奶的黑咖啡。

n. 黑；黑色；（大寫時）指黑人

▶The lady in black is my girlfriend.
那位穿黑色衣服的女生是我的女友。

blackboard
◀€Track 0524

[`blæk͵bord] **n.** 黑板

▶The teacher wrote a sentence on the blackboard.
老師在黑板寫了一個句子。

blacksmith
◀€Track 0525

[`blæk͵smɪθ] **n.** 鐵匠

▶He is a blacksmith by trade.
他以做鐵匠謀生。

blade [bled]
◀€Track 0526

n. 刀片；鋒刃

▶Be careful of the scissor blades.
小心剪刀的刀片。

blame [blem]
◀€Track 0527

v 責怪；責罵

▶She blamed her unhappiness on her mother-in-law. 她把自己不快樂歸咎於婆婆。

n. 指責；責備；責任

▶They put the blame on a newcomer.
他們把罪過怪到一名公司新人身上。

中級

blank [blæŋk]
◀€Track 0528

adj. 空白的；無表情的

▶It was a blank check. 這是一張空白支票。

n. 空白；空格處

▶Please sign your name in the blank.
請在空格處簽名。

blanket [`blæŋkɪt]
◀€Track 0529

n. 毛毯；毯子

▶He wrapped the abused dog in a blanket.
他把受虐的狗用毯子裹著。

blast [blæst]
◀€Track 0530

n. 疾風；爆破；突然吹奏（樂器）；猛然一擊；狂歡

▶Ten people died in the blast. 爆炸中有十人喪生。

v 炸開；吹奏；強烈譴責；轟擊

▶The president was blasted for being uncapable of ruling the country. 總統被抨擊沒有治國的能力。

blaze [blez]
◀€Track 0531

n. 火焰；強光；（情緒的）爆發；猛烈掃射

▶In a blaze of fury, he shouted at his violent father. 盛怒之下，他對著暴力的父親吼叫。

v 燃燒；閃耀；迸發

▶Her face blazed with enthusiasm. 她的臉閃耀著熱誠。

bleach [blitʃ] ◀ Track 0532
v 將……漂白；漂洗；使脫色

▶He bleached the quilt. 他用漂白粉漂洗被子上的污漬。

n 漂白劑

▶Diluted household bleach can be used for the disinfection of facilities. 稀釋後的漂白劑可以用來殺菌各種物品。

bleak [blik] ◀ Track 0533
adj 荒涼的；寒冷刺骨的；冷峻的；無希望的

▶The economic future looked bleak. 經濟前景看起來很黯淡。

bleed [blid] **v** 流血；出血 ◀ Track 0534
▶His nose was bleeding. 他在流鼻血。

blend [blɛnd] ◀ Track 0535
v 混和；使混雜；使交融

▶She blended flour and egg together. 她把麵粉和蛋混合在一起。

bless [blɛs] ◀ Track 0536
v 為……祈福；保佑。

▶May God bless all of us. 願上帝保佑我們大家。

blessing [`blɛsɪŋ] ◀ Track 0537
n 上帝的賜福；祝福；幸事；福氣

▶His divorce was a blessing in disguise. 他離婚反倒是幸事。

blind [blaɪnd] ◀ Track 0538
adj 盲的；視而不見的

▶He was born blind. 他天生視盲。

blink [blɪŋk] ◀ Track 0539
v 眨眼睛；（燈光）閃爍

▶He blinked his eyes in disbelief. 他不可置信地眨著眼睛。

n 一眨眼；一瞥；一瞬間

▶The cat disappeared on the street in a blink of an eye. 貓在街上一眨眼就消失了。

blizzard [`blɪzɚd] ◀ Track 0540
n 大風雪；暴風雪；暴風雪似的一陣；大量

▶They got stuck in a blizzard when they were hiking in the mountain. 他們在山中健行時受困於暴風雪中。

block [blɑk] ◀ Track 0541
n 塊狀物；街區

▶The school is two blocks away. 學校在距此的兩個街區外。

v 阻塞；堵住

▶An angry crowd blocked his way. 憤怒的群眾阻擋了他的去路。

blonde [blɑnd] ◀ Track 0542
adj 金黃色的；金髮碧眼的

▶She is naturally blond. 她天生金髮。

n 金髮碧眼的女子

▶He married a blonde. 他娶了一位金髮碧眼的女子。

相關片語 **dumb blonde** 漂亮無腦的金髮碧眼女子

▶The actress is not a dumb blonde at all. 這名女演員絕不是個空有臉蛋沒有頭腦的金髮女子。

blood [blʌd] **n.** 血　◀Track 0543

▶He donated blood every three months.
他每三個月捐血一次。

bloody [`blʌdɪ]　◀Track 0544

adj. 流血的；血淋淋的

▶Many soldiers died in this long and bloody battle. 許多士兵在這場漫長、血腥的戰爭中喪生。

bloom [blum]　◀Track 0545

n.（觀賞的）花；開花

▶The orchids are in full bloom.
蘭花盛開了。

補充片語 in full bloom 盛開

v. 開花

▶The orchids are beginning to bloom.
蘭花要開始開花了。

blossom [`blɑsəm]　◀Track 0546

n.（果樹的）花；開花

▶We went to Japan during the cherry blossom. 我們在櫻花季去日本。

v. 開花；生長茂盛

▶Never in their wildest thought had they imagined that their daughter would blossom into a royal bride. 他們想都沒想過女兒會成為飛上枝頭變王妃。

blouse [blaʊz]　◀Track 0547

n.（婦女或孩童的）短上衣

▶She wore a blouse and a denim skirt.
她穿了一件襯衫和牛仔裙。

blow [blo] **v.** 吹　◀Track 0548

▶A breeze blew over the park.
一陣微風吹過公園。

n. 吹氣；一擊；（口）強風；精神上的打擊

▶The death of his wife was a huge blow to him. 他妻子的死亡對他造成很大的打擊。

blue [blu]　◀Track 0549

adj. 藍色的；憂鬱的

▶She has blue eyes and blonde hair.
她有金髮藍眼。

n. 藍色；沮喪、憂鬱；藍調

▶He was dressed in blue.
他穿著藍色的衣服。

blunt [blʌnt]　◀Track 0550

adj. 鈍的；不利的；耿直的、直率的；（頭腦或感覺）遲鈍的

▶The journalist asked a blunt question to the mayor. 記者問了市長一個直率的問題。

blur [blɝ]　◀Track 0551

n. 模糊不清的事物；模糊；朦朧；污點

▶When she doesn't wear glasses, everything is a blur to her. 她不戴眼鏡時，看每樣東西都是模糊的。

v. 使模糊不清；使朦朧；弄髒

▶Tears blurred the little girl's eyes.
小女孩淚眼迷濛。

blush [blʌʃ] **v.** 臉紅；慚愧　◀Track 0552

▶He blushes whenever he sees Jenny.
他每次見到珍妮都會臉紅。

n. 臉紅；羞愧

▶A blush came into her cheeks.
她的臉頰紅了。

board [bord]　◀Track 0553

v. 上（船、車或飛機）

▶She already boarded the plane.
她已經登機了。

中級

n. 板子

▶He put a poster on the board.
他在告示牌上貼了一張海報。

boast [bost]　◀€Track 0554

v. 自吹自擂；吹噓；誇耀

▶He boasted of his feats.
他吹噓著自己的功績。

n. 自吹；大話；引以為豪的事物

▶Alice is full of boasts. 艾莉絲滿口大話。

boat [bot] **n.** 小船　◀€Track 0555

▶We will ship the goods by boat.
我們將用小船載運貨物。

body [`badɪ] **n.** 身體　◀€Track 0556

▶Antioxidants are good for our body.
抗氧化物對人體有益。

bodyguard　◀€Track 0557

[`badɪˌgard] **n.** 護衛者；保鏢

▶The billionaire has three bodyguards.
這位億萬富翁有三名保鏢。

boil [bɔɪl]　◀€Track 0558

v. （水等）沸騰；烹煮；煮沸

▶I boiled two eggs and added them into the salad. 我煮了兩顆蛋並把它們加入沙拉中。

bold [bold]　◀€Track 0559

adj. 英勇的；無畏的；大膽的；厚顏無恥的

▶He made a bold move to lead the development of the new product.
他大膽帶領研發這個新產品。

bolt [bolt] **n.** 門栓；門閂　◀€Track 0560

▶The tree was struck by a bolt of lightning.
樹木被閃電擊中了。

v. 拴上；閂上

▶She bolted all the windows and doors.
她閂上所有門窗。

bomb [bam] **n.** 炸彈　◀€Track 0561

▶The bomb exploded and injured hundreds.
炸彈引爆了，數百人受傷。

bond [band]　◀€Track 0562

n. 聯繫；結合；羈絆

▶They quickly formed a bond with their adopted child. 他們和收養的孩子很快就建立了感情。

v. 以……作保；使……黏合；團結在一起

▶The coach bonded the players into a closely knit team. 教練將球員們團結為情誼緊密的球隊。

bone [bon] **n.** 骨頭　◀€Track 0563

▶There was a fish bone stuck in his throat. 他的喉嚨卡了一根魚刺。

bonus [`bonəs]　◀€Track 0564

n. 獎金；紅利；分紅；津貼

▶We got a Christmas bonus from our company. 我們公司發了聖誕節獎金。

補充片語 Christmas bonus 聖誕節獎金

bony [`bonɪ]　◀€Track 0565

adj. 多骨的；瘦削的；骨瘦如柴的

▶She has long bony legs. 她有細長瘦削的腿。

book [bʊk] **n.** 書；書本　◀€Track 0566

▶They bought books and magazines online. 他們在線上買書和雜誌。

v. 預訂；登記

▶We booked our flight tickets two months ago. 我們兩個月前就預訂了機票。

bookcase [`bʊk͵kes] ◀Track 0567

n. 書架；書櫥

▶The bookcase is wobbly.
書架搖搖晃晃的。

booklet [`bʊklɪt] ◀Track 0568

n. 小冊子

▶We made a 10-page booklet to introduce the science fair. 我們製作了十頁的小冊子介紹科學博覽會。

bookshelf [`bʊk͵ʃɛlf] ◀Track 0569

n. 書架

▶There are many fashion magazines on the bookshelf. 書架上擺滿了時尚雜誌。

bookstore [`bʊk͵stor] =bookshop（英式英文） **n.** 書店 ◀Track 0570

▶She went to a bookstore to buy a novel.
她去書店買了一本小說。

boom [bum] ◀Track 0571

v. 發出隆隆聲；激增；迅速發展

▶The company's business boomed after surviving the financial tsunami. 這家公司挺過金融海嘯後生意興隆。

n. 隆隆聲；（商業）繁榮；（政治情況）好轉；激增、暴漲

▶He was born during the baby boom.
他是戰後嬰兒潮世代的一員。

boost [bust] ◀Track 0572

n. 推動；促進；提高；增加

▶The victory was a boost to their morale.
這次勝利對他們士氣大振。

v. 舉；推；抬；推動；促進；提高

▶The teacher tried to boost the student's confidence. 老師試著增強學生的自信心。

boot [but] ◀Track 0573

n. 靴子；一踢；解僱

▶She bought a pair of riding boots.
她買了一雙馬靴。

v. 使穿靴；猛踢；趕走

▶She booted the kids out of the kitchen.
她把孩子攆出廚房。

相關片語 **give sb. the boot** 解僱某人

▶His boss gave him the boot because he caught him stealing. 老闆會把他解僱，因為抓到他偷東西。

booth [buθ] ◀Track 0574

n. 售貨棚；電話亭；（餐廳的）雅座；包廂

▶She went to a telephone booth and called her parents. 她到電話亭打電話給父母。

border [`bɔrdɚ] ◀Track 0575

n. 邊緣；邊界；國界

▶We were near the border between France and Spain. 我們在法國和西班牙邊界附近。

v. 毗鄰；接界；與……接壤

▶Italy borders France. 義大利與法國接壤。

bore [bor] **v.** 使無聊 ◀Track 0576

▶The novel bores me. 這本小說讓我覺得很無聊。

n. 令人討厭的人

▶He is a huge bore. 他是很令人討厭的人。

中級

boredom [`bordəm]
n. 無聊；厭倦
▶She eats snacks out of boredom.
她純粹是出無聊而吃零食。

🔊 Track 0577

boring [`borɪŋ]
adj. 無趣的；乏味的
▶This movie is boring. 這部電影很無趣。

🔊 Track 0578

born [bɔrn]
adj. 出生的；天生的
▶He was born with a silver spoon.
他是含著金湯匙出生的。

🔊 Track 0579

borrow [`baro]
v. 借；向……借
▶I borrowed three books from the library. 我跟圖書館借了三本書。

🔊 Track 0580

boss [bɔs] **n.** 老闆；主管
▶Her boss is very demanding.
她的上司要求很多。

🔊 Track 0581

both [boθ]
adv. 並；又；兩者皆是
▶I like Jamie and Kelly both.
傑米和凱利我都喜歡。

🔊 Track 0582

adj. 兩個都
▶Both her hands were cold.
她的兩隻手都是冷的。

pron. 兩者；雙方
▶Both of them are my classmates.
他們兩者都是我的同學。

bother [`baðɚ]
v. 煩擾；打擾
▶The way he handled this matter bothered me. 他處理這件事的方式令我惱怒。

🔊 Track 0583

n. 煩惱；麻煩
▶He is a bother to his teacher.
他令老師感到很頭痛。

bottle [`batl] **n.** 瓶子
▶Plastic bottles can be recycled.
保特瓶是可以回收利用的。

🔊 Track 0584

bottom [`batəm]
n. 底部；底層
▶She pounded the chicken breast with the bottom of a glass. 她用玻璃杯底部敲打雞胸肉。

🔊 Track 0585

adj. 底部的；最底下的
▶The bottom layer of the cake was made of chocolate and blueberries. 蛋糕的底部是用巧克力和藍莓做成的。

boulevard
[`bulə͵vard] **n.** 林蔭大道；大道
▶They strolled along the boulevard.
他們沿著林蔭大道散步。

🔊 Track 0586

bounce [baʊns] **v.** 彈起
▶The boy was bouncing a basketball.
男孩在拍籃球。

🔊 Track 0587

n. 彈；跳；彈性
▶This soccer ball lost its bounce.
這顆足球失去彈性了。

相關片語 **get the bounce** 被解僱
▶They got the bounce and we didn't.
他們被解僱，而我們沒有。

bow [bo]
n. 船頭；前槳；蝴蝶結；鞠躬
▶He tied the ribbons in a bow.
他把緞帶打成蝴蝶結。

🔊 Track 0588

bowl [bol] n. 碗
Track 0589
▶I had a bowl of oatmeal.
我早餐吃了一碗燕麥片。

bowling [`bolɪŋ]
Track 0590
n. 保齡球
▶She enjoyed bowling, music, and dancing. 她喜歡打保齡球、聽音樂、跳舞。

box [baks] n. 盒子
Track 0591
▶He bought a box of chocolate for his girlfriend. 他買了一盒巧克力給女友。

boxing [`baksɪŋ]
Track 0592
n. 拳擊；拳術
▶It is against the rules of boxing to hit above or below the belt. 拳擊賽中打擊對手腰帶以上或以下的部位是違規的。

boy [bɔɪ] n. 男孩；兒子
Track 0593
▶The boy was playing jigsaw.
男孩在玩拼圖。

boycott [`bɔɪˌkat]
Track 0594
v. 聯合抵制；拒絕參加；杯葛
▶People were urged to boycott the import of pork from that country. 人們被鼓動起來杯葛那個國家進口豬肉到國內。

n. 聯合抵制；拒絕參加
▶The group proposed a trade boycott of the American goods. 那個團體提議針對美國商品做出貿易抵制。

boyfriend [`bɔɪˌfrɛnd]
Track 0595
n. 男朋友
▶She was on a vacation with her boyfriend.
她和男友去度假。

boyhood [`bɔɪhʊd]
Track 0596
n. 男子的童年；少年時代
▶He spent his boyhood in the farm.
他的童年是在農場度過的。

bra [bra]
Track 0597
=brassiere n. 胸罩
▶She bought a new bra in the lingerie store. 她在內衣專賣店買了一件新的胸罩。

bracelet [`breslɪt]
Track 0598
n. 手鐲
▶She wore a beautiful bracelet.
她帶著一條漂亮的手鐲。

braid [bred]
Track 0599
n. 辮子；髮辮
▶She wore her hair in a braid.
她紮著一條辮子。

v. 將頭髮編成辮子；編織
▶She showed us how to braid a rug.
她向我們示範如何編織地毯。

brain [bren] n. 腦；頭腦
Track 0600
▶He racked his brain and finally finished the dissertation.
他絞盡腦汁終於完成論文。

補充片語 racked one's brain 絞盡腦汁

brake [brek] n. 煞車
Track 0601
▶The car has an anti-lock brake system.
這部車配有防鎖死煞車系統。

v. 煞車
▶The government didn't do much to break inflation.
政府並未盡力抑制通貨膨脹。

中級

branch [bræntʃ]
🔈 Track 0602
n. 支線；分支；分店、分公司

▶The company has a branch in Tokyo.
這家公司在東京有分公司。

brand [brænd]
🔈 Track 0603
n. 品牌；商標

▶This brand of clothes is her favorite.
這個品牌的衣服是她的最愛。

v. 印商標於……；打烙印於……

▶The media branded him a man with the Midas touch. 媒體封他為點石成金的人。

補充片語 **Midas touch** 點石成金

brass [bræs]
🔈 Track 0604
n. 黃銅；銅器；銅管樂器

▶She polished the brass until it shone like new. 她擦拭銅器直到它像新的一樣發亮。

adj. 黃銅色的；黃銅製的；銅管樂器的

▶He is an excellent brass player.
他是傑出的銅管樂器樂手。

相關片語 **as bold as brass** 厚顏無恥的

▶Jack, as bold as brass, put the blame on the newcomer. 傑克厚顏無恥地把罪過推給新人身上。

brave [brev] **adj.** 勇敢的
🔈 Track 0605
▶They were praised for their brave actions. 他們因為英勇的行為而受到讚揚。

bravery [`brevərɪ]
🔈 Track 0606
n. 勇敢；勇氣

▶The student was praised for his bravery.
他因為很有勇氣而受到讚揚。

bread [brɛd] **n.** 麵包
🔈 Track 0607
▶She baked her own bread. 她自製麵包。

break [brek]
🔈 Track 0608
v. 打破；破壞

▶I broke my mother's favorite vase.
我把媽媽最心愛的花瓶打破了。

n. 休息

▶It's time to take a break.
該是休息的時候了。

breakdown
🔈 Track 0609
[`brek͵daʊn]
n. （機器）故障；（精神）衰弱、崩潰；（體力）衰竭

▶The truck had a breakdown on the highway. 卡車在公路上 錨了。

相關片語 **nervous breakdown** 精神崩潰

▶He had a nervous breakdown after the war. 他在戰後精神崩潰了。

breakfast [`brɛkfəst]
🔈 Track 0610
n. 早餐

▶I had a tuna sandwich for breakfast.
我早餐吃鮪魚三明治。

breakup [`brek`ʌp]
🔈 Track 0611
n. 中斷；中止；解體

▶He just had a breakup with his girlfriend.
他剛與女友分手。

breast [brɛst]
🔈 Track 0612
n. 乳房；胸部

▶The doctor found a tumor in her breast.
醫師發現她胸部有腫瘤。

breath [brεθ] n. 呼吸
◀Track 0613

▶He took a deep breath before the interview. 他面試前深深地吸了一口氣。

補充片語 take a deep breath 深呼吸

---

breathe [brið] v 呼吸
◀Track 0614

▶The man is still breathing. 男子仍有呼吸。

---

breed [brid]
◀Track 0615

n. （人工培育出來的動植物）品種

▶My favorite breed of dog is Maltese.
我最喜歡的狗是馬爾濟斯。

v. 養殖；飼養；孕育

▶Familiarity breeds contempt.
親不敬，熟生蔑。

---

breeze [briz]
◀Track 0616

n. 微風；輕而易舉的事；

▶Starting a business is by no means a breeze. 創業決非易事。

v. 吹著微風；輕鬆地通過；輕盈地經過

▶She breezed into the reading room.
她輕盈地走進書房。

相關片語 shoot the breeze 閒聊；聊天

▶They sat in the couch and shot the breeze. 他們坐在沙發上聊天。

---

bribe [braɪb]
◀Track 0617

n. 賄賂；行賄物

▶The officials in that country are notorious for taking bribes. 那個國家的官員以收賄而惡名昭彰。

v. 賄賂；收買

▶He bribed the officials in exchange for preferential treatment. 他賄賂官員以換取優惠待遇。

---

brick [brɪk] n. 磚塊
◀Track 0618

▶She bought a brick of cheese and a carton of milk.
她買了一塊乳酪和一盒牛奶。

---

bride [braɪd] n. 新娘
◀Track 0619

▶The bride is an American actress.
新娘是美國女演員。

相關片語 bride-to-be 準新娘

▶The bride-to-be loves her engagement ring. 準新娘很喜愛她的訂婚戒指。

---

bridegroom
◀Track 0620

[`braɪd͵grʊm]

=groom n. 新郎

▶The bridegroom was dressed in his royal marine uniform. 新郎身穿皇家海軍制服。

---

bridge [brɪdʒ] n. 橋
◀Track 0621

▶The Golden Gate Bridge is a famous tourist destination in San Francisco.
金門大橋是舊金山著名的觀光景點。

---

brief [brif]
◀Track 0622

adj. 簡短的；短暫的

▶The chairman delivered brief remarks before the meeting. 主席在會議開始前簡短致詞。

---

briefcase [`brif͵kes]
◀Track 0623

n. 公事包

▶He brought a briefcase to work.
他上班帶了一個公事包。

---

bright [braɪt]
◀Track 0624

adj. 明亮的；晴朗的；聰明的

中級

▶The talented young man will have a bright future. 這個很有天份的年輕男生將有美好的前程。

brilliant [`brɪljənt]
◀Track 0625

adj. 明亮的；優秀的；出色的；高明的

▶This is a brilliant idea. 這真是個好主意。

bring [brɪŋ] **v** 帶來
◀Track 0626

▶She brought twenty cupcakes to the party. 她帶了二十份杯子蛋糕到派對。

Britain [`brɪtən] **n** 英國
◀Track 0627

▶He's from Great Britain. 他來自英國。

British [`brɪtɪʃ]
◀Track 0628

adj. 英國的；英國人的

▶The American actress is a new member of the British royal family. 這位美國女演員成為英國皇室新成員。

n. 英國人

▶My sister married a British when she studied in the UK. 我妹妹在英國求學時嫁給一位英國人。

broad [brɔd]
◀Track 0629

adj. 寬闊的；廣泛的；遼闊的

▶He had a broad smile on his face. 他有開朗的笑容。

broadcast
◀Track 0630

[`brɔd͵kæst] **n** 廣播；廣播節目

▶There will be a live broadcast of the concert tonight. 今晚會有音樂會現場直播。

v 播送；廣播

▶The show was broadcast every Sunday morning. 這個節目每週日早上播出。

broke [brok]
◀Track 0631

adj. 破產的；身無分文的

▶The company was broke. 這家公司破產了。

相關片語 **go for broke** 孤注一擲

▶He went for broke and invested all his money on his business. 他孤注一擲，把所有錢全挹注在公司裡。

brook [brʊk]
◀Track 0632

n. 小河；小溪

▶There is a brook behind the house. 屋後有一條小河。

broom [brum]
◀Track 0633

n. 掃把；掃帚

▶She grabbed a brook and started sweeping. 她拿起掃把開始掃地。

brother [`brʌðɚ]
◀Track 0634

n. 兄；弟

▶The man standing over there is my brother. 站在那裡的人是我弟弟。

brow [braʊ]
◀Track 0635

n. 額頭；眉毛；面容、表情

▶H wrinkled his brow upon hearing the news. 他聽到新聞皺起眉頭。

補充片語 **wrinkle one's brows** 皺眉

brown [braʊn]
◀Track 0636

adj. 褐色的；棕色的

▶We saw a brown bear in the forest. 我們在森林裡看見一隻棕熊。

n. 褐色；棕色

▶The lady in brown is my sister. 身穿棕色衣服的是我的妹妹。

brownie [ˈbraʊnɪ]
◄€ Track 0637

n. 巧克力小方餅；果仁巧克力小方塊蛋糕

▶ I bought a brownie with strawberries for my daughter. 我給女兒買了一個草莓布朗尼蛋糕。

browse [braʊz]
◄€ Track 0638

v. 瀏覽；隨便翻閱；漫不經心地逛（商品）

▶ She browsed through the novel while waiting for the bus. 她在等公車時翻了一下小說。

n. 瀏覽

▶ She had a browse through the novel on the shelf. 她瀏覽了一下書架上的小說。

bruise [bruz]
◄€ Track 0639

n. 傷痕；青腫；擦傷；挫傷

▶ There are bruises on her face.
她的臉上有幾處淤傷。

v. 使受瘀傷；使青腫；使碰傷；使（情感）受挫

▶ He fell down from the stairs and bruised his leg. 他從樓梯摔了下來，腿撞得瘀青了。

brunch [brʌntʃ]
◄€ Track 0640

n. 早午餐

▶ They always have brunch together on Saturday morning. 他們每星期六早上總是一起吃早午餐。

brush [brʌʃ] **n.** 刷子
◄€ Track 0641

▶ We need a new toilet brush.
我們需一支新的馬桶刷。

v. 刷

▶ Brush your teeth before you go to bed.
睡前要刷牙。

brutal [ˈbrutl̩]
◄€ Track 0642

adj. 殘忍的；野蠻的；粗暴的；嚴酷的；殘酷的

▶ The battle was brutal and bloody.
這場戰爭很殘忍血腥。

bubble [ˈbʌbl̩]
◄€ Track 0643

n. 水泡；泡狀物；冒泡聲；泡影、虛幻之事

▶ Her bubble was burst. 她的幻想破滅了。

v. 沸騰；冒泡；發出沸騰聲；充滿生氣

▶ He was bubbling over with enthusiasm.
他充滿熱誠。

bucket [ˈbʌkɪt]
◄€ Track 0644

n. =pail 水桶

▶ The man kicked the bucket last night.
那名男子昨晚過世了。

補充片語 kick the bucket 過世

buckle [ˈbʌkl̩]
◄€ Track 0645

n. 帶釦；搭鉤

▶ He has a belt with a silver buckle.
他有一條帶有銀釦的皮帶。

v. 扣緊；扣住

▶ She buckled herself into the seat.
她坐在椅子上扣上安全帶。

bud [bʌd]
◄€ Track 0646

n. 芽；花苞、花蕾；萌芽；未成熟的事物；小孩

▶ The fruit trees are in bud. 果樹發芽了。

v. 發芽；開始生長

▶ The plants in the garden are budding.
花園裡的植物正在發芽。

相關片語 taste bud 味蕾

中級

▶There are 100 taste receptors on each taste bud. 每個味蕾都有一百個味覺接收器。

budget [`bʌdʒɪt] ◀Track 0647

n. 預算；經費

▶He managed to keep his monthly budget below $3,000. 他保持每個月開支限制在三千元以下。

v. 按預算計劃；編列預算；安排

▶My boss has a busy schedule and budgets his time carefully. 我的上司行程很緊湊，他很妥善規畫時間。

buffalo [`bʌfl̩ˏo] ◀Track 0648

n. 水牛；野牛；（美國城市）水牛城

▶I'll make some buffalo chicken wings for appetizer. 我會做些水牛城雞翅來當開胃菜。

buffet [bʌ`fe] ◀Track 0649

n. 自助餐；快餐

▶Let's go to the all-you-can-eat buffet. 我們去吃到飽的餐廳吧。

bug [bʌg] ◀Track 0650

n. 蟲子；（口）故障

▶There is a bug on this program. 這個程式有一個瑕疵。

build [bɪld] **v.** 興建；建立 ◀Track 0651

▶The house was built of bricks. 這棟房子是用磚塊建造的。

building [`bɪldɪŋ] ◀Track 0652

n. 建築物

▶The office building is only three blocks away from here. 辦公大樓只離這裡三條街的距離。

bulb [bʌlb] ◀Track 0653

n. 電燈泡；球莖；球狀物

▶Nickel is used to make the fuse of the light bulb. 鎳被用來做燈泡的保險絲。

bull [bʊl] ◀Track 0654

adj. 雄的；公牛的；行情看漲的

▶She took the bull by its horns and argued with the manager. 她下定決心和經理理論。

補充片語 take the bull by its horns
下定決心

相關片語 like a bull in a china shop 魯莽闖禍的人

▶His parents always worried about him because he was like a bull in a china shop. 他老是魯莽闖禍，讓他的父母很擔心他。

bullet [`bʊlɪt] **n.** 子彈 ◀Track 0655

▶The policeman got a bullet in his thigh. 警察的大腿被一顆子彈擊中。

相關片語 bullet train
高速火車（子彈列車）

▶He took a bullet train from London to Paris. 他從倫敦搭子彈列車到巴黎。

bulletin [`bʊlətɪn] ◀Track 0656

n. 公告；公報

▶The employees got an e-bulletin from the company every Monday. 那家公司的員工每週一都會收到電子公報告。

相關片語 bulletin board 佈告欄

▶The college's bulletin board is available to this community for free. 這所大學的佈告欄免費開放給這個社區使用。

bully [ˋbʊlɪ]
◀Track 0657

n. 惡霸；恃強凌弱者

▶The schoolyard bully is very obnoxious.
這個校園惡霸令人厭惡。

v. 威嚇；恃強凌弱；橫行霸道；霸凌

▶The boy didn't dare to go to the restroom alone because he was constantly bullied there. 男孩不敢一個人上廁所，因為他常在那裡被霸凌。

bump [bʌmp]
◀Track 0658

v. 碰；撞；重擊；撞傷

▶I bumped into Zoe when I was on a business trip in New York. 我在紐約出公差時巧遇柔伊。。

補充片語 bump into 巧遇

n. 重擊；猛撞；凸塊

▶He had a bump on his arm.
他的手臂上有個腫塊。

相關片語 goose bumps 雞皮疙瘩

▶Her angelic voice gave us goose bumps.
她天籟般的聲音讓我們全身起雞皮疙瘩。

bun [bʌn] **n.** 小圓麵包
◀Track 0659

▶I baked some buns and croissants in the oven. 我在烤箱烤了一些小圓麵包和牛角麵包。

bunch [bʌntʃ]
◀Track 0660

n. 一束；串；一群、一伙

▶He sent his girlfriend a bunch of flowers.
他送女友一束花。

bundle [ˋbʌndl]
◀Track 0661

n. 綑；束；大堆、大量

▶The teacher found a bundle of typos in the essay. 老師發現文章有大量錯字。

burden [ˋbɝdn]
◀Track 0662

n. 重擔；負擔；沉重的責任

▶The current national debt is a huge burden to the country. 這個國家目前的國債是很沈重的負擔。

v. 加負擔於；加負荷於

▶She always burdens people with her problems. 她總是拿自己的困擾麻煩別人。

bureau [ˋbjʊro]
◀Track 0663

n. 事務處；聯絡處；局，司，署，社

▶She was an agent of the Federal Bureau of Investigation. 她是美國聯邦調查局的探員。

中級

burger [ˋbɝgɚ]
◀Track 0664

n. 漢堡；漢堡牛肉餅；各種夾餅

▶He had a cheese burger and French fries for lunch. 他午餐吃起司漢堡和薯條。

burglar [ˋbɝglɚ]
◀Track 0665

n. 夜賊；破門竊盜者

▶A burglar broke into her house last night. 她家昨晚遭小偷闖空門。

burn [bɝn]
◀Track 0666

v. 燃燒；著火；燒傷；燒死

▶He burned his fingers when he was ironing his shirt. 他在燙襯衫時不小心燙傷手指。

burst [bɝst]
◀Track 0667

v. 爆炸；突然發生

▶She burst into tears when she heard the bad news. 她一聽到壞消息眼淚就潰堤了。

bury [ˋbɛrɪ]
◀Track 0668

v. 埋葬；使專心

▶They buried their dead dog in the forest. 他們把過世的狗埋在森林中。

相關片語 **bury oneself in** 埋首於某事

▶The professor buried himself in his research. 教授埋首於研究工作。

---

bus [bʌs] n. 公車
◀ Track 0669

▶We were waiting for our bus.
我們在等候公車。

---

bush [bʊʃ] n. 灌木叢
◀ Track 0670

▶She found her wedding ring under a lavender bush. 她在薰衣草灌木底下找到結婚戒指。

相關片語 **beat around the bush**
拐彎抹角地説

▶Stop beating around the bush. Just get to the point. 不要再拐彎抹角了，説重點。

---

business [`bɪznɪs]
◀ Track 0671
n. 職業；商業；生意；公司

▶The company is a family business.
這家公司是家族企業。

---

businessman
◀ Track 0672
[`bɪznɪsmən] n. 生意人；實業家

▶He is an inventor and a successful businessman.
他是發明家兼成功的實業家。

---

busy [`bɪzɪ]
◀ Track 0673
adj. 忙碌的；繁忙的

▶After a busy day, he slept like a log.
他忙完了一天，睡得很沈。

---

but [bʌt] conj. 但是；卻
◀ Track 0674

▶He is 25, but he looks like he's 35.
他二十五歲，但看起來像三十五歲。

---

prep. 除⋯⋯以外

▶She seldom talks about anything but pets. 她很少談到寵物以外的事情。

---

butcher [`bʊtʃə]
◀ Track 0675
n. 肉販；屠夫；劊子手

▶She bought some pork from the butcher. 她跟肉販買了一些豬肉。

v. 屠宰（牲口）；屠殺；蹧蹋

▶The ruthless dictator butchered innocent civilians. 無情的獨裁者屠殺了無辜的百姓。

---

butter [`bʌtə] n. 奶油
◀ Track 0676

▶He spread some peanut butter on the toast. 他在土司上抹了一些花生醬。

---

butterfly [`bʌtə‚flaɪ]
◀ Track 0677
n. 蝴蝶

▶My dog is chasing butterflies in the garden. 我的小狗在庭院追著蝴蝶跑。

---

button [`bʌtn]
◀ Track 0678
n. 鈕扣；按鈕

▶You can push this button to turn on the TV. 你可以按這個鈕來開電視。

v. 扣上；扣住

▶Button up you coat. It's cold outside.
把外套衣服扣好，外面很冷。

---

buy [baɪ] v. 買、購買
◀ Track 0679

▶She bought a birthday cake for her son. 她幫兒子買了一個生日蛋糕。

---

buzz [bʌz]
◀ Track 0680
v. 嗡嗡叫；按機器使發出信號；嘰嘰喳喳；給⋯⋯打電話

▶This is Natalie. Can you buzz me in?
我是娜塔莉。可以幫我開門嗎？

補充片語 **buzz sb. in**
按（開門）鈕讓某人進入

n. 嗡嗡聲；機器噪音；電話

▶I gave him a buzz when he was home.
他在家時，我打電話給他。

補充片語 **give sb. a buzz** 打電話給某人

---

by [baɪ]　◀€Track 0681

prep. 在……旁；在……（時間）之前；
透過；被

▶I go to school by bike. 我騎腳踏車上學。

adv. 經過；在旁邊

▶A car went by. 一輛車開過。

中級

▶ **Cc**

　　以下表格是全民英檢官方公告中級「聽、說、讀、寫」所須具備的能力，本書例句皆依此範疇特別設計，只要掃描右方QR code，就能搭配相對應的音軌實現「眼耳並用」方式，刺激左腦的語言學習功能；同時也可使用本書附贈的紅膠片，將其置於單字上，一面記憶一面自我挑戰，達到雙倍的學習成果！

聽 ▶	在日常生活中，能聽懂一般的會話；能大致聽懂公共場所廣播、氣象報告及廣告等。在工作時，能聽懂簡易的產品介紹與操作說明。能大致聽懂外籍人士的談話及詢問。
說 ▶	可在日常生活中，能以簡易英語交談或描述一般事物，能介紹自己的生活作息、工作、家庭、經歷等，並可對一般話題陳述看法。在工作時，能進行簡單的答詢，並與外籍人士交談溝通。
讀 ▶	在日常生活中，能閱讀短文、故事、私人信件、廣告、傳單、簡介及使用說明等。在工作時，能閱讀工作須知、公告、操作手冊、例行的文件、傳真、電報等。
寫 ▶	能寫簡單的書信、故事及心得等。對於熟悉且與個人經歷相關的主題，能以簡易的文字表達。

cabbage [`kæbɪdʒ]　🔊 Track 0682
n. 甘藍菜；捲心菜

▶She shredded the cabbage by hand and put the pieces into the salad. 她用手把甘藍菜撕成碎片並把它們放進沙拉裡。

cabin [`kæbɪn]　🔊 Track 0683
n. （船或飛機的）客艙；小木屋

▶They lived in the cabin for two years before moving into the large brick house. 他們住在小木屋兩年，後來搬到很大的磚房。

相關片語 **cabin crew** 客機航班服務員

▶The cabin crew of the airline are renowned for its professional service. 這家航空公司的客機航班服務員以專業服務著稱。

cabinet [`kæbənɪt]　🔊 Track 0684
n. 櫥；櫃

▶We have three filing cabinets in the office. 我們的辦公室有三個檔案櫃。

cable [`kebl]　🔊 Track 0685
n. 電纜；有線電視

▶The truck used a cable to tow the car. 卡車用電線拖走汽車。

cactus [`kæktəs]　🔊 Track 0686
n. 仙人掌

▶They planted the cacti along the fence. 他們沿著籬笆種植仙人掌。

café [kə`fe]　🔊 Track 0687
n. 咖啡廳；小餐館

▶We went to the café for brunch. 我們去小餐館吃早午餐。

cafeteria [ˌkæfə`tɪrɪə]　🔊 Track 0688
n. 自助餐廳

▶The food in school cafeteria is inexpensive.
學校自助餐廳的食物價格不貴。

caffeine [`kæfiɪn] ◀ Track 0689
n. 咖啡因

▶Caffeine is a stimulant that promotes alertness. 咖啡因是提神的興奮劑。

cage [kedʒ] n. 鳥籠；獸籠 ◀ Track 0690

▶She opened the cage and set the birds free. 她打開鳥籠釋放小鳥自由。

cake [kek] n. 蛋糕 ◀ Track 0691

▶I made a birthday cake for my daughter.
我為女兒做了一個生日蛋糕。

calculate [`kælkjə,let] ◀ Track 0692
v. 計算；估計；推測；（以某種目的）計劃

▶She calculated the cost of her trip.
她計算旅行的費用。

calculating ◀ Track 0693
[`kælkjə,letɪŋ]
adj. 計算的；慎重的；工於心計的

▶The murderer is callous and calculating.
這個謀殺犯很殘酷並工於心計。

calculation ◀ Track 0694
[,kælkjə`leʃən] n. 計算

▶She made a quick calculation on a piece of paper. 她在紙上很快地做了計算。

calculator ◀ Track 0695
[`kælkjə,letɚ] n. 計算機；計算者

▶May I borrow your calculator?
我可以跟你借計算機嗎？

calendar [`kæləndɚ] ◀ Track 0696
n. 月曆；行事曆

▶She wrote down the schedule in her calendar. 她把行程寫在行事曆上。

calf [kæf] n. 小牛 ◀ Track 0697

▶The calf is calling for its mother.
小牛在呼喚牛媽媽。

相關片語 calf love 年少的初戀

▶He spoke of a calf love that lasted for a year. 他提到一段長達一年的年少初戀。

call [kɔl] ◀ Track 0698
v. 喊叫；稱呼；打電話

▶You're drunk. Let me call a taxi for you.
你喝醉了，我幫你叫一部計程車。

n. 打電話

▶He made a call to his grandmother and said happy birthday to her. 他打電話給祖母並祝她生日快樂。

calligraphy ◀ Track 0699
[kə`lɪgrəfɪ] n. 書法；筆跡

▶We used to have calligraphy class when were young. 我們小時候有書法課。

中級

calm [kɑm] ◀ Track 0700
adj. 冷靜的；鎮定的

▶He remained calm even in the most difficult situation. 他在面對最艱困的時候依舊維持鎮定。

v. 使冷靜；使鎮定

▶Calm down. It's not the end of the world.
冷靜，這又不是世界末日。

calorie [`kælərɪ] ◀ Track 0701
n. 卡路里；（熱量單位）大卡

▶She burned 225 calories from exercise.
她透過運動燃燒了二千五百大卡。

camel [ˈkæml] n. 駱駝　◀Track 0702

▶It's the last straw that breaks a camel's back. 那是壓垮駱駝的最後一根稻草。

camera [ˈkæmərə] ◀Track 0703
n. 相機

▶Every smart phone has a built-in camera.
每支智慧型手機都有內建相機。

camp [kæmp] n. 露營活動 ◀Track 0704

▶We set up a camp in the middle of the woods. 我們在樹林中露營。

v. 露營

▶They camped in the mountains.
他們在山裡露營。

campaign [kæmˈpen] ◀Track 0705
n. 戰役；活動；運動；競選活動

▶He launched a campaign for tourism promotion. 他開始進行推銷觀光的運動。

v. 從事運動；參加競選；出征

▶The politician said that he will campaign for Brexit. 政治人物說他將致力於英國脫歐的運動。

camping [ˈkæmpɪŋ] ◀Track 0706
n. 露營

▶They went camping in the countryside.
他們在鄉間露營。

campus [ˈkæmpəs] ◀Track 0707
n. 校園

▶Students in that private school are required to wear uniforms on campus.
那所私立學校的學生在校園必須穿校服。

can [kæn] ◀Track 0708
aux. 表示「可以；能夠；可能」的助動詞

▶Can you speak French? 你會說法文嗎?

Canada [ˈkænədə] ◀Track 0709
n. 加拿大

▶They moved to Canada ten years ago.
他們十年前搬到加拿大。

Canadian [kəˈnedɪən] ◀Track 0710
adj. 加拿大的；加拿大人的

▶The Canadian actor was raised in Vancouver.
這名加拿大演員在溫哥華長大。

n. 加拿大人

▶My sister-in-law is a Canadian.
我的妹夫是加拿大人。

canal [kəˈnæl] ◀Track 0711
n. 運河；水道

▶They built a canal to turn the desert into a fertile land. 他們為了讓沙漠變成肥沃的土地而建了一條運河。

cancel [ˈkænsl] v. 取消 ◀Track 0712

▶They cancelled the meeting to make additional preparation for the event.
他們為了替盛會做額外的準備而取消會議。

cancer [ˈkænsɚ] n. 癌 ◀Track 0713

▶He was diagnosed with lung cancer.
他被診斷罹患肺癌。

candidate [ˈkændədet] ◀Track 0714
n. 候選人

▶We think he is the best candidate for the presidential election. 我們認為他是競選總統的最佳候選人。

candle [`kændl̩] n. 蠟燭 ◀ Track 0715

▶He has been burning his candle at both ends lately. 他最近忙到蠟蠋兩頭燒。

candy [`kændɪ] ◀ Track 0716
=sweet （英式英文）n. 糖果

▶You'd better brush your teeth after eating candy. 你吃完糖果後最好去刷牙。

cane [ken] n. 藤條；手杖 ◀ Track 0717

▶We made sugar canes and pretzels in the weekend. 我們週末做了拐杖糖和椒鹽捲餅。

cannon [`kænən] n. 大砲 ◀ Track 0718

▶They pointed the cannon west at a plywood target. 他們把大砲朝西對準一個三夾板的目標。

cannot [`kænɑt] ◀ Track 0719
abbr. 不能、不會

▶He cannot come to the party due to his busy schedule. 他因為行程緊湊而無法前來派對。

canoe [kə`nu] n. 獨木舟 ◀ Track 0720

▶They crashed their canoe and were forced to trek through the bushes. 他們撞毀了獨木舟，被迫在灌木間步行。

v. 划獨木舟

▶Food was canoed up the river into the tribe. 糧食由獨木舟運送到河的上游到那個部落。

相關片語 paddle one's own canoe
自力更生；獨立自主

▶She began paddling her own canoe when she turned 18. 她十八歲就開始自力更生了。

can't [kænt] ◀ Track 0721
abbr. 不能、不會

▶I can't wait for my birthday party. 我等不及要舉辦生日派對了。

canvas [`kænvəs] ◀ Track 0722
n. 帆布；油畫；風帆

▶He painted on canvas a beautiful oil painting. 他在帆布上畫了美麗的油畫。

canyon [`kænjən] ◀ Track 0723
n. 峽谷

▶They entered the canyon near the Buffalo Springs Lake. 他們在布法羅泉湖的附近進入峽谷。

中級

cap [kæp] ◀ Track 0724
n. 無邊便帽；制服帽

▶He wears a baseball cap whenever he goes. 他無論到哪裡都戴著棒球帽。

capability ◀ Track 0725
[ˌkepə`bɪlətɪ] n. 能力；才能；性能；潛力

▶She has the capability of being a good leader. 她有成為領導者的能力。

capable [`kepəbl̩] ◀ Track 0726
adj. 有能力做……的；能夠做……的；能幹的；有才華的

▶He is capable of conducting the research. 他有能力從事研究。

capacity [kə`pæsətɪ] ◀ Track 0727
n. 容量；能量；生產力；能力；資格

▶The auditorium has a seating capacity of 300. 這個禮堂可容納三百名觀眾。

cape [kep] n. 披肩；斗篷　◀Track 0728

▶Superman wears a cape and tights.
超人穿著披肩和緊身衣。

capital [`kæpətl̩]　◀Track 0729

n. 資金；資本；本錢；首都

▶Paris is the fashion capital of the world. 巴黎是國際時尚之都。

adj. 主要的；首位的；重要的

▶Capital punishment has caused heated debates among the public. 死刑長期以來在大眾引起熱烈的討論。

補充片語 capital punishment 死刑

capitalism　◀Track 0730

[`kæpətl̩ˌɪzəm] n. 資本主義

▶Some people claim that capitalism and globalization have led to wealth disparity. 有人認為資本主義和全球化導致貧富差距。

capitalist [`kæpətl̩ɪst]　◀Track 0731

adj. 資本主義的；資本家的；擁有資本的

▶In advanced capitalist societies, the necessaries of life include a heated dwelling, food, clothing, cars, and etcetera. 在先進資本主義社會中，生活的必需品包括具有暖氣的房子、豐盛的食物、衣服、汽車等。

n. 資本主義者；資本家；有錢人

▶Donald Trump is a capitalist.
唐納川普是個資本家。

captain [`kæptɪn]　◀Track 0732

n. 船長；機長；隊長；領隊

▶He is the captain of the basketball team. 他是籃球隊隊長。

caption [`kæpʃən]　◀Track 0733

n. 標題；字幕；說明

▶Her selfie captions are very interesting.
她的自拍標題很有趣。

v. 加標題於

▶She captioned the pictures with the timeline of their relationship. 她將照片加註標題並把他們的關係以時間表的方式呈現出來。

capture [`kæptʃɚ]　◀Track 0734

v. 捕獲；佔領；奪得；引起（注意）；（用照片）捕捉

▶The photographer successfully captured the beauty of the Grand Canyon. 攝影師成功地捕捉大峽谷的美。

n. 俘虜；佔領；捕獲物；戰利品

▶The refugees fled to escape capture.
難民逃亡以避免被逮。

car [kɑr] n. 汽車　◀Track 0735

▶He recently bought an electric car.
他最近買了一部電動車。

carbon [`kɑrbən] n. 碳　◀Track 0736

▶We need to reduce carbon emission before it is too late. 我們必須減少碳排放量，以免一切太遲了。

補充片語 carbon emissions 碳排放

card [kɑrd] n. 卡片　◀Track 0737

▶I received a birthday card from my boyfriend. 我收到男友送我的生日卡片。

cardboard　◀Track 0738

[`kɑrdˌbord] n. 硬紙板

▶The homeless man slept in a cardboard box. 這個無家可歸的男人睡在硬紙板箱裡。

adj. 硬紙板的；虛構的

▶The characters in her novel are too cardboard and emotional. 她的小說裡的角色都太做作又情緒化。

care [kɛr]　◀Track 0739

n. 看護；照料；所關心之事；用心

▶The patient is still in intensive care unit. 病人仍在加護病房。

v. 關心；在意；喜歡

▶Do you care for a beer? 你要不要喝點啤酒？

career [kə`rɪr]　◀Track 0740

n. 事業；（終身）職業

▶She started her modeling career at the age of 13. 她十三歲就開始模特兒的職業。

carefree [`kɛr,fri]　◀Track 0741

adj. 無憂無慮的；輕鬆愉快的

▶She lived a very carefree life when she was young.
她年輕時過著無憂無慮的生活。

careful [`kɛrfəl]　◀Track 0742

adj. 小心的；注意的

▶The vet gave the dog a careful examination.
獸醫幫狗兒做了詳細的檢查。

careless [`kɛrlɪs]　◀Track 0743

adj. 粗心的

▶His careless mistake caused the company to lose a huge sum of money. 他粗心的疏失造成公司損失巨額的金錢。

cargo [`kɑrgo]　◀Track 0744

n. （裝載的）貨物

▶This train was carrying a cargo of coal.
火車正在載運一批煤炭。

carnation [kɑr`neʃən]　◀Track 0745

n. 康乃馨

▶She planted some carnations and roses in her garden. 她在花園種了一些康乃馨和玫瑰。

carnival [`kɑrnəvl̩]　◀Track 0746

n. 嘉年華會

▶We went to see the carnival parade in Brazil. 我們去巴西觀賞嘉年華遊行。

補充片語 **carnival parade** 嘉年華會遊行

carpenter [`kɑrpəntɚ]　◀Track 0747

n. 木匠

▶Her husband is a skillful carpenter.
她的先生是個技藝非常高超的木匠。

carpet [`kɑrpɪt] **n.** 地毯　◀Track 0748

▶The children sat on the carpet playing cards. 孩子坐在地毯玩撲克牌。

carriage [`kærɪdʒ]　◀Track 0749

n. 四輪馬車；火車車廂；嬰兒車；運費

▶Princess Diana sat in a carriage during her wedding to Prince Charles. 黛妃搭乘馬車嫁給查爾斯王子。

相關片語 **baby carriage** 嬰兒車

▶She pushed her pet dog in a baby carriage along the street. 她用嬰兒車推著愛犬逛街。

carrier [`kærɪɚ]　◀Track 0750

n. 運送人；送信者；從事運輸事業者；（車上的）置物架；帶菌者

中級

▶When handled improperly, meat can be a lethal carrier of bacteria. 肉品若未經適當處理，可能會是致命的帶菌物。

相關片語 **mail carrier** 郵差；郵車

▶The devoted mail carrier never missed one delivery in six years. 這名敬業的郵差六年來從沒錯失送達任何的郵件。

carrot [`kærət] n. 紅蘿蔔
◀Track 0751

▶She made a beef stew with carrots in it. 她燉牛肉加了紅蘿蔔進去。

carry [`kærɪ]
◀Track 0752

v. 扛、抱、拿、背、提、搬等

▶The old man is too weak to carry the luggage. 這位年邁的男人太虛弱以致無法提行李。

cart [kɑrt] n. 推車
◀Track 0753

▶The shopping mall provides a lot of shopping carts for its customers. 購物中心提供很多推車供消費者使用。

v. 用運貨車裝運

▶He carted the produce he grew to the market. 他用運貨車裝運他種植的農作物到市場去。

carton [`kɑrtn]
◀Track 0754

n. 紙盒；紙板箱

▶Mom bought a carton of grape juice from the supermarket. 媽媽在超市買了一盒葡萄汁。

v. 用紙盒裝；製作紙盒

▶Cartoned eggs can last longer in a cool, dry room. 盒裝雞蛋可以在陰涼乾爽的地方保存比較久。

cartoon [kɑr`tun]
◀Track 0755

n. 卡通

▶The children are watching cartoons. 孩子們正在看卡通影片。

carve [kɑrv]
◀Track 0756

v. 雕刻；切開；開拓

▶The company has carved out a niche in the luxury goods market. 公司已在高檔精品市場中開拓出利基。

case [kes]
◀Track 0757

n. 箱子、盒子；事件、案例

▶Normally I would take the metro, but in this case, it would be more convenient to drive. 我平時會搭捷運，但這個情況下，開車比較方便。

cash [kæʃ] n. 現金
◀Track 0758

▶I'd like to pay in cash. 我想付現金。

v. 兌現

▶May I cash this check, please? 請問我可以兌現這張支票嗎

cashier [kæ`ʃɪr]
◀Track 0759

n. 出納；出納員

▶She was a cashier at Carrefour. 她在家樂福當出納員。

cassette [kə`sɛt]
◀Track 0760

n. 卡式錄音帶或錄影帶

▶People nowadays use thumb drives instead of video cassettes. 現代人都用隨身碟而不用卡式錄影帶了。

補充片語 **thumb drive** 隨身碟

cast [kæst]
◀Track 0761

n. 拋；擲；班底、演員陣容

▶It's a movie with great cast and amazing special effects. 那部電影演員陣容堅強並有很棒的特效。

v. 丟，擲；投射（光影或視線）；鑄造

▶He cast his vote at a polling station. 他在投票所投票。

補充片語 **polling station** 投票所

castle [ˋkæsl] **n.** 城堡
◀Track 0762

▶The princess lived in a strong castle. 公主住在一座堅固的城堡中。

casual [ˋkæʒʊəl]
◀Track 0763

adj. 偶然的；隨便的；不拘禮節的；非正式的

▶It's not a formal occasion. Casual wear will be fine. 那不是個正式的場合，穿休閒服就可以了。

casualty [ˋkæʒjʊəltɪ]
◀Track 0764

n. 傷亡人員；傷亡人數；受害者

▶The bombing caused many casualties and left thousands of civilians homeless. 這場轟炸造成很多傷亡人數，並導致數千名平民無家可歸。

cat [kæt] **n.** 貓
◀Track 0765

▶My cat purrs when I pet her. 我拍拍我的貓咪時，她會發出咕嚕咕嚕的聲音。

catalog [ˋkætəlɔg]
◀Track 0766
=cat·al·ogue (英式英文)

n. 目錄；型錄

▶Many stores have converted their printed catalog to an online catalog. 許多商店已將紙本印刷目錄改成線上目錄。

v. 編目錄；登記

▶The botanist found new plants and cataloged them in his journal. 植物學家發現新植物並把它們編錄在他的期刊中。

catastrophe
◀Track 0767
[kəˋtæstrəfɪ]

n. 大災難；慘敗；天翻地覆的事件

▶Hundreds of people were killed in the natural catastrophe. 數百人在這場天災中喪生。

catch [kætʃ]
◀Track 0768

v. 抓、接；趕上

▶The police already caught the bank robbers. 警方已逮捕銀行搶犯。

n. 抓、接

▶The job fair caught the interest of many young people. 這場就業博覽會吸引了很多年輕人的興趣。

補充片語 **job fair** 就業博覽會

category [ˋkætəˏgorɪ]
◀Track 0769

n. 種類；類目；範疇

▶Chamber music is a category of classical music. 室內樂歸在古典音樂類。

caterpillar
◀Track 0770
[ˋkætəˏpɪlə] **n.** 毛毛蟲

▶Monarch caterpillars have two sets of antennae. 帝王蝶的毛毛蟲有兩組觸角。

cattle [ˋkætl] **n.** 牛；牲畜
◀Track 0771

▶He raised cattle and chicken on the farm. 他在農場養牛和雞。

cause [kɔz]
◀Track 0772

v. 引起、導致

中級

▶I hope I didn't cause you too much inconvenience. 我希望我並沒有帶給你太多的不便。

n. 原因、起因；理由

▶The cause of his death remains unknown. 他的死因至今仍不明。

cave [kev] **n.** 洞穴；洞窟　◀€ Track 0773

▶We found a brown bear living in the cave. 我們發現洞穴住著一隻棕熊。

v. 塌陷；屈服

▶The teacher caved into the demands of the parents. 老師屈服於家長的要求。

cavity [`kævətɪ]　◀€ Track 0774

n. 洞；穴；（身體的）腔室；（牙的）蛀洞

▶The child has had cavities for a while and she really needs to see a dentist. 小孩牙齒有幾個蛀洞已長達一段時間，實在需要去看牙醫了。

CD [si-di]　◀€ Track 0775
=compact disk **n.** 光碟

▶He spent his pocket money on CDs. 他把零用錢花在買光碟。

cease [sis]　◀€ Track 0776

v. 停止；終止；結束

▶The two countries finally cease fire against each other.
這兩國終於彼此停火了。

n. 停止

▶The strong wind has blown without cease for two days. 強風已無停止地吹了兩天。

補充片語 without cease 不停地

ceiling [`silɪŋ] **n.** 天花板　◀€ Track 0777

▶The lobby has very high ceilings.
大廳的天花板很高。

celebrate [`sɛlə͵bret]　◀€ Track 0778

v. 慶祝

▶My grandparents are going to celebrate their wedding anniversary. 我的祖父母將慶祝他們的婚姻紀念日。

celebration　◀€ Track 0779

[͵sɛlə`breʃən] **n.** 慶祝

▶There are New Year celebrations all over the world. 全球都有慶祝新年的活動。

celebrity [sɪ`lɛbrətɪ]　◀€ Track 0780

n. 名流；名人

▶She became an Internet celebrity after several of her videos went viral on Youtube. 她的影片在Youtube被瘋傳而成為網紅。

補充片語 Internet celebrity 網路紅人；
go viral 影片像病毒一樣迅速增生、爆紅

cell [sɛl] **n.** 細胞　◀€ Track 0781

▶The new treatment can exclusively targets cancer cells. 新療法可以直接瞄準癌細胞。

cellar [`sɛlɚ]　◀€ Track 0782

n. 地下室；地窖；酒窖

▶He built a cellar to store potatoes, carrots, and red wine. 他蓋了一個地窖來存放馬鈴薯、胡蘿蔔和紅酒。

cello [`tʃɛlo] **n.** 大提琴　◀€ Track 0783

▶She teaches cello and chamber music. 她教授大提琴和室內樂。

cell phone [ˋsɛl-fon] ◀Track 0784
n. 行動電話

▶Please turn off your cell phone during the class. 上課中請關閉你的行動電話。

cement [səˋmɛnt] ◀Track 0785
n. 水泥

▶The cement has a mixed formula.
這包水泥有很多混合的成份。

v. 用水泥塗；用水泥接合

▶The two country signed an agreement to further cement their trade relations.
兩國簽署協定以促進君加強貿易關係。

cemetery [ˋsɛməˌtɛrɪ] ◀Track 0786
n. 墓地

▶He went to the cemetery to lay flowers on his father's grave. 他去墓園並在父親墓碑上放了鮮花。

cent [sɛnt] **n.** 一分（美元）◀Track 0787

▶The sugar cane cost me 80 cents.
這根拐杖糖花了我八十分美元。

center [ˋsɛntɚ] ◀Track 0788
=cent·re （英式英文）
n. 中心點；中央

▶It's a ten-minute walk from my office to the city center. 從我的辦公室到市中心走路要花十分鐘。

v. 以……為中心；使集中

▶Her talks always center around her children. 她的談話總是圍繞著她的孩子們。

centimeter ◀Track 0789
[ˋsɛntəˌmitɚ] =centimetre
（英式英文）**n.** 公分

▶The basketball player is 210 centimeters tall. 這名籃球員有二百一十公分高。

central [ˋsɛntrəl] ◀Track 0790
adj. 中心的；中央的

▶We took a walk at the Central Park in New York. 我們在紐約的中央公園散步。

century [ˋsɛntʃʊrɪ] ◀Track 0791
n. 世紀

▶She in particularly interested in the Spanish architecture of the 17th century.
她對十七世紀西班牙建築特別感興趣。

cereal [ˋsɪrɪəl] ◀Track 0792
n. 麥片；穀類加工食品

▶I had a bowl of cereal and a sandwich for breakfast.
我早餐吃一碗麥片和一個三明治。

ceremony ◀Track 0793
[ˋsɛrəˌmonɪ] **n.** 儀式；典禮

▶She was dressed to the nines for her first Golden Globes ceremony.
她盛裝出席她的第一場金球獎頒獎典禮。

補充片語 be dressed to the nines
穿著講究

certain [ˋsɝtən] ◀Track 0794
adj. 確信的；某……；某種程度的

▶He was not certain what to expect when he arrived at the party.
他到派對時，並不確定應抱有什麼樣的期待。

certainly [ˋsɝtənlɪ] ◀Track 0795
adv. 無疑地；當然

中級

▶He will certainly pass the difficult exam. 他無疑地會通過這個困難的考試。

certificate [sə`tɪfəkɪt] ◀ Track 0796

n. 證書；執照；憑證

▶She had a marriage certificate to show that she was the wife of the TV host. 她有結婚證書證明自己是這位電視節目主持人的妻子。

補充片語 **marriage certificate** 結婚證明

chain [tʃen] ◀ Track 0797

n. 鏈條；項圈；一連串；連鎖店

▶They are the world's biggest hotel chain and offer free parking for all guests. 他們是全球最大的飯店連鎖並提供所有客人免費停車的服務。

v. 用鏈拴住；拘禁

▶The man chained his dog outside without food and water. 男人把狗用鏈拴在屋外，且不提供食物和水。

相關片語 **chain smoker** 一根接著一根抽煙的人

▶He was a chain smoker before he got married. 他婚前是個菸抽個不停的人。

chair [tʃɛr] **n.** 椅子 ◀ Track 0798

▶My grandmother used to rock me to sleep in this rocking chair. 我祖母曾讓我坐在這張躺椅哄我入睡。

chairman [`tʃɛrmən] ◀ Track 0799

n. 主席；議長；（大學）系主任

▶He was appointed as the chairman of the commission. 他被指派擔任委員會的主席。

chalk [tʃɔk] **n.** 粉筆 ◀ Track 0800

▶The boy used a chalk to draw a dog on the blackboard. 男童用粉筆在黑板上畫了一隻狗。

challenge [`tʃælɪndʒ] ◀ Track 0801

n. 挑戰；艱鉅的事；異議、質疑

▶Building a railway in the mountain is a real challenge. 在山中建造一條鐵路是個挑戰。

v. 向……挑戰；對……提出異議；激發

▶An African-American student challenged her teachings on slave history. 非裔美籍學生向老師提出奴隸歷史的質疑。

chamber [`tʃembə] ◀ Track 0802

n. 房間；寢室；會場；會議廳；（體內的）腔室

▶This is a torture chamber during the Khmer Rouge takeover. 這是赤色高棉時期的刑訊室。

補充片語 **torture chamber** 刑訊室

champagne ◀ Track 0803

[ʃæm`pen] **n.** 香檳；香檳酒

▶We opened a bottle of champagne to celebrate our victory. 我們開了一瓶香檳酒慶祝勝利。

champion [`tʃæmpɪən] ◀ Track 0804

n. 冠軍；優勝者

▶The team was the champion of World Cup. 這支隊伍是世界盃的冠軍。

v. 擁護；支持；為……而戰

▶They have championed for judicial reform for years. 他們為了司法改革奮戰了好幾年。

championship
◀Track 0805

[`tʃæmpıən ʃıp] n. 優勝;冠軍地位;錦標賽

▶He won the diving championship of the Olympic Games. 他贏得奧林匹克的跳水冠軍。

chance [tʃæns] n. 機會
◀Track 0806

▶The scientist made a revolutionary discovery by chance. 科學家意外地做出革命性的發現。

change [tʃendʒ]
◀Track 0807

n. 改變;變化

▶A change is as good as a rest. 換個環境等於休息。

v. 改變;變動

▶Climate change poses a serious threat to the survival of mankind. 氣候變遷對人類的生存造成很嚴重的威脅。

changeable
◀Track 0808

[`tʃendʒəbl] adj. 易變的;不定的

▶She is the most changeable person I have ever seen. 她是我見過脾氣最陰晴不定的人。

channel [`tʃænl]
◀Track 0809

n. 水道;航道;頻道

▶He switched to another channel to watch sports. 他換到另一個頻道看運動賽事。

chant [tʃænt]
◀Track 0810

n. 歌;曲子;詠唱

▶The chant of the crowd was "Stop bullying now". 群眾喊叫的口號是「現在就停止霸凌」。

v. 吟誦;反覆地唱

▶The children are chanting Christmas carols. 孩子們正在唱聖誕歌曲。

chaos [`keas]
◀Track 0811

n. 混亂;雜亂的一團

▶The country was in a state of chaos during the civil war. 國家在內戰期間陷入一團混亂。

chapter [`tʃæptə]
◀Track 0812

n. (書籍的)章;回

▶Please preview Chapter 5 before we start our next class. 請在下次上課前先預習第五章。

character [`kærıktə]
◀Track 0813

n. (人的)性格;(事物的)特質;(戲劇 或小說的)人物角色

▶The characters in this novel are mysterious yet attractive. 這本小說的人物既神秘又吸引人。

中級

characteristic
◀Track 0814

[ˌkærəktə`rıstık]

n. 特性;特徵;特色

▶His sense of humor is a very attractive characteristic. 他的幽默感是特色。

adj. 特有的;表示特性的

▶The creamy taste is characteristic of this cheese. 這種起司的特性是擁有香濃的口感。

charge [tʃɑrdʒ]
◀Track 0815

n. 費用;掌管

▶A 5% service charge will be added to all bills at this café. 這間餐館的帳單要另收百分之五的服務費。

v. 索費;指控

▶How much do you charge for laundry service? 洗衣服務要收多少錢?

charity [`tʃærətɪ] ◀€ Track 0816

n. 慈悲；慈善；施捨；善舉；慈善事業

▶ She started the charity and raised more than $10,000 to help homeless people. 她成立慈善團體並募款一萬元幫助無家可歸的人們。

charm [tʃɑrm] ◀€ Track 0817

n. 魅力；符咒、護身符

▶ Princess Diana's compassion towards the sick and poor was her greatest charm. 黛妃對飽受貧病所苦的人們展現的同理心是她最迷人之處。。

v. 使陶醉；吸引；對……施魔法

▶ We were charmed by the magic show. 我們都被魔術表演給迷住了。

> 相關片語 **work like a charm**
> 十分奏效地；迅速地成功

▶ His strategy worked like a charm. 他的策略奏效。

charming [`tʃɑrmɪŋ] ◀€ Track 0818

adj. 迷人的；有魅力的

▶ The super model is stunning and charming. 這名超模既美麗又迷人。

chart [tʃɑrt] **n.** 圖表 ◀€ Track 0819

▶ The chart showed the average cost of living in this city over the years. 這張圖表顯示這座城市過去幾年來的平均生活費。

chase [tʃes] **v.** 追逐；追求 ◀€ Track 0820

▶ My cat is chasing his toy mouse. 我的貓在追牠的玩具老鼠。

chat [tʃæt] **n.** 聊天 ◀€ Track 0821

▶ He never really enjoyed water cooler chat or office politics. 他向來不喜歡辦公室閒聊或辦公室政治。

> 補充片語 **water cooler chat** 辦公室閒聊

v. 聊天

▶ My son is chatting with his cyber friends. 我兒子在和網友們聊天。

cheap [tʃip] ◀€ Track 0822

adj. 便宜的；廉價的

▶ Soy bean milk is cheap and nutritious. 豆漿便宜又營養。

cheat [tʃit] ◀€ Track 0823

v. 欺騙；行騙；作弊 **n.** 騙子；欺詐；作弊

▶ He was caught cheating on his exam. 他被抓到考試作弊。

check [tʃɛk] ◀€ Track 0824
=cheque （英式英文）

n. 支票

▶ The bank sent me a check by express mail. 銀行用快捷郵件寄給我一張支票。

checkout [`tʃɛkˌaʊt] ◀€ Track 0825

n. 結帳離開；付款櫃台

▶ When is the checkout time, please? 請問結帳退房的時間是幾點?

cheek [tʃik] ◀€ Track 0826

n. 臉頰；腮幫子；傲慢態度；厚臉皮

▶ She has chubby cheeks and a dimple chin. 她有圓潤的臉頰和酒窩頸。

> 相關片語 **have the cheek to do sth.** 厚者臉皮做某事

▶ She had the cheek to ask me for a favor. 她竟有臉要我幫她的忙。

> 補充片語 **ask sb. a favor** 請某人幫忙

cheer [tʃɪr] ◀Track 0827

v. 歡呼；使振奮、高興

▶It was out of place for you to cheer when the director was demoted to professor. 主任被降職為教授時，你在旁邊歡呼很不恰當。

n. 歡呼；喝彩；鼓勵

▶The crowd burst into cheers upon hearing the good news. 群眾聽到好消息後立即發出歡呼聲。

cheerful [`tʃɪrfəl] ◀Track 0828

adj. 興高采烈的；使人愉快的；樂意的

▶She has a radiant smile and a cheerful personality. 她擁有燦爛的笑容和使人愉快的個性。

cheese [tʃiz] ◀Track 0829

n. 乳酪；乾酪

▶The cheese is very tangy and full of flavor. 這個乳酪味道很香、口感豐富。

chef [ʃɛf] ◀Track 0830

n. （餐館的）主廚；廚師；大廚師

▶He is the chef of a five star hotel. 他是五星級飯店的主廚。

chemical [`kɛmɪkl̩] ◀Track 0831

n. 化學製品；化學藥品

▶Benzene is a toxic chemical. 苯是有毒的化學物質。

adj. 化學的；化學上的

▶It is very sad to see the country use chemical weapons against its own civilians. 看到這個國家使用化學武器對付自己的人民，讓人感到很難過。

chemist [`kɛmɪst] ◀Track 0832

n. 化學家

▶The chemist was so passionate about his experiments that he slept in the lab almost all year round. 這名化學家非常熱衷進行他的實驗，以致幾乎一年到頭都睡在實驗室。

chemistry [`kɛmɪstrɪ] ◀Track 0833

n. 化學；化學作用

▶He studied astrophysics and chemistry at college. 他在大學時學天體物理學和化學。

cherish [`tʃɛrɪʃ] **v.** 珍惜 ◀Track 0834

▶She cherished the memories she had with her parents. 她很珍惜與父母共同度過的時光。

cherry [`tʃɛrɪ] ◀Track 0835

n. 櫻桃；櫻桃樹；櫻桃色

▶We went to the orchard and picked cherries and raspberries. 我們去果園採櫻桃和覆盆子。

chess [tʃɛs] **n.** 西洋棋 ◀Track 0836

▶Alpha Go defeated the world chess champion. 阿法圍棋擊敗了世界西洋棋冠軍。

chest [tʃɛst] ◀Track 0837

n. 胸口、胸膛；五斗櫃

▶She coughed hard from deep inside the chest. 她從胸口用力地咳嗽。

相關片語 **get sth. off one's chest** 將某事傾吐出來

▶I finally feel better after I got it off my chest. 我把這件事說出來，心裡終於舒坦多了。

chew [tʃu] ◀Track 0838

v. 嚼；咀嚼；嚼碎；深思細想

中級

▶The boy chewed gum while playing baseball. 男孩打棒球時嚼著口香糖。

相關片語 **chew the fat** 閒聊；發牢騷

▶I met with my friends and we chewed the fat for hours. 我和朋友碰面並一起閒聊幾個小時。

chick [tʃɪk]
🔊Track 0839

n. 小雞；少女；小妞

▶*White Chicks* is a very funny movie. 《小姐好白》是部很好笑的電影。

chicken [ˋtʃɪkɪn]
🔊Track 0840

n. 小雞；雞肉

▶Mom made mashed potatoes and roast chicken for supper. 媽媽晚餐做了馬鈴薯泥和烤雞。

chief [tʃif]
🔊Track 0841

adj. 主要的；等級最高的

▶He is the chief financial officer of this company. 他是這間公司的財務長。

補充片語 **chief financial officer** 財務長

n. 首長；長官

▶The president is also the command-in-chief of the military. 總統也是三軍統率。

child [tʃaɪld] **n.** 孩子；孩童
🔊Track 0842

▶She is the only child in her family. 她是家中的獨生女。

childbirth
🔊Track 0843

[ˋtʃaɪldˏbɝθ] **n.** 分娩；生產

▶She shared her childbirth experience on her Facebook. 她在臉書分享生產時的經驗。

childhood
🔊Track 0844

[ˋtʃaɪldˏhʊd] **n.** 童年

▶The princess didn't have a happy childhood. 這位公主的童年並不愉快。

childish [ˋtʃaɪldɪʃ]
🔊Track 0845

adj. 孩子般的；幼稚的

▶Stop being so childish. You're already a grown-up. 別這麼幼稚，你已經是成年人了。

childlike [ˋtʃaɪldˏlaɪk]
🔊Track 0846

adj. 孩子般的；天真的；單純的

▶Although she's 20, she still has a childlike face. 她雖然已二十歲了，仍有一張孩子般天真的臉蛋。

chill [tʃɪl]
🔊Track 0847

n. 寒冷；寒氣；風寒；掃興

▶There was a chill in the air this morning. 今天早上寒氣很重。

adj. 冷颼颼的；冷淡的；使人寒心的；冷靜的

▶During the financial tsunami, many businesses felt the chill wind of the recession. 金融海嘯期間，許多企業都感受到景氣的蕭條。

相關片語 **catch a chill** 著涼

▶He caught a chill that turned into pneumonia. 他著涼後感染了肺炎。

chilly [ˋtʃɪlɪ]
🔊Track 0848

adj. 冷颼颼的；冷淡的；使人寒心的

▶The reporter was given a chilly reception and found few willing to speak to her. 這名記者受到冷淡的接待，並發現很少人願意和她說話。

chimney [`tʃɪmnɪ]
🔊 Track 0849

n. 煙囪

▶ The thief slipped into the chimney and became stuck halfway down.
小偷滑進煙囪並在半途被卡住。

chimpanzee
🔊 Track 0850

[ˌtʃɪmpænˋzi] n. 黑猩猩

▶ Keeping forests intact helps safeguard the chimpanzee habitat. 確保森林不被濫墾有助保護黑猩猩的棲息地。

chin [tʃɪn] n. 下巴
🔊 Track 0851

▶ My dog rested his chin on my lap.
我的狗把下巴托在我的大腿上。

china [`tʃaɪnə]
🔊 Track 0852

n. 瓷器；陶瓷器

▶ She bought a beautiful collection of fine china cups and saucers.
她買了一組漂亮的瓷杯和瓷碟。

Chinese [`tʃaɪˋniz]
🔊 Track 0853

adj. 中國的；中國人的；華人的

▶ Chinese New Year is the most important traditional holidays in the Chinese community.
中國新年是華人世界中最重要的傳統節日。

n. 中國人

▶ Jeremy Lin is an American Chinese.
林書豪是美籍華人。

chip [tʃɪp]
🔊 Track 0854

n. 碎片；炸洋芋片；瑣碎之物

▶ Fish and chips are one of Britain's national dishes.
炸魚薯條是英國的國民小吃。

v. 削；鑿；把……切成薄片

▶ She chipped a hole on the door.
她在門上鑿了一個洞。

相關片語 **chip in for** 為……而湊錢

▶ We chipped in for a rental car.
我們湊錢租了一輛車。

chirp [tʃɝp]
🔊 Track 0855

v. 發出啾啾聲；唧唧喳喳地說話

▶ I sat on the porch listening to birds chirping among the trees. 我坐在門廊聽著樹上的小鳥啾啾地叫著。

n. 啾啾聲；唧唧聲

▶ We heard the cheerful chirps of the birds outside the window. 我們聽到窗外小鳥開心的啾啾聲。

chocolate [`tʃɑkəlɪt]
🔊 Track 0856

n. 巧克力；巧克力糖；巧克力飲料

▶ She received a box of chocolate from her boyfriend on Valentine's Day.
她在情人節收到男友送的一盒巧克力。

choice [tʃɔɪs] n. 選擇
🔊 Track 0857

▶ You can't have your cake and eat it. You've got to make a choice. 魚與熊掌不可兼得，你得做出個選擇。

choir [kwaɪr]
🔊 Track 0858

n. 合唱團；唱詩班

▶ The Vienna Boys' Choir performed a series of concerts in Taiwan. 維也納少年合唱團在台灣舉辦一系列的演唱會。

choke [tʃok]
🔊 Track 0859

v. 使窒息；掐住脖子；哽住；說不出話來；塞住

▶ The family was almost choked by the heavy smoke. 這戶人家差點被濃煙窒息了。

中級

n. 窒息；嗆

▶What should we do during a food choke? 我們吃東西噎到時該怎麼處置？

cholesterol
Track 0860

[kə`lɛstə͵rol] **n.** 膽固醇

▶Our body needs cholesterol, but too much can raise the risk of heart disease. 我們的身體需要膽固醇，但過量會提高心臟病的風險。

choose [tʃuz] **v.** 選擇
Track 0861

▶He chose a ring for his fiancée. 他幫未婚妻選了一枚戒指。

chop [tʃap]
Track 0862

v. 砍；劈；切細、剁碎

▶She chopped up the nuts and added them to the dough. 她把堅果切碎混入麵團。

n. 砍；劈；剁；肋骨肉、排骨

▶The pork chops were tender and juicy. 這些豬排鮮嫩多汁。

chopstick [`tʃap͵stɪk]
Track 0863

n. 筷子

▶I can't use chopsticks. May I have a fork? 我不會用筷子，可以給我一支叉子嗎？

chore [tʃor]
Track 0864

n. 家庭雜務；日常瑣碎而例行的工作

▶A career woman, she's juggling between work and house chores everyday. 身為職業婦女，她每天都忙碌於工作和家務之中。

chorus [`korəs]
Track 0865

n. 合唱團；合唱曲；副歌

▶We burst into a chorus of Merry Christmas. 我們突然齊唱聖誕快樂歌。

Christian [`krɪstʃən]
Track 0866

adj. 基督教的

▶Red Cross is a Christian charity. 紅十字會是基督教慈善團體。

n. 基督教徒

▶My aunt is a devout Christian. 我的嬸嬸是虔誠的基督徒。

Christmas [`krɪsməs] =X·mas **n.** 聖誕節
Track 0867

▶As Christmas is approaching, many people are preparing gifts for their family and friends. 隨著聖誕節的來臨，許多人都在為親朋好友準備禮物。

chubby [`tʃʌbɪ]
Track 0868

adj. 豐腴的；圓胖的

▶She has chubby cheeks and some freckles on her nose. 她有豐腴的臉頰，鼻子上有些雀斑。

church [tʃɝtʃ] **n.** 教堂
Track 0869

▶She goes to church every Sunday morning. 她每個星期天早上都去教堂。

cigar [sɪ`gɑr] **n.** 雪茄煙
Track 0870

▶Grandpa, can I have a puff of your cigar? 阿公，我可以吸一口你的雪茄煙嗎？

cigarette [͵sɪgə`rɛt]
Track 0871

n. 香菸

▶Smoke cigarettes is an expensive habit. 抽菸是很花錢的習慣。

cinema [`sɪnəmə]
Track 0872

n. 電影院；一部電影

▶Do you want to go to the cinema with us after work? 你要和我們下班一起看電影嗎？

補充片語 go to the cinema 去看電影

---

circle [`sɝk!] n. 圓圈
◄Track 0873

▶He drew a circle on the sand.
他在沙子上畫了一個圓圈。

---

circular [`sɝkjələ]
◄Track 0874

adj. 圓的；迂迴的；拐彎抹角的

▶The company's logo is in circular shape. 公司的標識是圓形的。

---

circulate [`sɝkjə‚let]
◄Track 0875

v. 循環；傳播；流通

▶The news was instantaneously circulated around the world. 新聞即時在世界傳開了。

---

circulation
◄Track 0876

[‚sɝkjə`leʃən] **n.** 循環；（貨幣或消息的）傳播；（報刊的）發行

▶The circulation of the magazine was more than 500,000 last year. 這本雜誌的銷量去年超過五十萬本。。

---

circumstance
◄Track 0877

[`sɝkəm‚stæns] **n.** 情況；環境

▶Under no circumstances should you abuse animals. 無論在什麼樣的情況下，你都不應該虐待動物。

補充片語 under no circumstances
在任何情況下都不……

---

circus [`sɝkəs]
◄Track 0878

n. 馬戲團；馬戲表演

▶The show of the Circus du Soleil was absolutely amazing. 太陽馬戲團的表演真是太精彩了。

---

citizen [`sɪtəzn]
◄Track 0879

n. 市民；居民；公民

▶He emigrated to the United States and became the country's citizen. 他移民到美國並成為美國公民。

---

city [`sɪtɪ] n. 城市
◄Track 0880

▶She lives in Taipei City. 她住在台北市。

---

civil [`sɪv!]
◄Track 0881

adj. 市民的；民用的；民事的；文明的；國內的

▶Many people in that country were displaced because of the civil war. 那個國家許多人民因為內戰而流離失所。

補充片語 civil war 內戰

---

civilian [sɪ`vɪljən]
◄Track 0882

adj. 平民的；百姓的

▶A total of 3,680 civilian casualties was documented in the report. 報告記錄共有三千六百八十名老百姓傷亡。

n. 平民；百姓

▶The dictator used weapons of mass destruction against the civilians. 獨裁者用大規模毀滅性武器對付老百姓。

補充片語 weapons of mass destruction 大規模毀滅性武器

---

civilization
◄Track 0883

[‚sɪvlə`zeʃən]

n. 文明；文明國家；文明世界；文明設施；開化

▶The Maya civilizations was developed by the Maya peoples. 馬雅文明是由馬雅人發展出來的。

中級

civilize [`sɪvə‚laɪz] ◀Track 0884

v. 使文明；使開化；教化；熏陶；使有教養

▶Kyle is a civilized man.
凱爾是個有教養的人。

claim [klem] ◀Track 0885

v. 要求；主張；聲稱

▶He claimed that he was innocent.
他堅稱自己是無辜的。

n. 要求；主張；斷言

▶She made a claim to the property.
她主張她有權利獲得這筆財產。

clap [klæp] ◀Track 0886

v. 拍（手）；鼓（掌）

▶The audience clapped unwillingly.
觀眾不情願地拍手。

n. 拍手鼓掌；喝彩

▶We gave the pianist a big clap.
我們給鋼琴家熱烈的鼓掌。

clarify [`klærə‚faɪ] ◀Track 0887

v. 澄清；闡明

▶She issued a statement to clarify the mystery. 她發出聲明澄清這個謎團。

clash [klæʃ] ◀Track 0888

n. 碰撞聲；衝突；不協調

▶The negotiation ended up in a violent clash. 談判在激烈的衝突中結束。

補充片語 end up in 以⋯⋯結束

v. 碰地相撞；發生衝突；抵觸

▶The demonstrators clashed with the police, prompting the police to use water cannons to stop the riot. 示威者與警方發生衝突，使得警方動用水槍停止這場暴動。

class [klæs] ◀Track 0889

n. 班級；課；（社會）階級、等級

▶They played dodge ball in the PE class.
他們在體育課打躲閃球。

classic [`klæsɪk] ◀Track 0890

adj. 典型的；經典的

▶This is a classic example of Ponzi scheme. 這是典型龐氏騙局的例子。

補充片語 Ponzi scheme 龐氏騙局

n. 典型事物；著名事件；經典名著

▶*Les Misérables* is a literary classic.
《悲慘世界》是文學經典名著。

classical [`klæsɪkl] ◀Track 0891

adj. 經典的，古典的

▶Her favorite music genre is classical music. 她最喜歡的音樂類型是古典樂。

classification ◀Track 0892

[‚klæsəfə`keʃən] **n.** 分類；類別

▶Most public libraries use Dewey Decimal classifications to arrange books on the shelves. 大部分的公共圖書館是用杜威十進位圖書分類法將各類書歸在書架上。

classify [`klæsə‚faɪ] ◀Track 0893

v. 將⋯⋯分類；將⋯⋯歸類

▶Librarians usually spend a lot of time classifying books. 館員通常都花很多的時間在歸類書。

classmate ◀Track 0894

[`klæs‚met] **n.** 同班同學

▶Peter and I have been classmates since we were in kindergarten. 彼德和我從幼稚園就是同班同學。

classroom
◀Track 0895

[`klæs͵rʊm] n. 教室

▶The students are learning English in the classroom. 學生在教室學習英語。

claw [klɔ] n. 爪子；手
◀Track 0896

▶Tigers and lions have sharp claws.
老虎和獅子都有銳利的爪子。

v. 用爪子抓、撕、挖；費力奪回

▶My cat clawed the sofa and pulled the table cloth until everything fell down.
我的貓用爪子抓沙發，又把桌巾拉下來，把桌面的東西全翻倒了。

clay [kle] n. 黏土；泥土
◀Track 0897

▶She used a clay mask to purify her skin. 她用泥土面膜淨化皮膚。

clean [klin] v. 清潔
◀Track 0898

▶Mom cleaned the kitchen sink after dinner. 媽媽在晚餐後清洗廚房水槽。

adj. 乾淨的

▶His apartment is always neat and clean. 他的公寓總是整齊乾淨。

cleaner [`klinɚ]
◀Track 0899

n. 清潔工；乾洗店；清潔劑

▶She is an office cleaner.
她是辦公室的清潔工。

cleanse [klɛnz]
◀Track 0900

v. 清乾淨

▶She cleansed her face with this foaming gel. 她用這個會起泡的凝膠洗臉。

clear [klɪr]
◀Track 0901

adj. 清楚的；清澈的

▶After the rain, the sky was clear and blue. 下雨後，天空變得明朗又湛藍。

v. 清除；收拾；使乾淨；使清楚

▶He cleared the leftovers in the fridge.
他把冰箱的剩菜清掉。

clearance [`klɪrəns]
◀Track 0902

n. 清除；出空；清倉大拍賣

▶She bought the quilt at a clearance sale. 她在清倉特賣期間買了這件被子。

補充片語 clearance sale
清倉特賣；出清特賣

clerk [klɝk]
◀Track 0903

n. 店員；辦事員

▶He was a bank clerk. 他是銀行行員。

clever [`klɛvɚ]
◀Track 0904

adj. 聰明的；靈巧的

▶His dog is clever and can flip open a door handle. 他的狗很聰明，會用門把開門。

click [klɪk]
◀Track 0905

v. 發出咔嗒聲；按壓滑鼠以點選

▶Double-click the icon to start the program. 在電腦圖示點兩下，以驅動程式。

n. 咔嗒聲；按一下滑鼠

▶People nowadays are accustomed to everything being just a click away—be that online shopping, chatting, or music. 現代人很習慣透過按滑鼠完成事情，無論是網購、聊天或聽音樂。

client [`klaɪənt] n. 客戶
◀Track 0906

▶He is an important client of our company. 他是我們公司重要的客戶。

中級

cliff [klɪf] n. 懸崖
◀Track 0907

▶She jumped off the cliff and glided over the sea. 她在懸崖邊跳下，乘著划翔傘在海上翔翔。

climate [ˋklaɪmɪt]
◀Track 0908

n. 氣候

▶The climate in this country is mild. 這個國家的氣候很溫和。

climax [ˋklaɪmæks]
◀Track 0909

n. 頂點；最高點

▶The movie reached a climax when the audience discovered that the innocent lady was a double agent. 這部電影在觀眾發現這名無辜的女孩原來是雙面間諜時，達到了最高峰。

climb [klaɪm] v. 爬；攀爬
◀Track 0910

▶She was the first woman to climb up Mount Everest. 她是第一位登上聖母峰的女性。

climber [ˋklaɪmɚ]
◀Track 0911

n. 攀登者；登山者

▶The climbers stayed in a cave during a snow storm. 登山者在暴風雪降臨時待在洞穴中。

climbing [ˋklaɪmɪŋ]
◀Track 0912

n. 攀登

▶We went mountain climbing last weekend. 我們上個週末去登山。

clinic [ˋklɪnɪk]
◀Track 0913

n. 診所；臨床授課；會診

▶This is a walk-in eye clinic. 這是可以臨時看診的眼科診所。

clip [klɪp] n. 夾；迴紋針
◀Track 0914

▶He removed his tie clip and unknotted his tie. 他拿掉領帶夾並解開領帶。

v. 用夾子夾緊；用迴紋針夾住

▶He clipped the worksheets together. 他把活頁練習題用夾子夾在一起。

clock [klɑk] n. 時鐘
◀Track 0915

▶The clock is a bit fast. 時鐘有點走快了。

clockwise
◀Track 0916

[ˋklɑkˌwaɪz] adj. 順時針方向的

▶The fan runs at a slow speed in a clockwise direction. 電扇以順時針方向慢慢地轉著。

adv. 順時針方向地

▶Does the Milky Way rotate clockwise or counterclockwise? 銀河是以順時針方向或逆時針方向旋轉？

clone [klon]
◀Track 0917

n. 翻版；複製人；複製品；一味仿效的人

▶She looked like a clone of Angelina Jolie. 她看起來像是安潔莉娜 裘莉的翻版。

close [klos]
◀Track 0918

v. 關起；關閉；結束

▶Do you mind if I close the window? 你介意我把窗戶關起來嗎？

n. 結束；末尾

▶He made a short conclusion at the close of the meeting. 他在會議結束時做簡短的結論。

adj. （距離）近的；（關係）親近的

▶He is very close with his parents. 他和雙親關係很親近。

adv. 接近地；緊密地

▶The little girl held her teddy bear close.
小女孩緊抱著她的泰迪熊。

closet [`klɑzɪt] n. 衣櫃
◀Track 0919

▶There is a beautiful closet in the guest room.
客房有一個很漂亮的衣櫃。

cloth [klɔθ]
◀Track 0920

n. 布；織物；衣料

▶She used a cloth to wipe the table.
她用一塊抹布擦拭餐桌。

clothe [kloð]
◀Track 0921

n. 為……穿衣；為……提供衣服

▶His laughed when he saw how his wife clothed the children for the Halloween.
他看到妻子幫小孩穿了萬聖節服裝，不禁笑了出來。

clothed [kloðd]
◀Track 0922

adj. 穿……衣服的

▶The weather was so cold that even some dogs were clothed .
天氣太冷，甚至有些主人也幫狗穿了衣服。

clothes [kloz] n. 衣服
◀Track 0923

▶She made clothes for her children.
她幫自己的小孩做衣服。

clothing [`kloðɪŋ]
◀Track 0924

n. 衣服；衣著

▶He is the manager of a clothing company.
他是一家服飾公司的經理。

cloud [klaʊd] n. 雲
◀Track 0925

▶The white cloud looked like cotton candy. 白雲看起來很像棉花糖。

v. （煙霧）籠罩；瀰漫；使模糊；使混濁

▶His face was clouded with despair.
他的臉充滿著絕望感。

相關片語 **on cloud nine**
欣喜若狂；樂上雲霄

▶She was on cloud nine when she got the admission letter from Yale. 她收到耶魯大學的入學許可函時欣喜若狂。

cloudy [`klaʊdɪ]
◀Track 0926

adj. 多雲的；陰天的

▶It was a windy and cloudy day.
那是個風大又多雲的一天。

clover [`klovɚ]
◀Track 0927

n. 紅花草；苜蓿；三葉草

▶Four-leaf clovers are considered a sign of good luck. 四葉草被視為是幸運的象徵。

相關片語 **live in clover** 生活優逸

▶Since she became a super model, her family has lived in clover. 她成為超模後，家人從此過著安逸舒適的生活。

clown [klaʊn] n. 小丑
◀Track 0928

▶He is the family clown. 他是家裡的小丑。

v. 扮小丑；開玩笑；裝傻

▶The children clowned around when their parents were not home. 父母不在家，小孩在家一片胡鬧。

club [klʌb]
◀Track 0929

n. （運動、娛樂等的）俱樂部；會所

▶Do you want to join the tennis club?
你想參加網球社嗎？

clue [klu]
◀Track 0930

n. 線索；提示；跡象

中級

▶She had no clue that her boyfriend was a double agent. 她根本不知道男友是雙面間諜。

clumsy [`klʌmzɪ] ◀ Track 0931
adj. 笨拙的

▶The dog seemed weak, clumsy, and sad. 這隻小狗看起來很虛弱、肢體不靈活又傷心。

coach [kotʃ] ◀ Track 0932
n. （運動隊的）教練；巴士；長途公車

▶Jack is a basketball coach.
傑克是籃球教練。

coal [kol] ◀ Track 0933
n. 煤；煤塊；木炭

▶We added more coal into the fire.
我們在火堆中加入更多的煤炭。

coarse [kors] ◀ Track 0934
adj. 粗的；粗糙的；粗劣的；粗俗的

▶She had a cold and her voice became coarse. 她得了感冒，聲音變得很沙啞。

coast [kost] **n.** 海岸 ◀ Track 0935
▶New York is located in the eastern coast of the United States. 紐約位在美國東岸。

coat [kot] ◀ Track 0936
n. 外套；（動物的）皮毛

▶It's cold outside. Put on your coat before you leave the house. 外面很冷。出門前先把外套穿起來。

cock [kak] **n.** 公雞 ◀ Track 0937
▶I was woken up by the crowing of the cocks. 我被公雞的叫聲吵醒。

cockroach [`kak,rotʃ] ◀ Track 0938
=roach n. 蟑螂

▶I hate cockroaches, especially those that can fly. 我討厭蟑螂，特別是會飛的那種。

cocktail [`kak,tel] ◀ Track 0939
n. 雞尾酒

▶We invited him to the cocktail party.
我們邀請他參加雞尾酒會。

cocoa [`koko] **n.** 可可粉 ◀ Track 0940
▶She used cocoa when making a chocolate cake. 她用可可粉做巧克力蛋糕。

coconut [`kokə,nət] ◀ Track 0941
n. 椰子；椰子肉

▶He sold freshly picked coconuts in the market. 他在市場賣鮮採的椰子。

相關片語 **coconut milk** 椰奶

▶She added some coconut milk into the red bean soup.
她在紅豆湯裡加一些椰奶。

code [kod] **n.** 規則；代碼 ◀ Track 0942
▶The dress code for the banquet is formal. 這場晚宴的服裝規定是正式服裝。

補充片語 **dress code** 服裝規定

v. 為……編碼

▶The boy was coding his robot to walk to the destination. 男童正在編寫讓他的機器人走到目的地的程式碼。

coffee [`kɔfɪ] **n.** 咖啡 ◀ Track 0943
▶I'd like a cup of coffee without sugar.
我要一杯不加糖的咖啡。

coffin [`kɔfɪn] **n.** 棺材　　◀€Track 0944

▶His coffin was covered with the national flag. 他的棺材用國旗覆蓋著。

v. 入殮；將……放進棺材

▶The body of their dead child was coffined. 他們死去的孩子已經入殮。

相關片語 **drive a nail into one's coffin**
促死某人早死；加速某人死亡

▶A drug addict, he is literally driving a nail into his coffin. 他是吸毒成癮者，根本就是加速自己死亡。

coin [kɔɪn] **n.** 錢幣　　◀€Track 0945

▶Students donated coins to the charity. 學生捐贈錢幣到慈善機構。

coincidence　　◀€Track 0946

[ko`ɪnsɪdəns] **n.** 巧合；同時發生的事；符合

▶Do you think it was a coincidence that he was the person of interest in two identity theft investigations? 他在兩件身分竊盜案的調查都是嫌疑犯，你認為是純屬巧合嗎？

補充片語 **person of interest** 嫌疑犯

Coke [kok] **n.** 可樂　　◀€Track 0947

▶He drinks two bottles of coke everyday. 他每天都喝兩瓶可樂。

cold [kold] **adj.** 冷的　　◀€Track 0948

▶It was so cold during the New Year holidays. 新年假期期間天氣很冷。

n. 寒冷；感冒

▶He caught a cold and took a day-off. 他感冒請假了。

collapse [kə`læps]　　◀€Track 0949

v. 倒塌；崩潰；瓦解

▶The man suddenly collapsed and fell into a coma during his birthday party. 男子在慶生時突然倒下陷入昏迷。

n. 倒塌；崩潰；突然失敗；（健康）衰竭、垮掉

▶The collapse of the dilapidated building was inevitable. 這棟殘破的建築會倒塌是不可避免的。

collar [`kɑlɚ]　　◀€Track 0950

n. 衣領、領子；狗的項圈

▶There are many yellow stains on the collar of his shirt. 他的襯衫上有許多黃污漬。

相關片語 **get hot under the collar**
發怒

▶She got hot under the collar when she heard people speaking ill of her. 她聽到別人在她背後說她的壞話時，勃然大怒。

colleague [kɑ`lig]　　◀€Track 0951

n. 同事

▶He doesn't get along with his colleagues. 他跟同事處得不好。

collect [kə`lɛkt]　　◀€Track 0952

v. 收集；領取

▶She has the habit of collecting stamps. 她有收集郵票的習慣。

collection [kə`lɛkʃən]　　◀€Track 0953

n. 收集；收藏品

▶I have a collection of Marvel comic books. 我收藏了漫威的漫畫書。

collector [kə`lɛktɚ]　　◀€Track 0954

n. 收集者；收藏家；收費員；收票員

▶He is a collector of foreign coins. 他是個外幣收藏家。

中級

college [`kɑlɪdʒ] n. 大學 ◀Track 0955

▶He majored in physics and chemistry at college. 他大學主修物理學和化學。

collide [kə`laɪd] ◀Track 0956

v. 碰撞；相撞；衝突

▶The two cars collided at the intersection. 兩輛汽車在十字路口發生碰撞。

colony [`kɑlənɪ] ◀Track 0957

n. 殖民地；僑居地

▶Hong Kong used to be a colony of the United Kingdom.
香港曾是英國的殖民地。

color [`kʌlɚ] ◀Track 0958
=colour （英式英文） n. 顏色；色彩

▶My favorite color is green.
我最喜歡的顏色是綠色。

v. 著色；塗上顏色

▶The boy was coloring the picture with felt-tip pens. 男童用彩色筆在圖上著色。

補充片語 felt-tip pen 彩色筆

colored [`kʌlɚd] ◀Track 0959
adj. 有顏色的；彩色的；著色的；
　　經渲染的；帶有偏見的

▶The teacher used colored chalks to highlight key points.
老師用彩色粉筆強調重點。

colorful [`kʌlɚfəl] ◀Track 0960
=colourful （英式英文）
adj. 色彩豐富的；多彩多姿的

▶His paintings are colorful and full of life. 他的畫作色彩豐富、充滿生命力。

column [`kɑləm] ◀Track 0961
n.（報紙的）欄；（報紙、雜誌的）
　　短評欄、專欄

▶He is a freelance journalist for the science column of the daily newspaper. 他在這家每日發行的報紙擔任科技專欄的自由記者。

comb [kom] ◀Track 0962
n. 梳子；梳理

▶He always carries a comb in his pocket.
他的口袋總是攜帶一把梳子。

v. 梳頭

▶She combed her hair before leaving the house. 她出門前先梳理頭髮。

combination ◀Track 0963
[ˌkɑmbə`neʃən] n. 混合；混合體；組合

▶This medicine cannot be used in combination with sleeping pills. 這個藥不能和安眠藥混合服用。

combine [kəm`baɪn] ◀Track 0964
v. 使結合；兼有

▶The writer combined wit and humor in his novel. 作家在他的小說結合了詼諧和幽默。

combined [kəm`baɪnd] ◀Track 0965
adj. 聯合的；共同的；多功能組合的

▶What we have accomplished is the result of combined effort. 我們所成就的事情是大家共同努力的成果。

come [kʌm] v. 來 ◀Track 0966

▶Come here and join our chitchat.
來這裡加入我們的閒聊吧。

comedian ◀Track 0967

[kə`midɪən] n. 喜劇演員；逗人開心的人

▶Jack Black is my favorite comedian.
傑克・布萊克是我最喜歡的喜劇演員。

comedy [`kɑmədɪ] ◀Track 0968
n. 喜劇

▶*Shallow Hal* is one of my favorite comedies.
《情人眼裡出西施》是我最喜歡的喜劇之一。

comet [`kɑmɪt] n. 彗星 ◀Track 0969
▶Scientists still cannot predict the comet's orbit. 科學家仍無法預測這顆彗星的軌道。

comfort [`kʌmfɚt] ◀Track 0970
n. 安逸；舒適；使人舒服的設備；
　　給予安慰 的東西

▶She enjoyed the comfort of the bed, sofa, and appliances of the apartment.
她很享受公寓裡的床、沙發和電器。

v. 安慰；慰問

▶The social workers tried to comfort the grieving mother.
社工試著安慰這位悲傷的母親。

相關片語 **comfort food**
　　　　　讓人感到開心的食物；療癒食物

▶Pea crackers is the comfort food I need right now.
我現在最想吃的療癒食物是豌豆酥。

comfortable ◀Track 0971
[`kʌmfɚtəbl] **adj.** 舒適的；自在的

▶We felt comfortable at the party.
我們在派對感到很自在。

comfortably ◀Track 0972
[`kʌmfɚtəblɪ] **adv.** 舒適地；舒服地

▶My cat was lying comfortably on the sofa. 我的貓在沙發舒服地躺著。

相關片語 **comfortably off** 生活寬裕

▶She worked hard even though she was very comfortably off. 她生活很寬裕，但仍很努力工作。

comic [`kɑmɪk] ◀Track 0973
adj. 喜劇般的；連環漫畫的

▶The boy is reading Doraemon comic books. 男孩正在看《哆啦A夢》漫畫書。

n. 連環漫畫；連環漫畫書

▶I liked to read the comics on the newspaper. 我喜歡看報紙的連環漫畫。

coming [`kʌmɪŋ] ◀Track 0974
adj. 即將到來的

▶The meeting will be held this coming Friday. 會議在即將到來的星期五舉行。

comma [`kɑmə] ◀Track 0975
n. 逗號；停頓

▶Where should I put a comma in this sentence?
我應該在這個句子哪裡加逗號呢？

command [kə`mænd] ◀Track 0976
v. 命令，指揮

▶The general commanded the troops to cease fire. 將軍命令部隊停火。

commander ◀Track 0977
[kə`mændɚ] **n.** 指揮官；司令官

▶He was a commander of the US navy.
他是美國海軍的指揮官。

comment [`kɑmɛnt] ◀Track 0978
n. 批評；議論

▶I have no comment on this issue.
我對這個議題不予評論。

v. 發表意見；評論

▶He commented that the policy was not feasible. 他評論這個政策並不可行。

commerce [ˋkɑmɝs]　◀Track 0979
n. 商業；貿易；交易；（思想）交流

▶E-commerce is convenient and fast. 電子貿易很便利快速。

commercial　◀Track 0980
[kəˋmɝʃəl]
adj. 商業的；以營利為目的的；工業用的

▶The commercial airline is considered one of the safest in the world. 這家商業航空公司被視為擁有全球最安全的飛安紀錄之一。

n. 商業廣告

▶This TV commercial is controversial. 這支電視廣告很有爭議性。

相關片語 **commercial break** 播廣告的空檔

▶He stretched his limbs during the commercial break. 他趁播廣告的空檔伸展一下四肢。

commission　◀Track 0981
[kəˋmɪʃən] **n.** 佣金；（權限或任務的）委託

▶The modeling agency gets a 10% commission from booking shoots for its models. 模特兒經紀公司從為旗下模特兒安排的拍照工作中抽取百分之十的佣金。

v. 委任；委託；任命

▶The company was commissioned to build the metro transit system. 這家公司被委託製造大眾運輸系統。

相關片語 **out of commission** 退出現役；不工作

▶My cell phone is out of commission. 我的手機壞掉了。

commit [kəˋmɪt]　◀Track 0982
v. 做（錯事）；犯（罪）

▶The man confessed that he committed homicide. 男人坦承犯下殺人罪。

相關片語 **commit suicide** 自殺

▶Committing suicide will not solve your problems. 自殺是不會解決你的問題的。

commitment　◀Track 0983
[kəˋmɪtmənt] **n.** 承諾

▶Her commitment to Buddhism is apparent. 她很明顯地篤信佛教。

committee [kəˋmɪtɪ]　◀Track 0984
n. 委員會

▶The committee was convened by the director-general. 委員會是由局長召開。

common [ˋkɑmən]　◀Track 0985
adj. 一般的；共同的

▶John is a very common name. 約翰是很常見的名字。

commonplace　◀Track 0986
[ˋkɑmənˏples]
adj. 普通平凡的；陳腐的；平淡無味的

▶Laptops are commonplace these days. 筆電現在變得非常普遍。

n. 司空見慣的事；老生常談

▶Night markets are a commonplace here. 夜市在這裡是很常見的。

communicate　◀Track 0987
[kəˋmjunəˏket] **v.** 溝通

▶The manager tried to communicate with the difficult customer. 經理試著跟奧客溝通。

communication
◀€ Track 0988

[kə‚mjunə`keʃən] **n.** 溝通

▶Employees in that company are required to take a course on communication skills. 那家公司的員工被要求去上溝通技巧的課程。

communist
◀€ Track 0989

[`kamjʊ‚nɪst]

adj. 共產主義的；共產黨的；支持共產主義的

▶North Korea is a communist country. 北韓是個共產主義的國家。

n. 共產主義；共產黨員

▶The country's officials are all communists. 這個國家的官員都是共產黨員。

community
◀€ Track 0990

[kə`mjunətɪ]

n. 社區；共同社會；（一般）社會大眾；（財產）共有

▶She is an active volunteer in the community. 她在這個社區是很活躍的義工。

companion
◀€ Track 0991

[kəm`pænjən] **n.** 同伴；伴侶；朋友

▶My aunt is a good companion for my mother. 我的阿姨是我媽媽的好同伴。

相關片語 **travelling companion** 旅伴

▶Kathy is not only my soul mate, but also a good travelling companion. 凱西不僅是我的靈魂伴侶，也是很好的旅伴。

company [`kʌmpənɪ]
◀€ Track 0992

n. 公司

▶He established a company that manufactured lithium batteries. 他成立一家專門製造鋰電池的公司。

補充片語 **lithium battery** 鋰電池

comparative
◀€ Track 0993

[kəm`pærətɪv]

adj. 比較的；用比較方法的；比較而言的；相對的

▶She studied comparative literature at college. 她大學時曾學習比較文學。

compare [kəm`pɛr]
◀€ Track 0994

v. 比較；對照

▶He compared the prices of the same piece of furniture from different shops before placing an order. 他比較同件家具在不同店家的售價後，才決定下單。

compared [kəm`pɛrd]
◀€ Track 0995

adj. 比照的；對照的

▶Compared with her, I'm a terrible cook. 相較於她，我的烹飪技巧顯得拙劣。

comparison
◀€ Track 0996

[kəm`pærəsn] **n.** 比較

▶The students made a comparison of different countries' cultures in their presentations.
學生做報告比較不同國家的文化。

相關片語 **out of all comparison**
無與倫比

▶His magic show is out of all comparison. 他的魔術秀真是無與倫比。

compass [`kʌmpəs]
◀€ Track 0997

n. 羅盤；指南針

▶They brought a compass and a map when they went trekking. 他們旅行時帶了一個指南針和地圖。

中級

compete [kəmˋpit] 🔊 Track 0998

v 與……競爭；媲美、比得上

▶My calligraphy cannot compete with my grandfather's. 我的書法不及我祖父。

competition 🔊 Track 0999

[ˌkɑmpəˋtɪʃən] **n** 競爭；比賽；競爭對手

▶Alpha Go defeated the world's top chess player in a chess competition. 阿法圍棋在一場圍棋比賽中擊敗了世界頂尖的圍棋選手。

competitive 🔊 Track 1000

[kəmˋpɛtətɪv]

adj 競爭的；競爭性的；好競爭的

▶The entertainment industry is highly competitive. 演藝圈是高度競爭的行業。

competitor 🔊 Track 1001

[kəmˋpɛtətɚ] **n** 競爭者；對手

▶He is a formidable competitor. 他是個很難對付的競爭對手。

complain [kəmˋplen] 🔊 Track 1002

v 抱怨

▶She complained to the restaurant about their service. 她向餐廳抱怨服務不周。

complaint [kəmˋplent] 🔊 Track 1003

n 抱怨；投訴；怨言

▶The customer made a complaint about the car he just bought from a dealer. 顧客投訴有關最近向代理商買的車子。

complete [kəmˋplit] 🔊 Track 1004

v 完成；使完整

▶We completed the project before the deadline. 我們在期限前完成這項計畫。

adj 完整的；結束的；兼有的

▶The apartment is complete with furniture. 這棟公寓帶有家具。

completion 🔊 Track 1005

[kəmˋpliʃən] **n** 完整

▶The railway is due for completion today. 這條鐵路今天為完工期。

complex [ˋkɑmplɛks] 🔊 Track 1006

adj 錯綜複雜的；複合的、合成的

▶The structure of the organization is very complex. 這個機構的架構很複雜。

n 複合物；綜合體

▶The newly completed sports and leisure complex will open in May. 這座剛完工的運動休閒中心將在五月啟用。

complicate 🔊 Track 1007

[ˋkɑmpləˌket] **v** 使複雜

▶The reforms actually complicated the current situation. 這項改革實際上使目前的情勢更加複雜。

complicated 🔊 Track 1008

[ˋkɑmpləˌketɪd]

adj 複雜的；難懂的

▶This essay is complicated and difficult to understand. 這篇文章很複雜難懂。

compliment 🔊 Track 1009

[ˋkɑmpləmənt] **n** 讚美；恭維

▶Your compliment really elevated my spirits. 你的讚美真的提振了我的士氣。

v 讚美

▶I complimented him on his achievements. 我讚美他的成就。

compose [kəm`poz] ◀ Track 1010

v. 作（詩曲）；構（圖）；組成、構成；使鎮靜

▶ Carbon dioxide is composed of two oxygen atoms and one carbon atom.
二氧化碳是由兩個氧原子和一個碳原子所組成的。

補充片語 **be composed of** 由……組成

相關片語 **compose oneself** 使鎮定下來

▶ He managed to compose himself during the accident.
他在意外發生時，設法讓自己冷靜下來。

composer [kəm`pozə] ◀ Track 1011

n. 作曲家；調停者

▶ He is the lead singer and composer of the band. 他是樂團的主唱兼作曲家。

composition [ˌkɑmpə`zɪʃən] ◀ Track 1012

n. 寫作；作曲；作文；構圖；成分；合成物

▶ The teacher is correcting students' English compositions.
老師正在批改學生的英文作文。

compound [kɑm`paʊnd] ◀ Track 1013

n. 混合物；化合物

▶ His character was a singular compound of honesty and courage.
他的人格是誠實和勇氣的非凡組合。

adj. 複合的

▶ Here is the compound interest chart for your reference.
這張複利圖表可以供你參考。

補充片語 **compound interest** 複利

v. 使混合；用合成方法製作；加重

▶ The bad news only compounded the situation.
這個壞消息只是使情勢變得更惡劣。

comprehension [ˌkɑmprɪ`hɛnʃən] ◀ Track 1014

n. 理解；理解力

▶ The theory of relativity is beyond my comprehension.
相對論超過我能理解的範圍。

補充片語 **beyond one's comprehension** 某人難以理解的

compute [kəm`pjut] ◀ Track 1015

v. 計算；估算

▶ The judges computed the scores and announced the winner. 裁判計算分數並宣布冠軍得主。

computer [kəm`pjutə] ◀ Track 1016

n. 電腦

▶ Computers are a commonplace in our daily life.
電腦是我們日常生活很尋常的物品。

conceal [kən`sil] ◀ Track 1017

v. 隱藏；隱瞞

▶ She concealed her age in order to audition for the lead role of the musical. 她為了參加這個音樂劇的試鏡而隱瞞年齡。

concentrate [`kɑnsɛnˌtret] ◀ Track 1018

v. 集中；聚集；全力以赴；全神貫注

▶ He concentrated on his lab work.
他專注在實驗室的工作。

中級

concentration ◀€Track 1019

[ˌkɑnsɛn`treʃən] **n.** 集中；專心

▶I lost concentration when the TV was on. 電視開著時，我的注意力就分散了。

concept [`kɑnsɛpt] ◀€Track 1020

n. 概念；觀念；思想

▶The concept of beauty varies in different cultures. 在不同的文化對美的觀念各異。

concern [kən`sɝn] ◀€Track 1021

n. 關心的事；掛念

▶He expressed his concerns about the matter. 他表達這件事情的關心。

v. 關於；關係到；使關心、使擔心、使不安

▶The news concerned the elections. 這件新聞與選舉有關。

concerning ◀€Track 1022

[kən`sɝnɪŋ] **prep.** 關於

▶We received several e-mails concerning the animal cruelty case. 我們收到幾封與虐待動物相關案件的電郵。

concert [`kɑnsɝt] ◀€Track 1023

n. 音樂會；演奏會

▶The singer will hold a series of concerts in the stadium. 這名歌手將在體育館舉辦一系列的演唱會。

conclude [kən`klud] ◀€Track 1024

v. 結束；推斷出；最後決定為

▶The chairman of the committee concluded the meeting by 4:00 P.M. 委員會的主席在下午四點前結束會議。

conclusion ◀€Track 1025

[kən`kluʒən] **n.** 結論；結果；締結；議定

▶He jumped to a conclusion but later found he made the wrong judgment. 他倉促下結論後來發現他做了錯誤的判斷。

補充片語 jump to a conclusion/ conclusions 匆匆下結論

concrete [`kɑnkrit] ◀€Track 1026

adj. 有形的；具體的

▶Quilts and clothes are concrete objects. 被子和衣服是實體的物件。

n. 具體物；混凝土

▶The office building was built with concrete, steel, and composite materials. 這棟辦公室建築是用混凝土、鋼筋和複合材料所建造的。

condition [kən`dɪʃən] ◀€Track 1027

n. 狀況；條件；情況；環境、形式

▶The foreign labors worked in terrible conditions. 外籍勞工在很糟的情況下工作。

v. 決定；為……的條件；使處於良好狀態

▶The dog was conditioned to expect food upon hearing the bell. 小狗被制約一聽到鈴聲就會期待食物。

相關片語 in condition 身體健康

▶He was very muscular when he was in condition.
他的身體狀況好時，肌肉很壯碩。

conduct [kən`dʌkt] ◀€Track 1028

v. 引導；帶領；管理；處理；指揮

▶The research was conducted by Prof. Smith. 這個研究是由史密斯教授帶領進行的。

n. 品行；行為

▶The private school has a strict code of conduct. 這所私立學校有嚴格的行為準則。

conductor [kən`dʌktə] ◀ Track 1029
n. 領導人；（合唱團或樂隊）指揮

▶He is the principal conductor of the Berlin Symphony Orchestra. 他是柏林愛樂交響樂團的總指揮。

cone [kon] ◀ Track 1030
n. 圓錐體；錐形冰淇淋筒

▶She made ice cream cones and ice cream sandwiches at home. 她在家自製冰淇淋筒和冰淇淋三明治。

conference ◀ Track 1031
[`kɑnfərəns] **n.** 會議；會談

▶The International Conference on Machine Learning will be held in California in June. 機器學習國際會議將於六月在加州舉行。

相關片語 **press conference** 記者會

▶At the press conference, the singer announced that she will married a dancer. 歌手在記者會宣布將嫁給一位舞者。

confess [kən`fɛs] ◀ Track 1032
v. 坦白；承認；懺悔告解

▶She confessed that she poisoned her niece. 她承認對姪女下毒。

confidence ◀ Track 1033
[`kɑnfədəns] **n.** 自信；信心

▶I have complete confidence that you will make a wise decision. 我完全相信你能做出富有智慧的決定。

confident [`kɑnfədənt] ◀ Track 1034
adj. 自信的；有信心的

▶He is a confident and persuasive speaker. 他是個有自信又說服力的演講者。

confine [kən`faɪn] ◀ Track 1035
v. 限制；使侷限

▶AIDS is not merely confined to homosexuals.
愛滋病並不只侷限在同性戀者。

confirm [kən`fɝm] ◀ Track 1036
v. 確定；確認

▶Have you confirmed with the hotel we are going to stay? 你跟我們要留宿的飯店做確認了嗎?

conflict [kən`flɪkt] ◀ Track 1037
n. 衝突

▶The conflict between the two countries is getting out of control. 兩國的衝突日漸失控了。

confront [kən`frʌnt] ◀ Track 1038
v. 面對

▶The politician was confronted by a group of angry people who were upset by his rude remarks. 政治人物不得不面對被他無禮發言所激怒的人民。

confrontation ◀ Track 1039
[ˌkɑnfrʌn`teʃən] **n.** 對質；對抗；衝突

▶There was a verbal confrontation between the employee and his boss.
員工和老闆起了口頭衝突。

Confucius [kən`fjuʃəs] ◀ Track 1040
n. 孔子

▶Confucius was considered the greatest teacher in the Chinese history. 孔子被視為是華人史上最偉大的老師。

confuse [kən`fjuz] ◀ Track 1041
v. 使困惑；搞亂

中級

▶I confused Jack with his twin brother Joe. 我把傑克和他的雙胞胎弟弟喬伊搞混了。

confusion [kən`fjuʒən] ◀ Track 1042
n. 混亂;困惑;混淆

▶She labeled her bookcase to prevent confusion.
她把書包做記號以避免混淆。

congratulate ◀ Track 1043
[kən`grætʃə͵let] **v.** 恭喜

▶He congratulated the president-elect for his success to win the trust of the majority of people. 他恭喜總統當選人贏得大多數人的信任。

congratulation ◀ Track 1044
[kən͵grætʃə`leʃən] **n.** 恭喜

▶I extend my congratulations to you for your re-election. 我恭喜你連任成功。

congress [`kaŋgrəs] ◀ Track 1045
n. 正式會議;代表大會;立法機關;
美國國會;聚會

▶A medical congress on mental health will be held this coming March. 一場有關心理健康的醫學會議將在即將來臨的三月舉行。

conjunction ◀ Track 1046
[kən`dʒʌŋkʃən]
n. 連接詞;結合;連接;同時發生

▶They will work in conjunction with a number of charity organizations. 他們將與數個慈善機構進行工作。

補充片語 in conjunction with
與……一起

connect [kə`nɛkt] ◀ Track 1047
v. 連接;聯想;接通電話

▶With the access to the Internet, you can connect the world whenever you want. 有了網際網路,你可以在任何時間與世界連結。

connection ◀ Track 1048
[kə`nɛkʃən] **n.** 關聯

▶He was charged in connection with the death of his wife. 他因與妻子的死亡有關而被起訴。

補充片語 in connection with
與……有關

conquer [͵kaŋkə] ◀ Track 1049
v. 攻克;佔領;征服;得勝

▶Genghis Khan conquered Eurasia and had faced the challenge of ruling people with different religions. 成吉斯汗征服歐亞大陸並面對統治有各式宗教人民的挑戰。

conscience ◀ Track 1050
[`kanʃəns] **n.** 良心;道德心

▶She didn't show any conscience or remorse after committing the homicide.
她犯了殺人罪卻顯得毫無良知或悔意。

conscious [`kanʃəs] ◀ Track 1051
adj. 意識到的

▶She is health-conscious and eats many vegetables and fruit. 她很有健康意識並吃很多蔬果。

consequence ◀ Track 1052
[`kansə͵kwɛns] **n.** 結果;後果

▶He knew he broke the rule and took the consequence. 他知道自己違反規定,已經承擔後果了。

補充片語 take the consequences
承擔後果

consequent
◀Track 1053

[`kɑnsə͵kwɛnt]

adj. 作為結果的；隨之發生的

▶Due to the local culture, there was a consequent shortage of donor organs. 由於當地的文化，因此發生器官捐贈短缺的現象。

consequently
◀Track 1054

[`kɑnsə͵kwɛntlɪ] **adv.** 結果；因此；必然地

▶She woke up late this morning and consequently missed the train. 她早上晚起因此錯過了火車。

conservative
◀Track 1055

[kən`sɝvətɪv] **adj.** 保守的；守舊的；傳統的

▶She was so conservative that her friends found her difficult to get along with. 她是如此的保守以致於朋友覺得她很難相處。

n. 保守者；守舊派

▶The Conservatives are opposed to these changes in order to protect the middle class. 保守黨反對這些改變，以保障中等階級的民眾。

consider [kən`sɪdə]
◀Track 1056

v. 考慮；認為

▶They are considering moving to Cardiff. 他們考慮搬到卡地夫。

considerable
◀Track 1057

[kən`sɪdərəbl] **adj.** 相當大的；相當多的

▶He had considerable influence in politics. 他在政界有很大的影響力。

considerate
◀Track 1058

[kən`sɪdərɪt] **adj.** 週到的

▶My daughter is very sweet and considerate. 我的女兒很可愛又貼心。

consideration
◀Track 1059

[kənsɪdə`reʃən]

n. 考慮；需要考慮的事；體貼、關心

▶We took individual differences into consideration when we developed the products. 我們開發這些產品時，有把個別人的需求列入考慮。

補充片語 take sth. into consideration
考慮；將某事列入考慮

consist [kən`sɪst]
◀Track 1060

v. 組成；構成；存在於；符合

▶The elementary school consists of teachers, students, and a principal. 這所小學是由師生和校長所構成。

consistent
◀Track 1061

[kən`sɪstənt] **adj.** 始終如一的；前後一致的

▶His account is consistent with the information we have. 他的説法和我們握有的資訊一致。

補充片語 be consistent with
與……一致

consonant
◀Track 1062

[`kɑnsənənt] **n.** 子音

▶The teacher was teaching consonants and vowels. 老師正在教子音和母音。

constant [`kɑnstənt]
◀Track 1063

adj. 固定的；不停的、連續不斷的

中級

▶His wife's constant nagging was annoying. 他妻子嘮叨不休很令人厭煩。

constitute
Track 1064

[`kɑnstə͵tjut] **v** 構成;形成;
設立(機構);制定(法律)

▶What he did constituted the act of money laundering. 他所做的事構成了洗錢的行為。

constitution
Track 1065

[͵kɑnstə`tjuʃən] **n** 憲法、章程;體格;
(事物的)構造或組成方式

▶The Constitution of the United States was written and adopted in 1787.
美國憲法是在1787年起草並啟用的。

construct [kən`strʌkt]
Track 1066

v 建造;構成;創立(學說);構(詞)

▶The building was constructed as a garage. 這棟建築被建造來做為車庫。

n (複數)構想;概

▶This issue was merely a media construct. 這個議題是媒體杜撰出來的。

construction
Track 1067

[kən`strʌkʃən] **n** 建造;建設;建築

▶A major new hospital is under construction.
一所大型的新醫院正在建造中。

補充片語 under construction 在建造中

consult [kən`sʌlt] **v** 商量
Track 1068

▶After consulting with his parents, he decided to study in a vocational school. 他與父母商量後,決定去職業學校就讀。

consultant
Track 1069

[kən`sʌltənt] **n** 顧問;諮詢者

▶She is a finance consultant in the bank. 她在銀行擔任財經顧問。

補充片語 finance consultant
財經顧問問

consume [kən`sjum]
Track 1070

v 消耗;花費;吃完;喝光;揮霍;耗盡

▶The child consumed most of her time in reading fairy tales.
孩子把大部分的時間都花在看童話故事。

consumer
Track 1071

[kən`sjumɚ] **n** 消費者;顧客

▶In the digital age, you can be a smart consumer. 在這個數位時代,你可以成為聰明的消費高手。

contact [`kɑntækt]
Track 1072

n 接觸;聯繫

▶Take care. Let's keep in contact.
多保重,我們保持聯絡。

v 與……接觸;與……聯繫

▶You can contact us via e-mail.
你可以透過電郵與我們聯絡。

contagious
Track 1073

[kən`tedʒəs] **adj** 接觸傳染性的;感染性的

▶She took a day-off because she had contagious conjunctivitis.
她得了傳染性結膜炎,所以請假一天。

contain [kən`ten] **v** 包含
Track 1074

▶The beverage contains sugar and additives.
這個飲料包含糖和添加物。

container [kən`tenɚ] ◀≋Track 1075

n. 容器；貨櫃

▶She sliced the watermelons and put them into a container.
她切好西瓜並放入盒子中。

contemporary ◀≋Track 1076

[kən`tɛmpə͵rɛrɪ]

adj. 當代的；同時代的；同齡的

▶He was contemporary with Sir Nicholas Winton.
他與尼古拉斯‧溫頓爵士是同個時代的人。

n. 同時代的人；同齡的人；同時期的東西；當代人

▶His paintings were ignored by his contemporaries.
他的畫作被同時代的人忽略了。

content [kən`tɛnt] ◀≋Track 1077

adj. 滿足的；滿意的

▶He is content with his life.
他對他的生活很滿意。

v. 使滿足；使滿意

▶His answer didn't seem to content the customer.
他的回答似乎並未讓顧客感到滿意。

n. 滿足；內容物

▶The content of the book is very technical.
這本書的內容很技術性。

相關片語 **to one's heart's content**
盡情地

▶Let's go to the buffet and eat to our heart's content.
我們去吃到飽餐廳吃個痛快吧。

contest [kən`tɛst] ◀≋Track 1078

n. 比賽；競賽；競爭

▶She became a household name after the singing contest. 她參加歌唱比賽以後，成為家喻戶曉的人物。

v. 競爭；角逐

▶Three presidential candidates are contesting for the presidency. 有三位總統候選人在角逐總統大位。

contestant ◀≋Track 1079

[kən`tɛstənt] **n.** 參賽者

▶The talent show has contestants from all over the world. 這個達人秀有來自全球的參賽者。

context [`kantɛkst] ◀≋Track 1080

n. 上下文；（事件的）來龍去脈；背景

▶He took my words completely out of context. 他把我的話完全斷章取義了。

補充片語 **out of context** 斷章取義

continent [`kantənənt] ◀≋Track 1081

n. 大陸；陸地；洲

▶Germany dominates the European continent in economic terms.
德國在經濟上主導了歐洲大陸。

continual [kən`tɪnjʊəl] ◀≋Track 1082

adj. 多次重複的；連續的；不間斷的

▶The politician's continual tweeting and lies could lead to his downfall. 這名政治人物不斷推文和說謊可能會導致他的隕落。

continue [kən`tɪnjʊ] ◀≋Track 1083

v. 繼續

▶Against their parents' wishes, they continued meeting each other.
他們在父母反對之下仍繼續見面。

中級

continuous
◀Track 1084

[kən`tɪnjʊəs]

adj. 連續不間斷的；持久不鬆懈的

▶The company assured continuous supply of solar power energy.
這家公司保證能持續供應太陽能。

contract [kən`trækt]
◀Track 1085

n. 合約

▶She signed a contract with a famous modeling agency.
她與一家知名的模特兒經紀公司簽約了。

v. 訂契約

▶The company was contracted to build a stadium in the city center.
這家公司簽約要在市中心蓋一座體育館。

contrary [`kantrɛrɪ]
◀Track 1086

adj. 相反的；對比的；逆向的

▶Her position is contrary to mine.
她的立場跟我相反。

contrast [`kan͵træst]
◀Track 1087

n. 對比；對照

▶There was a sharp contrast between what she did and what she preached.
她說一套、做一套，形成強烈的對比。

v. 使對比；形成對照

▶His writing style contrasts sharply with mine.
他的寫作風格跟我的形成鮮明的對比。

contribute
◀Track 1088

[kən`trɪbjut] **v.** 貢獻；捐獻

▶He didn't contribute anything to this project.
他對這個計畫沒有做出任何貢獻。

contribution
◀Track 1089

[͵kantrə`bjuʃən] **n.** 貢獻；捐獻；捐獻的財物

▶One of Nikolas Tesla's greatest contributions was the invention of alternating current. 尼古拉‧特斯拉最偉大的貢獻之一是交流電的發明。

補充片語 alternating current 交流電

control [kən`trol]
◀Track 1090

n. 控制

▶When he found that his wife cheated on him, he lost his control.
他發現妻子外遇時，他失控了。

v. 控制

▶I don't know how to control my dog.
我不知道如何控制我的狗。

controller [kən`trolɚ]
◀Track 1091

n. 管理人；控制器；主計員

▶Her dad was an air-traffic controller.
她爸爸是航空交通指揮員。

convenience
◀Track 1092

[kən`vinjəns] **n.** 便利；方便；便利設施

▶The apartment has all the modern conveniences.
這棟公寓擁有一切現代化的設備。

相關片語 convenience store 便利商店

▶I bought a tuna sandwich in a convenience store.
我在便利商店買了一個鮪魚三明治。

convenient
◀Track 1093

[kən`vinjənt] **adj.** 方便的；便利的

▶It is very convenient to shop online.
網路購物很方便。

中級

conventional
🔊 Track 1094

[kən`vɛnʃənl] **adj.** 習慣的；慣例的；傳統式的；符合習俗的

▶She looked beautiful in the conventional dress. 她穿傳統的洋裝很漂亮。

conversation
🔊 Track 1095

[ˌkɑnvɚ`seʃən] **n.** 對話；對談

▶He practiced English conversation with his American cyber friends.
他和美國網友練習英文會話。

converse [kən`vɝs]
🔊 Track 1096

v. 交談；談話

▶The leaders of the two countries conversed for hours in the meeting.
兩國領袖在會議中交談好幾個小時。

convey [kən`ve]
🔊 Track 1097

v. 運送；傳達

▶Please convey my best regards to Mr. Jackson.
請幫我向傑克森先生傳達問候之意。

convince [kən`vɪns]
🔊 Track 1098

v. 說服；使相信

▶I was convinced that he was innocent.
我相信他是無辜的 。

cook [kʊk]
🔊 Track 1099

v. 烹煮；做菜

▶Mom was cooking dinner while I was doing homework.
媽媽在煮飯的同時，我在做功課。

n. 廚師

▶My husband is a good cook.
我先生的廚藝很好。

cooker [`kʊkɚ]
🔊 Track 1100

n. 炊具；爐灶；烹調器具

▶I steamed the buns in my rice cooker.
我用電鍋蒸小圓麵包。

cookie [`kʊkɪ]
🔊 Track 1101
=cooky **n.** 甜餅乾

▶We made chocolate cookies on Saturday afternoon. 我們星期六下午做巧克力餅乾。

cooking [`kʊkɪŋ]
🔊 Track 1102

n. 烹調；烹調術

▶I love my husband's cooking.
我喜歡先生煮的菜。

adj. 烹調用的

▶The chef used cooking wine to marinate fish. 大廚用烹調用的酒來 魚。

cool [kul]
🔊 Track 1103

adj. 涼爽的；冷靜的；冷淡的；（口）極好的

▶Yesterday was a cool and windy day.
昨天是個涼爽又風大的一天。

v. 使涼快；使冷卻；使（情緒）平息

▶She placed the cake on the table to cool.
她把蛋糕放在餐桌上放涼。

cooperate [ko`ɑpəˌret]
🔊 Track 1104
=cooperate **v.** 合作；配合

▶He cooperated with the police in the investigation. 他在調查中與警方配合。

cooperation
🔊 Track 1105

[koˌɑpə`reʃən] **n.** 協力；合作；配合

▶The project will foster cooperation and exchange between the two schools.
這個計畫有助兩所學校合作與交流。

cooperative
◀Track 1106

[ko`apə,retɪv] **adj.** 合作的；樂意配合的

▶The police said the young man was cooperative.
警方表示這名年輕人非常配合。

cope [kop] **v** 對付；處理
◀Track 1107

▶He coped with the difficult situation with ease. 他輕而易舉地處理這個困難的情況。

補充片語 cope with 處理；巧妙應付

copper [`kapə]
◀Track 1108

n. 銅；銅製品；銅幣

▶Copper can conduct heat and electricity.
銅可以傳導熱能和電力。

adj. 銅的；銅製的；紅銅色的

▶Her copper hair was tied back in a ponytail. 她把紅銅色的頭髮紮成馬尾。

copy [`kapɪ]
◀Track 1109

n. 抄本；複製品

▶She gave me a complimentary copy of her new book. 她贈送我一本她的新書。

v 抄寫；抄襲；模仿

▶She copied the file and uploaded it to Google Cloud Storage. 她複製這個檔案並把它上傳到谷歌的雲端儲存端。

copyright [`kapɪ,raɪt]
◀Track 1110

n. 版權；著作權

▶Record companies sued Napster for copyright infringement. 唱片公司集體訴訟Napster線上音樂服務犯了著作權侵權。

補充片語 copyright infringement
著作權侵權

adj. 有版權的

▶Copyright regulations provide principles for current copyright protection.
版權條例提供目前版權保護的原則。

v 取得版權

▶Pirating copyrighted software is a criminal activity. 盜版有版權的軟體是一種犯罪行為。

coral [`kɔrəl]
◀Track 1111

n. 珊瑚；珊瑚製品；珊瑚色

▶Corals are dying due to global warming.
珊瑚因為全球暖化而漸漸死亡。

adj. 珊瑚的；珊瑚製的

▶She is wearing a coral bracelet.
她戴著一條珊瑚手鍊。

cord [kɔrd]
◀Track 1112

n. 細繩；粗線；絕緣電線

▶She coiled an extension cord and put it in a drawer.
她把延長線捲起來並放進抽屜裡。

相關片語 emergency cord
（火車上的）緊急煞車繩

▶He pulled the emergency cord on the train as it entered the station. 火車進站時，他拉下緊急煞車繩。

core [kor] **n.** 果核；核心
◀Track 1113

▶She cut out the cores of several apples to make an apple pie. 她除去幾顆蘋果的果核來做蘋果派。

corn [kɔrn]
◀Track 1114

n. 小麥、穀物；玉米

▶I ate an ear of corn and an apple.
我吃了一根玉米和一顆蘋果。

corner [`kɔrnə]
◀Track 1115

n. 角、角落

▶There is a café just around the corner of this street. 街角有一家咖啡廳。

corporation
◀ Track 1116

[ˌkɔrpəˈreʃən]

n. 法人；社團法人；股份公司；大公司

▶She is a financial analyst in a large corporation.
她是一家大公司的財經分析師。

correct [kəˈrɛkt]
◀ Track 1117

adj. 正確的

▶The spelling of the word is correct.
這個字的拼法是正確的。

v. 糾正、訂正

▶The teacher was correcting the student's English pronunciation. 老師糾正學生的英文發音。

correspond
◀ Track 1118

[ˌkɔrɪˈspand] **v.** 符合；相應；一致

▶His account didn't correspond with the witness's version.
他的說詞與證人所述不符。

補充片語 correspond with 符合

correspondent
◀ Track 1119

[ˌkɔrɪˈspandənt]

n. 對應物；特派員、通訊記者；客戶

▶He is a BBC correspondent in the Vatican. 他是英國廣播公司派駐梵諦岡的特派記者。

corridor [ˈkɔrɪdɚ]
◀ Track 1120

n. 走廊；迴廊；通道

▶His studio is at the end of the corridor.
他的工作室在走廊盡頭。

cosmetics
◀ Track 1121

[kazˈmɛtɪks] **n.** 化妝品；美容品

▶She bought cosmetics and perfumes online. 她在網路購買化妝品和香水。

cost [kɔst]
◀ Track 1122

n. 費用；成本；代價

▶The cost of the advertisement is expensive. 這個廣告的成本很高。

v. 花費（時間、金錢、勞力等）

▶It cost me $100 to buy the pencil case.
我花了一百元買這個鉛筆盒。

costly [ˈkɔstlɪ]
◀ Track 1123

adj. 貴重的；昂貴的；代價高的

▶The diamond ring is costly.
這個鑽戒非常昂貴。

costume [ˈkɑstjum]
◀ Track 1124

n. 服裝；戲服

▶She dressed up as Peter Pan at the costume party.
她在變裝派對打扮成彼德潘。

補充片語 costume party
化妝舞會；變裝派對

cottage [ˈkɑtɪdʒ]
◀ Track 1125

n. 農舍；小屋；（度假）別墅

▶They spent their summer vacation at a beach cottage.
他們在海濱農舍度過暑假。

cotton [ˈkɑtn]
◀ Track 1126

n. 棉；棉花

▶This shirt is made of pure cotton.
這件襯衫是用純棉做成的。

中級

couch [kaʊtʃ] **n.** 長沙發 ◀⟨Track 1127

▶When I got home, I saw my dog sleeping comfortably on the couch. 我到家時看見我的舒適地在沙發上睡覺。

cough [kɔf] **v** 咳嗽 ◀⟨Track 1128

▶He coughed out a blood clot. 他咳出一個血塊。

n. 咳嗽；咳嗽聲

▶She had a bad cough last night. 她昨晚咳得很厲害。

could [kʊd] ◀⟨Track 1129

aux. 助動詞can的過去式；表示假設語氣的「可以、但願」

▶She wished she could have a daughter. 她但願能有個女兒。

couldn't [ˋkʊdnt] ◀⟨Track 1130

abbr. 不能（**could not**的縮寫）

▶He couldn't sleep well last night because it was too noisy outside the house. 他昨晚因為屋外太吵而沒睡好。

council [ˋkaʊnsḷ] ◀⟨Track 1131

n. 會議；政務會；協調會；議事、商討

▶UN General Secretary Antonio Guterres hosted the UN Security Council meeting on September 26, 2018 in New York. 聯合國秘書長古特瑞斯於2018年9月26日主持聯合國安理會會議。

補充片語 UN Security Council
聯合國安理會

count [kaʊnt] ◀⟨Track 1132

v 數；算；將……計算在內；有意義；依賴

▶My two-year old daughter can count from one to fifteen. 我的兩歲女兒可以從一數到十五。

n. 計算；總數

▶His white blood cell count is too low to fight germs. 他的白血球數量太少以致於無法抵抗細菌。

counter [ˋkaʊntɚ] ◀⟨Track 1133

n. 計數器；櫃台

▶She deposited a check at the bank counter. 她在銀行櫃台存了一張支票。

v 反抗；反擊

▶Hopefully, scientific advances could help counter global warming. 但願科技的進步有助抵抗全球暖化。

counterclockwise ◀⟨Track 1134

[ˌkaʊntɚˋklɑkˌwaɪz] **adj.** 逆時針的

▶He stirred the soup in a counterclockwise direction. 他以逆時針的方向攪拌湯。

country [ˋkʌntrɪ] ◀⟨Track 1135

n. 國家；鄉下、郊外

▶The United Kingdom is a country with monarchy. 英國是個君主政體的國家。

countryside ◀⟨Track 1136

[ˋkʌntrɪˌsaɪd] **n.** 鄉村；農間

▶The family lived in the countryside. 這戶人家住在鄉村。

county [ˋkaʊntɪ] **n.** 縣；郡 ◀⟨Track 1137

▶She came from Pingtung County. 她來自屏東縣。

couple [ˋkʌpḷ] ◀⟨Track 1138

n. 夫妻；一對

▶The young couple just got married and they were spending their honeymoon in Bali. 這對年輕夫妻剛結婚，在峇里島度蜜月。

coupon [`kupɑn] ◀€Track 1139

n. 聯票；減價優惠券

▶She collected coupons from newspapers and magazines and saved her own wages to buy a car. 她從報章雜誌收集折價卷，並把工資存下來買車。

courage [ˌkɝɪdʒ] ◀€Track 1140

n. 勇氣

▶He didn't have the courage to ask for a raise. 他沒有勇氣要求加薪。

courageous ◀€Track 1141

[kəˋredʒəs] **adj.** 英勇的；勇敢的

▶It was courageous of him to stay in the war zone and help the refugees. 他留在戰區幫助難民是非常勇敢的。

course [kors] ◀€Track 1142

n. 課程；習慣的程序；一道菜

▶He took a course in linguistics. 他修了一門語言學的課。

court [kort] **n.** 法庭；場地 ◀€Track 1143

▶The court declared him innocent. 法庭宣告他無罪。

courteous [`kɝtjəs] ◀€Track 1144

adj. 慇懃的；謙恭的；有禮貌的

▶She is courteous to her teachers. 她對老師很有禮貌。

courtesy [`kɝtəsɪ] ◀€Track 1145

n. 禮貌；禮節

▶He should at least have the courtesy to apologize to you. 他至少出於禮貌應向你道歉才是。

相關片語 **courtesy bus** 免費接駁車

▶The courtesy bus service operates between the train station and the department store. 這輛免費接駁車服務在火車站和百貨公司之間往返。

cousin [`kʌzn] ◀€Track 1146

n. 表或堂兄弟姐妹

▶My cousin is an American-born Chinese. 我的堂妹是華裔美籍人。

cover [`kʌvɚ] **v.** 覆蓋 ◀€Track 1147

▶She covered the pizza with a layer of cheese. 她在比薩上鋪了一層起士。

n. 遮蓋物；書皮（封面或封底）

▶The young model's face was on the cover of a fashion magazine. 這名年輕模特兒的臉孔出現在一本時尚雜誌的封面。

cow [kaʊ] **n.** 母牛；奶牛 ◀€Track 1148

▶He raised a few cows and sheep on the farm. 他在農場養了一些乳牛和綿羊。

coward [`kaʊɚd] ◀€Track 1149

adj. 膽小的；怯懦的

▶In The Wonderful Wizard of Oz, a coward lion desperately wanted to become courageous. 在《綠野仙蹤》這部童話故事裡，有一隻膽怯的獅子極度想要變得很勇敢。

n. 膽小鬼；懦夫

▶Bullies are in fact cowards. 霸凌者實際上是懦夫。

cowardly [`kaʊɚdlɪ] ◀€Track 1150

adj. 膽小的；懦弱的；卑劣的

▶It was a barbaric and cowardly attack. 這是野蠻又卑劣的攻擊。

adv. 膽小地；怯懦地；卑劣地

中級

▶After causing big trouble, he cowardly made a fast escape. 他製造了大麻煩後，膽怯地逃離了。

cowboy [`kaʊbɔɪ]　◀Track 1151
n. 牛仔；牧牛人

▶The cowboy had a strong Texan accent. 這位牛仔有很濃的德州口音。

cozy [`kozɪ]　◀Track 1152
adj. 舒適的；愜意的

▶The Victorian house is not grand but cozy. 這棟維多利亞式建築的房子雖非富麗堂皇但很舒適。

crab [kræb] **n.** 螃蟹；蟹肉　◀Track 1153
▶Crabs are crustaceans.
螃蟹是甲殼類動物。

crack [kræk]　◀Track 1154
n. 裂縫、裂痕；爆裂聲；猛烈一擊

▶There are many cracks on the wall of this old building. 這棟老舊建築的牆壁有許多裂痕。

v. 裂開；砸開；猛擊；爆裂；斷裂

▶A squirrel cracked a nut, ate the insides, and threw away the hard shell. 一隻松鼠把堅果砸開，吃掉裡面的果肉，然後把外殼丟掉。

相關片語 **a hard nut to crack**
棘手的事；難對付的人

▶I was told that Alice is a hard nut to crack. After working with her, I think what people said is true. 我被告知艾莉絲是個麻煩人物。與她共事後，我認為人們所言是實話。

cracker [`krækə]　◀Track 1155
n. 薄脆餅乾；鞭炮、爆竹

▶Pea crackers are delicious snacks.
豌豆酥是美味的零嘴。

cradle [`kredl]　◀Track 1156
n. 搖籃；嬰兒時期；發源地

▶Ancient China was the cradle of civilization. 古代中國是文明的發源地。

v. 輕輕抱著

▶He cradled the baby gently in his arms. 他輕柔地將寶寶抱在懷裡。

相關片語 **from cradle to grave**
生老病死

▶Identity theft is a problem from cradle to grave. 身分竊盜是人們從出生到其死亡都要小心的問題。

craft [kræft] **n.** 工藝；手藝　◀Track 1157
▶She taught arts and crafts to school children. 她教學校學生做手工藝品。

補充片語 **arts and crafts** 手工藝品

cram [kræm]　◀Track 1158
v. 把……塞進；擠滿；塞滿；
狼吞虎嚥地吃；死記硬背；填鴨式地教

▶He crammed for his geography exam.
他為了準備地理考試而臨時抱佛腳。

相關片語 **cram school** 補習班

▶Many students go to cram school in order to get into good colleges. 許多學生為了上好的大學而去補習班。

cramp [kræmp]　◀Track 1159
v. 用夾鉗夾緊；限制；約束；妨礙

▶His education was cramped by lack of money. 他因為缺錢而無法繼續受教育。

n. 鐵鉗；約束物；束縛；抽筋；痙攣

▶The rigid doctrines are cramps on free thinking. 這些嚴苛的教條對自由思想造成束縛。

crane [kren]
🔊 Track 1160

n. 鶴；起重機

▶They used a crane to lift up the beam. 他們用起重機把橫樑吊起來。

v. 用起重機搬運；伸長脖子看

▶The children craned their necks to see the magic show. 孩子們伸長脖子看魔術秀。

crash [kræʃ]
🔊 Track 1161

n. 相撞；墜毀；失敗；垮台

▶There was no survivors in the plane crash. 這起空難沒有倖存者。

補充片語 plane crash 飛機失事；空難

v. 相撞；墜毀；（電腦）當機

▶The computer crashed again. 電腦又當機了。

crawl [krɔl]
🔊 Track 1162

v. 爬行；蠕動；緩慢前進；爬滿

▶A snail crawled out from under the leaves. 一隻蝸牛從樹葉中爬了出來。

n. 爬行；緩慢前進

▶Highway traffic is at a crawl due to a two-vehicle crash. 因為兩輛車子相撞，高速公路的交通行進很緩慢。

crayon [`kreən] n. 蠟筆
🔊 Track 1163

▶The child drew a picture with crayons. 小孩用蠟筆畫圖。

crazy [`krezɪ]
🔊 Track 1164

adj. 瘋狂的；失常的

▶You must be crazy to work for that notorious organization. 你一定是瘋了才去那個惡名昭彰的機構上班。

creak [krik]
🔊 Track 1165

v. 發出軋吱聲

▶The desk creaked as I leaned against it for support. 我靠著書桌支撐時，它發出了軋吱聲。

n. 軋軋吱吱聲

▶I heard the creaks of the stairs as she walked upstairs. 她上樓時，我聽到了樓梯的軋吱聲。

cream [krim]
🔊 Track 1166

n. 奶油；乳脂食品；乳膏狀物

▶She put some cream and sugar in her coffee. 她在咖啡裡加入了奶油和糖。

create [krɪ`et]
🔊 Track 1167

v. 創造；創作

▶I was surprised to know that the life-saving app was created by a 14-year-old. 我很驚訝得知這個能救命的應用程式是由十四歲的青少年所創造的。

creation [krɪ`eʃən]
🔊 Track 1168

n. 創造；創立；宇宙；萬物

▶Service industry has strong potential to continuously create jobs. 服務業的就業機會持續有潛力地增長。

creative [krɪ`etɪv]
🔊 Track 1169

adj. 創意的；有創造力的

▶He is a very creative musician. 他是非常有創造力的音樂家。

creativity [ˌkrie`tɪvətɪ]
🔊 Track 1170

n. 創造力

中級

▶The young man is full of creativity and innovative ideas.
這個年輕人充滿創造力和創新的思想。

creature [`kritʃɚ] ◀≣Track 1171
n. 生物；動物

▶Elephants are the largest creatures on land. 大象是陸地上最大的生物。

credit [`krɛdɪt] ◀≣Track 1172
n. 賒賬；信譽；銀行存款；信用

▶She bought the car on credit.
她以賒賬的方式買這輛車。

補充片語 on credit
以賒帳方式；憑信用卡

v. 相信；將……記入貸方；將……歸於；記 學分

▶The actress credited her winning the award to her parents.
女演員將獲獎歸功於她的雙親。

creep [krip] ◀≣Track 1173
v. 躡手躡腳地走；緩慢前進；爬行；蔓延；起雞皮疙瘩

▶A smile crept on her face as she talked about her son.
她談到兒子時，臉上露出了笑容。

n. 爬；蠕動；毛骨悚然的感覺

▶The tattoos on his body gave me the creeps.
他身上的刺青讓我感到毛骨悚然。

補充片語 give sb. the creeps 讓某人感到毛骨悚然；使人汗毛直豎

crew [kru] ◀≣Track 1174
n. 一組工作人員；全體船員或機組人員

▶The maintenance crew will repair the conveyers in the factory as soon as possible.
維修組將儘快修理工廠的輸送帶。

補充片語 maintenance crew 維修組

crib [krɪb] ◀≣Track 1175
n. 小兒床；有欄杆的嬰兒床

▶They bought a convertible crib for their newborn baby. 他們幫新生的寶寶買了一個可折疊的嬰兒床。

cricket [`krɪkɪt] ◀≣Track 1176
n. 蟋蟀；板球；光明正大

▶He was playing cricket with his son.
他在和兒子玩板球。

crime [kraɪm] ◀≣Track 1177
n. 罪行；罪過

▶Stealing people's Identities is a crime.
盜用別人的身分是犯罪的一種。

criminal [`krɪmənl] ◀≣Track 1178
adj. 犯罪的；犯法的；刑事上的

▶The job fair was held for job seekers with criminal records. 這個就業博覽會是為有犯罪記錄的求職者所舉辦的。

補充片語 criminal record 犯罪記錄

n. 罪犯

▶The criminal is still at large.
罪犯還逍遙法外。

補充片語 at large 逍遙法外

cripple [`krɪpl] **n.** 跛子 ◀≣Track 1179
▶She is an emotional cripple.
她是感情有缺陷的人。

補充片語 emotional cripple
感情有缺陷的人

v 使成跛子；使陷入癱瘓

▶He was crippled in the accident.
他因意外而成為殘疾。

crisis [`kraɪsɪs]　◀ Track 1180
n 危機；危險期

▶The company survived the financial crisis in 2007. 這家公司在2007年的金融危機中存活了下來。

crisp [krɪsp]　◀ Track 1181
adj. 脆的；酥的；脆嫩的；清爽的；乾脆俐落的

▶The pickled cucumber is fresh and crisp. 這醃小黃瓜很新鮮脆　。

crispy [`krɪspɪ]　◀ Track 1182
adj. 酥脆的；清脆的；乾淨俐落的

▶This apple is crispy and juicy.
這顆蘋果很鮮脆多汁。

critic [`krɪtɪk]　◀ Track 1183
n 評論家；批評家；吹毛求疵的人

▶She is a record producer and a music critic. 她是唱片製作人，也是個音樂評論家。

critical [`krɪtɪkl̩]　◀ Track 1184
adj. 緊要的；關鍵性的；批判的；愛挑剔的

▶He is critical with his wife and children.
他對妻兒很挑剔。

criticism [`krɪtə͵sɪzəm]　◀ Track 1185
n 批評；評論；苛求；挑剔

▶Her acting in the film was beyond criticism. 她在這部片的演技無可挑剔。

補充片語 beyond criticism
無可挑剔；無從指責

criticize [`krɪtɪ͵saɪz]　◀ Track 1186
v 批評；非難；評論

▶Alice always criticizes people behind their back. 艾莉絲老在別人背後批評別人。

crocodile [`krɑkə͵daɪl]　◀ Track 1187
n 鱷魚；鱷魚皮革

▶I don't use accessories made from the skin of crocodiles or other animals.
我不用鱷魚或其他動物的皮所做的飾品。

相關片語 crocodile tears
鱷魚眼淚；假慈悲

▶She shed crocodile tears when she heard what happened to John. 她聽到約翰發生了事，虛情假意的掉了眼淚。

crooked [`krʊkɪd]　◀ Track 1188
adj. 歪曲的；變形的；不正當的

▶Her back is so crooked that she can not even sit straight.
她的背彎得她連坐都坐不直。

crop [krɑp]　◀ Track 1189
n 作物；莊稼；收成

▶Farmers harvested crops in autumn.
農民在秋天收割穀物。

v 剪短；種植、播種；收割

▶He cropped several acres of wheat and barley. 他種了幾英畝的小麥和大麥。

cross [krɔs]　◀ Track 1190
v 穿越；橫過

▶Look both ways before you cross the street. 過馬路前應先看兩邊的道路。

中級

n. 十字形；十字架

▶He wore a necklace with a cross on it.
他戴著一條有十字架的項鍊。

crossroad [`krɔsˌrod] ◀Track 1191
v. 十字路口；交叉點；轉折點

▶When she started her own business, it was definitely a crossroad in her life.
她創業時是她一生中重大的轉折點。

crouch [`kraʊtʃ] ◀Track 1192
adj. 蹲伏；彎腰；卑躬屈膝，諂媚

▶The cat was crouching in the armchair.
貓咪正蜷伏在扶手椅上。

crow [kro] n. 烏鴉 ◀Track 1193

▶A black crow was making loud squawking noises yesterday evening.
昨天傍晚有一隻黑烏鴉叫聲很吵。

v. （雞）報曉；啼

▶He was woken up by the rooster's crow this morning. 他早上被公雞叫聲吵醒。

crowd [kraʊd] n. 人群 ◀Track 1194

▶A crowd of people celebrated the festival on the street. 一群人在街上慶祝節慶。

crowded [`kraʊdɪd] ◀Track 1195
adj. 擁擠的

▶The famous scenic spot was crowded with tourists. 這個著名的景點擠滿了遊客。

crown [kraʊn] ◀Track 1196
n. 王冠；榮冠；王位

▶The queen wore a crown at official events. 女皇在正式場合戴著王冠。

v. 為……加冕；立……為王

▶The beauty queen was crowned when she was only 20. 這位選美皇后被封后時，芳齡才20歲。

crucial [`kruʃəl] ◀Track 1197
adj. 決定性的；嚴酷的

▶It is crucial that you be there before he arrives at the airport. 他抵達機場時你是在場的，這點很重要的。

cruel [`kruəl] ◀Track 1198
adj. 殘忍的；痛苦傷人的

▶It is very cruel of you to say that.
你説這種話很傷人。

cruelty [`kruəltɪ] ◀Track 1199
n. 殘酷；殘忍；殘酷的行為

▶Animal cruelty is a crime.
虐待動物是犯罪的一種。

cruise [kruz] ◀Track 1200
v. 巡航；航遊；緩慢巡行；乘船遊覽

▶They cruised along the coast and enjoyed the beautiful scenery. 他們沿著海岸航遊並欣賞著明媚的風光。

n. 巡航；巡邏；乘遊輪航遊

▶We went on a cruise round the Mediterranean. 我們搭遊輪航遊地中海。

補充片語 go on a cruise 搭遊輪航遊

crumb [krʌm] ◀Track 1201
n. 麵包、糕餅屑；碎屑；少許

▶She threw crumbs into the lake to feed the swans. 她丟了麵包屑到湖裡餵天鵝。

v. 捏碎；弄碎；把……裹上麵包屑

▶She crumbed the chicken before cooking. 她把雞肉裹上麵包屑後開始料理。

crunchy [`krʌntʃɪ]
◀ Track 1202

adj. 鬆脆的；易碎的

▶The celeries and cucumber are fresh and crunchy. 這芹菜和小黃瓜很新鮮爽脆。

crush [krʌʃ]
◀ Track 1203

v. 壓碎；壓壞；摧毀；擠、塞

▶She used the bottom of a glass to crush the garlic. 她用杯子底部來壓大蒜。

n. 壓碎；壓壞；極度擁擠；暗戀

▶He had a crush on Mary. 他暗戀瑪莉。

補充片語 **have a crush on sb.**
暗戀某人

crutch [krʌtʃ] **n.** 拐杖
◀ Track 1204

▶She has been on crutches since she broke her leg last month. 她上個月腿受傷後就一直拄著枴杖至今。

cry [kraɪ] **v.** 哭；哭泣；喊叫
◀ Track 1205

▶The baby cried when her mother was sleeping. 媽媽正在睡覺時，寶寶哭了。

n. 叫喊聲；哭

▶Did you hear the cries of the children? 你有聽到孩子們的哭叫聲嗎？

crystal [`krɪstl]
◀ Track 1206

n. 水晶；水晶飾品

▶The door knob is made of crystal. 這個門把是用水晶做成的。

adj. 水晶的；水晶製的；水晶般的

▶She has a set of crystal wine glasses. 她有一組水晶酒杯。

cub [kʌb]
◀ Track 1207

n. 幼獸（獅、虎、狼等）

▶The polar bear cub became an animal star of the zoo. 這隻小北極熊成了動物園的動物明星。

cube [kjub]
◀ Track 1208

n. 立方體；立方

▶The cube of 3 is 27. 三的三次方是二十七。

v. 使成立方體；使成小方塊

▶She cut the chicken into small cubes. 她把雞肉切成雞丁。

cucumber
◀ Track 1209

[`kjukəmbɚ] **n.** 黃瓜；胡瓜

▶She sliced some cucumber and a tomato and put them in the salad. 她切了一些小黃瓜和番茄加入沙拉裡。

cue [kju] **n.** 提示；暗示
◀ Track 1210

▶It's a cue for us to make sweeping changes. 這是我們該做全面改變的提示。

v. 給提示；給暗示

▶The director cued the extras to start acting. 導演暗示臨時演員開始演戲。

cuisine [kwɪ`zin]
◀ Track 1211

n. 烹飪；烹調法；菜餚

▶She learned about French cuisine and cooking techniques at a cooking school. 她在烹飪學校學習法式料理和烹飪技巧。

cultivate [`kʌltə͵vet]
◀ Track 1212

v. 耕種；栽培；陶冶；培養

▶The project aims to cultivate young talent. 這個計畫旨在培育年輕人才。

cultural [`kʌltʃərəl]
◀ Track 1213

adj. 文化的；人文的；修養的

中級

▶New York is a city full of cultural diversity.
紐約是多元文化的城市。

culture [ˋkʌltʃɚ] n. 文化 ◄Track 1214

▶Korean pop culture is popular around the world.
韓國的流行文化在世界很受歡迎。

cunning [ˋkʌnɪŋ] ◄Track 1215
adj. 狡猾的

▶She is cunning and manipulative.
她很狡猾又工於心計。

cup [kʌp] ◄Track 1216
n. 杯子；（一）杯

▶Would you like a cup of coffee?
你要不要喝杯咖啡?

cupboard [ˋkʌbɚd] ◄Track 1217
n. 食櫥；碗櫃

▶The china cups and saucers are in the kitchen cupboard.
瓷器杯和碟子放在廚房碗櫃裡面。

cure [kjʊr] ◄Track 1218
n. 治療；痊癒；療法

▶There is still no cure for this disease.
這個疾病仍沒有治癒的方法。

v. 治癒；消除（弊病等）

▶The new drug can cure chronic myeloid leukemia.
這個新藥可以治癒慢性骨髓性白血病。

curiosity [ˌkjʊrɪˋɑsətɪ] ◄Track 1219
n. 好奇；好奇心

▶The topic aroused his curiosity.
這個主題引起了他的好奇心。

curious [ˋkjʊrɪəs] ◄Track 1220
adj. 好奇的；渴望知道的

▶The baby is curious about everything around her.
寶寶對周圍的所有事物都很好奇。

curl [kɝl] ◄Track 1221
v. 捲曲；使捲起來

▶Sasha had curled her hair for the party. 莎夏為了派對而把頭髮燙捲。

n. 捲髮；捲狀物；捲曲

▶He ran his fingers through the loose curls of his girlfriend. 他輕撫摸著女友蓬鬆的捲髮。

current [ˋkɝənt] ◄Track 1222
adj. 現在的；當前的

▶He is the current manager of the company. 他是公司現任的經理。

n. 流動；氣流；潮流

▶Alternating current is better than direct current. 交流電比直流電好用。

curry [ˋkɝɪ] ◄Track 1223
n. 咖哩；咖哩菜餚

▶I put some coconut milk into the curry.
我在咖哩中加了一些椰奶。

curse [kɝs] ◄Track 1224
v. 詛咒；咒罵

▶She cursed everyone in the family.
她咒罵家中的每一個人。

n. 咒罵人的話；咒語；禍害

▶The evil fairy put a curse on the princess. 妖精對公主下了咒語。

補充片語 put a curse on sb.
對某人下咒

curtain [`kɝ·tn]
◀Track 1225

n. 窗簾；門簾；（舞台上的）幕

▶He closed the curtains and went to bed. 他把窗簾拉下後就去睡覺了。

curve [kɝv] **n.** 曲線；弧線
◀Track 1226

▶She does yoga every morning to enhance her curves. 她每天早上練瑜伽，使自己的曲線更漂亮。

v. 彎曲

▶The road curves to the east. 道路向東轉。

cushion [`kʊʃən]
◀Track 1227

n. 墊子；靠墊

▶She knelt on a cushion to pray.
她跪在跪墊上祈禱。

v. 裝上靠墊；緩和衝擊

▶The thick carpet cushioned her fall.
厚地毯緩和了她跌下的衝擊。

custom [`kʌstəm]
◀Track 1228

n. 習俗；習慣

▶It's a Chinese custom to celebrate Dragon Boat Festival.
華人的習俗會慶祝端午節。

customer [`kʌstəmɚ]
◀Track 1229

n. 顧客

▶Sometimes customers are not always right. 有時顧客不永遠是對的。

cut [kʌt] **v.** 剪；切
◀Track 1230

▶The boy happily cut his birthday cake.
男孩開心地切著生日蛋糕。

n. 剪、切的傷口，割痕

▶She put a bandage on the cut.
她在傷口上貼上繃帶。

cute [kjut]
◀Track 1231

adj. 可愛的；漂亮的

▶Pandas are very cute. 貓熊很可愛。

cycle [`saɪkl]
◀Track 1232

n. 週期；循環；腳踏車

▶We studied the life cycle of a butterfly in biology class.
我們生物課學習蝴蝶的生命週期。

v. 循環；輪轉；騎腳踏車

▶She cycled to the small town.
她騎腳踏車去這個小鎮。

cyclist [`saɪklɪst]
◀Track 1233

n. 騎腳踏車的人；自行車騎士

▶This road is hazardous for cyclists.
這條路對自行車騎士來説很危險。

中級

▶ Dd

　　以下表格是全民英檢官方公告中級「聽、說、讀、寫」所須具備的能力，本書例句皆依此範疇特別設計，只要掃描右方QR code，就能搭配相對應的音軌實現「眼耳並用」方式，刺激左腦的語言學習功能；同時也可使用本書附贈的紅膠片，將其置於單字上，一面記憶一面自我挑戰，達到雙倍的學習成果！

聽 ▶	在日常生活中，能聽懂一般的會話；能大致聽懂公共場所廣播、氣象報告及廣告等。在工作時，能聽懂簡易的產品介紹與操作說明。能大致聽懂外籍人士的談話及詢問。
說 ▶	可在日常生活中，能以簡易英語交談或描述一般事物，能介紹自己的生活作息、工作、家庭、經歷等，並可對一般話題陳述看法。在工作時，能進行簡單的答詢，並與外籍人士交談溝通。
讀 ▶	在日常生活中，能閱讀短文、故事、私人信件、廣告、傳單、簡介及使用說明等。在工作時，能閱讀工作須知、公告、操作手冊、例行的文件、傳真、電報等。
寫 ▶	能寫簡單的書信、故事及心得等。對於熟悉且與個人經歷相關的主題，能以簡易的文字表達。

dad [dæd] =dad·dy =pap·a=pa=pop n. 爸爸
◀ Track 1234

▶My dad is a physician. 我爸爸是醫生。

daffodil [`dæfədɪl]
◀ Track 1235

n. 黃水仙

▶She put a bouquet of daffodils in the vase. 她用一大束黃色水仙花佈置餐桌。

daily [`delɪ] adj. 每天的
◀ Track 1236

▶She made exercise her daily routine. 她把運動列為每日固定的行程。

adv. 每天

▶He takes a walk daily. 他每天散步。

dairy [`dɛrɪ]
◀ Track 1237

n. 製酪場；乳品店；牛奶與乳品業

▶Her son is allergic to dairy products. 她的兒子對乳製品過敏。

dam [dæm] n. 水壩；水堤
◀ Track 1238

▶A dam was built across the river. 水壩建在這條河流上。

v. 築壩於……

▶The lake was dammed to increase its storage capacity. 這個湖築了一個水壩以強化儲水功能。

damage [`dæmɪdʒ]
◀ Track 1239

n. 損害；損失

▶The tornado caused great damage to the state. 龍捲風造成這個州極大的損害。

v. 損害；毀壞

▶The museum was damaged in the bombing. 博物館在轟炸時遭到損壞。

damn [dæm]
◀ Track 1240

v. 咒罵；指責；罰……入地獄

▶The critics damned the politician. 評論們譴責這名政治人物。

n. 詛咒；絲毫；一點點

▶He didn't give a damn about what people said.
他一點都不在乎別人怎麼說。

相關片語 **damn the consequence**
不顧一切

▶There was a mad rush to make sweeping change and damn the consequence.
有些人極力呼籲不顧一切地全面改革。

damp [dæmp]　◀≋Track 1241

adj. 有濕氣的；潮濕的

▶It was a damp and cold day.
那是一個又濕又冷的一天。

n. 濕氣；潮濕

▶There was damp everywhere in the building. 這棟建築到處都是濕氣。

v. 使潮濕；弄濕

▶The failure did not damp her determination to solve the problem.
失敗並未降低她解決問題的決心。

相關片語 **something damp** 一杯酒

▶Let's have something damp.
我們去喝一杯酒吧。

dance [dæns] **v.** 跳舞　◀≋Track 1242

▶We danced to the music.
我們隨著音樂跳舞。

n. 跳舞

▶They went to a dance last Saturday night. 他們上週六去參加舞會。

dancer [`dænsə]　◀≋Track 1243

n. 舞者；舞蹈家

▶She is a world-renowned dancer.
她是世界知名的舞蹈家。

dancing [`dænsɪŋ]　◀≋Track 1244

n. 跳舞；舞蹈

▶She took classes in dancing and drama. 她修了舞蹈課和戲劇課。

danger [`dendʒə]　◀≋Track 1245

n. 危險

▶The patient is out of danger now.
病人已脫離危險。

dangerous　◀≋Track 1246

[`dendʒərəs] **adj.** 危險的

▶The product contains dangerous chemicals. 這個產品含有危險化學品。

dare [dɛr] **aux.** 敢；膽敢　◀≋Track 1247

▶She dares not to sleep alone.
她不敢單獨睡覺。

v. 敢；膽敢

▶He dared the wrath of his mother.
他不怕惹他母親發火。

dark [dɑrk]　◀≋Track 1248

adj. 暗的；黑的

▶The room was very dark. 房間很暗。

n. 黑暗

▶We couldn't see anything in the dark.
我們在黑暗中什麼也看不見。

darken [`dɑrkn]　◀≋Track 1249

v. 使變暗

▶Her face darkened, and I realized that I had probably said something wrong.
她氣得沉下臉來，我才了解剛剛可能說錯話了。

darling [`dɑrlɪŋ]　◀≋Track 1250

n. 心愛的人；寵兒

中級

▶Darling, could you please pass the jam? 親愛的，可以把果醬傳過來嗎？

adj. 親愛的；寵愛的；漂亮的

▶They went to airport to pick up their darling daughter.
他們去機場接寶貝女兒。

dart [dɑrt]　◀Track 1251

n. 標槍；投標遊戲；猛衝、飛奔

▶The thief made a dart for the exit.
小偷朝著出口衝去。

v. 擲飛鏢；猛衝

▶The chickens darted away on all sides. 雞朝四處奔逃而散。

dash [dæʃ]　◀Track 1252

v. 猛撞；急奔；潑灑；使（希望）破滅

▶The injury on her knees dashed her dream to become a ballet dancer. 她的膝蓋受傷，這使她成為芭蕾舞者的夢想破滅了。

n. 急衝；奔跑；短跑；破滅

▶He made a dash for home. 他猛衝回家。

補充片語 **make a dash for**
急奔某處；衝向某物

data [ˋdetə] **n.** 資料；數據　◀Track 1253

▶The data was collected by the graduate student. 這些資料是由研究生收集起來的。

date [det]　◀Track 1254

n. 日期；約會；約會對象

▶She had a date with Jamie yesterday afternoon. 她昨天下午與傑米約會。

v. 確定年代；註明日期；和……約會

▶The museum dates back to 1920.
這間博物館建於1920年。

daughter [ˋdɔtɚ]　◀Track 1255

n. 女兒

▶My daughter will turn 18 tomorrow.
我女兒明天就滿18歲了。

dawn [dɔn]　◀Track 1256

n. 黎明；破曉

▶They must leave for the airport at dawn. 他們必須天一亮就前晚機場。

v. 破曉；天亮

▶As Sunday morning was dawning, she went to the graveyard and put a bouquet of flowers at her father's tomb. 週日清晨剛破曉，她到墓園並放了一束鮮花在父親的基碑上。

day [de] **n.** 一天；日；白晝　◀Track 1257

▶There are seven days in a week.
一週有7天。

daybreak [ˋdeˏbrek]　◀Track 1258

n. 黎明；破曉

▶She left for the airport before daybreak.
她破曉之前就前往機場了。

daylight [ˋdeˏlaɪt]　◀Track 1259

n. 日光；白晝

▶He went to the train station before daylight. 他在天亮前就去火車站了。

補充片語 **before daylight** 天亮前

相關片語 **in broad daylight**
大白天地；光天化日之下

▶The terrorist attack occurred in broad daylight. 恐攻在光天化日之下發生了。

dazzle [ˋdæzl̩]　◀Track 1260

v. 使目眩；使眼花；使迷惑

▶The splendid palace dazzled him.
壯麗的皇宮使他目眩。

n. 耀眼的光；令人讚歎或迷惑的東西

▶She was dazzled by his charm and good heart. 她為他的魅力和善良所傾倒。

dead [dɛd] Track 1261

adj. 死的；無效的；已廢的

▶The battery is dead. 電池沒電了。

deadline [`dɛd͵laɪn] Track 1262

n. 截止期限；最後日期

▶The deadline for sending the application form is January 20. 函送申請表的截止日是一月二十日。

deadly [`dɛdlɪ] Track 1263

adj. 致命的；不共戴天的；死一般的；非常的

▶It is a deadly weapon. 這是致命的武器。

deaf [dɛf] **adj.** 聾的 Track 1264

▶My dog is deaf but he can respond to hand signals.
我的狗耳聾但可以回應手勢。

deal [dil] **v.** 處理；對付 Track 1265

▶He dealt with the problem with ease.
他從容地處理這個問題。

n. 交易

▶They considered it a good business deal. 他們認為這是筆划算的商業交易。

dealer [`dilɚ] Track 1266

n. 業者；商人；經銷商

▶She is a dealer in antiques.
她是個古董的經銷商。

相關片語 **drug dealer** 毒販

▶The drug dealer was sentenced to 30 years in prison. 那個毒販被判入獄服刑三十年。

dear [dɪr] **adj.** 親愛的 Track 1267

▶Her children are very dear to her.
她很看重她的孩子。

int. （感歎詞）哎呀；

▶Oh dear, I forgot to bring my wallet.
哎呀，我忘了帶錢包了。

n. 親愛的（人）

▶She was a dear to help me with my yard work. 她真好，幫我整理院子。

death [dɛθ] **n.** 死；死亡 Track 1268

▶We were shocked by his sudden death.
他的猝逝讓我感到震驚。

debate [dɪ`bet] Track 1269

n. 辯論；辯論會

▶The verdict sparked a nationwide debate. 這個判決引發全國的辯論。

v. 辯論；爭論

▶They debated on the issue until midnight.
他們就這個議題辯論到深夜。

debt [dɛt] **n.** 債；負債 Track 1270

▶She paid off her debts one year ago.
她一年前就把債務還清了。

decade [`dɛked] **n.** 十年 Track 1271

▶She has lived here for more than a decade. 她住在這裡超過十年了。

decay [dɪ`ke] Track 1272

v. 腐朽；蛀蝕；腐爛；衰敗；使蛀壞

▶Meat decays rapidly without refrigeration.
若沒有冷凍，肉類很快就會腐爛。

中級

n. 腐朽；腐爛；蛀牙

▶Tooth decay is easier to treat in its early stages. 蛀牙在早期治療較為容易。

deceive [dɪ`siv] **v.** 欺騙
◀Track 1273

▶I was deceived into thinking that she genuinely cared about me. 我上當受騙，以為她真誠關心我。

December [dɪ`sɛmbə-] =Dec. **n.** 十二月
◀Track 1274

▶They are going to Luxemburg in December. 他們十二月要去盧森堡。

decide [dɪ`saɪd] **v.** 決定
◀Track 1275

▶He decided to get the work done by Friday. 他決定在星期五前把工作完成。

decision [dɪ`sɪʒən]
◀Track 1276
n. 決定

▶It was his decision to use tear gas on protestors. 是他決定用催淚瓦斯驅散示威者。

deck [dɛk] **n.** 甲板
◀Track 1277

▶We sat on the upper deck of the bus. 我們坐在公車上層。

相關片語 deck shoe 平底帆布鞋

▶He slipped his foot out of his deck shoe. 他脫掉平底帆布鞋。

declaration
◀Track 1278
[ˌdɛklə`reʃən] **n.** 聲明

▶All employees of this company have signed a declaration of secrecy. 這家公司所有員工都簽了保密聲明。

補充片語 declaration of secrecy 保密聲明

declare [dɪ`klɛr]
◀Track 1279
v. 宣稱；宣告；申報（稅）

▶He declared himself an agnostic. 他宣稱自己是不可知論者。

相關片語 declare war 宣戰

▶The headmaster publicly declared war against drugs. 校長公開向毒品宣戰。

decline [dɪ`klaɪn]
◀Track 1280
v. 婉拒；婉謝

▶He declined to attend the ceremony. 他婉拒參加典禮。

decorate [`dɛkəˌret]
◀Track 1281
v. 裝飾；佈置

▶She decorated her room with roses. 她用玫瑰佈置她的房間。

decoration
◀Track 1282
[ˌdɛkə`reʃən] **n.** 裝飾；裝潢；裝飾物

▶I was impressed by the decorations of her room. 我對她房間的裝飾感到印象深刻。

相關片語 interior decoration 室內裝潢

▶She took a course in interior decoration after work. 她下班後去上室內裝潢課。

decrease [`dikris]
◀Track 1283
v. 減少；降低

▶The actor's popularity decreased after a scandal was revealed. 在醜聞被揭露後，這名演員受歡迎的程度下降。

n. 減少；降低

▶There has been a decrease in unemployment. 失業率減少了。

dedicate [`dɛdə͵ket]　◀⣂Track 1284

v 以……奉獻；獻（給）；題獻（著作）

▶She dedicated the award to her family.
她把獎項獻給家人。

deed [did] **n** 行為；行動　◀⣂Track 1285

▶Like many of us, she has done good deeds and made mistakes. 如同我們每人，她有做好事，也有犯錯。

補充片語 dirty deed 卑鄙行為

deep [dip] **adj** 深的　◀⣂Track 1286

▶He took a deep breath before the exam. 考前他做了深呼吸。

adv 深地

▶Still water runs deep. 靜水流深。（沉默寡言者可能胸藏丘壑。）

deer [dɪr] **n** 鹿　◀⣂Track 1287

▶The deer ran away at the sight of the lion. 鹿一看到獅子就跑開了。

defeat [dɪ`fit]　◀⣂Track 1288

n 失敗；挫折

▶He suffered a crushing defeat in the primary election. 他在初選遭遇慘敗。

v 戰勝；擊敗

▶They defeated the American team and went into the final.
他們擊敗美國隊，晉級決賽。

defend [dɪ`fɛnd]　◀⣂Track 1289

v 防禦；保衛

▶She went to martial arts class to learn how to defend herself. 她去武術課學習自我防衛。

defense [dɪ`fɛns]　◀⣂Track 1290
=defence （英式英文）

n 防禦；抵禦

▶Nutritions help build the body's natural defenses. 營養素有助身體的天然防禦力。

defensive [dɪ`fɛnsɪv]　◀⣂Track 1291

adj 防禦的

▶The US supplied defensive weapons to Ukraine. 美國提供烏克蘭防禦性武器。

deficit [`dɛfɪsɪt]　◀⣂Track 1292

n 不足額；赤字

▶The government is forecasting a foreign trade deficit of $50bn for 2020. 政府預期2020年外貿逆差將達到五千億元。

define [dɪ`faɪn]　◀⣂Track 1293

v 解釋；為……下定義；確定……的界限

▶The root cause of the problem was not clearly defined. 問題的根本並未被明確的界定。

definite [`dɛfənɪt]　◀⣂Track 1294

adj 明確的

▶He didn't give a definite answer to the journalist's question. 針對記者的提問，他沒有給予明確的回答。

definition [͵dɛfə`nɪʃən]　◀⣂Track 1295

n 定義

▶The teacher explained the definitions of each new word. 老師解釋每個生字的定義。

degree [dɪ`gri]　◀⣂Track 1296

n 程度；度數；學位

▶He had a bachelor's degree.
他有大學學歷。

中級

delay [dɪˋle]
◀︎Track 1297

n. 延遲;耽擱

▶His wife tried to persuade him to quit drinking without delay. 他妻子試圖說服他立即戒酒。

v. 延遲;耽擱

▶The bad weather delayed the plane. 由於天氣不好,造成班機延誤。

delegate [ˋdɛləˌget]
◀︎Track 1298

n. 代表;會議代表;代表團團員

▶At the end of the conference, delegates were asked to submit their feedback. 會議尾聲時,代表們被要求遞交回饋表。

v. 委派⋯⋯為代表;委派某人做⋯⋯;授權 給⋯⋯

▶The director has delegated Mike to attend the meeting. 主任已經委派麥可參加會議。

delete [dɪˋlit]
◀︎Track 1299

v. 刪除;劃掉;刪去

▶They deleted all the swear words from the article. 他們把文章中所有的髒話都刪掉了。

deliberate [dɪˋlɪbərɪt]
◀︎Track 1300

adj. 深思熟慮的;謹慎的;蓄意的

▶She is deliberate in every move she makes. 她的每個舉止都很謹慎。

v. 考慮;仔細思考

▶The manager was deliberating what to do next. 經理考慮接下來該怎麼做。

delicate [ˋdɛləkət]
◀︎Track 1301

adj. 精美的;精緻的;易碎的;需要小心處理的;鮮美的

▶The child has a delicate stomach. 這孩子腸胃很虛。

delicious [dɪˋlɪʃəs]
◀︎Track 1302

adj. 美味的

▶The pumpkin pie is delicious. 南瓜派真是美味。

delight [dɪˋlaɪt]
◀︎Track 1303

n. 欣喜;愉快;樂趣

▶She read the comic book with great delight. 她非常愉快地看著漫畫書。

v. 使高興;使感欣喜

▶He delights in making new friends. 他喜歡結交新朋友。

delighted [dɪˋlaɪtɪd]
◀︎Track 1304

adj. 高興的;快樂的

▶She was very delighted with the result of the exam. 她對考試結果感到非常滿意。

delightful [dɪˋlaɪtfəl]
◀︎Track 1305

adj. 令人高興的

▶It was a delightful Wednesday morning. 那是個令人愉快的星期三早晨。

delinquent
◀︎Track 1306

[dɪˋlɪŋkwənt] **adj.** 怠忽職守的;有過失的

▶Sociologists studied the causes of delinquent behavior among adolescents. 社會學家研究青少年違法行為的原因。

n. 違法者;有過失者

▶The juvenile delinquents were recidivists. 這些少年犯是慣犯。

補充片語 juvenile delinquent 少年犯

deliver [dɪˋlɪvɚ]
◀︎Track 1307

v. 運送;投遞

▶She delivered a speech in the meeting.
她在會議發表演說。

delivery [dɪ`lɪvərɪ] ◀≣Track 1308
n. 遞送

▶Payment will be made upon delivery.
貨到付款。

相關片語 **delivery room** 產房

▶Back then, fathers were barred from the delivery room.
在從前，爸爸是不能進產房的。

demand [dɪ`mænd] ◀≣Track 1309
n. 要求；請求

▶Demand exceeded supply in the market for solar energy.
市場對太陽能的需求超過供給。

v. 要求；請求

▶The boss demanded that we finish the task by Friday.
老闆要求我們星期五前完成這項工作。

相關片語 **in demand**
非常需要的；受歡迎的

▶Data scientists are in demand.
資料科學家是很多公司都需要的。

demanding ◀≣Track 1310
[dɪ`mændɪŋ] **adj.** 苛求的；高要求的；
使人需吃力應付的

▶He is very demanding and difficult to get along with. 他很苛刻，難以相處。

democracy ◀≣Track 1311
[dɪ`mɑkrəsɪ] **n.** 民主；民主政體；民主國家

▶The UK is a democracy with monarchy.
英國是具有君主體制的民主國家。

democrat ◀≣Track 1312
[`dɛmə,kræt] **n.** 民主主義者；（美國）民主黨人；民主黨 支持者

▶The Democrats was defeated in the last election. 民主黨在上次選舉被擊敗。

democratic ◀≣Track 1313
[,dɛmə`krætɪk] **adj.** 民主的；民主政體的

▶The United States is a democratic country. 美國是民主國家。

demonstrate ◀≣Track 1314
[`dɛmən,stret] **v.** 論證；證明；示範

▶The salesman demonstrated the new smart phone. 銷售員展示新款的智慧型手機。

demonstration ◀≣Track 1315
[,dɛmən`streʃən] **n.** 示範；論證；證明

▶She gave me a demonstration of how the new washing machine works. 她向我示範新的洗衣機怎麼操作。

denial [dɪ`naɪəl] ◀≣Track 1316
n. 否認；否定；拒絕承認

▶The suspect tried to interrupt the interrogator to make his denial. 嫌疑犯試著打斷訊問者，並予以否認。

dense [dɛns] ◀≣Track 1317
adj. 密集的；稠密的；濃密的

▶We were almost lost in the dense forest. 我們差點就在濃密的森林裡迷路了。

dental [`dɛntl̩] ◀≣Track 1318
adj. 牙齒的；牙科的

▶I made an appointment for a dental check-up. 我預約了檢查牙齒。

dentist [ˋdɛntɪst] n. 牙醫 ◀Track 1319

▶I visited my dentist for a check-up and cleaning. 我去看牙醫檢查牙齒以及洗牙。

deny [dɪˋnaɪ] v. 否認 ◀Track 1320

▶The singer denied the rumor that she was in love with an actor. 歌手否認她與男演員陷入熱戀的謠言。

depart [dɪˋpɑrt] ◀Track 1321

v. 分離；離開

▶The plane will depart at 8 P.M.
飛機將在晚上八點起飛。

department ◀Track 1322

[dɪˋpɑrtmənt] n. 部門

▶He worked at the company's HR department. 他在公司的人資部上班。

departure [dɪˋpɑrtʃɚ] ◀Track 1323

n. 出發；離開；啟程

▶The plane's departure was delayed twice. 飛機二度延遲起飛。

相關片語 departure lounge 候機室

▶We are in the departure lounge waiting for our next flight. 我們在候機室等候下一個班機。

depend [dɪˋpɛnd] ◀Track 1324

v. 依賴；信賴；視……而定

▶Whether we will go hiking tomorrow depends on the weather. 我們明天是否要健行取決於天氣。

dependable ◀Track 1325

[dɪˋpɛndəbḷ] adj. 可靠的；可信任的

▶She is a dependable companion.
她是可信賴的朋友。

dependent ◀Track 1326

[dɪˋpɛndənt] adj. 依靠的；依賴的

▶He was dependent on his wife after losing his job.
他失業後就依賴妻子的收入了。

n. 受撫養者；受撫養親屬

▶Her pension will provide for her dependents. 她靠養老金養家。

depict [dɪˋpɪkt] ◀Track 1327

v. 描畫；描述；描寫

▶The biography depicted the entrepreneur as a pioneer in the industry.
這本自傳描述這位企業家是業界的先驅。

deposit [dɪˋpɑzɪt] ◀Track 1328

n. 存款；保證金、押金、訂金；沈澱物

▶We paid a deposit to reserve a room in the hotel.
我們先付訂金，預訂這間旅館的房間。

v. 放下；放置、寄存

▶She deposited $3,000 in the post office. 她在郵局存了三千元。

相關片語 safe deposit 保險箱

▶She kept her jewelries in the safe deposit. 她把珠寶放在保險箱裡。

depress [dɪˋprɛs] ◀Track 1329

v. 使沮喪

▶The setback depressed her.
這個挫折使她沮喪。

depressed [dɪˋprɛst] ◀Track 1330

adj. 消沉的、沮喪的、抑鬱的；蕭條的

▶He was depressed upon hearing the bad news. 他聽到壞消息後，陷入沮喪。

depressing
◀Track 1331

[dɪ`prɛsɪŋ] adj. 令人沮喪的

▶It was depressing for him to watch the girl he liked flirt with other guys.
他看到心儀的女孩和其他男生打情罵俏，感到沮喪。

depression
◀Track 1332

[dɪ`prɛʃən] n. 沮喪、抑鬱；意志消沉；不景氣、蕭條

▶Taking drugs will only worsen your depression. 吸毒只會讓你的憂鬱更嚴重。

相關片語 **pregnancy depression** 孕期憂鬱症

▶She experienced pregnancy depression for a year. 她經歷了一年的孕期憂鬱症。

depth
◀Track 1333

[dɛpθ] n. 深度；厚度

▶I expressed the depth of our gratitude to him. 我向他表達我們深切的感謝。

相關片語 **out of one's depth** 非某人所能理解；非某人能力所及

▶Physics is out of my depth.
我對物理學一竅不通。

describe
[dɪ`skraɪb]
◀Track 1334

v. 形容；描述

▶Words cannot describe how sorry I was to hear the news. 我聽到這個消息時，心中的難過是言語無法形容的。

description
◀Track 1335

[dɪ`skrɪpʃən] n. 描述；敘述；說明

▶The witnesses gave the police a full description of the killer. 證人向警方詳述殺人犯的長相 。

descriptive
◀Track 1336

[dɪ`skrɪptɪv] adj. 描寫的；記敘的

▶His writing is very descriptive.
他的寫作風格很生動。

desert [`dɛzət]
◀Track 1337

v. 逃跑；拋棄；遺棄

▶He deserted his girlfriend for a rich woman. 他為了一位富有的女人而拋棄女友。

n. 沙漠

▶They crossed a large area of desert.
他們穿過一大片沙漠。

deserve [dɪ`zɝv]
◀Track 1338

v. 應受；值得

▶He deserved the award.
他是應該得到這個獎章。

design [dɪ`zaɪn] n. 設計
◀Track 1339

▶The design of the dress is exquisite.
這件洋裝的設計很精緻。

v. 設計

▶She designed the interiors of the department store. 她設計百貨公司的內部裝潢。

designer [dɪ`zaɪnə]
◀Track 1340

n. 設計師

▶Jason Wu is a fashion designer.
吳季剛一位知名服裝設計師。

desire [dɪ`zaɪr] n. 渴望
◀Track 1341

▶He had no desire for luxury goods.
他對奢侈品沒有任何慾望。

v. 渴望

▶She desired to be a famous actress.
她渴望成為知名的女演員。

中級

desk [dɛsk] n. 書桌
◀ Track 1342

▶The reporter had a piles of papers on her desk. 記者的書桌有一疊文件。

despair [dɪ`spɛr] n. 絕望
◀ Track 1343

▶He was in despair after his wife passed away. 他妻子過世後,他陷入絕望。

補充片語 in despair 絕望地

desperate [`dɛspərɪt]
◀ Track 1344
adj. 危急的;絕望的;極度渴望的

▶She was desperate when she lost her parents. 她慟失雙親時,深感絕望。

despise [dɪ`spaɪz]
◀ Track 1345
v. 鄙視;看不起

▶She despises anyone who abuses animals. 她鄙視任何虐待動物的人。

despite [dɪ`spaɪt]
◀ Track 1346
prep. 儘管

▶She took the exam despite her illness. 儘管生病,她仍去考試。

dessert [dɪ`zɝt]
◀ Track 1347
n. 甜點;餐後點心

▶I made an apple pie for dessert. 我做了一個蘋果派做為甜點。

destination
◀ Track 1348
[ˌdɛstə`neʃən] n. 目的地;終點

▶Taroko National Park is one of the tourist destinations in Taiwan. 太魯閣國家公園是台灣的觀光景點之一。

destiny [`dɛstənɪ]
◀ Track 1349
n. 命運

▶It was her destiny to meet him again. 命運注定她再度與他相見。

destroy [dɪ`strɔɪ]
◀ Track 1350
v. 破壞;摧毀

▶The tornado destroyed many houses. 龍捲風摧毀了許多房屋。

destruction
◀ Track 1351
[dɪ`strʌkʃən] n. 摧毀;破壞;毀滅

▶The typhoon caused serious destruction to the village. 颱風對這鄉村造成嚴重的破壞。

destructive
◀ Track 1352
[dɪ`strʌktɪv] adj. 破壞性的;毀滅性的;消極的、無幫助的

▶He never engaged in destructive criticism. 他從不發表有害評論。

detail [`ditel]
◀ Track 1353
n. 細節;詳情

▶He knew all the details of the project. 他知道計畫所有的細節。

v. 詳述;詳細說明

▶The report detailed the progress of the project. 這份報告詳述計畫的進度。

相關片語 in detail 詳細地

▶She described the incident in detail. 她詳細地描述事發狀況。

detailed [`di`teld]
◀ Track 1354
adj. 詳細的

▶They gave a detailed description of the robbers. 他們詳述搶匪的樣貌。

detect [dɪ`tɛkt]
◀ Track 1355
v. 發覺;察覺;看穿

▶She detected discomfort from his face.
她從男子的臉上察覺了他感到不舒服。

detective [dɪˋtɛktɪv] ◀Track 1356

n. 偵探

▶The amateur detective broke the case.
業餘偵探破了這個案子。

adj. 偵探的；偵探用的

▶His new detective series are a fabulous
read. 他新出的偵探系列小説很好看。

detergent [dɪˋtɝdʒənt] ◀Track 1357

n. 洗潔劑；去垢劑

▶The liquid detergent is more soluble in
water. 洗滌液較易溶於水。

adj. 洗滌的

▶The detergent effect is highly significant.
這個洗滌效果非常顯著。

determination ◀Track 1358
[dɪˌtɝməˋneʃən]

n. 決心；堅定、果斷；決斷力

▶He is a man of determination.
他是個果斷的人。

determine [dɪˋtɝmɪn] ◀Track 1359

v. 決心；決定

▶They determined to win the competition.
他們決心要贏得比賽。

determined ◀Track 1360

[dɪˋtɝmɪnd] **adj.** 下定決心的

▶He was determined to quit drugs.
他決心戒毒。

develop [dɪˋvɛləp] ◀Track 1361

v. 建立；發展

▶The teacher helped his students
develop reading habits. 老師幫助學生養
成閱讀習慣。

development ◀Track 1362

[dɪˋvɛləpmənt] **n.** 發展；發育；進展；開發

▶The government tried to strengthen the
country's economic development. 政府
試圖強化國家的經濟發展。

device [dɪˋvaɪs] ◀Track 1363

n. 設備；儀器；裝置

▶The hardware device is not connected
to the computer yet. 這個硬體裝置還沒有
連上電腦。

devil [ˋdɛvl] ◀Track 1364

n. 撒旦；魔鬼；惡魔；惡棍

▶Don't make deals with devils. 不要跟魔
鬼打交道。

相關片語 **devil's advocate**
故意唱反調的人

▶He wasn't really for euthanasia. He was
just playing the devil's advocate. 他並非
真正主張安樂死，只是故意唱反調罷了。

devise [dɪˋvaɪz] ◀Track 1365

v. 設計；發明

▶The boy devised a computer game and
sold it to a company. 男孩設計了一個電
腦遊戲並把它賣給一家公司。

devote [dɪˋvot] ◀Track 1366

v. 將……奉獻給

▶He devoted his life to helping the poor
and sick. 他把生命奉獻在幫助貧病的人。

補充片語 **devote oneself to**
專心於；獻身於

中級

devoted [dɪ`votɪd] ◀≣Track 1367

adj. 專心致志的；獻身的；摯愛的

▶ She was devoted to the study of philosophy. 她致力研究哲學。

devotion [dɪ`voʃən] ◀≣Track 1368

n. 獻身；奉獻

▶ His devotion to charity work was respected all over the world. 他獻身於慈善工作，並廣為世人景仰。

dew [dju] **n.** 露水；露 ◀≣Track 1369

▶ The petals glistened with dew. 花瓣上閃耀著露珠。

diabetes [ˌdaɪə`bitiz] ◀≣Track 1370

n. 糖尿病

▶ He has type 1 diabetes. 他是第1型糖尿病的病人。

diagnose [`daɪəgnoz] ◀≣Track 1371

v. 診斷

▶ She was diagnosed with lung cancer. 她被診斷罹患肺癌。

diagnosis ◀≣Track 1372

[ˌdaɪəg`nosɪs] **n.** 診斷；診斷結果；診斷書

▶ The doctor will give you a clear diagnosis when we get the results of your medical examination. 我們得到你的體檢報告時，醫生會給你明確的診斷。

diagram [`daɪəˌgræm] ◀≣Track 1373

n. 圖表；圖解

▶ She drew a diagram to help everyone follow her logic. 她畫了一張圖表，讓大家能了解她的邏輯。

v. 圖示；以圖解法表示

▶ He diagramed the floor plan of the building. 他畫了樓層的平面圖。

dial [`daɪəl] **v.** 撥打 ◀≣Track 1374

▶ When the accident happened, he quickly dialed 911. 意外發生時，他迅速撥打911。

n. 表盤；鐘盤

▶ There is a Hello Kitty on the dial of her watch. 她的手錶表盤上是一隻凱蒂貓。

dialect [`daɪəlɛkt] **n.** 方言 ◀≣Track 1375

▶ Hakka is one of the dialects in Taiwan. 客家話是台灣方言的一種。

dialogue [`daɪəˌlɔg] ◀≣Track 1376
=di·a·log （英式英文）**n.** 對話；交談

▶ The leaders had a pleasant dialogue. 領袖們對話愉快。

diamond [`daɪəmənd] ◀≣Track 1377

n. 鑽石

▶ She thinks that diamonds are women's best friend.
她認為鑽石是女人最好的朋友。

diaper [`daɪəpɚ] **n.** 尿布 ◀≣Track 1378

▶ The mother changed her baby's diaper in the room. 媽媽在房裡幫寶寶換尿布。

diary [`daɪərɪ] **n.** 日記 ◀≣Track 1379

▶ He kept a diary when he was young. 他小時候有寫日記的習慣。

dictionary ◀≣Track 1380

[`dɪkʃənˌɛrɪ] **n.** 字典

▶ She looked up the new word in the dictionary. 她用字典查生字。

didn't [`dɪdnt] ◀┋Track 1381
abbr. 未、沒有做（**did not**的縮寫）

▶We didn't do enough to stop climate change. 我們沒有盡力阻止氣候變遷。

die [daɪ] v. 死；死去 ◀┋Track 1382

▶He died of heart attack. 他死於心臟病。

diet [`daɪət] ◀┋Track 1383
n. 飲食；特種飲食

▶The diet is for people with diabetes. 這個飲食是為糖尿病的人設計的。

v. 飲食；特種飲食

▶She lost a lot of weight by extreme dieting. 她透過激烈節食，減了很多體重。

adj. 減重的；節食的

▶She drank diet cola throughout the day. 她一整天都喝健怡可樂。

differ [`dɪfə] ◀┋Track 1384
v. 不同；相異；分歧

▶Their viewpoints differ from each other. 他們的觀點各異。

補充片語 differ from 與……不同

difference [`dɪfərəns] ◀┋Track 1385
n. 不同；差異

▶I can't tell the difference between an ape and a gorilla.
我分不清楚猿和猩猩的差別。

different [`dɪfərənt] ◀┋Track 1386
adj. 不同的

▶Eastern culture is very different from western one. 東方文化和西方文化差有很大的不同。

difficult [`dɪfəˌkəlt] ◀┋Track 1387
adj. 困難的；難處理的；難對付的

▶The math problem is difficult to solve. 這題數學很難解。

difficulty [`dɪfəˌkʌltɪ] ◀┋Track 1388
n. 困難；難處

▶He overcame many obstacles to make great achievements in life. 他克服了許多困難才在生命中取得了重大成就。

dig [dɪg] v. 挖；掘 ◀┋Track 1389

▶A tunnel was dug through the hill.
一條貫通山丘的隧道已挖通了。

digest [daɪ`dʒɛst] ◀┋Track 1390
v. 消化；融會貫通

▶She sat in the couch and allowed meal to digest. 她坐在沙發上讓胃裡的食物消化。

n. 摘要；文摘

▶This is a digest of today's news.
這是今天新聞摘要。

digestion [də`dʒɛstʃən] ◀┋Track 1391
n. 消化；消化能力

▶Having midnight snacks is not good for digestion. 吃宵夜會消化不良。

digit [`dɪdʒɪt] ◀┋Track 1392
n. 數字；手指

▶As a kindergarten teacher, your salary will never reach 6 digits. 做一個幼稚園老師，你的薪水永遠不會達到六位數。

digital [`dɪdʒɪtl] ◀┋Track 1393
adj. 指狀的；數字的；數碼的

▶The number 7580 contains four digits.
數字7580是四位數。

中級

dignity [`dɪgnətɪ]
◀Track 1394

n. 尊嚴；莊嚴；高尚；尊貴

▶She wished to die with dignity.
她希望死得有尊嚴。

dilemma [də`lɛmə]
◀Track 1395

n. 進退兩難；困境

▶She was caught in a dilemma whether she should marry John or Peter. 她陷入了是該嫁給約翰或彼得的兩難局面。

補充片語 be caught in a dilemma
陷入兩難局面

diligent [`dɪlədʒənt]
◀Track 1396

adj. 勤勞的

▶He was diligent in his work.
他工作很勤勞。

dim [dɪm]
◀Track 1397

adj. 微暗的；暗淡的；朦朧的

▶His eyesight grew dim as he became older. 他隨著年齡增長，視力變模糊了。

v. 使變暗淡；使變模糊

▶The woman's eyes dimmed with tears.
女人的眼睛因淚水而變得模糊了。

dime [daɪm] **n.** 一角硬幣
◀Track 1398

▶The boy put some dimes into his piggy bank. 男孩丟了幾個一角硬幣到小豬撲滿。

dine [daɪn] **v.** 進餐；用餐
◀Track 1399

▶He dined with his parents last night.
他昨晚與父母用餐。

dinner [`dɪnɚ] **n.** 晚餐
◀Track 1400

▶We had spaghetti for dinner.
我們晚餐吃義大利麵。

dinosaur [`daɪnə͵sɔr]
◀Track 1401

n. 恐龍

▶Dinosaurs went into extinction long time ago. 恐龍很早就絕種了。

dip [dɪp] **v.** 浸染；浸洗
◀Track 1402

▶The chef dipped the chick in the batter and then fried it.
主廚把雞肉在麵糊中浸一下後再油炸它。

n. 浸泡；凹地；蘸濕；蘸醬

▶She took a dip in the ocean when it was 40 Celsius degrees.
氣溫四十度時，她去海邊浸泡在海裡。

相關片語 go for a dip 游個泳

▶The children went for a dip in the pool.
孩子們在泳池游泳。

diploma [dɪ`plomə]
◀Track 1403

n. 畢業文憑

▶She is a self-made millionaire although she doesn't have a college diploma.
她雖然沒有大學文憑，但白手起家成為百萬富翁。

diplomat [`dɪpləmæt]
◀Track 1404

n. 外交官

▶He was an extraordinary diplomat.
他是很傑出的外交官。

direct [daɪ`rɛkt]
◀Track 1405

adj. 直接的

▶We took a direct flight to Seoul.
我們搭乘直航班機到首爾。

v. 指揮；指導；指路

▶She directed us the way to the museum.
她指點我們怎麼到博物館。

direction [daɪˋrɛkʃən] ◀Track 1406
n. 方向

▶He gave us very clear directions.
他給我們很清楚的指示。

director [daɪˋrɛktɚ] ◀Track 1407
n. 主管;指揮;導演

▶He is the director of this film.
他是這部影片的導演。

dirt [dɝt] ◀Track 1408
n. 污物;泥土;爛泥

▶The table cloth was covered with dirt.
餐桌巾佈滿灰塵。

相關片語 **treat sb. like dirt**
待某人如糞土

▶She felt she was treated like dirt by her boyfriend. 她覺得男友待她如糞土。

dirty [ˋdɝtɪ] **adj.** 髒的 ◀Track 1409

▶Take off your dirty shirt and change a clean one. 脫下你的骯髒襯衫改換乾淨的。

v. 弄髒

▶The dog dirtied the carpet.
小狗把地毯弄髒了。

disability [dɪsəˋbɪlətɪ] ◀Track 1410
n. 無能;殘疾;不利條件

▶She didn't let physical disability hamper her life. 她並未讓身體的殘疾阻礙她的生命。

補充片語 **physical disability** 身體殘疾

disabled [dɪsˋeb!d] ◀Track 1411
adj. 有殘缺的;有殘疾的;殘廢的

▶Some people are mentally disabled.
有些人心理有殘缺。

相關片語 **learning-disabled**
有學習障礙的

▶We provide emotional support for the learning-disabled children. 我們提供有學習障礙的孩子心靈上的支援。

disadvantage ◀Track 1412
[ˌdɪsədˋvæntɪdʒ] **n.** 缺點;不利條件;損害

▶Her lack of experience was a disadvantage when she applied for the job. 她缺少經驗,對於應徵這份工作是一個不利條件。

v. 使處不利地位;損害

▶The charity intends to help the disadvantaged.
這個慈善團體旨在幫助弱勢群體。

disadvantaged ◀Track 1413
[ˌdɪsədˋvæntɪdʒd] **adj.** 弱勢的;貧困的

▶The program aims to help disadvantaged children. 這個計畫旨在幫助貧困兒童。

disagree [ˌdɪsəˋgri] ◀Track 1414
v. 意見不和;爭論;不一致

▶They disagreed on all kinds of foreign policy issues.
他們對各項外交政策議題都意見不一致。

disagreement ◀Track 1415
[ˌdɪsəˋgrimənt] **n.** 意見不一;爭論;不符

▶She had a loud disagreement with her sister. 她和妹妹大吵一架。

disappear [ˌdɪsəˋpɪr] ◀Track 1416
v. 消失;不見

▶The man disappeared long ago.
那個男子很久以前就杳無音訊了。

中級

disappoint
◀€Track 1417

[ˌdɪsəˈpɔɪnt] v. 使失望

▶The singer didn't want to disappoint her fans. 歌手不想讓粉絲失望。

disappointed
◀€Track 1418

[ˌdɪsəˈpɔɪntɪd] adj. 失望的

▶I was very disappointed with her. 我對她很失望。

disappointing
◀€Track 1419

[ˌdɪsəˈpɔɪntɪŋ] adj. 使人失望的

▶His answer to the customer's request was very disappointing. 他針對客戶詢問所做的回應令人失望。

disappointment
◀€Track 1420

[ˌdɪsəˈpɔɪntmənt] n. 失望；掃興；令人失望、掃興的人或事

▶The movie was a great disappointment. 這部電影令人掃興。

disapproval
◀€Track 1421

[ˌdɪsəˈpruvl] n. 不贊成；不喜歡

▶I could sense the director's disapproval of his proposal. 我可以感覺到主任不贊成他的提案。

disapprove
◀€Track 1422

[ˌdɪsəˈpruv] v. 不贊成；不同意

▶We strongly disapprove of drunk driving. 我們強烈反對酒駕。

disaster
[dɪˈzæstɚ]
◀€Track 1423

n. 災難；不幸

▶There were severe casualties when the natural disaster struck. 天災降臨時，造成嚴重的傷亡。

補充片語 natural disaster 天災；自然災難

discard
[dɪsˈkɑrd]
◀€Track 1424

v. 拋棄；摒棄；丟棄

▶She discarded all the old magazines. 她把所有舊雜誌都丟了。

n. 被拋棄的人；拋棄物

▶He collected all the discards and put them into trash can. 他把所有不要的東西都丟到垃圾筒。

discipline
[ˈdɪsəplɪn]
◀€Track 1425

n. 紀律；風紀

▶She doesn't have the discipline to save money. 她沒有存錢的紀律。

v. 訓練；使有紀律；懲戒

▶The mother tried to discipline her children to brush their teeth before going to bed. 媽媽試圖訓練小孩睡前刷牙。

disco
[ˈdɪsko]
=discotheque
◀€Track 1426

n. 小舞廳；迪斯可舞廳

▶They had a disco there last Saturday night. 他們上週六晚上有迪斯可舞會。

discomfort
◀€Track 1427

[dɪsˈkʌmfɚt] n. 不適，不安，不舒服；使人不舒服的事物

▶He felt a bit discomfort after the microsurgery. 他在微創手術後身體稍有一點不適。

v. 使不舒服；使不安

▶She was discomforted by his hysterical reaction. 他歇斯底里的反應使她感到很痛苦。

disconnect
🔊Track 1428

[ˌdɪskəˈnɛkt] **v.** 使分離

▶He disconnected the machine from the electricity supply. 他把機器的電源切斷。

discount
[ˈdɪskaʊnt]
🔊Track 1429

n. 折扣；不全信

▶His account must be taken at a discount. 他的說法我們不應盡信。

v. 將……打折扣；懷疑地看待；不全相信

▶The department store discounted the sale prices of winter coats. 百貨公司削價出售冬天外套。

discourage
🔊Track 1430

[dɪsˈkɝ·ɪdʒ] **v.** 使洩氣；使沮喪

▶He was discouraged by their criticism. 他對他們的批評感到喪氣。

discover
[dɪsˈkʌvɚ]
🔊Track 1431

v. 發現

▶Nikola Tesla made many scientific discoveries. 尼古拉·特斯拉有許多科學發現。

discovery
[dɪsˈkʌvərɪ]
🔊Track 1432

n. 發現

▶Scientists are excited about the discovery of a nearly complete dinosaur fossil. 科學家們對於發現一個幾乎完整的恐龍化石感到興奮不已。

補充片語 dinosaur fossil 恐龍化石

discrimination
🔊Track 1433

[dɪˌskrɪməˈneʃən]

n. 區別；歧視、不公平待遇

▶Let's hope that racial discrimination no longer exists. 希望種族歧視不再存在。

補充片語 racial discrimination 種族歧視

discuss [dɪˈskʌs]
🔊Track 1434

v. 討論

▶The first chapter discusses the origin of the universe. 第一章探討宇宙的由來。

discussion
🔊Track 1435

[dɪˈskʌʃən] **n.** 討論

▶The controversial issue is still under discussion.
這個爭議性的議題仍在討論中。

disease [dɪˈziz]
🔊Track 1436

n. 疾病

▶He contracted a lung disease.
他感染了肺病。

disguise [dɪsˈgaɪz]
🔊Track 1437

n. 假裝；掩飾；喬裝

▶His smile was a disguise for his depression.
他用笑容掩飾他的憂鬱。

v. 掩飾；隱瞞；把……喬裝起來

▶He disguised himself as a clown.
他把自己喬裝成一位小丑。

disgust [dɪsˈgʌst]
🔊Track 1438

v. 使作嘔；使討厭

▶The smell of the garbage disgusted the neighbors. 垃圾的味道讓鄰居作嘔。

n. 作嘔；厭惡；憎惡

▶He looked at the dirty tissues in disgust.
他厭惡地看著骯髒的衛生紙。

補充片語 in disgust 厭惡地

中級

dish [dɪʃ] **n.** 盤；碟；菜餚 ◀Track 1439

▶Would you help me do the dishes?
你可以幫我洗碗嗎?

dishonest [dɪsˋɑnɪst] ◀Track 1440
adj. 不誠實的

▶He was morally dishonest.
他的品行不端。

disk [dɪsk] ◀Track 1441
=**disc** **n.** 圓盤；盤狀物；光碟（電腦磁碟；唱片；影像圓盤）

▶He saved the photos in the disk.
他把照片都存在光碟裡。

dislike [dɪsˋlaɪk] ◀Track 1442
v. 不喜歡

▶She disliked the stiff doctrines.
她不喜歡僵硬的教義。

n. 不喜歡

▶He has a dislike for carrots.
他不喜歡胡蘿蔔。

補充片語 **have a dislike for** 不喜歡

相關片語 **likes and dislikes** 好惡

▶We all have our own likes and dislikes.
我們都各有好惡。

dismiss [dɪsˋmɪs] ◀Track 1443
v. 讓……離開；遣散

▶She was dismissed from the hospital a month later. 她住院一個月之後出院。

disorder [dɪsˋɔrdɚ] ◀Track 1444
n. 混亂；無秩序；失調；障礙

▶His dorm was in disorder. 他的宿舍很亂。

display [dɪˋsple] ◀Track 1445
v. 陳列；展出；顯示

▶She displayed interest in ballet.
她展現對芭蕾的興趣。

n. 展覽；陳列；陳列品

▶The displays of the paintings are elegant. 圖畫陳列的方式很雅緻。

disposable ◀Track 1446
[dɪˋspozəbl] **adj.** 用完即丟的；一次性使用的；可任意處置、使用的

▶Disposable cups are banned at certain schools. 有些學校禁用免洗杯。

disposal [dɪˋspozl] ◀Track 1447
n. 處置；處理；自由處置權

▶We spent a lot time on the disposal of furniture in the new office. 我們在新辦公室的傢具布置上花了很多時間。

dispose [dɪˋspoz] ◀Track 1448
v. 配置；處理；處置

▶The general disposed troops near the river. 將軍在河流附近布置軍隊。

dispute [dɪˋspjut] ◀Track 1449
v. 爭論；爭執

▶They disputed over the cost.
他們為了成本的事起爭執。

n. 爭論；爭執

▶They finally settled the dispute.
他們最後終於平息了爭執。

dissatisfaction ◀Track 1450
[ˌdɪssætɪsˋfækʃən] **n.** 不滿；不平

▶The beauty industry sells women's dissatisfaction with their appearances in order to make a profit. 美容業以推銷女性對外表的不滿來賺取利潤。

dissolve [dɪ`zɑlv]
◀Track 1451

v. 分解；使溶解；使融化；使終結；
解（謎）；（會議）解散

▶Honey dissolves in water. 蜂蜜溶於水。

distance [`dɪstəns]
◀Track 1452

n. 距離

▶It is a long distance from Taipei to Frankfurt. 台北離法蘭克福很遠。

distant [`dɪstənt]
◀Track 1453

adj. 遠的；遠離的；遠親的；冷淡的、疏遠的

▶She's very distant with Ellen. 她對艾倫很冷淡。

distinct [dɪ`stɪŋkt]
◀Track 1454

adj. 與其他不同的；清楚的

▶He and his wife had distinct tastes.
他和妻子嗜好不同。

distinction
◀Track 1455

[dɪ`stɪŋkʃən] **n.** 區別；區分；差別；不同點

▶She treated her employees without distinction. 她對每位員工的對待並無不同。

distinguish
◀Track 1456

[dɪ`stɪŋgwɪʃ] **v.** 區別

▶He can distinguish his classmates by their footsteps. 他能根據同學們的腳步聲辨認出他們。

distinguished
◀Track 1457

[dɪ`stɪŋgwɪʃt] **adj.** 卓越的；著名的

▶She is a distinguished researcher.
她是個知名的研究員。

distract [dɪ`strækt]
◀Track 1458

v. 轉移；岔開；使分心；使苦惱

▶The news distracted the manager.
那個消息使經理很苦惱。

distress [dɪ`strɛs]
◀Track 1459

n. 不幸；悲痛；貧困；引起痛苦的事物

▶The athlete showed signs of distress at the end of the race. 比賽接近尾聲時，選手表現出很痛苦的樣子。

v. 使悲痛；使苦惱；使憂傷

▶His father's death distressed him greatly. 他父親的離世使他很痛苦。

distribute [dɪ`strɪbjʊt]
◀Track 1460

v. 分發；分配

▶The government distributed the lands among the peasants.
政府把土地分給農民。

distribution
◀Track 1461

[ˌdɪstrə`bjuʃən] **n.** 分配；配給物

▶This specie has a wide distribution in this area. 這個物種在這區有很大的數量。

district [`dɪstrɪkt]
◀Track 1462

n. 地區；行政區

▶There is a shopping district near our house. 我們的房子附近有個商店區。

distrust [dɪs`trʌst]
◀Track 1463

v. 不信任

▶She distrusted Amy. 她不信任艾咪。

n. 不信任；懷疑

▶He looked at his business partner with distrust.
他用懷疑的目光看著他的生意夥伴。

disturb [dɪs`tɝb]
◀Track 1464

v. 打擾

中級

▶Please don't disturb me. I'm trying to concentrate on my work. 請不要打擾我，我正在專心工作。

disturbance
🔊Track 1465

[dɪs`tɝbəns] **n.** 打擾；擾亂；引起騷亂的事物

▶The rapid rise in the rice price had triggered the disturbances. 米價快速飆漲引發騷動。

ditch [dɪtʃ]
🔊Track 1466

n. 溝；壕溝；水道

▶The irrigation ditches are used to channel the water for irrigation. 水道是用來疏導水做為灌溉之用。

v. 掘溝；用溝渠圍住；（車）開入溝裡、（飛機）水上迫降、（火車）脫軌；拋棄、擺脫、甩掉

▶She ditched a broken radio. 她丟棄一台壞掉的收音機。

dive [daɪv] **v.** 跳水
🔊Track 1467

▶She dived into the pool from the diving board. 她從跳水板上跳水進池子裡。

diverse [daɪ`vɝs]
🔊Track 1468

adj. 不同的；互異的；各式各樣的；多變化的

▶Daphne and I have diverse interests. 黛芙妮和我的興趣截然不同。

divide [də`vaɪd]
🔊Track 1469

v. 分；劃分

▶The captain divided the team into two groups. 隊長把隊伍分為兩個小組。

divine [də`vaɪn]
🔊Track 1470

adj. 神性的；天賜的；神聖的；天才的；極好的

▶The singer's angelic voice was simply divine. 這個歌手天籟般的聲音真是棒極了。

division [də`vɪʒən]
🔊Track 1471

n. 部門

▶He worked at the sales division. 他在行銷部門上班。

divorce [də`vors] **n.** 離婚
🔊Track 1472

▶Their divorce was amicable. 他們友好地離婚了。

v. 與……離婚

▶She divorced her husband after he beat her. 她遭丈夫毆打後，與丈夫離婚了。

dizzy [`dɪzɪ] **adj.** 暈的
🔊Track 1473

▶He felt dizzy in the middle of the night. 他在半夜感到頭暈。

do [du] **v.** 做
🔊Track 1474

▶She has done a lot of house chores. 她做了許多家務。

aux. 構成疑問句、否定句、強調句或倒裝句的助動詞

▶Do you believe in life after death? 你相信有輪迴嗎？

dock [dɑk]
🔊Track 1475

n. 碼頭；港區；船塢

▶The fish boat was in dock for repairs. 漁船停在船塢進行維修。

v. 使靠碼頭

▶The ship was docked at San Francisco. 船停靠在洛杉磯。

doctor [`dɑktɚ]
🔊Track 1476

=doc.=physician=Dr

（英式英文）**n.** 醫生

▶Dr. Lee is an expert in pediatrics.
李醫師是小兒科的專家。

document
Track 1477

[`dɑkjəmənt] n. 文件

▶The historical documents were kept in the museum.
這些歷史文件被存放在博物館。

documentary
Track 1478

[͵dɑkjə`mɛntərɪ] adj. 文件的；記錄的

▶The documentary film will be premiered this coming Sunday.
這部紀錄片將於本週日首播。

補充片語 **documentary film**
紀錄片；文獻片

n. 紀錄片；紀實節目

▶The documentary is about the life of Princess Diana.
這部紀錄片是關於黛妃的一生。

dodge [dɑdʒ]
Track 1479

v. 閃開；躲避；巧妙迴避

▶The prime minister had to dodge a flying shoe. 總理不得不閃避飛來的一隻鞋子。

n. 託詞；推託的妙計

▶He bought the property as a tax dodge. 為了逃稅，他買下這個房地產。

doesn't [`dʌznt]
Track 1480

abbr. 不（**does not**的縮寫）

▶He doesn't like parties at all.
他一點也不喜歡派對。

dog [dɔg] n. 狗
Track 1481

▶Have you walked the dog? 你去遛狗了嗎?

doll [dɑl] n. 洋娃娃
Track 1482

▶The little girl put her doll in a cradle.
小女孩把洋娃娃放進搖籃裡。

dollar [`dɑlɚ]
Track 1483
=buck n. 元；美元、加幣

▶The coat cost me $590. 這件外套花了我
五百九十元。

dolphin [`dɑlfɪn] n. 海豚
Track 1484

▶We saw a school of dolphins in the sea. 我們在海上看到一群海豚。

dome [dom]
Track 1485

n. 圓頂屋；半球形物；蒼穹

▶The dome of the stadium is under maintenance. 體育館的圓屋頂正在維修中。

domestic [də`mɛstɪk]
Track 1486

adj. 家庭的；家事的；國內的

▶The domestic policy achieved much success. 這個國內政策獲得很大的成功。

相關片語 **domestic violence** 家庭暴力

▶Verbal abuse is also domestic violence.
言語虐待也是家庭暴力。

dominant [`dɑmənənt]
Track 1487

adj. 佔優勢的；具支配地位的；統治的

▶Brexit was the dominant issue in the debate. 英國脫歐是辯論的主要議題。

dominate [`dɑmə͵net]
Track 1488

v. 支配；統治；處於支配地位；控制

▶I didn't get to talk to him because his brother dominated the conversation. 我沒什麼機會和他聊到天，因為他弟弟主導了整場對話。

中級

donate [`donet`]
◀Track 1489

v 捐獻；捐贈

▶She donates $1,000 to the burn center each month. 她每個月捐贈一千元給燒燙傷中心。

donation [do`neʃən]
◀Track 1490

n 捐贈物；捐獻；捐款

▶He made a donation of $2,000 to the charity organization. 他捐了二千元給那間慈善機構。

相關片語 **organ donation card**
器官捐贈同意卡

▶I have an organ donation card. 我有一張器官捐贈同意卡。

donkey [`dɑŋkɪ]
◀Track 1491

n 驢子；傻瓜

▶She tied the little donkey to a pole outside. 她把驢子繫在外面的竹竿。

don't [dont]
◀Track 1492

abbr 不（do not的縮寫）

▶I don't like watching TV news. 我不喜歡看電視新聞。

doom [dum]
◀Track 1493

n 厄運；毀滅；末日審判

▶The news channels are full of doom and gloom. 新聞頻道充斥不幸的消息。

v 註定；命定；使失敗；使毀滅

▶The reforms are doomed to failure. 這些改革註定會失敗。

door [dor] **n** 門
◀Track 1494

▶He lives six doors from Charlie. 他住的地方與查理隔了六家住戶。

doorstep [`dor,stɛp]
◀Track 1495

n 門階

▶He sat on the doorstep reading a magazine. 他坐在門階上看雜誌。

相關片語 **on/at one's doorstep**
在某人家附近

▶When a handsome mailman showed up on her doorstep, Chelsea's heart stuttered. 一位英俊的郵差出現在崔兒喜的家附近時，她的心小鹿亂撞了。

doorway [`dor,we]
◀Track 1496

n 出入口；門口；門路；途徑

▶They hugged each other at the doorway. 他們在門口擁抱彼此。

dorm [dɔrm] **n** 宿舍
◀Track 1497

▶She lives in the dorm and has two roommates. 她住在宿舍，有兩名室友。

dormitory [`dɔrmə,torɪ]
◀Track 1498
=dorm **n** 宿舍

▶My sister will move to the college dormitory before school begins. 我姊姊在開學前要搬到大學宿舍裡去住。

dosage [`dosɪdʒ]
◀Track 1499

n （藥的）劑量；服用方式

▶When taking the medicine, do not exceed the recommended dosage. 服用這個藥物時，不可超過醫師建議的劑量。

dose [dos]
◀Track 1500

n （藥物的）一劑；劑量

▶He took a dose of penicillin under medical observation without a reaction. 他在醫療人員監視下服用一劑盤尼西林，所幸無不良反應。

相關片語 **like a dose of salts**
很快地；一下子

▶He finished the house chores like a dose of salts. 他很快就把家務做完了。

dot [dɑt] n. 點；小圓點　◀Track 1501

▶Her apron was pink with white dots.
她的粉紅色圍裙有白色小圓點。

double [`dʌbl̩]　◀Track 1502

adj. 兩倍的；成雙的；雙人的

▶The society has double standards for women. 社會對女性有雙重標準。

v. 使加倍；增加一倍

▶The profit this year has doubled.
今年的利潤成長一倍。

n. 兩倍數量；加倍

▶Her rent is the double of mine.
她的房租是我的兩倍。

doubt [daʊt]　◀Track 1503

n. 懷疑；疑慮

▶There is no doubt that she is hard-working. 她無疑地是勤奮的人。

v. 懷疑；疑慮

▶They doubted what he said was true.
他們懷疑他所說的話是否真實。

doubtful [`daʊtfəl]　◀Track 1504

adj. 懷疑的；疑惑的

▶He is doubtful about whether to take on this job. 他很遲疑是否該接下這份工作。

dough [do] n. 生麵糰　◀Track 1505

▶She is making dough to make bagels.
她正在揉麵糰準備做貝果。

相關片語 **earn one's own dough**
自己掙錢

▶He earned his own dough when he was in senior high school.
他從高中起就自己掙錢了。

doughnut [`do͵nʌt]　◀Track 1506
=donut n. 油炸圈餅；炸麵圈

▶He earns his living by selling doughnuts.
他靠賣甜甜圈維生。

dove [dʌv]　◀Track 1507

n. 鴿；溫和派人士

▶The doves were kept in a cage.
鴿子被關在籠子裡。

down [daʊn]　◀Track 1508

adv. 向下地；（程度、數量）減緩、減少地

▶They went down to California last summer. 他們去年夏天南下去加州。

prep. 在⋯⋯下方；沿著

▶They rowed down the river.
他們沿著河流向下划。

n. 下降；失敗；蕭條

▶The famous actress had her ups and downs. 知名的女演員有過得意之時，也有過不順遂之日。

adj. 向下的；（情緒）低落的

▶He seemed to be a bit down.
他似乎有點悶悶不樂。

download [`daʊn͵lod]　◀Track 1509

v. （電腦）下載

▶You can download the app from your cell phone.
你可以在手機下載這個應用程式。

n. 下載；下載的文件

▶The software is available for download.
這個軟體可供使用者下載。

中級

downstairs
◀Track 1510

[͵daʊn`stɛrz] **adv.** 在樓下；往樓下

▶She went downstairs to answer the door. 她下樓去應門。

adj. 樓下的

▶The number of the downstairs fax machine is 5172-6391. 樓下的傳真機號碼是5172-6391。

downtown
◀Track 1511

[͵daʊn`taʊn] **adv.** 往城市商業區

▶We went downtown to see an opera. 我們進城去看歌劇。

adj. 城市商業區的

▶She works in a company located in downtown Los Angeles. 她在洛杉磯市中心的公司上班。

n. 城市商業區；鬧區

▶Bankruptcy ended the company's presence in downtown. 這家公司破產，在城市的鬧區消失了。

downwards
◀Track 1512

[`daʊnwədz] **adv.** 向下地；朝下地

▶The sales figures were revised downwards. 銷售數字被往下修正了。

doze [doz]
◀Track 1513

v. 打瞌睡；打盹

▶The movie was so boring that I dozed off. 這部電影太悶，以致於我打瞌睡了。

n. 瞌睡；假寐

▶She had a little doze in the rocking chair. 她在搖椅上打瞌睡了。

dozen [`dʌzn]
◀Track 1514

n. 一打；許多

▶I bought a dozen of eggs in the supermarket. 我在超市買了一打雞蛋。

Dr. [`dɑktə]=doc·tor
◀Track 1515

n. 博士；醫生；大夫；學者；教師

▶Dr. Smith is an expert in biology. 史密斯博士是生物學的專家。

draft [dræft]
◀Track 1516

n. 草稿，草圖

▶She sketched a draft with a pencil. 她用鉛筆快速畫了一張草稿。

v. 起草；設計

▶They drafted a proposal for the project. 他們草擬了一個企劃案草案。

drag [dræg]
◀Track 1517

v. 拉；拖；拖曳；慢吞吞地進行

▶He dragged his luggage up the stairs. 他把行李拖到樓上去。

n. 拖曳；拉；累贅；拖後腿的事；令人厭倦的事

▶The welcoming banquet was a drag. 這場歡迎晚宴很無趣。

相關片語 **drag one's feet** 拖拖拉拉

▶The prime minister seemed to drag his feet on these issues. 總理似乎將這些議題一直拖延擱置。

dragon [`drægən] **n.** 龍
◀Track 1518

▶Dragons are considered auspicious in the Chinese culture. 龍在中華文化被視為吉祥的象徵。

Dragon Boat Festival
◀Track 1519

[`drægən-bot-`fɛstəvl] **n.** 端午節

▶The Dragon Boat Festival will take place next Saturday. 下週六是端午節。

中
級

dragonfly
◀ᛔTrackᛔTrack 1520

[`dræɡənˌflaɪ] **n.** 蜻蜓

▶A dragonfly just flew into my room.
有隻蜻蜓剛剛飛進我的房間。

drain [dren]
◀Track 1521

v. 排出、排掉（液體）；喝乾；耗盡

▶He drained a bottle of mineral water.
他喝光一瓶礦泉水。

n. 排水管

▶All their efforts went down the drain.
他們的努力都白費了。

補充片語 **go down the drain** 付諸東流

相關片語 **laugh like a drain** 放聲大笑

▶She laughed like a drain when a bird
pooped on her friend. 小鳥在她朋友身上
便便時，她放聲大笑。

drama [`drɑmə]
◀Track 1522

n. 戲劇；戲劇性

▶Many people are crazy about Korean
dramas. 很多人都很迷韓劇。

dramatic [drə`mætɪk]
◀Track 1523

adj. 戲劇的；劇本的；戲劇般的；戲劇性
的；引人注目的

▶Excessive carbon emissions have a
dramatic impact on our climate. 過量的
碳排放對我們的氣候造成戲劇化的影響。

drape [drep] **n.** 簾；幔
◀Track 1524

▶She drew the drapes and went to bed.
她拉上窗簾就去睡覺了。

v. 覆蓋；垂掛

▶He draped his coat over the back of his
chair. 他把外套披掛在椅背上。

draw [drɔ] **v.** 畫
◀Track 1525

▶The boy drew an airplane on the
blackboard. 男孩在黑板畫一架飛機。

drawer [`drɔɚ] **n.** 抽屜
◀Track 1526

▶She put the car key in the drawer.
她把車鑰匙放在抽屜裡。

drawing [`drɔɪŋ]
◀Track 1527

n. 描繪；圖畫

▶He made a drawing of a seal.
他畫了一隻海豹。

dread [drɛd]
◀Track 1528

n. 害怕；畏懼；恐怖

▶He has a dread of spiders. 他懼怕蜘蛛。

補充片語 **have a dread of** 對……懼怕

v. 害怕；擔心；畏懼

▶She dreads to see her ex-husband
again. 她害怕再見到前夫。

dreadful [`drɛdfəl]
◀Track 1529

adj. 可怕的

▶It was a dreadful car crash.
這真是一場可怕的交通事故。

dream [drim]
◀Track 1530

n. 夢；夢想

▶He realized his dream of becoming a
singer. 他實現成為歌手的夢想。

v. 做夢；夢到

▶I dreamed that I could fly last night.
我昨晚夢見自己可以飛。

dress [drɛs]
◀Track 1531

v. 給……穿衣；使穿著；穿衣；打扮

▶The mother was dressing her child.
媽媽正為小孩穿衣服。

n. 衣服；女裝；連身裙

▶You look gorgeous in this dress.
你穿這件洋裝真美。

dresser [`drɛsɚ] ◀ Track 1532
n. 附有鏡子的衣櫥；附有抽屜的梳妝台

▶She kept her engagement ring in a drawer of the dresser. 她把訂婚戒放在衣櫥的抽屜裡。

dressing [`drɛsɪŋ] ◀ Track 1533
n. 服飾、打扮；梳理；敷藥包紮；醬料

▶I want Caesar dressing on my salad.
我的沙拉上面要加凱撒沙拉醬。

drift [drɪft] ◀ Track 1534
v. 漂流；漂泊；遊蕩；吹積成堆

▶Many young people drifted into Taipei City to seek jobs. 許多年輕人北漂到台北找工作。

n. 漂流；漂移；漂流物；緩流

▶There was a drift of farmers to big cities. 農民流向大城市。

drill [drɪl] ◀ Track 1535
n. 鑽頭；操練、訓練

▶He had lots of drill in algebra.
他在代數方面受過許多訓練。

v. 鑽孔；操練、訓練

▶The teacher drilled the class in reading comprehension.
老師訓練學生閱讀理解力。

drink [drɪŋk] **v.** 喝 ◀ Track 1536

▶I drank a glass of orange juice.
我喝了一杯柳橙汁。

n. 飲料

▶After being diagnosed with liver cancer, he never touched a drop of drink. 他被診斷罹患肝癌後，再也不喝酒了。

drinking [`drɪŋkɪŋ] ◀ Track 1537
n. 喝，喝酒

▶Binge drinking can lead to health problems. 過量飲酒可能導致健康問題。

drip [drɪp] **v.** 滴下；滴落 ◀ Track 1538

▶The petals dripped with dew. 花瓣掛滿露珠。

n. 滴下；滴水聲；點滴；水滴

▶He was put on a drip after the surgery.
他手術後就打著點滴。

drive [draɪv] ◀ Track 1539
v. 開車；駕駛

▶They drove to the shopping mall.
他們開車到購物中心。

n. 開車兜風；駕車旅行

▶It was a long drive from Taipei to Kaohsiung. 從台北開車到高雄要花很久的時間。

driver [`draɪvɚ] ◀ Track 1540
n. 駕駛人；司機

▶He is a taxi driver. 他是一位計程車司機。

driveway [`draɪˌwe] ◀ Track 1541
n. 私人車道；馬路；車道

▶The chauffeur picked up the billionaire on the driveway. 司機在車道上接送這位億萬富翁。

drop [drɑp] ◀ Track 1542
v. 滴下；丟下；下（車）

▶He dropped the letter into the mail box. 他把這封信投到郵筒中。

n. 滴;落下;降落

▶The drop in prices was the result of different factors. 價格的下跌是不同因素造成的結果。

---

drought [draʊt] 🔊 Track 1543

n. 乾旱;旱災

▶The drought ruined the crops.
乾旱把莊稼給毀了。

---

drown [draʊn] **v** 溺死 🔊 Track 1544

▶He fell into the lake and drowned.
他掉進湖裡溺死了。

相關片語 **look like a drowned rat**
濕得像落湯雞

▶After the heavy rain, she looked like a drowned rat. 大雨過後,她全身都濕透了。

---

drowsy [`draʊzɪ] 🔊 Track 1545

adj. 昏昏欲睡的;睏倦的;無活力的;呆滯的

▶I felt drowsy in the afternoon.
我下午覺得昏昏欲睡的。

---

drug [drʌg] **n.** 藥;毒品 🔊 Track 1546

▶The new drug can cure this disease.
新藥可以治癒這個疾病。

---

drugstore [`drʌg͵stor] 🔊 Track 1547

n. 藥局

▶Could you buy some bandages for me when you go to the drugstore?
你到藥局可以幫我買一些繃帶嗎?

---

drum [drʌm] **n.** 鼓 🔊 Track 1548

▶He played the drums in the band.
他在樂團裡打鼓。

---

drunk [drʌŋk] 🔊 Track 1549

adj. 喝醉酒的

▶He is drunk. Let's get him a taxi.
他喝醉了,我們幫他叫一部計程車吧。

n. 醉漢;酒鬼

▶His father was a drunk.
他的父親是個酒鬼。

相關片語 **drunk driving** 酒後駕駛

▶The country will introduce a stricter law to punish drunk driving. 這個國家要引進更嚴格的法律來懲罰酒駕。

---

dry [draɪ] **adj.** 乾的 🔊 Track 1550

▶The country has a dry climate in winter. 這個國家冬天氣候乾燥。

v 弄乾;使乾燥

▶He dried his tears with a tissue.
他用面紙擦乾了眼淚。

---

dryer [`draɪɚ] 🔊 Track 1551

n. 乾燥器;吹風機;烘乾機

▶She bought a new hair dryer.
她買了一支新的吹風機。

---

duck [dʌk] **n.** 鴨子;鴨肉 🔊 Track 1552

▶The ducks quacked loudly on the grass. 鴨子在草地上大聲地呱呱叫。

---

duckling [`dʌklɪŋ] 🔊 Track 1553

n. 小鴨

▶The ugly duckling turned out to be a swan. 那隻醜小鴨原來是隻天鵝。

---

due [dju] 🔊 Track 1554

adj. 應支付的;到期的;預定應到的;應有的

▶They are due to leave tomorrow.
他們預定明天離開。

中級

相關片語 **due date** 期限；到期日；預定日期；預產期

▶His wife's due date is only five days away. 他妻子的預產期是五天之後。

dull [dʌl] ◀┋Track 1555

adj. 晦暗的；模糊的；陰沈的；乏味的、單調的

▶The movie was so dull that many people fell asleep. 這電影沉悶到許多人都睡著了。

dumb [dʌm] ◀┋Track 1556

adj. 啞的；不能說話的；沉默寡言的；愚笨的

▶She did a dumb thing.
她做了一件愚蠢的事。

dump [dʌmp] ◀┋Track 1557

v. 傾倒；拋棄

▶She dumped the garbage into the garbage truck. 她把垃圾倒進垃圾車。

n. 垃圾場

▶The cabinet is about ready for the dump. 這櫥櫃破爛不堪快要送垃圾場了。

相關片語 **down in the dumps** 沮喪的；抑鬱的

▶He's been down in the dumps since he lost his job. 他失業之後就一直很抑鬱。

dumpling [`dʌmplɪŋ] ◀┋Track 1558

n. 餃子；水煎包等

▶The dumplings at that restaurant are delicious. 那家餐廳的餃子很好吃。

durable [`djʊrəbl̩] ◀┋Track 1559

adj. 經久的；耐用的

▶The kitchen wares are made of durable materials.
這些餐具是用非常耐用的材質做的。

duration [djʊ`reʃən] ◀┋Track 1560

n. （時間）持續；持久；持續時間

▶The duration of the award ceremony will last for one hour. 頒獎典禮的持續時間是一小時。

during [`djʊrɪŋ] ◀┋Track 1561

prep. 在……期間

▶He was born during World War II.
他在第二次世界大戰時期出生。

dusk [dʌsk] ◀┋Track 1562

n. 薄暮；黃昏

▶She worked from dusk till dawn.
她從晚上工作到清晨。

dust [dʌst] **n.** 灰塵 ◀┋Track 1563

▶His coat was covered with dust.
他的外套全是灰塵。

v. 除去灰塵；打掃

▶She dusted the room.
她把房間灰塵擦拭掉。

相關片語 **bite the dust** 被拒絕；倒地而死；陣亡；掛點

▶He bit the dust when he heard the gunfire. 他聽到槍響時即倒地身亡。

dusty [`dʌstɪ] ◀┋Track 1564

adj. 滿是灰塵的；塵狀的

▶The attic was very dusty.
閣樓積了很多灰塵。

duty [`djutɪ] ◀┋Track 1565

n. 職責；任務

▶The police was injured when he was on duty. 警察執勤時受傷了。

dwarf [dwɔrf]
◀ Track 1566

n. 侏儒；矮子；矮小的動物

▶*Snow White and the Seven Dwarfs* is a fairy tale. 《白雪公主和七位小矮人》是一部童話故事。

adj. 矮小的；發育不全的

▶She grew some dwarf trees in the garden. 她在庭院種了一些矮樹。

v 使矮小；萎縮；阻礙生長

▶Lack of food dwarfed the children. 缺乏食物阻礙了這些孩子的生長發育。

dye [daɪ] **n.** 染料；染色
◀ Track 1567

▶The hair dye is chemical-free. 這個頭髮染料不含化學物質。

v 染髮

▶She dyed her hair blond. 她把頭髮染成金色。

dynamic [daɪ`næmɪk]
◀ Track 1568

adj. 動力的；力學的；動態的；有活力的；機能的

▶He is a dynamic young entrepreneur. 他是有活力的年輕企業家。

dynamite
◀ Track 1569

[`daɪnə͵maɪt] **n.** 炸藥

▶The issue of abortion is political dynamite. 墮胎議題是一顆政治炸彈。

v 用炸藥爆破；炸毀

▶They dynamited an old bridge. 他們炸毀一座老舊的橋。

dynasty [`daɪnəstɪ]
◀ Track 1570

n. 王朝；朝代

▶Du Fu was a Chinese poet of the Tang dynasty. 杜甫是中國唐朝的詩人。

中級

Ee

　　以下表格是全民英檢官方公告中級「聽、說、讀、寫」所須具備的能力，本書例句皆依此範疇特別設計，只要掃描右方QR code，就能搭配相對應的音軌實現「眼耳並用」方式，刺激左腦的語言學習功能；同時也可使用本書附贈的紅膠片，將其置於單字上，一面記憶一面自我挑戰，達到雙倍的學習成果！

聽	在日常生活中，能聽懂一般的會話；能大致聽懂公共場所廣播、氣象報告及廣告等。在工作時，能聽懂簡易的產品介紹與操作說明。能大致聽懂外籍人士的談話及詢問。
說	可在日常生活中，能以簡易英語交談或描述一般事物，能介紹自己的生活作息、工作、家庭、經歷等，並可對一般話題陳述看法。在工作時，能進行簡單的答詢，並與外籍人士交談溝通。
讀	在日常生活中，能閱讀短文、故事、私人信件、廣告、傳單、簡介及使用說明等。在工作時，能閱讀工作須知、公告、操作手冊、例行的文件、傳真、電報等。
寫	能寫簡單的書信、故事及心得等。對於熟悉且與個人經歷相關的主題，能以簡易的文字表達。

each [itʃ] pron. 每一個　◀Track 1571
▶Each did his best.
　每個人都竭力所能。

adj. 每一的；各自的
▶Each child got a Christmas gift.
　每個孩子都得到一份聖誕禮物。

adv. 每一
▶The sugar canes are twenty cents each.
　拐杖糖每個售價二十美分。

eager [`igɚ]　◀Track 1572
adj. 熱心的；熱切的；渴望的；急切的
▶He is eager to get a job.
　他渴望找到一份工作。

eagle [`igl] n. 老鷹　◀Track 1573
▶I saw eagles flying over the Grand Canyon. 我在大峽谷看到老鷹在飛翔。

ear [ɪr] n. 耳；聽力　◀Track 1574
▶He whispered a secret in my ear.
　他貼著我的耳朵小聲說了一個秘密。

early [`ɝlɪ] adj. 早的　◀Track 1575
▶Early bird gets the worm.
　早起的鳥兒有蟲吃。

adv. 早地
▶She got up early this morning.
　她今早很早起。

earn [ɝn] v. 賺得；贏得　◀Track 1576
▶His heroic deeds earned him worldwide respect. 他英勇的事蹟贏得舉世敬重。

earnest [`ɝnɪst]　◀Track 1577
adj. 認真的
▶She is an earnest teacher.
　她是一個認真的老師。

n. 誠摯

▶She wasn't kidding. She was in earnest.
她不是在開玩笑的，她是認真的。

相關片語 **earnest money deposit**
保證金

▶It is necessary to put up an earnest money deposit when you buy real estate. 買房地產時需要付保證金。

earnings [`ɝnɪŋz]
◀Track 1578
n. 收入；工資

▶He saved most of his earnings.
他把大部分的收入都存了起來。

earphone [`ɪr‚fon]
◀Track 1579
n. 耳機；聽筒

▶He placed earphones on his head and pressed the start button of his smart phone. 他戴起耳機，按下智慧型手機的開始鍵。

earring [`ɪr‚rɪŋ] **n.** 耳環
◀Track 1580

▶She wore a pair of pearl earrings to the party. 她戴著一對珍珠耳環到派對。

earth [ɝθ] **n.** 地球；泥土
◀Track 1581

▶It is one of the most pristine places on earth. 這是地球上最純淨的地方之一。

earthquake
◀Track 1582
[`ɝθ‚kwek] **n.** 地震

▶There was an earthquake last night.
昨晚發生了地震。

ease [iz]
◀Track 1583
v. 減輕；緩和；使安心

▶She used a natural remedy to ease her headache. 她使用天然療法減緩頭痛。

n. 舒適；悠閒；容易；放鬆；自在

▶After working for 35 years, they now live a life of ease.
他們工作了三十五年後，現在過著安逸的生活。

easily [`izɪlɪ]
◀Track 1584
adv. 容易地；輕易地

▶He was easily distracted. 他很容易分心。

east [ist] **n.** 東方
◀Track 1585

▶The sun rises in the east and sets in the west. 太陽東升西落。

adv. 東邊地，往東邊地

▶The train headed east. 火車朝著東方行進。

adj. 東邊的

▶She lives in East London. 她住在倫敦東部。

Easter [`istɚ] **n.** 復活節
◀Track 1586

▶The children were painting Easter eggs and making Easter Bonnets. 孩子們在畫復活節彩蛋並製作復活節帽子。

eastern [`istɚn]
◀Track 1587
adj. 東邊的

▶She is interested in eastern cultures.
她對東方文化很感興趣。

easy [`izɪ]
◀Track 1588
adj. 容易的；輕鬆的

▶He came from a wealthy family and lived an easy life.
他出生富裕的家庭，過著舒適的生活。

eat [it] **v.** 吃
◀Track 1589

▶She ate lunch in the cafeteria.
她在自助餐廳吃午餐。

echo [ˋɛko]　◀ Track 1590

n. 回聲；共鳴；應聲蟲

▶The song aroused echo in the audience's hearts. 這首歌在觀眾心中引起了共鳴。

v. 發出回聲；產生迴響；重複他人的話

▶His voice echoed in the mountains. 他的聲音在山中迴蕩。

eclipse [ɪˋklɪps]　◀ Track 1591

n. （天）蝕；（聲望等）失色

▶There was a solar eclipse at noon. 今天中午有日蝕。

補充片語 solar eclipse 日蝕

v. 蝕；遮蔽……的光；對……投下陰影

▶The moon was eclipsed at 11:20 P.M. last night. 昨晚十一點二十分出現月蝕。。

economic [͵ikəˋnɑmɪk]　◀ Track 1592

adj. 經濟上的

▶The country was facing an economic crisis. 這個國家面臨經濟危機。

economical　◀ Track 1593

[͵ikəˋnɑmɪkl] **adj.** 經濟的；節約的；節儉的

▶He is an economical shopper. 他是個節儉的購物者。。

economics　◀ Track 1594

[͵ikəˋnɑmɪks] **n.** 經濟學

▶Prof. Nye is an expert in economics. 奈伊教授是經濟學的專家。

economist　◀ Track 1595

[ɪˋkɑnəmɪst] **n.** 經濟學者

▶Many economists expected the Fed to hike rates in September. 許多經濟學家預測聯準會於九月將調高利率。

economy [ɪˋkɑnəmɪ]　◀ Track 1596

n. 節約；節省；經濟；經濟情況

▶This country's economy has made great strides since 1980. 這個國家的經濟自從1980年起已大幅改善。

edge [ɛdʒ] **n.** 邊；邊緣　◀ Track 1597

▶She sliced some cucumbers and arranged them around the edge of the dish. 她切了一些小黃瓜並把它們排列在菜餚的四周。

edible [ˋɛdəbl]　◀ Track 1598

adj. 可食的

▶Few people know that this plant is edible. 很少人知道這種植物是可食用的。

edit [ˋɛdɪt] **v.** 編輯；校訂　◀ Track 1599

▶She spent the whole day editing this article. 她花了一整天編輯這篇文章。

edition [ɪˋdɪʃən]　◀ Track 1600

n. 版本；發行數

▶The dictionary has a pocket edition. 這本字典有袖珍版。

editor [ˋɛdɪtə] **n.** 編輯　◀ Track 1601

▶He is an editor for this fashion magazine. 他是時尚雜誌的編輯。

editorial [͵ɛdəˋtorɪəl]　◀ Track 1602

adj. 編輯的；編者的

▶Most of the editorial staff quit their jobs this week. 大部分的編輯人員這週都離職了。

n. （報刊的）社論；（電台、電視的）重要評論

▶His editorials are insightful and timely. 他所寫的社論很有見解並及時性。

educate [`ɛdʒə,ket]
◀≋Track 1603

v. 教育

▶She was educated in Canada and the UK. 她在加拿大和英國受教育。

education
◀≋Track 1604

[,ɛdʒʊ`keʃən] **n.** 教育

▶He has had a good education.
他受過良好的教育。

educational
◀≋Track 1605

[,ɛdʒʊ`keʃənl]

adj. 有教育意義的；與教育有關的；教育的

▶The science fair is both entertaining and educational. 這個科學博覽會既有娛樂性，也富教育意義。

eel [il] **n.** 鰻；鰻魚
◀≋Track 1606

▶The eel was at least five feet in length.
這隻鰻魚至少有五呎長。

effect [ɪ`fɛkt]
◀≋Track 1607

n. 影響；作用

▶The medicine will take effect within 30 minutes.
這個藥在三十分鐘內會開始起作用。

v. 造成；達到（目的）；產生

▶They effected a number of important reforms. 他們完成了許多重要的改革。

effective [ɪ`fɛktɪv]
◀≋Track 1608

adj. 有效的

▶He was an effective teacher.
他課教得很好。

efficiency [ɪ`fɪʃənsɪ]
◀≋Track 1609

n. 效率

▶The technology has greatly increased our work efficiency. 這個科技大大提升我們的工作效率。

efficient [ɪ`fɪʃənt]
◀≋Track 1610

adj. 效率高的

▶This is an efficient solar panel.
這是很有效率的太陽能板。

effort [ɛ`fɚt] **n.** 努力
◀≋Track 1611

▶It requires a team effort to achieve this task. 要完成這項工作，需要團隊努力。

egg [ɛg] **n.** 蛋
◀≋Track 1612

▶She boiled an egg and mixed it in the salad. 她水煮一顆蛋，把它拌入沙拉裡。

ego [`igo]
◀≋Track 1613

n. 自我；自我意識；自尊心

▶The setback was a blow to her ego.
這個挫折對她的自尊心是個打擊。

補充片語 a blow to one's ego 對某人自尊心的一個打擊

eight [et] **pron.** 八個
◀≋Track 1614

▶The police solved eight of the twelve murders which occurred last year. 去年發生的十二起謀殺案中，警方破獲了八件。

n. 八；八個

▶Eight plus ten equals eighteen.
八加十等於十八。

adj. 八的；八個的

▶I bought eight books from the bookstore.
我在書店買了八本書。

eighteen [`e`tin]
◀≋Track 1615

pron. 十八（個）

中級

▶Eighteen of the most vulnerable families in the city will be able to move in new apartments. 這個城市最弱勢的十八戶人家將能搬進全新的公寓。

n. 十八；十八個

▶My son will be at the age of eighteen tomorrow. 我兒子明天就滿十八歲了。

adj. 十八的；十八個的

▶There are eighteen members in the club. 俱樂部有十八個會員。

eighty [`etɪ] ◀Track 1616
pron. 八十（個）

▶Eighty minus ten equals seventy.
八十減十等於七十。

n. 八十；八十個

▶The man is in his eighties.
這位男士已八十多歲了。

adj. 八十的；八十個的

▶My grandmother is eighty.
我的祖母八十歲。

either [`iðɚ] ◀Track 1617
adv. 也（用於否定句）

▶If she doesn't take the course, I won't either. 如果她不選這門課，我也不會。

pron. （兩者中）任一

▶He may not agree with either of them on this issue. 在這個議題上，他可能都不同意他們兩位的看法。

adj. （兩者中）任一的

▶She held a torch in either hand.
她不是左手就是右手拿著一個火把。

conj. 或者

▶He will come here either today or tomorrow.
他不是今天就是明天會來這裡。

elaborate [ɪ`læbə͵ret] ◀Track 1618
adj. 精心製作的；精巧的；煞費苦心的

▶He made an elaborate hairstyle for the model. 他幫模特兒做了很精巧的髮型。

v. 精心製作；詳盡闡述；詳細說明

▶He elaborated on his inspirations for this novel. 他詳細說明這本小說的靈感來源。

補充片語 elaborate on 詳細說明

elastic [ɪ`læstɪk] ◀Track 1619
adj. 有彈性的；可伸縮的；能恢復的

▶The trousers are not elastic at all.
這件褲子完全沒有彈性。

elbow [`ɛlbo] ◀Track 1620
n. 肘；肘部；彎頭；（椅子的）扶手

▶Her elbow was injured after her fall.
她跌倒後手肘受傷。

v. 用手肘推擠著前進

▶It was so crowded that he had to elbow his way to the exit. 人實在太多了，以至於他必須用手肘推擠才能到出口。

相關片語 up to one's elbows 非常忙

▶She has been up to her elbows with the children lately. 她最近忙著顧小孩。

elder [`ɛldɚ] ◀Track 1621
n. 長者；前輩

▶She is my elder by three years.
她大我三歲。

adj. 年紀較大的

▶His elder son is in graduate school.
他的長子在唸研究所。

elderly [`ɛldɚlɪ] ◀Track 1622
adj. 年長的

▶She is elderly but her heart and mentality are still strong. 他雖年長，但心智狀態仍然良好。

elect [ɪˈlɛkt] ◀Track 1623
v. 選舉；推選；選擇

▶He was elected the class leader. 他被選為班長。

election [ɪˈlɛkʃən] ◀Track 1624
n. 選舉；當選

▶The presidential election is held every four years. 總統選舉每四年舉辦一次。

electric [ɪˈlɛktrɪk] ◀Track 1625
adj. 電的；導電的；電動的

▶She bought an electric car to reduce carbon emission. 她為了減少碳排放而買了一台電動車。

electrical [ɪˈlɛktrɪkl] ◀Track 1626
adj. 與電有關的；電器科學的；電的

▶He is an electrical engineer with more than 20 years of experience. 他是電機工程師，擁有超過二十年的資歷。

electrician ◀Track 1627
[ˌɪlɛkˈtrɪʃən] **n.** 電工；電氣技師

▶He is a great electrician with lots of experience. 他是能力很強的電機技師，擁有豐富的經驗。

electricity ◀Track 1628
[ˌɪlɛkˈtrɪsətɪ] **n.** 電；電流；電力；電學

▶Electricity and sustainable energy are the main driving force behind an economy. 電和永續能源是經濟成長的主要驅動力。

electronic [ɪlɛkˈtranɪk] ◀Track 1629
adj. 電子的

▶He teaches electronic keyboard and piano at a music academy. 他在音樂學院教電子琴和鋼琴。

electronics ◀Track 1630
[ɪlɛkˈtranɪks] **n.** 電子學

▶He teaches electronics and woodworking. 他教電子學和木工。

elegant [ˈɛləgənt] ◀Track 1631
adj. 雅緻的，優美的，優雅的

▶Princess Diana was beautiful and elegant. 黛妃既美麗又優雅。

element [ˈɛləmənt] ◀Track 1632
n. （化）元素；成分；要素

▶Kindness and compassion are elements of a two-way street benefiting both givers and receivers. 仁慈和同情心是使施予者和受惠者都獲益的雙向元素。

elementary ◀Track 1633
[ˌɛləˈmɛntərɪ] **adj.** 基本的

▶She teaches in the elementary school. 她在小學教書。

補充片語 elementary school 小學

elephant [ˈɛləfənt] ◀Track 1634
n. 大象

▶The population of African elephants is decreasing due to poaching. 由於盜獵，非洲大象數量正在減少中。

elevator [ˈɛləˌvetɚ] ◀Track 1635
n. 電梯

中級

▶The elevator finally came down.
電梯終於下來了。

eleven [ɪ`lɛvn]
◀€Track 1636

pron. 十一（個）

▶The reporter interviewed eleven of the world's top design teams. 記者訪問全球前十一個最佳設計團隊。

n. 十一；十一個

▶Her sister is at the age of eleven. 她的妹妹十一歲。

adj. 十一的；十一個的

▶There are eleven students in my class. 我的班上有十一個學生。

eliminate [ɪ`lɪmə͵net]
◀€Track 1637

v. 排除；消除；（比賽中）淘汰

▶The project aims to eliminate illiteracy. 這個計畫旨在消除文盲。

else [ɛls] **adv.** 其他；另外
◀€Track 1638

▶There is nothing else left to eat. 已經沒有任何剩餘的食物了。

conj. 其他的；另外的

▶We must be there by seven, or else we'll miss the train. 我們一定要在七點前趕到那裡，要不然就會錯過火車。

elsewhere
◀€Track 1639

[`ɛls͵hwɛr]

adv. 在別處；往別處；到別處

▶She lived elsewhere during winter vacation. 她寒假住在別處。。

e-mail [`i͵mel]
◀€Track 1640

n. 電子郵件

▶Have you received my e-mail? 你收到我寄的電郵了嗎？

v. 用電子郵件發送；寄電子郵件給……

▶The department store e-mailed its catalogues to the customers. 百貨公司以電郵方式將目錄寄給顧客。

embarrass
◀€Track 1641

[ɪm`bærəs] **v.** 使困窘

▶He seemed embarrassed by all the attention. 他對於受到這麼大的關注似乎感到很尷尬。

embarrassment
◀€Track 1642

[ɪm`bærəsmənt]

n. 窘；難堪；使人難堪的事物

▶He smiled with embarrassment. 他笑得很尷尬。

embassy [`ɛmbəsɪ]
◀€Track 1643

n. 大使館

▶The ambassador was dispatched to the American Embassy in Cairo, Egypt. 大使被調派到美國駐埃及的開羅大使館工作。

emerge [ɪ`mɝdʒ]
◀€Track 1644

v. 浮現；（問題）發生；顯露；（事實）暴露；（從困境中）露頭

▶The actress emerged unscathed from the sex scandal. 這位女演員安然走出了性醜聞。

emergency
◀€Track 1645

[ɪ`mɝdʒənsɪ] **n.** 緊急情況

▶During the emergency many people volunteered to help. 緊急發生時，許多人志願出來協助。

相關片語 **emergency room** 急診室

▶The emergency room was filled with people who didn't have medical emergencies. 急診室充滿了不需要緊急醫療的民眾。

emotion [ɪ`moʃən]
◀ Track 1646

n. 情緒；情感

▶He tends not to show too much emotion in front of people. 他在人面前通常不展露太多情緒。

emotional [ɪ`moʃənl]
◀ Track 1647

adj. 感情（上）的；易情緒激動的；感情脆弱的

▶She was very emotional when she heard the news. 她聽到這個消息，情緒很激動。

emperor [`ɛmpərɚ]
◀ Track 1648

n. 皇帝

▶Tsar Paul I, the Russian emperor, was assassinated on 23 March, 1801. 俄國沙皇於1801年3月23日遭到暗殺。

emphasis [`ɛmfəsɪs]
◀ Track 1649

n. 強調；重視

▶The manager put much emphasis on customer service. 經理很重視我們的客服。

補充片語 put emphasis on 重視

emphasize
◀ Track 1650

[`ɛmfə‚saɪz]=**emphasise**

（英式英文）**v.** 強調

▶The teacher emphasized that he did not tolerate plagiarism. 老師強調他不容許抄襲。

empire [`ɛmpaɪr]
◀ Track 1651

n. 帝國；皇權

▶When Constantine was born, the Roman Empire was already a vast and sprawling domain. 康士坦丁出生時，羅馬帝國已是幅員廣大的國度了。

employ [ɪm`plɔɪ]
◀ Track 1652

v. 聘雇；雇用

▶Most companies prefer to employ young people. 大部分的公司都傾向雇用年輕人。

employee [‚ɛmplɔɪ`i]
◀ Track 1653

n. 員工

▶He was a hardworking and capable employee. 他是勤奮又能幹的員工。

employer [ɪm`plɔɪɚ]
◀ Track 1654

n. 雇主

▶The new employer was considered fair and responsible. 新雇主被大家認為他的為人公正並有責任感。

employment
◀ Track 1655

[ɪm`plɔɪmənt] **n.** 雇用；職業、工作

▶She found employment as a secretary. 她找到了一份秘書的工作。

相關片語 employment agency 職業介紹所

▶She went to an employment agency to find a temporary job for the summer. 她到職業介紹所找暑期臨時工讀的機會。

empty [`ɛmptɪ]
◀ Track 1656

adj. 空的；未占用的

▶He collected empty bottles for recycling. 他收集空瓶拿去回收。

v. 使成為空的

▶She emptied the suite and moved to an apartment. 她把小套房清空，搬到一間公寓。

enable [ɪn`ebl̩] **v.** 使能夠
◀ Track 1657

▶Good team work will enable you to finish the project before the deadline. 好的團隊能使你在期限內完成計畫。

中級

enclose [ɪnˋkloz] ◀Track 1658
v. 圍住；隨函附上

▶I enclosed a file in the e-mail to him.
我在寄給他的電郵中附加一份檔案。

enclosed [ɪnˋklozd] ◀Track 1659
adj. 與世隔絕的；封閉的

▶The mansion was enclosed by a high wall. 豪宅被高牆圍住。

encounter ◀Track 1660
[ɪnˋkaʊntɚ] **v.** 遭遇（敵人）；偶然相遇

▶She encountered great difficulties in learning physics. 她學物理遇到了很大的困難。

n. 遭遇；衝突

▶She had a chance encounter with David Beckham. 她巧遇大衛・貝克漢。

補充片語 chance encounter 巧遇

encourage [ɪnˋkɝɪdʒ] ◀Track 1661
v. 鼓勵

▶His mother encouraged him to participate in the singing contest. 他媽媽鼓勵他參加歌唱比賽。

encouragement ◀Track 1662
[ɪnˋkɝɪdʒmənt] **n.** 鼓勵；獎勵

▶She owed her winning the award to her father's encouragement. 她把贏得獎項歸功於爸爸的鼓勵。

encyclopedia ◀Track 1663
[ɪnˌsaɪkləˋpidɪə] **n.** 百科全書

▶The encyclopedia only has electronic version now.
這部百科全書現在只有電子版本了。

相關片語 walking encyclopedia 活百科全書；學識極為淵博的人

▶If you have any questions, ask Elon. He is a living encyclopedia. 如果你有任何問題，去問伊隆，他是部活百科全書。

end [ɛnd] ◀Track 1664
n. 結局；終點；盡頭；結束

▶There is no end to her complaints.
她的抱怨沒完沒了。

v. 結束；了結；作為……的結尾

▶The movie ended in a stupid way.
這部電影以愚蠢的方式結尾。

endanger [ɪnˋdendʒɚ] ◀Track 1665
v. 危及；危害

▶The construction of the dam will endanger the rich biodiversity of this pristine area. 水壩的建造將危害這個純淨地區的生物多樣性。

ending [ˋɛndɪŋ] ◀Track 1666
n. 結局；結尾

▶We were pleased to see that the movie had happy ending. 我們很高興這部電影有個快樂的結局。

endurance ◀Track 1667
[ɪnˋdjʊrəns] **n.** 忍耐；耐久力

▶The agony was beyond endurance.
這種痛苦令人難以承受。

endure [ɪnˋdjʊr] ◀Track 1668
v. 忍耐；忍受；持久；持續

▶I can't endure to see her pine away.
我不忍看到她日漸憔悴。

enemy [ˋɛnəmɪ] **n.** 敵人 ◀Track 1669

▶She had a few enemies in her class.
她在班上和幾個同學結怨了。

energetic
Track 1670

[ˌɛnɚˋdʒɛtɪk] **adj.** 精力旺盛的；精神飽滿的

▶Although my grandfather is 84, he is still energetic.
我祖父雖已高齡84，仍精神飽滿。

energy [ˋɛnɚdʒɪ]
Track 1671

n. 精力；活力；能量

▶She devoted all her energy to her family. 她把所有精力投入家庭。

enforce [ɪnˋfors]
Track 1672

v. 實施；執行；強制；強迫

▶Traffic radars are installed to help enforce the law. 交通管制雷達被裝設以協助執法。

engage [ɪnˋgedʒ]
Track 1673

v. 佔用；聘雇；使訂婚；使從事、忙於

▶Peter is engaged to Victoria.
彼得和維多莉亞訂婚了。

engine [ˋɛndʒən]
Track 1674

n. 引擎；發動機

▶The engine is making a strange noise.
引擎在發出奇怪的噪音。

engineer [ˌɛndʒəˋnɪr]
Track 1675

n. 工程師

▶My father is a civil engineer.
我爸爸是土木工程師。

engineering
Track 1676

[ˌɛndʒəˋnɪrɪŋ] **n.** 工程；工程學

▶His major was mechanical engineering.
他主修機械工程。

England [ˋɪŋglənd]
Track 1677

n. 英國；英格蘭

▶The family settled down in England.
這戶人家在英格蘭定居。

English [ˋɪŋglɪʃ]
Track 1678

adj. 英文的；英國的；英國人的

▶Our English teacher is an Australian.
我們的英文老師是澳洲人。

n. 英語；英國人

▶My cousin married a British when she studied in the UK. 我表妹在英國讀書時，嫁給了一位英國人。

Englishman
Track 1679

[ˋɪŋglɪʃmən] **n.** 英國人

▶He is a 30-year old Englishman who now lives in Croatia. 他是三十歲的英國人，現住在克羅埃西亞。

enhance [ɪnˋhæns]
Track 1680

v. 提高；增加（價值、品質、吸引力等）

▶Getting the right treatment will enhance your quality of sleep. 獲得正確的治療將提升你的睡眠品質。

enjoy [ɪnˋdʒɔɪ]
Track 1681

v. 喜愛；享受

▶Children enjoyed reading fairy tales.
小孩喜愛看童話故事。

enjoyable [ɪnˋdʒɔɪəbl̩]
Track 1682

adj. 快樂的

▶It was an enjoyable movie.
這是部令人快樂的電影。

enjoyment
Track 1683

[ɪnˋdʒɔɪmənt] **n.** 樂趣；享受；令人愉快的事

中級

▶Listening to classical music is one of my greatest enjoyments. 聽古典音樂對我來說是最大的享受之一。

enlarge [ɪn`lardʒ]
◀┋Track 1684
v 擴大；擴展；放大；詳述

▶They enlarged the living room by extending it into what was a porch. 他們佔用原先的門廊擴建了客廳。

enlargement
◀┋Track 1685
[ɪn`lardʒmənt]
n. 擴大；擴展；擴充；增建；放大的照片

▶They sent their mother an enlargement of their baby's photo. 他們給母親寄了一張寶寶的放大照片。

enormous [ɪ`nɔrməs]
◀┋Track 1686
adj. 巨大的；龐大的

▶The master bedroom was enormous. 主臥室很大。

enough [ə`nʌf]
◀┋Track 1687
adv. 足夠地

▶She is old enough to make the decision. 她已夠大，可以做這個決定了。

adj. 足夠的

▶We have enough food for our guests. 我們有足夠的食物提供客人享用。

pron. 足夠的東西

▶I love the cheese cake, and I can't get enough of it. 我愛吃起司蛋糕，怎麼也吃不夠。

enroll [ɪn`rol]
◀┋Track 1688
=enrol （英式英文）
v 登記；註冊；使入會、入伍、入學；招生

▶The private school enrolls students with different needs. 這所私立學校招收有不同需求的學生。

enrollment
◀┋Track 1689
[ɪn`rolmənt] **n.** 登記；入會；入伍

▶The kindergarten enrollment begins tomorrow. 這所幼稚園明天開始招生。

ensure [ɪn`ʃʊr]
◀┋Track 1690
v 保證；擔保

▶We will make improvements to ensure that such incident will not happen again. 我們會改進，以確保類此事件不再發生。

enter [`ɛntə] **v** 進入
◀┋Track 1691

▶We entered the theater from the back door. 我們從後門進入戲院。

enterprise
◀┋Track 1692
[`ɛntə,praɪz] **n.** （冒險性）事業；企業；公司

▶Taipower is a state-owned enterprise. 台電是國營事業。

相關片語 private enterprise 私人企業；民營企業

▶Foxconn is one of the largest private enterprises in the world. 富士康是全球最大的民營企業之一。

entertain [,ɛntə`ten]
◀┋Track 1693
v 使歡樂；娛樂

▶They hired a magician to entertain their guests. 他們雇了一位魔術師娛樂賓客。

entertainer
◀┋Track 1694
[,ɛntə`tenə] **n.** 款待者；請客者；表演者

▶She is an all-round entertainer and actress. 她是全方位的藝人和女演員。

entertainment
🔊 Track 1695

[ˌɛntɚˋtɛnmənt] **n.** 招待；款待；娛樂；消遣

▶He danced for our entertainment.
他跳舞為我們助興。

補充片語 for sb's entertainment 為某人提供娛樂；給某人助興

enthusiasm
🔊 Track 1696

[ɪnˋθjuzɪˌæzəm] **n.** 熱心；熱情

▶He has great enthusiasm for jazz.
他對爵士樂有很大的熱情。

相關片語 brief period of enthusiasm 三分鐘熱度

▶She showed only a brief period of enthusiasm for dancing.
她對舞蹈只有三分鐘熱度。

enthusiastic
🔊 Track 1697

[ɪnˌθjuzɪˋæstɪk] **adj.** 熱情的；熱心的

▶He is very enthusiastic about the project. 他對這項計畫很有熱誠。

entire [ɪnˋtaɪr]
🔊 Track 1698

adj. 整個的；全部的

▶I ate an entire pizza.
我把整個比薩都吃掉了。

entitle [ɪnˋtaɪtl̩]
🔊 Track 1699

v. 給予權利；給予資格；為書題名；給稱號

▶Children and Students are entitled to a discount. 小孩和學生有打折扣的權利。

補充片語 be entitled to 給予權利、使有資格

entrance [ˋɛntrəns]
🔊 Track 1700

n. 入口；進入；入學

▶We immediately noticed her entrance because she was absolutely gorgeous.
她一進來我們就注意到了，因為她實在美極了。

entry [ˋɛntrɪ]
🔊 Track 1701

n. 入場；出賽；進入權；入口；參賽者（作品）

▶We were denied entry because we didn't have tickets.
我們因為沒票，所以不能入場。

補充片語 deny entry 拒絕入場；拒絕入境

envelope [ˋɛnvəˌlop]
🔊 Track 1702

n. 信封

▶This is a self-addressed envelope.
這是一件回郵信封。

envious [ˋɛnvɪəs]
🔊 Track 1703

adj. 嫉妒的；羨慕的

▶He is envious of his little sister.
他很嫉妒他的妹妹。

environment
🔊 Track 1704

[ɪnˋvaɪrənmənt] **n.** 環境

▶The working environment is an important factor in influencing the performance and health of workers in the workplace.
職場環境對於影響員工表現和健康是很重要的因素。

environmental
🔊 Track 1705

[ɪnˌvaɪrənˋmɛntl̩] **adj.** 環境的；有關環境的

▶We should do something to address environmental issues.
我們應該針對環境議題做些努力。

中級

相關片語 **environmental protection** 環境保護

▶She shared photos on how she implements environmental protection at home. 她分享照片，展示如何在家落實環保。

envy [`ɛnvɪ] n. 羨慕；妒忌 ◀Track 1706

▶Her face is the envy of all the girls in the school. 她的美貌令學校所有女生好生羨慕。

v. 羨慕；妒忌

▶The married man started to envy his single friends. 這個已婚男士羨慕起他的單身朋友。

equal [`ikwəl] ◀Track 1707
adj. 平等的；相等的

▶The supply is equal to the demand. 供給等於需求。

v. 等於；比得上

▶Five plus three equals eight. 五加三等於八。

n. （地位或能力）相同的人；相等的事物

▶He had no equals when it came to horsemanship. 在馬術方面，他沒有對手。

equality [i`kwɑlətɪ] ◀Track 1708
n. 相等；平等；均等

▶The school is committed to the ideal of equality. 這所學校致力推動平權的理念。

equip [ɪ`kwɪp] ◀Track 1709
v. 裝備；配備

▶The hospital is well-equipped. 這所醫院設備十分完善。

equipment ◀Track 1710
[ɪ`kwɪpmənt]
n. 配備、裝備、設備；用具；才能知識

▶The equipment of the office was significantly improved. 辦公室設備大幅改善了。

equivalent ◀Track 1711
[ɪ`kwɪvələnt]
adj. 相等的；等同的；等價的；等效的

▶He is doing the equivalent job in the new company but for lower wages. 他在新公司做同樣的工作，但薪水比之前低。

n. 相等物；等價物；對應詞

▶McDonald's have no Chinese equivalents that can compete with it. 麥當勞在華人餐飲業沒有可與之匹敵的對手。

era [`ɪrə] ◀Track 1712
n. 時代；年代；紀元

▶Artificial intelligence has ushered in a new era. 人工智慧開啟了一個新時代。

erase [ɪ`res] ◀Track 1713
v. 擦去；抹掉；清除

▶She erased the diagram on the blackboard. 她把黑板上的示意圖擦掉。

eraser [ɪ`resə] ◀Track 1714
n. 橡皮擦；板擦

▶He rubbed out the mistakes with an eraser. 他把錯誤用橡皮擦擦掉。

erect [ɪ`rɛkt] ◀Track 1715
v. 豎立；使直立；建立；安裝

▶A memorial was erected in memory of the unsung heroes. 這座紀念碑是為了紀念一群無名英雄而豎立的。

補充片語 **in memory of** 為了紀念……；
unsung hero 無名英雄

errand [`ɛrənd]
◀ Track 1716

n. 差事；差使

▶He ran errands for his mother after school. 他下課後幫媽媽跑腿辦事。

補充片語 run errands 跑腿辦事

---

error [`ɛrə] **n.** 錯誤；失誤
◀ Track 1717

▶There was an error in the calculation. 計算過程中有個錯誤。

---

erupt [ɪ`rʌpt]
◀ Track 1718

v. 噴出；迸發；爆發；發疹

▶If the volcano erupts, the aftermath will be very serious. 如果這座火山爆發，後果會很嚴重。

---

escalator [`ɛskə͵letə]
◀ Track 1719

n. 電扶梯

▶He walked up an up-going escalator at the rate of one step per second. 他以每秒一台階的速度在往上的手扶梯走著。

---

escape [ə`skep] **v.** 逃跑
◀ Track 1720

▶He left his family to escape his violent parents. 他離家以逃避暴力的雙親。

n. 逃跑；逃避

▶He had a narrow escape in the car crash. 他在車禍事故中逃過一劫。

相關片語 escape one's notice 疏忽；沒注意到

▶It didn't escape her notice that I was distracted. 她注意到我分心了。

---

escort [`ɛskɔrt] **n.** 護衛隊
◀ Track 1721

▶She asked if I could be her escort for the evening. 她問我晚上是否可以當她的舞伴。

v. 護航；護送

▶We escorted the child home. 我們護送這個小孩回到家。

---

especially [ə`spɛʃəlɪ]
◀ Track 1722

adv. 尤其；特別是

▶The course is designed especially for beginners. 這堂課是特別為初學者所設計的。

---

essay [`ɛse]
◀ Track 1723

n. 論說文；散文

▶He helped proofread my essay before I submitted it to the professor. 我把論文交給教授之前，他幫我做了校對。

---

essence [`ɛsns]
◀ Track 1724

n. 本質；要素；本體；精髓

▶The essence of this essay is that climate change is irreversible. 這篇論文的核心就是氣候變化是不可逆的。

---

essential [ɪ`sɛnʃəl]
◀ Track 1725

adj. 必要的

▶Water is essential to sustain life. 水對於維持生命是不可或缺的。

---

essentially [ɪ`sɛnʃəlɪ]
◀ Track 1726

adv. 實質上；本來；本質上

▶The book is essentially a story of his life. 這本書基本上是寫他一生的故事。

---

establish [ə`stæblɪʃ]
◀ Track 1727

v. 建立；設立；創辦

▶The non-profit organization was established to help orphans. 這所非營利機構是為幫助孤兒而創辦的。

中級

establishment ◀❬Track 1728

[ɪsˋtæblɪʃmənt] **n.** 建立；創立；建立的機構

▶This nursing home is a well-run establishment. 這間安養院是經營良好的機構。

estate [ɪsˋtet] ◀❬Track 1729

n. 地產；財產；資產

▶He will inherit his mother's estate when he is 25. 他二十五歲將繼承母親的遺產。

相關片語 **real estate** 不動產

▶He began his real estate career when he was 20. 他在二十歲開始經營不動產的事業。

estimate [ˋɛstəˌmet] ◀❬Track 1730

v. 估計；估量

▶The building cost is estimated at $5 billion. 建築這棟大樓的成本預估要五十億元。

n. 估計；估價；評斷；看法

▶His estimate of the situation was not quite accurate. 他對情勢的預估不是那麼精確。

etc. [ɛtˋsɛtərə] ◀❬Track 1731
=et cetera **adv.** 等等

▶They went to the zoo and saw tigers, penguins, polar bears, etc. 他們去動物園看到老虎、企鵝、北極熊等等。

eternal [ɪˋtɝnḷ] ◀❬Track 1732

adj. 永恆的；無窮的；無休止的

▶The kind princess is the epitome of eternal beauty. 這位仁慈的公主是永恆美麗的象徵。

eternity [ɪˋtɝnətɪ] ◀❬Track 1733

n. 永恆；不朽；來世；永恆的真理；無終止的一段時間

▶The pastor talked about eternity and repentance. 牧師談論有關永生和懺悔。

Europe [ˋjʊrəp] **n.** 歐洲 ◀❬Track 1734

▶As she traveled across Europe, she worked as a babysitter and a waitress. 她旅歐期間，曾擔任保姆和女服務生。

European [ˌjʊrəˋpiən] ◀❬Track 1735

adj. 歐洲的；歐洲人的

▶The professor currently teaches European Union law, criminal law and human rights law. 教授目前教歐盟法律、刑法和人權法。

n. 歐洲人

▶My son-in-law is a European. 我的女婿是歐洲人。

evacuate [ɪˋvækjʊˌet] ◀❬Track 1736

v. 撤離；撤空；疏散；避難

▶Holidaymakers were evacuated when the fire threatened the hotel property. 當火勢延燒危及旅館時，所有遊客都被撤離了。

evaluate [ɪˋvæljʊˌet] ◀❬Track 1737

v. 估……的價；評估

▶The company encourages users to evaluate its software tools and give feedback to them. 這家公司鼓勵用戶評估其所推出的軟體工具並給予回饋。

eve [iv] ◀❬Track 1738

n. （節日的）前夕；（大事發生的）前一刻

▶They went to a party on New Year's Eve. 他們在除夕去參加派對。

even [ˋivən] ◀❬Track 1739

adj. 平坦的，平等的；一致的；對等的

▶The desk is not even. 這張書桌不平整。

相關片語 **break even**
不賺不賠；收支平衡的

▶The company has started to break even on a quarterly basis. 這家公司每一季都開始收支平衡。

evening [`ivnɪŋ] Track 1740
n. 夜晚；晚上

▶They went to see a movie yesterday evening. 他們昨晚去看電影了。

event [ɪ`vɛnt] Track 1741
n. 事件；項目

▶The golden couple's wedding was considered the social event of the year. 這對金童玉女的婚禮被視為是當年社交界的盛事。

eventual [ɪ`vɛntʃʊəl] Track 1742
adj. 最終發生的；最後的；結果的

▶The eventual design of the stadium was inspired by the work of a German architect. 體育館最後的設計是從一位德國建築師的作品獲得啟發。

eventually Track 1743
[ɪ`vɛntʃʊəlɪ] **adv.** 最終地、最後

▶Her parents eventually accepted her career choice and supported her decision. 她的父母最接受她的職業選擇並支持她的決定。

ever [`ɛvɚ] Track 1744
adv. 從來；任何時候；究竟

▶Have you ever been to Sweden? 你曾去過瑞典嗎?

every [`ɛvrɪ] Track 1745
adj. 每一個；一切的

▶The talk show is broadcasted every Friday evening. 這個脫口秀每週五晚間播出。

everybody Track 1746
[`ɛvrɪˌbɑdɪ] **pron.** 每個人；人人；各人

▶You need to get real. You can't please everybody. 你要實際點，你無法取悅每個人。

everyday [`ɛvrɪ`de] Track 1747
adj. 每日的，平常的

▶My brother wears his everyday clothes to work. 我弟弟每天穿休閒服上班。

補充片語 **everyday clothes** 便裝

everything [`ɛvrɪˌθɪŋ] Track 1748
pron. 每件事；事事

▶Money can't buy everything.
金錢並不能買到一切。

everywhere Track 1749
[`ɛvrɪˌhwɛr] **adv.** 到處；處處；每個地方

▶Her parents looked everywhere for her, but eventually lost hope. 她的雙親到處找她，但最終失去了希望。

evidence [`ɛvədəns] Track 1750
n. 證據；證人；證詞

▶There is no concrete evidence against him. 沒有對他不利的具體證據。

v. 證明；顯示；表明

▶His class is extremely interesting, as evidenced by the fact that the clip of it has very much gone viral on YouTube. 他的課非常有趣，從課堂的片段在YouTube上被瘋傳可見。

補充片語 **as evidenced by**
由……可證明

中級

evident [`ɛvədənt] ◀Track 1751

adj. 明顯的

▶It was evident that she was unhappy.
她很顯地不快樂。

evil [`ivl] **n.** 邪惡；禍害 ◀Track 1752

▶When his evil acts were revealed, his wife left him immediately. 當他邪惡的行徑被揭發後，妻子立刻離他而去。

adj. 邪惡的；惡毒的

▶The Evil Queen tricked Snow White into eating the apple that she poisoned. 邪惡的王后騙白雪公主吃下被下毒的蘋果。

evolution [ˌɛvə`luʃən] ◀Track 1753

n. 發展；進展；演化

▶His book is about the evolution of the universe. 他的書是有關宇宙的演化。

evolve [ɪ`vɑlv] ◀Track 1754

v. 使逐步成形；發展；進化；成長

▶His company has evolved over the years into a conglomerate. 他的公司幾年內就發展成為一個大型企業集團。

exact [ɛg`zækt] ◀Track 1755

adj. 精確的；確切的

▶We still don't know the exact casualties of this conflict. 我們仍不知道這場衝突中確切的傷亡人數。

exactly [ɪg`zæktlɪ] ◀Track 1756

adv. 正是；的確是

▶I need to know what exactly happened. 我需要知道實際上到底發生什麼事了。

exaggerate ◀Track 1757

[ɪg`zædʒəˌret] **v.** 誇張；誇大；言過其實

▶He exaggerated the truth about reading all of the Narnia series of books. 他誇大真相，表示已讀完《納尼亞傳奇》系列小説。

exaggeration ◀Track 1758

[ɪgˌzædʒə`reʃən]

n. 誇張；誇大；誇張的言語

▶She is a drama queen. She is prone to exaggeration. 她很容易小題大做，傾向誇大其詞。

補充片語 drama queen 小題大做的人

exam [ɛg`zæm] ◀Track 1759

n. 考試；測驗

▶He burned the midnight oil for his physics exam. 他為了物理考試而開夜車了。

補充片語 burn the midnight oil 開夜車

examination ◀Track 1760

[ɪgˌzæmə`neʃən] **n.** 考試

▶The child had a medical examination and it came back that there were no signs of abuse against him. 孩童做了體檢，報告結果並無任何受虐的跡象。

examine [ɛg`zæmɪn] ◀Track 1761

v. 檢查

▶The dentist examined his teeth and did an X-ray. 牙醫檢查了他的牙齒並照了X光。

examiner [ɪg`zæmɪnə] ◀Track 1762

n. 主考人；檢查人

▶The examiner was running the test properly. 主考官妥當地檢視考場。

相關片語 medical examiner 驗屍官

▶According to the medical examiner, the man's death was ruled a homicide. 根據驗屍官的説法，男子死因是他殺。

example [ɛg`zæmpl̩] ◀ Track 1763
n. 例子；榜樣

▶He was a perfect example of someone who wanted to live a simple life. 他是那些想過簡單生活的人的最佳典範。

excel [ɪk`sɛl] ◀ Track 1764
v. 勝過他人；優於；突出

▶She excelled the rest of the class in calculus. 她的微積分在班上勝過所有同學。

excellence [`ɛksl̩əns] ◀ Track 1765
n. 優秀

▶The college is well-known for its academic excellence. 這所大學以學生成績優異而著稱。

excellent [`ɛksl̩ənt] ◀ Track 1766
adj. 出色的；優秀的

▶He is an excellent writer. 他是很優秀的作家。

except [ɛk`sɛpt] ◀ Track 1767
conj. 除了；要不是

▶He was honored everywhere except in his homeland. 他在各地都備受景仰，除了祖國以外。

prep. 除……之外

▶We all left the party that night except Amy. 我們那晚都離開派對了，除了艾咪以外。

exception [ɪk`sɛpʃən] ◀ Track 1768
n. 例外

▶Her movies are mostly entertaining but this one is an exception. 她的電影大多很有娛樂性，惟獨這部例外。

exceptional ◀ Track 1769
[ɪk`sɛpʃən] **adj.** 例外的；特殊的；異常的

▶He is an exceptional firefighter. 他是卓越的消防員。

exchange [ɪks`tʃendʒ] ◀ Track 1770
n. 交換；交流；交易所

▶I was an exchange student in Germany and it was awesome. 我到德國當交換學生，是很美的經驗。

v. 交換；兌換；調換

▶The leaders of the two countries shook hands and exchanged ideas. 兩國元首握手並交換意見。

相關片語 **exchange angry words** 爭吵

▶They exchanged angry words a few days ago, but now it's all water under the bridge. 他們前幾天吵了幾句，不過現在已經事過境遷了。

excite [ɛk`saɪt] ◀ Track 1771
v. 刺激；使激動

▶Her lecture on movie special effects excited the audience's interest. 她有關電影特效的講座引起了聽眾的興趣。

excited [ɛk`saɪtɪd] ◀ Track 1772
adj. 感到興奮的

▶He was excited about the new job. 他對於新工作感到很興奮。

excitedly [ɪk`saɪtɪdlɪ] ◀ Track 1773
adv. 興奮地；激動地

中級

▶She talked excitedly about her coming wedding.
她興奮地談論著即將舉辦的婚禮。

excitement　🔊 Track 1774
[ɪk`saɪtmənt] **n.** 刺激；興奮；令人興奮的事

▶The little boy was jumping up and down with excitement. 小男孩興奮地跳上跳下。

exciting [ɛk`saɪtɪŋ]　🔊 Track 1775
adj. 刺激的；令人激動的

▶The action movie was really exciting.
這部動作片真是刺激。

exclaim [ɪks`klem]　🔊 Track 1776
v. 呼喊；驚叫；（抗議地）大聲叫嚷；大聲說出

▶She exclaimed in delight when she saw her baby.
她看到自己的寶寶時，欣喜地驚呼。

exclusive [ɪk`sklusɪv]　🔊 Track 1777
adj. 除外的；唯一的；獨有的；獨家的

▶The journalist had an exclusive interview with Princess Diana. 那位記者獨家採訪到黛妃。

n. 獨家新聞；獨家產品

▶The breaking news was a *New York Times* exclusive. 這則即時新聞是《紐約時報》的獨家新聞。

excursion [ɪk`skɝʒən]　🔊 Track 1778
n. 遠足；短途旅行

▶They are planning for the excursion next month. 他們正在規劃下個月的遠足。

excuse [ɛk`skjuz]　🔊 Track 1779
n. 理由；藉口

▶He wrote an excuse for his absence from work. 他寫了一張請假條，說明曠職的原因。

v. 原諒；辯解

▶Excuse me. I need to go to the restroom.
不好意思，我必須去化妝間。

executive [ɪg`zɛkjʊtɪv]　🔊 Track 1780
n. 執行者；高級官員；經理；業務主管

▶She was on the executive committee.
她是執行委員會的委員。

adj. 執行的；經營管理的；行政的

▶He was the chief executive officer of the transnational company. 他是這家跨國公司的最高執行長。

補充片語 chief executive officer =CEO 最高執行長；首席執行長

exercise [`ɛksɚ͵saɪz]　🔊 Track 1781
n. 運動；練習；習題

▶The doctor suggested that she should do exercise. 醫師建議她要運動。

v. 做運動

▶He exercises on a regular basis.
他經常運動。

exhaust [ɪg`zɔst]　🔊 Track 1782
v. 用完；耗盡；使精疲力盡；使排出氣體

▶Cleaning the entire house exhausted her. 打掃整間屋子令她精疲力盡。

n. 廢氣

▶Car exhaust fumes contain poisonous chemicals. 汽車廢氣黑煙含有毒化學物質。

exhibit [ɪg`zɪbɪt]　🔊 Track 1783
v. 展示；陳列

▶The museum exhibited Millet's paintings.
博物館展出米勒的畫。

n. 展示品；陳列品

▶There will be an exhibit of oil paintings at the art gallery. 美術館舉辦油畫展。

exhibition
◀Track 1784

[ˌɛksə`bɪʃən] **n.** 展覽

▶I went to an exhibition of Monet's paintings at the museum. 我去博物館參觀莫內畫展。

exile [`ɛksaɪl]
◀Track 1785

n. 流亡；離鄉背井；被流放者；離鄉背井者

▶She spent 15 years in exile. 她曾經流亡十五多年。

v. 流放；放逐；使離鄉背井

▶He was exiled because of his religious belief. 他因宗教信仰而被迫流亡。

相關片語 **live in exile** 過流亡生活

▶Snowden is wanted by the US and lives in exile in Russia. 史諾登被美國通緝，目前流亡蘇俄。

exist [ɛg`zɪst] **v.** 存在
◀Track 1786

▶Slavery still exists in that country. 那個國家仍有奴隸制度。

existence [ɪg`zɪstəns]
◀Track 1787

n. 存在；實在

▶Cell phones have become part of our everyday existence. 手機已成為我們每天日常生活的一部分。

exit [`ɛksɪt] **n.** 出口
◀Track 1788

▶There are two exits at the ground floor. 在一樓有兩個出口。

v. 出去；離去

▶We exited the auditorium by the rear door. 我們從禮堂的後門出去。

exotic [ɛg`zɑtɪk]
◀Track 1789

adj. 異國情調的；奇特的；外國的

▶These exotic flowers are breathtakingly beautiful. 這些奇花異草美得令人屏息。

expand [ɪk`spænd]
◀Track 1790

v. 展開；擴充；擴展

▶The company plans to expand its presence in the US. 公司計畫將在美國擴展業務。

expansion
◀Track 1791

[ɪk`spænʃən] **n.** 擴展

▶The remodeling and expansion of the factory will take place between 2019 and 2022. 工廠的改造和擴充將於2019年到2022年之間進行。

expect [ɛk`spɛkt]
◀Track 1792

v. 期待；預期

▶That's not what she expected. 那不是她期待的結果。

expectation
◀Track 1793

[ˌɛkspɛk`teʃən] **n.** 期待

▶The result fell short of their expectations. 結果不符合他們的期待。

補充片語 **fall short of one's expectations** 不符合某人的期待

expedition
◀Track 1794

[ˌɛkspɪ`dɪʃən] **n.** 遠征；考察；探險隊

▶They were on an expedition to explore the center of the Australian continent. 他們到澳州大陸中心進行了一次遠征考察。

補充片語 **go on an expedition** 去探險、進行遠征考察

中級

相關片語 **go on a shopping expedition** 上街購物

▶We plan to go on a shopping expedition this Saturday. 我們計畫這個週六要上街購物。

expel [ɪk`spɛl]
◀Track 1795

v 驅逐;趕走;排出(氣體等);把……除名、開除

▶The class bully was expelled. 這個班級的惡霸被學校開除了。

expense [ɪk`spɛns]
◀Track 1796

n 花費;費用

▶Their biggest expenses was children's education. 他們最大的開銷是孩子的教育費。

expensive
◀Track 1797

[ɛk`spɛnsɪv] **adj** 昂貴的;高價的

▶Houses in big cities are very expensive. 大城市的房價很高。

experience
◀Track 1798

[ɛk`spɪrɪəns] **n** 經驗;經歷

▶He had a near-death experience before. 他曾有過瀕死經驗。

v 經歷;體驗

▶She had no experience in this kind of job. 她沒有這類工作的經驗。

experiment
◀Track 1799

[ɪk`spɛrəmənt] **n** 實驗

▶Gardening is something I've learned by experiment. 我透過實驗學習精進園藝。

v 做實驗

▶They are experimenting the use of drones to deliver their products. 他們在實驗利用無人機運送產品。

experimental
◀Track 1800

[ɪk͵spɛrə`mɛntl] **adj** 實驗性的;根據實驗的;實驗用的

▶This is an experimental technology. 這是個實驗性的科技。

expert [`ɛkspɚt]
◀Track 1801

n 專家;能手

▶He is an expert in biopharmaceutical science. 他是生技醫藥的專家。

expiration
◀Track 1802

[͵ɛkspə`reʃən] **n** 終結;期滿;吐氣;死亡

▶The temperature of storage will affect the expiration date of the milk. 儲藏溫度將影響牛奶的有效日期。

補充片語 **expiration date** 到期日;有效日期

expire [ɪk`spaɪr]
◀Track 1803

v 期滿;屆期;呼氣;斷氣

▶The contract between the two companies will expire at the end of the month. 這兩家公司的合約在月底就要到期了。

explain [ɛk`splen]
◀Track 1804

v 解釋;說明

▶He explained how the washing machine worked. 他解釋這台新衣機如何使用。

explanation
◀Track 1805

[͵ɛksplə`neʃən] **n** 說明;解釋

▶You owe me an explanation for your absence from the meeting. 你必須向我解釋缺席會議的原因。

explode [ɪk`splod]
◀Track 1806

v 爆炸;使爆炸

▶The car exploded soon after it bumped into the tree. 汽車撞到樹之後不久就爆炸了。

exploit [ɪk`splɔɪt]　◀⁞Track 1807

v. 剝削；利用；開發；開拓

▶The restaurant was accused of exploiting underage workers. 這家餐廳被控剝削未成年員工。

補充片語 be accused of 被控……

explore [ɪk`splor]　◀⁞Track 1808

v. 探測；探勘；探討

▶They explored the possibility of further cooperation. 他們探討進一步合作的可能性。

explorer [ɪk`splorɚ]　◀⁞Track 1809

n. 探險家；勘探者

▶He was an explorer from Greece. 他是從希臘來的探險家。

explosion [ɪk`sploʒən]　◀⁞Track 1810

n. 爆發；爆炸

▶There was a terrible explosion and the whole sky lit up. 一起可怕的爆炸事故發生了，連整片天空都亮了。

explosive [ɪk`splosɪv]　◀⁞Track 1811

adj. 爆炸（性）的

▶Gas is highly explosive. 瓦斯具高度爆炸性。

n. 爆炸物

▶Nitroglycerin is a powerful explosive. 硝化甘油是一種強有力的爆炸物。

export [ɛks`port]　◀⁞Track 1812

n. 出口；出口產品

▶The export of rhino horns are strictly prohibited. 犀牛角出口被嚴格禁止。

v. 出口

▶Korean pop culture has been exported to many countries. 韓國流行文化已經傳到很多國家了。

expose [ɪk`spoz]　◀⁞Track 1813

v. 使暴露於；使接觸到；揭露；揭發；

▶The politician's corruption was exposed. 政治人物貪污的行徑被揭發了。

exposure [ɪk`spoʒɚ]　◀⁞Track 1814

n. 暴露；曝曬；揭露；揭發；曝光

▶Too much exposure to the sun can dehydrate the skin. 過度曝曬在陽光下可能造成肌膚缺水。

express [ɛk`sprɛs]　◀⁞Track 1815

v. 表達

▶He expressed congratulations on her new position. 他向她榮膺新職表達祝賀。

n. 特快車

▶They took express train to Naples. 他們搭特快車到那不勒斯。

adj. 特快的

▶She sent the parcel by express delivery. 她用快遞寄送包裹。

expression　◀⁞Track 1816

[ɪk`sprɛʃən] **n.** 表達

▶She gave him a gift as an expression of thanks. 她送他禮物表達感謝。

extend [ɪk`stɛnd] **v.** 延長　◀⁞Track 1817

▶We extended our gratitude to their help. 我們對他的協助表達謝意。

中級

173

extension [ɪk`stɛnʃən] ◀Track 1818
n. 延長；伸展；延期；增設部分

▶My neighbor just built an extension to their house. 我的鄰居剛剛擴建了他們的房屋。

extensive [ɪk`stɛnsɪv] ◀Track 1819
adj. 廣大的；廣闊的；廣泛的；大規模的

▶The hurricane brought extensive damage to the city. 颶風為城市帶來巨大的損害。

extent [ɪk`stɛnt] ◀Track 1820
n. 廣度；寬度；長度；程度；範圍

▶Some people are biased to some extent. 有些人在某個程度上有偏見。

exterior [ɪk`stɪrɪə] ◀Track 1821
adj. 外部的；外表的；外用的；對外的

▶The seed of dove tree has a hard exterior covering. 珙桐樹的種子外殼很硬。

n. 外部；外表

▶Behind that cold exterior is a sensitive and serious man. 外表冷酷的背後，他是個敏感又正經的男人。

extinct [ɪk`stɪŋkt] ◀Track 1822
adj. 熄滅了的；已消亡的；絕種的；滅絕的

▶The West African black rhino is extinct. 西非黑犀牛已經絕種了。

extra [`ɛkstrə] **adj.** 額外的 ◀Track 1823

▶The teacher punished the class by giving them extra homework. 老師給全班額外的功課，做為處罰。

extraordinary [ɪk`strɔrdn͵ɛrɪ] **adj.** 異常的；非凡的 ◀Track 1824

▶The world is full of extraordinary women. 這個世界充滿傑出的女人。

extreme [ɪk`strim] ◀Track 1825
adj. 末端的

▶They took extreme measures to end the riot. 他們採取極端的手端來終止這場暴動。

n. 極端

▶She went to extremes to please everybody. 她為了討好每個人，已到太過極端的地步。

extremely [ɪk`strimlɪ] ◀Track 1826
adv. 極度地；非常地

▶We were extremely exhausted fortunate. 我們極度地幸運。

eye [aɪ] **n.** 眼睛 ◀Track 1827

▶His eyes are mesmerizing. 他的眼睛很迷人。

eyebrow [`aɪ͵braʊ] ◀Track 1828
n. 眉；眉毛

▶Her caustic remarks raised eyebrows. 她尖酸刻薄的言語引起眾人的側目。

補充片語 raise eyebrows
引起側目、驚訝；招致不滿

eyelash [`aɪ͵læʃ] **n.** 睫毛 ◀Track 1829

▶She put on her false eyelashes to complete her makeup. 她戴上假睫毛完成妝容。

eyelid [`aɪ͵lɪd] ◀Track 1830
n. 眼皮；眼瞼

▶Her eyelids are golden brown with eye shadow. 她在眼皮上塗了金黃色的眼影。

eyesight [`aɪ͵saɪt] ◀Track 1831
n. 視力；視

▶He had poor eyesight. 他的視力很差。

▶ Ff

以下表格是全民英檢官方公告中級「聽、說、讀、寫」所須具備的能力，本書例句皆依此範疇特別設計，只要掃描右方**QR code**，就能搭配相對應的音軌實現「眼耳並用」方式，刺激左腦的語言學習功能；同時也可使用本書附贈的紅膠片，將其置於單字上，一面記憶一面自我挑戰，達到雙倍的學習成果！

聽 ▶	在日常生活中，能聽懂一般的會話；能大致聽懂公共場所廣播、氣象報告及廣告等。在工作時，能聽懂簡易的產品介紹與操作說明。能大致聽懂外籍人士的談話及詢問。
說 ▶	可在日常生活中，能以簡易英語交談或描述一般事物，能介紹自己的生活作息、工作、家庭、經歷等，並可對一般話題陳述看法。在工作時，能進行簡單的答詢，並與外籍人士交談溝通。
讀 ▶	在日常生活中，能閱讀短文、故事、私人信件、廣告、傳單、簡介及使用說明等。在工作時，能閱讀工作須知、公告、操作手冊、例行的文件、傳真、電報等。
寫	能寫簡單的書信、故事及心得等。對於熟悉且與個人經歷相關的主題，能以簡易的文字表達。

中級

fable [`febl̩] 🔊 Track 1832

n. 寓言；虛構的故事

▶ The Tortoise and the Hare is one of the classic tales in Aesop's Fables. 《龜兔賽跑》是伊索寓言的經典故事之一。

補充片語 Aesop's Fables 伊索寓言

fabric [`fæbrɪk] 🔊 Track 1833

n. 織品；布料

▶ The clothes are made of synthetic fabrics. 這些衣服是用合成布料做成的。

fabulous [`fæbjələs] 🔊 Track 1834

adj. 驚人的；難以置信的；極好的

▶ You look fabulous in this dress! 你穿這件洋裝漂亮極了！

face [fes] n. 臉；面子 🔊 Track 1835

▶ She slapped the pervert across the face.
她甩了變態一記耳光。

v. 面對

▶ We need to face the truth.
我們必須面對真相。

facial [`feʃəl] 🔊 Track 1836

adj. 臉的；面部的

▶ This facial mask will leave your face smoother and brighter.
這款面膜能讓你的臉更光滑明亮。

補充片語 facial mask 面膜

相關片語 facial expression 面部表情

▶ He has changed over all these years, but his facial expression is pretty much the same. 他這幾年變了，惟獨面部表情幾乎沒什麼變。

facility [fə`sɪlətɪ] ◀Track 1837
n. 能力、技能；設備、設施

▶The non-profit organization's emergency assistance facility will be expanded to cover countries in post-conflict situations. 這個非營利組織的緊急服務設施將擴展到發生衝突後的國家。

補充片語 emergency assistance facility 緊急服務設施

fact [fækt] n. 事實，實情 ◀Track 1838

▶We need to face the fact that this project doesn't seem to work. 我們必須面對現實，那就是這個計畫似乎不可行。

factory [`fæktərɪ] n. 工廠 ◀Track 1839

▶He works in a clothing factory. 他在成衣工廠工作。

faction [`fækʃən] ◀Track 1840
n. 派系；小集團；派系之爭；內鬨

▶The crisis divided the party into factions. 這場危機使黨內分成好幾個派系。

factor [`fæktɚ] ◀Track 1841
n. 因素；要素

▶Price was a major factor in the purchasing decision. 價格是採購決定的重要因素。

faculty [`fækḷtɪ] ◀Track 1842
n. （身體的）機能；技能；（大學的）全體教職員

▶She has been a faculty member in this high school for 10 years. 她在這所高中擔任教職員已十年。

fad [fæd] ◀Track 1843
n. 一時的流行；一時的風尚

▶People scurry around looking for the latest health fad to make them healthier and younger. 人們忙於尋找最新的保健時尚，讓自己更健康、年輕。

fade [fed] ◀Track 1844
v. 凋謝；枯萎；褪去；逐漸消失

▶The sound of her footsteps faded away. 她的腳步聲逐漸消失了。

Fahrenheit ◀Track 1845
[`færən͵haɪt] adj. 華氏溫度的；華氏的

▶Celsius and Fahrenheit are different scales to measure temperature. 攝氏和華氏是測量溫度的不同計量。

fail [fel] v. 失敗；不及格 ◀Track 1846

▶He failed his calculus exam. 他的微積分不及格。

failure [`feljɚ] n. 失敗 ◀Track 1847

▶She was upset by her failure in the election. 她因選舉失敗而感到沮喪。

faint [fent] ◀Track 1848
adj. 頭暈的；行將昏厥的；微弱的；虛弱的；軟弱無力的

▶A faint blush appeared on her cheeks. 她的雙頰出現淡淡的紅暈。

v. 昏厥；暈倒

▶She couldn't stop shaking and feeling like she was about to faint. 她無法停止顫抖，感覺快要昏過去了。

n. 昏厥

▶He felt quite shocked and fell into a faint. 他感到很震驚，昏厥倒在地上了。

fair [fɛr] ◀Track 1849
adj. 公平的；公正的

▶It's not fair to blame her entirely.
把一切都怪她並不公平。

n. 集市；露天的娛樂集會；廟會

▶There will be a job fair at the city call this weekend. 週末在市政大廳會有就業博覽會。

fairly [`fɛrlɪ]　◀ Track 1850

adv. 公平地；正當地；相當地；完全地

▶He is a fairly good comedian.
他是一個相當不錯的喜劇演員。

fairy [`fɛrɪ]　◀ Track 1851

n. 小妖精；仙女；仙子

▶The fairy told Cinderella that she should return home before midnight. 仙女告訴灰姑娘她必須在午夜前回家。

adj. 仙女的；小妖精的；幻想中的

▶The children are reading fairy tales in the reading room. 孩子們在閱讀室看童話故事。

補充片語 fairy tale 童話故事

相關片語 fairy godmother （女）恩人

▶Mother Teresa was a fairy godmother to the poor and sick. 德蕾莎修女是貧病人士的恩人。

faith [feθ]　◀ Track 1852

n. 信念；信任；信仰

▶Some people lost their faith in the judicial system. 有些人對司法體制失對信心了。

faithful [`feθfəl]　◀ Track 1853

adj. 忠誠的；忠貞的；忠實的

▶He is a faithful, kind, and thoughtful husband.
他是個忠誠、仁慈又體貼的丈夫。

fake [fek]　◀ Track 1854

adj. 假的；冒充的

▶It was a fake passport. 這是本假護照。

n. 冒牌貨；仿冒品

▶The jeweler determined that the diamond was a fake. 珠寶商鑑定這顆鑽石是假的。

v. 假裝；做假動作；偽造；捏造；冒充

▶He didn't want to go to school, so he faked a headache. 他不想去上學，所以假裝頭痛。

相關片語 fake note 假鈔；偽鈔

▶They were found to use fake notes for their entrance fees. 他們被發現持偽鈔支付入場費。

fall [fɔl]　◀ Track 1855
=autumn n. 秋天

▶We planted a maple tree last fall.
我們去年秋天種了一顆楓樹。

v. 落下；跌倒；下降

▶She fell down from the stairs and broke her leg. 她從樓梯跌了下來，腿都跌斷了。

false [fɔls]　◀ Track 1856

adj. 假的，不正確的

▶The president claimed that the media kept releasing fake news. 總統堅稱媒體不斷發佈假新聞。

fame [fem] n. 聲譽　◀ Track 1857

▶For her, the sudden fame was difficult to deal with, and she began to develop panic attack. 她無法應付突如其來的名聲，開始有恐慌症。

相關片語 come to fame 出名

▶She came to fame during the 1990s.
她在1990年代出名。

中級

familiar [fə`mɪljɚ] ◀€Track 1858

adj. 世所周知的；熟悉的；常見的；親近的

▶Have we met before? You look familiar.
我們曾見過面嗎？你看起來很面熟。

familiarity ◀€Track 1859

[fə͵mɪlɪ`ærətɪ] **n.** 熟悉；通曉；親近；親暱

▶Familiarity with Vietnamese is required for this job.
這個工作要求通曉越語。

family [`fæməlɪ] ◀€Track 1860

n. 家庭；家人

▶She is a new member of the British royal family. 她是英國皇室的新成員。

famous [`feməs] ◀€Track 1861

adj. 有名的

▶She was famous for her angelic face.
她以擁有天使般的臉孔出名。

fan [fæn] ◀€Track 1862

n. 風扇；狂熱愛好者；粉絲

▶She is a fan of Lady Gaga.
她是女神卡卡的粉絲。

fanatic [fə`nætɪk] ◀€Track 1863

n. 狂熱者；極端分子

▶He is a fitness fanatic. 他是健身迷。

adj. 入迷的；狂熱的

▶She is fanatic about Hello Kitty.
她對凱蒂貓很著迷。

fancy [`fænsɪ] ◀€Track 1864

adj. 別緻的；花俏的；特級的

▶They went to a fancy restaurant last night. 他們昨晚去高檔餐廳用餐。

fantastic [fæn`tæstɪk] ◀€Track 1865

adj. 極好的；了不起的

▶She looked fantastic in the evening gown.
她穿晚禮服美極了。

fantasy [`fæntəsɪ] ◀€Track 1866

n. 空想；幻想；夢想

▶When she wrote this novel, she retreated into a fantasy world.
她寫這本小說時，遁入了幻想世界。

far [fɑr] **adv.** 遠地 ◀€Track 1867

▶She went far into the forest to study gorillas.
她深入森林去研究大猩猩。

adj. 遠的

▶How far is it from London to Bath?
倫敦到巴斯距離多遠？

fare [fɛr] ◀€Track 1868

n. （交通工具的）票價；車（船）費

▶Taxi fares are expected to increase in the wake of the fuel price hike. 燃料費上漲後，計程車費預期也將隨之調漲。

相關片語 **fare card** 儲值卡

▶She put twenty bucks in the machine and bought a fare card.
她在機器投幣二十元，買了一張儲值卡。

farewell [`fɛr`wɛl] ◀€Track 1869

n. 告別；送別演出

▶We waved farewell to our host family.
我們向寄宿家庭揮手道別。

adj. 告別的

▶Kevin suggested that we throw a farewell party for May.
凱文建議我們會幫梅伊辦一場餞別派對。

補充片語 throw a party 辦一場派對；
farewell party 歡送會

farm [fɑrm] n. 農場
◀Track 1870

▶He raised cattle and horses on his farm. 他在農場養了牛和馬。

farmer [`fɑrmɚ] n. 農夫
◀Track 1871

▶She enjoys being a farmer.
她很享受當農夫。

farther [`fɑrðɚ]
◀Track 1872

adj. （距離、時間）更遠的，更往前的

▶It was father to the train station than we expected. 去火車站的路程比我們預期的遠。

adv. 更遠地，更進一步地

▶The new telescope allows us to see farther than we've ever seen before. 這個新的望遠鏡能讓我們看到比以前更遠的地方。

fascinate [`fæsn͵et]
◀Track 1873

v. 迷住；使神魂顛倒

▶Space exploration has always fascinated him. 太空探險一直令他著迷。

fascinated
◀Track 1874

[`fæsn͵etɪd] **adj.** 著迷的

▶She was fascinated by his kindness and pleasant personality. 她被他的仁慈和宜人的個性給迷住了。

fascinating
◀Track 1875

[`fæsn͵etɪŋ] **adj.** 迷人的；優美的；極好的

▶This is one of the most fascinating castles I have ever seen. 這是我見過最迷人的城堡之一。

fashion [`fæʃən]
◀Track 1876

n. 時尚；流行；風行一時的人或事物

▶Bell bottoms have gone out of fashion.
喇叭褲已經退流行了。

v. 使成形；把……塑造成

▶He fashioned a heart from a river pebble. 他用河邊的小卵石做成一顆心。

fashionable
◀Track 1877

[`fæʃənəbl] **adj.** 流行的；時尚的；趕時髦的

▶The couple is active in fashionable circle. 這對夫妻在時尚圈很活躍。

fast [fæst]
◀Track 1878

adj. 快的；迅速的

▶He bought a hamburger and some French fries at a fast food restaurant. 他在速食店買了一個漢堡和一些薯條。

adv. 快地

▶She walked fast and expected me to do the same. 她走路很快，也期望我跟她一樣走得那麼快。

fasten [`fæsn]
◀Track 1879

v. 扣緊；閂住

▶We fastened our seatbelts before the plane took off. 飛機起飛前，我們把安全帶扣緊。

fat [fæt]
◀Track 1880

adj. 肥的；胖的；高脂的

▶He is not fat, but he can eat a lot.
他不胖，但很能吃。

n. 脂肪；油脂

▶Although artificial trans fats are edible, they are not good for our health. 雖然人工反式脂肪可食用，但它們對健康無益。

補充片語 trans fats 反式脂肪

中級

fatal [`fetl]
🔊 Track 1881

adj. 命運的；命中註定的；無可挽回的；致命的

▶He suffered fatal injuries and died in the hospital. 他遭受致命的傷，於醫院往生。

fate [fet] **n.** 命運
🔊 Track 1882

▶She realized that her fate was not in her own hands. 她了解到她的命運並不是由自己掌控。

相關片語 **as sure as fate**
毫無疑問；千真萬確；命中注定

▶My dog can dance, but he as sure as fate can't sing. 我的狗會跳舞，但毫無疑問地牠也不會唱歌。

father [`faðɚ] **n.** 父親
🔊 Track 1883

▶His father is a financial analyst for World Bank. 他爸爸是世界銀行的財經分析師。

faucet [`fɔsɪt] **n.** 水龍頭
🔊 Track 1884

▶Turn off the faucet when you brush your teeth. 刷牙時把水龍頭關掉。

fault [fɔlt] **n.** 缺點；錯誤
🔊 Track 1885

▶The boss kept finding fault with her work. 老闆一直在挑她工作上的毛病。

faulty [`fɔltɪ]
🔊 Track 1886

adj. 有缺點的；不完美的；有缺陷的

▶We will replace a faulty item if a replacement is in stock. 若這款商品有庫存，我們會將有瑕疵的產品汰換掉。

favor [`fevɚ]
🔊 Track 1887

=favour （英式英文）

v. 贊同；偏愛、偏袒

▶The father favored his eldest son. 爸爸偏袒大兒子。

n. 贊成；偏愛；恩惠；幫忙

▶Could you do me a favor? 你可以幫我一個忙嗎？

favorable [`fevərəbl]
🔊 Track 1888

adj. 贊同的；順利的；適合的；討人喜歡的

▶The movie received a favorable review. 這部電影獲得好評。

favorite [`fevərɪt]
🔊 Track 1889

=favourite （英式英文）

adj. 最喜歡的

▶My favorite movie is Along with the Gods. 我最喜歡的電影是《與神同行》。

n. 最喜歡的人或事物

▶Ivanka is her father's favorite. 伊凡卡是爸爸最寵的孩子。

fax [fæks]
🔊 Track 1890

=facsimile **n.** 傳真機；傳真通信

▶You can send your request to us by fax. 你可以用傳真的方式把需求傳給我們。

v. 傳真

▶I faxed the letter yesterday. 我昨天已把信傳真過去了。

相關片語 **junk fax** 垃圾傳真（以傳真方式大量傳出的廣告資料）

▶You can delete junk faxes by using this software. 你可以用這個軟體刪除垃圾傳真。

fear [fɪr] **n.** 恐懼
🔊 Track 1891

▶He has a great fear of being alone. 他很怕落單。

v. 恐懼

▶Investigators feared that no passengers would survive the air crash. 調查人員擔心可能沒有乘客在這場空難倖存。

fearful [ˋfɪrfəl]　◀Track 1892

adj. 可怕的；擔心的、害怕的

▶She was fearful that she might say something wrong. 她害怕會説錯話。

feast [fist] **n.** 盛宴　◀Track 1893

▶We are going to attend our friends' wedding feast. 我們要去參加朋友的喜宴。

v. 盛宴款待；盡情地吃；使感官得到享受

▶They feasted on the delicious cheese cake. 他們盡情地吃著美味的起士蛋糕。

相關片語 **feast one's eyes on** 欣賞某物之美；一飽眼福

▶We feasted our eyes on the ancient architecture. 我們欣賞著古代建築之美。

feather [ˋfɛðɚ] **n.** 羽毛　◀Track 1894

▶The owl ruffled its feathers. 貓頭鷹豎起了羽毛。

feature [ˋfitʃɚ]　◀Track 1895

n. 特徵；特色；面貌

▶The latest tablet computer has many new features. 這款最新的平板電腦有許多新特點。

v. 以……為特色；以……為號召；起重要作 用

▶The movie features Mackenzie Foy and Helen Mirren. 這部電影由麥肯基·弗依和海倫·米蘭出演。

February [ˋfɛbrʊˏɛrɪ] =Feb. **n.** 二月　◀Track 1896

▶They moved to California last February. 他們去年二月搬到加州。

federal [ˋfɛdərəl]　◀Track 1897

adj. 聯邦政府的，國家的

▶Germany is a federal republic. 德國是個聯邦共和國。

相關片語 **Federal Bureau of Investigation (FBI)** 美國聯邦調查局

▶Her father is an FBI agent specializing in violent crimes. 她爸爸是美國聯邦調查局探員，專門調查暴力犯罪。

fee [fi] **n.** 費用　◀Track 1898

▶The registration fee of the private school is expensive. 這所私立學校註冊費很貴。

feeble [ˋfibl]　◀Track 1899

adj. 衰弱無力的；（智力、性格）軟弱的；拙劣無效而站不住腳的；微弱的

▶The patient is very feeble after the operation. 病人術後非常虛弱。

feed [fid] **v.** 餵食　◀Track 1900

▶Please do not feed animals in the zoo. 在動物園請勿餵食動物。

feedback [ˋfidˏbæk]　◀Track 1901

n. 反饋；反饋信息；一個人對某人或事物的反應

▶Since its publication, the author has received a lot of positive feedback from his readers. 自從這本書出版了之後，作者接獲許多讀者正面的回饋。

feel [fil] **v.** 感覺；覺得　◀Track 1902

▶She felt the quilt to see its quality. 她摸摸被子感覺它的品質。

中級

feeling [`filɪŋ] ◀Track 1903

n. 感覺；看法；預感

▶The trip helped her develop a feeling for the beauty of nature. 那段旅程讓她培養對大自然美的鑑賞力。

feelings [`filɪŋz] ◀Track 1904

n. 感情；感性

▶He had mixed feelings about meeting his ex-girlfriend again. 他對於再度見到前女友感到很矛盾。

fellow [`fɛlo] ◀Track 1905

n. 男人；傢伙；同事；伙伴

▶He is a jolly good fellow. 他是個樂觀的好人。

adj. 同伴的；同事的

▶He had great support from his fellow soldiers. 他從同袍中得到很大的支持。

female [`fimel] ◀Track 1906

adj. 女的；雌的

▶The female elephant is very protective of its calf. 母象很保護小象。

n. 女性；雌性動物

▶The puppy is a female, not male. 這隻小狗是母的，不是公的。

feminine [`fɛmənɪn] ◀Track 1907

adj. 女性的；婦女的；女孩子氣的；陰性的

▶He was constantly bullied because of his feminine appearance. 他因為女性化的外表而經常被霸凌。

n. 女性；陰性；陰性詞

▶In French, "class" is feminine. 在法語，「班級」是個陰性詞。

fence [fɛns] **n.** 柵欄；籬笆 ◀Track 1908

▶She planted cacti as a fence around the garden. 她在庭院種植仙人掌做為籬笆。

ferry [`fɛrɪ] **n.** 擺渡；渡輪 ◀Track 1909

▶They took the ferry to the island. 他們搭渡輪到那座小島。

v. （乘渡輪）渡過

▶Small boats were used to ferry the goods to their destination. 小船被用來戴運貨物到目的地。

fertile [`fɝtl̩] ◀Track 1910

adj. 多產的；繁殖力強的；富饒的；能生育的

▶The once fertile land is turning into a desert. 這片曾經是肥沃的土地逐漸變成沙漠了。

fertilizer [`fɝtl̩ˌaɪzɚ] ◀Track 1911

n. 肥料

▶Organic farmers use fertilizer from natural source, such as compost. 有機農夫使用源自天然的肥料，比方堆肥。

festival [`fɛstəvl̩] ◀Track 1912

n. 節慶；節日

▶Moon Festival is an important holiday celebrated by the Chinese community. 中秋節是華人世界的重要節慶。

fetch [fɛtʃ] ◀Track 1913

v. （去）拿來；去請……來；給……以

▶He had to fetch his son from the airport. 他要去機場接兒子。

相關片語 **fetch and carry** 跑腿；做家務；當聽差；聽某人支使辦事

▶She expected her daughter to fetch and carry for her at any time. 她期待女兒無論何時都要聽她使喚。

fever [`fivə] ◀€Track 1914

n. 發燒；發熱

▶She got a sore throat and a fever.
她喉嚨痛，還有發燒。

few [fju] ◀€Track 1915

pron. 幾個；很少數

▶Only a few of the students passed the physics exam. 只有少數學生通過物理學考試。

adj. 幾個的；幾乎沒有的；少數的

▶Few people survived the earthquake.
這場地震只有少數人倖存。

fiancé [‚fiən`se] **n.** 未婚夫 ◀€Track 1916

▶She showed off her diamond ring given by her fiancé. 她炫耀未婚夫送給她的鑽戒。

fiber [`faɪbə] ◀€Track 1917

n. 纖維；纖維物質；性格、素質

▶The doctor suggested that he eat more dietary fiber to prevent bowel cancer. 醫師建議他多食膳食纖維，以避免罹患腸癌。

fiction [`fɪkʃən] ◀€Track 1918

n. 小說；虛構的事

▶She is a big fan of science fictions.
她是科幻小說迷。

補充片語 **science fiction** 科幻小說

fiddle [`fɪdl] ◀€Track 1919

v. 拉小提琴；胡來；亂動；盲目擺動；浪費時間；遊蕩

▶The accountant had been fiddling the company's finances for years. 會計多年來一直在偽造公司的財務狀況。

n. 小提琴；瑣事；欺詐；騙局

▶Joe discovered that two of his colleagues were on the fiddle. 喬伊發現他的兩個同事在搞欺詐。

相關片語 **fit as a fiddle** 非常健康

▶Although my grandmother is 80, she is fit as a fiddle. 我祖母雖然高齡八十，身體仍非常健康。

field [fild] ◀€Track 1920

n. 原野；運動場；領域

▶The field was planted with lemon trees. 這片原野種滿了檸檬樹。

fierce [fɪrs] ◀€Track 1921

adj. 兇猛的；好鬥的；狂熱的；激烈的；糟透的

▶The singing competition was getting fierce. 歌唱比賽越來越激烈了。

fifteen [`fɪf`tin] ◀€Track 1922

pron. 十五（個）

▶Fifteen of the participants have never used cannabis. 十五位實驗參與者從沒吸過大麻。

n. 十五；十五歲

▶The talented young actress just turned fifteen last month. 這位很有天份的年輕女演員上個月剛滿十五歲。

adj. 十五的；十五個的

▶There are fifteen pencils in the drawer.
抽屜裡有十五枝鉛筆。

fifty [`fɪftɪ] **pron.** 五十（個） ◀€Track 1923

▶Fifty of the employees are female while others are male. 五十名員工是女性，其餘是男性。

n. 五十

中級

▶She is in her fifties, but she still looks beautiful. 她已五十來歲了，但看起來仍很美。

adj. 五十的；五十個的

▶The documentary was made about fifty years ago. 這部紀錄片大約是五十年前拍的。

fight [faɪt]　🔊 Track 1924

v. 打架；搏鬥；爭吵

▶The couple fought like cats and dogs last night. 這對夫妻昨晚吵得很激烈。

n. 打架；爭吵

▶She passed away after a long fight with colon cancer. 她與直腸癌進行了長期的搏鬥後，最後不敵病魔去世了。

fighter [`faɪtɚ]　🔊 Track 1925

n. 戰士；鬥士

▶She is a fighter for women's rights. 她是女權的鬥士。

相關片語 **firefighter** 消防員

▶It took the firefighters several days to extinguish the forest fires. 消防員花了好幾天才撲滅了森林大火。

figure [`fɪgjɚ]　🔊 Track 1926

n. 外形；體形；數字；人物

▶The model has a slender figure. 模特兒擁有苗條的身材。

v. 計算；認為；料到

▶I figure that she will succeed in the modeling industry. 我認為她在模特兒界會成功。

file [faɪl] **n.** 文件夾；檔案　🔊 Track 1927

▶She deleted the file by accident. 她不小心刪掉檔案了。

v. 把……歸檔；提出（申請）；提起（訴訟）

▶The company filed for bankruptcy. 這家公司申請破產。

補充片語 **file for** 提起訴訟

fill [fɪl] **v.** 裝滿；充滿　🔊 Track 1928

▶She filled the bathtub with hot water. 她在浴缸注滿了熱水。

film [fɪlm]　🔊 Track 1929

n. 影片；電影；底片

▶The film was shot in Prague. 影片是在布拉格拍攝的。

filter [`fɪltɚ]　🔊 Track 1930

n. 濾（光、波等）器；多孔過濾材料

▶This water filter can remove chemicals and heavy metals. 這個淨水器可以移除化學物質和重金屬。

v. 過濾；滲透；（消息等）走漏

▶The water is filtered through a reverse osmosis system. 這些水是經由逆滲透系統過濾的。

fin [fɪn] **n.** 鰭；鰭狀物　🔊 Track 1931

▶The five-star hotel has removing shark's fin from its restaurant menus. 這家五星級飯店已將魚翅相關菜餚從菜單中移除了。

補充片語 **shark's fin** 鯊魚鰭、魚翅

final [`faɪnl]　🔊 Track 1932

adj. 最後的；確定的

▶The CEO will make the final decision. 執行長將做最後的決定。

n. 決賽；期末考

▶He burned the midnight oil for his finals. 他開夜車準備期末考。

finally [`faɪnḷɪ]
🔊Track 1933

adv. 最後地；終於

▶She finally realized her potential as a smart and independent woman. 她最終實踐了自己具有成為聰明、獨立女性的潛力。

finance [faɪ`næns]
🔊Track 1934

n. 財政；金融

▶The company's finances are properly documented. 這家公司的財務狀況有被妥善記錄下來。

v. 籌措資金

▶The city government is financing for the housing project. 市政府為住宅計畫籌措資金。

financial [faɪ`nænʃəl]
🔊Track 1935

adj. 財政的

▶The company struggled to survive during the financial crisis of 2008. 這家公司於2008年金融海嘯期間撐得很辛苦。

find [faɪnd] **v.** 發現；找到
🔊Track 1936

▶I found the course difficult to comprehend. 我發現這門課很難理解。

fine [faɪn]
🔊Track 1937

adj. 美好的；很好的

▶She is a fine educator. 她是很傑出的教育家。

v. 處以罰金

▶He was fined for speeding. 他因超速而被罰款。

n. 罰鍰

▶The maximum penalty for animal cruelty is a $100,000 fine. 虐待動物最高可判罰十萬元。

finger [`fɪŋgɚ] **n.** 手指
🔊Track 1938

▶She cut her finger while chopping an onion. 她在切洋蔥時切到手指。

finish [`fɪnɪʃ]
🔊Track 1939

v. 結束；完成

▶We have to finish the project by Friday. 我們星期五以前要完成這個計畫。

n. 結束；終結；最後階段

▶The team fought to the finish. 這支隊伍堅持戰鬥到底。

finished [`fɪnɪʃt]
🔊Track 1940

adj. 完成的；結束了的

▶Are you finished with the paper shredder? 你用完碎紙機了嗎？

補充片語 **paper shredder** 碎紙機

fire [faɪr] **n.** 火
🔊Track 1941

▶Someone set the house on fire. 有人縱火燒這間房子。

v. 開火射擊；解僱；起火燃燒

▶The gunman fired five shots at the president. 持槍歹徒向總統開了五槍。

firecracker
🔊Track 1942

[`faɪrˌkrækɚ] **n.** 鞭炮、爆竹

▶They let off firecracker and fireworks. 他們燃放鞭炮和煙火。

fireman [`faɪrmən]
🔊Track 1943

n. 消防隊員；救火隊員

▶The fireman risked his life to save the old lady. 這名消防員冒著生命危險拯救老婦人。

中級

185

fireplace [`faɪr͵ples] ◀Track 1944

n. 壁爐

▶He removed the ashes from the fireplace. 他清除了壁爐的灰燼。

fireproof [`faɪr`pruf] ◀Track 1945

adj. 防火的、耐火的

▶He kept the confidential documents in a fireproof safe. 他把機密文件放在防火的保險箱裡。

v. 使具防火性能；為……安裝防火設施

▶The school was fireproofed before this became mandatory. 這所學校在強制規定安裝防火設施之前，就已這麼做了。

firewoman ◀Track 1946

[`faɪrwʊmən] **n.** 女消防員

▶A firewoman is climbing the ladder. 一名女消防員正在爬消防梯。

firework [`faɪr͵wɝk] ◀Track 1947

n. 煙火

▶The celebration ended with a spectacular display of fireworks. 慶典以精彩的煙火結束。

firm [fɝm] **n.** 商行；公司 ◀Track 1948

▶She has been working for an accountancy firm for more than a decade. 她在一家會計事務所工作逾十年。

adj. 牢固的；堅定的

▶He prefers to sleep on a soft mattress to a firm one. 相較硬床墊，他更喜歡睡軟床墊。

first [fɝst] ◀Track 1949

adj. 第一的；最前面的

▶She took the first train to Cambridge. 她搭最早的一班火車去劍橋。

adv. 最先；首先

▶They first met in a blind date. 他們是在相親頭一次見面。

n. 第一；第一個

▶I was the first to be in the classroom. 我是第一個進教室的學生。

fish [fɪʃ] **n.** 魚 ◀Track 1950

▶He caught a lot of fish today. 他今天捕獲很多魚。

v. 釣魚

▶They fished the river for catfish. 他們在這條河捕鯰魚。

fisherman [`fɪʃ-mən] ◀Track 1951

n. 漁夫

▶He has been a fisherman for almost his entire life. 他幾乎一生都是漁夫。

fishing [`fɪʃɪŋ] **n.** 釣魚 ◀Track 1952

▶The family depends on fishing for their income. 這戶人家依賴捕魚為生。

fist [fɪst] **n.** 拳頭 ◀Track 1953

▶He shook his fist at the robber. 他向搶劫犯揮拳頭。

補充片語 shake one's fist at sb. 向某人揮拳

相關片語 make money hand over fist 賺大錢、發大財

▶She succeeded in her business and made money hand over fist. 她經商成功發大財了。

fit [fɪt] **n.** 一陣；（病）發作 ◀Track 1954

▶He had a fit of apoplexy. 他中風了。

相關片語 in a fit of rage 一怒之下

▶The boy was were arrested for killing the old lady in a fit of rage. 男孩在一怒之下殺了老太太而被逮捕。

five [faɪv] **pron.** 五（個） ◀ Track 1955

▶Five of the students failed the chemistry exam. 五個學生化學考試不及格。

n. 五；五歲

▶My daughter is eight and my son is five. 我的女兒八歲，兒子五歲。

adj. 五的；五個的

▶There are five people in her family. 她的家有五個人。

fix [fɪks] ◀ Track 1956

v. 修理；處理；安排

▶She had the refrigerator fixed. 她請人把冰箱修好了。

flag [flæg] **n.** 旗子 ◀ Track 1957

▶The tank carried the national flag of the US. 那部坦克車懸著美國國旗。

flake [flek] **n.** 小薄片 ◀ Track 1958

▶Flakes of snow slowly fell down from the sky. 片片雪花從天空落下來。

v. 成薄片；（成片）剝落

▶He flaked the chicken and rolled it up in the bread. 他把雞肉切片，再用麵包把它捲起來。

相關片語 flake out 累癱；入睡；昏倒

▶She came home and flaked out on the couch. 她一到家就睡倒在沙發上。

flame [flem] ◀ Track 1959

n. 火焰；火舌；光輝

▶The cabin was in flames. 小木屋著火了。

補充片語 be in flames 著火；失火

v. 發出火焰；燃燒

▶His face flamed with humiliation. 他的臉因受羞辱而滿臉通紅。

flap [flæp] ◀ Track 1960

v. 拍打；拍擊；振（翅）

▶The swan flapped its wings over the lake. 天鵝在湖上拍動牠的翅膀。

n. 拍動；拍打聲；蓋口；激動慌亂（狀態）

▶She was in a flap when the accident happened. 意外發生時，她慌亂了起來。

補充片語 be in a flap 處於慌亂之中

flare [flɛr] ◀ Track 1961

v. （火焰）閃耀；燃燒；突然發怒

▶The comet flared brightly enough to be seen by telescopes. 這顆彗星閃耀到可以被望眼鏡觀察到。

n. 閃耀的火光；閃光信號；照明燈；（怒氣的）爆發

▶The sailors set off a flare to call for help. 水手發射了一顆照明彈求救。

相關片語 flare up （火）突然變旺；（人）突然發怒

▶He flares up easily when people let him down. 別人讓他失望時，他很容易因此而發怒。

flash [flæʃ] ◀ Track 1962

n. 閃光；燈光的一閃；閃光燈

▶After she saw a flash of lightning, she counted the number of seconds until she heard the thunder. 她看到一道閃電後，開始數秒數直到聽到打雷。

v. 使閃光；閃出；閃爍；（想法）閃現

▶An idea flashed through his mind.
他的腦子裡閃過一個點子。

相關片語 **in a flash** 很快；立刻

▶This recipe can help you prepare breakfast in a flash.
這份食譜可以幫你很快就準備好早餐。

flashlight [`flæʃˌlaɪt]
🔊 Track 1963
n. 手電筒；閃光燈

▶The power is out. Do you have a flashlight?
停電了，你有手電筒嗎？

flat [flæt]
🔊 Track 1964
=apartment **n.** 一層樓；一層公寓

▶She lived in the flat her mother bought her. 她住在媽媽幫她買的公寓裡。

adj. 平坦的；單調無聊的

▶The colors of the painting is a bit flat.
這幅畫的色彩有些平淡。

flatter [`flætɚ]
🔊 Track 1965
v. 諂媚；奉承；使高興

▶He flattered his boss because he wanted to get a promotion.
他因為想升遷而討好上司。

flavor [`flevɚ]
🔊 Track 1966
=flavour （英式英文）

n. 味；味道

▶I like the flavor of goat cheese.
我喜歡羊乳酪的味道。

v. 給……調味

▶She flavored the chicken with tomatoes and onions. 她以番茄和洋蔥為雞肉調味。

相關片語 **flavor of the month**
風靡一時的人或物；時尚

▶The romantic comedy was flavor of the month. 這部浪漫喜劇片曾經風靡一時。

flaw [flɔ]
🔊 Track 1967
n. 缺點；瑕疵；裂縫

▶The proposal is full of flaws.
這份提案充滿錯誤。

v. 使破裂；使有缺陷

▶The education system is flawed in many ways. 教育體制在很多方面都有缺陷。

flea [fli] **n.** 跳蚤
🔊 Track 1968

▶He saw a flea on the cat's head.
她看見貓咪的頭上有一隻跳蚤。

相關片語 **flea market** 跳蚤市場

▶She bought a pin at the flea market.
她在跳蚤市場上買了一個別針。

flee [fli] **v.** 逃；逃走
🔊 Track 1969

▶When the gangsters fled, the guard raised the alarm.
幫派份子逃竄時，警衛按了警報器。

flesh [flɛʃ]
🔊 Track 1970
n. 肉；肌肉；（供食用的）獸肉、果肉；肉體

▶The spirit is willing but the flesh is weak. 力不從心。

相關片語 **flesh and blood** 血肉之軀

▶We are only flesh and blood.
我們只是血肉之軀。

flexible [`flɛksəbl]
🔊 Track 1971
adj. 可彎曲的；有彈性的

▶We are quite flexible on scheduling.
我們對於時程安排是相當有彈性的。

flight [flaɪt] n. 班機；飛航 ◀ Track 1972

▶ Flight 245 will arrive in Dublin at 2:00 P.M..
第二四五班機將於下午兩點抵達都柏林。

flip [flɪp] ◀ Track 1973

v. 擲；輕拋；輕彈；快速翻（頁）

▶ She flipped through the brochure till she found what she was looking for.
她快速翻閱小冊子直到看到想找的資訊。

n. 輕彈；輕拋；（跳水或體操的）空翻

▶ The girl was doing cartwheels, somersaults and flips.
女孩在做側手翻、翻筋斗和空翻。

相關片語 flip one's lid 發瘋；失去自制力

▶ He flipped his lid when he found his dog messed up the living room. 當他發現他的狗把客廳搞得一團亂時，忍不住發飆了。

float [flot] v. 浮；漂浮 ◀ Track 1974

▶ A boat was floating in the middle of the sea. 一艘船浮在海面的中央。

n. 漂流物；浮標；浮板

▶ They swam with floats and flippers.
他們用浮板和蛙鞋游泳。

flock [flɑk] ◀ Track 1975

n. 群；人群；群眾

▶ A flock of tourists entered the museum.
一群觀光客湧進了博物館。

v. 聚集；成群

▶ Birds of a feather flock together.
物以類聚。

flood [flʌd] n. 洪水；水災 ◀ Track 1976

▶ The flood damaged the infrastructure.
洪水毀損了基礎建設。

v. 淹沒；使氾濫

▶ The road was flooded. 道路被水淹沒了。

flooding [`flʌdɪŋ] ◀ Track 1977

n. 氾濫；產後出血；水災

▶ Classes were canceled because of flooding. 由於水災，學校停課了。

floor [flor] n. 地板；樓層 ◀ Track 1978

▶ Marble floor brings a sense of elegance to your living room. 大理石地板為你的客廳帶來一種高雅的格調。

flour [flaʊr] ◀ Track 1979

n. 麵粉；（穀類磨成的）粉

▶ She mixed the flour with butter and raisins in a bowl.
她在碗裡將麵粉和奶油、葡萄乾充分混合在一起。

flourish [`flɝɪʃ] ◀ Track 1980

v. （植物）茂盛；繁茂；（事業等）興旺；炫耀、誇耀

▶ Impressionism flourished in that period.
印象派在那個時期十分興盛。

n. 揮舞；炫耀；華麗的詞藻

▶ This article was full of flourish and drama.
這篇文章充滿華麗的詞藻和戲劇性。

flow [flo] n. 流動；流暢 ◀ Track 1981

▶ The system helps track the flow of tourists in and out of the airport.
這套系統有助於記錄在機場出入的遊客。

v. 流動；湧（進或出）

▶ Many rivers flow into the Atlantic Ocean.
許多小河匯入大西洋。

中級

flower [`flauɚ] n. 花
◄€ Track 1982
▶She planted a lot of flowers in the garden. 她在庭院種了很多的花。

flu [flu] n. 流行性感冒
◄€ Track 1983
▶Many people were hospitalized because of the flu. 很多人因為這個流感而住院。

fluent [`fluənt]
◄€ Track 1984
adj. 流利的
▶She can speak very fluent German. 她會說非常流利的德語。

fluid [`fluɪd]
◄€ Track 1985
adj. 流動的；液體的；不固定的；易變的；流暢的
▶Her fluid movements reminded him of a dancer he had dated several years ago. 她優雅流暢的動作使他想起幾年前曾約會過的舞者。

n. 流體
▶Researchers have developed a new method to detect bodily fluids and estimate their age. 研究人員研發了一種新方法來偵測體液並推算人的年齡。

flunk [flʌŋk] v. 使不及格
◄€ Track 1986
▶He flunked his final. 他的期末考不及格。

flush [flʌʃ]
◄€ Track 1987
v. 用水沖洗；（臉）發紅；漲紅；使興奮
▶Excitement flushed his cheeks. 他興奮地臉都漲紅了。

n. 沖洗；紅光；興奮、激動
▶He felt a flush of excitement when his girlfriend said yes to his proposal. 他向女友求婚成功，感到一陣興奮。

flute [flut] n. 長笛；橫笛
◄€ Track 1988
▶How he played the flute was really cool. 他吹長笛的方式很酷。

flutter [`flʌtɚ]
◄€ Track 1989
v. 振翼；拍翅；（旗幟）飄揚；（脈搏）跳動；顫動、發抖
▶Her heart fluttered with emotions. 她的心隨著情緒起伏。

n. 振翼；飄動；興奮；激動；（心臟）振顫
▶The good news caused a flutter of excitement among the public. 這個好消息引起大眾一陣轟動。

fly [flaɪ]
◄€ Track 1990
v. 飛；駕駛飛機；搭飛機旅行
▶He will fly to Paris tomorrow. 他明天搭飛機去巴黎。

n. 蒼蠅
▶The flies were everywhere in that restaurant. 那家餐廳到處都是蒼蠅。

foam [fom] n. 泡沫
◄€ Track 1991
▶This facial foam is very effective yet mild. 這牌子的潔面泡沫洗淨力很好又溫和。

補充片語 facial foam 洗面乳

v. 起泡沫
▶The kitten foamed at the mouth when we gave her the medication for an infection. 我們給這隻小貓服用治療感染的藥物時，牠口吐白沫。

補充片語 foam at the mouth 口吐白沫

focus [`fokəs]
◄€ Track 1992
v. 使集中；使聚焦

▶She focused on her work instead of gossiping with colleagues. 她專注工作，而不去和同事八卦。

n. 焦點；重點

▶Death penalty has been the focus of public debate. 死刑一直是大眾討論的焦點。

foe [fo] ◀Track 1993

n. 敵人；仇敵；危害物

▶The two countries were bitter foes for years. 這兩國多年來都是仇敵。

fog [fɑg] **n.** 霧 ◀Track 1994

▶It's dangerous to drive when the fog is too dense. 霧太濃時，開車很危險。

foggy [`fɑgɪ] ◀Track 1995

adj. 有霧的；多霧的；朦朧的

▶It was a foggy day, and the tops of the buildings disappeared into the mist. 那天霧很濃，建築物的頂端都消失在濃霧中。

foil [fɔɪl] **n.** 金屬薄片；箔紙 ◀Track 1996

▶She wrapped the chocolate in foil to keep it fresh. 她將巧克力用箔紙包起來，以保新鮮。

fold [fold] **v.** 對折；摺疊 ◀Track 1997

▶He folded up the letter and put it into an envelope. 他把信摺起來放進信封裡。

n. 摺疊；摺痕

▶Rip the paper along the fold. 沿著摺痕把紙撕下。

folk [fok] ◀Track 1998

n. 人們；各位；雙親

▶I went home to see my folks. 我回家看父母。

adj. 民間的；民眾的；通俗的

▶She started folk dance and ballet training at the age of six. 她八歲時開始民俗舞蹈和芭蕾的訓練。

補充片語 **folk dance** 民俗舞蹈

follow [`falo] ◀Track 1999

v. 跟隨；跟著；接著

▶He followed his father's advice. 他聽從爸爸的勸告。

follower [`faləwɚ] ◀Track 2000

n. 追隨者；信徒；擁護者；侍從；部下

▶She is a follower of the Korean boy band. 她是這個韓國男團的追隨者。

following [`faləwɪŋ] ◀Track 2001

adj. 接著的；其次的；下述的

▶He finished school in 1998 and the following year he joined the army. 他於1998年完成學業，次年從軍。

prep. 在……以後

▶Following the reception, there will be a press conference. 招待會後將有一場記者會。

n. 追隨者；下列人員或事物

▶The restaurant has a loyal following. 這家餐廳有一批老顧客。

fond [fɑnd] ◀Track 2002

adj. 喜歡的；喜好的

▶She is fond of singing old songs. 她喜歡唱老歌。

補充片語 **be fond of** 喜歡；愛好

中級

food [fud] **n.** 食物　　◀◣Track 2003
▶I love Thai food. 我喜歡泰式食物。

fool [ful] **n.** 笨蛋；傻瓜　　◀◣Track 2004
▶She is a chronic liar. You are a fool if you believe in her. 她是慣性撒謊者，如果你相信她的話，你就是笨蛋。

v. 愚弄；鬼混
▶He was fooled by her appearance. 他被她的外表給騙了。

foolish [`fulɪʃ]　　◀◣Track 2005
adj. 愚蠢的；荒謬可笑的
▶It was so foolish of you to buy that stuff. 你買這個東西很愚蠢。

foot [fʊt] **n.** 腳；英尺　　◀◣Track 2006
▶My office isn't far from where I live, so I go to work on foot. 我的辦公室離住處不遠，所以我走路上班。

football [`fʊt͵bɔl]　　◀◣Track 2007
n. 足球
▶That was the most exciting football game I had ever seen. 那是我看過最刺激的足球賽。

for [fɔr] **prep.** 為了　　◀◣Track 2008
▶He bought the diamond ring for his fiancée. 他買了一只鑽戒給未婚妻。

conj. 因為；由於
▶We are all happy for her, for she finally found someone who truly loves her. 我們都很替她高興，因為她終於找到真心愛她的人。

forbid [fə`bɪd]　　◀◣Track 2009
v. 禁止；不許

▶The law forbids smoking in public places. 法律禁止在公共場合吸烟。

force [fors]　　◀◣Track 2010
n. 力量；武力；勢力
▶The police used force to quell the protestors. 警方使用武力驅散抗議者。

v. 強迫；迫使；強行攻佔
▶She had to force herself to be nice to him. 她必須強迫自己對他和顏悅色。

forecast [`for͵kæst]　　◀◣Track 2011
n. 預測；預報；預料
▶The economic forecast is positive for the next few years. 未來幾年的經濟預測很正面。

v. 預測；預報；預示；預言
▶Heavy rain has been forecasted for tomorrow. 預報明天有大雨。

forehead [`for͵hɛd] **=brow**（英式英文）　　◀◣Track 2012
n. 額；前額；前部
▶He kissed his son's forehead. 他親了兒子的額頭。

foreign [`fɔrɪn]　　◀◣Track 2013
adj. 外國的；外來的
▶He works at the Ministry of Foreign Affairs. 他在外交部工作。

foreigner [`fɔrɪnɚ]　　◀◣Track 2014
n. 外國人
▶Generally speaking, Taiwanese are friendly to foreigners. 大致上來說，台灣人對外國人很友善。

foresee [for`si]　◀﹦Track 2015

v 預見；預知

▶As a doctor, he foresaw that the patient would not have many years left.
身為醫師，他預知這位病患壽命不多了。

forest [`fɔrɪst] **n** 森林　◀﹦Track 2016

▶We nearly got lost in the forest.
我們差一點就在森林裡迷路了。

forever [fə`ɛvɚ]　◀﹦Track 2017

adv 永遠

▶I will remember him forever.
我永遠會記得他。

forget [fə`gɛt] **v** 忘記　◀﹦Track 2018

▶Oops, I forgot to bring my purse.
糟了，我忘了帶錢包。

forgetful [fə`gɛtfəl]　◀﹦Track 2019

adj 健忘的

▶He became forgetful and had trouble memorizing new things. 他變得健忘，無法記住新發生的事。

forgive [fə`gɪv] **v** 原諒　◀﹦Track 2020

▶Sometimes it's very hard to forgive.
有時饒恕是很困難的。

fork [fɔrk] **n** 叉子　◀﹦Track 2021

▶He used a fork to eat pizza.
他用叉子吃比薩。

form [fɔrm]　◀﹦Track 2022

n 外形；類型；表格

▶He filled in the online application form and e-mailed it to the company.
他填好線上表格並用電郵寄給公司。

v 形成；塑造；養成

▶The students quickly formed into lines.
學生們很快就排好隊了

formal [`fɔrml]　◀﹦Track 2023

adj 正式的

▶He was invited to attend a formal function. 他受邀參加一場正式的活動。

formation [fɔr`meʃən]　◀﹦Track 2024

n 形成；構成；構成物；結構

▶The coach asked the players to try new formations.
教練要求隊員嘗試新陣型。

former [`fɔrmɚ]　◀﹦Track 2025

pron 前者

▶Of the two computer systems, he preferred the former.
這兩套電腦系統中，他比較喜歡前者。

adj 從前的；前者的；前任的

▶Willy Brandt was the former chancellor of Germany. 威利‧布蘭特是德國前總理。

formula [`fɔrmjələ]　◀﹦Track 2026

n 慣例；常規；配方；方程式

▶The company changed the formula of its shampoo. 公司更換了洗髮精的配方。

fort [fɔrt] **n** 堡壘；要塞　◀﹦Track 2027

▶The soldiers defended the fort from the enemy forces.
士兵抵禦堡壘，避免敵兵攻擊。

相關片語 **hold the fort** 代為照料

▶Henry will hold the fort while our boss is on the business trip.
亨利會在老闆出差期間代理他的工作。

中級

forth [forθ] ◀ Track 2028

adv. （空間）向前、向外；（時間）從……以後

▶From that day forth we became friends. 從那天以後，我們成為朋友了。

fortunate [`fɔrtʃənɪt] ◀ Track 2029

adj. 幸運的

▶She was fortunate to be alive after the severe injuries. 她在遭受這麼嚴重的受傷還能存活，非常幸運。

fortunately ◀ Track 2030

[`fɔrtʃənɪtlɪ] **adv.** 幸運地

▶Fortunately, we didn't make any mistakes during the presentation. 幸運地，我們在報告中沒有犯任何錯誤。

fortune [`fɔrtʃən] ◀ Track 2031

n. 財產；財富

▶She made a fortune when the company went public in 2010. 公司在2010年上市時，她發了大財。

補充片語 make a fortune 致富；發大財

forty [`fɔrtɪ] ◀ Track 2032

pron. 四十（個）

▶She has thirty books, and he has forty. 她有三十本書，而他有四十本。

n. 四十

▶He became a world-renowned neurologist by the time he was forty. 他四十歲時成為世界知名的神經科醫師。

adj. 四十的；四十個的

▶There are forty employees in the company. 公司有四十名員工。

forward [`fɔrwəd] ◀ Track 2033

adv. 向前；提前；今後

▶He leaned forward to give his daughter a kiss. 他向前傾，親他的女兒一下。

adj. 前面的；早的；早熟的

▶He is forward thinking, ambitious, and committed. 他很有前瞻性、具上進心，並且很熱誠。

forwards [`fɔrwədz] ◀ Track 2034

adv. 往前的

▶Please move forwards. 請往前進。

fossil [`fɑsl] ◀ Track 2035

n. 化石；頑固不化的人；守舊的事物

▶A team of international scientists discovered the fossils of the world's first reptile. 一個國際科學家團隊發現了世界上最早的爬蟲類化石。

adj. 化石的；成化石的

▶Solar energy is a sustainable alternative to fossil fuels. 太陽能是取代化石燃料的永續替代方式。

補充片語 fossil fuel 化石燃料（天然氣、石油等）

相關片語 old fossil 頑固不化的人

▶He is an old fossil. 他是個頑固的人。

foster [`fɑstə] ◀ Track 2036

v. 養育；領養

▶They consider fostering a child overseas. 他們打算跨國領養一個小孩。

adj. 收養的；領養的

▶The couple have four foster children. 這對夫妻有四個領養的孩子。

補充片語 foster child 養子

foul [faʊl] ◀Track 2037

adj. 骯髒的；惡臭的；邪惡的；下流的；惡劣的；犯規的

▶The foul smell causes nuisances to local residents. 惡臭的氣味讓居民很困擾。

n. 犯規

▶The play has five technical fouls this postseason. 這名選手在季後賽有兩次技術性犯規。

v. 弄髒；玷污；污染；使壅塞

▶Heavy pollution has marred the landscape and fouled the waters. 重污染毀損了景觀也污染了水源。

相關片語 **through fair and foul** 在任何情況下

▶He promised he would stand by his friend through fair and foul. 他承諾不管在任何情況下，都會站在朋友這一邊。

found [faʊnd] ◀Track 2038

v. 建立；建造；創辦

▶The organization was founded in 1995. 這個機構是在1995年創辦的。

foundation ◀Track 2039

[faʊnˋdeʃən] **n.** 建立；創辦；基礎；基金會；地基

▶Gratitude is the foundation of happiness. 感恩是快樂的基礎。

founder [ˋfaʊndɚ] ◀Track 2040

n. 創立者；創建者；奠基者

▶He is the founder and CEO of this company. 他是這家公司的創辦人暨執行長。

fountain [ˋfaʊntɪn] ◀Track 2041

n. 噴水池；噴泉；噴泉式飲水器；（知識的）泉源

▶There is a beautiful fountain in the middle of the garden. 庭院的中央有一座美麗的噴水池。

相關片語 **water fountain** 飲水器

▶There are water fountains at the visitor center. 在遊客中心有很多個飲水器。

four [for] **pron.** 四個 ◀Track 2042

▶I ate three hamburgers, and he ate four. 我吃了三個漢堡，他吃了四個。

n. 四；四個

▶My son is nearly four. 我的兒子快要四歲了。

adj. 四的；四個的

▶The village has four temples. 這個村莊有四間廟宇。

fourteen [ˋforˋtin] ◀Track 2043

pron. 十四（個）

▶He has fifteen dollars, and I have fourteen. 他有十五元，而我有十四元。

n. 十四

▶Seven times two equals fourteen. 七乘二等於十四。

adj. 十四個

▶The handbag cost fourteen pounds. 這個手提包要價十四英鎊。

fox [fɑks] ◀Track 2044

n. 狐狸；狡猾的人

▶The politician is sly like a fox. 這名政客像狐狸一樣狡猾。

補充片語 **sly like a fox** 非常狡猾

fragile [ˋfrædʒəl] ◀Track 2045

adj. 易碎的；脆弱的；易損壞的

中級

195

▶She has a very fragile and sensitive skin. 她的皮膚很脆弱敏感。

fragrance [`fregrəns] ◀Track 2046
n. 芬芳；香氣；香味

▶The company launched a new fragrance for teenage girls. 這家公司推出專為青少女設計的新香水。

frail [frel] ◀Track 2047
adj. 身體虛弱的；意志薄弱的；易損壞的

▶He is too fail to live by himself. 他身體太虛弱，無法獨居。

frame [frem] ◀Track 2048
v. 為……加框；塑造；製定；構想出

▶She framed her family photo and put it on her office desk. 她把全家福的照片裱框，並將它放在辦公桌上。

n. 架構；框架；（人或動物的）骨骼；機構

▶The basketball player has a large frame. 這名籃球員的身材魁梧。

相關片語 **frame of mind**
　　　　心境；思想狀態；情緒

▶She was in a really good frame of mind. 她的心情很好。

France [fræns] **n.** 法國 ◀Track 2049

▶I bought this fragrance in France. 我在法國時買了這瓶香水。

frank [fræŋk] ◀Track 2050
adj. 老實的；坦白的

▶To be frank, she is very clever. 坦白說，她相當聰明。

fraud [frɔd] ◀Track 2051
n. 欺騙；詐騙；騙局；騙子

▶The jewelry store confirmed the receipt was a fraud. 珠寶店證實那張收據是假的。

相關片語 **commit fraud** 詐騙

▶The company committed securities fraud by not following the rules. 這家公司因未遵循規定而犯了證券詐騙罪。

freak [frik] ◀Track 2052
n. 怪誕的舉動；畸形的人；反常現象；奇怪念頭；背離社會習俗的人

▶Snowing in June is a real freak. 六月下雪很反常。

adj. 反常的；怪異的

▶The town was hit by a freak snowstorm. 這個小鎮被一場異常的暴風雪侵襲。

相關片語 **freak of nature**
　　　　不正常的事物；畸形的事物

▶A chicken with two heads is a freak of nature. 有兩個頭的雞是畸形的。

free [fri] ◀Track 2053
adj. 自由的；免費的；不受限制的

▶I have some free tickets for Céline Dion's concert. 我有一些席琳·迪翁的演唱會免費門票。

v. 釋放；使自由

▶The hostages were freed after a two-day siege. 人質經過兩天的圍困後獲釋。

freedom [`fridəm] ◀Track 2054
n. 自由

▶People enjoy much more freedom these days. 現在的人們自由多了。

freeway [`fri,we] ◀Track 2055
=mo·tor·way （英式英文）
n. 高速公路

▶An ambulance was speeding on the freeway.
一台救護車在高速公路超速行駛。

freeze [friz]　🔊Track 2056
v. 結冰；凝固

▶When the pool freezes, it becomes an excellent ice rink for skaters. 當池子結冰後，它就變成溜冰者絕佳的溜冰場了。

相關片語 freeze out 凍死

▶The vegetables froze out overnight.
蔬菜在一夜之間凍死了。

freezer [`frizɚ]　🔊Track 2057
n. 冰箱；冷藏箱；冷凍櫃

▶She bought a frost-free freezer from a local supply store.
她在當地供應商店買了一個無霜冷凍櫃。

freezing [`frizɪŋ]　🔊Track 2058
adj. 凍極的；極冷的

▶It was a freezing winter.
那是個極凍的冬天。

相關片語 freezing point 冰點

▶The freezing point of water is 32°F.
水的結冰點是華氏三十二度。

freight [fret]　🔊Track 2059
n. 貨物；運費；貨運

▶The goods will be sent by sea freight.
這些貨物將以海運的方式送到目的地。

v. 裝貨於；運輸（貨物）；運貨

▶They freighted the ship with goods.
他們把貨物裝船。

French [frɛntʃ]　🔊Track 2060
adj. 法國的；法國人的；法語的

▶We spent our summer vacation in a small French town. 我們暑假在一個法國小鎮度假。

n. 法國人；法語

▶Can you speak French? 你會說法文嗎？

frequency　🔊Track 2061
[`frikwənsɪ] **n.** 頻繁；屢次；頻率；次數

▶The radio station broadcasts at a frequency of 92.0 MHz. 這家電臺以九十二兆赫的頻率廣播。

frequent [`frikwənt]　🔊Track 2062
adj. 頻繁的；時常發生的；屢次的

▶She is a frequent customer of the organic store. 她是這家有機商店的常客。

v. 常到；時常出入

▶He likes to frequent masquerade balls.
他喜歡出入化妝舞會。

fresh [frɛʃ] **adj.** 新鮮的　🔊Track 2063

▶He is fresh out of college and very diligent. 他剛剛大學畢業，為人很勤奮。

freshman [`frɛʃmən]　🔊Track 2064
n.（大學等的）一年級生；新生；新手；新人

▶She is a freshman at Princeton.
她是普林斯頓大學的一年級新生。

Friday [`fraɪˌde]　🔊Track 2065
=Fri. **n.** 星期五

▶Thank God it's Friday. Let's go to the movie after work. 感謝老天終於星期五了，我們下班去看電影吧。

fridge [frɪdʒ]　🔊Track 2066
=re·fri·ger·a·tor **n.** 冰箱

中級

▶Fruit and vegetables keep much longer in a fridge. 蔬果在冰箱可以保存比較久。

friend [frɛnd] n. 朋友 ◀Track 2067

▶Amy is my bosom friend.
艾咪是我的閨密。

friendly [`frɛndlɪ] ◀Track 2068

adj. 友善的；友好的

▶I met many friendly German when I traveled there. 我在德國旅行時，遇到很多友善的德國人。

friendship [`frɛndʃɪp] ◀Track 2069

n. 友誼

▶Christy and John's friendship blossomed into love. 克莉斯蒂和約翰的友誼升級成戀人關係。

fright [fraɪt] ◀Track 2070

n. 驚嚇；恐怖

▶The cat ran off in fright.
貓咪受到驚嚇跑走了。

相關片語 **fright mail** 恐嚇信件

▶They send fright mail to senior citizens to scare them into donating to the group. 他們發送恐嚇信件給年長者，使他們心生恐懼而將錢捐給這個團體。

frighten [`fraɪtn] ◀Track 2071

v. 使驚嚇；使害怕

▶The ghost movie frightened the children. 這部鬼片嚇壞孩子們了。

frightened [`fraɪtnd] ◀Track 2072

adj. 受驚的，害怕的

▶The child were frightened by the tornado.
這個孩子被龍捲風嚇到了。

frightening [`fraɪtnɪŋ] ◀Track 2073

adj. 令人恐懼的，使人驚嚇的，駭人的

▶It was the most frightening experience I've ever had. 這是我經歷過最嚇人的經驗。

frisbee [`frɪzbi] n. 飛盤 ◀Track 2074

▶They are playing frisbee in the yard.
他們在院子裡玩飛盤。

frog [frɑg] n. 青蛙 ◀Track 2075

▶I refused to dissect a frog in our biology class. 我拒絕在生物課解剖青蛙。

from [frɑm] **prep.** 從 ◀Track 2076

▶She came from London to visit us.
她從倫敦來看我們。

front [frʌnt] n. 前方 ◀Track 2077

▶The front of the Sun Yat-sen Memorial Hall is magnificent. 國父紀念館的正面很壯觀。

adj. 前面的

▶Two of her front teeth are missing.
她的兩顆門牙掉了。

frost [frɑst] ◀Track 2078

n. 霜；冰凍；（態度）冷淡；失敗

▶The frost ruined the orchards.
寒霜毀了這座果園。

v. 結霜；凍壞；受凍

▶More than half of the grains were frosted.
超過一半的穀物都結霜了。

frosty [`frɑstɪ] ◀Track 2079

adj. 霜凍的；結霜的；嚴寒的

▶It was a cloudy and frosty day.
那是個多雲又嚴寒的一天。

frown [fraʊn]
🔊 Track 2080

v. 皺眉;用皺眉表示不滿

▶He sat frowning while listening to his patient's complaints. 他皺著眉坐著傾聽病人的抱怨。

n. 皺眉;不悅之色

▶The governor read the missive with a frown. 州長皺眉看著公文。

frozen [`frozn]
🔊 Track 2081

adj. 冷凍的;凍僵的;冷淡的;嚇呆的

▶She microwaved the frozen food and ate it for dinner. 她用微波爐加熱冷凍食物,把它當晚餐吃了。

補充片語 frozen food
　　冷凍食品;冷凍食物

fruit [frut] **n.** 水果
🔊 Track 2082

▶What's your favorite fruit?
你最喜歡吃哪一種水果?

frustrate [`frʌs‚tret]
🔊 Track 2083

v. 使挫敗;阻撓;使心煩

▶He was frustrated to find he flunked the finals. 他得知期末考不及格,感到很挫敗。

fry [fraɪ] **v.** 炸;煎;炒
🔊 Track 2084

▶I fried an egg and made a hamburger for the homeless young man. 我煎了一顆蛋並做了一個漢堡給那位無家可歸的年輕男子。

n. 油炸物;薯條

▶French fries are tasty, but they contain too many calories. 薯條很美味,但卡路里太高。

fuel [`fjʊəl] **n.** 燃料
🔊 Track 2085

▶They stopped for fuel on the way to the shopping mall. 他們在前往購物中心的路上停下來加油。

v. 給……加油;提供燃料

▶The rapid promotion of the young man in the foreign affairs ministry has fueled resentment of the public. 這位年輕人在外交部迅速升遷引起公眾的厭惡。

fulfill [fʊl`fɪl]
🔊 Track 2086
=fulfil （英式英文）**v.** 執行（命令等）;服從;符合

▶She fulfilled herself as an actress.
她發揮了女演員的潛力。

full [fʊl] **adj.** 滿的;吃飽的
🔊 Track 2087

▶The metro was full of people during the New Year's Eve. 新年前夕期間,捷運裡滿滿的都是人。

fully [`fʊlɪ]
🔊 Track 2088

adv. 完全地;徹底地;充分地

▶We fully understand your point of view.
我們完全理解你的觀點。

fun [fʌn] **n.** 樂趣
🔊 Track 2089

▶They had a lot of fun in the prom.
他們在畢業舞會玩得很開心。

adj. 有趣的;開心的

▶We had a fun shopping last night.
我們昨晚購物很開心

function [`fʌŋkʃən]
🔊 Track 2090
n. 功能

▶The new cell phone features functions that match its rival brands but comes at a lower price. 這款新手機具有與競爭品牌同樣的功能,但價格較低廉。

中級

v. 作用；運作

▶The laptop functioned normally until yesterday. 筆電在昨天之前都還運作正常。

functional [`fʌŋkʃənl] ◀Track 2091

adj. 機能的；職務上的；功能上的；有起作用的；實用的

▶The software is functional and user-friendly. 這套軟體很實用，也對使用者很友善。

fund [fʌnd] **n.** 資金；基金 ◀Track 2092

▶They raised funds to help a student attend the field trip. 他們為了幫一名學生參加戶外教學而募款。

v. 提供資金

▶The company funded his business trip to Finland. 公司資助他到芬蘭出差。

fundamental ◀Track 2093

[ˌfʌndə`mɛntl] **adj.** 基本的；根本的；關鍵的

▶Human rights are a fundamental part of a civilized society. 人權是文明社會的根本部分。

funeral [`fjunərəl] ◀Track 2094

n. 喪葬；葬禮

▶Her funeral was held last week. 她的葬禮在上週舉行了。

funny [`fʌnɪ] ◀Track 2095

adj. 有趣的；可笑的；古怪的

▶His reaction was so funny that I couldn't contain myself from laughing. 他的反應太好笑了，以致於我無法控制大笑。

fur [fɝ] **n.** 毛；皮毛 ◀Track 2096

▶He ran through his finger through the cat's fur. 他順著貓的毛撫摸著牠。

furious [`fjʊərɪəs] ◀Track 2097

adj. 狂怒的；狂暴的；猛烈的

▶They had a furious debate about project. 他們為了這個計畫吵得很兇。

furnish [`fɝnɪʃ] ◀Track 2098

v. 給（房間）配置傢俱；供應；提供

▶She furnished the house in a unique and contemporary style. 她把房子布置得很獨特又具當代的風格。

furnished [`fɝnɪʃt] ◀Track 2099

adj. 配有傢俱的

▶The apartment is fully furnished with elegant and new furniture. 這間公寓配有全新典雅的傢俱。

furniture [`fɝnɪtʃɚ] ◀Track 2100

n. 傢俱

▶They just bought the furniture for their new house. 他們剛為新家添購這些傢俱。

further [`fɝðɚ] ◀Track 2101

adv. 進一步地；更遠地

▶We've got to do something. We can't just sit there and see her sink further and further into depression.
我們要做點事情，不能坐視她一天天消沉下去。

adj. 更遠的；更深層的；進一步的

▶Was that you at the further end of the hall? 當時走廊另一頭那個人是你嗎？

furthermore ◀Track 2102

[`fɝðɚ`mor] **adv.** 而且；此外

▶The hotel is near the train station. Furthermore, it provides excellent food and service. 這間飯店位在火車站附近，而且它提供美味的食物和的完善的服務。

fuss [fʌs]　◀╪ Track 2103

n. 忙亂；大驚小怪；異議；爭論

▶She made a fuss when things didn't go her way. 如果事情不如她的願，她就會小題大做。

v. 忙亂；大驚小怪；過分講究；抱怨；為小事煩惱

▶Stop fussing and whining.
別瞎忙和抱怨了。

future [`fjutʃɚ] **n.** 未來　◀╪ Track 2104

▶He plans to study in Denmark in the future. 他計畫未來要去丹麥求學。

adj. 未來的

▶We studied future tense in our grammar class. 我們在文法課學習將來式。

▶ Gg

　　以下表格是全民英檢官方公告中級「聽、說、讀、寫」所須具備的能力，本書例句皆依此範疇特別設計，只要掃描右方QR code，就能搭配相對應的音軌實現「眼耳並用」方式，刺激左腦的語言學習功能；同時也可使用本書附贈的紅膠片，將其置於單字上，一面記憶一面自我挑戰，達到雙倍的學習成果！

聽 ▶	在日常生活中，能聽懂一般的會話；能大致聽懂公共場所廣播、氣象報告及廣告等。在工作時，能聽懂簡易的產品介紹與操作說明。能大致聽懂外籍人士的談話及詢問。
說 ▶	可在日常生活中，能以簡易英語交談或描述一般事物，能介紹自己的生活作息、工作、家庭、經歷等，並可對一般話題陳述看法。在工作時，能進行簡單的答詢，並與外籍人士交談溝通。
讀 ▶	在日常生活中，能閱讀短文、故事、私人信件、廣告、傳單、簡介及使用說明等。在工作時，能閱讀工作須知、公告、操作手冊、例行的文件、傳真、電報等。
寫 ▶	能寫簡單的書信、故事及心得等。對於熟悉且與個人經歷相關的主題，能以簡易的文字表達。

gain [gen] ⓥ 贏得；得到
◀Track 2105

▶She gained a lot of weight during pregnancy. 她懷孕時增加了很多體重。

ⓝ 獲得；獲利；收益

▶He told a big lie for his personal gain. 他為了個人利益而撒了一個大謊。

galaxy [ˋgæləksɪ] ⓝ 銀河
◀Track 2106

▶There are many galaxies besides ours. 除了我們所處的銀河，宇宙還有很多的銀河。

gallery [ˋgælərɪ]
◀Track 2107

ⓝ 畫廊，美術館

▶The gallery is frequented by art lovers. 這間美術館經常有藝術愛好者前來。

gallon [ˋgælən]
◀Track 2108

ⓝ 加侖（液量單位；美制等於785升；英制等於546升）

▶She drinks 1.5 gallons of water each day. 她每天喝一點五加侖的水。

gallop [ˋgæləp]
◀Track 2109

ⓝ（馬）疾馳；騎馬奔馳

▶He went for a gallop this morning. 他早上騎著馬奔馳了一番。

補充片語 go for a gallop 騎馬奔馳

相關片語 at a gallop
　　飛快地；以最快速度地

▶She disappeared at a gallop on the driveway. 她在車道上飛快地消失了。

gamble [ˋgæmbl]
◀Track 2110

ⓥ 打賭

▶Her husband had gambled away all their money.
她先生把家裡所有的錢都賭光了。

補充片語 gamble away
賭博輸掉某物；輸光

n. 賭博；打賭

▶She took a gamble to exercise leadership without losing her feminine nature. 她在不失去女性特質的前提下，為了行使領導權豁出去了。

補充片語 take a gamble 冒險而為

---

gambler [`gæmblə]
🔊 Track 2111
n. 賭徒

▶He is a habitual gambler.
他是個慣性賭徒。

---

gambling [`gæmblɪŋ]
🔊 Track 2112
n. 賭博

▶He quit gambling for a couple of years.
他戒賭已好幾年了。

相關片語 gambling man 賭徒

▶Gambling men are more likely to act violently toward others.
賭徒對他人比較容易有暴力傾向。

---

game [gem]
🔊 Track 2113
n. 遊戲；比賽

▶His knee injury forced him to withdraw from the game.
他的膝蓋傷迫使他退出比賽。

---

gang [gæŋ]
🔊 Track 2114
n.（歹徒的）一幫；一群人、一夥人

▶A gang of criminals committed a burglary. 一群罪犯犯下竊盜罪。

v. 使結成一夥；成群結隊

▶Officials have ganged up against the president. 官員結成一夥對抗總統。

---

gangster [`gæŋstə]
🔊 Track 2115
n. 歹徒、流氓

▶These gangsters were locked up in jail.
這些流氓已入獄服刑了。

---

gap [gæp]
🔊 Track 2116
n. 缺口；分歧；間斷；差距

▶The widening gap between the rich and poor needs to be addressed urgently.
貧富差距的擴大需要被緊急處理。

補充片語 gap between rich and poor 貧富差距

---

garage [gə`rɑʒ] n. 車庫
🔊 Track 2117

▶He built a garage next to his house.
他在房子旁建了一座車庫。

---

garbage [`gɑrbɪdʒ]
🔊 Track 2118
n. 垃圾

▶Would you help me take out the garbage? 你能幫我把垃圾拿出去嗎?

---

garden [`gɑrdn] n. 花園
🔊 Track 2119

▶She planted roses and petunias in the garden. 她在花園種了玫瑰和牽牛花。

---

gardener [`gɑrdənə]
🔊 Track 2120
n. 園丁；花匠

▶There are butterflies and bees flitting in the garden. 蝴蝶和蜜蜂在花園飛來飛去。

---

garlic [`gɑrlɪk]
🔊 Track 2121
n. 大蒜；蒜頭

▶He crushed four cloves of garlic into the olive oil and heated them until golden. 他搗碎四瓣蒜頭放入橄欖油，並把它加熱到呈現金黃色。

中級

gas [gæs] n. 氣體；瓦斯 ◀ Track 2122

▶ I used gas for cooking but now I use an electric stove. 我以前用瓦斯煮飯，現在我電磁爐。

gasoline [`gæsə‚lin] ◀ Track 2123
=gas=petrol n. 汽油

▶ The price of gasoline has fluctuated recently. 汽油價格最近波動不定。

gasp [gæsp] ◀ Track 2124

v. 倒抽一口氣；喘氣；喘著氣說

▶ He gasped in surprise at the sight of his girlfriend's new haircut. 他看到女友的新髮型，驚得倒吸了一口氣。

n. 倒抽一口氣；喘息；喘氣

▶ At his last gasp, he confessed the crime. 男子在他剩下最後一口氣時，坦承了罪刑。

補充片語 **at one's last gasp** 在奄奄一息時；在剩下最後 一口氣時

gate [get] n. 大門；登機門 ◀ Track 2125

▶ The sign of the gate said "No Trespassing". 大門的標示寫著「不准擅自進入」。

gather [`gæðɚ] ◀ Track 2126

v. 聚集；收集；召集

▶ They gathered the information from the local library. 他們在當地圖書館收集了這些資訊。

gathering [`gæðərɪŋ] ◀ Track 2127

n. 集會；聚會

▶ He met Christy at a social gathering. 他是在社交聚會上認識克莉斯汀的。

補充片語 **social gathering** 社交聚會

gay [ge] ◀ Track 2128

adj. 同性戀的；快樂的；輕快的；尋歡作樂的

▶ His offensive remarks caused outrage among gay communities. 他冒犯性的言論造成同性戀社群的憤慨。

gaze [gez] ◀ Track 2129

v. 凝視；注視；盯

▶ The boy gazed at the stars. 男孩凝視著星星。

n. 凝視；注視

▶ Her gaze fell on a stray puppy on the street. 她的目光落到了路邊一隻流浪狗的身上。

gear [gɪr] ◀ Track 2130

n. 齒輪；傳動裝置；工具；設備；家用器具

▶ Police in riot gear used water cannons to disperse the demonstrators. 身著防暴衣的警察用水柱驅散示威者。

v. 用齒輪使轉動；搭上齒輪；使準備好

▶ Evidence showed that they geared up for a fight. 證據顯示他們準備要抗爭。

補充片語 **gear up for sth.** 為某事做好準備

gender [`dʒɛndɚ] ◀ Track 2131

n. 性，性別

▶ The candidate said he is gender neutral. 這名候選人說他對性別抱持中立的態度。

gene [dʒin] ◀ Track 2132

n. 基因；遺傳因子

▶ The mutant gene is believed to cause Parkinson's disease. 這個突變的基因被認為是造成帕金森氏症的原因。

general [`dʒɛnərəl] ◀Track 2133

adj. 一般的；普通的；大體的；全體的；大眾性的

▶He is the general manager of the fast food chain.
他是這間連鎖速食店的總經理。

n. 一般；一般情況

▶In general, we had a fruitful discussion in the meeting. 大致上來説，我們在會議的討論很有成果。

generally [`dʒɛnərəlɪ] ◀Track 2134

adv. 通常；一般地；廣泛地；普遍地；大體而言

▶Generally speaking, she is a good cook.
大致上來説，她的廚藝還不錯。

generate [`dʒɛnə,ret] ◀Track 2135

v. 產生；引起；生育

▶The company's latest advertisement has generated a lot of debate.
這家公司最新的廣告引發了很多的辯論。

generation ◀Track 2136

[,dʒɛnə`reʃən] **n.** 世代

▶Many people in Generation Z are unsure what the future will be like.
許多Z世代的人們對於未來抱持著不確定感。

generator ◀Track 2137

[`dʒɛnə,retɚ] **n.** 製造機；製造者；發電機

▶The backup generator will automatically restore the power and provide electricity for several days. 這個備用的發電機可以自動恢復電力並提供好幾天的電力。

generosity ◀Track 2138

[,dʒɛnə`rasətɪ] **n.** 寬宏大量；慷慨

▶Many people benefited from her compassion and generosity. 許多人受惠於她的同理心和慷慨行為。

generous [`dʒɛnərəs] ◀Track 2139

adj. 慷慨的；大方的

▶She is generous and thoughtful.
她很慷慨又體貼。

genetics [dʒə`nɛtɪks] ◀Track 2140

n. 遺傳學

▶He studied genetics, genomics, and evolutionary biology at college. 他在大學研究遺傳學、基因組研究和演化生物學。

genius [`dʒinjəs] ◀Track 2141

n. 天才；天賦才能

▶The boy was a genius in calculus without any formal training. 這個男孩在沒接受正式的訓練下，在微積分展現過人的天賦。

gentle [`dʒɛntl̩] ◀Track 2142

adj. 溫和的；輕柔的；有教養的；文靜的

▶The babysitter was very gentle to children. 這位保姆對孩子們很溫和。

gentleman ◀Track 2143

[`dʒɛntl̩mən] **n.** 紳士；男士

▶The gentleman talking to the president was an ambassador. 跟總統交談的這位紳士是大使。

genuine [`dʒɛnjʊɪn] ◀Track 2144

adj. 真的；非偽造的；名副其實的；真誠不造作的

▶The certificate was confirmed genuine.
這張證書被證實是真的。

中級

geography
◀Track 2145

[`dʒɪ`ɑgrəfɪ] **n.** 地理學；地勢；地形

▶The geography of the country is diverse.
這個國家的地形很多元。

geometry [dʒɪ`ɑmətrɪ]
◀Track 2146

n. 幾何學

▶Dan is nine, and he studies algebra, geometry, and Latin. 丹九歲，正在學習代數、幾何學，和拉丁文。

germ [dʒɝm]
◀Track 2147

n. 微生物；細菌；萌芽

▶The teacher taught the pupils how to control germs and prevent the spread of illnesses. 老師教導學生如何控制細菌及避免疾病的傳染。

German [`dʒɝmən]
◀Track 2148

adj. 德國的；德語的；德國人的

▶This documentary was produced by a German broadcaster called ARD. 這部紀錄片是由德國公共廣播聯盟所製作。

n. 德語；德國人

▶Her boyfriend is a German.
她的男友是德國人。

Germany [`dʒɝmənɪ]
◀Track 2149

n. 德國

▶Germany is one of the world's major economic powers. 德國是世界重要的經濟強國之一。

gesture [`dʒɛstʃɚ]
◀Track 2150

n. 姿勢；手勢

▶He greeted the crowd with a triumphant gesture at Madison Square. 他在麥迪遜廣場以勝利之姿迎接群眾。

v. 用手勢表示

▶She gestured to Charlie to remain in his seat. 她比了手勢叫查理維持坐在位子上。

get [gɛt]
◀Track 2151

v. 得到；理解；到達

▶He got the chance to audition for *Britain's Got Talent*. 他獲得《英國達人秀》的試鏡機會。

ghost [gost] **n.** 鬼
◀Track 2152

▶The children were frightened by the ghost story. 小孩被鬼故事嚇著了。

giant [`dʒaɪənt]
◀Track 2153

adj. 巨大的

▶A giant oil painting was hung in the hallway. 大廳掛著一幅巨大的油畫。

n. 巨人；偉人

▶The basketball player looks like a giant. He's 210 centimeters tall. 這位籃球選手看起來像巨人，他有210公分高。

gift [gɪft] **n.** 禮物；天賦
◀Track 2154

▶His Christmas gift was a pair of sneakers. 他的聖誕禮物是一雙球鞋。

gifted [`gɪftɪd]
◀Track 2155

adj. 有天資的；有天賦的

▶She is a gifted musician. 她是個有天份的音樂家。

gigantic [dʒaɪ`gæntɪk]
◀Track 2156

adj. 巨人的

▶The growth of the company under his leadership has been gigantic. 在他的領導之下，這家公司的成長幅度巨大。

giggle [ˋgɪgl̩] ◀ Track 2157

v. 咯咯地笑；咯咯笑著說

▶When he sang, we all started giggling.
他唱歌時，我們都開始咯咯地笑了起來。

n. 咯咯的笑；傻笑；可笑的人或事物；
玩笑、趣事

▶He burst into giggles at the sight of
Stephanie's shocked face. 他一看見史蒂
芬妮震驚的表情，就咯咯地笑了起來。

補充片語 **burst into giggles** 咯咯地笑起
來；**at the sight of** 一看見……就

ginger [ˋdʒɪndʒə] ◀ Track 2158

n. 生薑

▶I like ginger beer because it is a non-
alcoholic beverage with an aromatic
flavor. 我喜歡薑汁啤酒因為它是不含酒精又
帶有香氣的飲料。

giraffe [dʒəˋræf] ◀ Track 2159

n. 長頸鹿

▶We saw baboons, zebras, giraffes, and
gazelles in the zoo. 我們在動物園裡看到
狒狒、斑馬、長頸鹿和瞪羚。

girl [gɝl] **n.** 女孩；女兒 ◀ Track 2160

▶The little girl was playing with her dog.
小女孩在跟她的小狗玩耍。

girlfriend [ˋgɝlˌfrɛnd] ◀ Track 2161

n. 女朋友

▶The billionaire's girlfriend is a British
actress. 這位億萬富翁的女友是位英國女演
員。

give [gɪv] **v.** 給予 ◀ Track 2162

▶It's better to give than to receive.
施比受更有福。

glacier [ˋgleʃə] **n.** 冰河 ◀ Track 2163

▶Glaciers are melting faster than expected
due to global warming. 由於全球暖化，冰
河比人類原本預期的要溶解得更快。

glad [glæd] **adj.** 高興的 ◀ Track 2164

▶He was very glad to visit Taiwan again.
他很高興再度來訪台灣。

glance [glæns] ◀ Track 2165

v. 粗略看一下；一瞥；掃視

▶She glanced briefly at the newspapers.
她大略看了一下報紙。

n. 一瞥；掃視

▶He took a glance at the report and noticed
a mistake. 他掃視了報告，發現一個錯誤。

glass [glæs] ◀ Track 2166

n. 玻璃；玻璃杯

▶I drank a glass of orange juice.
我喝了一杯柳橙汁。

glasses [ˋglæsɪz] ◀ Track 2167

n. 眼鏡

▶She wore glasses to correct nearsighted
vision. 她戴眼鏡矯正近視。

相關片語 **field glasses** 望遠鏡

▶He used field glasses to observe distant
mountains. 他用望遠鏡觀察遠山。

glee [gli] **n.** 快樂；歡欣 ◀ Track 2168

▶We celebrated our daughter's birthday
with glee. 我們興高采烈地慶祝女兒的生日。

glide [glaɪd] **v.** 滑動 ◀ Track 2169

▶This ball pen glides over the paper.
這枝原子筆書寫起來流暢極了。

中
級

n. 滑動；滑行

▶They took a glide in a hang glider.
他們搭乘滑翔翼滑行一番。

補充片語 **take a glide** 滑行一番

glimpse [glɪmps] ◀ Track 2170

n. 瞥見；一瞥；少許

▶She caught a glimpse of a robber as he
ran out of the bank. 當搶匪逃離銀行時，
她瞥見了那名搶匪。

補充片語 **catch a glimpse of** 一眼瞥見

v. 看一眼；瞥見

▶From a window inside, he glimpsed a
village at a distance. 他從屋內的窗戶看見
遠處有一個小村莊。

glitter [`glɪtɚ] ◀ Track 2171

v. 閃耀；閃亮

▶All that glitters is not gold.
閃光的東西並非都是金子。。

global [`globl] ◀ Track 2172

adj. 球狀的；全世界的；總體的

▶Global warming is happening faster
than we think. 全球暖化比我們想像得還要
快發生。

globe [glob] ◀ Track 2173

n. 球狀物；地球儀；地球

▶Neuschwanstein Castle attracts tourists
from all around the globe. 新天鵝堡吸引
了來自全球的觀光客。

gloom [glum] ◀ Track 2174

n. 黑暗；陰暗；憂鬱的心情

▶The novel is full of gloom and sadness.
這本小說充滿沮喪和悲傷。

v. 變陰暗；顯得悶悶不樂；使憂鬱

▶She gloomed over her dead dog.
她因為狗狗過世而悶悶不樂。

gloomy [`glumɪ] ◀ Track 2175

adj. 陰暗的；陰沉的；憂鬱的；陰鬱的

▶They landed in Sydney on a really
gloomy winter day. 他們在一個十分陰鬱
的冬日抵達雪梨。

glorious [`glorɪəs] ◀ Track 2176

adj. 光榮的；榮譽的；壯觀的；極好的

▶The team celebrated their glorious
victory. 這支隊伍慶祝他們光榮的勝利。

glory [`glorɪ] ◀ Track 2177

n. 光榮；榮譽；可誇耀的事

▶The smart library is the glory of the
city. 這座智慧型圖書館是城市的驕傲。

相關片語 **morning glory**
牽牛花；虎頭蛇尾的人

▶A few morning glories have blossoms
up to 8 inches wide in my garden. 我的
花園裡有些牽牛花已經開到八英吋寬了。

glove [glʌv] **n.** 手套 ◀ Track 2178

▶She wore gloves to protect her elaborately
painted fingernails. 她戴手套保護精心擦好的
指甲油。

glow [glo] ◀ Track 2179

v. 發熱、發光、發怒

▶Her face glowed with joy.
她愉悅得容光煥發。

n. 光輝；喜悅

▶He felt a glow of pride at his son's
courageous performance. 他為兒子的表
現感到自豪。

glue [glu] n. 膠水；黏著劑　◀ Track 2180

▶She used super glue to repair the tent.
她用強力膠來修理帳篷。

v. 黏牢；緊附；如用黏著劑固定

▶My husband kept his eyes glued to the television when I stepped into the room.
我走進房間時，我先生眼睛仍緊盯著電視。

go [go]　◀ Track 2181

v. 去；離去；行走；從事（活動）

▶We are going shopping this Saturday.
我們星期六要去購物。

n. 輪到的機會；嘗試；進行

▶OK, let's have another go.
好吧，我們再試一次。

goal [gol] n. 目標　◀ Track 2182

▶She planned to achieve her goal of losing three kilos in two months. 她計畫兩個月要達到減少兩公斤體重的目標。

goat [got] n. 山羊　◀ Track 2183

▶He raised goats and chicken on the farm.
他在農場養了群山羊和雞。

god [gɑd]　◀ Track 2184

n. 上帝；造物主；神祇

▶May God keep us from all harm. 願上帝保佑我們出入平安。

goddess [`gɑdɪs]　◀ Track 2185

n. 女神；受尊崇或仰慕的女子

▶When he met his goddess Mackenzie Foy, he went as red as a beetroot. 當他見到他的女神麥肯基・弗依時，他的臉都脹紅了。

gold [gold]　◀ Track 2186

n. 金；金色；金牌

▶He took the gold at the Olympic Games of London in 2016. 他奪得2016年奧運金牌。

golden [`goldn]　◀ Track 2187

adj. 金的；金色的；黃金般的；絕好的；珍貴的

▶The cathedral was crowned with a golden dome. 這座教堂有個金色的圓頂。

golf [gɑlf] n. 高爾夫球運動　◀ Track 2188

▶They played golf while discussing a few business deals. 他們邊打高爾夫球邊商討生意。

good [gʊd]　◀ Track 2189

adj. 好的；愉快的；令人滿意的；擅長的

▶They had a good time when they first met. 他們第一次見面時，度過了愉快的時光。

n. 利益；好處；善事

▶It will do you good to do some exercise every morning. 每天早上做點運動對你是有好處的。

goodbye [gʊd`baɪ]　◀ Track 2190

n. 再見；道別

▶She said goodbye to her boyfriend and left for England. 她向男友道再見後即前往英國。

goodness [`gʊdnɪs]　◀ Track 2191

n. 良善；仁慈；美德；精華

▶Please have the goodness to help me. 請你大發慈悲幫助我吧。

補充片語 have the goodness to do sth. 懇請做某事

中級

goods [gʊdz] n. 商品
◄€Track 2192
▶They will deliver the goods by air freight. 他們將以空運寄送商品。

goose [gus] n. 鵝；鵝肉
◄€Track 2193
▶I fed the goose with some bread. 我拿了一些麵包餵鵝。

gorgeous [`gɔrdʒəs]
◄€Track 2194
adj. 燦爛的；華麗的；令人愉快的；極美的
▶She looked absolutely gorgeous in the wedding gown. 她穿這件婚紗看起來真是美極了。

gorilla [gə`rɪlə]
◄€Track 2195
n. 大猩猩；彪形大漢
▶She has studied gorilla in the wild for 20 years. 她在野外研究大猩猩已長達二十年。

gossip [`gɑsəp]
◄€Track 2196
n. 閒話；流言蜚語；小道新聞
▶The gossip was spread to slander or defame an individual. 這個閒話被傳播開來，以誹謗或破壞某人的名聲。

n. 閒聊；說長道短
▶They gossiped about the manager. 他們在聊經理的八卦。

govern [`gʌvən]
◄€Track 2197
v. 統治；管理；控制
▶The country was governed by a corrupt autocracy. 這個國家被一個貪腐的獨裁政府所統治。

government
◄€Track 2198
[`gʌvənmənt] n. 政府
▶The government faces a furious backlash from the public over its judicial reform. 政府面臨民眾對於司改憤怒的反彈。

governor [`gʌvənə]
◄€Track 2199
n. 州長；地方行政長官；總督；主管；（公共機構的）董事；老闆
▶Bill Clinton was elected Governor of Arkansas. 比爾‧柯林頓選上阿肯色州州長。

gown [gaʊn]
◄€Track 2200
n. （女生的）禮服
▶She designed the evening gown for the royal bride. 她幫皇室新娘設計晚禮服。

grab [græb]
◄€Track 2201
v. 攫取；抓取；奪取；匆忙地做
▶We grabbed a bite at the café near our office. 我們在辦公室附近的咖啡廳吃了一些小點心。

n. 抓住；奪取之物
▶They both made a grab for the same piece of cheese cake. 他們倆都想拿同一塊起司蛋糕。

grace [gres]
◄€Track 2202
n. 優美；風度；恩惠
▶She battled cancer with grace and dignity. 她優雅且不失尊嚴地對抗癌症。

v. 使優美；使增光
▶The model has graced many covers of fashion magazines. 這位模特兒替許多時尚雜誌的封面增添光彩。

graceful [`gresfəl]
◄€Track 2203
adj. 優美的；得體的
▶The actress was beautiful and graceful. 那名女演員非常美麗優雅。

gracious [`greʃəs]
◄€Track 2204
adj. 親切的

▶The chef was gracious enough to take a selfie with us. 那名主廚很親切地與我們一起自拍。

grade [gred]
Track 2205

n. 分數；年級；等級

▶Her dream was to become a teacher ever since she was in third grade. 她讀三年級時，就夢想成位一名老師。

gradual [ˋgrædʒʊəl]
Track 2206

adj. 逐漸的；逐步的

▶His conversion to the religion was a gradual process. 他對這個信仰的皈依是漸進的過程。

gradually [ˋgrædʒʊəlɪ]
Track 2207

adv. 逐漸地

▶They gradually became good friends. 他們逐漸地變成好朋友。

graduate [ˋgrædʒʊ͵et]
Track 2208

n. 畢業生

▶He was an Eton College graduate. 他是伊頓公學的畢業生。

v. 畢業

▶I started to look for a job before I graduated from college. 我在大學畢業前就開始找工作了。

graduation
Track 2209

[͵grædʒʊˋeʃən] **n.** 畢業

▶She is scheduled for graduation the first week of June. 她預定六月第一週畢業。

grain [gren]
Track 2210

n. 穀粒；穀類；細粒；一點

▶He grew grains and raised sheep. 他種穀養羊。

相關片語 **with a grain of salt**
有保留地；不完全相信地

▶She took the gossip with a grain of salt. 她不完全相信這個八卦。

gram [græm] **n.** 克
Track 2211

▶The wok weighs 850 grams. 這個鍋子重八百五十公克。

grammar [ˋgræmə]
Track 2212

n. 文法

▶He taught English grammar, spelling, and creative writing. 他教英文文法、拼字，和創意寫作。

grand [grænd]
Track 2213

adj. 雄偉的；偉大的；重要的

▶The manager has a grand vision for the company. 經理對公司抱有遠大的願景。

grandchild
Track 2214

[ˋgrænd͵tʃaɪld] **n.** 孫子（女）；外孫（女）

▶His grandchildren are adorable. 他的孫子女很可愛。

granddaughter
Track 2215

[ˋgræn͵dɔtə] **n.** 孫女；外孫女

▶She smiled from ear to ear when she saw her granddaughter. 她看見孫女時，笑得合不攏嘴。

grandfather
Track 2216

[ˋgrænd͵faðə] **n.** 祖父；外祖父

▶We are going to celebrate our grandfather's birthday tomorrow. 我們明天要慶祝祖父的生日。

中級

grandmother
◀Track 2217

[ˋɡrændˏmʌðɚ] n 祖母；外祖母

▶Her grandmother was the headmaster of a private school. 她的祖母是私立學校的校長。

grandparent
◀Track 2218

[ˋɡrændˏpɛrənt] n 祖父母；外祖父母

▶My maternal grandparents were British. 我的外公婆都是英國人。

grandson
◀Track 2219

[ˋɡrændˏsʌn] n 孫子；外孫

▶Her grandson is an architect. 她的孫子是位建築師。

grant [ɡrænt] v 同意
◀Track 2220

▶He was granted a parole. 他被獲允假釋出獄。

n 授與物；獎學金；補助金；同意

▶They gave him a grant to study in Japan for a year. 他們給他一筆獎學金去日本留學一年。

grape [ɡrep] n 葡萄
◀Track 2221

▶She offered them a bunch of grapes in return for removing a snake from her back yard. 她送他們一串葡萄，回報他們幫她從後院除掉一條蛇。

補充片語 a bunch of grapes 一串葡萄

grapefruit
◀Track 2222

[ˋɡrepˏfrut] n 葡萄柚

▶She ate grapefruit just because she enjoyed the taste. 她吃葡萄柚純粹是因為喜歡它的味道。

graph [ɡræf]
◀Track 2223

n 曲線圖；圖表；標繪圖

▶The graph shows the birth rate of this country over the past ten years. 這曲線圖顯示了這個國家過去十年的出生率。

v 用圖表表示

▶He graphed the company's profits and losses on a chart. 他以圖表顯示公司的獲利與損失。

graphic [ˋɡræfɪk]
◀Track 2224

adj 生動的；寫實的；繪畫的；平面藝術的

▶The book gave a graphic description of World War II. 這本書對第二次世界大戰做了生動的描述。

grasp [ɡræsp]
◀Track 2225

v 抓牢；握緊；領會

▶She grasped the chance to prove her talent for singing. 她抓住證明她的歌唱天份的機會。

n 緊握；抓；理解；控制

▶He finally felt that true happiness might be within his grasp. 他終於覺得真正的幸福可能是觸手可及的事了。

grass [ɡræs] n 草；草地
◀Track 2226

▶They had a picnic on the grass. 他們在草地上野餐。

grasshopper
◀Track 2227

[ˋɡræsˏhɑpɚ] n 蚱蜢

▶I saw a grasshopper on a flower in my garden. 我看見一隻蚱蜢停在我庭院的花朵上。

grassy [ˋɡræsɪ]
◀Track 2228

adj 長滿草的；草綠色的；有草味的

▶She took pictures of the grassy knoll. 她把綠草如茵的小丘拍照了下來。

grateful [ˋgretfəl] ◀€Track 2229
adj. 感謝的

▶She was grateful to him for his help.
她很感謝他的幫助。

gratitude [ˋgrætəˌtjud] ◀€Track 2230
n. 感激之情

▶I baked a cake for him to express my gratitude. 我烤了一個蛋糕給他以示感激。

grave [grev] ◀€Track 2231
n. 墓穴；埋葬處

▶You are digging your own grave if you keep drinking too much alcohol. 如果你繼續過量飲酒，就等於是在自掘墳墓。

補充片語 **dig one's own grave**
自掘墳墓、自取滅亡

adj. 嚴肅的；認真的；嚴重的

▶He knew the family's situation was grave and he immediately took action. 他知道這家人的狀況很嚴重，便立刻行動援助。

gravity [ˋgrævətɪ] ◀€Track 2232
n. 地心引力；重量；嚴重性；嚴肅

▶Does he realize the gravity of the situation? 他明白到局勢的嚴重性了嗎？

gray [gre] ◀€Track 2233
adj. 灰色的；灰的；蒼白的；頭髮灰白的

▶Her hair turned gray overnight after the traumatic experience. 她經歷精神創傷後，頭髮一夕之間變灰白了。

n. 灰色；灰色衣服

▶He was dressed in gray in the funeral.
他在葬禮穿著灰色衣服。

grease [gris] ◀€Track 2234
n. 動物脂；油脂；賄賂

▶The pot was thick with grease.
這個鍋子上有厚厚的一層油。

v. 塗油脂於；賄賂

▶He did an overhaul of the bicycle and greased everything. 他把腳踏車做了大整修，並把該上油的零件都上油了。

相關片語 **grease sb.'s palm**
賄賂某人；打點

▶He greased the palm of an official with US$1000 so that the police station staff would not come down hard on his son. 他用一千美元賄賂一位官員，如此一來警察局才不會為難他的兒子。

greasy [ˋgrizɪ] ◀€Track 2235
adj. 油污的；油膩的；油滑奉承的

▶I'm looking for a shampoo to control my greasy hair. 我在找能控油的洗髮精。

相關片語 **greasy spoon** 廉價小飯館

▶We went to a greasy spoon for lunch.
我們在一家廉價小飯館吃午餐。

great [gret] ◀€Track 2236
adj. 棒的；極好的；偉大的

▶Hubert de Givenchy was one of the greatest designers of all time. 于貝爾·紀梵希是最偉大的時裝設計師之一。

補充片語 **of all time** 永遠的，無論何時的

greatly [ˋgretlɪ] ◀€Track 2237
adv. 極其；大大地；非常

▶We were greatly impressed by their warm hospitality. 他們溫暖的款待讓我們非常感動。

greedy [ˋgridɪ] ◀€Track 2238
adj. 貪婪的；貪吃的

中級

▶The ruling party is greedy for power.
執政黨貪圖權力。

green [grin]　◀€ Track 2239

adj. 綠色的；（臉色）發青的

▶The green bean casserole tastes delicious. 焗烤四季豆真美味。

n. 綠色

▶The playroom was decorated in bright green and yellow. 兒童遊樂室以鮮豔的綠色和黃色裝飾著。

greenhouse　◀€ Track 2240

[`grin͵haʊs] **n.** 溫室

▶She grows a lot of potatoes in the greenhouse. 她在溫室種植很多馬鈴薯。

相關片語 **greenhouse effect** 溫室效應

▶The greenhouse effect is changing our climate now. 溫室效應正在改變我們的氣候。

greet [grit]　◀€ Track 2241

v. 迎接；問候；打招呼

▶He greeted the guests at the door.
他在門口迎接客人。

greeting [`gritɪŋ]　◀€ Track 2242

n. 問候

▶She brightened my day with a cheerful greeting card. 她寄來的問候卡，讓我整天都很開心。

grief [grif] **n.** 悲痛　◀€ Track 2243

▶She buried her cat with grief.
她悲慟地埋葬她的貓。

相關片語 **come to grief**
終歸失敗；以失敗告終；出事故

▶Their marriage came to grief after six years. 他們的婚姻經過六年以失敗告終。

grieve [griv] **v.** 悲傷　◀€ Track 2244

▶She was grieved to know that her friend became a drug addict. 她得知朋友吸毒成癮，感到非常哀傷。

grill [grɪl]　◀€ Track 2245

v. （用烤架）烤；拷問；被炙烤

▶He grilled chicken with a special sauce.
他用特製的醬汁烤雞。

n. 烤架；燒烤的肉類食物

▶Put the corn on the grill.
把玉米放到烤架上。

grim [grɪm]　◀€ Track 2246

adj. 無情的；嚴厲的；殘酷的；猙獰的；可怕的

▶The medical prognosis was grim.
醫學預後的評估令人擔憂。

grin [grɪn] **v.** 露齒而笑　◀€ Track 2247

▶She grinned from ear to ear when her boyfriend gave her a diamond ring. 她的男友給她鑽戒時，她露齒而笑。

補充片語 **grin from ear to ear** 咧著嘴笑

n. 露齒的笑

▶He returned home with a broad grin on his face. 他回家時滿臉笑容。

相關片語 **grin and bear it** 逆來順受

▶Sometimes we just need to grin and bear it. 有時我們必須逆來順受。

grind [graɪnd]　◀€ Track 2248

v. 磨碎；用力擠壓；磨光；咬牙

▶She ground the nuts finely.
她把堅果磨得很細。

n. 磨；苦差事

▶He found learning physics a grind.
他覺得學物理是件苦事。

相關片語 **have an axe to grind**
有私心；另有企圖

▶The whistle blower has an ax to grind.
這個告密者是另有企圖的。

補充片語 **whistle blower** 告密者

---

groan [gron]　◀Track 2249
n. 呻吟聲；哼聲；抱怨聲

▶The paramedics could hear the groans of someone trapped in the overturned car. 急救人員能聽到困在翻覆車子裡的人的呻吟聲。

v. 呻吟；抱怨；呻吟著說

▶The wounded soldier groaned in pain.
這名傷兵痛苦地呻吟著。

---

grocery [ˈɡrosərɪ]　◀Track 2250
n. 食品；雜貨

▶She bought a basket of groceries.
她買了一籃子的雜貨。

相關片語 **grocery store** 雜貨店

▶The boy went to the grocery store to run errands for his mom. 男孩去雜貨店幫媽媽跑腿買東西。

---

groom [grum] **n.** 新郎　◀Track 2251

▶Prince Harry, the groom, choose to wear a military uniform. 身為新郎的哈利王子選擇穿著軍裝。

---

gross [gros]　◀Track 2252
adj. 總計的；顯著的；粗俗的；令人討厭的

▶The piles of dirty dishes look gross.
一堆堆骯髒的碗盤看起來很噁心。

---

ground [graʊnd] **n.** 地面　◀Track 2253

▶He sat down on the ground and trembled.
他坐在地上發抖。

---

group [grup]　◀Track 2254
n. （一）群；類；組

▶A group of tourists visited the Presidential Office Building this afternoon. 今天下午有一群觀光客參觀總統府。

---

grow [gro]　◀Track 2255
v. 生長；成長；種植

▶She grew vegetables and an apple tree in the garden. 她在庭院種了一些蔬菜和一顆蘋果樹。

---

growl [graʊl]　◀Track 2256
v. 咆哮；嗥叫；（雷、砲等）轟鳴

▶The manager growled at the assistant by his side. 經理對著坐在旁邊的助理咆哮。

n. 咆哮聲；轟鳴聲；嗥叫

▶He gave a growl of frustration.
他挫敗地咆哮著。

---

grown-up [ˈɡron ˌʌp]　◀Track 2257
n. 成年人

▶Her children are all grown-ups.
她的孩子都已是成年人了。

---

growth [groθ]　◀Track 2258
n. 成長；發育；生長物；種植

▶Good nutrition is important for healthy growth. 營養對於健康發育是很重要的。

---

grumble [ˈɡrʌmbl̩]　◀Track 2259
v. 發牢騷；抱怨；咕噥

中級

▶They grumbled about the increased work load. 他們抱怨工作量增加。

n. 怨言；牢騷

▶He is full of grumbles about his job. 他對工作牢騷滿腹。

guarantee [ˌgærən`ti] ◀Track 2260
v. 保證

▶The food is guaranteed to be fresh and delicious in that restaurant. 那家餐廳的食物保證新鮮又美味。

n. 保證

▶The company offers a money-back guarantee if customers are not satisfied with their products. 若客戶不滿意這家公司的商品，它們提供退款保證。

補充片語 money-back guarantee 退款保證

guard [gɑrd] ◀Track 2261
n. 警衛；看守員；護衛隊

▶The security guards were vigilant and asked people to extinguish their cigarettes. 保安維持警戒，並要求民眾把香菸熄滅。

v. 保衛；防衛

▶She is a celebrity that carefully guards her privacy. 她是一位極力保護自己隱私的名人。

guardian [`gɑrdɪən] ◀Track 2262
n. 保護員；守護員；管理員；（律）監護人

▶Tom's grandparents became the legal guardians of him and his two brothers. 湯姆的祖父母成了他和兩個兄弟的法定監護人。

補充片語 legal guardian 法定監護人

guava [`gwɑvə] n. 芭樂 ◀Track 2263

▶He brought guavas on his way back from the office. 他回辦公室的途中買了一些芭樂。

guess [gɛs] v. 猜；猜想 ◀Track 2264

▶I guess you are right. She is in a bad mood. 我想你是對的，她的心情很不好。

n. 猜；猜想

▶My guess is that she was too shy to ask for help. 我猜她太害羞而不敢求助。

guest [gɛst] n. 客人；賓客 ◀Track 2265

▶We have distinguished guests from home and abroad to attend this important event. 我們有來自海內外的貴賓參加這場重要的盛會。

guidance [`gaɪdns] ◀Track 2266
n. 指導

▶His math has improved dramatically under his teacher's guidance. 在他的老師指導下，他的數學大幅進步。

guide [gaɪd] ◀Track 2267
n. 導遊；嚮導；指導者；指南

▶Our tourist guide was very nice and helpful. 我們的嚮導很隨和而且很樂於助人。

v. 領路；帶領；引導

▶The librarian guided us through the smart library. 館員帶領我們參觀這座智慧圖書館。

guideline [`gaɪdˌlaɪn] ◀Track 2268
n. 指導方針

▶The guideline is based on scientific evidence. 這指導方針是依據科學實證所制定的。

guilt [gɪlt]
◀Track 2269

n. 有罪；過失；內疚

▶She felt a sense of guilt for ignoring her children.
她對於疏忽了孩子而感到罪惡。

guilty [ˋgɪltɪ]
◀Track 2270

adj. 有罪的；有罪惡感的；內疚的

▶He felt guilty about cheating on his wife. 他因對妻子不忠而他深感罪惡。

guitar [gɪˋtɑr] **n.** 吉他
◀Track 2271

▶She sang while playing the guitar.
她邊唱歌邊彈著吉他。

gulf [gʌlf]
◀Track 2272

n. 海灣；巨大分歧、鴻溝

▶It is hoped that the peace accord will bridge the gulf between the two ethnic groups.
大眾希望和平協定能縮小兩個族群之間的巨大分歧。

gulp [gʌlp]
◀Track 2273

v. 狼吞虎嚥地吃；大口地飲；喘不過氣；哽住

▶He gulped down a bottle of mineral water. 他將礦泉水一飲而盡。

n. 吞嚥；一大口

▶Fred drank the whisky in one gulp.
佛列德將威士忌一飲而盡。

gum [gʌm]
◀Track 2274

n. 樹脂；黏合劑；口香糖

▶He chewed gum to help quit smoking.
他嚼口香糖是為了戒菸。

gun [gʌn] **n.** 槍
◀Track 2275

▶Privately-owned guns should be banned.
私人擁有槍枝的情形應該被禁止。

gut [gʌt]
◀Track 2276

n. 腸子；內臟；膽量

▶He is a man with plenty of guts.
他是很有魄力的男人。

v. 取出內臟；損毀（屋內）裝置

▶She gutted the fish before frying them. 她炸魚之前先取出魚的內臟。

相關片語 **sweat one's guts out**
拼命工作

▶The man sweats his guts out to raise his family. 男人拼命工作以養家活口。

guy [gaɪ]
◀Track 2277

n. 傢伙；朋友；人

▶She fell in love with the guy she met in the cocktail party. 她愛上了在雞尾酒會遇到的一名男士。

gym [dʒɪm]
◀Track 2278

n. 體育館；健身房

▶He works out to keep his body in the best condition.
他為了保持最佳的體態而健身。

補充片語 **work out** 進行體能鍛鍊

gypsy [ˋdʒɪpsɪ]
◀Track 2279

n. 吉普賽人；吉普賽語；流浪者

▶She is a gypsy. 她是個吉普賽人。

adj. 吉普賽人的；吉普賽的

▶A gypsy boy was falsely accused of the attempted murder. 一個吉普賽男孩被錯誤地指控犯下這起企圖謀殺。

中級

▶ Hh

　　以下表格是全民英檢官方公告中級「聽、說、讀、寫」所須具備的能力，本書例句皆依此範疇特別設計，只要掃描右方QR code，就能搭配相對應的音軌實現「眼耳並用」方式，刺激左腦的語言學習功能；同時也可使用本書附贈的紅膠片，將其置於單字上，一面記憶一面自我挑戰，達到雙倍的學習成果！

聽 ▶	在日常生活中，能聽懂一般的會話；能大致聽懂公共場所廣播、氣象報告及廣告等。在工作時，能聽懂簡易的產品介紹與操作說明。能大致聽懂外籍人士的談話及詢問。
說 ▶	可在日常生活中，能以簡易英語交談或描述一般事物，能介紹自己的生活作息、工作、家庭、經歷等，並可對一般話題陳述看法。在工作時，能進行簡單的答詢，並與外籍人士交談溝通。
讀 ▶	在日常生活中，能閱讀短文、故事、私人信件、廣告、傳單、簡介及使用說明等。在工作時，能閱讀工作須知、公告、操作手冊、例行的文件、傳真、電報等。
寫 ▶	能寫簡單的書信、故事及心得等。對於熟悉且與個人經歷相關的主題，能以簡易的文字表達。

habit [ˋhæbɪt] n. 習慣
◀ Track 2280

▶She buys the same brand of shampoo out of habit.
她習慣買同一個牌子的洗髮精。

habitual [həˋbɪtʃʊəl]
adj. 習慣的
◀ Track 2281

▶He is a habitual criminal. 他是慣犯。

hack [hæk]
◀ Track 2282
v. 劈；砍；亂砍；當駭客；侵入

▶The company's official website was hacked. 這家公司的官網被駭客入侵了。

hacker [ˋhækɚ]
◀ Track 2283
n. 駭客；企圖不法侵入他人電腦系統的人

▶The hacker was hired by the government for his exceptional skills.
這名駭客因技術高超而被政府雇用。

hadn't [ˋhædnt]
◀ Track 2284
abbr. 未曾、還沒（had not的縮寫）

▶He hadn't seen his mom for a while.
他已有一段時間沒見到媽媽了。

hair [hɛr] n. 頭髮
◀ Track 2285

▶She has rich auburn hair.
她有一頭豐盈的赤褐色頭髮。

haircut [ˋhɛrˌkʌt]
◀ Track 2286
n. 剪髮

▶His Mohawk haircut is very cool.
他的龐克頭髮型很酷。

hairdresser
◀ Track 2287
[ˋhɛrˌdrɛsɚ] n. 美髮師

▶He is a seasoned hairdresser.
他是一位技術純熟的美髮師。

hairstyle [`hɛr,staɪl]

🔊 Track 2288

n. 髮型

▶She giggled at the sight of his new hairstyle. 她看到他的新髮型，忍不住吱喀喀地笑了。

half [hæf]

🔊 Track 2289

pron. 半；一半；二分之一

▶Out of 100 students, only half passed the math exam. 在一百個學生之中，只有一半的人數學及格。

adj. 一半的；二分之一的

▶They drove half a mile along the main street. 他們沿著大街開了半英里。

n. 半；二分之一

▶A half of 30 is 15. 三十的一半是十五。

adv. 一半地；相當地

▶The glass is half full. 杯子有一半是滿的。

halfway [`hæf`we]

🔊 Track 2290

adv. 在中途；到一半

▶She met her classmate halfway between her house and the school. 她在家和學校的中間處與同學碰面。

hall [hɔl] **n.** 會堂；大廳

🔊 Track 2291

▶They just laid a new carpet in the hall. 他們剛在大廳鋪了新地毯。

Halloween [,hælo`in]

🔊 Track 2292

n. 萬聖節

▶He wore a Wolverine costume for Halloween.
他在萬聖節穿著金剛狼服裝。

hallway [`hɔl,we]

🔊 Track 2293

n. 玄關；門廳；走廊

▶The hallway is elegant and nicely decorated.
房子的玄關很典雅且佈置得很美。

halt [hɔlt]

🔊 Track 2294

v. 停止行進；停止；使終止

▶Production was halted because of the failure of the computer system. 因為電腦系統故障，生產停止了。

n. 停止；暫停；終止

▶The truck came to a halt to avoid hitting a school bus.
卡車停下來以避免撞到校車。

> **補充片語** come to a halt
> 停止前進；陷入停頓

ham [hæm] **n.** 火腿

🔊 Track 2295

▶Mom made a ham sandwich and sliced some apples for my breakfast. 媽媽做了火腿三明治又切了蘋果當作我的早餐。

hamburger

🔊 Track 2296

[`hæmbɚgɚ]=**burger** **n.** 漢堡

▶He made himself a hamburger and some French fries. 他為自己做了一個漢堡和一些薯條。

hammer [`hæmɚ]

🔊 Track 2297

n. 槌頭；鎚子

▶The criminal used a hammer to destroy the building's doorbell. 這名罪犯用鎚子敲壞大樓的門鈴。

hand [hænd] **n.** 手

🔊 Track 2298

▶For someone his size, he has big hands. 以他的體型來看，他有一雙大手。

v. 遞交；傳遞

中級

▶She handed me a glass of grape juice. 她遞給我一杯葡萄汁。

handbag [`hænd͵bæg] ◀ Track 2299
n. 手提包

▶Inside her handbag are cosmetics and a wallet. 她的手提包裡有化妝品和錢包。

handful [`hændfəl] ◀ Track 2300
n. 一把；一握；少量

▶They invited 200 guests to the party, but only a handful showed up.
他們邀請了兩百名客人到派對，但只有少數人出席。

handicap [`hændɪ͵kæp] ◀ Track 2301
n. 障礙；不利條件；殘障

▶She never let her physical handicap hampers her life.
她從不讓生理上的障礙限制她的生命。

v. 妨礙；使不利

▶Medical assistance was hadicapped due to the narrow fire lane, and the old man passed away at the end.
因為狹窄防火巷的關係，醫療救援大為不利，這名老人最後過世了。

handicapped ◀ Track 2302
[`hændɪ͵kæpt] **adj.** 有生理缺陷的；殘障的；智力低下的

▶She was physically handicapped.
她有生理上的殘缺。

handkerchief ◀ Track 2303
[`hæŋkɚ͵tʃɪf] **n.** 手帕

▶She used a handkerchief to dry her tears when she heard the bad news.
她聽到壞消息時，用手帕擦乾眼淚。

handle [`hændl̩] ◀ Track 2304
v. 處理；對待；操作

▶We need to handle this issue carefully.
我們要小心地處理這個議題。

n. 把手；柄狀物；落人口實的把柄

▶The door handle was made of gold and porcelain. 這個門把是用金子和陶瓷做的。

handsome [`hænsəm] ◀ Track 2305
adj. 英俊的；可觀的

▶Jonathon is the most handsome man I have ever met.
強納生是我遇過最英俊的男人。

handwriting ◀ Track 2306
[`hænd͵raɪtɪŋ] **n.** 筆跡；筆法；書寫

▶His handwriting is illegible.
他的筆跡很難讀。

handy [`hændɪ] ◀ Track 2307
adj. 手邊的；便利的；手巧的

▶There is a café near our office, so it's quite handy when we are hungry. 辦公室附近有間小餐館，當我們肚子餓時，吃東西很方便。

相關片語 come in handy
遲早有用；派得上用場

▶The reference book may come in handy. 這本參考書可能派得上用場。

hang [hæŋ] ◀ Track 2308
v. 懸掛；吊起

▶She hung an oil painting on the wall.
她在牆上掛了一幅油畫。

hanger [`hæŋɚ] ◀ Track 2309
n. 衣架；掛鉤

▶I bought some velvet hangers to keep my closet neat and organized. 我買了一些絨面衣架讓衣櫥保持乾淨整齊。

happy ['hæpən] v 發生 ◀Track 2310

▶The witness told the police what happened. 目擊證人告訴警方事發的來龍去脈。

happily ['hæpɪlɪ] ◀Track 2311

adv 快樂地

▶She is happily married and has two young children. 她的婚姻幸福，並有兩個年幼的小孩。

happy ['hæpɪ] ◀Track 2312

adj 高興的；樂意的；滿意的

▶He was a happy child before his mom passed away. 在媽媽過世前，他是個快樂的小孩。

harassment ◀Track 2313

['hærəsmənt] n 煩擾；騷擾

▶Sher learned taekwondo to protect herself from sexual harassment. 她學習跆拳道以保護自己免受性騷擾。

harbor ['harbə] ◀Track 2314

n 港灣；避難所

▶Shanghai is a big harbor. 上海是個巨大的海港。

v 庇護；藏匿；（船）入港停泊；躲藏

▶She was charged with harboring the criminal. 她因藏匿罪犯而被起訴。

hard [hard] ◀Track 2315

adj 堅硬的；困難的；努力的

▶He is a hard nut to crack. 他是很難應付的人。

補充片語 **a hard nut to crack**
難以對付的人

adv 努力地；困難地；猛烈地

▶The single mother worked hard to support her family. 這位單親媽媽努力工作養家。

harden ['hardn] ◀Track 2316

v 使變硬；變堅固；變得冷酷；變麻木

▶Poverty hardened his determination to improve his knowledge and life. 貧窮使他堅定要精進知識，改善生活。

hardly ['hardlɪ] ◀Track 2317

adv 幾乎不；簡直不

▶She has hardly eaten anything since she broke up with her boyfriend. 她和男友分手後，幾乎不吃東西了。

hardship ['hardʃɪp] ◀Track 2318

n 艱難

▶He overcame a lot of hardships in life. 他克服了很多人生中的艱難。

hardware ['hard,wɛr] ◀Track 2319

n 五金器具；武器、軍事裝備；（電腦）硬體；裝備、設備

▶The country has upgraded its military hardware. 這個國家已升級軍事裝備了。

hardworking ◀Track 2320

[,hard'wɜkɪŋ] adj 勤勉的；努力的

▶She is a bright and hardworking student. 她是聰明又勤奮的學生。

hardy ['hardɪ] ◀Track 2321

adj 能吃苦耐勞的；強壯的；堅強的

中級

▶He is very hardy and resourceful.
他很吃苦耐勞又足智多謀。

harm [hɑrm] n. 傷害

◀Track 2322

▶The herbal repellant will not do harm to your body. 這個植物配方的驅蟲劑不會對身體造成傷害。

補充片語 do harm to 對……造成傷害

▶Under no circumstances will I allow anyone to harm my family. 無論在什麼情況下，我都不允許任何人傷害我的家人。

補充片語 under no circumstances
無論在什麼情況下都不

harmful [`hɑrmfəl]

◀Track 2323

adj. 有害的

▶Smoking is harmful to your health.
抽菸對健康有害。

harmonica

◀Track 2324

[hɑr`mɑnɪkə] n. 口琴

▶He treasured the harmonica given by his dad. 他很珍惜爸爸送他的口琴。

harmony [`hɑrmənɪ]

◀Track 2325

n. 和睦；融洽；一致

▶Humans must live in harmony with nature. 人類應該與大自然和平共處。

補充片語 in harmony with
與……協調一致

harsh [hɑrʃ]

◀Track 2326

adj. 粗糙的；刺耳的；刺鼻的；澀口的；
刺眼的；嚴厲的；惡劣的

▶You need to relax. Don't be too harsh on yourself. 你應該放輕鬆，不要對自己太嚴苛。

harvest [`hɑrvɪst]

◀Track 2327

n. 收獲；收成；成果

▶We had an awesome harvest this year. 我們今年有個大豐收。

v. 收獲；收割；獲得

▶They just harvested the vegetables fresh from the garden. 他們剛剛從庭院採了鮮蔬。

hasn't [`hæznt]

◀Track 2328

abbr. 還沒、未曾（has not的縮寫）

▶He hasn't finished his breakfast.
他還沒吃完早餐。

hassle [`hæsl]

◀Track 2329

n. 激烈爭論；口角；困難；麻煩

▶It was a real hassle to find a good mortgage broker. 要找個好的房屋仲介是一件很麻煩的事情。

v. 找麻煩

▶She kept hassling him about his personal love life . 她一直煩問他的個人感情生活。

haste [hest]

◀Track 2330

n. 急忙；迅速；慌忙

▶More haste, less speed. 欲速則不達。

hasty [`hestɪ]

◀Track 2331

adj. 匆忙的，倉促的；輕率的

▶They regretted their last hasty telephone call with their mother. 他們很後悔與媽媽最後一次的電話交談過於倉促。

hat [hæt] n. 帽子

◀Track 2332

▶She wore a pale pink hat in the official occasion. 她在正式場合戴了一頂淺粉紅色的帽子。

hatch [hætʃ] ◀Track 2333

v. 孵出；孵化

▶The eggs are hatched with the help of an incubator. 這些蛋是靠孵卵器孵化出來的。

n. （蛋的）孵化；（小雞等）一窩

▶There are three birds in this hatch. 這一窩有三隻小鳥。

hate [het] **v.** 厭惡；討厭 ◀Track 2334

▶She hates being treated like a servant in her sister's home. 她討厭在姊姊家被當做僕人般對待。

n. 仇恨；厭惡；反感

▶He looked at the killer with hate in his eyes. 他用憎恨的目光看著這個殺人犯。

hateful [`hetfəl] ◀Track 2335

adj. 可憎的；討厭的

▶Washing dishes is a hateful chore. 洗碗是令人討厭的家務事。

hatred [`hetrɪd] ◀Track 2336

n. 憎恨；敵意

▶He was detained for spreading racial hatred. 他因散布種族仇恨而被拘留。

haunt [hɔnt] ◀Track 2337

v. （鬼魂）常出沒於；（思想）縈繞心頭；使困擾；纏住某人

▶People said the building was haunted by ghosts. 人們說那棟建築有鬼魂出沒。

n. 常去的地方

▶The pub is one of his haunts. 那間酒館是他常去的地方。

have [hæv] ◀Track 2338

v. 有；吃；使做……

▶I have two pair of sunglasses. 我有兩副太陽眼鏡。

aux. 已經（完成式的助動詞）

▶I have finished my homework. 我已寫完功課了。

haven't [`hævnt] ◀Track 2339

abbr. 還沒、未曾（have not的縮寫）

▶We haven't been to the Palace of Fine Arts. 我們還沒去過藝術宮。

hawk [hɔk] ◀Track 2340

n. 鷹，隼；貪婪的傢伙；騙子

▶The teacher watched the students like a hawk to make sure they focused on their studies. 老師目光犀利地看著學生，以確保他們專注在學習上。

hay [he] ◀Track 2341

n. （飼料用的）乾草

▶Make hay while the sun shines. 趁有陽光照耀時弄好乾草（打鐵趁熱，勿失良機）。

相關片語 **hit the hay** 去睡覺

▶I hit the hay early last night. 我昨晚很早就睡覺。

hazard [`hæzɚd] ◀Track 2342

n. 危險；危害物

▶The flood caused serious hazards to the downstream areas. 洪水對下游地區造成嚴重的危害。

v. 冒險做出；大膽嘗試；冒……的危險；使冒危險

▶Binge drinking will hazard your health. 過量飲酒會危害你的健康。

中級

he [hi] **pron.** 他　　◀ Track 2343

▶He is smart and charming.
他既聰明又迷人。

head [hɛd] **n.** 頭　　◀ Track 2344

▶She has a good head for physics.
她很擅長物理。

v. 前往

▶The ship headed north to Newcastle.
船朝北開到新堡。

headache [ˋhɛdͺek]　◀ Track 2345

n. 頭痛；令人頭痛的事

▶He took an aspirin to relieve his headache.
他服用一顆阿司匹林來緩解頭痛。

headline [ˋhɛdͺlaɪn]　◀ Track 2346

n. 標題；頭條新聞

▶The political scandal has been in the headlines for days. 這則政治醜聞已經上了好幾天的頭條新聞。

v. 給……加標題；使成頭條；使成注意焦點

▶The newspapers headlined the official's bribery scandal. 報紙以官員的賄賂醜聞作為頭條新聞。

相關片語 **hit the headlines** 上頭條

▶The air crash will definitely hit the headline. 這起空難一定會上頭條。

headmaster　◀ Track 2347

[ˋhɛdͺmæstɚ] **n.** 美國私立學校校長

▶The headmaster will retire next year.
這位私立學校的校長明年即將退休。

headphones　◀ Track 2348

[ˋhɛdͺfonz] **n.** 頭戴式耳機

▶My headphones don't work.
我的頭戴式耳機故障了。

headquarters　◀ Track 2349

[ˋhɛdˋkwɔrtɚz] **n.** 總部；總公司

▶The company's headquarters is located in Helsinki.
這家公司的總部位於赫爾辛基。

headset [ˋhɛdͺsɛt]　◀ Track 2350

n. 戴在頭上的收話器；雙耳式耳機

▶I don't wear headsets when driving.
我開車時不戴耳機。

heal [hil]　◀ Track 2351

v. 治癒；使恢復健康；（傷口）癒合；痊癒

▶It took a long time for the wound to heal.
這個傷口花了很長的時間才癒合。

health [hɛlθ] **n.** 健康　◀ Track 2352

▶Drinking too much alcohol is not good for your health.
喝太多酒對你的健康無益。

healthy [ˋhɛlθɪ]　◀ Track 2353

adj. 健康的

▶My grandmother is healthy and energetic.
我的祖母很健康、精力充沛。

heap [hip]　◀ Track 2354

n. 一堆；堆積；大量

▶He had heaps of work to do.
他有一大堆工作要做。

v. 堆積；積聚；裝滿

▶The laundry basket was heaped with dirty clothes. 洗衣籃裡堆滿了髒衣服。

hear [hɪr] **v** 聽到；聽見　◀Track 2355

▶They heard a noise from the attic.
他們聽到閣樓傳來吵嘈聲。

heart [hɑrt] **n** 心；心臟　◀Track 2356

▶She has a weak heart. 她的心臟很虛弱。

heartbreak　◀Track 2357

[`hɑrt͵brek] **n** 心碎；難忍的悲傷或失望

▶He had never experienced heartbreak
like this before. 他過去從沒經歷過像這樣
的心碎感覺。

heat [hit]　◀Track 2358

n 熱；熱氣；高溫

▶They hope the heat of the sun can
warm up the room. 他們希望陽光的熱能
可以讓房間暖和起來。

v 加熱；使變熱

▶We heated up the pizza and the soup
for lunch. 我們熱點比薩和湯作為午餐。

heater [`hitɚ]　◀Track 2359
n 暖氣機；加熱器

▶The heater didn't work, so he crawled
into a sleeping bag. 暖氣故障了，所以他
窩進了睡袋裡。

heaven [`hɛvən]　◀Track 2360
n 天國；極樂之地；天堂

▶May his journey to Heaven be blessed.
願他前往天堂的旅途受到上天祝福。

相關片語 **seventh heaven**
極樂；歡天喜地

▶They've been in seventh heaven since
they won the lottery. 他們自從贏得樂透
後，高興得不得了。

heavenly [`hɛvənlɪ]　◀Track 2361
adj 天空的；天堂般的；極好的；美好的

▶The dessert is heavenly.
這點心真在太美味了。

heavy [`hɛvɪ]　◀Track 2362
adj 沉重的；大的；繁忙的

▶The suitcase was too heavy for me.
我覺得這個行李箱太重了。

he'd [hid]　◀Track 2363
abbr 他會（he would、he had的縮寫）

▶He'd done everything he could to
protect his children. 他已竭盡所能地保護
他的孩子。

heed [hid] **v** 留心；注意　◀Track 2364

▶She didn't heed her father's advice.
她不聽從父親的勸告。

n 留心；注意

▶Tom paid no heed to her warnings.
湯姆沒把她的警告放在心上。

補充片語 **pay heed to** 留心；注意

heel [hil]　◀Track 2365
n 腳後跟；高跟鞋

▶She is obsessed with high heels.
她很愛穿著高跟鞋。

相關片語 **down at heel**
衣衫襤褸的；穿著寒酸的

▶When I first met him, he looked down at
heel. 我第一次遇見他時，他衣衫襤褸。

height [haɪt] **n** 高；高度　◀Track 2366

▶She reached the heights of her career
when she was 40. 她在40歲時達到事業的
高峰。

中級

heir [ɛr]
Track 2367

n. 繼承人；嗣子；（性格、技能等的）繼承者

▶Prince William is the second heir, right after his father Prince Charles. 威廉王子是王位的第二繼承人，排在他的父親查爾斯王子之後。

helicopter
Track 2368

[`hɛlɪkɑptɚ] **n.** 直升機

▶They rushed the sick child to the children's hospital by helicopter. 他們趕緊把病童以直升機送往兒童醫院。

hell [hɛl]
Track 2369

n. 地獄、冥府；人間煉獄；極大困境；悲慘境地；（加強語氣）究竟

▶The company was in production hell to meet the ever-growing demand of the new model car. 這家公司為製造出日益增加的新款車需求量，而處在生產地獄。

相關片語 give sb. hell
怒斥某人；騷擾某人；困擾某人

▶He didn't tell you the truth because he was afraid you'd give him hell. 他不敢跟你說實話因為他怕你會把他狠狠數落了一頓。

he'll [hil]
Track 2370

abbr. 他會（he will的縮寫）

▶He is in the restroom. He'll come back soon. 他在廁所，很快就會回來。

hello [hə`lo]
Track 2371

n. 表示問候的招呼；哈囉

▶I just called her to say hello and that I missed her. 我剛剛打電話問候她並告訴她我想念她。

interj. 喂；你好；哈囉

▶Hello, may I speak to Jenny? 你好，我可以跟珍妮說電話嗎？

helmet [`hɛlmɪt]
Track 2372

n. 頭盔；安全帽

▶You must wear a helmet when you ride a scooter. 你騎機車時一定要戴安全帽。

help [hɛlp] **v.** 幫助
Track 2373

▶He donated a lot of money to help AIDS patients. 他捐了很多錢幫助愛滋病病患。

n. 幫助

▶We appreciate your help. 我們很感激你的幫助。

helpful [`hɛlpfəl]
Track 2374

adj. 有幫助的

▶The Internet is very convenient and helpful. 網路既方便又有幫助。

hen [hɛn] **n.** 母雞
Track 2375

▶He raised cattle and hens on his farm. 他在農場養了牛和母雞。

hence [hɛns]
Track 2376

adv. 因此；從現在起

▶She aced the final; hence, she was in a good mood. 她期末考考得很好，因此心情很飛揚。

her [hɝ] **pron.** 她
Track 2377

▶Her parents gave her a new laptop. 她的父母送她一台新的筆電。

herb [hɝb]
Track 2378

n. 草本植物；藥草

▶This herb has a medicinal effect. 這個藥草具有醫用的療效。

herd [hɝd] ◀ Track 2379

n. 畜群；牧群；放牧人

▶He came across a herd of goats when he was hiking. 他在健行時遇到一群山羊。

v. 放牧；把……趕在一起；聚在一起；成群

▶The dog was herding sheep for the rancher. 這隻狗在幫牧場主人牧羊。

here [hɪr] **adv.** 這裡 ◀ Track 2380

▶Come here and let's have some chitchat. 過來跟我們一起閒聊。

hermit [`hɝmɪt] ◀ Track 2381

n. 隱士；遁世者

▶She became a hermit after quitting the job. 她離職後變成了隱士。

hero [`hɪro] ◀ Track 2382

n. 英雄；受崇拜的人

▶My dad is my hero. 我爸爸是我的英雄。

heroic [hɪ`roɪk] ◀ Track 2383

adj. 英勇的；英雄的；記述英雄及其事跡的

▶His heroic deeds were unknown until 1990.
他英勇的事蹟直到1990年才為人所知。

heroin [`hɛroˏɪn] ◀ Track 2384

n. 海洛因

▶His drug-addicted brother died due to overdose of heroin. 他吸毒成癮的弟弟因為吸食海洛因過量而死亡。

heroine [`hɛroˏɪn] ◀ Track 2385

n. 女英雄；女傑；受崇拜的女子

▶Every woman is a heroine in her own life. 每個人女人都是自己生命中的女英雄。

hers [hɝz] **pron.** 她的 ◀ Track 2386

▶I have an apartment, but hers is much larger than mine. 我有一間公寓，但她的公寓比我的大間多了。

herself [hɚ`sɛlf] ◀ Track 2387

pron. 她自己

▶She doesn't have much confidence in herself. 她對自己不太有自信。

he's [hiz] ◀ Track 2388

abbr. 他是、他已（ **he is** 、 **he has** 的縮寫）

▶He's an outstanding scholar.
他是位傑出的學者。

hesitate [`hɛzəˏtet] ◀ Track 2389

v. 躊躇；猶豫

▶If you have any questions, please do not hesitate to let us know. 若你有任何問題，請不要猶豫讓我們知道。

hey [he] **interj.** 嘿 ◀ Track 2390

▶Hey, I haven't seen you for ages.
嘿，我好久沒看到你了。

hi [haɪ] **interj.** 嗨（招呼語） ◀ Track 2391

▶Hi, Larry. How are you?
嗨，賴瑞。你好嗎？

hidden [`hɪdn] ◀ Track 2392

adj. 隱藏的；隱秘的

▶He had no hidden agenda to stifle press freedom.
他對於要扼止新聞自由毫無掩飾。

> **補充片語** **hidden agenda** 隱藏的議程；未公開的計劃；引申為別有心機、有幕後動機

中級

hide [haɪd] v 藏；躲藏 ◀Track 2393

▶She hid her diary under the mattress.
她把她的日記藏床墊下。

high [haɪ] ◀Track 2394

adj. 高的；（價值）高的；高速的

▶He put the medicine on a high shelf so
that his children couldn't reach it. 他把
藥放在高架上，這樣他的小孩才拿不到。

adv. 高地

▶The new drone flew much higher than the
old one. 新型無人機飛得比舊型還要高。

highlight [`haɪ͵laɪt] ◀Track 2395

v 用強光照射；用強光突出；使顯著；使突
出

▶Her speech highlighted the problem of
racial discrimination. 她的演說強調了種族
歧視的問題。

n 強光（效果）；最精彩的部分；最重要的
部分

▶The Grand Canyon trip was the
highlight of our trip in the US. 大峽谷是
我們美國之旅最精彩的部分。

highly [`haɪlɪ] **adv.** 非常 ◀Track 2396

▶She was highly intellectual and much
ahead of her classmates. 她智力非常
高，超越同班同學的程度。

high-rise [`haɪ`raɪz] ◀Track 2397

n 高樓

▶The ten-story high-rise is located in the
heart of the city. 這棟十層樓高的大樓位在
市中心。

highway [`haɪ͵we] ◀Track 2398

n 公路；道路

▶The speed limit of the highway is 120
kilometers per hour. 這條公路的時速是
120公里。

hijack [`haɪ͵dʒæk] ◀Track 2399

v 劫持；攔路搶劫

▶Four terrorists hijacked the airplane.
四名恐怖份子劫機。

hijacker [`haɪ͵dʒækɚ] ◀Track 2400

n 強盜；劫機者；劫持者；劫盜

▶Hijackers crashed the plane into the
World Trade Center. 劫機犯將飛機撞向世
貿中心大樓。

hijacking [`haɪdʒækɪŋ] ◀Track 2401

n 攔路搶劫；劫持

▶The 911 attack in the US is considered
as the most severe incident of aircraft
hijacking in aviation history. 發生在美國
的911恐攻事件被視為是飛航史最嚴重的劫機
事件。

補充片語 aircraft hijacking 劫機

hike [haɪk] ◀Track 2402

n 徒步旅行；健行

▶They went on a five-mile hike in the
forest. 他們在森林裡步行五英里。

v 徒步旅行；健行

▶Whether we will go hiking tomorrow
depends on the weather. 我們明天是否
要徒步旅行取決於天氣。

hiker [`haɪkɚ] ◀Track 2403

n 徒步旅行者；遠足者

▶The national park is full of hikers on the
weekend. 這座國家公園在週末有絡繹不絕
的健行者。

hiking [`haɪkɪŋ]
◀Track 2404

n. 徒步旅行；健行

▶My daughter went hiking with her friends. 我女兒跟朋友一起徒步旅行。

---

hill [hɪl] **n.** 小山；丘陵
◀Track 2405

▶We saw a herd of goats on the hill.
我們在丘陵看到一群山羊。

---

him [hɪm] **pron.** 他
◀Track 2406

▶I haven't seen Ben for a while. Have you heard from him lately? 我有一陣子沒看到班恩了。你最近有聽到他的消息嗎?

---

himself [hɪm`sɛlf]
◀Track 2407

pron. 他自己

▶The little boy just lost him mom and cried himself to sleep. 小男孩剛剛失去母親，他是哭著入睡的。

---

hint [hɪnt]
◀Track 2408

n. 暗示；建議；指點；少許、微量

▶I dropped a hint to my husband that I wanted a candle-lit dinner on our wedding anniversary. 我向先生暗示我想要一頓燭光晚餐來慶祝我們的結婚紀念日。

補充片語 drop a hint to sb.
給予某人暗示

v. 暗示；示意

▶He hinted that I should be wary of the woman sitting next to me. 他暗示我應該要提防坐在我身旁的女人。

相關片語 take a hint
領會別人的暗示；看眼色

▶She just couldn't take a hint and kept eating with her mouth open. 她就是不明白別人的暗示，還一直張著嘴吃東西。

---

hip [hɪp] **n.** 臀部；屁股
◀Track 2409

▶The old man had a rheumatic hip.
這位老翁的髖關節患了風濕病。

---

hippopotamus
◀Track 2410

[ˌhɪpə`patəməs]=**hippo n.** 河馬

▶The baby hippopotamus attracts many visitors to the zoo. 這隻河馬寶寶吸引很多遊客去動物園看牠。

---

hire [haɪr] **v.** 雇用；租用
◀Track 2411

▶He hired a butler to take care of his house. 他雇用一名管家打理房子。

n. 雇用；租用

▶The bus station has bikes for hire.
巴士站有腳踏車供人租用。

---

his [hɪz]
◀Track 2412

det. 他的；他的東西

▶His favorite food is cheeseburger.
他最喜愛的食物是起司漢堡。

---

hiss [hɪs]
◀Track 2413

v. 發出嘶嘶聲；發出噓聲（表示不滿）；

以噓聲表示；嘶嘶地說出

▶The politician was hissed and hooted.
這名政治人物被噓又被呵斥。

n. 嘶嘶聲；噓聲

▶I heard a hiss and saw a snake coming out of the bushes. 我聽到嘶嘶聲，然後看到一隻蛇從灌木裡爬出來。

---

historian [hɪs`torɪən]
◀Track 2414

n. 歷史學家

▶His father is a renowned historian.
他的爸爸是知名的歷史學家。

中級

historic [hɪs`tɔrɪk]　◀Track 2415

adj. 歷史上著名的；具重大歷史意義的

▶This is a historic moment for our country. 對我們國家來説，這是個具有歷史紀念性的一刻。

historical [hɪs`tɔrɪk!]　◀Track 2416

adj. 歷史的；史學的；有關歷史的

▶*A Tale of Two Cities* is a historical novel by Charles Dickens. 《雙城記》是查爾斯‧狄更斯所著的歷史小説。

補充片語 historical novel 歷史小説

history [`hɪstərɪ]　◀Track 2417

n. 歷史；由來；過去的經歷；故事

▶He is an expert in Middle East history. 他是中東歷史的專家。

hit [hɪt] **v.** 打；打擊；碰撞　◀Track 2418

▶The death of his wife hit him hard. 他妻子的離世對他打擊很大。

n. 打擊；碰撞；成功而風行一時的事物

▶Jolin Tsai's new album is a hit. 蔡依林的新專輯很暢銷。

hive [haɪv]　◀Track 2419

n. 蜂窩；蜂巢；熱鬧的場所；蜂群；喧嚷的人群

▶To express her gratitude, she gave them a bunch of grapes for removing a bee hive for her. 她為了感謝他們幫她移除蜂窩，便送了一串葡萄給他們。

hoarse [hors]　◀Track 2420

adj. 嘶啞的；嗓子粗啞的

▶His voice became hoarse because of too much shouting in the game. 他因為在比賽喊叫太頻繁，所以聲音變得很沙啞。

hobby [`habɪ] **n.** 嗜好　◀Track 2421

▶Zoe's hobby is cooking. 柔伊的嗜好是烹飪。

hockey [`hakɪ] **n.** 曲棍球　◀Track 2422

▶Basketball, soccer, and hockey are all team sports. 籃球、足球、曲棍球都是團隊運動。

hold [hold]　◀Track 2423

v. 握住；抓住；舉行

▶She held her little son in her arms. 她把小兒子抱在懷裡。

n. 抓住；支撐

▶He grabbed hold of Kelly before she fell down the stairs. 他在凱莉要跌下樓梯前抓住了她。

holder [`holdɚ]　◀Track 2424

n. 持有者；保有者；支托物

▶She bought a toothbrush holder and put it in the bathroom. 她買了一個牙刷架，並把它放在浴室裡。

hole [hol] **n.** 洞　◀Track 2425

▶His wife mended the hole in his trousers. 他的妻子把他的褲洞縫補了起來。

holiday [`halə,de]　◀Track 2426

n. 假日；節日；休假日

▶We plan to go to Switzerland during the Christmas holidays. 我們計畫在聖誕節假期去瑞士。

hollow [`halo]　◀Track 2427

adj. 中空的；凹陷的；空洞的；空虛的

▶She had anorexia, and her cheeks were hollow. 她有厭食症，雙頰都凹陷了。

n. 窪地；洞；坑；山谷

▶He found a hollow in a tree and squeezed inside of it. 他在樹裡發現了一個洞，於是將自己擠了進去。

holy [`holɪ] ◀Track 2428
adj. 神聖的；虔誠的；獻身於宗教的；聖潔的

▶The city is a holy site for this religion. 這座城市是這個信仰的聖地。

home [hom] **n.** 家 ◀Track 2429
▶He went home early to watch the football game.
他為了看足球賽很早就回家了。

adv. 在家；回家；到家

▶You can't leave young children home alone. It's too dangerous. 你不能把小孩獨自留在家裡，這樣太危險了。

adj. 家庭的；本國的；總部的

▶May I have your home telephone number? 我可以跟你要家裡的電話號碼嗎?

homeland ◀Track 2430
[`hom͵lænd] **n.** 祖國；家鄉

▶They left their homeland and moved to Australia. 他們離開祖國，搬到澳洲了。

homesick [`hom͵sɪk] ◀Track 2431
adj. 想家的

▶She got terribly homesick when she worked overseas.
她在國外工作時非常想家。

homework ◀Track 2432
[`hom͵wɝk] **n.** 回家作業

▶Our teacher gave us piles of homework yesterday. 老師昨天給我們一大堆的功課。

honest [`ɑnɪst] ◀Track 2433
adj. 誠實的；用正當手段取得的；坦白的

▶To be honest with you, I'm fed up with your lies.
坦白跟你說，我已受夠了你的謊言。

honestly [`ɑnɪstlɪ] ◀Track 2434
adv. 誠實地；老實說；實在

▶Honestly, you're the best magician I have ever seen on the show. 老實說，你是我在這個節目看到最好的魔術師。

honesty [`ɑnɪstɪ] **n.** 誠實 ◀Track 2435
▶Her honesty and genuine concern for those who are in need won his respect. 她的誠實和對需要幫助的人發出的的真誠關心贏得了他的敬重。

honey [`hʌnɪ] **n.** 蜂蜜 ◀Track 2436
▶I poured some honey on my muffin. 我在鬆餅上淋了一些蜂蜜。

honeymoon ◀Track 2437
[`hʌnɪ͵mun] **n.** 蜜月；蜜月假期

▶We went to Paris for our honeymoon. 我們去巴黎度蜜月。

v. 度蜜月

▶They honeymooned in New Zealand. 他們到紐西蘭度蜜月。

Hong Kong [hɔŋ-kɔŋ] ◀Track 2438
n. 香港

▶The couple settled down in Hong Kong. 這對夫妻在香港定居下來。

honk [hɔŋk] **n.** 汽車喇叭聲 ◀Track 2439
▶She gave us a honk and a wave as she drove away. 她駕車離開時，向我們鳴了一聲喇叭並揮手道別。

中級

v. 鳴（汽車）喇叭

▶A 5-year-old boy left inside a car kept honking the horn until he was rescued by a passerby. 一名被留在車上的五歲男童不斷按喇叭，直到被一名路人援救。

honor [ˋɑnɚ]

🔊Track 2440

=honour （英式英文） **n.** 榮譽；面子；光榮的人或事；禮儀；敬意

▶She graduated with honors.
她以優等成績畢業。

v. 使增光；給⋯⋯以榮譽；尊敬

▶He honored his parents.
他很尊敬他的父母。

相關片語 **in honor of**
紀念；以表敬意；以慶祝

▶The award was in honor of his grandfather for his heroic deeds during the war. 這個獎項是為紀念他祖父在戰爭時所做的英勇事蹟而頒發。

honorable [ˋɑnɚəbl]

🔊Track 2441

adj. 可尊敬的；高尚的；光榮的；榮譽的；表示尊敬的；體面的

▶The soldiers were given an honorable burial. 這些士兵被光榮下葬。

hood [hʊd]

🔊Track 2442

n. 頭巾；兜帽；風帽；罩；車蓋

▶She bought a down coat with a removable hood. 她買了一件有可拆風帽的羽絨衣。

v. 罩上風帽；裝上車蓬；覆蓋

▶Clouds hooded the hilltop.
雪覆蓋著山丘頂。

hoof [huf]

🔊Track 2443

n. （馬）蹄；人的腳

▶She loves her horse and always makes sure that the horse's hooves are healthy. 她很愛護她的馬，總是確保牠的馬蹄是健康的。。

v. 用腳踢；步行

▶He hoofed to the supermarket to get some chocolates. 他走路到超市買了一些巧克力。

相關片語 **on the hoof**
即興地；事先無準備地

▶He wrote the play on the hoof.
他在即興地情況下寫了這個劇本。

hook [hʊk] **n.** 鉤；掛鉤

🔊Track 2444

▶She hung the coat on the hook.
她把外套掛在鉤子上。

v. 用鉤子鉤住；引人上鉤

▶He hooked a fish. 他釣到一條魚。

相關片語 **by hook or by crook**
不擇手段

▶She was determined to get what she wanted by hook or by crook. 她決心要得到想要的東西，即使是以不擇手段的方式也一樣。

hop [hɑp]

🔊Track 2445

v. （人）單足跳；（動物）齊足跳；跳舞

▶The boy hopped on the train.
男童跳上火車。

n. 跳躍

▶Paris to London is actually a short hop by plane. You don't need to worry about getting exhausted. 巴黎到倫敦其實是很短的飛行旅程，你不用擔心勞累。

hope [hop] **v.** 希望

🔊Track 2446

▶She hopes she will achieve her dreams. 她希望能完成她的夢想。

中
級

n. 希望

▶It is my father's hope that I will become a doctor. 我的爸爸希望我以後成為醫師。

---

hopeful [`hopfəl]
🔊 Track 2447

adj. 抱有希望的；充滿希望的

▶He was hopeful that they could reach an agreement. 他對於他們能達成協議充滿希望。

---

hopefully [`hopfəlɪ]
🔊 Track 2448

adv. 希望地

▶Hopefully my sister will win the competition. 希望我妹妹能贏得這場比賽。

---

horizon [hə`raɪzn]
🔊 Track 2449

n. 地平線；（知識、經驗）眼界、視野

▶Good books can broaden our horizons. 好書能開拓我們的視野。

相關片語 **a cloud on the horizon** 預期未來可能發生的困難或關卡；大難臨頭

▶He found himself preoccupied by a cloud on the horizon. 他發現自己就要大難臨頭了。

---

hormone [`hormon]
🔊 Track 2450

n. 荷爾蒙；激素

▶Lack of sleep may impair the secretion of growth hormone. 睡眠不足會阻礙生長激素的分泌。

補充片語 **growth hormone** 生長激素

---

horn [hɔrn]
🔊 Track 2451

n. 角；喇叭；管樂器；小號、號角

▶A shipment of illegal rhino horns was seized by the police. 一個載有非法犀牛角的貨運被警方攔截了。

相關片語 **blow one's own horn** 吹噓

▶Pay no attention. She is blowing her own horn again. 別理她，她又再吹噓了。

---

horrible [`hɔrəbl̩]
🔊 Track 2452

adj. 可怕的；糟透的

▶It's sad to see horrible news about child abuse cases. 看到可怕的虐童案新聞，真令人難過。

---

horrify [`hɔrə͵faɪ]
🔊 Track 2453

v. 使恐懼；使驚訝；使反感

▶People were horrified by the Hiroshima atomic bombing on Aug. 6, 1945. 人們對於1945年8月6日的廣島原子彈事件感到震驚恐懼。

---

horror [`hɔrɚ] n. 恐怖
🔊 Track 2454

▶I don't watch horror movies because they are scary. 我不看恐怖片，因為它們太嚇人了。

補充片語 **horror movie** 恐怖片

---

horse [hɔrs] n. 馬
🔊 Track 2455

▶She learned how to ride a horse when she was in high school. 她在中學時學會了騎馬。

---

hose [hoz] n. 水管
🔊 Track 2456

▶Firefighter tested the fire hoses in the building.
消防員測試了這棟建築的消防水管。

v. 用水管淋澆或沖洗

▶She was hosing the garden when her neighbor dropped by. 她的鄰居來訪時，她正在用水管澆花。

hospital [`hɑspɪtḷ]
◀Track 2457
n. 醫院

▶My father is a pediatrician in a general hospital. 我爸爸在一間綜合醫院擔任小兒科醫師。

hospitalize
◀Track 2458
[`hɑspɪtḷˌaɪz] **v** 使住院治療

▶She was hospitalized for a congenital heart defect.
她因先天心臟缺陷而住院治療。

host [host]
◀Track 2459
n. 主人；東道主；主持人

▶The host of the show was hilarious.
這個節目的主持人很爆笑。

v 主持；主辦；以主人身分招待

▶They attended the banquet hosted by a rich businessman. 他們參加由一名富商所主辦的晚宴。

hostage [`hɑstɪdʒ]
◀Track 2460
n. 人質；抵押品

▶The hijackers held all the passengers as hostages.
劫機犯將所有乘客當作人質。

補充片語 take sb. hostage/hold sb. hostage 抓住某人以當作人質

hostel [`hɑstḷ]
◀Track 2461
n. 旅社；青年旅社

▶The hostel is well equipped with a laundry room. 這間旅社設備很好，附有洗衣間。

hostess [`hostɪs]
◀Track 2462
n. 女主人；旅館女老闆；女服務員

▶The hostess prepared a lot of food to make sure it was sufficient for her guests.
女主人準備了很多食物，確保份量足夠賓客食用。

hostile [`hɑstɪl]
◀Track 2463
adj. 敵人的，敵方的；懷敵意的、不友善的

▶There was a hostile reaction to the government's reforms.
人民對政府的改革懷有敵意。

hot [hɑt] **adj.** 熱的；辣的
◀Track 2464

▶It was a hot and humid day.
那是個炎熱又潮濕的一天。

hotel [ho`tɛl] **n.** 飯店
◀Track 2465

▶The five-star hotel received complaints from its customer. 這間五星級飯店接獲客人的抱怨。

hound [haʊnd]
◀Track 2466
n. 獵犬；卑劣的人；有癮的人、瘋狂追求某事的人

▶Celebrities are followed by paparazzi and gossip hounds wherever they go.
名人不論去哪裡都被狗仔隊和八卦迷跟蹤。

hour [aʊr] **n.** 小時
◀Track 2467

▶It took him only half an hour to finish the oil painting.
他只用了半個小時就完成了這幅油畫。

hourly [`aʊrlɪ]
◀Track 2468
adj. 每小時的

▶It is difficult for hourly employees to save money and support their family.
時薪人員要存錢和維持家計有其困難。

補充片語 **hourly employee**
鐘點工；時薪人員

adv. 每小時地；頻繁地

▶In this remote rural area, buses come hourly.
在這偏遠的農村地帶，公車每小時才會來一次。

house [haʊs]　Track 2469
n. 屋子；房子

▶They bought a house in London.
他們在倫敦買了一間房子。

v. 給……房子住；將……收藏在屋內

▶The library houses a number of ancient Islamic manuscripts. 這間圖書館收藏了許多古代伊斯蘭手稿。

household　Track 2470
[`haʊsˌhold] **n.** 一家人；家庭；戶

▶Nowadays, most households have computers.
現在絕大多數家庭都擁有電腦。

adj. 家庭的；家用的

▶These household appliances are designed to be more energy-efficient.
這些家電用品都被設計得更節能省電。

補充片語 **household appliance**
家電產品；家用電器

housekeeper　Track 2471
[`haʊsˌkipɚ] **n.** 管家；傭人領班

▶He hired a housekeeper to help him with the house chores. 他請了一個管家幫他打理家事。

housewife　Track 2472
[`haʊsˌwaɪf] **n.** 家庭主婦

▶She is happy to be a housewife and takes care of her family. 她樂於當家庭主婦照顧全家人。

housework　Track 2473
[`haʊsˌwɝk] **n.** 家事

▶I love listening to music when I'm doing housework. 我做家事時喜歡邊聽音樂。

housing [`haʊzɪŋ]　Track 2474
n. 住房供給；房屋；住宅

▶High housing prices make it difficult for young people to start their own family. 高房價使得年輕人難以成家。

how [haʊ]　Track 2475
adv. 怎樣；多麼；為何

▶How is Prof. Jones?
瓊斯教授近來好嗎？

conj. 如何；怎麼

▶That was how we became close friends. 我們就是這樣成為親密的好友。

however [haʊˋɛvɚ]　Track 2476
adv. 無論如何；不管用什麼方法

▶He mustn't have any more red meat, however much he feels like it. 他不能再吃紅肉了，無論他有多想吃。

conj. 然而

▶She is a superstar. However, she is very modest.
她是巨星，然而她非常謙虛。

howl [haʊl]　Track 2477
v. 嗥叫；怒吼；吼叫著說，狂喊

▶We heard a wolf howl in the midnight.
我們在深夜聽到狼在嚎叫。

n. 嗥叫；怒吼；號啕大哭；大笑

中級

▶He let out a howl of pain when a brick fell on his foot. 一顆磚塊落在他的腳上，他發出痛苦的叫喊聲。

補充片語 let out a howl 發出喊叫

how's [haʊz]
◀≣Track 2478

abbr. 如何（**how is**的縮寫）

▶How's it going? 一切都好嗎？

Hualian [`hwɑ`liɛn]
◀≣Track 2479

n. 花蓮

▶They went to Hualian and Taitung last summer. 他們去年夏天去花蓮和台東。

hug [hʌg] **n.** 擁抱
◀≣Track 2480

▶He gave his son a hug and promised him they would see each other soon. 他給兒子一個擁抱並承諾兩人很快會再見面。

v. 擁抱

▶They hugged each other before saying goodbye. 他們互道再見前互相擁抱。

huge [hjudʒ]
◀≣Track 2481

adj. 巨大的；龐大的

▶The United States is a huge country. 美國是個幅員遼闊的國家。

hum [hʌm]
◀≣Track 2482

v. 發嗡嗡聲；發哼聲；哼曲子

▶She hummed as she did the house chores. 她一邊做家事一邊哼著歌。

n. 哼聲；哼曲子的聲音；嗡嗡聲

▶They heard the hum of bees and smelled the fragrance of flowers in the garden. 他們在花園聽著蜜蜂嗡嗡叫，聞著花朵的芳香。

human [`hjumən]
◀≣Track 2483

adj. 人的；人類的；有人性的

▶The drought caused widespread human suffering. 這場旱災造成眾多人受苦。

n. 人；人類

▶There is no doubt that humans should be responsible for global warming. 無疑地，人類應為全球暖化負責任。

humanity [hju`mænətɪ]
◀≣Track 2484

n. 人性；人道；人類

▶Human trafficking is a crime against humanity. 人口走私是有違人道的罪行。

humble [`hʌmbl̩]
◀≣Track 2485

adj. 謙遜的；卑微的；簡陋的

▶In my humble opinion, we should streamline our processes to achieve better outcomes. 依我個人淺見，我們應簡化流程以達到更好的結果。

humid [`hjumɪd]
◀≣Track 2486

adj. 潮濕的

▶The room is dark and humid. 這個房間陰暗又潮濕。

humidity [hju`mɪdətɪ]
◀≣Track 2487

n. 濕氣；濕度

▶The humidity of this area is high all year round. 這個地區整年濕氣都很重。

humiliate [hju`mɪlɪˌet]
◀≣Track 2488

v. 羞辱；使蒙恥辱；使丟臉

▶Cyber bullying has humiliated people to the point of suicide. 網路霸凌已羞辱別人到自殺的地步了。

humor [`hjumɚ] **n.** 幽默
◀≣Track 2489

▶My father has a very good sense of humor. 我爸爸很有幽默感。

humorous [`hjumərəs] ◀≋Track 2490

adj. 幽默的；詼諧的

▶Mark Twain is famous for his humorous writing.
馬克‧吐溫以幽默的寫作風格著稱。

hunch [hʌntʃ] ◀≋Track 2491

n. 預感；直覺

▶I have a hunch that she is telling lies again. 我直覺她又在說謊了。

v. 弓起；聳起；隆起；彎成弓狀

▶The cat hunched its back and meowed threateningly. 貓弓起身體，帶著威脅的音調喵喵叫。

hundred [`hʌndrəd] ◀≋Track 2492

n. 一百

▶Hundreds of people showed up to donate blood after the huge earthquake. 大地震後有數百人出來捐血。

adj. 一百的；一百個的

▶We invited one hundred guests to the party. 我們邀請一百位賓客參加派對。

hunger [`hʌŋgɚ] ◀≋Track 2493

n. 饑餓；渴望

▶They felt hunger when they burned the midnight oil for their finals. 他們開夜車準備期末考時，感到飢腸轆轆。

hungry [`hʌŋgrɪ] ◀≋Track 2494

adj. 餓的；饑餓的；渴望的

▶After an exhausting day, she felt very hungry. 她忙了一天後，感到很飢餓。

hunt [hʌnt] ◀≋Track 2495

v. 追獵；獵取；尋找；追求

▶He is hunting a job.
他在找工作。

n. 打獵；搜索

▶The police is on the hunt for the bomber.
警方正在搜捕那個炸彈客。

hunter [`hʌntɚ] ◀≋Track 2496

n. 獵人；追求者；搜尋者

▶The young man is a good hunter.
這個年輕人很擅長打獵。

hurricane [`hɝɪ͵ken] ◀≋Track 2497

n. 颶風；暴風雨

▶The hurricane caused serious damage to the entire state. 這個颶風讓整個州遭受嚴重的損失。

hurry [`hɝɪ] ◀≋Track 2498

v. 使趕快；催促；趕緊；匆忙

▶The man who had a heart attack was hurried to the hospital.
這名心臟病發的男子被緊急送到醫院。

n. 急忙；倉促

▶He was in a hurry to go to school.
他趕著去上課。

hurt [hɝt] ◀≋Track 2499

v. 傷害；使疼痛；疼痛

▶Her knee hurts.
她的膝蓋在痛。

husband [`hʌzbənd] ◀≋Track 2500

n. 丈夫；老公

▶My husband is an obstetrician.
我先生是產科醫師。

中級

hush [hʌʃ]

v 使沉默；使安靜；安靜下來；沉默

▶The nanny hushed the crying baby.
保姆使啼哭的寶寶安靜下來。

n 靜寂；沉默

▶When she stepped into the room, there
was a deathly hush. 她走進房間時，現場
一片死寂。

相關片語 **hush money** 遮口費

▶The politician paid the woman hush
money to cover up their affair. 這名政治
人物付該女遮口費，要她為他們的風流韻事
保密。

hut [hʌt] **n** （簡陋的）小屋
Track 2502

▶They stayed in a hut when the rain
fell. 他們在下雨時留在小屋裡。

hydrogen
Track 2503

[ˈhaɪdrədʒən] **n** 氫

▶Hydrogen can be produced from
diverse resources.
氫能從多種資源中製造出來。

hypocrite [ˈhɪpəkrɪt]
Track 2504

n 偽君子；偽善者

▶Their boss is a hypocrite. He talks about
environmental issues but his factories
produce a lot of pollution. 他們的老闆是
偽君子，他談了很多環境議題，但他的工廠
製造很多污染。

▶ Ii

以下表格是全民英檢官方公告中級「聽、說、讀、寫」所須具備的能力，本書例句皆依此範疇特別設計，只要掃描右方QR code，就能搭配相對應的音軌實現「眼耳並用」方式，刺激左腦的語言學習功能；同時也可使用本書附贈的紅膠片，將其置於單字上，一面記憶一面自我挑戰，達到雙倍的學習成果！

聽 ▶	在日常生活中，能聽懂一般的會話；能大致聽懂公共場所廣播、氣象報告及廣告等。在工作時，能聽懂簡易的產品介紹與操作說明。能大致聽懂外籍人士的談話及詢問。
說 ▶	可在日常生活中，能以簡易英語交談或描述一般事物，能介紹自己的生活作息、工作、家庭、經歷等，並可對一般話題陳述看法。在工作時，能進行簡單的答詢，並與外籍人士交談溝通。
讀 ▶	在日常生活中，能閱讀短文、故事、私人信件、廣告、傳單、簡介及使用說明等。在工作時，能閱讀工作須知、公告、操作手冊、例行的文件、傳真、電報等。
寫 ▶	能寫簡單的書信、故事及心得等。對於熟悉且與個人經歷相關的主題，能以簡易的文字表達。

中級

I [aɪ] **pron.** 我　　　◀ Track 2505

▶ I was over the moon when I won the lottery. 我贏得樂透時，開心得不得了。

ice [aɪs] **n.** 冰　　　◀ Track 2506

▶ Sea ice plays a fundamental role in polar ecosystems. 海冰在北極生態系統扮演很重要的角色。

iceberg [ˋaɪsˌbɝg] ◀ Track 2507
n. 冰山

▶ The increasing number of reported cases of child abuse is only the tip of the iceberg compared with the real number of cases. 與實際發生的虐童案量相比，越來越多件獲報的虐童案只是冰山的一角。

icy [ˋaɪsɪ] ◀ Track 2508
adj. 多冰的；結滿冰的；覆蓋著冰的；冰冷的

▶ The man slipped on an icy pavement. 這名男士在結冰的人行道滑倒了。

ID [aɪ-di] ◀ Track 2509
n. 身分證明；身分證

▶ Do not give someone your ID or a copy of your ID. 不要隨便給人你的身份證或身份證影本。

I'd [aɪd] ◀ Track 2510
abbr. 我會、我已（I would或I had的縮寫）

▶ I'd like a cup of coffee, please. 我想要一杯咖啡，麻煩了。

idea [aɪˋdɪə] ◀ Track 2511
n. 想法；主意；計劃；打算；概念

▶ This is a fantastic idea. 這是個絕佳的點子。

ideal [aɪ`diəl]
◀ Track 2512
adj. 理想的；完美的

▶He is an ideal candidate for the job.
他是這份工作的理想人選。

identical [aɪ`dɛntɪkl]
◀ Track 2513
adj. 完全相同的；完全相似的

▶She has two identical pairs of shoes.
她有兩雙完全相同的鞋子。

相關片語 identical twin 同卵雙生

▶Johnny and Jack are identical twins.
強尼和傑克是同卵雙胞胎。

identification
◀ Track 2514
[aɪ,dɛntəfə`keʃən]
n. 認出；識別；身分證明；身分證

▶They were asked by the security guards to show some identification at the entrance. 他們在入口處被保安人員要求出示身分證明。

identify [aɪ`dɛntə,faɪ]
◀ Track 2515
v. 確認；識別；鑑定

▶The police is trying to identify a suspect possibly involved in a robbery. 警方正在鑑別一個可能涉及搶案的嫌疑犯。

identity [aɪ`dɛntətɪ]
◀ Track 2516
n. 身分；特點；特性

▶The undercover agent finally discovered the identity of the killer. 臥底警探終於發現兇手的身分了。

idiom [`ɪdɪəm]
◀ Track 2517
n. 慣用語；成語；（個人特有）用語

▶"In a nutshell" is an idiom. 「總而言之」
（in a nutshell）是一個慣用語。

idiot [`ɪdɪət]
◀ Track 2518
n. 白癡；傻瓜；笨蛋

▶She is not an idiot. She knows what her problem is. 她不是笨蛋。她知道自己的問題是什麼。

idle [`aɪdl]
◀ Track 2519
adj. 不工作的；閒置的；無所事事的；無目的的

▶After working for 30 years, they now live an idle life. 他們工作了三十年後，現在過著悠閒的生活。

v. 無所事事；閒逛；閒混；虛度（光陰）

▶He didn't learn anything and simply idled away his time. 他什麼都不學，只是虛度著光陰。

補充片語 idle away 虛度（時光）

idol [`aɪdl]
◀ Track 2520
n. 偶像；受崇拜的人；紅人

▶She was a pop idol in Japan.
她在日本曾是流行偶像。

if [ɪf] **conj.** 如果；是否
◀ Track 2521

▶I you were me, what would you do?
如果你是我，你會怎麼做？

ignorance [`ɪgnərəns]
◀ Track 2522
n. 無知

▶He spoke nonsense out of ignorance.
他出於無知而說了愚蠢的話。

補充片語 out of ignorance 出於無知

ignorant [`ɪgnərənt]
◀ Track 2523
adj. 無知的，不學無術的；沒有受教育的；無知造成的

▶The child was ignorant of what just happened. 小孩不知道剛剛發生什麼事了。

ignore [ɪg`nor]　🔊 Track 2524
v. 不顧；忽視

▶He ignored the advice from his doctor and kept working overtime. 他不顧醫師的建議，仍持續加班。

I'll [aɪl]　🔊 Track 2525
abbr. 我會（I will的縮寫）

▶Of course I'll go to your birthday party. 我當然會參加你的生日派對。

ill [ɪl]　🔊 Track 2526
adj. 病的；不健康的；壞的；邪惡的

▶Ill news runs apace. 惡事傳千里。

illegal [ɪ`ligl]　🔊 Track 2527
adj. 不合法的，違法的

▶It is illegal to trade ivory in Taiwan. 在台灣，買賣象牙是不合法的。

illness [`ɪlnɪs]　🔊 Track 2528
n. 病；患病（狀態）；身體不適

▶After the traumatic experience, he suffered from some form of mental illness.
經歷這個精神創傷後，他遭受到某種精神疾病的折磨。

illustrate [`ɪləstret]　🔊 Track 2529
v. （用圖、實例等）說明；插圖於，圖解說明

▶The professor illustrated his points with clips from TV news.
教授用電視新聞影片的片段來說明他的觀點。

illustration　🔊 Track 2530
[ɪ,lʌs`treʃən] **n.** 說明，圖解，圖示，插圖，圖表，圖案

▶This children's book is full of illustrations that are richly detailed and classically drawn. 這本童書充滿細節豐富又經典的插圖。

I'm [aɪm]　🔊 Track 2531
abbr. 我是（I am的縮寫）

▶I'm so glad to see you again.
我好高興再看到你。

image [`ɪmɪdʒ]　🔊 Track 2532
n. 肖像；形象；印象；概念

▶Public image of the company is generally negative after the tainted oil scandal. 在爆發黑心油醜聞後，大眾對這家公司的形象普遍感覺是負面的。

imaginable　🔊 Track 2533
[ɪ`mædʒɪnəbl]
adj. 能想像的；可想像得到的

▶The bakery offers cakes of every imaginable flavor. 顧客想像得到的口味蛋糕，這家烘焙坊都有提供。

imaginary　🔊 Track 2534
[ɪ`mædʒə,nɛrɪ] **adj.** 想像中的；虛構的；幻想的

▶Totoro is an imaginary animal.
龍貓是虛構的動物。

imagination　🔊 Track 2535
[ɪ,mædʒə`neʃən] **n.** 想像力；空想；幻想；妄想

▶The writer has a great imagination.
這名作家很有想像力。

中級

imaginative
◀Track 2536

[ɪ`mædʒə͵netɪv]

adj. 虛構的;幻想的;有想像力的

▶He is a talented and imaginative designer.
他是很有才華又富有想像力的設計師。

imagine [ɪ`mædʒɪn]
◀Track 2537

v. 想像

▶Imagine the world where we could only see souls, not the outward appearances. 想像一下我們只能看見靈魂而非外表的世界。

imitate [`ɪmə͵tet]
◀Track 2538

v. 模仿;以……做為範例,仿效

▶The little girl imitated her mother by pretending to feed a stuffed animal. 小女孩模仿媽媽,假裝餵食玩具動物。

imitation [͵ɪmə`teʃən]
◀Track 2539

n. 模仿,模擬;仿造;偽造;仿製品;贗品

▶She took taekwondo lessons, apparently in imitation of the movie's heroine. 她很明顯地是為了仿效電影裡的女英雄而去上跆拳道課。

補充片語 in imitation of 為了仿效

immediate [ɪ`midɪɪt]
◀Track 2540

adj. 立即的

▶They prepare shelters and food to meet the refugees' immediate needs. 他們準備了庇護空間和食物以因應難民當下的需求。

immediately
◀Track 2541

[ɪ`midɪtlɪ] **adv.** 立刻地

▶When we heard the fire alarm go off, we left the office building immediately. 我們一聽到消防警報器響,就立刻離開辦公大樓。

immigrant
◀Track 2542

[`ɪməgrənt] **n.** (外來)移民

▶During the country's civil war, a huge number of illegal immigrants flocked to Europe to seek a better life. 在這個國家的內戰期間,大量非法移民湧入歐洲尋求更好的生活。

補充片語 illegal immigrant 非法移民

immigrate [`ɪmə͵gret]
◀Track 2543

v. 遷居;遷入;從外地移居

▶The Turkish family immigrated to Germany ten years ago. 這個土耳其家庭十年前就移居德國了。

immigration
◀Track 2544

[͵ɪmə`greʃən] **n.** 移居;移民入境;(總稱)外來移

▶The country has adopted a conservative position on immigration. 該國對移民入境採取保守的立場。

immune [ɪ`mjun]
◀Track 2545

adj. 免疫的;不受影響的;有免疫力的

▶I am totally immune to his flirting. 我對他的調情完全無動於衷。

相關片語 immune system 免疫系統

▶The treatment damaged her immune system severely. 這個治療嚴重損害她的免疫系統。

impact [ɪm`pækt]
◀Track 2546

n. 衝擊;對……產生影響

▶The policy will have a positive impact on our environment. 這項政策將對我們的環境將帶來正面影響。

v. 衝擊;產生影響

▶AI has already impacted a variety of industries. 人工智慧已對許多產業造成衝擊。

impatient [ɪm`peʃənt] ◀ Track 2547
adj. 沒耐心的；不耐煩的

▶She is very impatient with her own children. 她對自己的孩子很沒耐心。

imperial [ɪm`pɪrɪəl] ◀ Track 2548
adj. 帝國的；帝王的；威嚴宏大的

▶He studied at Imperial College London and graduated magna cum laude. 他就讀倫敦帝國大學並以極為優異的成績畢業。

impersonal ◀ Track 2549
[ɪm`pɝsn̩l] **adj.** 非個人的；非針對人的；客觀的；無人情味的；不具人格的

▶The teacher tried to keep the discussion impersonal so that no one would feel discriminated. 老師試圖讓討論不帶個人色彩，避免有人覺得受到歧視。

implement ◀ Track 2550
[`ɪmpləmənt] **v.** 執行；實施

▶They are raising funds to implement the project. 他們正在募款以實行這個計畫。

implication ◀ Track 2551
[ˌɪmplɪ`keʃən]
n. 牽連；含義；言外之意；暗示

▶He explained by implication why the principal characters in the story had to be anonymous. 他含蓄地解釋為何故事的主要角色必須匿名。

補充片語 by implication 含蓄地；暗示地

imply [ɪm`plaɪ] ◀ Track 2552
v. 暗指；暗示；意味著

▶The jury believed his silence implied that he was guilty. 陪審團相信他的沈默暗示他是有罪的。

impolite [ˌɪmpə`laɪt] ◀ Track 2553
adj. 無禮的

▶It is impolite to ask a person's salary. 問別人的薪水是不禮貌的。

import [`ɪmport] ◀ Track 2554
n. 進口；輸入；進口商品

▶The import of crude oil went up last year. 去年原油進口量增加。

v. [ɪm`port] 進口；輸入；引進

▶The company imported cars from Germany. 該公司從德國進口汽車。

importance ◀ Track 2555
[ɪm`pɔrtn̩s] **n.** 重要性

▶He attaches a lot of importance to health. 他很重視健康。

important [ɪm`pɔrtnt] ◀ Track 2556
adj. 重要的

▶A balanced diet is important to our health. 均衡的飲食對我們的健康是很重要的。

impose [ɪm`poz] ◀ Track 2557
v. 徵（稅）；加負擔於……；把……強加於

▶High taxes have been imposed on alcohol. 酒精近來被課以重稅。

impossible ◀ Track 2558
[ɪm`pasəbl] **adj.** 不可能的

▶It is impossible for her to change. 她永遠都不可能改變了。

中級

impress [ɪm`prɛs] ◀€Track 2559

v. 給……極深的印象

▶I was deeply impressed by his kindness and generosity. 我對他的仁慈和慷慨印象深刻。

impression ◀€Track 2560

[ɪm`prɛʃən] **n.** 印象

▶He tried to make a good impression on the interviewers. 他試圖給面試官留下好印象。

補充片語 **make a good impression on sb.** 給某人留下好印象

相關片語 **first impression** 第一印象

▶Her first impression of the town was positive. 她對這個城鎮的第一印象很正面。

impressive ◀€Track 2561

[ɪm`prɛsɪv] **adj.** 予人深刻印象的；令人欽佩的

▶The cathedral is very impressive. 這間教堂令人印象非常深刻。

improve [ɪm`pruv] ◀€Track 2562

v. 進步；改進；改善

▶The teacher is helping her students improve their English pronunciation. 這名老師正在幫學生改善英文發音。

improvement ◀€Track 2563

[ɪm`pruvmənt] **n.** 改進；改善

▶Their child has made a lot of improvement since they moved to the farm. 自從他們搬到農場，孩子的行為就改善很多了。

impulse [`ɪmpʌls] ◀€Track 2564

n. 衝動；一時的念頭

▶He bought the car on an impulse. 他一時衝動買了一輛車。

補充片語 **on (an) impulse** 一時衝動

in [ɪn] ◀€Track 2565

prep. 在……裡；在…… 方面；穿著

▶She is dressed in pink. 她穿粉紅色的衣服。

adv. 進；在裡頭

▶Summer is in, and the children can't wait for the summer vacation. 夏天來了，孩子們等不及要放暑假了。

adj. 在裡面的；流行的

▶She only wears the in things in the season because she likes to draw attention. 她只穿當季流行的衣服，因為她喜歡受人注目。

inadequate ◀€Track 2566

[ɪn`ædəkwɪt] **adj.** 不充分的；貧乏的；不適當的；不能勝任的

▶She is inadequate for the task of raising her own children. 她不能勝任養育子女的任務。

incense [`ɪnsɛns] ◀€Track 2567

n. 香；焚香時的煙；香味；香氣

▶She burned incense and prayed to Buddha for guidance and help. 她燒香並向佛陀祈求指引和幫助。

v. 焚香；向……敬香；用香薰；激怒；使憤怒

▶He became incensed at her rudeness. 他被她的無禮給激怒了。

inch [ɪntʃ] **n.** 英吋 ◀€Track 2568

▶He is six feet and ten inches tall. 他有六呎十吋高。

incident [`ɪnsədnt] ◀Track 2569
n. 事件

▶The incident has caught nationwide attention. 這起事件引起全國關注。

include [ɪn`klud] ◀Track 2570
v. 包含；包括

▶The bill includes meals and service. 帳單包括餐費和服務費。

included [ɪn`kludɪd] ◀Track 2571
adj. 包含的；被包括的

▶Decorations and furniture are included in the price. 裝潢和家具都被包含在價格裡。

including [ɪn`kludɪŋ] ◀Track 2572
prep. 包含

▶Many dignitaries will attend the banquet, including the prime minister and ambassadors. 許多重要人士都將出席晚宴，包括總理和大使群。

income [`ɪn͵kʌm] ◀Track 2573
n. 收入

▶The non-profit organization aims to help children from families with low income. 這個非營利性組織旨在幫助低收入家庭的孩子。

incomplete ◀Track 2574
[͵ɪnkəm`plit] **adj.** 不完全的；不完整的；未結束的

▶The report is incomplete due to lack of accurate statistics. 這篇報告因為缺乏精確的統計數據而顯得不完整。

inconvenient ◀Track 2575
[͵ɪnkən`vinjənt] **adj.** 不方便的；不便的

▶It's inconvenient to go to work without public transportation. 上班沒有大眾運輸很不方便。

increase [ɪn`kris] ◀Track 2576
v. 增加；增長

▶We need to increase public awareness of global warming. 我們必須增進大眾對全球暖化的認知。

n. 增加；增長

▶Childhood diabetes is on the increase. 孩童糖尿病有增加的趨勢。

increasingly ◀Track 2577
[ɪn`krisɪŋlɪ] **adv.** 漸漸地；越來越多地

▶She became increasingly difficult to get along with. 她變得越來越難相處了。

indeed [ɪn`did] ◀Track 2578
adv. 真正地；確實；更確切地

▶A friend in need is a friend indeed. 患難見真情。

independence ◀Track 2579
[͵ɪndɪ`pɛndəns] **n.** 獨立；自立

▶The United States issued the Declaration of Independence on July 4, 1776. 美國於1776年7月4日發表獨立宣言。

independent ◀Track 2580
[͵ɪndɪ`pɛndənt] **adj.** 獨立的

▶She has been financially independent since she graduated from high school. 她自從高中畢業後，在經濟上一直是自食其力。

index [`ɪndɛks] ◀Track 2581
n. 索引；標誌；跡象；指示符號；指數；指標

中級

▶He looked up "pneumonia" in the index. 他在索引中尋找「肺炎」這個條目。

v 將……編入索引；表明；指示

▶This dictionary is properly indexed. 這本字典的索引編排得很恰當。

相關片語 **index finger** 食指

▶She put her index finger on her lip. 她把食指放在嘴唇邊。

India [ˋɪndɪə] **n.** 印度　　　🔊Track 2582

▶This article discussed gender inequality and women's rights in India. 這篇文章探討印度性別不平等和女權問題。

Indian [ˋɪndɪən]　　　🔊Track 2583
adj. 印度的；印第安的

▶Indian food is delicious. 印度食物很美味。

n. 印度人；印第安人

▶She married an Indian and lived in India for more than two decades. 她嫁給了印度人而且在印度住了超過二十年。

indicate [ˋɪndəˌket]　　　🔊Track 2584
v. 指示；指出；表明

▶The research indicated that more needed to be done to support people experiencing mental illness. 研究指出我們應有更多作為以支援受到心理疾病困擾的人們。

indication　　　🔊Track 2585

[ˌɪndəˋkeʃən] **n.** 指示；跡象、徵兆

▶There is every indication that he will recover from the illness soon. 所有的跡象都表示他很快將從這個疾病復原。

補充片語 **there is every indication that...** 所有跡象表明……

indifferent　　　🔊Track 2586

[ɪnˋdɪfərənt] **adj.** 冷淡的

▶The mother is very indifferent to her own children. 這個母親對親生孩子很冷淡。

individual　　　🔊Track 2587

[ˌɪndəˋvɪdʒʊəl] **adj.** 個人的；個體的；特有的

▶The psychiatrist handled the case on an individual basis. 精神分析師單獨處理每個個案。

n. 個人；個體

▶Every individual should be treated equally. 每個人都應被平等對待。

indoor [ˋɪnˌdor]　　　🔊Track 2588
adj. 室內的

▶Table tennis is an indoor sport. 桌球是室內的運動。

indoors [ˋɪnˋdorz]　　　🔊Track 2589
adv. 在室內

▶The activity was held indoors due to the heavy rain. 這個活動因為大雨而在室內舉辦。

indulge [ɪnˋdʌldʒ]　　　🔊Track 2590
v. 沉迷於；滿足；使高興；使享受一下；縱容；遷就

▶He indulged himself with snacks and junk food. 他放縱自己吃零食和垃圾食物。

industrial [ɪnˋdʌstrɪəl]　　　🔊Track 2591
adj. 工業的

▶The company has many partners in Hsinchu Science-based Industrial Park. 這家公司在新竹科學工業園區有很多合夥的夥伴。

補充片語 industrial park 工業園區

industrialize　🔊Track 2592

[ɪnˋdʌstrɪəlˌaɪz] **v** 使工業化

▶Germany is an industrialized country with a relatively high standard of living. 德國是工業化國家，生活水平很高。

industry [ˋɪndəstrɪ]　🔊Track 2593

n 工業；企業；行業

▶The auto industry is moving towards electric cars. 汽車業正在轉型發展電動車。

inevitable [ɪnˋɛvətəbl]　🔊Track 2594

adj 不可避免的

▶The company's bankruptcy was inevitable. 該公司倒閉是不可避免的。

infant [ˋɪnfənt] **n** 嬰兒　🔊Track 2595

▶The mother gazed at her newborn infant lovingly. 母親慈愛地注視著她的新生兒。

infect [ɪnˋfɛkt]　🔊Track 2596

v 傳染；感染；使受影響；污染

▶His happiness infected everyone around him. 他的愉悅感染了周圍的每個人。

infection [ɪnˋfɛkʃən]　🔊Track 2597

n 傳染；感染；傳染病

▶The nurse drew her blood to check if there were any signs of infection. 護士幫她抽血檢查是否有任何感染的徵兆。

infer [ɪnˋfɝ]　🔊Track 2598

v 推斷；推論；意味著

▶He inferred from the customer's facial expression that she was not pleased with their service. 他從客戶表情推斷她並不滿意他們的服務。

inference [ˋɪnfərəns]　🔊Track 2599

n 推論；推斷

▶The police made the inference that her son was abducted. 警方推斷她的兒子被綁架了。

inferior [ɪnˋfɪrɪə]　🔊Track 2600

adj （地位、品質）低等的；較差的；次於的

▶In some countries, women are considrered inferior to men. 在有些國家，女性獲得比男性更低等的對待。

n （地位等）低於他人者；部下；次級品

▶She is ruthless with her inferiors. 她對下屬很無情。

inflation [ɪnˋfleʃən]　🔊Track 2601

n 通貨膨脹

▶The government's priority is to reduce inflation. 政府的當務之急是減少通膨。

influence [ˋɪnflʊəns]　🔊Track 2602

n 影響；作用；影響力

▶Alice is a bad influence on her. 艾莉絲對她有不良的影響。

v 影響

▶The media has tried to influence every election. 媒體一直在試圖影響每場選舉。

influential　🔊Track 2603

[ˌɪnflʊˋɛnʃəl] **adj** 有影響力的；有權勢的

▶Jack Ma's speech was influential and inspiring. 馬雲的演講很有影響力並具啟發性。

中級

inform [ɪn`fɔrm] **v** 通知 ◀ Track 2604

▶Have you informed him of our decision?
你有通知他我們的決定了嗎？

informal [ɪn`fɔrml̩] ◀ Track 2605
adj. 非正式的

▶The president held an informal meeting
with the head of Egypt. 這名總統與埃及
領袖舉辦非正式會談。

information ◀ Track 2606

[͵ɪnfɚ`meʃən] **n.** 資料；資訊；消息

▶The Internet contains all kinds of
information. 網路包含各式各樣的資訊。

informative ◀ Track 2607

[ɪn`fɔrmətɪv] **adj.** 情報的；教育性的

▶The guide book is very informative.
這本旅遊指南資訊很豐富。

補充片語 guide book 旅遊指南

informed [ɪn`fɔrmd] ◀ Track 2608
adj. 消息靈通的；根據情報的；有教養或見
識的；收到通知的

▶Our opponents in the debate contest
gave really informed opinions. 我們在辯
論比賽中的對手真的給出了相當具有見解的
評論。

ingredient ◀ Track 2609

[ɪn`gridɪənt] **n.** 組成部分；原料；（構成）
要素

▶Artificial ingredients and trans fats are
not good for health. 人工原料和反式脂肪
對健康無益。

inhabitant ◀ Track 2610

[ɪn`hæbətənt] **n.** 居民；居住者；棲息的動物

▶The Indians are the native inhabitants
of America. 印第安人是美國的原住民。

inherit [ɪn`hɛrɪt] ◀ Track 2611

v 繼承；遺傳；成為繼承人；獲得遺傳

▶She inherited her mother's beauty.
她遺傳了母親的美貌。

initial [ɪ`nɪʃəl] ◀ Track 2612
adj. 開始的，最初的

▶His initial reaction was joy and excitement
when he heard the good news. 他聽到這
個好消息的最初反應是喜悅和興奮。

n. 首字母

▶She wrote her initials on her photos and
gave them to her fans. 她在照片上寫了
名字的首字母並把照片送給粉絲。

v 簽姓名的首字母於

▶He initialed the questionnaire's cover
sheet. 他在問卷封面簽上姓名的首字母。

inject [ɪn`dʒɛkt] ◀ Track 2613

v 注射；插話；投入

▶Highly allergic to peanuts, he has to
inject himself with the prescription
drug if he eats anything that contains
nuts. 他對花生高度過敏，若吃到任何有堅
果的食物，就必須自行注射處方藥。

injection [ɪn`dʒɛkʃən] ◀ Track 2614

n. 注射；注射劑；引入；投入；
（人造衛星）射入軌道

▶She was given an injection to reduce
the symptoms of hay fever. 她被注射一
針以減緩花粉熱的症狀。

injure [`ɪndʒɚ] **v** 使受傷 ◀ Track 2615

▶He was injured at work.
他在工作時受傷了。

injured [`ɪndʒɚd] ◀Track 2616
adj. 受傷的

▶The injured stray dog was sent to the hospital by a kind-hearted man. 一名善心男子將這隻受傷的流浪狗送去了醫院。

injury [`ɪndʒərɪ] ◀Track 2617
n. 傷害；損害

▶The tennis player was forced to retire due to his knee injury. 這名網球選手因為膝蓋受傷而被迫退休。

ink [ɪŋk] **n.** 墨水 ◀Track 2618

▶ My hands were stained with ink from the printer, for I was trying to fix the glitch. 我的手因為修理印表機的問題而沾滿了墨水。

inn [ɪn] **n.** 小旅館 ◀Track 2619

▶The couple ran an inn and a tavern in the town. 這對夫妻在小鎮經營小旅館和小酒館。

inner [`ɪnɚ] ◀Track 2620
adj. 內部的；裡面的；核心的；精神的；內心的；隱晦的

▶An elegant lady, she exudes inner beauty and confidence. 她是優雅的淑女，散發著內在美和自信。

innocence [`ɪnəsns] ◀Track 2621
n. 無罪；純真

▶The suspect pleaded innocence and provided an alibi. 嫌犯辯稱他是清白的，並提供不再場證明。

innocent [`ɪnəsnt] ◀Track 2622
adj. 無辜的；無罪的；清白的；天真的；單純的；無害的

▶The puppy looks so innocent and adorable. 這隻小狗看起來好無辜又討人喜歡。

input [`ɪnˌpʊt] ◀Track 2623
n. 投入；輸入；意見

▶She didn't have much input in the group and simply followed what people told her to do. 她在團體的參與度不多，只是遵照別人告訴她怎麼做。

v. 將……輸入

▶I have inputed all the correct information and saved it in the cloud. 我已輸入所有正確的資訊並把它儲存在雲端。

inquire [ɪn`kwaɪr] ◀Track 2624
=enquire **v.** 訊問；查問；調查

▶He wrote an e-mail inquiring about the wages of this job. 他寫電郵詢問這份工作的薪資。

inquiry [ɪn`kwaɪrɪ] ◀Track 2625
=enquiry **n.** 詢問；打聽；質詢；調查；探索

▶He made an inquiry about the progress of the case. 他詢問案子的進度。

insect [`ɪnsɛkt] **n.** 昆蟲 ◀Track 2626

▶Butterflies are beautiful insects. 蝴蝶是美麗的昆蟲。

insert [ɪn`sɝt] ◀Track 2627
v. 插入；嵌入

▶They inserted an advertisement in the magazine. 他們在雜誌刊登了廣告。

inside [`ɪn`saɪd] ◀Track 2628
prep. 在……裡面

中級

▶She parked her car inside the garage. 她把車停在車庫裡。

adv. 在裡面;往裡面

▶The police went inside and found that the curtain was stained with blood in the room. 警方走進房間,發現窗簾上有血漬。

n. 裡面;內部;內側

▶The is no door knob on the inside of the bathroom. 浴室那一側沒有門把。

insist [ɪn`sɪst] **v.** 堅持　◀€ Track 2629

▶She insisted on cleaning my flat every Saturday. 她堅持每週六要幫我打掃公寓。

inspect [ɪn`spɛkt] ◀€ Track 2630

v. 檢查;審查;檢閱;進行檢查

▶The FBI agents inspected the crime scene. 美國聯邦調查局探員檢查了犯案現場。

inspector [ɪn`spɛktɚ] ◀€ Track 2631
n. 檢查員;視察員;督察員

▶The school inspector said the exam results of the high school were the worst he had ever seen. 督學說這所中學的考試成績是他見過最糟的。

補充片語 school inspector 督學

inspiration ◀€ Track 2632

[͵ɪnspə`reʃən] **n.** 靈感;鼓舞人心的人事物;吸入、吸氣

▶The musician took his inspiration from four seasons. 這位音樂家從四季取得靈感。

inspire [ɪn`spaɪr] ◀€ Track 2633
v. 鼓舞;激勵

▶When he was a fifth grader, he was inspired by his math teacher to be a scientist. 他小學五年級時,受到數學老師鼓勵成為一名科學家。

install [ɪn`stɔl] ◀€ Track 2634
v. 安裝;設置;安頓

▶They installed a heater in the room. 他們在房間安裝了暖氣機。

instance [`ɪnstəns] ◀€ Track 2635
n. 例子;實例

▶The idiom "so far so good" means that things are going well so far. For instance, you might use it to refer to your studies at school. 「目前為止一切順利」(so far so good)這個慣用語是目前為止都還好。例如,你可以用來指在學校學習的狀況。

instant [`ɪnstənt] ◀€ Track 2636
adj. 立即的;緊迫的;速食的

▶We need to take instant measures to tackle the issue. 我們必須採取即刻行動來處理這個問題。

n. 剎那;頃刻

▶He fell in love with Gemma the instant he saw her. 他一看到潔瑪的剎那間,就愛上她了。

instead [ɪn`stɛd] ◀€ Track 2637
adv. 作為替代;反而;卻

▶Instead of working, he played video games all day. 他不去上班,反而整天打電動。

instinct [`ɪnstɪŋkt] ◀€ Track 2638
n. 本能;天性;直覺

▶Her instinct told her to lock the doors of her car immediately. 她的直覺告訴她立刻把所有的車門鎖上。

institute [ˋɪnstətjut]　◀Track 2639

n. 學會；協會；（專科性的）學校；（教師的）講習會；機構

▶His alma mater is the Massachusetts Institute of Technology. 他的母校是麻省理工學院。

補充片語 the Massachusetts Institute of Technology 麻省理工學院

institution　◀Track 2640

[ˌɪnstəˋtjuʃən] **n.** 公共團體；機構；制度；習俗

▶The patient was hospitalized in an institution. 該病患被安置在療養院。

instruction　◀Track 2641

[ɪnˋstrʌkʃən] **n.** 教學；講授；教導；命令；指示；用法說明

▶Please read the instructions before operating the bread machine. 操作麵包機前，請先閱讀操作說明。

instructor [ɪnˋstrʌktɚ]　◀Track 2642

n. 教員；教練；指導者；大學講師

▶She is a yoga instructor. 她是瑜伽教練。

instrument　◀Track 2643

[ˋɪnstrəmənt] **n.** 儀器；器具；樂器

▶How many musical instruments can you play? 你會彈奏幾種樂器?

insult [ɪnˋsʌlt]　◀Track 2644

n. 辱罵；侮辱

▶Her colleagues made insults about her appearance. 她的同事說了侮辱她外表的話。

v. 侮辱；羞辱

▶It was sad to see her mother insult her and curse at her. 看到她媽媽羞辱、咒罵她，真叫人難過。

insurance [ɪnˋʃʊrəns]　◀Track 2645

n. 保險；保險契約；保險業；保險金；預防措施；安全保證

▶He bought travel insurance with trip cancellation coverage. 他買了旅遊險，其中包含旅遊取消的賠償。

intellectual　◀Track 2646

[ˌɪntlˋɛktʃʊəl] **adj.** 智力的；理智的；需要智力的；智力發達的

▶This article lacked intellectual depth. 這篇文章缺乏知識的深度。

n. 高智力的人；知識份子

▶He was too much of an intellectual and too little of a leader. 他太書卷氣，缺乏領袖的特質。

intelligence　◀Track 2647

[ɪnˋtɛlədʒəns] **n.** 智慧；智能；理解力；情報

▶Artificial intelligence is changing the way we live. 人工智慧正在改變我們的生活型態。

intelligent　◀Track 2648

[ɪnˋtɛlədʒənt] **adj.** 有才智的；聰明的；有理性的

▶Dolphins are intelligent animals. 海豚是很聰明的動物。

intend [ɪnˋtɛnd]　◀Track 2649

v. 想要；打算

▶The prime minister intended to handle the protest peacefully. 這名總理打算以和平的方式處理這場抗爭。

中級

intense [ɪn`tɛns]　◀Track 2650

adj. 強烈的；劇烈的；極度的

▶She felt an intense pain on her leg.
她感到腿部劇烈疼痛。

intensify [ɪn`tɛnsə͵faɪ]　◀Track 2651

v. 加強；增強；加劇

▶The turmoil intensified. 動亂變得劇烈了。

intensive [ɪn`tɛnsɪv]　◀Track 2652

adj. 加強的；密集的；特別護理的；
集約栽培的

▶The athlete is under intensive training.
運動員正在接受密集訓練。

intention [ɪn`tɛnʃən]　◀Track 2653

n. 意圖

▶It was not my intention to offend you.
我並沒有意圖要冒犯你。

interact [͵ɪntə`rækt]　◀Track 2654

v. 互動；互相作用；互相影響；交流

▶The volunteers interacted with the children and handed out schoolbags and stationery items to underprivileged children. 志工與孩子們互動，並發書包及文具用品給清寒學生。

interest [`ɪntərɪst]　◀Track 2655

n. 興趣；愛好

▶She developed an interest in investment.
她對投資產生了興趣。

v. 使感興趣；使發生興趣

▶Hockey has never really interested him. 他從沒對曲棍球感到有興趣過。

interested [`ɪntərɪstɪd]　◀Track 2656

adj. 感興趣的

▶She is very interested in Korean culture.
她對韓國文化很感興趣。

interesting [`ɪntərɪstɪŋ] **adj.** 有趣的　◀Track 2657

▶He is definitely one of the most interesting people I have ever met. 他絕對是我所遇過最有趣的人之一。

interfere [͵ɪntə`fɪr]　◀Track 2658

v. 妨礙；干預；干涉

▶China has repeatedly warned the US not to interfere in its relationship with Taiwan. 中國一再警告美國不要干涉其與台灣的關係。

interference [͵ɪntə`fɪrəns] **n.** 阻礙；抵觸；干擾；干預　◀Track 2659

▶She left home to escape her mother's interference in her life. 她離家以逃避母親對她生活的干預。

intermediate [͵ɪntə`midɪət] **adj.** 居中的；中等程度的；中型的　◀Track 2660

▶The course was designed for students with intermediate level of English. 這堂課是為英文中級程度的學生所設計。

internal [ɪn`tɝnḷ]　◀Track 2661

adj. 內部的；內在的；固有的；國內的；內政的；體內的

▶He suffered a seizure and an internal bleeding in the brain. 他心臟病突發並有腦出血的症狀。

international [͵ɪntə`næʃənḷ] **adj.** 國際的　◀Track 2662

▶He was the CEO of a big international company. 他是一家大型國際公司的執行長。

Internet [ˋɪntəˌnɛt] ◀ Track 2663

n. 網路

▶He met his wife through the Internet. 他透過網路遇見現在的妻子。

interpret [ɪnˋtɝprɪt] ◀ Track 2664

v. 解釋；說明；理解；口譯；做翻譯

▶She interpreted his frown as a sign of worry. 她把他的皺眉解讀為憂心。

interpretation ◀ Track 2665

[ɪnˌtɝprɪˋteʃən] **n.** 解釋；說明；翻譯；口譯；詮釋

▶His interpretation of the poem is profound. 他針對這個詩篇的解釋很具深度。

interpreter ◀ Track 2666

[ɪnˋtɝprɪtə] **n.** 口譯員；翻譯員

▶She is a simultaneous interpreter. 她是一名同步口譯員。

interrupt [ˌɪntəˋrʌpt] ◀ Track 2667

v. 打斷

▶He kept interrupting our conversation. 他不斷地打斷我們的對話。

interval [ˋɪntəvl] ◀ Track 2668

n. 間隔；距離；（音樂會等的）中場休息時間

▶The palm trees were planted at seven-inch intervals. 這些棕櫚樹以七英吋的間隔栽種。

interview [ˋɪntəˌvju] ◀ Track 2669

n. 訪談；面談；接見

▶He had butterflies in his stomach before the interview. 他在面試前感到很不安。

v. 會見；訪談；採訪

▶The CNN journalist will interview the British prime minister at 10:00 A.M. (Eastern Standard Time). 美國有線電視新聞的記者將於美國東部時間早上十點訪問英國首相。

intimate [ˋɪntəmɪt] ◀ Track 2670

adj. 親密的；熟悉的；氣氛融洽的；精通的；私密的

▶She has an intimate knowledge of ancient Chinese literature. 她精通中國古代文學。

n. 至交；密友

▶Intimates of the singer said that she was depressed by her father's death and she needed some time to heal. 該名歌手的密友表示，她因父親過世而感到沮喪，需要一些時間治療傷痛。

into [ˋɪntu] ◀ Track 2671

prep. 到……裡；進入到；成為

▶She walked into the room silently. 她默默地走進房間裡。

introduce [ˌɪntrəˋdjus] ◀ Track 2672

v. 介紹

▶Can you introduce yourself? 你可以自我介紹嗎？

introduction ◀ Track 2673

[ˌɪntrəˋdʌkʃən] **n.** 介紹；正式引見；引進

▶The public called for the introduction of harsher sentences for drunk driving. 大眾要求針對酒駕引進更嚴的刑罰。

中級

intrude [ɪn`trud]
◀€Track 2674

v. 侵入；闖入；打擾

▶It would be better not to intrude people's privacy. 最好不要侵入別人的隱私。

intruder [ɪn`trudə]
◀€Track 2675

n. 侵入者；闖入者；干擾者

▶An intruder entered the house through the basement. 一名盜賊從地下室闖入了民宅。

invade [ɪn`ved]
◀€Track 2676

v. 侵入；侵略；侵犯；大批進入；侵襲

▶Napoleon's armies invaded the city in 1810. 拿破崙的軍隊於1810年侵略這座城市。

invasion [ɪn`veʒən]
◀€Track 2677

n. 入侵；侵略；侵犯；侵佔

▶The overnight invasion took the country by surprise. 該國出乎意料地在一夜之間遭到侵襲。

invent [ɪn`vɛnt] **v.** 發明
◀€Track 2678

▶Nikola Tesla invented alternating electrical current. 尼古拉・特斯拉發明交流電。

invention [ɪn`vɛnʃən]
◀€Track 2679

n. 發明；創造；發明物；發明才能

▶The invention of the Internet has totally changed our lifestyle. 網際網路的發明完全改變了我們的生活風格。

inventor [ɪn`vɛntə]
◀€Track 2680

n. 發明者

▶Alexander Graham Bell is the inventor of telephone. 亞歷山大・格拉漢姆・貝爾是電話的發明者。

invest [ɪn`vɛst] **v.** 投資
◀€Track 2681

▶She invested a lot of money in real estate. 她花很多錢投資房地產。

investigate
◀€Track 2682

[ɪn`vɛstə‚get] **v.** 調查

▶The police is investigating an armed robbery that happened yesterday. 警方正在調查昨天發生的武裝搶劫。

investment
◀€Track 2683

[ɪn`vɛstmənt] **n.** 投資；投資額；投資物；（時間、精神 的）投入

▶Foreign investment has improved the economy of Shenzhen in recent years. 外資改善了深圳近幾年的經濟。

investor [ɪn`vɛstə]
◀€Track 2684

n. 投資者；出資者

▶An investor offered to acquire Tesla's shares for US$14 each. 一名投資者提出以每股十四美元的價格收購特斯拉。

invisible [ɪn`vɪzəbl̩]
◀€Track 2685

adj. 看不見的

▶It is said that free markets are driven by the "invisible hand" theory. 有人說自由市場的運作是由「一隻看不見的手」的理論所驅使。

invitation [‚ɪnvə`teʃən]
◀€Track 2686

n. 邀請；邀請函；請帖

▶I received an invitation to his wedding. 我接獲了他的婚禮邀請函。

invite [ɪn`vaɪt] **v.** 邀請
◀€Track 2687

▶The singer was invited to perform at the Oscars. 這名歌手獲邀在奧斯卡頒獎典禮演出。

involve [ɪnˈvɑlv]　Track 2688
v. 使捲入；連累；牽涉；需要；包含

▶It's not proper for me to involve in your family's quarrel. 我不便牽扯進你們的家族爭端裡。

involved [ɪnˈvɑlvd]　Track 2689
adj. 複雜的；有關的

▶He is not involved in the assault of the journalist. 他跟那位記者受到攻擊的事件無關。

IQ [ˈaɪˈkju] **n.** 智力商數　Track 2690
▶Stephen Hawking had an IQ of 160. 史蒂芬·霍金擁有160的智商。

iron [ˈaɪɚn]　Track 2691
n. 鐵；鐵質；熨斗

▶Strike the iron while it is hot. 打鐵要趁熱。

v. 用熨斗燙平

▶He is ironing his shirt. 他正在熨燙他的襯衫。

irony [ˈaɪrənɪ]　Track 2692
n. 反語；冷嘲；諷刺

▶The irony is that the expert's advice only made things worse. 諷刺的是該專家的意見卻導致事情惡化了。

irregular [ɪˈrɛgjələ]　Track 2693
adj. 不規則的

▶An irregular heartbeat is a sign of a serious disease. 不規律的心跳是嚴重疾病的警訊。

irritate [ˈɪrəˌtet]　Track 2694
v. 使惱怒；使煩躁；使難受

▶Her rude behavior began to irritate her teacher. 她的無禮行為開始讓老師惱火了。

is [ɪz]　Track 2695
v. 是（用於第三人稱單數現在式）

▶What is your opinion on this? 你對這件事的看法如何？

island [ˈaɪlənd]　Track 2696
n. 島；島嶼

▶The island of Ibiza is located off the coast of Spain. 伊比薩島是西班牙離岸的島嶼。

isle [aɪl] **n.** 小島　Track 2697
▶The isle cannot be seen from this shore. 從這個海岸看不到那座小島。

isn't [ˈɪznt]　Track 2698
abbr. 不是（is not的縮寫）

▶The patient's vital sign isn't getting stronger. 病人的生命跡象並沒有增強。

isolate [ˈaɪslˌet]　Track 2699
v. 使孤立

▶The village was isolated due to landslides. 這個村莊因為土石流而被隔絕。

isolation [ˌaɪslˈeʃən]　Track 2700
n. 隔離；孤立；脫離

▶Doctors Without Borders helped establish Ebola treatment centers and isolation wards in the city, Mbandaka, in 2018. 無國界醫生組織在2018年於姆班達卡協助設立伊波拉治療中心和隔離病房。

issue [ˈɪʃʊ]　Track 2701
n. 發行物；發行量；問題；爭議

中級

▶This book explored a lot of controversial issues. 這本書探索了很多具有爭議性的議題。

v. 發行；發佈；由……產生；使流出；核發

▶The post office issued commemorative stamps in honor of the outstanding teacher. 郵局發行紀念郵票向這位傑出的教師致敬。

it [ɪt] **pron.** 它；牠　　◀€Track 2702

▶This is my new tablet computer. I just bought it today. 這是我的新平板電腦。我今天才買的。

itch [ɪtʃ] **v.** 發癢；渴望　◀€Track 2703

▶Jennifer's hands itched. 珍妮佛的雙手發癢。

n. 癢；渴望

▶He had an itch on his scalp for years. 他的頭發癢多年。

item [`aɪtəm]　◀€Track 2704
n. 項目；品項

▶How many items do we have on the agenda? 我們的議事行程上有幾個項目?

it'll [`ɪtl]　◀€Track 2705
abbr. 它會（it will的縮寫）

▶It'll be hard to make it to the meeting on time if you get up too late. 如果你太晚起床的話，準時到達會議場所會很困難。

its [ɪts] **det.** 它的；牠的　◀€Track 2706

▶Do you think my cat licks its paws and body too much? 你覺得我的貓會不會太常舔牠的腳掌和身體?

it's [ɪts]　◀€Track 2707
abbr. 它是（it is的縮寫）

▶It's a rainy day, and we should stay in the classroom for today's PE class. 今天是個雨天，我們的體育課應該要留在教室內。

itself [ɪt`sɛlf]　◀€Track 2708
pron. 它自己；牠自己

▶ The elephant was trying to hurt itself after being injected with a strong dose of medicine. 這隻大象在被注射高劑量藥物之後試圖傷害自己。

I've [aɪv]　◀€Track 2709
abbr. 我已、我有（I have的縮寫）

▶I've never seen the movie before. 我從沒看過這部電影。

ivory [`aɪvərɪ]　◀€Track 2710
n. 象牙；象牙色；象牙製品

▶Ivory trade is banned in several countries to save the elephants. 象牙買賣在數個國家被禁止，以拯救大象。

adj. 象牙的；象牙製的；象牙色的

▶You look gorgeous in this ivory dress. 你穿這件象牙白的禮服真美。

ivy [`aɪvɪ] **n.** 常春藤　◀€Track 2711

▶I love how the ivies covered the hostel. 我喜歡這間旅舍被常春藤包覆住的外觀。

▶ Jj

以下表格是全民英檢官方公告中級「聽、説、讀、寫」所須具備的能力，本書例句皆依此範疇特別設計，只要掃描右方QR code，就能搭配相對應的音軌實現「眼耳並用」方式，刺激左腦的語言學習功能；同時也可使用本書附贈的紅膠片，將其置於單字上，一面記憶一面自我挑戰，達到雙倍的學習成果！

聽 ▶	在日常生活中，能聽懂一般的會話；能大致聽懂公共場所廣播、氣象報告及廣告等。在工作時，能聽懂簡易的產品介紹與操作説明。能大致聽懂外籍人士的談話及詢問。
説 ▶	可在日常生活中，能以簡易英語交談或描述一般事物，能介紹自己的生活作息、工作、家庭、經歷等，並可對一般話題陳述看法。在工作時，能進行簡單的答詢，並與外籍人士交談溝通。
讀 ▶	在日常生活中，能閱讀短文、故事、私人信件、廣告、傳單、簡介及使用説明等。在工作時，能閱讀工作須知、公告、操作手冊、例行的文件、傳真、電報等。
寫 ▶	能寫簡單的書信、故事及心得等。對於熟悉且與個人經歷相關的主題，能以簡易的文字表達。

中級

---

jacket [`dʒækɪt]
◀ Track 2712

n. 夾克；上衣

▶She wore a denim jacket and a black skirt.
她穿了一件牛仔夾克和黑裙。

---

jade [dʒed]
◀ Track 2713

n. 翡翠；玉；玉製品；綠玉色

▶The Buddha statue is made of jade.
這尊佛像是玉製的。

adj. 玉的；玉製的；綠玉色的

▶He gave me a jade ring.
他送我一個玉戒指。

---

jail [dʒel] **n.** 監獄
◀ Track 2714

▶The man spent ten years in jail for a crime he didn't commit.
這名男子為了一件未犯的案而入獄十年。

v. 監禁

▶He was jailed for twenty years.
他被關在牢裡二十年。

---

jam [dʒæm]
◀ Track 2715

v. 塞進；塞住；堵住；使擠滿

▶Tens of thousands of people jammed the square. 數萬人把廣場擠得滿滿的。

---

janitor [`dʒænɪtə]
◀ Track 2716

n. 門警；看門人；門房；照看房屋的工友

▶The school janitor was responsible for overseeing the safety of the school.
學校的門警負責學校的安全。

January [`dʒænjʊˌɛrɪ]
=Jan **n.** 一月
◀ Track 2717

▶We are going to Hokkaido in January.
我們一月要去北海道。

Japan [dʒəˋpæn] **n.** 日本 ◀ Track 2718
▶She studied medicine in Japan.
她在日本學醫。

Japanese [ˌdʒæpəˋniz] ◀ Track 2719
n. 日語；日本人
▶He married a Japanese.
他取了一位日本妻子。

adj. 日本的；日本人的；日語的
▶We bought a Japanese car.
我們買了一輛日本車。

jar [dʒɑr] ◀ Track 2720
n. 罐；罈（寬口的）瓶
▶She bought a jar of honey from the supermarket. 她從超市買了一罐蜂蜜。

jasmine [ˋdʒæsmɪn] ◀ Track 2721
n. 茉莉花；茉莉花茶；淡黃色
▶The gardener planted jasmine and roses around the courtyard. 園丁在庭中種植茉莉花和玫瑰。

jaw [dʒɔ] **n.** 下巴；頜；顎 ◀ Track 2722
▶Her jaw dropped when her crush asked her to the prom. 她暗戀的人約她去畢業舞會時，她吃驚地下巴都掉下來了。

補充片語 **one's jaw drop**
（因吃驚而）下巴掉下來

v. 閒聊；嘮叨；數落
▶They spent the whole afternoon jawing with each other. 他們整個下午都在閒聊。

相關片語 **wag one's jaw** 喋喋不休
▶My mother often wags her jaw when the final exams come. 在期末考期間，我媽媽老是喋喋不休的。

jazz [dʒæz] ◀ Track 2723
n. 爵士樂；爵士舞
▶New Orleans is the cradle of jazz.
紐奧良是爵士樂的發源地。

jealous [ˋdʒɛləs] ◀ Track 2724
adj. 妒忌的；吃醋的
▶She is jealous of Amy's beautiful figure. 她很嫉妒艾咪的姣好身材。

jealousy [ˋdʒɛləsɪ] ◀ Track 2725
n. 妒忌；猜忌
▶She insulted him in a fit of jealousy over his attraction to another woman. 她因為他對別的女人傾心而心生妒忌地羞辱他。

jeans [dʒinz] **n.** 牛仔褲 ◀ Track 2726
▶Steve always wears jeans to work.
史蒂夫總是穿牛仔褲上班。

jeep [dʒip] **n.** 吉普車 ◀ Track 2727
▶They drove a jeep across the desert.
他們開著吉普車穿越沙漠。

jelly [ˋdʒɛlɪ] ◀ Track 2728
n. 果凍；果醬；膠狀物
▶She made a blueberry jelly for dessert.
她做了藍莓果凍當甜點。

jet [dʒɛt] ◀ Track 2729
n. 噴射機；噴射器；噴出物
▶He flew to London by jet.
他搭飛機到倫敦。

v. 噴出；射出；搭飛機旅行
▶We are jetting off to Zimbabwe next month. 我們下個月要去辛巴威。

相關片語 **jet lag** 時差

▶He got jet lag for a week after traveling overseas. 他從國外旅遊回來後，過了一個禮拜才把時差調回來。

jewel [`dʒuəl]
Track 2730

n. 寶石；寶石飾物；首飾

▶She wore no jewels or costly diamonds on the red carpet. 她走紅毯時既沒戴寶石沒也戴昂貴的鑽石。

jewelry [`dʒuəlrɪ]
Track 2731

n. 珠寶

▶She studied jewelry design in Florence, Italy. 她在義大利佛羅倫斯學習珠寶設計。

jingle [`dʒɪŋgl]
Track 2732

v. 發出叮噹聲

▶The coins jingled in his pocket as he hurried to the grocery store. 他急忙趕去雜貨店時，硬幣在他的口袋裡叮噹作響。

n. 叮噹聲；琅琅上口的（廣告）歌

▶The commercial jingle is repeated again and again on the radio. 這支洗腦的廣告歌曲不斷地在收音機放送。

job [dʒɑb]
Track 2733

n. 工作；分內事情；成果

▶She gave up her job to have a baby. 她為了生小孩而放棄工作。

jog [dʒɑg] **v.** 慢跑
Track 2734

▶He jogs every evening after work. 他每晚下班後都去慢跑。

join [dʒɔɪn] **v.** 加入；參加
Track 2735

▶He joined the army after graduating from high school. 他高中畢業後就從軍了。

joint [dʒɔɪnt]
Track 2736

adj. 聯合的；連接的；合辦的

▶The couple opened a joint account at Barclays. 這對夫妻在巴克萊銀行開了一個共同帳戶。

n. 接合點；關節

▶She had pain and swelling in her leg joints. 她的腿關節疼痛腫脹。

joke [dʒok] **n.** 笑話；玩笑
Track 2737

▶She hates dirty jokes. 她討厭聽黃色笑話。

v. 開玩笑

▶We joked and laughed at the family gathering. 我們在家族聚會開玩笑地大笑。

jolly [`dʒɑlɪ]
Track 2738

adj. 快活的；高興的；令人愉快的；歡樂的

▶He had an attractive and jolly personality. 他具有很吸引人及開朗的個性。

v. 用好話哄勸；用好話使高興；開玩笑；戲弄

▶She jollied me into going for a walk with her. 她哄我跟她一起去散步。

journal [`dʒɝnl]
Track 2739

n. 日誌；日報；雜誌；期刊

▶He kept a travel journal, which is now a book. 他會寫旅遊日誌，現在已出書了。

相關片語 **medical journal** 醫學期刊

▶Her paper was published in a medical journal. 她的論文被刊登在一本醫學期刊上。

journalist [`dʒɝnəlɪst]
Track 2740

n. 新聞工作者；新聞記者

中級

▶The journalist was killed in the bombing. 這名新聞記者在爆炸中身亡。

journey [`dʒɚnɪ]　◀Track 2741
n. 旅行；旅程；行程

▶Have a happy journey! 祝旅途愉快！

v. 旅行

▶At the age of 18, she journeyed to New York City to pursue her modeling career. 她十八歲旅行到紐約去追尋模特兒的生涯。

相關片語 **break one's journey** 中途下車

▶They decided to break their journey in Cambridge. 他們決定在劍橋中途下車。

joy [dʒɔɪ] n. 歡樂；樂趣　◀Track 2742

▶He brought a lot of joy to his family to liven the atmosphere when his father became ill. 當他的父親生病時，他替家裡帶來了很多歡樂，鼓舞氣氛。

joyful [`dʒɔɪfəl]　◀Track 2743
adj. 高興的

▶He was joyful about his memory of his wife. 對妻子的回憶，他滿懷喜悅。

judge [dʒʌdʒ]　◀Track 2744
n. 法官；裁判

▶The judge revealed her own thoughts and feelings about the case. 這名法官表達了她對該案的想法和感受。

v. 判決；判斷；評斷

▶If you judge a book by its over, you may miss many good opportunities. 如果你以貌取人，你可以會錯失掉很多好的機會。

judgement　◀Track 2745
[`dʒʌdʒmənt] n. 審判；判斷；判斷力；看法

▶He let his emotions cloud his judgment. 他讓情感影響了他的判斷力。

jug [dʒʌg] n. 水罐；甕；壺　◀Track 2746

▶The cat was licking a milk jug. 這隻貓在舔牛奶罐。

juice [dʒus] n. 果汁　◀Track 2747

▶He gulped down a glass of grape juice. 他一口氣喝完一杯葡萄汁。

juicy [`dʒusɪ] adj. 多汁的　◀Track 2748

▶The fresh orange is organically planted, and is very juicy. 這個新鮮的柳橙是有機的，而且非常多汁。

July [dʒu`laɪ] n. 七月　◀Track 2749

▶They will go to Hungary in July. 他們七月會去匈牙利。

jump [dʒʌmp] v. 跳　◀Track 2750

▶Don't jump to conclusions. 不要草率地下結論。

n. 跳躍；跳一步的距離

▶The dog jumped over the fence. 小狗躍過了籬笆。

June [dʒun] n. 六月　◀Track 2751

▶She will marry in June. 她會在六月結婚了。

jungle [`dʒʌŋgl] n. 叢林　◀Track 2752

▶They were stranded in the jungle. 他們被困在叢林裡。

中級

junior [`dʒunjɚ]　◀Track 2753

adj. 年紀較輕的；資淺的；地位較低的；
大學三年級的

▶She studies in a junior college.
她就讀專科學校。

n. 較年少者；較資淺者；等級較低者；
晚輩；大學三年級生

▶ This activity is for juniors only, others
should stay in the classrrom. 這個活動
是給初級者的，其他人應留在教室內。

junk [dʒʌŋk]　◀Track 2754

n. 廢棄的舊物；垃圾

▶There is too much junk on TV these
days. 現在電視上有太多亂七八糟的節目。

相關片語 **junk mail** 垃圾郵件

▶She tossed the junk mail into the
recycle trash bin. 她把垃圾郵件丟進垃圾
回收桶。

jury [`dʒʊrɪ] **n.** 陪審團　◀Track 2755

▶The jury was in deliberation for several
hours. 陪審團進行討論好幾個小時。

just [dʒʌst]　◀Track 2756

adv. 僅；只是；正好

▶He just came back from New Zealand.
他剛從紐西蘭回來。

justice [`dʒʌstɪs]　◀Track 2757

n. 正義；公平；正當的理由；合法；司法；
審判

▶The family wants justice for their son.
這家人希望司法還兒子公道。

相關片語 **bring sb. to justice** 使某人受
到制裁；使某人歸案受審

▶Perpetrators must be brought to
justice. 犯罪者必須受到制裁。

justify [`dʒʌstə͵faɪ]　◀Track 2758

v. 證明無罪；證明……為正當；為……辯駁

▶The end can't justify the means. 行事不
能不擇手段。

▶ Kk

　　以下表格是全民英檢官方公告中級「聽、說、讀、寫」所須具備的能力，本書例句皆依此範疇特別設計，只要掃描右方QR code，就能搭配相對應的音軌實現「眼耳並用」方式，刺激左腦的語言學習功能；同時也可使用本書附贈的紅膠片，將其置於單字上，一面記憶一面自我挑戰，達到雙倍的學習成果！

聽 ▶	在日常生活中，能聽懂一般的會話；能大致聽懂公共場所廣播、氣象報告及廣告等。在工作時，能聽懂簡易的產品介紹與操作說明。能大致聽懂外籍人士的談話及詢問。
說 ▶	可在日常生活中，能以簡易英語交談或描述一般事物，能介紹自己的生活作息、工作、家庭、經歷等，並可對一般話題陳述看法。在工作時，能進行簡單的答詢，並與外籍人士交談溝通。
讀 ▶	在日常生活中，能閱讀短文、故事、私人信件、廣告、傳單、簡介及使用說明等。在工作時，能閱讀工作須知、公告、操作手冊、例行的文件、傳真、電報等。
寫 ▶	能寫簡單的書信、故事及心得等。對於熟悉且與個人經歷相關的主題，能以簡易的文字表達。

kan·ga·roo
🔊 Track 2759

[ˌkæŋgəˋru] **n.** 袋鼠

▶Some local residents spotted kangaroos wandering on the road.
有些當地居民在路上看到袋鼠在閒晃。

Kaoh·siung
🔊 Track 2760

[ˋkauˋʃɔŋ] **n.** 高雄

▶I visited Fisherman's Wharf in Kaohsiung with my family.
我和家人一起去了高雄的漁人碼頭。

keen [kin]
🔊 Track 2761

adj. 熱衷的；渴望的，極想的

▶He is keen to get scholarship.
他很積極要獲得這筆獎學金。

Keep [kip]
🔊 Track 2762

v. 保持；持有；繼續不斷

▶He keeps a habit of reading international news every day.
他保有每天閱讀國際新聞的習慣。

keeper [ˋkipɚ]
🔊 Track 2763

n. 飼養人；保管者；看守人

▶The old man used to be a lighthouse keeper.
這位老先生以前是一位燈塔看守人。

ketch·up [ˋkɛtʃəp]
🔊 Track 2764

n. 番茄醬

▶You can add some ketchup to the omelet rice to add flavor to it.
你可以加些番茄醬到蛋包飯裡來增加風味。

ket·tle [ˋkɛtḷ] **n.** 水壺
🔊 Track 2765

▶The camping kettle is made of stainless steel.
這個露營用的水壺是不鏽鋼做成的。

相關片語 **a fine kettle of fish**
亂七八糟，很令人不愉快的事

▶The mischievous kid made the solemn occasion a fine kettle of fish. 這個頑皮的小孩把這個莊嚴的場合弄得一團亂。

key [ki] **n.** 鑰匙；關鍵
◀Track 2766

▶The entrepreneur shared his thoughts on the key to success.
商人分享了他對成功關鍵的看法。

adj. 主要的；關鍵的

▶The Key Performance Indicator is a reference for us to know about the working efficiency of a company. 績效指標是用來看一間公司的效率的參考數據。

keyboard [`ki,bord]
◀Track 2767
n. 鍵盤

▶It is said that the Bluetooth keyboard may have several drawbacks.
據說藍芽鍵盤有一些缺點。

kick [kɪk] **v.** 踢
◀Track 2768

▶The toddler kicked away the quilt in his sleep.
這個小朋友在睡覺時把被子踢掉了。

n. 踢；一時的愛好或狂熱

▶Do you get a kick out of teaching Mandarin to the exchange students?
你喜歡上教交換學生中文了嗎？

相關片語 **kick the bucket** 死去

▶It is said that the villain has kicked the bucket. 據說那個惡棍已經翹辮子了。

kid [kɪd] **n.** 小孩；年輕人
◀Track 2769

▶Don't be so harsh on him. He is just a kid. 別對他那麼嚴厲。他只是個孩子。

kidnap [`kɪdnæp]
◀Track 2770
v. 誘拐；綁架

▶The wealthy man's daughter was kidnapped by a masked man.
這名有錢人的女兒被蒙面男子綁架了。

kidney [`kɪdnɪ] **n.** 腎臟
◀Track 2771

▶He suffers from chronic kidney disease.
他因為慢性腎臟疾病而受苦。

kill [kɪl] **v.** 殺死；引起死亡
◀Track 2772

▶Mom killed the cockroach with pesticide.
媽媽拿殺蟲劑來殺死蟑螂。

相關片語 **kill time** 打發時間

▶Karen sometimes likes to binge-watch Korean Dramas to kill time on the weekend.
凱倫有時候喜歡在周末看韓劇打發時間。

kilogram [`kɪlə,græm]
◀Track 2773
n. 公斤

▶The parcel weighs two kilograms.
這個小包裹重兩公斤。

kilometre [`kɪlə,mitɚ]
◀Track 2774
n. 公里

▶The distance between Taipei and Kaohsiung is 297 kilometers.
台北到高雄的距離是297公里。

kin [kɪn]
◀Track 2775
n. 家族；親戚；同類

▶That man is no kin to me.
那個男人和我沒有親屬關係。

adj. 有親屬關係的

中級

▶People say that Kate and I look alike, but she is not kin to me.
人們說凱特和我長得很像，但是她和我沒有親屬關係。

kind [kaɪnd]　◀≣Track 2776

adj. 親切的；有同情心的

▶It was kind of you to help me overcome the predicament.
你人真好，幫助我克服難關。

n. 種類

▶There are several kinds of fishes in the fish pod.
這個魚缸裡面有好幾種魚。

kindergarten　◀≣Track 2777

[`kɪndɚ͵gɑrtn] **n.** 幼稚園

▶Rita will go to the kindergarten when she is three years old.
瑞塔三歲的時候會去幼兒園上學。

kindle [`kɪndl̩]　◀≣Track 2778

v. 激起；點燃；煽動

▶The politician's speech kindled the people's enthusiasm.
政客的演講激發了民眾的熱情。

kindly [`kaɪndlɪ]　◀≣Track 2779

adj. 親切的；和藹的；善良的；宜人的

▶Your kindly deeds have relieved their nervousness.
你親切的話語舒緩了他們的緊張情緒。

adv. 親切地；和藹地；好心地；令人愉快地

▶An elderly lady kindly offered me the direction to my destination.
一位老太太好心地指引我到目的地。

kindness [`kaɪndnɪs]　◀≣Track 2780

n. 仁慈；好意；友好的行為；好心

▶I will never forget the kindness and hospitality of my host family in Canada.
我永遠不會忘記在加拿大的寄宿家庭對我的好意和熱情招待。

king [kɪŋ]　◀≣Track 2781

n. 國王；某領域中最有勢力的人；大王

▶The Lion King is a famous musical animated film.
獅子王是一部有名的音樂動畫電影。

kingdom [`kɪŋdəm]　◀≣Track 2782

n. 王國

▶Laura learned about the geography of the United Kingdom when she was an exchange student there.
蘿拉去英國做交換學生時，學習了當地的地理。

kiss [kɪs] **v./n.** 親吻　◀≣Track 2783

▶Due to the hygienic reasons, you had better not kiss a new-born baby on the cheek. 因為衛生問題，你最好不要親新生兒的臉頰。

kit [kɪt]　◀≣Track 2784

n. 成套工具（或物件等）；工具箱

▶She has a first-aid kit in her house.
她在家裡放了一個急救箱。

補充片語 emergency / survival / first-aid kit 急救箱／緊急工具箱

▶The official advocated that every family should keep a survival kit in the house.
官員倡導每個家庭都應該在房子裡放一個緊急工具箱。

kitchen [`kɪtʃɪn] n. 廚房 ◀Track 2785
▶Gina dreams to have an outdoor kitchen in her garden.
吉娜想要有一個在花園裡的室外廚房。

kite [kaɪt] n. 風箏 ◀Track 2786
▶The kids seem to enjoy flying a kite.
小朋友似乎放風箏放得很開心。

kitten [`kɪtn] n. 小貓 ◀Track 2787
▶Hank was surprised when his daughter brought a kitten home and kept it as a pet.
漢克看到他女兒帶小貓回家當寵物的時候很驚訝。

kitty [`kɪtɪ] n. 小貓；貓咪 ◀Track 2788
▶Jenny is a die-hard fan of Hello Kitty.
珍妮是凱蒂貓的忠實粉絲。

knee [ni] n. 膝蓋；膝關節 ◀Track 2789
▶Jerry hurt his knee when he fell off his bike yesterday.
傑瑞昨天騎腳踏車時跌倒，導致他的膝蓋受傷。

kneel [nil] v. 跪（下） ◀Track 2790
▶He found that he could not kneel down, for his left knee was so painful.
他發現他的左腳膝蓋痛到令他無法跪下。

補充片語 kneel down 跪下

knife [naɪf] n. 刀；刀子 ◀Track 2791
▶The old master has been sharpening knives for the local chefs for twenty years.
老師傅已經為本地的廚師們磨刀二十年了。

knight [naɪt] n. 武士 ◀Track 2792
▶The king dubbed him a knight after he won the victory in the battle.
在他於戰場上贏得勝利之後，國王便封他為騎士。

knit [nɪt] v. 編織 ◀Track 2793
▶Maggie decided to knit a scarf for her boyfriend as a birthday gift.
梅姬決定要為男友織一條圍巾作為生日禮物。

n. 編織衣物；編織法
▶The store is having a sale of sweater knits.
這家店的編織毛衣在特價。

knob [nɑb] n. 門把 ◀Track 2794
▶Gary thinks that there are so many germs on the door knob that he wouldn't touch it.
蓋瑞覺得門把上有很多細菌，所以不願意碰它。

knock [nɑk] v. 敲；擊打 ◀Track 2795
▶Remember to knock on the door before you enter the manager's office.
進到經理辦公室之前記得要敲門。

knot [nɑt] n. 結 ◀Track 2796
▶The instructor showed the kids how to tie and untie the knots in the rope.
講師教小朋友如何將繩子打結和解結。

相關片語 tie the knot 結婚

▶When are you two going to tie the knot?
你們兩個什麼時候要結婚呀？

v. 打結；綑紮

中級

▶Ryan learned to knot shoe laces in the kindergarten.
雷恩是在幼兒園學習怎麼綁鞋帶的。

know [no]　◀Track 2797

v. 知道；認識；理解

▶He knows well about the intellectual property laws.
他熟知智慧財產權的相關法律。

相關片語 **know the ins and outs**
知道詳細情況

▶The janitor knows all the ins and outs of the school building.
管理員知道學校大樓的所有情況。

knowledge [`nɑlɪdʒ]　◀Track 2798
n. 知識；學問；了解

▶Hank is keen to explore new fields and gain more knowledge.
漢克熱衷於探索新領域以及獲取新知識。

knowledgeable
[`nɑlɪdʒəbḷ]　◀Track 2799
adj. 有知識的；博學的；有見識的

▶Tom is so knowledgeable that we call him a walking encyclopedia. 湯姆是如此博學，我們都稱他為行動百科全書。

knuckle [`nʌkḷ]　◀Track 2800
n. 指（根）關節；（四足動物的）膝關節

▶The boy cracked his knuckles when he fell. 男孩跌倒時弄傷了他的手指關節。

相關片語 **rap on the knuckle**
責備；訓斥

▶The teacher gave me a rap on the knuckle for my bad grades in the exam.
老師因為我在考試中成績太差而訓斥了我一頓。

koala [ko`ɑlə] **n.** 無尾熊　◀Track 2801

▶The health of the koalas may be harmed if they are hugged by too many tourists.
如果被太多遊客抱，無尾熊的健康可能會受損。

Korea [ko`riə] **n.** 韓國　◀Track 2802

▶Korea has been a popular destination for tourists from other Asian countries.
韓國一直是很受其他亞洲國家歡迎的旅遊目的地。

Korean [ko`riən]　◀Track 2803
adj. 韓國的；韓語的；韓國人的
n. 韓語；韓國人

▶Thomas is preparing for the Korean Proficiency Test.
湯瑪士正在準備韓國語言能力測驗。

KTV [ke-ti-vi] **n.** 卡拉OK　◀Track 2804

▶Why do people like to sing old songs in the KTV?
為什麼人們會喜歡在卡拉OK唱老歌呢？

▶ Ll

　　以下表格是全民英檢官方公告中級「聽、説、讀、寫」所須具備的能力，本書例句皆依此範疇特別設計，只要掃描右方QR code，就能搭配相對應的音軌實現「眼耳並用」方式，刺激左腦的語言學習功能；同時也可使用本書附贈的紅膠片，將其置於單字上，一面記憶一面自我挑戰，達到雙倍的學習成果！

聽 ▶	在日常生活中，能聽懂一般的會話；能大致聽懂公共場所廣播、氣象報告及廣告等。在工作時，能聽懂簡易的產品介紹與操作説明。能大致聽懂外籍人士的談話及詢問。
説 ▶	可在日常生活中，能以簡易英語交談或描述一般事物，能介紹自己的生活作息、工作、家庭、經歷等，並可對一般話題陳述看法。在工作時，能進行簡單的答詢，並與外籍人士交談溝通。
讀 ▶	在日常生活中，能閱讀短文、故事、私人信件、廣告、傳單、簡介及使用説明等。在工作時，能閱讀工作須知、公告、操作手冊、例行的文件、傳真、電報等。
寫 ▶	能寫簡單的書信、故事及心得等。對於熟悉且與個人經歷相關的主題，能以簡易的文字表達。

中級

lab [læb] n 實驗室　◀Track 2805

▶Kevin stayed in the lab until eleven p.m. yesterday to finish the experiment.
凱文為了把實驗做完，昨天在實驗室待到晚上十一點。

label [ˋlebḷ] n 貼紙；標籤　◀Track 2806

▶Lena always read the labels on food packages to see the ingredients of the foods.
麗娜總是會看食品包裝上的標籤來了解食物的食材。

v 貼標籤

▶The specimens of butterflies were labeled with their scientific names. 這些蝴蝶標本都有貼標籤標示出他們的學名。

labor [ˋlebɚ]
=labour（英式英文）n 勞工　◀Track 2807

▶The immigrant labors have become the major work force in some regions of the country.
移工已經成為某些地區的主要勞動力來源。

v 勞動；努力幹活；費力前進

▶My mother labored in the garden to plant flowers.
我媽媽在花園裡費勁地種花。

laboratory　◀Track 2808
[ˋlæbrəˌtorɪ] n 實驗室

▶The students have to follow safety protocols when doing experiments in the laboratory. 學生在實驗室裡做實驗時，要遵守安全守則。

lace [les] n 鞋帶；帶子　◀Track 2809

▶Gary stepped on his shoe laces and fell down.
蓋瑞踩到自己的鞋帶，跌倒了。

v. 繫上；束緊

▶The arrogant boy asked his friend to lace his shoes.
這名高傲的男孩叫自己的朋友幫他綁鞋帶。

lack [læk] ◀≣Track 2810

n. 缺少；不足；**v.** 缺乏，沒有

▶He was not employed by the big company for his lack of working experience in this industry.
他因為缺乏產業工作經驗的關係，沒有被這個大公司錄取。

lad [læd] ◀≣Track 2811

n. 男孩，少年，小伙子；老弟，伙伴

▶Hey, lad! Don't be so harsh.
老弟！說話別那麼尖酸刻薄嘛！

ladder [`lædə-] **n.** 梯子 ◀≣Track 2812

▶Doris climbed up the ladder to change the bulb.
桃樂絲為了換燈泡爬上梯子。

lady [`ledɪ] **n.** 女士；小姐 ◀≣Track 2813

▶The lady over there is a well-known stage performer.
那位女士是一位著名的舞台表演者。

ladybird [`ledɪˌbɜ-d] ◀≣Track 2814

n. 瓢蟲（英）

▶The kid caught a ladybird and wanted to keep it as a pet.
小朋友抓了一隻瓢蟲，說要把它當寵物。

ladybug [`ledɪˌbʌg] ◀≣Track 2815

n. 瓢蟲（美）

▶A ladybug stopped on the windowsill.
有一隻瓢蟲停在窗台上。

lag [læg] ◀≣Track 2816

v. 走得慢；落後；延遲

▶The soldiers were tired after marching for eight hours and began to lag.
軍人們行軍八小時後變得疲倦，走路速度變慢。

n. 落後；遲滯；衰退

▶The brochure included some tips to overcome the jet lag.
這本小冊子包含一些克服時差的秘訣。

lake [lek] **n.** 湖 ◀≣Track 2817

▶The famous writer, David Thoreau, once stayed by the Walden Lake for two years.
知名作家大衛・梭羅曾經住在華登湖旁兩年。

lamb [læm] ◀≣Track 2818

n. 小羊；羔羊；容易受騙上當的人

▶The naive tourist was like a lamb to the slaughter in the con man's eyes.
那個搞不清楚狀況的遊客在詐騙份子的眼裡就像一隻待宰的羔羊。

lame [lem] ◀≣Track 2819

adj. 跛腳的，瘸的；站不住腳的，沒有說服力的

▶His performance was so lame that some of the audience left the theater before the show ended.
他的表演如此差勁以至於有些觀眾在他表演結束前就離場了。

v. 使跛腳；使無力

▶He was lamed when he fell down the ski slope in the competition.
他在比賽中從滑雪山坡上面跌下來的時候跛腳了。

lamp [læmp] n. 燈
◀€Track 2820
▶David has a customized lamp in his living room.
大衛的客廳裡有一盞特別設計的燈。

land [lænd] n. 陸地；土地
◀€Track 2821
▶The soldier was very excited when he stepped on his home land after staying overseas for ten years.
這名士兵在海外駐守十年後，於踏上自己的家鄉土地時感到非常激動。

v. 登陸；降落
▶Ladies and gentlemen, we are going to land in ten minutes. Please fasten your seatbelt.
各位先生、女士，我們十分鐘後即將降落。請繫好您的安全帶。

landlady [`lænd͵ledɪ]
◀€Track 2822
n. 女房東；女地主
▶My landlady is a thrifty and conservative old lady.
我的房東是一位節儉而且保守的老太太。

landlord [`lænd͵lɔrd]
◀€Track 2823
n. 房東；地主
▶The landlord said the rent would cover the utility fees.
房東說房租會包含水電費。

landmark
◀€Track 2824
[`lænd͵mɑrk] n. 地標
▶This office building is not only the tallest building in the city but also a famous landmark in the downtown area.
這棟辦公大樓不僅是市內最高的建築物，也是市中心區有名的地標。

landscape
◀€Track 2825
[`lænd͵skep] n. （陸上的）風景；景色
▶The beautiful landscape of Scandinavia was very impressive to many tourists.
北歐的風景令許多遊客難忘。

v. 在陸上造景；從事景觀美化工作
▶They had landscaped their front yard with shrubs and lawns.
他們用矮樹叢和草坪為前院造景。

landslide [`lænd͵slaɪd]
◀€Track 2826
n. 山崩；坍方；（選舉）壓倒性大勝利
▶The government evacuated the villagers for possible massive landslides.
政府因可能的大型山崩而撤離了這些村民。

相關片語 **mudflows and landslides** 土石流

▶Some of the villagers were left homeless because of the mudflows and landslides after the typhoon.
有些村民因為颱風過後的土石流而無家可歸。

lane [len]
◀€Track 2827
n. 小路；巷；車道；跑道
▶There are several food delis in the quiet lane.
在這條安靜的小巷子裡有幾家熟食店。

language [`læŋgwɪdʒ]
◀€Track 2828
n. 語言
▶The kid can speak two languages, for his father is German and his mother is Japanese.
因為爸爸是德國人、媽媽是日本人，所以這個小孩會說兩種語言。

中級

lantern [ˋlæntɚn] ◀ Track 2829
n. 燈籠；提燈

▶Thousands of people came to the festival to appreciate the hand-made traditional lanterns.
數千人來參加這個慶典，欣賞手工製作的傳統燈籠。

Lantern Festival ◀ Track 2830
[ˋlæntɚn-ˋfɛstəv] **n.** 元宵節

▶Chinese people eat sticky rice dumplings on Lantern Festival.
華人會在元宵節吃湯圓。

lap [læp] ◀ Track 2831
n. （跑場的）一圈；（泳池的）一個來回

▶The marathon runner was ahead of the other participants in the first lap, but he fell behind in the middle of the race.
這位馬拉松跑者在第一圈的時候領先其他的參加者，但是在賽跑中間的時候落後了。

large [lɑrdʒ] **adj.** 大的 ◀ Track 2832

▶He doesn't have any experience managing large projects.
他沒有任何管理大型計畫案的經驗。

largely [ˋlɑrdʒlɪ] ◀ Track 2833
adv. 大部份的；主要地；大量地

▶Vicky largely commutes to work by MRT.
薇琪大部分都是搭捷運通勤去上班。

laser [ˋlezɚ] **n.** 雷射 ◀ Track 2834

▶Betty is searching for information about laser surgery for eyes.
貝蒂正在查眼睛雷射手術的相關資訊。

last [læst] **v.** 持續 ◀ Track 2835

▶Children's attention span could only last for about ten minutes.
小朋友的專注力只能持續十分鐘。

late [let] **adj.** 晚的；遲的 ◀ Track 2836

▶Edward was late for the meeting and he got scolded by the manager.
愛德華會議遲到，被經理責罵了。

adv. 晚地

▶Frank came home late yesterday, so his mother was quite worried.
法蘭克昨天很晚才回家，所以他的媽媽很擔心。

lately [ˋletlɪ] **adv.** 近來 ◀ Track 2837

▶I haven't heard anything from my high school classmates lately.
我最近都沒有聽到高中同學的消息。

later [ˋletɚ] ◀ Track 2838
adv. 較晚地；以後

▶Mr. Hsu is not in the office now. Please leave a message of call back later. 徐先生目前不在辦公室。請留言或者晚點再打。

latest [ˋletɪst] **adj.** 最新的 ◀ Track 2839

▶Dozens of people lined up in front of the store to buy the latest version of iPhone. 數十人在店家前面排隊要買最新版的蘋果手機。

latitude [ˋlætəˌtjud] ◀ Track 2840
n. 緯度

▶Seattle and Paris are cities on approximately the same latitude.
西雅圖和巴黎是兩座緯度差不多的城市。

latter [`lætɚ]
◀ Track 2841

adj. 後面的;後半的;後者的;最近的

▶I haven't finished watching the film, so I don't know the latter part of the story.
我沒有看完這部電影,所以我不曉得後半段的故事。

laugh [læf] **v** 笑
◀ Track 2842

▶No one else laughed at Brian's joke except himself.
除了布萊恩自己以外,沒有人因為他的玩笑發笑。

n. 笑;笑聲;樂趣;令人發笑的人事物

▶Hank listened to the ridiculous story and had a good laugh.
漢克聽了這個荒謬的故事,而且被逗樂了。

laughter [`læftɚ]
◀ Track 2843

n. 笑;笑聲

▶Mrs. Jean's class is always full of joy and laughter.
琴女士的課堂總是充滿歡樂和笑聲。

launch [lɔntʃ]
◀ Track 2844

v 發射;使(船)下水;發動;開始從事;出版;投放市場

▶It is said that Space X will launch a tourist spaceship in about ten years.
據說太空探索技術公司將會在十年後發射載客的太空船。

n. 發射;(船)下水;發行;投放市場

▶The product launch luncheon will be held on January 1st.
產品發表午餐會將會在一月一日舉行。

laundry [`lɔndrɪ]
◀ Track 2845

n. 洗衣店;待洗的衣服;洗好的衣服

▶I was so tired after work that I decided to send all my clothes to the laundry downstairs.
我下班後太累了,以至於我決定把所有衣服都送到樓下的洗衣店洗。

相關片語 **do the laundry** 洗衣服

▶The housemaster showed the new students where to do the laundry and dine.
舍監告訴新生們要在哪裡洗衣服和用餐。

lava [`lɑvə] **n.** 熔岩
◀ Track 2846

▶Most of the landscape in this area was ruined by the lava from the volcano. 這個地區大部分的景觀都被火山岩漿給破壞掉了。

lavatory [`lævə,torɪ] =toilet **n.** 廁所
◀ Track 2847

▶The flight attendant cleaned the lavatory an hour ago.
空服員一個小時前有打掃過廁所。

law [lɔ] **n.** 法律;定律
◀ Track 2848

▶Murphy's law, "If something can go wrong, it will," may be believed by people in technical industries.
「只要可能出錯,就會出錯」這個莫非定律,是很多科技產業人相信的事情。

lawful [`lɔfəl] **adj.** 合法的
◀ Track 2849

▶It is not lawful to violate other people's privacy. 侵犯別人隱私權是違法的。

lawn [lɔn] **n.** 草坪
◀ Track 2850

▶Aaron mows the lawn for his neighbor to earn some extra money.
艾倫為鄰居除草來賺點外快。

中級

lawyer [ˋlɔjɚ] n 律師　◀ Track 2851

▶Dereck is a lawyer who always fights for women's right.
德瑞克是一位總是替婦女爭取權利的律師。

lay [le] v 放；鋪設；產卵　◀ Track 2852

▶The salmons swim upstream in the river to lay eggs every year.
每年鮭魚都在這條河流中逆流上游去產卵。

layer [ˋleɚ]　◀ Track 2853
n 層；階層；地層

▶The ozone layer depletion would leave creatures on Earth exposed to harmful radiation emitted by the sun.
臭氧層空洞會導致地球上的生物暴露於太陽的有害輻射。

lazy [ˋlezɪ]　◀ Track 2854
adj 懶惰的；懶洋洋的

▶The sloth moved slowly; it looked quite lazy.
樹懶動作很慢，看起來懶洋洋的。

lead [lid] n 鉛　◀ Track 2855

▶It is said that the color paint of the toy contains lead which may cause harm to children's health.
據說這種玩具的顏料含鉛，會對幼兒的健康造成傷害。

leader [ˋlidɚ]　◀ Track 2856
n 領導者；領袖

▶Karen was elected as the leader of the student association.
凱倫被選為學生會的領導者。

leadership [ˋlidɚʃɪp]　◀ Track 2857
n 領袖特質

▶Mr. Smith showed great leadership when he managed this project.
史密斯先生在管理這項計畫時，展現很好的領導者特質。

leading [ˋlidɪŋ]　◀ Track 2858
adj 領導的；主要的；飾演主角的

▶This company is a leading manufacturer of smartphones in the country.
這間公司在這個國家是智慧型手機的領導性製造商。

相關片語 occupy a leading position 執牛耳地位

▶Foxconn is a Taiwanese semi-conductor manufacturer which occupies the leading position in its industry.
富士康是一間台灣的半導體製造商，在該產業占有龍頭地位。

leaf [lif] n 葉子　◀ Track 2859

▶The leaves of maple trees turn red in autumn.
楓葉在秋天變紅。

leaflet [ˋliflɪt]　◀ Track 2860
n 傳單；單張印刷品

▶Helen took a part time job of distributing leaflets of a local restaurant.
海倫打工，幫一間本地的餐廳發傳單。

league [lig]　◀ Track 2861
n 同盟；聯盟；聯合會

▶Many baseball players dream of playing in the Major League Baseball Games.
許多棒球選手想要去參加大聯盟棒球比賽。

leak [lik] **v** 滲漏；洩漏　◀≡Track 2862

▶The confidential information was leaked by the employee of the company.
這個機密資訊是被自家公司的員工外洩的。

n. 漏洞；裂縫；漏出（水、電、瓦斯等）；（秘密）洩漏

▶The leak of the pipe was fixed within thirty minutes.
這個管線的裂縫在三十分鐘之內就修好了。

lean [lin]　◀≡Track 2863

v 傾斜；傾身；倚靠；依賴

▶It is dangerous to lean against the automatic doors.
倚靠著自動門是很危險的。

adj. 無脂肪的；精瘦的；貧瘠的；收益差的

▶The dish is made of lean meat and vegetables.
這道菜是由瘦肉和蔬菜製成的。

leap [lip]　◀≡Track 2864

v 跳；跳躍；迅速進行；立即著手

▶Look before you leap.
請三思而後行。

n. 跳；跳躍；飛躍；躍進

▶The manufacturing technology has improved by leaps and bounds in the past decade.
製造科技在過去十年快速地躍進。

learn [lɝn] **v** 學習　◀≡Track 2865

▶The student learned to speak three languages in the International School.
這名學生在國際學校學了三種語言。

learned [`lɝnɪd]　◀≡Track 2866

adj. 有學問的；博學的；學術性的；透過學習而獲得的

▶Mr. Han is a learned man; we used to call him a walking library.
韓先生博學多聞。我們以前都稱他為行動圖書館。

learner [`lɝnɚ] **n.** 學習者　◀≡Track 2867

▶The scholar researched about the cognitive process that learners go through when picking up a new language.
學者研究學習者在學習新語言時，會經過什麼認知過程。

learning [`lɝnɪŋ]　◀≡Track 2868

n. 學習；學問；學識

▶A little learning is no better than knowing nothing.
一知半解沒有比什麼都不懂好。

least [list] **adv.** 最少；最不　◀≡Track 2869

▶He is the least popular boy in the class.
他是班上最不受歡迎的男孩子。

adj. 最少的；最不重要的

▶Last but not least, the conference will be postponed to next week.
最後重要的一點是，研討會要延後到下周舉行。

pron. 最少；最少的東西

▶I wouldn't trust anyone in the group, you the least of all.
我不會相信這個團體裡的任何人，尤其是你。

n. 最少；最小

▶She is slow and inefficient, but at least she is meticulous and reliable.
她動作慢沒效率，但至少她謹慎又可靠。

leather [`lɛðɚ]　◀≡Track 2870

n. 皮革；皮革製品

中級

▶These shoes are made of genuine cow leather.
這雙鞋子是真牛皮製作成的。

adj. 皮革製的；皮的

▶Gina spent thirty thousand NT dollars on this leather handbag.
吉娜花了三萬元台幣買這個皮製手提包。

leave [liv] **v.** 離開；留下　◀Track 2871

▶We will leave for New York tomorrow.
我們明天會前往紐約。

n. 休假

▶Tom will be on personal leave tomorrow.
明天湯姆會請事假。

lecture [`lɛktʃɚ]　◀Track 2872

n. 授課；演講；冗長的訓話；告誡；責備

▶The lecture was about the archeological discoveries in a remote town in Russia.
這場演講是關於俄國偏遠小鎮的考古學發現。

v. 演講；講課；教訓；訓斥

▶My mentor lectured me for not following the academic protocol.
我的導師訓斥我沒有遵守學術規範。

lecturer [`lɛktʃərɚ]　◀Track 2873

n. 演講者；講師

▶The lecturer is a veteran engineer who just retired from NASA.
這名講者是才剛從美國國家太空總署退休的工程師。

left [lɛft] **adj.** 左邊的　◀Track 2874

▶The kid is used to writing with his left hand.
這個小孩習慣用左手寫字。

n. 左邊；左側

▶When you get off the bus, you will see the museum on your left.
當你下公車之後，你就會看到博物館在你的左手邊。

adv. 向左地

▶Turn left at the next intersection.
在下個路口右轉。

leg [lɛg] **n.** 腳　◀Track 2875

▶Jeff broke his leg when he fell off the cliff.
傑夫跌下懸崖時摔斷了腿。

legal [`ligl] **adj.** 合法的　◀Track 2876

▶Is it legal to sell medicine online?
線上販售藥品是合法的嗎？

legend [`lɛdʒənd]　◀Track 2877

n. 傳說；傳奇故事；傳奇人物

▶Legend has it that couples who visit this temple together would break up soon.
有傳説來這間廟的情侶都會很快就分手。

legendary
[`lɛdʒəndˌɛrɪ]　◀Track 2878

adj. 傳說的；傳奇的；赫赫有名的

▶Dozens of people lined up to see the legendary dinosaur egg.
許多人排隊要看傳奇的恐龍蛋。

leisure [`liʒɚ]　◀Track 2879

n. 閒暇；空閒時間；悠閒；安逸

▶Helen likes to read popular science books at her leisure.
海倫喜歡在閒暇時間閱讀科學書籍。

adj. 空暇的；有閒的；不以工作為主的

▶The actress was spotted going to the gym without any makeup in her leisure time.
這名女演員被看到在閒暇時素顏上健身房。

leisurely [ˋliʒɚlɪ] ◀Track 2880

adj. 從容不迫的；悠閒的；慢慢的

▶We like have a leisurely dinner after work on Fridays.
我們喜歡在周五下班後悠閒地吃頓晚餐。

adv. 從容不迫地；悠閒地

▶The lady picked flowers leisurely in her garden.
這位女士從容不迫地在她的花園裡摘花。

lemon [ˋlɛmən] **n.** 檸檬 ◀Track 2881

▶Remove the lemon from the pot before the bitter taste of lemon is released into the dish.
在檸檬的苦味釋放到菜餚裡之前，要將其從鍋中取出。

lemonade [ˏlɛmənˋed] ◀Track 2882

n. 檸檬水

▶The kid saved up a fortune by peddling honey lemonade in the tourist spot.
這個小孩靠著在觀光景點叫賣蜂蜜檸檬水而存下一大筆錢。

lend [lɛnd] **v.** 借予；借出 ◀Track 2883

▶Would you lend me a hand?
你可以幫忙我一下嗎？

length [lɛŋθ] ◀Track 2884

n. （距離或時間的）長度

▶You can look up the information of this movie on the website, including the length. 妳可以在這個網站上面查到這部電影的資訊，包括它的長度。

lengthen [ˋlɛŋθən] ◀Track 2885

v. 增長；使變長

▶Do not try to lengthen your speech by adding some unnecessary information.
不要為了增加演講的長度，納進一些沒用的資訊。

lengthy [ˋlɛŋθɪ] ◀Track 2886

adj. 長的；冗長的；囉唆的

▶Mr. Trump's son dozed off during his lengthy speech. 川普先生的兒子在他冗長的演講中間打了瞌睡。

lens [lɛnz] ◀Track 2887

n. 鏡片；鏡頭；透鏡

▶It is important to cleanse your contact lens before wearing it.
仔細清洗隱形眼鏡後再戴上是很重要的。

leopard [ˋlɛpɚd] **n.** 豹 ◀Track 2888

▶Is that giant feline over there a leopard or a jaguar?
那個大型貓科動物是豹還是美洲虎？

less [lɛs] ◀Track 2889

adv. 較少地；不如

▶This lake is very beautiful, but it's less known to the foreign tourists.
這個湖很美，但比較不為外國遊客所知。

adj. 較少的；較小的

▶This machine uses less electricity than that one.
這個機器使用的電力比那個少。

lesson [ˋlɛsn] **n.** 課；教訓 ◀Track 2890

▶The teacher will start a new lesson in the class today.
老師會在今天的課堂開始教新的一課。

let [lɛt] v 使；讓
Track 2891

▶Jane's mother doesn't let her stay at her friend's place overnight.
珍的媽媽不讓她在朋友家過夜。

let's [lɛts]
Track 2892

abbr. 讓我們來……（let us的縮寫）

▶Let's start the concert now.
我們現在開始音樂會吧！

letter [ˋlɛtɚ] n 信
Track 2893

▶Fiona has replied twelve complaint letters this afternoon.
今天下午，費歐娜已經回覆12封抱怨信了。

lettuce [ˋlɛtɪs] n 萵苣
Track 2894

▶Emily bought some lettuce and cabbage to make salad for dinner.
艾蜜莉買一些萵苣和包心菜做晚餐沙拉。

level [ˋlɛv!]
Track 2895

n. 水平面；程度；級別

▶The students were assigned to different classes according to their level of English proficiency.
學生們依照英語程度被分到不同的班級。

adj. 水平的；同高度的；同程度的；平穩冷靜的

▶I think the floor is not level.
我覺得地面有點傾斜。

liar [ˋlaɪɚ] n 說謊的人
Track 2896

▶Never trust a stranger; some liars do look sincere. 別相信陌生人。有些說謊的人看起來很誠懇。

liberal [ˋlɪbərəl]
Track 2897

adj. 心胸寬闊的；開明的；允許變革的，不守舊的；通才教育的

▶David remained liberal when it comes to politics.
講到政治，大衛是保持著開明的態度的。

n. 自由主義者

▶Many of the students in this university are liberals.
這間大學有許多學生是自由主義者。

liberate [ˋlɪbəˌret]
Track 2898

v. 解放；使獲自由

▶The slaves were liberated after the Civil War. 南北戰爭之後，奴隸被解放了。

liberty [ˋlɪbɚtɪ]
Track 2899

n. 自由；自由權；許可；自由活動或使用某物的權利

▶Many tourists came to New York to see the Statue of Liberty.
許多觀光客來到紐約看自由女神像。

librarian [laɪˋbrɛrɪən]
Track 2900

n. 圖書館員

▶The librarian sometimes reads stories for toddlers.
這名圖書館員有時會讀故事給小朋友聽。

library [ˋlaɪˌbrɛrɪ]
Track 2901

n. 圖書館

▶There is an automatic check-out machine in the first floor of the library.
圖書館一樓有一台自動借書機。

license [ˋlaɪsns]
=li·cence （英式英文）
Track 2902

v. 許可；特許；發許可證給

▶This medical intern is not licensed to perform surgeries on patients. 這名實習醫師沒有證照，不能對病人施以手術。

n. 許可；特許；許可證；執照

▶Helen's driver's license was suspended because of drunk driving.
海倫的駕照因為酒駕而吊銷。

----

lick [lɪk] **v.** 舔　　◀€Track 2903

▶The dog licked the baby's cheeks to show its affection to her.
狗狗舔了小寶寶的臉頰，表示對小寶寶的感情。

n. (舔)一口；少許

▶The kids don't have a lick of common sense.
這些小孩一點常識都沒有。

----

lid [lɪd] **n.** 蓋子　　◀€Track 2904

▶Can you open the lid of the jar for me?
你可以幫我打開罐子的蓋子嗎？

----

lie [laɪ] **v.** 躺；說謊；欺騙　　◀€Track 2905

▶Jenny's husband likes to lie on the couch and do nothing on the weekend.
珍妮的老公週末喜歡躺在沙發上耍廢。

n. 謊言

▶Don't tell a lie; I can tell the truth from a story.
別說謊；我分辨得出事實和捏造的故事。

----

life [laɪf]　　◀€Track 2906

n. 生命；性命；生活（狀態）；人生

▶Have you found the purpose of your life?
你有找到人生的目標了嗎？

----

lifetime [ˈlaɪfˌtaɪm]　　◀€Track 2907

n. 一生；終身的

▶This old couple have seen and experienced a lot in their lifetime.
這對老夫婦在他們的一生當中見過許多大風大浪。

相關片語 **the chance of a lifetime**
千載難逢的機會

▶You should go to the concert; don't miss the chance of a lifetime to see your idol in person!
你應該要去演唱會的；別錯過這個千載難逢的機會，去看你的偶像！

----

lift [lɪft]　　◀€Track 2908

v. 舉起；提高；升起

▶The athlete lifted the dumbbells with ease.
運動員輕鬆就舉起了啞鈴。

n. 提；升；振奮；（英）電梯；順便搭載

▶People lined up to take the lift to the top floor.
人們排隊搭電梯去頂樓。

----

light [laɪt] **n.** 燈；光線　　◀€Track 2909

▶There is no light in this room!
這個房間怎麼這麼暗！

v. 照亮；點燃；

▶You light up my life!
你照亮我的生命！

adj. 亮的；淺色的；

▶Do wear light-colored clothes when you go out in the evening.
晚上出門的時候記得要穿淺色的衣服。

adv. 輕便地；少負擔地

▶Tina likes to travel light; she doesn't have a lot of baggage.
蒂娜喜歡輕便地旅行；她沒有很多隨身行李。

lighten [`laɪtn̩]
🔊 Track 2910

v. 變亮、發亮；減輕重量

▶She used a flashlight to lighten the gloomy basement.
她使用一個手電筒照亮晦暗的地下室。

lighthouse
🔊 Track 2911

[`laɪt͵haʊs] **n.** 燈塔

▶The captain steered toward the shore when he saw the lighthouse.
船長看到燈塔的時候就駛向海岸。

lightning [`laɪtnɪŋ]
🔊 Track 2912

n. 閃電

▶The lightning was scary for toddlers.
小朋友覺得閃電很可怕。

like [laɪk]
🔊 Track 2913

prep. 像；如；和……一樣

▶Fiona wants to be a nurse like her mother.
費歐娜想要像她的母親一樣成為一個護士。

v. 喜歡

▶Hank doesn't like the taste of coriander.
漢克不喜歡香菜的味道。

likely [`laɪklɪ]
🔊 Track 2914

adj. 很可能的

▶It is likely that Sarah will give up participating in this contest.
莎拉可能會棄權，不參加比賽。

lily [`lɪlɪ] **n.** 百合；百合花
🔊 Track 2915

▶The fragrance of the lilies is really enchanting.
百合花的香味真的很迷人。

limb [lɪm] **n.** 肢；臂；腳
🔊 Track 2916

▶He has an artificial limb.
他裝有義肢。

相關片語 **out on a limb**
處於困境；處於孤立無援的境地

▶After his failure in starting his own business, he was left out on a limb.
他在創業失敗之後，就陷入困境。

limit [`lɪmɪt] **v.** 限制
🔊 Track 2917

▶Don't limit yourself; make a breakthrough!
不要設限，自我突破吧！

n. 限制；界限；限度

▶There is a ninety-minute dining time limit in this reataurant.
這家餐廳限制用餐90分鐘。

limitation
🔊 Track 2918

[͵lɪmə`teʃən] **n.** 限制；限制因素；侷限

▶There is no limitation on the topics of the final report; you can write about any topic that you like.
期末報告的主題沒有限制，你可以寫任何你想要寫的主題。

limp [lɪmp]
🔊 Track 2919

v. 一瘸一拐地走；跛行

▶The driver limped to the hospital after the accident.
車禍之後，駕駛自己跛行走到醫院去。

line [laɪn]
🔊 Track 2920

n. 線；排；路線；行列

▶I was astonished to see the long line in front of the local deli.
看到地方小吃店外面這麼多人排隊，我感到很驚訝。

v 排隊

▶The students were asked to line up before entering the auditorium.
學生們被要求進禮堂之前先排成一列。

linen [ˋlɪnən]
🔊 Track 2921
n 亞麻布；亞麻布製品

▶This outfit for babies is made of linen.
這件給小寶寶的衣服是亞麻布做的。

相關片語 **dirty linen** 家醜

▶Don't wash your dirty linen in the public.
家醜不要外揚。

link [lɪŋk] n 環節；連結
🔊 Track 2922

▶For more information, please click the link below.
如需更多資訊，請點下列的連結。

v 結合；連接；勾住

▶Are these two projects linked to each other?
這兩個專案是互相關聯的嗎？

lion [ˋlaɪən] n 獅子
🔊 Track 2923

▶The lion in the cage looks quite depressed.
關在籠子裡的獅子看起來很悶。

lip [lɪp] n 嘴唇
🔊 Track 2924

▶Use some lip balm; it will make your complexion better.
請用一些唇蜜；它會讓你看起來氣色更好。

lipstick [ˋlɪpˏstɪk]
🔊 Track 2925
n 口紅

▶She never goes out without wearing any make-up or lipstick.
她從來不會沒化妝、沒擦口紅就出門。

liquid [ˋlɪkwɪd] n 液體
🔊 Track 2926

▶Wendy was shocked when someone splashed unknown liquid at her.
有人向溫蒂潑灑不明液體時，她整個花容失色。

adj 液體的；流動的

▶You can add some water to make the paint more liquid
你可以加一點水讓油漆變得液體一點。

liquor [ˋlɪkɚ]
🔊 Track 2927
=spir·its （英式英文）
n 含酒精飲料

▶Students under eighteen are not allowed to purchase liquor in the store.
十八歲以下的學生不能在商店裡買酒。

list [lɪst] n 名冊；清單
🔊 Track 2928

▶Pearl couldn't find the strange woman one the guest list; it turned out that she just showed up at the wrong venue.
寶兒在賓客名單上面找不到這個女士的名字；結果是她跑錯場了。

v 列舉

▶The teacher listed some forms of clouds as examples.
老師列出一些雲的形態作為例子。

listen [ˋlɪsn] v 聽
🔊 Track 2929

▶The kids have a habit of listening to classical music in the morning.
孩子們有早晨聽古典音樂的習慣。

中級

listener [`lɪsnə]
🔊 Track 2930

n. 聆聽者

▶ You best friend will be a good listener and a shoulder to cry on.
你最好的朋友會是你最好的聽眾，也是安慰你的人。

liter [`litə]
🔊 Track 2931

=litre （英式英文） n. 公升

▶ It takes about twenty liters of water to flush the toilet once.
沖一次馬桶大約會用掉20公升的水。

literary [`lɪtəˌrɛrɪ]
🔊 Track 2932

adj. 文學的

▶ The professor will spend a few sessions to talk about the literary theories.
教授會花幾節課的時間介紹文學理論。

literature [`lɪtərətʃə]
🔊 Track 2933

n. 文學

▶ Students in this department will study about American literature and linguistics.
這個系的學生會學習美國文學和語言學。

litter [`lɪtə]
🔊 Track 2934

n. 垃圾；廢棄物；雜亂

▶ Gary's mother was upset when she saw his room in a litter.
蓋瑞的媽媽看到他房間一團亂，很不開心。

v. 把……弄得亂七八糟；亂丟（雜物或廢棄物）

▶ The sign says "Do not litter."
標語上寫「請勿亂丟垃圾」。

little [`lɪtl̩]
🔊 Track 2935

adj. 小的；少的；年幼的

▶ When I was little, I like to watch airplanes taking off and landing at the airport.
我小的時候喜歡在機場看飛機起降。

adv. 少；毫不

▶ She is a little drunk; let's send her home. 她有點喝醉；我們送她回家吧。

live [lɪv]
🔊 Track 2936

adj. 活的；實況的；即時的；現場的

▶ She sells things through live streaming on the Internet to make money.
她透過網路直播賣東西來賺錢。

lively [`laɪvlɪ]
🔊 Track 2937

adj. 精力充沛的；愉快的

▶ Mr. Tomson is a lively instructor; students love his class.
湯森先生是一位活力充沛的講師；學生們都喜歡他的課程。

liver [`lɪvə] n. 肝；肝臟
🔊 Track 2938

▶ Human beings can not live without livers.
人類沒有肝臟便不能存活。

補充片語 terminal liver cancer
末期肝癌

▶ He lost a lot of weight, for he suffered a great deal from the terminal liver cancer.
他因為末期肝癌受苦而瘦了不少。

lizard [`lɪzəd]
🔊 Track 2939

n. 蜥蜴；類蜥蜴爬行動物

▶ Can you tell the difference between a lizard and a salamander?
你能分辨蜥蜴和蠑螈的差別嗎？

load [lod] n. 裝載；重擔；裝載量；（一車或一船）貨物；工作量
🔊 Track 2940

▶ The maximum load of this newly-built bridge is 100 people.
這座新橋的最大乘載人數是一百人。

相關片語 **be a load off one's mind**
使如釋重負

▶ Finally completing the project is a load off my mind.
終於完成計畫，使我如釋重負。

v. 裝載；裝貨；（把彈藥）裝入；使充滿；大量給予

▶ The truck was loaded with books that will be donated to kids in the remote area.
卡車裝滿了要捐贈給偏遠地區小朋友的書籍。

loaf [lof] n. 一條
🔊 Track 2941

▶ Sean Van Jean was sentenced to prison, for he stole a loaf of bread.
尚萬強因為偷了一條麵包而入監服刑。

loan [lon] n. 借出；貸款
🔊 Track 2942

▶ Brian mortgaged the car to apply for a loan from the bank.
布萊恩抵押車子向銀行貸款。

v. 借出；貸與

▶ The bank loaned our company three million dollars.
銀行貸款給我們公司三百萬元。

lobby [`labɪ]
🔊 Track 2943

n. 門廊；大廳

▶ The tour guide asks us to meet in the lobby after putting our luggage in the room.
導遊要我們把行李放進房間之後到大廳集合。

lobster [`labstɚ] n. 龍蝦
🔊 Track 2944

▶ The lobster was freshly caught from the bay this morning.
這隻龍蝦是今天早上才在海灣裡面抓到的，相當新鮮。

local [`lokl]
🔊 Track 2945

adj. 地方性的；當地的；本地的

▶ The local government asked residents in the low land to evacuate after the torrential rain. 大雨之後，當地政府要求低窪地區的居民撤離。

n. 當地居民；本地人

▶ Let's ask the locals for directions.
我們向當地人問路好了。

locate [lo`ket]
🔊 Track 2946

v. 使⋯⋯座落於；找出⋯⋯所在位置；定居

▶ It's quite easy to locate the department store; it's in the tallest building in the downtown area.
要找到這間百貨公司很容易；它就在市中心最高的建築物裡。

location [lo`keʃən]
🔊 Track 2947

n. 位置；場所；所在地

▶ The location of the exhibition will be announced on the official website.
展覽的位置會公告在官方網站上面。

lock [lɑk] v. 鎖；鎖住
🔊 Track 2948

▶ Remember to lock the door before you leave.
你離開之前記得要鎖門喔。

n. 鎖

▶ The electronic lock is said to be unbreakable
這個電子鎖據説是無法被破壞的。

中級

locker [`lɑkɚ] **n.** 衣物櫃 🔊 Track 2949
▶The bully left some mean messages with paint in David's locker.
惡棍用噴漆在大衛的衣物櫃裡面留下一些惡意的訊息。

lodge [lɑdʒ] 🔊 Track 2950
n. 守衛室；旅社；山林小屋
▶The small room in the lodge made the guard with claustrophobia feel uncomfortable.
守衛室裡的狹小空間讓有幽閉恐懼症的守衛感到很不舒服。

v. 供……臨時住所；租房間給……住；暫住；投宿
▶Is it convenient for you to lodge us for a night?
你方便讓我們住宿一宿嗎？

log [lɔg] **n.** 原木；木料 🔊 Track 2951
▶The coffee table made of log is my favorite piece of furniture in the living room.
原木咖啡桌是客廳裡我最喜歡的一件家具。

v. 伐木；採伐林木
▶Some people were caught logging illegally in the forest.
有一些人被抓到在森林裡違法伐木。

logic [`lɑdʒɪk] 🔊 Track 2952
n. 邏輯；道理；理由
▶The communist's speech was completely out of logic.
這位共產主義者的演說完全沒有邏輯可言。

logical [`lɑdʒɪkl̩] 🔊 Track 2953
adj. 合邏輯的；合理的；（邏輯上）當然的、必然的

▶It is logical that she would turn down your request.
按理說，她應該會拒絕你的要求。

logo [`logo] **n.** 標識 🔊 Track 2954
▶The logo of the product was designed by a student in the art school. 這個標語是在藝術學校就讀的學生所設計的。

lollipop [`lɑlɪ͵pɑp] 🔊 Track 2955
n. 棒棒糖
▶The old man in the suit of Santa gave the toddler a lollipop.
穿著聖誕老人裝的老人給了這名小孩一個棒棒糖。

London [`lʌndən] 🔊 Track 2956
n. 倫敦
▶Tina's dream is to study visual arts in London. 緹娜的夢想是到倫敦學視覺藝術。

lone [lon] 🔊 Track 2957
adj. 孤單的；無伴的；單一的
▶Being lone is not good for the elderly woman's health.
孤獨一人對於這位老太太的健康有害。

loneliness [`lonlɪnɪs] 🔊 Track 2958
n. 孤獨；寂寞
▶Mr. Robinson felt his loneliness most keenly on holidays.
羅賓森先生每到假日就感到特別寂寞。

lonely [`lonlɪ] 🔊 Track 2959
adj. 孤單的；寂寞的
▶Tony sometimes felt lonely when he studied abroad.
東尼在國外留學，有時會感到寂寞。

long [lɔŋ] v 期盼；渴望　◀ Track 2960

▶He longed for some company when he traveled abroad alone. 他獨自一人到國外旅行時，很希望有人陪伴。

longing [ˈlɔŋɪŋ] n 渴望　◀ Track 2961

▶The kid gazed at the biscuit with longing.
這名小朋友帶著渴望看著那個餅乾。

long-term [ˈlɔŋˌtɝm] ◀ Track 2962
adj. 長期的

▶We plan to build a long-term cooperative relationship with your company.
我們計畫能和貴公司建立長期的企業關係。

look [lʊk] ◀ Track 2963
v 看；看著；看起來

▶Why does he look so nervous?
他為什麼看起來這麼緊張？

n 看；臉色；外表；面容

▶She said something inappropriate, so the other employees gave her funny looks.
她說了不恰當的話，所以其他的員工用奇怪的表情看著她。

loop [lup] ◀ Track 2964
n 圈，環，環狀物；環路，環線

▶My grandmother made three loops of ribbons as an amulet for me. 我的外婆將緞帶繞成三圈，送給我當作護身符。

相關片語 out of the loop 不清楚狀況

▶She felt isolated, for she was out of the loop when her colleagues were chatting about institutional affairs.
當同事們在討論機構事務時，她因進入不了狀況而感到孤立。

v 打成環，使成圈；用環扣住；纏繞；使（飛機）翻筋斗

▶The witness saw the plane loopping in the air before it crashed nearby.
目擊者看到飛機在空中盤旋，然後墜毀在這附近。

loose [lus] adj. 鬆的　◀ Track 2965

▶The nails in the wall have gone loose over the passage of time.
牆上的釘子隨時間流逝變鬆了。

相關片語 at loose ends
無事可做；不知做什麼好

▶The school instructor asked the students who were at loose ends to help him tidy up the garden on campus.
學校的教官叫一些無所事事的學生來幫他整理校園的花圃。

loosen [ˈlusn̩] ◀ Track 2966
v 解開；鬆開；放鬆（限制）

▶The man loosened his tie when he got home, and made himself a nice cup of hot tea.
男子在回家後鬆開領帶，並替自己泡了一杯不錯的熱茶。

相關片語 loosen one's tongue
使某人鬆口；使人無拘束地說話

▶A cup of wine loosened his tongue; he revealed some confidential information of his company to me.
一杯酒就讓他鬆口了；他告訴了我一些他們公司的機密資訊。

lord [lɔrd] n 統治者；君王 ◀ Track 2967

▶Anciant lords usually demand absolue obedience from their people.
古代的君王通常都會要求百姓的絕對服從。

中級

相關片語 **as drunk as a lord** 酩酊大醉

▶Teddy was as drunk as a lord; he couldn't even walk in a straight line.
泰迪喝的酩酊大醉；他甚至無法好好地走路。

lorry [ˋlɔrɪ] ◀Track 2968
=truck （美式英文）
n. 卡車；運貨車

▶Gary makes a living by driving a lorry to deliver goods for big manufacturers.
蓋瑞開大卡車替大型製造商送貨，藉以維生。

lose [luz] ◀Track 2969
v. 丟；失去；輸掉；損失

▶Hank lost about one million dollars on the stock market.
漢克在股票市場輸掉一百萬元左右。

loser [ˋluzɚ] ◀Track 2970
n. 失敗者；失主

▶David was upset when the bullies called him a "loser" or an "underdog."
大衛聽到小惡霸叫他「失敗者」和「輸家」，覺得很不開心。

loss [lɔs] n. 損失；喪失 ◀Track 2971

▶We express condolence for your loss.
我們為您痛失親人表達哀痛。

lot [lɑt] n. 很多；一塊地 ◀Track 2972

▶There is a parking lot in front of the office building.
這棟大樓前面有一個停車場。

adv. 很多地；非常

▶Thanks a lot! 非常謝謝！

lotion [ˋloʃən] ◀Track 2973
n. 乳液（霜）；塗劑；護膚液

▶Apply some suntan lotion. It can protect your skin from the harmful radiations in the sunlight.
擦一些防曬霜吧。它可以保護你的皮膚不受太陽光中的有害輻射傷害。

loud [laʊd] adj. 大聲的 ◀Track 2974

▶Don't be so loud; you may wake the sleeping baby!
不要這麼大聲；你可能會吵醒小寶寶！

adv. 大聲地

▶Speak out loud so that the audience can hear you clearly.
大聲一點，觀眾才能聽見你說什麼。

loudspeaker ◀Track 2975
[ˋlaʊdˋspikɚ] n. 擴聲器；揚聲器；喇叭

▶The cheerleaders used a loudspeaker to cheer the players on their team.
啦啦隊成員用擴音器幫隊上的選手加油。

lounge [laʊndʒ] ◀Track 2976
v. 懶洋洋地倚靠；懶散地消磨時間；閒蕩

▶Some tourists lounged at the outdoor seats of the café.
有些觀光客在這家咖啡廳的室外座位休息。

n. 閒蕩；（飯店、旅館的）休息室、會客廳；（機場的）候機室；客廳

▶Mr. Chang told his assistant to wait for him at the lounge room of the hotel. 張先生要他的助理在飯店的休息室等他。

lousy [ˋlaʊzɪ] adj. 糟透的 ◀Track 2977

▶The professor said the report was lousy and asked the student to reorganize it. 教授說這份報告寫得爛透了，要學生重新組織一次。

love [lʌv] **v** 愛；喜好　◀Track 2978

▶Helen wrote her son a letter to tell him how much she loved him.
海倫寫了一封信給兒子，告訴他，她有多愛他。

n. 愛

▶His love for photography gave him the courage to explore unknown places to shoot beautiful pictures.
他對攝影的愛，讓他有勇氣去未知的地方探索，以拍攝美麗的照片。

lovely [`lʌvlɪ]　◀Track 2979
adj. 可愛的；令人愉快的；美好的

▶This is a lovely party! Everyone is having a good time.
這是一個很美好的派對！每個人都玩得很開心。

lover [`lʌvɚ]　◀Track 2980
n. 戀人；情人（尤指男性）；愛好者

▶Diana is a lover of books; she has a collection of books regarding different fields.
黛安娜是書的愛好者；她蒐集了各種不同主題的書籍。

low [lo]　◀Track 2981
adj. 低的；低調的；情緒低落的

▶My supervisor asked me to keep a low profile.
我的主管要我行事低調。

lower [`loɚ]　◀Track 2982
v. 放下；降低

▶This exercise can help you lower your body fat percentage.
這種運動可以幫助你降低體脂率。

loyal [`lɔɪəl]　◀Track 2983
adj. 忠誠的；忠心的

▶Gary vowed to be loyal to the leader of the nation.
蓋瑞發誓要對國家領導人效忠。

loyalty [`lɔɪəltɪ]　◀Track 2984
n. 忠誠；忠心

▶To show his loyalty to his wife, Ryan vowed that he will never conceal anything to her.
為了表示對妻子的忠誠，萊恩發誓不會對她隱瞞任何事情。

luck [lʌk] **n.** 運氣；好運　◀Track 2985

▶The athlete prayed for good luck before he attended the competition.
這名選手參賽前為自己祈求好運。

luckily [`lʌkɪlɪ]　◀Track 2986
adv. 幸運地

▶The car was hit by a falling rock, but luckily, the driver wasn't hurt. 這台車被落石擊中，但幸運地，駕駛沒有受傷。

lucky [`lʌkɪ]　◀Track 2987
adj. 幸運的

▶Yellow is a lucky color for Leo today.
今天獅子座的幸運顏色是黃色。

luggage [`lʌgɪdʒ]　◀Track 2988
n. 行李

▶Jerry waited at the carousel to pick up his luggage.
傑瑞在行李轉盤那邊等著領行李。

lullaby [`lʌlə͵baɪ]　◀Track 2989
n. 催眠曲；搖籃曲

中級

▶She hummed a lullaby for her baby.
她輕輕哼搖籃曲給寶寶聽。

v. 唱搖籃曲使入睡

▶Tina lullabied her baby to sleep every night.
緹娜每天晚上唱搖籃曲哄寶寶入睡。

lunar [`lunɚ]　◀Track 2990
adj. 月球上的；月的；按月球的運轉測定的；陰曆的

▶Chinese Valentine's Day is on the 7th day of the 7th Chinese lunar month.
七夕情人節是在農曆的七月七日。

lunch [lʌntʃ] n. 午餐　◀Track 2991

▶Hank is so busy with his work that he sometimes skips lunch.
漢克有時候會忙到沒空吃午餐。

lung [lʌŋ] n. 肺，肺臟　◀Track 2992

▶Overexposure to secondhand smoke may result in damaged lungs in people who don't smoke.
過度暴露於二手菸可能會讓不抽菸的人的肺遭受損害。

相關片語 **at the top of one's lungs**
聲嘶力竭地

▶The girl cried for help at the top of her lung.
那個女孩聲嘶力竭地喊救命。

luxurious [lʌgˈʒʊrɪəs]　◀Track 2993
adj. 奢侈的

▶The retired baseball player led a luxurious life and spent all his savings.
退休的棒球員過著奢侈的生活，花光了積蓄。

luxury [`lʌkʃərɪ] n. 奢侈　◀Track 2994

▶David had been living in luxury since he hit the jackpot and won a huge sum of prize money.
大衛贏得頭獎彩金後，就過著奢侈的生活。

lychee [`laɪtʃi]　◀Track 2995
=litchi n. 荔枝

▶The popsicles come in different flavors such as lychee, pineapple, and strawberry.
這個冰棒有不同的口味，包括荔枝、鳳梨、草莓。

lyric [`lɪrɪk] adj. 抒情的　◀Track 2996

▶The lyric poem was composed by a British poet.
這首抒情詩是由一位英國詩人創作的。

n. 抒情作品；歌詞

▶The lyricist expressed his love to his wife in the lyrics.
這個作詞者在歌詞中表達對他妻子的愛。

▶ **Mm**

　　以下表格是全民英檢官方公告中級「聽、說、讀、寫」所須具備的能力，本書例句皆依此範疇特別設計，只要掃描右方QR code，就能搭配相對應的音軌實現「眼耳並用」方式，刺激左腦的語言學習功能；同時也可使用本書附贈的紅膠片，將其置於單字上，一面記憶一面自我挑戰，達到雙倍的學習成果！

聽 ▶	在日常生活中，能聽懂一般的會話；能大致聽懂公共場所廣播、氣象報告及廣告等。在工作時，能聽懂簡易的產品介紹與操作說明。能大致聽懂外籍人士的談話及詢問。
說 ▶	可在日常生活中，能以簡易英語交談或描述一般事物，能介紹自己的生活作息、工作、家庭、經歷等，並可對一般話題陳述看法。在工作時，能進行簡單的答詢，並與外籍人士交談溝通。
讀 ▶	在日常生活中，能閱讀短文、故事、私人信件、廣告、傳單、簡介及使用說明等。在工作時，能閱讀工作須知、公告、操作手冊、例行的文件、傳真、電報等。
寫 ▶	能寫簡單的書信、故事及心得等。對於熟悉且與個人經歷相關的主題，能以簡易的文字表達。

中級

ma'am [`mæəm]　◀ Track 2997

n. 閣下；女士（對女性的禮貌稱謂）

▶ What would you like to order, ma'am?
女士，您要點什麼菜呢？

machine [mə`ʃin]　◀ Track 2998

n. 機器

▶ This article is about how machine learning is used in the development of search engine.
這篇文章是關於機械學習是如何應用在發展搜尋引擎上的。

machinery [mə`ʃinərɪ]　◀ Track 2999

n. 機器；機械系統

▶ The packaging is completed by machinery rather than manual labor.
包裝都是透過機械進行，而非人工。

mad [mæd]　◀ Track 3000

adj. 發狂的；惱火的

▶ Calm down! Don't be so mad.
冷靜下來！別那麼生氣。

madam [`mædəm]　◀ Track 3001

n. （對婦女的恭敬稱呼）夫人，太太，小姐

▶ As you wish, madam. 悉聽尊便，夫人。

magazine [ˌmægə`zin]　◀ Track 3002

n. 雜誌

▶ Fiona is a subscriber of this famous fashion magazine.
費歐娜是這個知名時尚雜誌的訂閱者。

magic [`mædʒɪk]　◀ Track 3003

adj. 魔術的；有魔力的；不可思議的

▶ Edward likes to do magic tricks to entertain his guests.
愛德華喜歡變魔術來娛樂自己的客人。

n 魔法;巫術;神奇的力量

▶When the car touches water, it changes into a boat like magic. 這台車碰到水就成為一艘船,就像魔法一樣。

magical [`mædʒɪkl]
◀Track 3004

adj. 魔術的,有魔力的,用魔法的;迷人的

▶The concert was a fantastic and magical show that is unforgettable to everyone who attended it.
這場演唱會是一場精彩又迷人的表演,令所有觀眾難忘。

magician [mə`dʒɪʃən]
◀Track 3005

n 魔術師

▶The magician pulled out a rabbit from his hat, which stunned the kids in the audience. 魔術師從帽子裡拉出一隻兔子,讓觀眾裡的小朋友嚇了一跳。

magnet [`mægnɪt]
◀Track 3006

n 磁鐵;磁石;有吸引力的人或物

▶Hollywood has always been a magnet for young actors. 好萊塢一直以來都像磁鐵般吸引著年輕的演員們。

相關片語 **gossip magnet**
話題人物;焦點話題

▶The private life of the actor's son somehow became a gossip magnet.
這名演員兒子的私生活,不知為何成為焦點話題。

magnetic [mæg`nɛtɪk]
◀Track 3007

adj. 磁鐵的;有磁性的;有吸引力的;有魅力的

▶Gina is magnetic to kids; she seems to be kind and attractive to toddlers.
吉娜對小朋友很有吸引力;她似乎在小朋友眼中很和善、很有吸引力。

magnificent
◀Track 3008

[mæg`nɪfəsənt] **adj.** 壯麗的;宏偉的;華麗的

▶The tourists looked in awe at the magnificent pyramid.
遊客們帶著敬畏神情看著宏偉的金字塔。

maid [med]
◀Track 3009

n 少女,未婚女子;侍女,女僕

▶The rich man hired several maids to clean his grand mansion. 這位有錢人請了好幾位女傭來打掃他的豪宅。

相關片語 **old maid** 老處女

▶The unmarried woman was upset when she was called an old maid by her neighbor. 這名未婚的女人被鄰居說是老處女,很不開心。

mail [mel] **n** 郵件
◀Track 3010

▶I sent the document to my client by registered mail. 我用掛號把文件寄給客戶。

v. 郵寄

▶The staff of the train station mailed me the Mi bracelet that I left on the train. 火車站的工作人員幫我把我遺留在火車上的小米手環寄還給我。

mailman [`mel͵mæn]
◀Track 3011

=postman **n** 郵差

▶The mailmen were requested to wear the uniform when they are on duty.
郵差被要求在上班時穿著制服。

main [men] **adj.** 主要的
◀Track 3012

▶The main entrance is being renovated, so we entered the building through the side door. 主要入口正在整修,所以我們從側門進入大樓。

mainland [`menlənd] ◄Track 3013
n. 大陸；本土

▶Mr. Coney came to the mainland and established his own pertolium company. 康尼先生來到本土大陸，並建立一家石油公司。

mainly [`menlɪ] ◄Track 3014
adv. 主要地

▶The speech is mainly about the struggle of the immigrants in the U.S. 這部電影主要在講述居住在美國的移民者的辛苦之處。

maintain [men`ten] ◄Track 3015
v. 維持；維修；保養；繼續

▶The machine costs thirty thousand dollars to maintain its function every year. 這台機器每年需要花三萬元來保養。

majestic [mə`dʒɛstɪk] ◄Track 3016
adj. 雄偉的；壯觀的；莊嚴的；威嚴的

▶The Great Wall in China is such a majestic architecture that it attracts millions of visitors each year.
長城是如此宏偉的一座建築，每年吸引數百萬遊客來參觀。

major [`medʒɚ] ◄Track 3017
adj. 主要的；較多的；主修的；重要的

▶How to support yourself financially is a major issue.
要如何養活你自己是重要的客題。

n. 主修科目；主修學生

▶Hank has double majors: Chemistry and Electronics.
漢克主修兩個學科：化學和電子學。

v. 主修

▶I majored in American Literature in university.
我大學時主修美國文學。

majority [mə`dʒɔrətɪ] ◄Track 3018
n. 多數；過半數；大多數

▶The majority of the residents in this city are of the middle class.
這個城市的居民主要屬於中產階級。

make [mek] ◄Track 3019
v. 做；製造；使

▶The video shows how to make a quiche at home.
這支影片教導如何在家製作法式鹹派。

maker [`mekɚ] ◄Track 3020
n. 製作者；製造廠；製造業者

▶The maker of the down jacket is located in mainland China.
這件羽絨衣的製造商位在大陸。

make-up [`mek͵ʌp] ◄Track 3021
n. 構成；化妝；補考

▶Jerry has to take the make-up test, for he got a very low score in the final exam.
傑瑞期末考分數太低，所以得要去參加補考。

male [mel] ◄Track 3022
adj. 男性的；雄的；公的；**n.** 男子；雄性動物

▶It is said that male penguins would spend about two months to hatch the eggs.
據説雄性的企鵝會花兩個月的時間來孵蛋。

mall [mɔl] ◄Track 3023
n. 大規模購物中心

中級

▶Helen often drives to the mall and shops for groceries.
海倫常會開車到購物中心去採購日用品。

mammal [`mæml] ◀Track 3024

n. 哺乳動物

▶Platypus a kind of mammal that lays eggs. 鴨嘴獸是一種會下蛋的哺乳動物。

man [mæn] ◀Track 3025

n. （成年的）男人；人

▶Take the responsibility. You are a grown-up man. 負起責任來。你是大人了。

manage [`mænɪdʒ] ◀Track 3026

v. 管理；經營；駕馭；設法做到

▶Ivanka managed the affairs of the election campaign for her father.
伊凡卡為父親處理參選的事宜。

manageable ◀Track 3027
[`mænɪdʒəbl]

adj. 易辦的；可管理的；可控制的

▶The updated system is more manageable than the old one.
升級過後的系統比舊的版本好管理多了。

management ◀Track 3028
[`mænɪdʒmənt] **n.** 管理；經營

▶Vicky's positive personality is helpful in class management.
維琪正向的性格對班級經營很有幫助。

manager [`mænɪdʒə] ◀Track 3029

n. 商店，公司等的）負責人；主任，經理

▶He was promoted as the regional manager last month.
他上個晉升為區經理。

Mandarin [`mændərɪn] ◀Track 3030

n. 中文

▶Kevin went to Beijing to study Mandarin.
凱文到北京學習中文。

mango [`mæŋgo] **n.** 芒果 ◀Track 3031

▶We had a shaved ice with mango jelly for dessert.
我們吃刨冰配芒果果凍當點心。

mankind [`mæn͵kaɪnd] ◀Track 3032

n. 人類；男人；男子

▶It is said that mankind would be doomed if the asteroid hits the Earth.
據說這個小行星如果撞擊地球的話，人類就會滅絕。

man-made ◀Track 3033
[`mæn͵med] **adj.** 人造的；人工的；人為的

▶Numerous man-made satellites have been launched in the past two decades.
過去二十年來，有很多人造衛星被發射出去。

manner [`mænə] ◀Track 3034

n. 態度；方式；禮貌；舉止

▶The tourists strolled down the street in a leisurely manner.
這群觀光客用緩慢的步調走過街道。

mansion [`mænʃən] ◀Track 3035

n. 大廈；大樓；公寓；公寓大樓

▶After divorce, my mother still ran into my father a lot because they live in the same mansion.
雖然離婚了，我的母親還是很常碰到我的父親，因為他們仍住在同一棟公寓。

補充片語 **run into** 偶然碰到

manual [ˋmænjʊəl]　◀﹦Track 3036

n. 手冊，簡介

▶ The manual offers detailed instructions about how to operate the machine.
手冊中提供這台機器操作方法的詳細說明。

adj. 手的；手工的；用手操作的；用體力的

▶ This manuel television is quite vintage and exquisite.
這個手動電視相當復古精緻。

manufacture　◀﹦Track 3037

[ˌmænjəˋfæktʃə] **v.** 製造

▶ The company had an outsourcing contractor to manufacture the electronic gadget. 這家公司請外包的廠商大量生產這個電子產品。

n. 製造；製造業；製品

▶ The company has engaged in the manufacture of handsets for more than a decade.
這家公司製造手機已經超過十年了。

manufacturer　◀﹦Track 3038

[ˌmænjəˋfæktʃərə] **n.** 製造業者；廠商

▶ The manufacturer was accused of being negligent in product inspections.
這家製造商被指控說品檢不夠仔細。

many [ˋmɛnɪ]　◀﹦Track 3039

adj. 很多的；許多的

▶ Many people came to return the formula after they heard about the scandal of heavy metal contamination.
許多人聽說了重金屬汙染的醜聞之後，便前來將奶粉退貨。

pron. 許多人；很多

▶ Some of the volunteers in this organization didn't say a word, but many were unsatisfied with the way the leader dealt with the donation.
有些在這個組織裡的志工沒有表達意見，但是許多對於領導者處理善款的方式很不滿。

map [mæp] **n.** 地圖　◀﹦Track 3040

▶ The tourist carried a camera and had a map in his hands, which shows to everyone that he is not familiar with this town.
這位遊客帶著相機，手上拿著地圖，很明顯就是對這個城鎮不熟的。

maple [ˋmepl] **n.** 楓樹　◀﹦Track 3041

▶ In this tour, you can experience collecting the maple syrup. 這個旅行中，你可以體驗自己採集楓樹糖漿。

marathon　◀﹦Track 3042

[ˋmærəˌθɑn] **n.** 馬拉松賽跑

▶ There are several booths along the road which provides water supplies for the marathon runners.
沿途有好幾個亭子會提供水給馬拉松跑者。

marble [ˋmɑrbl]　◀﹦Track 3043

n. 大理石

▶ The sculptor carved a statue of Guanyin out of the marble.
雕刻師傅用大理石雕刻出一個觀音雕像。

march [mɑrtʃ]　◀﹦Track 3044

v. 前進；行軍

▶ The troop marched for miles to the front line of the battle.
軍隊走了好幾英里到達戰場的前線。

中級

n 行軍，行進；進行曲

▶The march in Paris was a massive protest against the rise in fuel tax.
在巴黎的遊行是針對燃料稅上漲的大型抗議活動。

相關片語 **steal a march on sb./sth.**
搶在某人或某事之前

▶They planned to steal a march on their rivals by releasing the new product before the New Year.
他們計畫搶在對手之前，在新年之前發行新產品。

margin [`mɑrdʒɪn] Track 3045

n 邊，邊緣；頁邊空白；極限；餘地

▶You can write down your notes on the blank margin of the paper.
你可以在紙上的白色邊緣。

相關片語 **by a narrow margin** 勉強

▶The sprinter won the race by a narrow margin.
這名短跑選手以些許之差贏得賽跑。

mark [mɑrk] Track 3046

v 做記號；打分數

▶Mark my words, or you will regret later.
記住我的話，不然你之後會後悔的。

n 記號；符號

▶Follow the mark on the floor, and you will find the venue of the conference.
跟著地上的標記，就可以找到研討會的會場了。

marker [mɑrkɚ] Track 3047

n 記號筆；馬克筆

▶Rita highlighted the key words on the page with a marker.
瑞塔用馬克筆把書頁上的重點字做記號。

market [`mɑrkɪt] Track 3048

n 市場；股票市場

▶This is the latest version of smartphone on the market.
這是市場最新版本的智慧型手機。

v 在市場上銷售

▶The company markets various office supplies. 這家公司銷售各種辦公室用品。

marriage [`mærɪdʒ] Track 3049

n 婚姻；婚姻生活

▶George's marriage didn't last long. He got divorced within a year.
喬治的婚姻沒有持續很久。他一年之內就離婚了。

married [`mærɪd] Track 3050

adj 已婚的；婚姻的

▶Frank and Nina have been married for more than thirty years.
法蘭克和妮娜已經結婚超過三十年了。

marry [`mærɪ] Track 3051

v 嫁；娶；和……結婚；嫁女兒

▶Marry in hast, repent at leisure.
匆匆結婚，慢慢後悔。

marvelous [`mɑrvələs] Track 3052
=marvellous（英式英文）

adj 令人驚歎的；極好的

▶May gave a marvelous performance on the New Year's Eve Party.
梅伊在跨年派對上有令人驚嘆的表演。

mask [mæsk] Track 3053

n 面具；口罩

▶The PM 2.5 reading is quite high today, so you had better wear a mask when you go out today.
懸浮粒子的指數偏高，所以今天你出門的時候記得戴口罩。

mass [mæs] ◀Track 3054
n. 團；塊；大量

▶There was a mass of earthworms in the yard after the rain.
下雨之後，院子裡有很多蚯蚓。

adj. 大眾的

▶The mass media is a strong force in terms of influencing the public's view on controversial issues.
大眾媒體對人們看待爭議議題的方式影響很大。

massage [mə`sɑʒ] ◀Track 3055
n. 按摩，推拿

▶Having a full body massage can help you to release stress.
去做全身按摩可以幫助你紓解壓力。

v. 給……按摩，為……推拿

▶I often massage my mother's shoulders after she comes home from work.
我媽下班回家之後，我常會幫她按摩肩膀。

massive [`mæsɪv] ◀Track 3056
adj. 大而重的；厚實的；魁偉的；大量的，大規模的

▶The tsunami caused massive destruction in the seashore town.
海嘯大規模摧毀了這個海邊的小鎮。

master [`mæstɚ] n. 主人 ◀Track 3057

▶The shepherd dog can understand every command of its master.
這隻牧羊犬可以聽得懂她主人的所有指令。

masterpiece [`mæstɚ,pis] n. 傑作；名作 ◀Track 3058

▶The Persistence of Memory is a masterpiece of Salvador Dali.
時間靜止是達利的傑作。

mat [mæt] n. 草蓆 ◀Track 3059

▶The monk sat on the mat and meditated.
和尚坐在草蓆上靜思。

match [mætʃ] ◀Track 3060
n. 火柴；配對

▶The match didn't work due to the moisture in the air.
因為空氣中的濕氣，火柴點不著。

v. 配對；搭配

▶The Denim jacket can match with your skirt.
這件牛仔外套可以搭配你的裙子。

mate [met] ◀Track 3061
n. 同伴；伙伴；配偶

▶Hi mate! How's the world treating you these days? 嗨，伙伴！最近過得如何？

相關片語 soul mate
靈魂相契、性情相投的人

▶If you can feel the natural affinity to someone, that person may be your soul mate.
如果你覺得自然地受到一個人的吸引，那個人可能就是你的靈魂伴侶了。

v. 使成配偶；使配對；使交配；成伙伴

▶My pet dog is not mature enough to mate.
我的寵物狗發育還不夠完全，無法配種。

material [mə`tɪrɪəl] ◀€Track 3062
n. 材料；材質

▶The material of the toy is not specified on the label.
這個玩具的材質沒有在標籤上註明。

math [mæθ] ◀€Track 3063
=mathematics **n.** 數學

▶The kids in the primary school learned about the basic mathematics.
這間小學的學生會學到基礎的數學。

mathematical ◀€Track 3064
[ˌmæθə`mætɪkl] **adj.** 數學的

▶The teacher explained the mathematical equation in a simple and funny way.
老師用簡單又幽默的方式解釋數學公式。

matter [`mætɚ] ◀€Track 3065
n. 事情；問題；毛病

▶What is the matter with you?
你有什麼毛病啊？

v. 要緊；有關係；重要

▶All that matters is that you should come back safe and sound. 最重要的事情是，你必須要平安無事地回來。

mattress [`mætrɪs] ◀€Track 3066
n. 褥墊，床墊

▶The princess suffered from insomnia before she couldn't tolerate any dust in the mattress. 公主因為受不了床墊上面有一點點灰塵而失眠。

mature [mə`tjʊr] ◀€Track 3067
adj. 成熟的

▶After studying abroad for about three years, Jerry became more mature and reliable. 出國留學大約三年之後，傑瑞變得更加成熟、可靠。

maturity [mə`tjʊrətɪ] ◀€Track 3068
n. 成熟

▶Tom showed his maturity in the face of the predicament.
湯姆面對困難的時候，表現出成熟的態度。

maximum ◀€Track 3069
[`mæksəməm] **adj.** 最大的

▶The maximum capacity of this conference room is 80 people.
這間會議室的最大容量是80人。

n. 最大數；最大限度；最高極限；

▶I can carry two boxes of books; this is the maximum.
我可以搬兩箱書；這是極限了。

may [me] ◀€Track 3070
aux. （表示可能性）也許；（表示允許）可以

▶He may not show up at the awarding ceremony this evening.
今晚他也許不會出席頒獎典禮。

n. 五月（首字大寫）

▶Diana's baby is due in May.
黛安娜的寶寶預計五月出生。

maybe [`mebɪ] ◀€Track 3071
adv. 大概；可能；或許

▶Maybe she will come back later; I can't tell you the exact time.
也許她晚點會回來，我無法告訴你確切的時間。

mayonnaise
◀Track 3072

[ˌmeə`nez] **n.** 美乃滋，蛋黃醬

▶You can make mayonnaise at home with room-temperature egg yolks and oil with natural flavors.
妳可以用室溫的蛋黃和具有自然風味的油在家自製美乃滋。

mayor [`meə]
◀Track 3073

n. 市長；鎮長

▶The mayor promised to lower the unemployment rate in the urban area to under 1 percent.
市長承諾要讓市內的失業率降到百分之一以下。

me [mi] **pron.** 我
◀Track 3074

▶The "Me Too" campaign was initiated to support the women who were harassed or mistreated.
「Me Too」運動是為了聲援遭受騷擾或不當對待的女性而發起的活動。

meadow [`mɛdo]
◀Track 3075

n. 草地

▶Some cattle and sheep were grazing on the meadow.
有些牛群和羊群在草地上吃草。

meal [mil]
◀Track 3076

n. 一餐；（進）餐

▶It's not healthy to skip meals for losing weight.
為了減重不吃正餐是不健康的。

mean [min]
◀Track 3077

adj. 吝嗇的；低劣的

▶Don't be so mean to your peer classmate. 不要對你的同學那麼小氣。

meaning [`minɪŋ]
◀Track 3078

n. 意思；含義；意義，重要性

▶There is a deep meaning behind the lines of the movie.
這部電影的對白有很深的意涵。

meaningful
◀Track 3079

[`minɪŋfəl] **adj.** 意味深長的

▶The charity campaign is a meaningful activity.
這個慈善活動很有意義。

means [minz]
◀Track 3080

n. 方法；手段；工具

▶The villain was arrested for making profits through illegal means.
這個惡人因為透過非法方式獲得利益而遭逮捕。

meantime [`min‚taɪm]
◀Track 3081

n. 期間，同時

▶Can you check if the water is boiling? In the meantime, I will prepare the ingredients for the soup.
妳可以看一下水是否滾了嗎？我會在同時準備湯的其他材料。

meanwhile
◀Track 3082

[`min‚hwaɪl] **adv.** 其間，同時

▶Some of the students were decorating the classroom; meanwhile, some were chatting.
有些學生在裝飾教室；同時，有些學生在聊天。

measurable
◀Track 3083

[`mɛʒərəbl]
adj. 可測量的；可預見的；顯著的

中級

▶It is expected that the project may bring measurable effects in terms of improving the middle school students' English proficiency.
預計這個計畫可以為增進中學生的英語能力帶來顯著的效果。

measure [`mɛʒɚ]　◀Track 3084
n. 度量單位；尺寸；分量

▶The measure of a man is what he does with power.
衡量一個人的方式，就是看他有權勢時的所做所為。

v. 測量；計量

▶The kid is leaning to use a ruler to measure the length of the pencil.
這個小朋友正在學習如何用尺測量鉛筆的長度。

measurement
[`mɛʒɚmənt] **n.** 尺寸、測量　◀Track 3085

▶Without a time piece, the measurement of time is not easy.
沒有鐘錶，就會比較難測量時間。

meat [mit] **n.** 肉　◀Track 3086

▶Gina is a vegan; she excludes all kinds of meat from her diet.
吉娜是素食者；她完全不吃肉。

mechanic　◀Track 3087
[mə`kænɪk] **n.** 技工；修理工

▶There are some glitches in the manufacturing system. Can you call the mechanic?
生產的系統有些問題。妳可以打電話請修理工過來嗎？

mechanical　◀Track 3088
[mə`kænɪkl] **adj.** 機械的；機械學的；機器驅動的；無感情的

▶After repeating the same routines day after day, Betty is tired of doing the mechanical tasks every day.
每天重複同樣的流程，貝蒂對機械化的工作感到厭倦。

medal [`mɛdl]　◀Track 3089
n. 獎章；紀念章

▶Troy hung the medals that he won in the swimming contests in his room.
特洛伊將他在游泳比賽中得到的獎牌掛在房間裡。

medical [`mɛdɪkl]　◀Track 3090
adj. 醫學的

▶Helen is a medical intern in the regional hospital.
海倫在一個地區醫院當實習醫生。

medicine [`mɛdəsn]　◀Track 3091
n. 藥

▶Mr. Freeman brings his medicine for the heart disease wherever he goes.
費里曼先生無論走到哪裡都帶著心臟病的藥物。

meditate [`mɛdə,tet]　◀Track 3092
v. 沉思，深思熟慮；計劃，打算

▶Jerry spent two weeks meditating upon his choice of career path.
傑瑞花了兩個星期思考他未來的生涯規劃。

medium [`midɪəm]　◀Track 3093
（複數為mediums/media）
n. 中間；媒介物；手段；工具；傳播媒介

▶The government is promoting the use of English as a medium of teaching.
政府正在宣導用全英語教學。

adj. 中間的；中等的

▶I registered for the medium-level Japanese class.
我註冊去參加中級的日文課程。

meet [mit] ◀ Track 3094

v. 遇見；認識；迎接

▶It is in the Astronomical Conference that I met Mr. Thomson for the first time.
我第一次遇到湯普先生，是在一場天文學的研討會上。

meeting [`mitɪŋ] ◀ Track 3095

n. 會議；聚會

▶The meeting was dismissed after we went through all the issues on the agenda.
討論完議程上面所有的議題之後，我們就散會了。

mellow [`mɛlo] ◀ Track 3096

adj. 成熟的；香醇的；圓潤的；老練的；肥沃的；極好的

▶The mellow voice of the jazz singer was enchanting to the audience.
這位爵士歌手的成熟嗓音令觀眾沉迷。

melody [`mɛlədɪ] ◀ Track 3097

n. 旋律；悅耳的聲音；曲調

▶The melody of the folk song reminds me of the old days when I often hung out with my childhood sweetheart.
這首民俗歌謠的旋律，使我想起我和青梅竹馬在一起的時光。

melon [`mɛlən] **n.** 甜瓜 ◀ Track 3098

▶The town is famous for producing sweet and juicy honeydew melons.
這個小鎮以出產香甜多汁的香瓜聞名。

melt [mɛlt] ◀ Track 3099

v. 使融化；使熔化；使溶解

▶The Japanese scientist invented ice cream that is melt-resistant.
日本科學家發明了不會融化的冰淇淋。

member [`mɛmbɚ] ◀ Track 3100

n. 成員；會員

▶The members of the non-governmental organization volunteered to help the victims of the tsunami. 這個非政府組織的成員自願幫忙海嘯的受害者。

membership ◀ Track 3101

[`mɛmbɚ‿ʃɪp] **n.** 會員身份；會員資格

▶The membership of the gym costs about five hundred dollars per month.
這個健身房的會員每個月要繳500元。

memorable ◀ Track 3102

[`mɛmərəbḷ] **adj.** 值得懷念的

▶This videotape contains footages of some memorable moments for Sean, like the birth of his first baby. 這個影帶中包含了一些對西恩來說相當值得懷念的片段，像是他第一個小孩出生的時候。

memorandum ◀ Track 3103

[ˌmɛmə`rændəm] **n.** 備忘錄；聯絡便條；（公司的）章程

▶The memorandum of the monthly meeting was sent to all the employees of the company. 每月例會的備忘錄已經寄給公司所有的員工了。

中級

memorial [məˋmorɪəl] ◀€Track 3104

n. 紀念物;紀念碑;紀念館

▶The memorial hall of the martyr will be completed before the end of this year. 這個烈士的紀念館將在年底前完工。

adj. 紀念的;追悼的;記憶的

▶Mr. Bush gave a memorial speech on his father's funeral.
布希先生在他父親的喪禮上致悼詞。

memorize ◀€Track 3105

[ˋmɛməˌraɪz] **v.** 記住

▶The master of the ceremony memorized the rundown of the event so as to make things go smoothly.
為了讓活動進行更順利,司儀把整個流程都背起來了。

memory [ˋmɛmərɪ] ◀€Track 3106

n. 記憶;記憶力;回憶

▶Watching Ultraman gives many people fond memories of their heroic childhood. 看鹹蛋超人卡通令許多人想起童年崇拜英雄的回憶。

mend [mɛnd] ◀€Track 3107

v. 修理;修正、改善

▶My father tried to mend the faucet but repeatedly failed. We had to hire a plumber at the end.
我的父親試著要修理水龍頭,但一直失敗。我們最後只好請水電工。

相關片語 **mend one's ways** 改過、改正自己的缺點;改過自新

▶The inmates were given a chance to mend their ways; they could work in the shelter factory.
受刑人有改過自新的機會;他們可以在庇護工廠工作。

mental [ˋmɛntḷ] ◀€Track 3108

adj. 精神的;心理的

▶The counselor mentioned that mental health includes one's emotional, psychological, and social well-being.
這名諮商師提到,心理健康包括一個人的情緒、心理,以及社交的健全狀態。

mention [ˋmɛnʃən] ◀€Track 3109

v. 提到;說起

▶He seldom mentions personal things; we don't know much about his background. 他很少提到自己的事情;我們不太清楚他的背景為何。

n. 提及;說起

▶She doesn't make any mention about her resignation from the company.
她完全沒有提到向公司辭職的事情。

menu [ˋmɛnju] **n.** 菜單 ◀€Track 3110

▶The menu of this restaurant has three versions: Chinese, English, and Japanese. 這家餐廳的菜單有三種版本:中文、英文、和日文。

merchant [ˋmɝtʃənt] ◀€Track 3111

n. 商人;零售商

▶The Persian merchant traveled to the Middle East to introduce his products.
這名波斯商人旅行至中東地區推銷他的商品。

mercy [ˋmɝsɪ] ◀€Track 3112

n. 慈悲;仁慈;憐憫;仁慈行為;寬容

▶The philanthropist has mercy for the poor kids, so he built a school and shelter for them.
這位慈善家憐憫這些貧窮的小孩,所以他為他們建造了一個學校和庇護所。

mere [mɪr]
🔊 Track 3113

adj. 僅僅的；只不過的

▶The mere thought of the delicacies at the market made me hungry.
只不過想到夜市的美食，我就肚子餓了。

merit [ˋmɛrɪt] **n.** 價值
🔊 Track 3114

▶Rita's book has the merit of being both informative and organized.
瑞塔的書的價值在於其具知識性又有清楚的架構。

mermaid [ˋmɝˌmed]
🔊 Track 3115

n. 美人魚；女游泳健將

▶The Little Mermaid was Gina's favorite fairy tale story.
《小美人魚》是吉娜最喜歡的童話故事。

merry [ˋmɛrɪ] **adj.** 歡樂的
🔊 Track 3116

▶The live band's performance created a merry atmosphere at the party.
這個樂團的現場表演為派對創造歡樂的氣氛。

mess [mɛs]
🔊 Track 3117

n. 混亂；凌亂的狀態；髒亂的東西

▶At the initial stage of the project, everything was in a mess, but it went back on track within two weeks.
在這個計畫的初期，所有東西都一團亂，不過兩個星期內就上軌道了。

message [ˋmɛsɪdʒ]
🔊 Track 3118

n. 訊息；口信；消息

▶Edward is not in office right now. Do you want to leave a message?
愛德華目前不在辦公室。你需要留言給他嗎？

messenger
🔊 Track 3119

[ˋmɛsndʒɚ] **n.** 送信者；信差

▶The messenger carried the diplomatic letter for his emperor.
信差為君主遞送外交的信件。

messy [ˋmɛsɪ]
🔊 Track 3120

adj. 混亂的

▶Ted plans to tide up his messy room during the winter break.
泰德想要利用寒假的時間好好整理凌亂的房間。

metal [ˋmɛtl̩] **n.** 金屬
🔊 Track 3121

▶Tina is a fan of heavy metal rock music.
蒂娜喜歡重金屬搖滾樂。

meter [ˋmitɚ]
🔊 Track 3122

v. 計量；用儀表測量

▶Our science teacher taught us how to meter the flow of the river with some really interesting tools.
我們的科學老師教我們如何用一些非常有趣的工具測量這個水的流動。

method [ˋmɛθəd]
🔊 Track 3123

n. 方法；方式

▶The book introduces several innovative teaching methods.
這本書介紹了幾種創新的教學法。

metro [ˋmɛtro]
🔊 Track 3124

=Metro **n.** 地下鐵道；捷運；地鐵

▶The metro system made it very convenient to travel around the metropolitan area.
這個地鐵系統使在市區移動相當方便。

中級

microphone
🔊 Track 3125
[`maɪkrə͵fon] =mike
n. 擴音器;麥克風

▶The microphone stopped working when the principal was about to start his lecture. 校長就要開始演講的時候,麥克風就失靈了。

microscope
🔊 Track 3126
[`maɪkrə͵skop] **n.** 顯微鏡

▶We observed the cells of the fungi with the microscope.
我們使用顯微鏡觀察菌類的細胞。

microwave
🔊 Track 3127
[`maɪkro͵wev] **n.** 微波爐

▶Gina doesn't have a kitchen in the apartment; she only has a microwave oven and an electronic stove.
吉娜公寓沒有廚房;她只有一個微波爐和一個電磁爐。

v. 微波

▶The dish has been microwaved.
這菜已經微波好了。

midday
🔊 Track 3128
[`mɪd͵de]
n. 正午,中午,日正當中

▶It is said that the temperature in the midday here is so high that you can fry an egg on the roof of your car. 據說這裡的溫度高到正午時可以在車頂煎蛋。

middle
🔊 Track 3129
[`mɪdl]
adj. 中間的;中等的

▶According to the witness of the robbery, the robber was a middle-aged man who was about 180 centimeters tall.
根據搶案目擊者的說法,搶匪是一個身高約180公分的中年男子。

n. 中部;中途

▶The runner hurt his ankle and gave up in the middle of the race.
跑者傷了腳踝,就在半途放棄比賽。

midnight
🔊 Track 3130
[`mɪd͵naɪt]
n. 午夜

▶Did you hear someone crying upstairs in the midnight yesterday?
你昨天半夜有聽到有人在樓上哭嗎?

adj. 半夜的

▶It's unhealthy to have midnight snacks every day.
每天都吃宵夜不太健康。

might
🔊 Track 3131
[maɪt]
n. 力量;力氣

▶Hank fought back with all his might when he realized that someone tried to put a slur on him. 漢克一發現有人惡意中傷他,就決定全力反擊。

mightn't
🔊 Track 3132
[`maɪtnt]
abbr. 可能不會(**might not**的縮寫)

▶He mightn't agree with our proposal, but it's worth a try. 他也許不會同意我們的提案,但是值得一試。

mighty
🔊 Track 3133
[`maɪtɪ]
adj. 強大的;強而有力的

▶Pen is mightier than the sward.
筆墨勝刀劍。

相關片語 **high and mighty** 神氣活現

▶Laura is sluggish in class, but she is high and mighty when joining extracurricular activities.
蘿拉上課時很懶散,參加課外活動很神氣活現。

mild [maɪld] adj. 溫和的 🔊 Track 3134

▶We should try to accept either mild or strong criticism in order to grow up.

為了成長，無論是溫和和尖銳的批評，我們都應試著接受。

相關片語 meek and mild 逆來順受的

▶Karen's mother is a traditional Chinese housewife who always appeared to be meek and mild.

凱倫的媽媽是一位傳統中國家庭主婦，總是逆來順受的樣子。

mile [maɪl] n. 英里；哩 🔊 Track 3135

▶The highest speed of this car is 90 miles per hour.

這輛車的最高時速是每小時90公里。

military [ˈmɪləˌtɛrɪ] 🔊 Track 3136
adj. 軍事的；軍用的；軍人的

▶The government has cut down the annual expenses on military equipment.

政府已經減少每年軍事設備的花費了。

n. 軍人；軍隊

▶Edward decided to join the military and become a professional soldier.

愛德華決定加入軍隊並且成為職業軍人。

milk [mɪlk] n. 奶 🔊 Track 3137

▶Do you want some milk in your coffee?

你想在咖啡裡加些牛奶嗎？

milkshake [ˌmɪlkˈʃek] 🔊 Track 3138
n. 奶昔

▶The strawberry milkshake of this cafeteria has sold out.

這個餐廳的草莓奶昔已經賣完了。

mill [mɪl] 🔊 Track 3139
n. 磨坊；麵粉廠；工廠

▶Sean worked in a steel mill in his twenties.

西恩二十幾歲的時候在一家煉鋼廠工作。

v. 碾碎；將……磨成粉

▶The coffee beans were milled into the powder in this workshop.

咖啡豆是在這間工作坊裡面磨成粉的。

million [ˈmɪljən] 🔊 Track 3140
n. 百萬；百萬元；無數

▶Jerry hit the jackpot and won the prize money of one million.

傑瑞中了彩券頭獎，贏得一百萬獎金。

mind [maɪnd] 🔊 Track 3141
n. 頭腦；智力；意向；心意

▶Owen changed his mind and decided to decline the company's offer.

歐文改變心意，婉拒了這家公司的工作機會。

v. 在意；介意

▶Do you mind if I use some air fresher in the room?

你介意我在房子裡用一些空氣清新劑嗎？

mine [maɪn] 🔊 Track 3142
n. 礦；礦井；寶庫

▶It is said that the biggest diamond mine is in South Africa.

據說最大的鑽石礦在南非。

v. 採礦

▶This website contains everything you need to know about Bitcoin mining.

這個網站包含所有你要挖礦賺比特幣所需要知道的事情。

中級

miner [`maɪnɚ] **n.** 礦工　◀ミTrack 3143

▶The movie depicts the miseries of miners who were forced to work for low wages.
這部電影描述被迫為了低薪而工作的礦工們悲慘的處境。

mineral [`mɪnərəl]　◀ミTrack 3144
n. 礦物

▶Scientists found some rare minerals in the meteorite discovered in Western Australia.
科學家在澳洲西部發現的隕石裡找到稀有的礦物。

adj. 礦物的，礦物質的

▶The merchant bought this land, for it was said to have rich mineral resources.
商人買下這塊土地，因為聽説這裡礦物資源豐富。

補充片語 **mineral resource** 礦物資源

minimum [`mɪnəməm]　◀ミTrack 3145
adj. 最小的，最少的，最低的

▶The minimum hourly wage has been adjusted to 150 dollars.
最低時薪已經調整為150元了。

minister [`mɪnɪstɚ]　◀ミTrack 3146
n. 部長，大臣，公使

▶The Minister of Education was forced to resign after he appointed a problematic public figure as the principal of a national university.
教育部長在任命一位爭議人物為國立大學校長之後，被迫辭職。

ministry [`mɪnɪstrɪ]　◀ミTrack 3147
n. 全體閣員；部

▶The Ministry of Foreign Affairs announced that it will assist those who were trapped in the foreign country which was struck by a severe earthquake.
外交部宣布會全力協助被困在受地震襲擊國家的我國旅客。

minor [`maɪnɚ]　◀ミTrack 3148
adj. 較少的；次要的；不重要的；年幼的；副修的

▶We shall leave the minor issues to the next meeting.
我們把次要的議題留到下次會議再討論。

n. 未成年人；副修科目

▶We cannot sell alcohol and cigarettes to minors who are under eighteen.
我們不能販賣酒和菸給12歲以下的未成年者。

v. 副修；兼修

▶Terry's major is electronics, and he minors in chemistry.
泰瑞主修電子學，副修化學。

minority [mar`nɔrətɪ]　◀ミTrack 3149
n. 少數（派）；少數民族；未成年

▶Myanmar Muslim minorities were said to be persecuted by the government.
據説緬甸的少數回教族群受到政府迫害。

mint [mɪnt]　◀ミTrack 3150
n. 薄荷；薄荷糖

▶I planted mint on my balcony.
我在陽台種植薄荷植物。

adj. 薄荷的

▶The mint chocolate flavored ice cream tastes wonderful.
薄荷巧克力口味的冰淇淋真好吃。

minus [`maɪnəs]
◀€ Track 3151

prep. 減去

▶ Ten minus three equals seven.
十減三等於七。

adj. 負的；

▶ It is minus twenty degree Celsius outside. 外面溫度是攝氏零下二十度。

n. 負號、減號；負數；不利

▶ The equation is rendered impossible by the replacement of a minus sign with a plus.
如果把減號換成加號這個等式就不成立了。

minute [maɪ`njut]
◀€ Track 3152

adj. 極細微的，細瑣的

▶ A minute problem may cause severe consequences.
微小的問題可能會導致嚴重的後果。

miracle [`mɪrəkl̩]
◀€ Track 3153

n. 奇蹟，奇蹟般的人或物

▶ It's a miracle that the kid can wake up from coma. 這個小朋友可以從昏迷當中甦醒，真是奇蹟。

mirror [`mɪrɚ] **n.** 鏡子
◀€ Track 3154

▶ It is said that the magic mirror can show your destiny.
據說這個魔鏡可以顯現出你的命運。

mischief [`mɪstʃɪf]
◀€ Track 3155

n. 頑皮；惡作劇；淘氣鬼

▶ Kevin was such a mischief that he was a pain in the neck in his teachers' eyes. 凱文以前是如此調皮以至於他的老師們都討厭他。

相關片語 **make mischief** 挑撥離間

▶ Don't make mischief among friends.
不要在朋友之間挑撥離間。

miserable [`mɪzərəbl̩]
◀€ Track 3156

adj. 悲慘的，痛苦的；不幸的

▶ He was compassionated for the miserable experience of the immigrant kids. 他很同情移民孩童的悲慘經驗。

misery [`mɪzərɪ] **n.** 痛苦
◀€ Track 3157

▶ Misery loves company. 同病相憐。

misfortune
◀€ Track 3158
[mɪs`fɔrtʃən]

n. 不幸；惡運；不幸的事；災難

▶ He never considered the things he encountered to be misfortunes; he thought of them as blessings in disguise.
他從來不會把遇到的事情當作是惡運；他認為那些都是偽裝的祝福。

mislead [mɪs`lid]
◀€ Track 3159

v. 把……帶錯方向；把……引入歧途，把……帶壞

▶ Don't be misled by the fake news. Be sure to verify the source of information.
不要被假新聞誤導了。一定要查證資訊的來源。

misleading
◀€ Track 3160
[mɪs`lidɪŋ] **adj.** 使人誤解的；騙人的

▶ The misleading information did harm to the celebrity's reputation. 這個誤導人的訊息對這位名人的聲譽造成損害。

中級

miss [mɪs] **v** 錯過;想念 ◀ Track 3161

▶I miss the old days when people can trust and help each other.
我想念那個人們可以互相信任、互相幫助的年代。

n. (首字大寫)小姐;女士(對未婚女子的稱謂)

▶Miss Chang was promoted as the manager of the Marketing Department last month.
張小姐上個月晉升為行銷部經理。

missile [`mɪsl] **n** 飛彈 ◀ Track 3162

▶The intercontinental ballistic missiles of North Korea were considered to be a great threat to the U.S. 北韓的彈道導彈被視為是對美國的極大威脅。

missing [`mɪsɪŋ] ◀ Track 3163
adj. 缺掉的;失蹤的

▶I think there is something missing in the piece of artwork, but I can't tell exactly what it is.
我感覺這個藝術作品好像少了什麼,但是我現在無法明確說出是缺了什麼。

mission [`mɪʃən] ◀ Track 3164
n. 外交使團;使命,任務;傳教團;天職

▶The soldiers came back home after they completed their mission.
這些士兵完成任務之後回到家鄉。

mist [mɪst] ◀ Track 3165
n. 薄霧;靄;霧狀物;噴霧;朦朧;模糊不清

▶The article explains the difference between fog, mist, and haze.
這篇文章解釋了霧、薄霧、煙霧的差別。

v 被蒙上薄霧;使變得模糊

▶Tears misted my eyes as I saw the sad movie. 看這部悲傷電影的時候,淚水模糊了我的眼睛。

mistake [mɪ`stek] ◀ Track 3166
n. 錯誤;失誤

▶The package was sent to my house by mistake.
這個包裹寄錯地址,被送到我家來了。

v 弄錯;誤解

▶It wasn't Hank who spread the rumor about you; he was mistaken.
不是漢克在散布謠言的,他被誤解了。

mister [`mɪstɚ] ◀ Track 3167
n. 先生(常縮寫為Mr.)

▶Diana likes the bakery products of Mister Donut.
黛安娜喜歡甜甜圈先生店的烘焙產品。

mistress [`mɪstrɪs] ◀ Track 3168
n. 女主人,主婦;女能手;女教師;女主管;情婦

▶The mistress of the former president became a famous talk show host.
前總統的情婦後來成為一位知名的談話節目主持人。

misunderstand ◀ Track 3169
[`mɪsʌndɚ`stænd] **v** 誤會,誤解

▶He misunderstood the message and thought that she was trying to insult him.
他誤解了訊息,以為她是在污辱他。

mix [mɪks] **v** 混合;拌和 ◀ Track 3170

▶Mix the milk, butter, and flour to make the paste.
把牛奶、奶油和麵粉混和成麵糊。

n. 混合；混合物；調配好的材料
▶There was an odd mix of people at Peter's party.
彼得的派對上面有形形色色的人。

mixture [`mɪkstʃɚ]
◀ Track 3171

n. 混合，混合物，混合料
▶The interview was conducted in mixture of Korean, Japanese, and English.
這場訪談是混雜著韓文、日文、和英文來進行的。

moan [mon]
◀ Track 3172

n. 呻吟聲；（風或樹葉的）蕭蕭聲；悲歎，發牢騷
▶The patient with terminal cancer let out a moan with pain.
這名患有癌症末期的人病人痛苦地呻吟著。

v. 呻吟；悲歎，抱怨
▶Pearl always moans about her lousy roommate.
寶兒總是抱怨她那個很髒亂的室友。

mob [mɑb]
◀ Track 3173

n. 暴民；烏合之眾；（貶）人群，民眾
▶The mob looted the stores and hurt some innocent passers-by.
暴民掠奪了一些店家，還傷了一些無辜的路人。

v. 成群襲擊，圍攻
▶The factory owner was mobbed by the laborers who had not received their wages for months.
這名工廠老闆被那些好幾個月沒拿到薪水的勞工給圍攻了。

mobile [`mobɪl]
◀ Track 3174

adj. 可動的；移動式的
▶There is a mobile toilet near the venue of the outdoor event.
這個戶外活動場地的附近有一個移動式的廁所。

mock [mɑk]
◀ Track 3175

v. 嘲笑；（為取笑而）模仿；使無效，挫敗
▶The actress was mocked for her unique accent during the audition.
女演員在試鏡期間因為特殊的口音遭到嘲笑。

n. 嘲弄；笑柄；贗品
▶Jerry did the mock exam before he took the actual exam.
傑瑞在正式考試之前有做過模擬試題。

補充片語 mock exam 模擬考試

model [`mɑdl]
◀ Track 3176

n. 模型；模範；模特兒
▶Helen worked as a model for the fashion magazine.
海倫過去曾當流行雜誌的模特兒。

v. 做……的模型；當模特兒
▶Gary modeled a skyscraper out of bits of wood.
蓋瑞用木片製作一個摩天大樓的模型。

moderate [`mɑdərɪt]
◀ Track 3177

adj. 中等的，適度的，不過分的
▶The marathon runner proceeded at a moderate speed so that he could last until the end.
這位馬拉松跑者維持適中的速度，好讓自己能夠支撐到終點。

中級

modern [`madən]
◄Track 3178

adj. 現代（化）的

▶The birth of modernism and *modern art* can be traced back to the Industrial Revolution.
現代主義和現代藝術的誕生可追溯至工業革命時期。

modest [`madɪst]
◄Track 3179

adj. 謙虛的，審慎的；適度的；有節制的

▶He remained modest at the press conference after he won the championship. 他在贏得比賽冠軍之後的記者會上仍保持謙虛。

modesty [`madɪstɪ]
◄Track 3180

n. 謙遜

▶Modesty is a virtue while arrogance may lead to failure.
謙虛是美德，而傲慢可能導致失敗。

moist [mɔɪst]
◄Track 3181

adj. 潮濕的；濕潤的

▶After hearing about the touching story, her eyes were moist with tears.
聽過這個感人故事之後，她的眼眶泛淚。

moisture [`mɔɪstʃə]
◄Track 3182

n. 濕氣，潮氣；水分；水氣

▶The moisture of the area made me feel uncomfortable.
這個地區的溼氣讓我覺得很不舒服。

moment [`momənt]
◄Track 3183

n. 瞬間；片刻

▶At that moment, I felt that all the efforts paid off.
在那個瞬間，我覺得所有努力都值得了。

mommy [`mamɪ] **n.** 媽媽
◄Track 3184

▶The toddler cried when he couldn't find his mommy by his side.
那位小朋友在身邊找不到媽媽時就大哭了起來。

Monday [`mʌnde] =Mon. **n.** 星期一
◄Track 3185

▶I have the Monday blues; I don't feel like going to work.
我有星期一症候群；真不想去上班。

money [`mʌnɪ]
◄Track 3186

n. 錢；金錢

▶The business was so profitable that he made a lot of money within one year.
這種生意很有利可圖，所以他一年之內就賺了很多錢。

monitor [`manətə]
◄Track 3187

v. 監控；監聽

▶Everything the inmates did was monitored by the prison guard.
受刑人的一舉一動都受到獄卒的監控。

n. 監聽員；監測器；班長、級長；（電腦）顯示器；螢幕

▶The superintendent saw someone break into the building through the monitor.
管理員透過監視器螢幕看到有人闖進了這棟大樓。

monk [mʌŋk] **n.** 僧侶
◄Track 3188

▶It is said that all teenage boys have to become a monk in the temple for three months in this Buddhist country.
據說在這個佛教國家，所有青少年男孩都要在寺廟裡當和尚三個月。

中級

monkey [ˋmʌŋkɪ]　◀€ Track 3189
n. 猴子

▶The monkeys in the national park would snatch food from the visitors' hands. 這個國家公園裡的猴子會從遊客手中搶走食物。

monster [ˋmɑnstɚ]　◀€ Track 3190
n. 怪獸；怪物

▶Pocket Monster is a very popular cartoon.
《口袋怪獸》是一部很受歡迎的卡通。

month [mʌnθ]　◀€ Track 3191
n. 月；月份

▶In Taiwan, there are a lot of taboos in the seventh month of the lunar calendar.
在台灣，農曆的七月有很多禁忌。

monthly [ˋmʌnθlɪ]　◀€ Track 3192
adj. 每月的；每月一次的

▶Fiona will be briefing the sales figure of the last season in the monthly meeting.
費歐娜會在月會上簡報上一季的銷售數字。

adv. 每月；每月一次

▶I visit my grandparents in the country monthly.
我每個月都會去鄉下探視我的祖父母。

monument　◀€ Track 3193
[ˋmɑnjəmənt] **n.** 紀念碑；紀念館；
歷史遺跡

▶Taj Mahal is a monument built by Emperor Shah Jahan for his second wife. 泰姬瑪哈陵是泰國國王沙賈汗為了他的第二任妻子所建造的紀念碑。

mood [mud]　◀€ Track 3194
n. 心情；心境；情緒

▶Her mood changed so fast that I became tired of pleasing her.
她的情緒變化之大，以致於我開始懶得討好她。

相關片語 **in the mood to/for**
有做……的心情

▶I am in the mood for singing. Let's go to the KTV!
我忽然想唱歌。去KTV吧！

moon [mun]　◀€ Track 3195
n. 月亮；月球

▶Neil Armstrong is the first human to step on the moon.
阿姆斯壯是第一位踏上月球的人類。

moonlight [ˋmunˌlaɪt]　◀€ Track 3196
n. 月光

▶The castle bathed in the moonlight — it was a tranquil and peaceful scene.
城堡沐浴在月光下 —— 真是寧靜又祥和的景象。

mop [mɑp] **n.** 拖把　◀€ Track 3197

▶The mop and the broom are in the cupboard at the corner.
拖把和掃把在牆角的櫥櫃裡。

v. 用拖把拖；擦乾

▶Someone spilled the coffee, so I had to mop the floor.
有人把咖啡打翻了，所以我得要去拖地。

moral [ˋmɔrəl]　◀€ Track 3198
adj. 道德上的；品行端正的；精神上的；道義上的

▶He is a hateful person, for he doesn't have any moral principles.
他是個令人討厭的人，因為他沒有一點道德原則。

相關片語 **moral support** 精神上的支持

▶I can't do much for you, but I can give you moral support.
我沒辦法為你做太多，但我可以給你精神上的支持。

n. 道德；品行；道德寓意；道德規範

▶Those people who try to smuggle produces harmful to the domestic agricultural industry have no morals at all.
那些想要偷渡會危害本地農業的農產品入境的人，真的很沒良心。

more [mor] ◀ Track 3199

adv. 更多；更大程度地；再

▶No one can be more generous than Mrs. Bronte; she gave everything she had to the underprivileged students.
沒有人能比夏綠蒂女士更大方了；她把自己所有的財產都給了貧困的學生。

pron. 更多的數量；更多的人或事物；

▶This soup tastes good. Can I have some more?
這個湯真好喝。我可以多要一些嗎？

adj. 更多的

▶I thought the bus is already crowed; it turned out there were more passengers in the metro system.
我以為公車已經很擠了；結果地鐵系統裡的乘客更多。

moreover [mor`ovɚ] ◀ Track 3200

adv. 並且；此外

▶He is a lawyer; moreover, he is an amateur soccer player.
他是一位律師。此外，他也是一位業餘的足球選手。

morning [`mɔrnɪŋ] ◀ Track 3201

n. 早晨；上午

▶I was stuck in the traffic jam this morning, so I was late for work.
我早上被卡在車陣裡，所以上班遲到了。

mortgage [`mɔrgɪdʒ] ◀ Track 3202

n. 抵押；抵押借款

▶It took Henry twenty years to pay off his house mortgage.
亨利花了二十年才還完房屋貸款。

v. 抵押；以……做擔保

▶He mortgaged his apartment to the bank in order to buy a luxurious car.
他把公寓抵押給銀行，貸款買名貴車。

mosquito [məs`kito] ◀ Track 3203

n. 蚊子

▶There is a mosquito bite on the arm of the toddler.
這個小朋友的手臂上面有一個蚊子咬的痕跡。

moss [mɔs] **n.** 苔蘚 ◀ Track 3204

▶A rolling stone gathers no moss.
滾石不生苔，轉業不聚財。

most [most] ◀ Track 3205

adv. 最；最大程度地；非常

▶That was the most ridiculous thing I've ever heard.
那是我聽過最荒謬的事情了。

pron. 最大量；最多數；大部分

▶Most of the students in this class have smartphones.
這班上大部分的學生都有智慧型手機。

adj. 最多的；多數的

▶Of all kinds of food, delicate desserts have the most calories per serving.
在所有種類的食物當中，精緻點心每份所含的熱量是最高的。

mostly [`mostlɪ]
🔊 Track 3206

adv. 大部分地，大多數地，主要地

▶The viewers of wrestling games, mostly men, would know about WWE.
摔角比賽的觀眾，主要是男性，都會聽過世界摔角比賽。

motel [mo`tɛl]
🔊 Track 3207

n. 汽車旅館

▶Ryan stayed at a motel during the road trip. 雷恩在公路旅行的時候，於一間汽車旅館住宿。

moth [mɔθ] **n.** 蛾；蠹
🔊 Track 3208

▶A moth was darting into the fire.
飛蛾撲火。

mother [`mʌðɚ]
🔊 Track 3209
=mommy=mom
=momma=mamma

n. 媽媽；母親

▶The single mother struggled to raise up her three kids.
這位單親媽媽努力撫養三個孩子長大。

Mother's Day
🔊 Track 3210

[`mʌðɚz-de] **n.** 母親節

▶We celebrated Mother's Day by cooking dinner for our mom at home.
我們在家煮晚餐給媽媽，慶祝母親節。

motion [`moʃən]
🔊 Track 3211

n. （物體的）移動、運行；動作、姿態

▶The players watched the footage of the basketball game in slow motion and discussed the strategies.
球員把比賽影片慢速撥放來看，並且討論戰術。

v. 打手勢；做動作示意

▶The singer motioned his bodyguard to step back.
歌手示意他的保鑣，要他們後退。

motivate [`motə,vet]
🔊 Track 3212

v. 給……動機；刺激；激發

▶The teacher devised some interesting activities to motivate his students to learn geography.
老師設計一些有趣的活動來激勵學生學習地理。

motivation
🔊 Track 3213

[,motə`veʃən] **n.** 刺激；推動

▶His motivation toward learning comes from his desire to pursue higher scores in the exams.
他學習的動機就是要在考試中得高分。

motor [`motɚ]
🔊 Track 3214

n. 馬達；發動機；電動機

▶The motor of the electric car would not make any noises.
這種電動車的馬達不會發出噪音。

中級

motorcycle
[`motə͵saɪkl̩] **=motorbike**
（英式英文）摩托車
🔊 Track 3215

▶Kevin took a motorcycle as his major traffic tool.
凱文以一台摩托車作為主要的交通工具。

mountain [`maʊntn̩]
🔊 Track 3216
n. 山

▶Helen got lost in the mountain; fortunately, she was rescued within two days.
海倫在山裡迷路了；幸運地，她在兩天之內就獲救了。

mountainous
🔊 Track 3217
[`maʊntənəs] adj. 多山的

▶The eastern area of the island is mountainous.
這個島嶼的東部是個多山的地區。

mouse [maʊs]
🔊 Track 3218
n. 鼠；膽小如鼠的人

▶He is as poor as a church mouse.
她一貧如洗。

moustache [məs`tæʃ]
🔊 Track 3219
=mustache n. 髭，小鬍子

▶The man with a mustache is our new PE teacher. 這個留著小鬍子的男人是我們的新體育老師。

mouth [maʊθ] n. 嘴
🔊 Track 3220

▶The dentist asked the patient to open his mouth. 這名牙醫師叫病人張開嘴巴。

movable [`muvəbl̩]
🔊 Track 3221
adj. 可動的；可移動的

▶The manual shows you how to build a moveable model robot.
這個說明手冊教你如何組裝一個可移動的機器人模型。

move [muv]
🔊 Track 3222
v. 移動；搬動；遷移

▶The freelance translator moved overseas last month.
這位自由譯者上個月搬到海外去了。

n. 移動；措施

▶The thermos sensor can detect every move that you make in the room.
這個熱感應器可以偵測到你在這個房間裡的一舉一動。

movement
🔊 Track 3223
[`muvmənt] n. 運動；活動；行動

▶The students initiated a movement to fight for gender equality on campus.
這些學生發起一個活動，爭取校園內的性別平等。

movie [`muvɪ]
🔊 Track 3224
=film=cinema=picture
n. 電影

▶The movie was adapted from a science fiction.
這部電影是改編自一部科幻小說。

mow [mo]
🔊 Track 3225
v. （用鐮刀等）刈（草等）

▶He mowed the lawn for his neighbor to earn some pocket money.
他替鄰居除草，賺點外快。

Mr. [`mɪstə]
🔊 Track 3226
=Mr n. 先生（用於男士稱謂）

▶Mr. Gibson won the honorable diploma of Harvard University for his contribution for the society.
吉勃遜先生因為對社會有很大的貢獻，獲得了哈佛的榮譽學位。

Mrs. [`mɪsɪz]
=Mrs n. 太太；夫人
◀Track 3227

▶Mrs. Curie was an outstanding physicist and chemist.
居里夫人是一位傑出的物理學家和化學家。

MRT [ɛm-ɑr-ti]
◀Track 3228
=mass rap·id tran·sit
=sub·way
=un·der·ground
=me·tro n. 大眾捷運系統

▶It's convenient to get around in the metropolitan area by taking the MRT system.
搭乘大眾捷運系統在都會區裡移動真的很方便。

Ms. [mɪz]
◀Track 3229
n. 女士（用於婚姻狀態不明的女性稱謂）

▶Ms. Clinton will introduce our new product on the Consumer Electronics Show.
柯林頓女士將會在消費電子展上介紹我們的新產品。

MTV [ɛm-ti-vi] n. 音樂電視
◀Track 3230

▶The popular singer's MTV has been viewed for more than one million times on Youtube.
這個流行歌手的音樂視頻在Youtube上面已經被觀看超過一百萬次。

much [mʌtʃ]
◀Track 3231
pron. 許多；大量的事物

▶Much of his fortune was inherited form his father.
他大部分的財產都是繼承自他的父親。

adv. 非常；很

▶He likes parkour sports very much.
他非常喜歡跑酷運動。

adj. 許多；大量的

▶I don't have much money, but I can donate some daily necessities to the refugees.
我沒有很多錢，但是我可以捐贈一些日常用品給難民。

mud [mʌd] n. 泥；泥漿
◀Track 3232

▶The puppies played in the mud and made a mess.
小狗狗跑到泥巴裡玩，弄得髒兮兮。

muddy [`mʌdɪ]
◀Track 3233
adj. 泥濘的；多泥的；渾濁的

▶It was not easy to drive through the muddy road.
開車行過泥濘的道路很不容易。

mug [mʌg]
◀Track 3234
n. 大杯子，馬克杯；嘴臉；鬼臉；搶劫

▶The clerk of the café said if you use a mug instead of a disposable cup, you can get one refill for free.
咖啡店的店員說如果你用馬克杯而不是使用一次性的杯子，就可以免費續杯一次。

v. 扮鬼臉，做怪相；給……拍照

▶The naughty boy mugged when taking a photo with his family.
頑皮的小男孩跟家人一起拍照的時候扮鬼臉。

中級

mule [mjul]
◀Track 3235

n. 騾子;固執的人

▶Don't waste your breath trying to persuade him; he is as stubborn as a mule.
不用浪費唇舌想去說服他;他像騾子一樣固執。

multiple [`mʌltəpl̩]
◀Track 3236

adj. 複合的,多樣的

▶There are multiple gun shots on the back of the elephant; the culprit may be a poacher. 這頭大象的背上有多處槍傷,可能是盜獵者做的。

multiply [`mʌltəplaɪ]
◀Track 3237

v. 乘;相乘;使成倍增加;繁殖

▶Termites multiply quickly.
白蟻繁殖是很快的。

murder [`mɝdɚ]
◀Track 3238

v. 殺害,謀殺

▶It is said that the correspondent journalist was murdered by a local gangster. 據說這位駐外記者是被當地的流氓給殺害的。

n. 謀殺,殺害

▶The villain confessed that he committed the murder of his mortal enemy. 這名惡棍坦承謀殺他的死對頭這件事情是他做的。

murderer [`mɝdərɚ]
◀Track 3239

n. 謀殺犯;兇手

▶The lawyer was criticized for defending for the merciless murderer on court. 這名律師因為在法庭上替冷血的殺手辯護而遭到批評。

murmur [`mɝmɚ]
◀Track 3240

n. 低語聲;低聲抱怨;輕柔而持續的聲音;心臟雜音

▶The employees of Romsey's restaurant had murmurs for working overtime every day. 拉姆齊餐廳的員工們因為每天都在加班而頗有微詞。

v. 輕聲細語;私語;小聲說話

▶The actor murmured his line on the stage, and the audience couldn't hear him.
演員在台上小聲地說出台詞,而觀眾無法聽見他說什麼。

muscle [`mʌsl̩]
◀Track 3241

n. 肌,肌肉

▶Regular exercise can strengthen your muscles.
規律運動可以幫你鍛練肌肉。

muse [mjuz]
◀Track 3242

v. 沉思,冥想;若有所思地說

▶I mused about the structure of my final report.
我在構思期末報告的架構要怎麼寫。

museum [mju`zɪəm]
◀Track 3243

n. 博物館

▶My uncle has a private museum where he displays his collection of paintings and sculptures.
我叔叔有一間私人的博物館,他在那裡展示他自己蒐集的畫和雕像。

mushroom
◀Track 3244

[`mʌʃrʊm] **n.** 蘑菇,蕈

▶It is said that colorful mushrooms are not edible.
據說顏色鮮豔的蘑菇是不能吃的。

v. 採蘑菇；雨後春筍般迅速增長

▶The convenience stores mushroomed in the downtown area in the past decade.
過去十年來，便利商店在城區如雨後春筍般成長。

---

music [`mjuzɪk] **n.** 音樂
🔊 Track 3245

▶What is your favorite genre of music?
你最喜歡的音樂類型是什麼？

---

musical [`mjuzɪkl]
🔊 Track 3246

adj. 音樂的

▶Jerry can play several musical instruments, including harmonica, cello, and accordion.
傑瑞會演奏好幾種樂器，包括口琴、大提琴，以及手風琴。

n. 歌舞劇；音樂片

▶My favorite musical is *Into the Woods*.
我最喜歡的音樂劇是《拜訪森林》。

---

musician [mju`zɪʃən]
🔊 Track 3247

n. 音樂家

▶The classical musician was said to be conservative and stubborn in private.
據說這位古典音樂家私下很保守又固執。

---

must [mʌst]
🔊 Track 3248

aux. 必定；必須

▶We must figure something out to solve the problem before we can call it a day.
我們在今天結束之前一定要想出解決的辦法。

---

mustache [`mʌstæʃ]
🔊 Track 3249

n. 小鬍子

▶The actor is satisfied with his mustache, but it was not well-received by his fans.
這名演員對自己的小鬍子很滿意，但是他的粉絲不太能接受。

---

mustn't [`mʌsnt]
🔊 Track 3250

abbr. 不可（**must not**的縮寫）

▶You mustn't step into the forbidden zone.
絕對不可以踏入禁區。

---

mute [mjut]
🔊 Track 3251

adj. 沉默的；啞的，不會說話的

▶The girl was born deaf and mute.
那個女孩出生就又聾又啞。

n. 啞巴；靜音

▶Please put your cell phone on mute.
請把手機關靜音。

v. 消音；降低、減輕（聲音）

▶The staff of the theater reminded the audience to mute their cell phones.
劇院的工作人員提醒觀眾將手機關成靜音。

---

mutter [`mʌtɚ]
🔊 Track 3252

v. 低聲嘀咕；低聲抱怨

▶Tom Sawyer muttered as he painted the fence for his uncle.
湯姆在幫叔叔粉刷圍籬時，一面低聲抱怨。

n. 咕噥，抱怨

▶I heard the diners' mutters when they tasted our new dish.
我聽見用餐客人在嘗試我們新菜色時發出的抱怨聲。

---

mutual [`mjutʃʊəl]
🔊 Track 3253

adj. 相互的

中級

▶Negotiation is necessary for mutual understanding.
溝通協調才能達到互相理解。

my [maɪ] det. 我的
◀╡Track 3254

▶This is my first time to visit the national space station.
這是我第一次參觀國家太空站。

myself [maɪˋsɛlf]
◀╡Track 3255
pron. 我自己

▶I can't forgive myself for making such a stupid mistake.
我無法原諒自己犯下這麼愚蠢的錯誤。

mysterious
◀╡Track 3256
[mɪsˋtɪrɪəs] adj. 神秘的；故弄玄虛的；詭異的

▶The mysterious unidentified flying object has aroused his curiosity.
這個神祕的不明飛行物體引起他的好奇心。

mystery [ˋmɪstərɪ]
◀╡Track 3257
n. 神秘的事物；難以理解的事物

▶This show introduced some unsolved mysteries around the world.
這個節目介紹一些世界各地的未解謎題。

myth [mɪθ]
◀╡Track 3258
n. 神話；虛構的人事物；無事實根據的觀點

▶The book is a collection of Greek myths.
這本書蒐集了許多希臘神話。

▶ Nn

　　以下表格是全民英檢官方公告中級「聽、說、讀、寫」所須具備的能力，本書例句皆依此範疇特別設計，只要掃描右方QR code，就能搭配相對應的音軌實現「眼耳並用」方式，刺激左腦的語言學習功能；同時也可使用本書附贈的紅膠片，將其置於單字上，一面記憶一面自我挑戰，達到雙倍的學習成果！

聽	在日常生活中，能聽懂一般的會話；能大致聽懂公共場所廣播、氣象報告及廣告等。在工作時，能聽懂簡易的產品介紹與操作說明。能大致聽懂外籍人士的談話及詢問。
說 ▶	可在日常生活中，能以簡易英語交談或描述一般事物，能介紹自己的生活作息、工作、家庭、經歷等，並可對一般話題陳述看法。在工作時，能進行簡單的答詢，並與外籍人士交談溝通。
讀	在日常生活中，能閱讀短文、故事、私人信件、廣告、傳單、簡介及使用說明等。在工作時，能閱讀工作須知、公告、操作手冊、例行的文件、傳真、電報等。
寫 ▶	能寫簡單的書信、故事及心得等。對於熟悉且與個人經歷相關的主題，能以簡易的文字表達。

中級

nail [nel] n. 釘子；指甲　◀ Track 3259

▶Terry bites his nail when he is embarrassed or nervous.
泰瑞在尷尬或者緊張的時候會咬指甲。

v. 釘；釘牢

▶A painting had been nailed up on the wall by the artist.
這名畫家把一幅畫釘在牆上。

相關片語 nail down the deal 達成協議

▶The negotiators spent ten hours to nail down the deal.
協商者花了十個小時才達成協議。

naive [na`iv]　◀ Track 3260
adj. 天真的，幼稚的

▶The naive little girl still believes in the existence of Santa Claus.
這個天真的小女孩仍然相信聖誕老人的存在。

naked [`nekɪd]　◀ Track 3261
adj. 裸身的；光禿禿的；赤裸裸的

▶Some naked young men jumped into the icy river; it is said to be a coming-of-age ceremony in the local custom.
有些年輕男子裸身跳進冰河裡；據說這是當地的成年禮儀式。

name [nem] n. 名字　◀ Track 3262

▶Fill in your name, age, and ID number in this form.
在這張表格上填寫您的姓名、年紀、以及身分證字號。

v. 命名；為……取名

▶The asteroid was named after the astronomer who discovered it.
這個小行星是以發現它的天文學家命名的。

namely [`nemlɪ]　◀ Track 3263
adv. 即；那就是

▶Only one person has the ability to deal with this problem, namely you.
只有一個人可以處理這個問題，也就是你。

nanny [`nænɪ] ◀Track 3264

n. 母山羊；保姆

▶Helen has a professional nanny certificate. 海倫有專業保母人員證照。

nap [næp] **n.** 打盹兒，午睡 ◀Track 3265

▶It is time for a nap after lunch.
到了午餐之後的午睡時間了。

v. 打盹兒，午睡

▶Mrs. Thompson napped in his armchair.
湯普森先生在他的扶手椅上睡了一下。

napkin [`næpkɪn] **n.** 餐巾 ◀Track 3266

▶The waitress placed napkins on the seats of the table.
服務生將餐巾放置在座位上。

narrator [næ`retɚ] ◀Track 3267

n. 解說員，講述者，旁白

▶The famous voice actor will be the narrator of the radio drama. 這位知名的聲優演員會擔任這個廣播劇的旁白。

narrow [`næro] ◀Track 3268

adj. 窄的；狹窄的

▶It was challenging for me to drive through this narrow lane.
開車通過這個窄巷子對我來說是個挑戰。

v. 使變窄；縮小、限制（範圍等）

▶The researcher narrowed down the potential targets for the study to make the objective more specific.
這位研究者縮小了這個研究的潛在目標群，讓研究目的更明確。

nasty [`næstɪ] ◀Track 3269

adj. 齷齪的；使人難受的；淫穢的；惡劣的；難處理的；惡意的

▶It was nasty for him to spread the rumors about his opponents.
他實在很惡毒，散播關於對手的謠言。

nation [`neʃən] **n.** 國家 ◀Track 3270

▶The president addressed to the nation on the issue of immigrants.
這位總統對全國發表關於移民的演說。

national [`næʃənl] ◀Track 3271

adj. 全國性的；國家的；國有的

▶Jerry subscribed the National Geographic Channel.
傑瑞訂閱國家地理頻道。

nationality ◀Track 3272

[ˌnæʃə`nælətɪ] **n.** 國籍；民族

▶Please fill in your name, ID number, and nationality in the Declaration Form.
請在申報單上填寫您的名字、身分證號，以及國籍。

native [`netɪv] ◀Track 3273

adj. 天生的；出生地的；祖國的；家鄉的；土著的；天然的

▶The private school claims that the English classes are conducted by native speakers. 這所私立學校宣稱其英語課程都是由英文為母語者教授的。

n. 本地人；本國人；土著，原住民

▶The natives on the island didn't understand English, so the sailors communicated with them through body language.
這個島上的原住民不懂英文，所以水手們用肢體語言與他們溝通。

natural [`nætʃərəl`]
🔊 Track 3274

adj. 自然的

▶The natural disasters caused great loss to the country last year. 去年，自然災害對這個國家造成了嚴重的損失。

naturalist
🔊 Track 3275

[`nætʃərəlɪst] **n.** 自然主義者；博物學家

▶The naturalist did not believe the existence of heaven and hell. 這名自然主義者不相信天堂和地獄的存在。

naturally [`nætʃərəlɪ`]
🔊 Track 3276

adv. 自然地，天生地；當然

▶Helen is new in the company; naturally, she knows little about the latent culture of the organization. 海倫剛來這家公司；自然地，她不太了解這個組織的潛在文化。

nature [`netʃə`]
🔊 Track 3277

n. 自然（狀態）；自然界

▶Aaron likes to go hiking and get close to nature on the weekend. 亞倫喜歡在週末的時候去踏青並接近大自然。

naughty [`nɔtɪ`]
🔊 Track 3278

adj. 頑皮的；淘氣的

▶The naughty boy broke the window by accident and ran away. 這名頑皮的男孩子不小心打破窗戶，然後逃跑了。

naval [`nevl`]
🔊 Track 3279

adj. 海軍的，軍艦的，船的

▶My brother worked as a naval engineer. 我哥哥以前是航海工程師。

navy [`nevɪ`] **n.** 海軍
🔊 Track 3280

▶Tina has served in the Navy for seven years. 緹娜已經在海軍服役七年了。

near [nɪr]
🔊 Track 3281

prep. 在……附近

▶There is as aquarium near the observatory museum. 在天文館的附近有一間水族館。

adj. 近的；

▶It takes about three minutes to walk to the university; it's actually quite near. 走路到大學只花大約三分鐘。其實很近。

adv. 近；接近；幾乎

▶As the date of our graduation ceremony drew near, we became less attentive to exams. 隨著畢業典禮逐漸靠近，我們對考試也越來越不在意。

v. 靠近

▶The cancer patient felt desperate, for he was nearing death. 這名癌症病患感到很絕望，因為他是如此接近死亡。

nearby [`nɪrˌbaɪ`]
🔊 Track 3282

adj. 附近的

▶Tina studied at a nearby high school. 緹娜念的是附近的國中。

adv. 在附近

▶We worked nearby so that we can go hom and rest in a shorter period of time. 我們在附近工作，如此一來，我們就可以在更短的時間內回家休息。

nearly [`nɪrlɪ`]
🔊 Track 3283

adv. 幾乎；差不多

中級

▶The girl was nearly dead when she was deserted by her biological mother.
被親生母親遺棄的時候，這個女孩子幾乎要死了。

nearsighted　◀Track 3284

[`nɪr`saɪtɪd] adj. 近視的；目光短淺的

▶More than half of the students in this class are nearsighted.
這個班上有超過一半的學生都有近視。

neat [nit]　◀Track 3285

adj. 整齊的；工整的；整潔的

▶Her neat hand writing left a good impression on the client.
她整齊的筆跡讓客戶留下很好的印象。

necessarily　◀Track 3286

[`nɛsəsɛrɪlɪ] adv. 必然地

▶War necessarily causes injuries and deaths.
戰爭必定會造成傷亡。

necessary [`nɛsəˌsɛrɪ]　◀Track 3287

adj. 必須的；必要的

▶It is necessary that you have the required certificate before you run a clinic.
你如果要自己開設診所，擁有所需執照是必須的。

necessity [nə`sɛsətɪ]　◀Track 3288

n. 需要

▶We donated some daily necessities to the victims of the tsunami.
我們捐贈了一些日常用品給海嘯的難民。

neck [nɛk] n. 脖子；頸　◀Track 3289

▶Teddy is a pain in the neck for many teachers, for he often plays trick on his peers. 泰迪是令老師們頭大的人物，因為他都會捉弄同學。

necklace [`nɛklɪs]　◀Track 3290

n. 項鍊

▶Fiona was very upset for she lost the necklace that her fiancé gave her. 費歐娜把未婚夫送她的項鍊弄丟了，很難過。

necktie [`nɛkˌtaɪ]　◀Track 3291

n. 領帶

▶The yellow necktie doesn't go with the blue shirt.
黃色的領帶跟這件藍色的襯衫不搭。

need [nid] v. 需要　◀Track 3292

▶I need a screwdriver to fix the machine.
我需要一個螺絲起子才能修理這個機器。

n. 需要；貧窮；困窘

▶The refugees are in need of clean water and daily necessities.
這些難民需要乾淨的水和日常生活用品。

aux. 必須

▶You need not worry about Tom. He is a grown up.
你不需要擔心湯姆。他是大人了。

needle [`nidl̩]　◀Track 3293

n. 針；指針

▶The kid cried as soon as he saw the needle on the nurse's hand.
小朋友看到護士手上的針，就哭了。

v. 用針縫；用針刺；用話刺激

▶Jerry tried to needle his friend into doing something dangerous. 傑瑞想要說一些話刺激他的朋友去做危險的事情。

中級

needy [`nidɪ] adj. 貧窮的 ◀Track 3294

▶The philanthropist would donate money to help the needy people in the underdeveloped area. 這位慈善家會捐款幫助落後地區的貧窮人家。

negative [`nɛgətɪv] ◀Track 3295

adj. 否定的；負面的、消極的

▶Three years ago, when Pearl suffered from depression, she held a negative attitude toward everything.
寶兒三年前患憂鬱症的時候，對任何事情都抱持負面的態度。

n. 否定；否定的回答；拒絕

▶The result of the referendum was a negative to the proposal.
公民投票的結果是對提案的否決。

neglect [nɪg`lɛkt] ◀Track 3296

v. 忽視；忽略；忘了做；疏於照管

▶Don't neglect your duty of attending to the residents in the nursing home.
不要忘記你照顧療養院居民的職責。

negotiate [nɪ`goʃɪ,et] ◀Track 3297

v. 談判

▶We spent three hours negotiating on the terms of the contract.
我們花了三個小時針對合約條款進行談判。

negotiation [nɪ,goʃɪ`eʃən] n. 談判，協商 ◀Track 3298

▶Being open and assertive is important during the negotiation. 談判時，保持開放和果斷的態度是很重要的。

neighbor [`nebɚ] ◀Track 3299
=neighbour （英式英文）n. 鄰居

▶Helen invited her neighbors to her house warming party.
海倫邀請鄰居參加她的新居落成派對。

v. 住在附近；與……為鄰

▶Our orchard neighbored with theirs.
我們的果園和他們的相鄰。

neighbourhood ◀Track 3300
[`nebɚ,hʊd] n. 鄰近地區

▶There is a park in the neighborhood where kids can hang out afterschool.
社區裡有一個公園，小朋友放學之後都會去那邊玩。

neither [`niðɚ] adv. 也不 ◀Track 3301

▶Rita doesn't like coriander, and neither do I.
瑞塔不喜歡香菜，我也不喜歡。

pron. 兩個中沒有一個

▶Neither of the twins has met their biological parents.
兩個雙胞胎都沒有見過他們的親生父母。

adj. 兩者都不

▶Neither party should violate the terms in the contract.
兩方都不應該違背合約的條款。

conj. 既不……，也不……

▶Neither Jack nor Jerry will attend the meeting. 傑克和傑瑞都不會來開會。

nephew [`nɛfju] ◀Track 3302
n. 姪兒；外甥

▶My nephew worked part time at the cafeteria.
我姪子在這間餐廳打工。

nerve [nɝv] ◀Track 3303
n. 神經；憂慮；勇敢

▶It really takes a lot of nerve to go into that haunted house at night. 在晚上進入那間鬼屋真的需要鼓起很大的勇氣。

相關片語 **get on one's nerves**
令人煩躁

▶The passengers on the train keep elbowing the way when they need to get of the cart; these people really get on my nerves.
火車上的乘客要下車時都用手肘推擠別人；這些人真令人煩躁。

nervous [`nɝvəs] ◀Track 3304
adj. 緊張的

▶Tina was very nervous when she gave a commencement speech.
緹娜在畢業典禮上致詞時非常緊張。

nest [nɛst] **n.** 巢；窩；穴 ◀Track 3305

▶The swallow built a nest in the barn.
這隻燕子在穀倉裡面築巢。

v. 築巢；將……比鄰放置在一起

▶He nested the glass tumblers in a crate.
他把玻璃酒杯一個一個放在箱子裡。

net [nɛt] **n.** 網狀物；網 ◀Track 3306

▶The fisherman built a net with wide meshes so that small fishes can escape.
漁夫造了一個空隙比較大的網子，讓小魚可以逃出去。

v. 用網捕

▶The kids were netting the tadpoles in the pond.
小朋友在池塘裡用網子抓蝌蚪。

network [`nɛt,wɝk] ◀Track 3307
n. 網；網狀物；網狀系統；廣播網，電視網；電腦網路

▶You can transmit the file to your colleague through the network in the office.
妳可以利用辦公室裡的網路系統把檔案傳給你的同事。

v. 用網覆蓋；在廣播網聯播；建立關係網

▶Kevin would network with some of his friends in college who took different career paths.
凱文和走上不同行業的大學同學建立關係網。

never [`nɛvɚ] ◀Track 3308
adv. 從不；永不；絕不

▶You should never embezzle the charity funds.
你永遠都不應該挪用慈善捐款。

nevertheless ◀Track 3309
[,nɛvɚðə`lɛs] **adv.** 仍然

▶She is only a nodding acquaintance of mine; nevertheless, I invited her to the party.
我跟她不是很熟；不過，我還是請她來參加派對了。

new [nju] **adj.** 新的 ◀Track 3310

▶Everything in this town remains the same; there is nothing new.
這個小鎮一切照舊，沒有什麼新的事物。

New Year's Day ◀Track 3311
[nju-jɪrz-de] **n.** 元旦

▶Many people attended the flag raising ceremony on the New Year's Day.
許多人在元旦時參加升旗典禮。

中級

New Year's Eve　◀ Track 3312
[nju-jɪrz-iv] **n.** 除夕

▶The count-down party on New Year's Eve was really fantastic.
除夕夜的倒數派對太棒了。

New York [nju-jɔrk]　◀ Track 3313
n. 紐約

▶Many immigrants entered the United States through the harbor in New York.
許多移民是從紐約的港口進入美國的。

newcomer　◀ Track 3314
[`nju`kʌmɚ] **n.** 新手，新到者，新生

▶Frank is a newcomer in the company. Can you show him around?
法蘭克是新進員工。你可以幫他介紹一下環境嗎？

news [njuz] **n.** 新聞；消息　◀ Track 3315

▶It is said that some hackers were spreading malicious fake news on the Internet.
據說有些駭客在網路上散布惡意的假消息。

newscaster　◀ Track 3316
[`njuz͵kæstɚ] **n.** 新聞廣播員

▶Ms. Pan used to be a newscaster, and now she is a host of a travel show.
潘小姐以前是一位新聞播報員，現在她是一位旅遊節目的主持人。

newspaper　◀ Track 3317
[`njuz͵pepɚ] **n.** 報紙

▶The scholar writes a column for the local newspaper.
這位學者為本地的報紙寫專欄。

next [`nɛkst]　◀ Track 3318
adj. 緊鄰的；接下來的；居次的

▶The next session of the conference will begin in twenty minutes.
這個研討會的下一節議程會在二十分鐘後開始。

adv. 接下來；次於

▶The author of the book made prediction about human's destiny; he claims that he can see what comes next.
這本書的作者預測了人類的命運，他聲稱可以看到接下來會發生什麼事情。

nice [naɪs]　◀ Track 3319
adj. 好的；美好的；好心的

▶She is an organized worker; she keeps her desk nice and neat.
她是很有組織規劃的員工；她的桌子總是整理得很好。

nickname [`nɪk͵nem]　◀ Track 3320
n. 暱稱，小名，綽號

▶Mary gave her little brother a nickname.
瑪莉幫她的弟弟取了一個綽號。

v. 給……起綽號

▶He was nicknamed "walking encyclopedia," for he is very knowledgeable.
他因為很博學，被取了一個綽號叫做行走百科全書。

niece [nis]　◀ Track 3321
n. 姪女；外甥女

▶My brother sent my niece to a boarding school when she was fourteen.
我哥在我姪女十四歲的時候，送她去念寄宿學校。

night [naɪt] n. 夜晚
◀Track 3322
▶The town becomes tranquil at night.
這個城鎮在晚上變得很寂靜。

nightmare [`naɪt‚mɛr]
◀Track 3323
n. 噩夢，夢魘
▶The night after seeing the horror movie, the girl had a nightmare.
看過恐怖電影後，女孩在晚上就做了惡夢。

nine [naɪn] n. 九
◀Track 3324
▶Four plus five equals nine.
四加五等於九。

adj. 九的
▶Nine people were injured in this accident.
這場意外中有九人受傷。

nineteen [`naɪn`tin]
◀Track 3325
n. 十九
▶Ted started to work when he was nineteen.
泰德十九歲就開始工作。

adj. 十九的；十九個的
▶There are nineteen departments in this organization.
這個組織中有十九個部門。

ninety [`naɪntɪ] n. 九十
◀Track 3326
▶My grandmother passed away when she was ninety.
我祖母在九十歲時過世。

adj. 九十的；九十個的
▶Ninety journalists attended the press conference.
有九十位記者參加了這場記者會。

no [no] adv./adj. 沒有
◀Track 3327
▶I have no excuses; I will take full responsibility for the mistake.
我沒有藉口，我會為這次的錯誤負全責。

n. 不；沒有；拒絕
▶The man shook his head, which signified a "no" to your request.
這個人搖頭，表示拒絕你的要求。

noble [`nobl]
◀Track 3328
adj. 高尚的；貴族的；顯貴的
▶The noble man was said to be raised up in a peasant's family. 這位高尚的男人據說是在農民的家庭長大的。

n. 貴族
▶She keeps a low profile about her background, so none of her schoolmates knows she is actually a noble.
她很低調，所以學校同學都不知道她其實是一位貴族。

nobody [`nobɑdɪ]
◀Track 3329
pron. 沒有人；無人
▶He didn't contact with anyone; nobody knows his whereabouts. 他沒有和任何人連絡，沒有人知道他的下落。

n. 無足輕重的小人物
▶I am just nobody. Would the government take my plea? 我只是個無名小卒。政府會接受我的請願嗎？

nobody's [`nobɑdɪz]
◀Track 3330
abbr. 沒有人的、沒有人是（nobody的所有格，或nobody is的縮寫）
▶Everybody's business is nobody's business.
大家的事，最後都會沒人管。

nod [nɑd] v. 點頭;打盹 ◀€ Track 3331

▶David nodded off during the archeological scholar's speech.
大衛在這位考古學者的演講中間打瞌睡。

n. 點頭;打瞌睡

▶I won't give the nod to treating conspiracy theories as facts.
我是不會同意將陰謀論視為事實的。

noise [nɔɪz] n. 噪音 ◀€ Track 3332

▶The noise on the street kept me up all night. 街上的噪音讓我整晚都睡不著。

noisy [`nɔɪzɪ] ◀€ Track 3333

adj. 吵鬧的;喧鬧的;充滿噪聲的

▶She is not into heavy metal rock music, for she thinks it's noisy.
她不喜歡重金屬音樂,她認為那很吵。

none [nʌn] ◀€ Track 3334

pron. 一個也無;沒有任何人或物;無一人

▶None of my friends support the bill; they think the draft is neither comprehensive nor sophisticated.
我沒有一個朋友支持這項法案;他們認為這個法案既不周全也不完整。

nonetheless ◀€ Track 3335

[ˌnʌnðə`lɛs] adv. 但是,仍然;儘管如此

▶Kevin had a tight schedule; nonetheless, he still visited his grandparents in the uptown. 凱文行程緊湊;儘管如此,他還是抽空去郊區探望他的祖父母。

nonsense [`nɑnsɛns] ◀€ Track 3336

n. 胡說;無意義的廢話

▶Stop talking about nonsense; make some constructive suggestions.
不要再胡說八道了;做些有意義的建議吧。

non-stop [`nɑn-stɑp] ◀€ Track 3337

adj. 直達的

▶The nonstop flight will reach Moscow in eight hours.
這班直搭飛機八小時後會到莫斯科。

adv. 不停地

▶The band will perform nonstop for three hours in the concert.
這個樂團在演唱會上會不停演奏三個小時。

noodle [`nudl] n. 麵 ◀€ Track 3338

▶The homemade noodles of this deli are made with buckwheat.
這家熟食店的自製麵條是蕎麥製成的。

noon [nun] n. 中午;正午 ◀€ Track 3339

▶The temperature reached 35 degrees Celsius at noon.
正午的溫度達到攝氏三十五度。

nor [nɔr] conj. 也不 ◀€ Track 3340

▶Neither Bart nor his brother will take over the family business.
巴特和他的哥哥都不會繼承家業。

normal [`nɔrml̩] ◀€ Track 3341

adj. 正常的

▶Water would freeze at zero degree Celsius in a normal state.
正常狀態下,水會在零度結冰。

normally [`nɔrml̩ɪ] ◀€ Track 3342

adv. 正常地;按照慣例地;通常

▶Hank keeps regular hours; normally, he goes to bed before midnight.
漢克作息規律;通常,他都在午夜之前就寢。

中級

north [nɔrθ] n. 北方
◀Track 3343

▶The weather in the north is quite chilly today.
今天北部的天氣會有點涼。

adj. 北部的；北方的；

▶The north part of the island is in the Arctic Circle.
這個島的北部在北極圈當中。

adv. 向北；在北方；自北方

▶According to the witness, the robber headed north after he left the bank.
目擊者指出，這位搶匪在離開銀行之後就往北方前進。

north-east [`nɔrθ`ist]
◀Track 3344

n. 東北，東北方；東北部

▶The cold from in the north-east of the island will cause the temperature to drop in the following days.
來自本島東北方的冷鋒會造成未來幾天的氣溫下降。

adv. 在東北；向東北；來自東北

▶The train headed northeast to the biggest harbor city in the country.
這班火車往東北方前進，前往本國最大的港口城市。

adj. 東北的；來自東北的；朝東北的

▶Due to the monsoon, we will be affected by the dust storm in the northeast area.
因為季風的關係，我們會受到來自東北區沙塵暴的影響。

northern [`nɔrðɚn]
◀Track 3345

adj. 北方的

▶People from the northern area speak their own dialect.
來自北方的人説自己的方言。

north-west
◀Track 3346

[`nɔrθ`wɛst] n. 西北，西北方；西北部

▶The county in the north-west are famous for producing peaches.
在西北方的縣以出產桃子著名。

adv. 在西北；向西北；來自西北

▶The bus will head northwest to another century-old town.
這個巴士會往西北方走，去一個百年老鎮。

adj. 西北的；來自西北的；朝西北的

▶The landscape in the northwest area is covered with forest.
西北方地區的景觀被森林覆蓋。

nose [noz] n. 鼻子
◀Track 3347

▶Don't pick your nose at the dinner table.
不要餐桌上挖鼻孔。

nostril [`nɑstrɪl] n. 鼻孔
◀Track 3348

▶The fragrance of the lilies comes to the nostrils.
百合花香撲鼻而來。

not [nɑt] adv. 不
◀Track 3349

▶I would rather not think of the past.
我寧願不要回想過去。

note [not] n. 筆記；便條
◀Track 3350

▶Remember to take notes during the lecture. 演講中記得要做筆記。

v. 注意

▶Note that you should enclose the application form to the email.
注意要將申請表附加在電子郵件中。

notebook [`not͵bʊk]
◀Track 3351

n. 筆記本；筆記型電腦

▶Attendants of the workshop should bring their notebook with them.
參加這場工作坊的人需要自備筆電。

nothing [`nʌθɪŋ]
◀ Track 3352

pron. 沒什麼;什麼事物都沒有

▶Nothing can stop him from going on a grand tour.
沒有什麼事情可以阻止他去壯遊。

n. 微不足道的事或物

▶What I need is nothing but a few days of rest.
我只不是想休息幾天而已。

notice [`notɪs]
◀ Track 3353

n. 公告;通知;注意;察覺

▶The notice said the service of the elevator won't resume until tomorrow morning. 這則通知說電梯要到明天早上才會恢復運作。

v. 注意;提到

▶Tina didn't notice the grammatical mistake and handed in the flawed report.
緹娜沒有注意到這個文法錯誤,交了有錯誤的報告出去。

notorious [no`torɪəs]
◀ Track 3354

adj. 惡名昭彰的,聲名狼藉的

▶The merchant was notorious, for he monopolized the row material for the textile industry.
這個商人因為壟斷紡織業的原料而惡名昭彰。

noun [naʊn] **n.** 名詞
◀ Track 3355

▶Money is an uncountable noun.
錢是不可數名詞。

nourish [`nɝɪʃ]
◀ Track 3356

v. 養育,滋養;培育

▶The book introduces some good foods to nourish children.
這本書介紹一些適合養育小孩的食物。

novel [`nɑvl̩]
◀ Track 3357

n. (長篇)小說

▶The movie was adapted from a best-selling novel.
這部電影是由暢銷小說改編的。

adj. 新奇的

▶In the international CES (Consumer Electronic Show), you can see some innovative inventions and some novel idea. 在國際客製化科技展,你可以看到一些創新的發明,以及新奇的想法。

novelist [`nɑvl̩ɪst]
◀ Track 3358

n. 小說家

▶The novelist is known for his works of fantasies. 這位小說家以奇幻小說著名。

November
◀ Track 3359

[no`vɛmbɚ] **n.** 十一月

▶He finally completed his doctoral thesis last November.
他終於在去年十一月完成博士論文。

now [naʊ]
◀ Track 3360

adv. 現在;此刻;馬上

▶The live broadcast of the football game is on TV now.
現在電視上撥出足球比賽的現場轉播。

n. 現在;目前;此刻

▶If you have a goal, pursue it. Now is the best time. 如果你有目標,就去追求。現在就是最適合的時機。

中級

nowadays [ˋnauəˏdez] ◀Track 3361

adv. 今日，現在

▶Smartphones have become a daily necessity for many people nowadays.
現在對許多人來説，手機是一項必須品。

nowhere [ˋnoˏhwɛr] ◀Track 3362

adv. 任何地方都不

▶What we've done was in vain. We are getting nowhere.
我們做的事情都白費了。什麼事情也沒達成。

相關片語 **in the middle of nowhere**
偏遠的某地

▶We got lost in the middle of nowhere; what's worse, there was no signal.
我們在窮鄉僻壤中迷路，更糟的是，我們收不到訊號。

nuclear [ˋnjuklɪə] ◀Track 3363

adj. 核心的，中心的；原子彈的

▶North Korea has promised to destroy the nuclear weapons it possesses.
北韓承諾要銷毀所擁有的核子武器。

補充片語 **nuclear weapon** 核子武器

number [ˋnʌmbə] ◀Track 3364

n. 數字；數量

▶Can you tell me the extension number of Mr. Chang's office?
你可以告訴我張先生辦公室的分機號碼嗎？

v. 編號；給號碼

▶Steve has terminal pancreas cancer; his days are numbered.
史提夫換了末期胰臟癌；他日子所剩無幾了。

numerous [ˋnjumərəs] ◀Track 3365

adj. 許多的；為數眾多的

▶There are numerous skyscrapers in the downtown area.
市區有許多摩天大樓。

nun [nʌn] **n.** 修女，尼姑 ◀Track 3366

▶The nuns are reciting the secrete scripture.
尼姑們正在念經。

nurse [nɜs] **n.** 護士 ◀Track 3367

▶The nurses in the emergency room have worked for more than ten hours today. 急診室的護士們今天已經工作超過12個小時了。

v. 看護；護理

▶The stray dog was meticulously nursed back to health by the kind young lady.
那名善良年輕的女性將這隻流浪狗仔細地照顧，使它恢復健康。

nursery [ˋnɜsərɪ] ◀Track 3368

n. 托兒所

▶Children are taught basic table manners in the nursery.
小朋友在這間托兒所學到基本的餐桌禮儀。

nursing [ˋnɜsɪŋ] ◀Track 3369

n. 看護，護理

▶Sarah got a certificate for nursing.
莎拉有看護的證照。

adj. 看護的，護理病人的

▶She attended a nursing school before she started to work in the nursing home. 在到護理之家工作之前，她有去上護理學校。

相關片語 **nursing home**
養老院；照料老人或病患的地方

▶The residents in the nursing home are being taken good care of.
這間養老院的住戶都被照顧得很好。

nut [nʌt]
◀⹇ Track 3370

n. 堅果；核果；難事；難對付的人

▶You can sprinkle some nuts to add flavors to the cake.
你可以在蛋糕上灑一點堅果來添加風味。

相關片語 **go nuts** 發怒；氣炸

▶My sister will go nuts when she finds that I deleted the file of her master's thesis by accident.
當我妹妹發現我不小心把她的碩士論文電子檔刪掉的時候，一定會暴跳如雷。

nutrient [`njutrɪənt]
◀⹇ Track 3371

n. 營養物，滋養物

▶The nutrients of the food product are listed on the label on the package.
這個食品的營養素有標示在包裝的標籤上。

nutrition [nju`trɪʃən]
◀⹇ Track 3372

n. 營養，滋養；營養物，滋養物

▶Inadequate nutrition may lead to poor health.
營養不足可能會導致健康不良。

nylon [`naɪlɑn] **n.** 尼龍
◀⹇ Track 3373

▶Materials like nylon, acrylic, or polyester are ignition-resistant.
尼龍、壓克力纖維、或聚酯纖維等材質是不可燃的。

中級

▶ Oo

　　以下表格是全民英檢官方公告中級「聽、說、讀、寫」所須具備的能力，本書例句皆依此範疇特別設計，只要掃描右方QR code，就能搭配相對應的音軌實現「眼耳並用」方式，刺激左腦的語言學習功能；同時也可使用本書附贈的紅膠片，將其置於單字上，一面記憶一面自我挑戰，達到雙倍的學習成果！

聽 ▶	在日常生活中，能聽懂一般的會話；能大致聽懂公共場所廣播、氣象報告及廣告等。在工作時，能聽懂簡易的產品介紹與操作說明。能大致聽懂外籍人士的談話及詢問。
說 ▶	可在日常生活中，能以簡易英語交談或描述一般事物，能介紹自己的生活作息、工作、家庭、經歷等，並可對一般話題陳述看法。在工作時，能進行簡單的答詢，並與外籍人士交談溝通。
讀 ▶	在日常生活中，能閱讀短文、故事、私人信件、廣告、傳單、簡介及使用說明等。在工作時，能閱讀工作須知、公告、操作手冊、例行的文件、傳真、電報等。
寫 ▶	能寫簡單的書信、故事及心得等。對於熟悉且與個人經歷相關的主題，能以簡易的文字表達。

oak [ok] n. 橡樹
◀ Track 3374

▶My parents planted an oak tree in the front yard.
我父母親在前院種植一棵橡樹。

oasis [o`esɪs]
◀ Track 3375
n.（沙漠中的）綠洲；（困境中）令人寬慰的事物或地方

▶The small park is a welcome oasis amid the city's many factories.
這個小公園在到處都是工廠的城市裡是一座小小的綠洲。

obedient [ə`bidjənt]
◀ Track 3376
adj. 順從的，服從的

▶To the conservative man, filial piety means being absolutely obedient to the parents.
對這個保守的男人來說，孝道就是對父母絕對的服從。

obey [ə`be] v. 遵守；服從
◀ Track 3377

▶We are supposed to obey the regulations of the organization.
我們應該要遵從這個機構的規定。

object [`abdʒɪkt]
◀ Track 3378
n. 物體；對象；目標；目的

▶The teenager claimed that he saw the unidentified flying object in the mountain.
這個青少年說他在山上看到不明飛行物體。

v. 反對

▶We objected his proposal, for it is not practical.
我們反對他的提案，因為那不實際。

objection [əb`dʒɛkʃən]
◀ Track 3379
n. 反對；異議

▶The construction of the incinerator was faced with strong objection of the local residents.
建造焚化爐的議題遭到當地居民強烈反對。

objective [əb`dʒɛktɪv] ◀Track 3380
n. 目標，目的；受格

▶His objective is to walk across the Antarctic continent without any assistance.
他的目標就是不靠任何協助徒步橫越南極洲大陸。

adj. 客觀的，無偏見的；客觀存在的

▶They gave us objective opinions about the curriculum design.
他們給了我們一些關於課程設計的客觀建議。

observation ◀Track 3381
[,ɑbzɚ`veʃən] **n.** 觀察；觀測力；監視；（觀察後的）意見或看法

▶With the space telescope, the observation of the remote galaxy became possible.
因為有太空望遠鏡，觀察遙遠的銀河系變得可能。

observe [əb`zɝv] ◀Track 3382
v. 注意；觀察；監視

▶Jenny went to the Republic of Congo to observe the habituated gorillas.
珍妮去剛果共和國去觀察當地的猩猩。

obstacle [`ɑbstək!] ◀Track 3383
n. 障礙物，妨礙

▶The habit of procrastination will become an obstacle to his success.
拖延的習慣會成為他成功的阻礙。

obtain [əb`ten] ◀Track 3384
v. 獲得，得到

▶Emily obtained the certificate after she finished the online courses.
艾蜜莉在上完線上課程之後獲得了這個證照。

obvious [`ɑbvɪəs] ◀Track 3385
adj. 明顯的

▶The sign that he was not eligible for this job is very obvious.
他不適任這個工作的徵兆是很明顯的。

obviously [`ɑbvɪəslɪ] ◀Track 3386
adv. 明顯地，顯然地

▶Obviously, he isn't keen for getting this job.
明顯地，他並不是很積極想要獲得這份工作。

occasion [ə`keʒən] ◀Track 3387
n. 場合；時機

▶It is inappropriate for you to crack jokes on the solemn occasion.
這這樣莊嚴的場合講笑話不太適合。

occasional [ə`keʒən!] ◀Track 3388
adj. 偶爾的；特殊場合的；臨時的

▶I have occasional lunch with the colleague sitting next to me.
我偶爾會和坐隔壁的同事一起吃午餐。

occupation ◀Track 3389
[,ɑkjə`peʃən] **n.** 工作，職業；日常事務；佔領

▶She is an engineer by occupation.
她的職業是工程師。

中級

occupy [`akjə,paɪ]　◀Track 3390
v. 佔領，佔據

▶Excuse me, is the seat occupied?
不好意思，請問這個位子有人坐嗎？

occur [ə`kɝ] **v.** 發生　◀Track 3391
▶Something unexpected occurred so we had to change our original plan.
有意料之外的事情發生，所以我們必須更改計畫。

ocean [`oʃən] **n.** 海洋　◀Track 3392
▶It is said that there are a lot of unexplored resources in the ocean.
據說在海洋中有很多未被開發的資源。

o'clock [ə`klɑk]　◀Track 3393
adv. ……點鐘

▶At five o'clock, most of the cleric workers would clock out.
五點鐘一到，大部分事務員就會打卡下班。

October [ak`tobə]　◀Track 3394
=Oct. **n.** 十月

▶There are two national holidays in October. 十月有兩個國定假日。

octopus [`aktəpəs]　◀Track 3395
n. 章魚

▶It is said that Paul the Octopus can precisely predict the champion of FIFA.
據說章魚保羅可以精準預測世足賽的冠軍。

odd [ad] **adj.** 古怪的　◀Track 3396
▶An odd-looking old man is walking toward us.
有個奇怪的老頭子朝我們走過來。

相關片語 odd job 零工

▶Ted hopes that he could find a decent job instead of doing odd jobs.
泰德希望他可以找到一份穩定的工作，而不是只有打零工。

of [av]　◀Track 3397
prep. 屬於；……的；因為

▶The stage play was said to be the greatest show of all time.
這個舞台劇被譽為是有史以來最好的表演。

off [ɔf]　◀Track 3398
adv. 離開；隔開；關掉

▶Please turn off the computer before you leave the laboratory.
離開實驗室之前記得要關掉電腦。

prep. 在……下方；往……下面；離開

▶I want this incident to be off the record. 我希望這次的事件不要公開。

adj. 偏離的；較遠的；不正常的

▶The power of the machine is off.
機器的電源關閉了。

offend [ə`fɛnd]　◀Track 3399
v. 冒犯，觸怒，使不舒服

▶The celebrity was offended by the post, and he claimed to file a suit against the person who left the comment.
這位名人覺得這篇貼文冒犯到他了，揚言要對貼文者提告。

offense [ə`fɛns]　◀Track 3400
=offence **n.** 罪過；觸怒

▶Don't take it personally. I mean no offense. 請不要在意。我無意冒犯。

offensive [ə`fɛnsɪv]　◀⋲ Track 3401

adj. 冒犯的；討厭的；進攻的

▶Many of the messages on Twitter were considered offensive.
許多推特上的留言都有冒犯人的意味。

n. 進攻，攻勢

▶It's not an appropriate occasion to take the offensive.
現在不是發動攻勢的適當時機。

offer [`ɔfə]　◀⋲ Track 3402

v. 提供；提議；給予

▶Our homeroom teacher offered us some pieces of advices about how to choose our career path.
我們班導師提供給我們一些如何選擇職涯方向的建議。

n. 提議；機會

▶Gina turned down the job offer, for she decided to study overseas.
吉娜因為想要去海外念書所以婉拒了這個工作機會。

office [`ɔfɪs]　◀⋲ Track 3403

n. 辦公室；公司

▶You can call the customer representatives during office hours.
妳可以在上班時間打電話給客服人員。

officer [`ɔfəsə]　◀⋲ Track 3404

n. 官員（軍官；警官）；公務員

▶The police officers came to the crime scene and took down the gangster.
警察到達犯罪現場並把壞人制伏了。

official [ə`fɪʃəl]　◀⋲ Track 3405

n. 官員；公務員

▶The official made a formal announcement for the implementation of the new policy.
官員發表正式聲明，說明新政策要執行了。

adj. 官方的

▶There is a recruiting announcement on the official website of the national park.
這個國家公園的官方網站上面有徵人的公告。

often [`ɔfən]　**adv.** 時常　◀⋲ Track 3406

▶Do you often download free movies on the Internet?
你常常從網路上下載免費的電影嗎？

oh [o]　◀⋲ Track 3407

interj.（表示驚訝，恐懼）哦，噢

▶Oh, what a pity.
噢，真可惜。

oil [ɔɪl]　**n.** 油　◀⋲ Track 3408

▶There is too much oil in this dish; it's greasy.
這道菜裡太多油了，整個油膩膩。

v. 給……上油；塗油

▶The mechanic oiled the machine to make it work more smoothly.
師傅給機器上油，讓它運作更順暢。

相關片語 **oil the wheels** 使事情變容易

▶An aid program was established to oil the wheels of economic reform in the region.
有一個輔助計畫已經被創建來讓當地的經濟改革更加順利。

OK [`o`ke]＝O.K.＝ok　◀⋲ Track 3409
＝o.k.＝okay　**adj.** 可以的；不錯的

中級

▶It is OK for you to make that choice.
你這樣選擇是還可以。

adv. 尚可

▶The dancer performed okay, but most of the audience wasn't impressed.
這位舞者表現得還可以，但是觀眾大部分並沒有特別感動。

n. 認可；

▶I need the okay from my supervisor to proceed with my plan.
我需要主管批准才可以進行計畫的下一步。

v. 批准；認可

▶Who okayed this? 是誰説可以的？

old [old] **adj.** 老的；舊的　◀Track 3410

▶The old building needs some renovations.
這棟老建築物需要翻修一番。

Olympic [o`lɪmpɪk]　◀Track 3411
adj. 奧林匹克（競賽）的

▶To the retired athlete, the Olympic medal was reminiscent of the past glory.
對這位退休運動員來説，奧運獎牌使他想起光榮的過去。

omit [o`mɪt]　◀Track 3412
v. 遺漏；省略；忽略不做

▶Every step is important; if you omit the details, there will be severe consequences.
每個步驟都很重要；如果你省略細節，會有嚴重的後果。

on [ɑn] **prep.** 在……上　◀Track 3413

▶There are dozens of patients on the waiting list of organ donation.
有好幾十個人在器官捐贈的等待名單上。

adv. 繼續；（穿）上；開著

▶The show must go on even one of our performers was injured.
儘管我們有一位表演者受傷了，表演還是要繼續。

once [wʌns]　◀Track 3414
adv. 一次；曾經

▶I have visited the Grand Canyon once.
我去過大峽谷一次。

conj. 一旦；一……便……

▶Once you pass the exam, you can be admitted to the program.
一旦通過測驗，你就可以修習這個課程了。

one [wʌn] **n.** 一；一歲　◀Track 3415

▶We had a party when our baby was one. 寶寶滿周歲的時候，我們辦了一個派對慶祝。

adj. 一的；一個的

▶Is one bottle of milk enough?
一罐牛奶夠嗎？

oneself [wʌn`sɛlf]　◀Track 3416
pron. 自己

▶Always doing something for oneself is against the altruistic spirit.
總是為自己做事情，違背利他的精神。

one-sided　◀Track 3417
[`wʌn`saɪdɪd] **adj.** 單側的；片面的；一面倒的

▶The comment of the conservative politician was considered to be one-sided and biased.
這位保守派政客的意見，被認為是片面又偏頗的。

onion [ˋʌnjən] n. 洋蔥 🔊 Track 3418

▶ The chef added some shredded onions to increase the flavor of the fried rice. 廚師加了一些切碎的洋蔥來增加炒飯的風味。

on·ly [ˋonlɪ] adv. 僅；只 🔊 Track 3419

▶ I know him only by name; I haven't met him in person. 我只知道他的名字，我沒見過他本人。

adj. 唯一的；

▶ He is the only person who knows about this traditional craftiness. 他是唯一知道這個傳統工藝的人。

conj. 可是；不過

▶ He is not only reliable but also capable. 他既可靠又有能力。

onto [ˋɑntu] 🔊 Track 3420
prep. 到……之上

▶ Please walk onto the stage and receive the award. 請上台領獎。

open [ˋopən] v. 開；打開 🔊 Track 3421

▶ I asked my brother to open the lid of the jar for me. 我請我哥哥幫我打開罐子的蓋子。

adj. 開放的；打開的

▶ He holds an open attitude towards his daughter's career orientation. 他對於女兒的職涯取向抱持開放的態度。

opener [ˋopənɚ] 🔊 Track 3422
n. 開啟的工具；開端；開啟者

▶ Please fetch the can opener in the cupboard for me. 請幫我拿櫥櫃裡面的開罐器。

opening [ˋopənɪŋ] 🔊 Track 3423
n. 開幕

▶ Special discounts will be offered at our grand opening. 在我們盛大開幕期間，商品特價供應。

adj. 開幕的，開始的

▶ The mayor will attend the opening ceremony of the local art center. 市長會出席本地藝術中心的開幕典禮。

opera [ˋɑpərə] n. 歌劇 🔊 Track 3424

▶ The Phantom of the Opera is my favorite musical. 歌劇魅影是我最喜歡的音樂劇。

operate [ˋɑpəˌret] 🔊 Track 3425
v. 運轉；營運；操作；動手術

▶ The automatic train can operate by itself. 這種自動列車可以自己運轉。

operation [ˌɑpəˋreʃən] 🔊 Track 3426
n. 操作；運轉；經營；手術

▶ The operation to remove the patient's brain tumor lasted for more than ten hours. 這場切除病人腦瘤的手術持續了超過十個小時。

operator [ˋɑpəˌretɚ] 🔊 Track 3427
n. 操作者；經營者；施行手術的醫生

▶ The monthly wage of the machine operator is rather high. 這位機械操作員每個月的薪水滿高的。

opinion [əˋpɪnjən] 🔊 Track 3428
n. 意見；看法

▶In my opinion, you should weigh the pros and cons before you make the final decision.
就我的意見來看，你應該先權衡利弊再做最後的決定。

opponent [ə`ponənt] ◀Track 3429
n. 對手，敵手

▶He was collecting the information of his opponents to figure out the best strategy to win the game.
他蒐集對手的資料，想要擬出一個贏得比賽的策略。

opportunity ◀Track 3430
[ˌɑpɚ`tjunətɪ] **n.** 機會

▶Dozens of performers joined the audition for the opportunity to act in the movie. 好幾十位表演者參加試鏡要爭取在電影中演出的機會。

oppose [ə`poz] **v.** 反對 ◀Track 3431

▶The merger case was opposed by many employees of the company.
這件合併案遭到許多員工的反對。

opposite [`ɑpəzɪt] ◀Track 3432
adj. 相反的，對立的；對面的

▶We took the wrong route; our destination was in the opposite direction.
我們走錯方向了；我們的目的地在反方向。

n. 對立面，對立物

▶His viewpoint on this issue is the opposite of mine.
他對這個議題的看法跟我完全相反。

prep. 在……對面

▶We sat opposite each other when we were in the library.
在圖書館裡，我們坐在彼此對面。

adv. 在對面
▶The two stores stood opposite at the street.
這兩家店就在彼此對面。

opposition ◀Track 3433
[ˌɑpə`zɪʃən] **n.** 反對，反抗，敵對，對立

▶Do you have anything in opposition to say? 你有任何反對意見要表達嗎？

option [`ɑpʃən] **n.** 選擇 ◀Track 3434
▶They had no option but to reconcile with each other.
他們別無選擇，只能對彼此妥協。

or [ɔr] **conj.** 或者；否則 ◀Track 3435
▶You have to get up early, or you will miss the school bus.
你得早點起床，不然會趕不上校車。

oral [`orəl] ◀Track 3436
adj. 口頭的，口述的

▶He passed the written test but failed the oral test.
他的筆試通過，但是口試沒過。

n. 口試
▶The oral of the entrance exam will take about thirty minutes.
這個入學考的口試大約要30分鐘。

orange [`ɔrɪndʒ] ◀Track 3437
n. 柳橙；橙色

▶We picked the oranges in the orchard.
我們在果園裡面摘柳橙。

adj. 橙色的
▶The candy with a new flavor came in an orange package.
這個新口味的糖果是使用橘色的包裝。

中級

orbit [`ɔrbɪt] n. 運行軌道　◀Track 3438

▶The orbit of an asteroid is not fixed.
小行星的運行軌道可能會改變。

v 環繞（天體等）的軌道運行

▶The moon orbits the earth.
月亮繞地球運行。

orchard [`ɔrtʃəd]　◀Track 3439
n. 果園

▶Visitors can pick the strawberries directly from the orchard.
遊客可以直接在果園裡面採草莓。

orchestra [`ɔrkɪstrə]　◀Track 3440
n. 管弦樂隊

▶Diana is the principal violinist in the orchestra. 黛安娜是這個管弦樂團裡面的首席小提琴手。

or·der [`ɔrdə]　◀Track 3441
n. 次序；命令；訂購

▶After we received the quotation, we decided to place an order.
收到報價單之後，我們就決定要下訂單了。

v 命令；訂購；點菜

▶Are you ready to order? 您要點餐了嗎？

orderly [`ɔrdəlɪ]　◀Track 3442
adj. 整齊的，有條理的，守秩序的

▶Terry has a collection of CDs, and he put them in an orderly way in the closet. 泰瑞有許多CD，他把它們整齊地收在櫃子裡。

n. （醫院的）護理員；勤務兵，傳令兵

▶The orderly on duty kept the record of the patient's vital signs.
值班的護理員紀錄了病人的生命徵象。

ordinary [`ɔrdn,ɛrɪ]　◀Track 3443
adj. 平凡普通的；平常的

▶He is just an ordinary salaryman; he works for more than ten hours a day and seldom has any recreation.
他是一個平凡的上班族；每天工作超過十個小時，沒有什麼娛樂可言。

organ [`ɔrgən] n. 器官　◀Track 3444

▶It is said that scientists can now 3D print functional organs.
據說科學家現在可以用3D列印出功能性器官。

organic [ɔr`gænɪk]　◀Track 3445
adj. 有機的

▶The restaurant claims that it only uses organic food ingredients.
這家餐廳聲稱他們只用有機的食材。

organiza·tion　◀Track 3446
[,ɔrgənə`zeʃən] **=or·gani·sation**
（英式英文）**n.** 組織；機構

▶My dream is to work for a non-governmental organization for a meaningful cause.
我的夢想就是為一個非政府組織工作，做有意義的事情。

organize [`ɔrgə,naɪz]　◀Track 3447
=organise （英式英文）

v 組織；安排；籌劃；使有條理

▶The wedding planner will organize all the details of the ceremony and the reception party.
這名婚秘會籌畫典禮及接待宴會的所有細節。

origin [`ɔrədʒɪn] **n.** 起源 ◀€Track 3448

▶The Big Bang Theory explains the origin of the universe.
大爆炸理論解釋了宇宙的起源。

original [ə`rɪdʒənl] ◀€Track 3449
adj. 最初的，原始的；有獨創性的

▶We had to change our original plan due to some unexpected accidents.
因為一些意外，我們必須更改原本的計畫。

ornament [`ɔrnəmənt] ◀€Track 3450
n. 裝飾品；裝飾；增添光彩的人或事物

▶The splendid ornament in the lobby was very impressive.
大廳裡金光閃閃的裝飾令人印象深刻。

v. 美化；裝飾

▶The tree is ornamented with Christmas tinsels.
這棵樹有聖誕彩帶裝飾。

orphan [`ɔrfən] **n.** 孤兒 ◀€Track 3451

▶The panda cub became an orphan when its parents were shot by the poachers.
小熊貓變成孤兒，因為牠的父母親被盜獵者給槍殺了。

orphanage [`ɔrfənɪdʒ] ◀€Track 3452
n. 孤兒院；孤兒身份；孤兒（總稱）

▶Gina volunteers to teach the kids in the orphanage English on the weekend.
吉娜周末會去孤兒院做志工教小朋友英文。

ostrich [`ɑstrɪtʃ] ◀€Track 3453
n. 鴕鳥；鴕鳥般的人（以為不正視危險就能躲開危險的人）

▶The ostrich ran away as soon as it saw the cheetah.
鴕鳥一看到美洲豹就趕快逃跑。

other [`ʌðə] ◀€Track 3454
adj. 其他的；其餘的；（兩者中）另一個的

▶He never cares about other people; he only tries to get the upmost benefit for himself.
他從來不在乎別人；他只想要為自己謀取最大的利益。

pron. （兩者中的）另一方；其餘的人或事物

▶Students chose different activities during the recess; some stayed in the classroom phubbing on their smartphones, while others play sports outside.
學生們在休息時間選擇不同的活動，有些人在教室裡低頭用手機，其他人則是在操場上運動。

otherwise ◀€Track 3455
[`ʌðə,waɪz] **adv.** 否則，不然；用別的方法

▶You had better check whether there are any typos in your report; otherwise, it may be returned by the professor.
你最好檢查報告中是否有錯字，否則的話，教授會退回你的報告。

ought [ɔt] ◀€Track 3456
aux. （表示義務、責任等）應當

▶We ought to send these animals back to their natural habitat.
我們應該把這些動物送回牠們的自然棲息地。

ounce [aʊns] ◀€Track 3457
n. 盎司，英兩；一點點，少量

▶How many tablespoons are in an ounce of butter?
一盎司的奶油是多少茶匙呢？

our [`aʊr] det. 我們的　◀Track 3458

▶Our goal for this quarter is to develop a new market in Southeast Asia.
我們本季的目標就是在東南亞地區發展新市場。

ours [`aʊrz]　◀Track 3459
pron. 我們的（東西）

▶Their reimbursement policies are stricter than ours.
他們的報帳規定比我們的嚴格。

ourselves [ˌaʊr`sɛlvz]　◀Track 3460
pron. 我們自己

▶If we choose to believer in the flattery advertisement, we are deceiving ourselves.
如果我們選擇相信浮誇的廣告，我們就是在欺騙自己。

out [aʊt]　◀Track 3461
adv. 出外；向外；在外

▶I'm going out. Do you want me to bring something back for you?
我要出門了。你有要我幫你帶什麼東西回來嗎？

adj. 外側的；向外的；用完的；不流行的

▶He is now out of danger.
他現在已脫離險境。

prep. 通過……而出

▶The cork won't come out of the bottle.
這個軟木塞卡在瓶子拔不出來。

outcome [`aʊtˌkʌm]　◀Track 3462
n. 結果

▶The outcome of the exam will be announced next Monday. You will know whether you pass the first stage. 這個考試的結果下週一就會公布。你便能得知你有沒有通過第一階段。

outdoor [`aʊtˌdor]　◀Track 3463
adj. 戶外的

▶Terry often does some outdoor activities with his son, such as rock climbing, hiking, or fishing.
泰瑞會和他兒子一起做一些戶外運動，像是攀崖、健行、或釣魚。

outdoors [`aʊt`dorz]　◀Track 3464
adv. 在戶外

▶They are chatting outdoors.
他們在外面聊天。

outer [`aʊtɚ]　◀Track 3465
adj. 在外的，外圍的，外面的

▶They bought a mansion at the outer circle of the city.
他們在城市外圍買了棟豪宅。

相關片語 outer space 外太空

▶The scientist gave a speech on the benefits of outer space explorations.
這位科學家發表一個演講，說明探索外太空的好處。

outfit [`aʊtˌfɪt]　◀Track 3466
n. 全套服裝；全套裝備

▶The motorcycle outfits cost him about nine thousand dollars.
這套機車裝備花了他快九千元。

v. 裝備，配備；獲得裝備

▶They outfitted the long journey to the Arctic Circle. 他們為北極圈長途旅行整裝。

中級

outgoing [`aʊt͵goɪŋ] ◀╪Track 3467

adj. 外向的，活潑的；離開的

▶She has an outgoing personality, so I think she can manage to be a good sales representative.
她有外向的個性，所以我想她應該可以當一個很好的銷售員。

outlet [`aʊt͵lɛt] ◀╪Track 3468

n. 出口；排氣口；（感情）發洩途徑；銷路，商店

▶I bought this down jacket at the outlet store; it was a good bargain.
我是在貨暢商店買這件羽絨衣的；很划算。

outline [`aʊt͵laɪn] ◀╪Track 3469

n. 外形，輪廓；提綱，概要

▶We only had an outline for this report; we are still working on the details.
我們只寫出這個報告的綱要，目前還在想細節的內容。

v. 畫出……的輪廓；概述

▶The kid outlined the vase, and then he got distracted and gave up the sketch.
小朋友畫出了花瓶的輪廓，接著他就分心然後放棄這幅素描了。

output [`aʊt͵pʊt] ◀╪Track 3470

n. 出產，生產；輸出；作品；產量

▶When acquiring a new language, you need enough input before you can have any output. 學習新語言的時候，你需要足夠的輸入，才能有產出。

outside [`aʊt`saɪd] ◀╪Track 3471

prep. 在……之外

▶There is a giant graffiti on the wall outside the building.
這棟大樓外面牆上有一個巨大的塗鴉。

adv. 在外面

▶The smell of the insect repellent in the house was so strong that we chose to stay outside.
房子裡的殺蟲劑味道太重了，所以我們選擇待在外面。

adj. 外面的；外部的

▶Reports on outside reading materials will bring you extra credits for this course.
課外閱讀的報告可以幫你在這堂課加分。

n. 外面；外部；外觀

▶On the outside, she is indifferent; on the inside, she is actually enthusiastic.
她外表冷漠，但是內心熱情。

outstanding ◀╪Track 3472

[`aʊt`stændɪŋ] **adj.** 顯著的，傑出的

▶The outstanding physicist received an award from the president for his contribution to the nation.
這名傑出的物理學家因為他對國家的貢獻獲頒總統獎。

outward [`aʊtwɚd] ◀╪Track 3473

adj. 向外的；外面的，外表的

▶I purchased a train ticket for an outward journey.
我買了一張單程旅行的票。

adv. 向外；（船）出海，出港；顯而易見地

▶A ship would shift outward during a turn.
船在轉彎的時候會向外飄。

oval [`ovl] **adj.** 卵形的 ◀╪Track 3474

▶I found an oval stone in the garden.
我在花園裡面發現一個卵形的石頭。

n. 卵形物

▶ Many things are in the shape of an oval, such as a kiwi, an egg, a tennis rack, etc.

許多東西都是卵形的，像是奇異果、蛋、網球拍等等。

oven [`ʌvən] n. 爐；烤箱
◀ Track 3475

▶ Place the cake in the oven at 180°C for twelve minutes.

將蛋糕放置在180度的烤箱中烤12分鐘。

over [`ovɚ]
◀ Track 3476

adv. 在上方；在上空；超過；遍及

▶ The helicopter was hovering over in this area.

直升機在這個地區上空盤旋。

adj. 結束了的

▶ We walked out of the theater slowly after the movie was over.

電影結束後，我們慢慢地走出戲院。

prep. 在上方；在上空

▶ The projector is over the seats of the audience.

投影機在觀眾座位的上方。

overall [`ovɚ,ɔl]
◀ Track 3477

adj. 從頭到尾的；總的，全部的

▶ This is the overall illustration of the theory.

這是這個理論的大致說明。

adv. 從頭到尾；大體上，總的來說

▶ She is not against the project overall.

整體來說，她不反對這個計畫。

n. 工裝褲

▶ The construction worker wears an overall when he is on duty.

這名建築工人在上班的時候會穿工裝褲。

overcoat [`ovɚ,kot]
◀ Track 3478

n. 外套

▶ The concierge held the overcoat for the guest.

服務人員替顧客拿著大衣。

overcome [,ovɚ`kʌm]
◀ Track 3479

v. 得勝；克服

▶ You have to learn to overcome the difficulties on your own.

你必須要學習靠自己的力量解決問題。

overeat [`ovɚ`it]
◀ Track 3480

v. 吃得過飽

▶ Overeating at the buffet restaurant is not good for your health.

在吃到飽餐廳吃太多東西對你的健康不好。

overflow [,ovɚ`flo]
◀ Track 3481

v. 充滿，洋溢；氾濫；從……溢出

▶ The waiter poured the water in the glass until it overflowed.

服務生倒水在杯子裡面直到它滿出來。

n. 溢出，過剩；氾濫

▶ The airline staff was anxious about the overflow of passengers in the airport.

機場旅客暴增，讓航空公司員工覺得很焦慮。

overhead [`ovɚ`hɛd]
◀ Track 3482

adj. 在頭頂上的；高架的；頭上的

▶ Where is the remote control for the overhead projector?

上頭投影機的遙控器在哪裡呢？

adv. 在頭頂上；在上頭；高高地

▶ A helicopter hovered overhead.

有一台直升機在頭頂盤旋。

中級

overlook [ˌovəˈlʊk] ◀€Track 3483

v. 眺望，俯瞰；看漏；寬容；監視；高聳於……之上

▶Money laundry problem has been overlooked for many years.
洗錢的問題已經被忽視很久了。

overnight [ˈovəˈnaɪt] ◀€Track 3484

adj. 通宵的，一整夜的；一夜間的

▶Taking overnight jobs may bother your circadian rhythm.
做通宵的工作可能會擾亂你的作息規律。

adv. 通宵，一整夜；一夜間

▶My friend is staying overnight with us this Saturday.
我朋友這個週末要跟我們一起過夜。

overpass [ˌovəˈpæs] ◀€Track 3485

n. 天橋

▶There are some graffiti on the balustrade of the overpass.
天橋的欄杆上面有些塗鴉。

overseas [ˈovəˈsiz] ◀€Track 3486

adj. 海外的

▶The overseas students will go back to their hometown in three months. 這些海外交換學生再過三個月就會回去家鄉。

adv. 在海外

▶Finding a job overseas may be a time-consuming process.
在海外找工作是一個很花時間的過程。

oversleep [ˈovəˈslip] ◀€Track 3487

v. 睡過頭

▶I overslept and missed the school bus. 我睡過頭結果錯過了公車。

overtake [ˌovəˈtek] ◀€Track 3488

v. 追上；超過；突然侵襲

▶We have to overtake the car in front of us because it was driving slowly.
我們必須超前面那台車，因為他開得太慢了。

overthrow [ˈovəθro] ◀€Track 3489

v. 打倒；推翻；廢除

▶The tyrant was overthrown by the long-oppressed people.
暴君被長期受壓榨的人民推翻了。

n. 打倒，推翻

▶The overthrow of the autocratic monarch was a huge international news. 這個專制君主被推翻是一個很大的國際新聞。

over-weight ◀€Track 3490

[ˈovəˌwet] **adj.** 體重過重的

▶Being overweight may lead to some health problems such as cardiovascular diseases, diabetes, or high blood pressure.
體重過重可能會導致一些健康的問題，像是心臟疾病、糖尿病、或者高血壓。

owe [o] ◀€Track 3491

v. 歸功於；欠；應給予

▶You did a big favor for me; I owe you once.
你幫了我一個大忙；我欠你一次。

owl [aʊl] ◀€Track 3492

n. 貓頭鷹；常熬夜的人

▶It is said that deforestation has caused the habitat of owls to shrink.
據說森林濫伐的現象已經造成貓頭鷹棲息地的縮減。

own [on]

◀ Track 3493

pron. 自己的（東西）

▶This is the first time that I travel abroad on my own.
這是我第一次自己出國。

v. 擁有

▶The wealthy man owns three mansions in the most prosperous district of the city.
這位富翁在城市裡最繁榮的地區有三棟豪宅。

adj. 自己的

▶It's my dream to have my own apartment.
擁有我自己的公寓是我的夢想。

owner [ˋonɚ]

◀ Track 3494

n. 所有人；物主

▶The police will inform the owner of the bag to retrieve it.
警察會通知這個袋子的所有人將它取回。

ownership [ˋonɚ ʃɪp]

◀ Track 3495

n. 所有權，物主身份

▶The property's ownership tax will increase next year.
財產所有權的稅率明年會增加。

ox [ɑks] **n.** 牛；閹牛

◀ Track 3496

▶The oxen are grazing on the field.
牛在牧場上吃草。

oxygen [ˋɑksədʒən]

◀ Track 3497

n. 氧，氧氣

▶Put on the emergency oxygen mask first and then assist the other passengers.
先戴上緊急氧氣面罩，再幫助其他的乘客。

中級

▶ Pp

　　以下表格是全民英檢官方公告中級「聽、說、讀、寫」所須具備的能力，本書例句皆依此範疇特別設計，只要掃描右方**QR code**，就能搭配相對應的音軌實現「眼耳並用」方式，刺激左腦的語言學習功能；同時也可使用本書附贈的紅膠片，將其置於單字上，一面記憶一面自我挑戰，達到的雙倍的學習成果！

聽 ▶	在日常生活中，能聽懂一般的會話；能大致聽懂公共場所廣播、氣象報告及廣告等。在工作時，能聽懂簡易的產品介紹與操作說明。能大致聽懂外籍人士的談話及詢問。
說 ▶	可在日常生活中，能以簡易英語交談或描述一般事物，能介紹自己的生活作息、工作、家庭、經歷等，並可對一般話題陳述看法。在工作時，能進行簡單的答詢，並與外籍人士交談溝通。
讀 ▶	在日常生活中，能閱讀短文、故事、私人信件、廣告、傳單、簡介及使用說明等。在工作時，能閱讀工作須知、公告、操作手冊、例行的文件、傳真、電報等。
寫 ▶	能寫簡單的書信、故事及心得等。對於熟悉且與個人經歷相關的主題，能以簡易的文字表達。

P.M. [`pi`ɛm] =p.m.=PM adv. 下午；午後
◀ Track 3498

▶The service of the elevator will be suspended between 2:00 P.M. and 5:00 P.M. today.
今天下午兩點到五點之間，電梯暫停運作。

pace [pes]
◀ Track 3499

n. 一步；步調；進度；步法

▶I am getting used to the fast pace of the metropolitan area.
我慢慢習慣大都會地區快速的步調了。

v. 踱步；慢慢地走

▶The leopard paced back and forth in the cage. 美洲豹在籠子裡來回踱步。

相關片語 **at a snail's pace** 非常緩慢地

▶The project is progressing at a snail's pace. 這個計畫進行非常緩慢。

Pacific [pə`sɪfɪk]
◀ Track 3500

n. （大寫）太平洋

▶The counrties on the Ring of Fire around the Pacific are often struck by earthquakes.
環太平洋火山帶上的國家常受到地震襲擊。

adj. 太平洋的

▶The peaceful condition in the Asia Pacific region is vital for the world economy. 亞太地區維持和平的狀態對於世界的經濟來說相當重要。

pack [pæk] v 裝箱；打包
◀ Track 3501

▶Have you packed for your honeymoon trip? 你已經打包準備好去蜜月旅行了嗎？

n. 包；綑；包裹

▶I ordered two packs of snacks at Amazon.com.
我用亞馬遜網站訂了兩包餅乾。

package [`pækɪdʒ]
◀Track 3502

n. 包裹

▶A package thief wondered around this neighborhood and took away the goods that people left at their doors.
包裹小偷在這附近遊蕩，偷拿別人還沒拿進屋子裡的包裹。

packet [`pækɪt]
◀Track 3503

n. 小包、小捆；小袋；一批（信）；
一大筆（錢）

▶My mom hid a packet of money under her pillow, but she totally forgot about it. 我媽在枕頭底下藏了一小包錢，但她完全忘記這件事情。

pad [pæd]
◀Track 3504

n. 低沉的腳步聲；輕拍聲

▶I can hear the pad of the old man who lives next door.
我聽到住隔壁的老先生低沉的腳步聲。

v. 步行；放輕腳步走；墊

▶We padded cross the hall decorated with a glamorous chandelier.
我們走過擁有一盞美麗大吊燈的大廳。

page [pedʒ] **n.** 頁
◀Track 3505

▶I am turning over a new page—I am going to quit the video games.
我要改過自新—不再玩電玩了。

pain [pen]
◀Track 3506

n. 疼痛、痛苦；辛苦

▶Do you feel pain in the neck?
你脖子會痛嗎？

painful [`penfəl]
◀Track 3507

adj. 疼痛的、令人不快的

▶It's really painful to give up your favorite job.
放棄你喜歡的工作真的很痛苦。

paint [pent]
◀Track 3508

v. 油漆；漆上顏色；畫

▶Gina painted the wall in her room ivory white.
吉娜把她房間的牆面漆成象牙白色。

n. 油漆

▶The pungent smell of the paint makes me feel nauseous.
油漆的刺鼻味讓我覺得很噁心。

painter [`pentɚ]
◀Track 3509

n. 油漆工；畫家

▶The painter steeped on the ladder to paint the top of the fence.
油漆工站到梯子上去漆圍籬的頂部。

painting [`pentɪŋ]
◀Track 3510

n. 上油漆；繪畫

▶The artist's oil paintings will be displayed in this exhibition.
這位藝術家的油畫作品將在這次展覽中展出。

pair [pɛr] **n.** 一對；一雙
◀Track 3511

▶I purchased a pair of tickets for the show through the Internet.
我在網路上買了這場表演的對票。

pajamas [pə`dʒæməs]
◀Track 3512
=pyjamas （英式英文）**n.** 睡衣

▶The girls will have a pajama party this weekend.
這些女孩這周末會辦一個睡衣派對。

中級

pal [pæl] n. 好朋友
◀Track 3513

▶Gary will meet his net pal in person this Saturday.
蓋瑞這個星期六會和他的網友見面。

palace [`pælɪs] n. 宮殿
◀Track 3514

▶The National Palace Museum is a scenic spot which many tourists would visit when they come to Taiwan.
故宮博物院是一個許多外國觀光客來台灣時會去參觀的景點。

pale [pel] adj. 蒼白的
◀Track 3515

▶The patient suffers from dehydration and looked very pale.
這名病患有脫水現象，看起來臉色蒼白。

palm [pɑm] n. 手掌；手心
◀Track 3516

▶The fortune teller claimed that he is good at palm reading.
算命師宣稱他擅長看手相。

相關片語 have an itching palm
貪財，收賄

▶The politician who has an itching palm is accused to be morally corrupted.
這名收賄的政治人物被指控道德喪失。

pan [pæn] n. 平底鍋
◀Track 3517

▶You can download the recipe for pan-fried salmon from the website. 妳可以在這個網站上面下載鍋煎鮭魚的食譜。

pancake [`pæn͵kek]
n. 薄煎餅
◀Track 3518

▶Pancake muffins are the perfect lazy morning breakfast or afternoon snack.
薄餅是很容易做的早餐或者下午的點心。

panda [`pændə] n. 貓熊
◀Track 3519

▶Bamboo shoots are panda's staple food. 竹子是熊貓的主食。

panel [`pæn!]
◀Track 3520

n. 專案小組，專題討論小組；嵌板，鑲板；儀表板

▶The committee will have a panel discussion about the curriculum design of the program. 委員會將召開座談會來討論此企畫的課程設計。

補充片語 panel discussion
座談會，小組討論會

panic [`pænɪk] n. 驚慌
◀Track 3521

▶She was in a panic when she realized that her purse was stolen.
發現錢包被偷的時候，她相當恐慌。

v. 驚慌

▶Tina panicked when she realized that she didn't bring the PowerPoint file for the presentation with her.
緹娜發現她忘記帶報告用的投影片檔案時，感到慌張。

相關片語 panic buying 瘋狂搶購

▶It is reported that there was panic buying after the news, which said that the price of tissues was going to rise, was released.
據說衛生紙價格即將上漲的消息一釋出，就造成了瘋狂搶購。

pants [pænts]
=trousers （英式英語）n. 褲子
◀Track 3522

▶There are some patches on the poor kid's pants.
這個貧窮小孩的褲子上面有一些補丁。

papa [`pɑpə]=father ◀Track 3523
n. 爸爸

▶Helen missed the old days when she and her papa would go hiking together on the weekend. 海倫想念她和她爸爸周末一起爬山的那些日子。

papaya [pə`paɪə] **n.** 木瓜 ◀Track 3524

▶I made some papaya milk smoothie for my kids.
我做了一些木瓜牛奶奶昔給小孩。

paper [`pepɚ] ◀Track 3525
n. 紙；報紙；試卷；報告

▶Students have to submit their final papers for this course before January 9th. 學生們必須要在一月九日之前繳交這堂課的期末報告。

parachute [`pærə͵ʃut] ◀Track 3526
n. 降落傘

▶The soldiers learned how to fold and load a parachute.
士兵們在學如何摺疊和裝載降落傘。

v. 跳傘，跳傘降落；傘降

▶Some young people consider going parachuting or skydiving an exciting activity.
有些年輕人認為跳傘是一種刺激的活動。

parade [pə`red] ◀Track 3527
n. 遊行，行進行列

▶There are grand parades during the Brazilian carnival.
在巴西嘉年華期間會有盛大的遊行活動。

v. 在……遊行；炫耀，標榜；使列隊行進

▶The marching band paraded through the street of Paris.
這個室外樂隊遊行經過巴黎的街道。

paradise [`pærə͵daɪs] ◀Track 3528
n. 天堂，樂園，像天堂一樣的地方

▶The kids had a lot of fun in the Lego Paradise Playground.
小朋友們在樂高樂園玩得很開心。

paragraph ◀Track 3529
[`pærə͵græf] **n.** （文章的）段，節

▶The professor expected to see a concluding sentence at the end of the paragraph.
教授會希望在段落的結尾看到總結的句子。

parallel [`pærə͵lɛl] ◀Track 3530
adj. 平行的，同方向的；相同的

▶Are the two lines parallel to each other?
這兩條線有互相平行嗎？

n. 平行線；類似的人或事物；相似處

▶The rails are not in parallel with each other.
這兩個軌道並非互相平行的。

v. 與……平行；與……相比；與……相似

▶This cannot be paralleled with the other.
這不能與另一個相比。

parcel [`pɑrs!] ◀Track 3531
n. 小包，包裹

▶You can check the table and find the right price for your parcel.
你可以對照這個表格，然後找到你的包裹的郵資費用。

v. 分配；把……包起來

▶The bigger farms were parceled out to the peasants after the revolution.
革命之後，較大的農地就被分配給農民了。

中級

pardon [`pɑrdn] ◀ Track 3532

n. 原諒；寬恕

▶I beg your pardon?
不好意思，可以再說一次嗎？

v. 原諒；寬恕

▶They may be pardoned for the mistake as long as they try to mend it.
他們如果願意改正，犯錯就能被原諒。

parent [`pɛrənt] ◀ Track 3533

n. 父親；母親

▶Compared with our parents' generation, we enjoy much more convenience in our daily life.
和父母親那一代相比，我們享有更多生活上的便利。

Paris [`pærɪs] **n.** 巴黎 ◀ Track 3534

▶Thousands of demonstrators gathered on the streets of Paris, protesting against the rise of the tax.
有數千名抗議者聚集在巴黎的街頭，抗議賦稅增加。

park [pɑrk] ◀ Track 3535

n. 公園；遊樂場

▶Ted worked part time as a mascot in the amusement park.
泰德在遊樂園打工當吉祥物。

v. 停車

▶You can not park your car here.
你不能在這裡停車。

parking [`pɑrkɪŋ] ◀ Track 3536

n. 停車，停車處

▶There is no parking in this area.
這一個地區禁止停車。

相關片語 **parking space** 停車位

▶The parking space is reserved for physically-challenged drivers.
這個停車位是殘障人士專用的。

parliament ◀ Track 3537

[`pɑrləmənt] **n.** 國會，議會

▶The meeting of the parliament was live streaming on the Internet.
國會的會議正在網路上面直播。

parrot [`pærət] **n.** 鸚鵡 ◀ Track 3538

▶Peter has a talking parrot as a pet.
彼得養了一隻會說話的鸚鵡當寵物。

part [pɑrt] ◀ Track 3539

v. 分開；告別；使分開

▶The couple left each other amulets when they parted with each other.
這對夫妻分開的時候留給彼此一個護身符。

partial [`pɑrʃəl] ◀ Track 3540

adj. 部分的，不完全的；偏袒的

▶This is only a partial answer to the question, so some points were deducted.
這個答案不完全，所以有些分數被扣掉了。

participant ◀ Track 3541

[pɑr`tɪsəpənt] **n.** 參與者

▶The participants of this activity were requested to put on safety gears.
這個活動的參加者被要求要配戴安全裝置。

participate ◀ Track 3542

[pɑr`tɪsə,pet] **v.** 參與，參加

▶All students were requested to participate in the camping activity.
所有的學生都需要參加這個露營的活動。

participle [`pɑrtəsəp!] ◀≣ Track 3543

n. 分詞

▶ The present participle of this verb can serve as an adjective.
這個動詞的現在分詞可以當成形容詞用。

particular ◀≣ Track 3544

[pə`tɪkjələ] **adj.** 特殊的；特定的

▶ Are there any particular requirement for the applicants of the job vacancy?
這個職缺的應徵者有需要符合什麼特殊的要求嗎？

particularly ◀≣ Track 3545

[pə`tɪkjələlɪ]
adv. 特別，尤其；具體地；詳盡地

▶ They are particularly concerned about the information security.
他們特別擔心資訊安全的問題。

partner [`pɑrtnɚ] ◀≣ Track 3546

n. 夥伴；拍檔；合夥人

▶ They used to be opponents, but now they are business partners.
他們以前是對手，但現在他們是商業夥伴。

partnership ◀≣ Track 3547

[`pɑrtnɚ ʃɪp] **n.** 合夥；合作關係

▶ Their partnership lasted for two years.
他們的合作關係維持了兩年。

party [`pɑrtɪ] ◀≣ Track 3548

n. 派對；聚會；政黨

▶ The candidate runs the campaign by himself; he is not supported by any particular political party.
這位候選人是獨立參選的；他不受特定政黨支持。

pass [pæs] ◀≣ Track 3549

v. 前進；通過；死亡；（考試）及格

▶ He didn't pass the certificate test for a chef.
他沒有通過廚師的證照考試。

n. 通行證

▶ We went to fetch the fast pass of our favorite ride as soon as we entered the amusement park.
我們一進遊樂園就去拿最喜歡的遊樂設施的快速通關券。

passage [`pæsɪdʒ] ◀≣ Track 3550

n. 通道；通行；走廊；（文章或樂曲的）段落

▶ Which of the following statement best summarized the passage?
下列敘述何者最能適當地總截此段落的內容？

passenger ◀≣ Track 3551

[`pæsndʒɚ] **n.** 乘客；旅客

▶ Passengers transferring to the south-bound train should change trains at this station.
要轉搭南向列車的旅客請在本站換車。

passion [`pæʃən] ◀≣ Track 3552

n. 熱情

▶ She has a passion for design, and aspires to be a fashion magazine editor.
她對設計充滿熱情，並立志當一個流行雜誌編輯。

相關片語 **passion fruit** 百香果

▶ The popsicles with a passio fruit flavor are sold out.
百香果口味的冰棒賣完了。

中級

passive [`pæsɪv] ◀Track 3553
adj. 被動的，消極的；順從的

▶The passive-aggressive behavior is to attack others in an implicit or indirect way.
消極的攻擊行為就是用間接的方式去攻擊別人。

passport [`pæs͵port] ◀Track 3554
n. 護照

▶The criminal used a counterfeit passport to enter the country.
罪犯使用假護照進入到這個國家。

past [pæst] ◀Track 3555
prep. 經過；通過；超過

▶It's a quarter past five now.
現在是五點十五分。

adv. 經過；越過

▶People who are on their way to work rushed past.
要去上班的人們匆匆經過。

n. 過去；昔日；往事

▶In the past, people didn't have to worry about identity theft.
在過去，人們不太需要擔心個人資訊被盜用。

adj. 過去的

▶Use the past tense when you describe something that has happened.
用過去式動詞時態來描述已經發生過的事情。

pasta [`pɑstə] ◀Track 3556
n. 義大利麵（細麵或通心粉等）

▶The homemade pasta is the most famous dish in the restaurant.
自製的義大利麵是這家餐廳最有名的菜餚。

paste [pest] **n.** 漿糊；麵糰 ◀Track 3557

▶Mix the room-temperature egg, the flour, and the milk to make the paste.
將室溫的蛋、麵粉、牛奶混和，做成麵糊。

v. 用漿糊黏貼

▶Paste the receipt to the form so that you can reimburse it.
把收據黏貼在表格上，才可以報帳。

pastry [`pestrɪ] ◀Track 3558
n. 油酥麵糰，酥皮點心

▶The puff pastry is quite easy to make.
這個泡芙酥皮糕點很容易製作。

pat [pæt] **v.** 輕拍；輕撫 ◀Track 3559

▶Ted's uncle patted him on the shoulder.
泰德的叔叔輕拍了他的肩膀一下。

n. 輕拍；輕打

▶Joe gave her a pat on the back to encourage her.
喬伊輕拍她的背，表示鼓勵。

path [pæθ] **n.** 小徑；小路 ◀Track 3560

▶They walked along the path through the woods. 他們沿著森林裡的小路走。

patience [`peʃəns] ◀Track 3561
n. 耐心，耐性

▶The nurse in the nursing home has great patience for the elderly residents.
這位護士對於療養院中的老年人很有耐心。

patient [`peʃənt] ◀Track 3562
adj. 有耐心的；有耐性的

▶The application procedure may take some time, so you need to be patient.
這個申請的程序可能會花一些時間，所以你需要有耐心一點。

n. 病人

▶The patient was transferred to the municipal hospital.
這名病人被轉診到市立醫院。

---

patriotic [ˌpetrɪˋɑtɪk]
◀€ Track 3563

adj. 愛國的

▶The patriotic soldiers were not willing to surrender to the enemy.
愛國的士兵們不願向敵方投降。

---

pattern [ˋpætɚn]
◀€ Track 3564

n. 花樣；圖案

▶The pattern on the knight's shield is the family crest.
這個騎士盾牌上面的圖案是他的家徽。

---

pause [pɔz]
◀€ Track 3565

v. 停頓；暫停

▶I paused the video to answer the phone. 我把影片暫停，去接電話。

n. 停頓；中斷

▶The whole project came to a pause because one of the researchers had to drop out. 因為有一位研究者必須要退出，所以整個計畫暫時中斷了。

---

pave [pev]
◀€ Track 3566

v. 舖路；舖設；舖滿

▶We bought some bricks to pave the front yard. 我們買了一些磚塊鋪在前院。

相關片語	pave the way for...
	為……鋪路，為……做準備

▶The pioneers' efforts paved the way for women to have careers in various professional fields.
先進者的努力為婦女們鋪路，使她們得以在各種專業領域發展職涯。

---

pavement [ˋpevmənt]
◀€ Track 3567

n. 人行道

▶The heavy rain fell down on the pavement.
大雨落在人行道上。

---

paw [pɔ]
◀€ Track 3568

n. 腳爪；【口】手

▶The paws of the puppy were covered with mud.
這隻小狗的爪子沾滿了泥巴。

v. 用腳爪抓；笨拙地觸摸；翻找

▶He pawed through the drawers frantically, looking for the stamp.
他拼命翻找抽屜，想要找到他的印章。

---

pay [pe]
◀€ Track 3569

v. 支付；付錢；償還

▶It took him three years to pay off the debt.
他花了三年才清償債務。

n. 薪水；報酬

▶I don' think he deserves the high pay.
我覺得他不值得領這麼高的薪水。

---

payment [ˋpemənt]
◀€ Track 3570

n. 支付；付款；支付的款項

▶When you open an account, you can make an online payment.
開通帳號之後，就可以在線上付款。

PE [pi-i]=physical education
◀€ Track 3571

n. 體育；體能教育

▶We will have the PE class at the gym, not in the playground.
我們會在體育館上體育課，而不是在操場。

pea [pi] n. 豌豆
◀₣Track 3572

▶There are some tips of growing peas in your home garden.
在家裡的花園種植碗豆有一些訣竅。

peace [pis]
◀₣Track 3573

n. 和平；平靜；治安

▶May he rest in peace. 願他安息。

peaceful [`pisfəl]
◀₣Track 3574

adj. 平靜的；和平的；寧靜的

▶The peaceful atmosphere in this small town made my sojourn here rather pleasant.
這個小鎮和平的氣氛讓我在這裡居住的期間很開心。

peach [pitʃ]
◀₣Track 3575

n. 桃子；桃樹；桃色

▶The peach candy tastes quite artificial.
這個桃子口味的糖果吃起來很像是人工香料做的。

peacock [`pikɑk]
◀₣Track 3576

n. 孔雀；愛炫耀的人，愛虛榮的人

▶The fable story is about an arrogant peacock.
這個寓言故事是關於一隻高傲的孔雀。

peak [pik]
◀₣Track 3577

n. 山頂，山峰；高點

▶They were exhilarated when they reached the peak of the mountain.
他們爬到山頂之後覺得相當興奮。

adj. 最高的

▶The peak season of tourism in the country is in December and January.
這個地區的旅遊旺季是在十二月和一月。

v. 達到高峰

▶The sales of the handsets peaked in the first quarter of this year.
這款手機在今年第一季賣得最好。

peanut [`pi͵nʌt] n. 花生
◀₣Track 3578

▶Some kids are allergic to peanuts.
有些小孩對花生過敏。

pear [pɛr] n. 洋梨；洋梨樹
◀₣Track 3579

▶Jenny made some pear jelly with ripe pears.
珍妮用熟透的梨子做了一些梨子果凍。

pearl [pɝl]
◀₣Track 3580

n. 珍珠；珠狀物；珍珠色；珍品

▶The necklace is made of artificial pearls. 這條項鍊是用人造珍珠做的。

相關片語 **pearls of wisdom**
智慧結晶；金玉良言

▶His advice was the pearls of wisdom.
他的建議是金玉良言。

adj. 珍珠的，珍珠色的

▶Diana wore a pearl necklace on her wedding reception party.
黛安娜在她的婚宴上戴著一條珍珠項鍊。

peasant [`pɛznt]
◀₣Track 3581

n. 農夫，小耕農；粗野人，鄉下人

▶The peasants from the rural area spoke vernacular.
這些鄉下的農人說著方言。

pebble [`pɛb!] n. 小卵石
◀₣Track 3582

▶The trails in the mountain were covered with pebbles.
這座山裡的步道鋪著小鵝卵石。

peculiar [pɪ`kjuljɚ] ◀ Track 3583

adj. 奇怪的；乖僻的；獨特的，罕見的

▶He holds a peculiar view toward friendship. 他對於友誼的看法很奇怪。

pedal [`pɛd!] ◀ Track 3584

n. 踏板，腳蹬

▶He mistook the accelerator as the brake pedal and caused an accident.
他錯把油門當剎車，造成了車禍。

v. 踩踏板；騎腳踏車

▶He kept pedaling so that the bicycle would move forward.
他持續踩著踏板，讓腳踏車前進。

peddler [`pɛdlɚ] n. 小販 ◀ Track 3585

▶The peddler sold some popcorns and soda to the viewers of the baseball game.
小販賣一些爆米花和汽水給棒球賽的觀眾。

pedestrian ◀ Track 3586

[pə`dɛstrɪən] **adj.** 步行的，行人的

▶The pedestrian crossing was decorated with LED lights so people can see it at night. 行人穿越道裝有LED燈，人們在晚上也可以看到它。

補充片語 pedestrian crossing
行人穿越道

n. 步行者，行人

▶The jaywalking pedestrian will be fined from 300 to 500 dollars.
違規穿越馬路的行人會遭罰款300至500元。

peek [pik] v. 偷看，窺視 ◀ Track 3587

▶The thief peeked through the fence to see whether the housekeeper was in the house. 小偷透過圍籬偷看管家是否在家。

n. 偷看一下，一瞥

▶Aaron tried to take a peek at his coworkers' salary slip.
艾倫想要偷看同事的薪水條。

peel [pil] ◀ Track 3588

n. （果、菜的）皮

▶The boy stepped on the banana peel and fell down.
小男孩踩到香蕉皮，跌倒了。

v. 剝皮、削皮、剝殼，脫去（衣服）

▶The squadron peeled off to attack enemy bombers.
一架中隊戰機脫離編隊，攻擊敵軍的轟炸機。

peep [pip] ◀ Track 3589

v. 窺視，偷看

▶In the medieval times, a thief may lose a hand, and a peeping Tom may lose an eye.
在中世紀時期，小偷會失去一隻手，而偷窺者則會失去一隻眼睛。

n. 窺視，偷看

▶Jack took a peep at his baby daughter sleeping in the cot.
傑克偷看了一下睡在搖籃裡的小女兒。

peer [pɪr] ◀ Track 3590

v. 與……相比，與……同等；凝視

▶She peered at me over the window.
她透過窗戶偷看我。

n. 同輩的人，同事，同僑

▶She worried about peer pressure on her child.
她擔心同僑壓力對她小孩的影響。

補充片語 peer pressure 同僑壓力

中級

pen [pɛn] n. 筆；鋼筆
◄ Track 3591

▶The pen is mightier than the sward.
輿論比刀劍更有殺傷力。

penalty [`pɛn!tɪ] n. 懲罰
◄ Track 3592

▶Washington is one of the states in the U.S. that abandoned death penalty.
華盛頓是美國廢除死刑的其中一個州。

補充片語 death penalty 死刑

pencil [`pɛns!] n. 鉛筆
◄ Track 3593

▶The pencil sharpener was fixed on the desk. 這個削鉛筆機是固定在桌上的。

penguin [`pɛngwɪn]
n. 企鵝
◄ Track 3594

▶Visitors to the zoo were amused when they saw the penguins wobbling around. 動物園的遊客看到企鵝搖搖晃晃地四處走，都覺得被逗樂了。

penny [`pɛnɪ] n. 一分錢
◄ Track 3595

▶I won't lend a penny to John; he is the least trust-worthy man in the company.
我一分錢都不會借給約翰；他是全公司最不能信任的人。

people [`pip!]
n. 人們；人民；民族
◄ Track 3596

▶The nomadic people are communities who move from one place to another.
遊牧民族是四處遷移的群體。

pepper [`pɛpɚ] n. 胡椒
◄ Track 3597

▶White pepper is a common seasoning used in Chinese cuisines.
白胡椒是常用在中國菜當中的調味料。

per [pɚ] prep. 每
◄ Track 3598

▶The highest speed of the car is about 120 kilometers per hour.
這輛車最高的速度是每小時120公里。

percent [pɚ`sɛnt]
=per cent n. 百分之一；百分比
◄ Track 3599

▶More than thirty percent of the students in this high school have a part-time job.
這所高中有超過百分之三十的學生在打工。

percentage
◄ Track 3600

[pɚ`sɛntɪdʒ] n. 百分率，百分比；比例

▶The percentage of students from single-parent family is getting higher in recent years.
來自單親家庭學生的比率在近年來有增加的趨勢。

perfect [`pɝfɪkt]
◄ Track 3601

adj. 完美的；理想的

▶She is the perfect candidate as a wedding planner.
作為婚禮秘書，她是一位完美的人選。

perfection
◄ Track 3602

[pɚ`fɛkʃən] n. 完美

▶The performers rehearsed for many times so that the show can reach perfection.
這些表演者排演了很多次，希望讓表演可以臻於完美。

perfectly [`pɝfɪktlɪ]
◄ Track 3603

adv. 完美無缺地；完全地

▶I think they match each other perfectly.
我覺得他們真是天作之合。

perform [pə`fɔrm] ◀🔊 Track 3604

v. 演出；表演；執行

▶The doctors always perform their duties faithfully.
醫生們總是忠實地執行任務。

performance ◀🔊 Track 3605

[pə`fɔrməns] **n.** 表現；表演；演出

▶Some of the viewers left the theater during the intermittence halfway through the performance.
有些觀眾在表演到一半的中場休息時就離開劇院了。

performer ◀🔊 Track 3606

[pə`fɔrmə] **n.** 表演者，演奏者，演出者

▶The performers of the show wore special make-up to create the dramatic effect.
這場演出的表演者們用特別的妝容表現戲劇效果。

perfume [pə`fjum] ◀🔊 Track 3607

n. 香水；香味，芳香

▶The employees of the company are not encouraged to wear perfume to work.
這家公司不太鼓勵員工上班時間用香水。

v. 灑香水於，使充滿香氣；散發香氣

▶He perfumed himself with some delicate dabs of cologne. 他使用了一點古龍水，讓自己身上留有香味。

perhaps [pə`hæps] ◀🔊 Track 3608

adv. 也許；大概

▶She didn't show much enthusiasm to this activity; perhaps she would just skip it. 她對這個活動沒有很熱衷；也許她不會來參加。

period [`pɪrɪəd] ◀🔊 Track 3609

n. 時期；時代；週期；生理期

▶She said she is not feeling well, for she was on her period.
她說她因為生理期而感到不適。

permanent ◀🔊 Track 3610

[`pɝmənənt] **adj.** 永久的；固定的

▶The injury may leave a permanent scar on your skin. 這個傷口可能會在你的皮膚上留下永久的疤痕。

n.【口】燙髮

▶She got a permanent in order to look more stylish.
她想要看起來更有型，所以去燙了頭髮。

permission ◀🔊 Track 3611

[pə`mɪʃən] **n.** 允許，許可，准許

▶I need my supervisor's permission to take a personal leave.
我請事假需要我主管的同意。

permit [pə`mɪt] ◀🔊 Track 3612

v. 允許，許可，准許

▶The students were not permitted to stay out overnight unless they are permitted by the superintendent. 除非有舍監同意，否則學生們不能在外面過夜。

n. 許可證，執照

▶I need the permit from the board to access the confidential data. 我需要董事會的同意才能取得這份機密的資料。

persist [pə`sɪst] ◀🔊 Track 3613

v. 堅持，固執；持續，存留

▶She persisted that she had nothing to do with the theft case.
她堅稱自己和此起竊盜案件無關。

中級

person [`pɝ·sn] n. 人
◀Track 3614

▶The only person who witnessed the criminal case was abducted by the culprit.
唯一目擊這樁犯罪行動的人被歹徒綁架了。

personal [`pɝ·sn!]
◀Track 3615
adj. 個人的；私人的；涉及私事的

▶The guest felt offended when the host of the show asked about her personal affairs. 談話節目主持人問到來賓的私事時，她覺得受到冒犯。

personality
◀Track 3616

[ˌpɝ·sn`ælətɪ] n. 性格

▶Her positive personality made her one of the most popular figures in the community. 她樂觀的個性使她成為社區裡最受歡迎的人物之一。

persuade [pə`swed]
◀Track 3617
v. 說服

▶We tried to persuade the old man that the woman was a con artist, but in vain. 我們試圖說服老人說這個女人是騙子，但沒用。

相關片語 persuade sb. into doing...
說服某人做某事

▶The salesperson tried to persuade me into buying the robot vacuum cleaner.
推銷員想要說服我去買這個掃地機器人。

persuasion
◀Track 3618

[pə`sweʒən] n. 說服，勸說；信仰，信念

▶It is my persuasion that the human rights of the immigrants should be protected.
我相信移民者的人權也應該受到保護。

persuasive
◀Track 3619

[pə`swesɪv] adj. 有說服力的

▶She is considered to be one of the most persuasive millennial politicians.
她被認為是千禧世代最有說服力的政治人物之一。

pessimistic
◀Track 3620

[ˌpɛsə`mɪstɪk] adj. 悲觀的

▶She always looks at things from a pessimistic point of view; she would think about the worst situation.
她總是用悲觀的角度看事情；她會考慮到最糟糕的情況。

pest [pɛst]
◀Track 3621

n. 害蟲，有害的動植物；討厭的人

▶The farmer used chemical insecticide to get rid of the pests.
農夫用化學殺蟲劑消滅害蟲。

pet [pɛt] n. 寵物
◀Track 3622

▶There is a newly-opened pet beauty salon in my neighborhood.
我家附近新開一家寵物美容店。

petal [`pɛt!] n. 花瓣
◀Track 3623

▶The staff of the hotel decorated the bathtub in the room with some rose petals.
這間飯店的員工用一些玫瑰花瓣來裝飾房間裡的浴缸。

petrol [`pɛtrəl]
◀Track 3624
=gas, gasoline （美式英文）
n. 汽油

▶The price of the petrol has been fluctuating this year.
今年油價一直浮動。

相關片語 petrol station 加油站

▶ We were looking for a petrol station because we were running out of gas.
因為要沒油了，所以我們正在尋找加油站。

pharmacy [`farməsɪ] ◀ Track 3625
n. 藥局；藥房；配藥學

▶ You can get medication for chronic diseases at a local pharmacy.
你可以在本地的藥房買到慢性疾病的藥物。

phenomenon ◀ Track 3626
[fə`namə,nan]
n. 現象；稀有的事；非凡的人才

▶ The cause of the phenomenon of aurora, also known as polar lights, is not fully understood now.
目前人們還不清楚造成極光現象的原因。

Philippines ◀ Track 3627
[`filə,pinz] **n.** 菲律賓

▶ Quezon City is the largest city in Philippines by population. 就人口數來説，奎松市是菲律賓最大的城市。

philosopher ◀ Track 3628
[fə`lasəfɚ] **n.** 哲學家

▶ Socrates was a Greek philosopher who is considered as the father of western philosophy. 蘇格拉底是一位希臘哲學家，他被認為是西方哲學之父。

philosophical ◀ Track 3629
[,filə`safɪk!] **adj.** 達觀的；哲學性的

▶ The professor wants the students to discuss the unsolved philosophical problems to train their critical-thinking ability. 教授要學生討論尚未解決的哲學議題，藉以訓練他們的批判思考能力。

philosophy [fə`lasəfɪ] ◀ Track 3630
n. 人生觀；哲學

▶ His philosophy is to seize the moment and enjoy life.
他的人生觀就是要把握當下，享受人生。

phone [fon] ◀ Track 3631
=telephone **n.** 電話

▶ I looked up the phone number of the university on the Internet.
我上網查了這所大學的電話號碼。

v. 打電話

▶ A con artist phoned me and claimed that he kidnapped my son.
有一個詐騙份子打電話給我，聲稱説他綁架了我兒子。

photo [`foto] ◀ Track 3632
n. 相片；照片

▶ Jack uploaded a photo to the social media website, and it received a lot of likes from his friends.
傑克上傳一張照片到社群網站上，而且他的很多朋友都去按讚。

photograph ◀ Track 3633
[`fotə,græf]=pho·to **n.** 相片；照片

▶ The pixel is the basic unit of the digital photograph.
像素是數位相片最基本的元素。

photographer ◀ Track 3634
[fə`tagrəfɚ] **n.** 攝影師

▶ The war-zone photographer risked his life to take photos of real-life battles.
這名戰地攝影師冒生命危險拍攝真實戰場上的相片。

中級

photographic
◀ Track 3635

[ˌfotəˈgræfɪk] adj. 攝影的；生動的，逼真的

▶The editor of the magazine put a lot of emphasis on photographic image quality.
這個雜誌編輯相當重視攝影照片的影像品質。

photography
◀ Track 3636

[fəˈtɑgrəfɪ] n. 攝影

▶This book is a guide to photography for beginners.
這本書是給攝影初學者的指引。

phrase [frez]
◀ Track 3637

n. 片語；詞組；措辭，說法

▶The students tried to memorize the short phrases in France.
這些學生們努力背誦法文片語。

相關片語 have a nice turn of phrase 善於辭令，很會說話

▶The eloquent man has a nice turn of phrase.
這名口才很好的男人相當能言善道。

v. 用言詞表達

▶Some con artists used beautifully-phrased sentences to fool the victims.
有些詐騙份子會用花言巧語欺騙受害者。

physical [ˈfɪzɪk!]
◀ Track 3638

adj. 身體的，肉體的；物質的；物理的；按自然法則的

▶Mr. Chang keeps exercise to maintain a good physical condition.
張先生持續運動以保持健康的身體狀態。

physician [fɪˈzɪʃən]
◀ Track 3639

n.（內科）醫生

▶The Good Doctor is a medical drama about the story of a physician.
《良醫》是一部講述醫生故事的醫療戲劇。

physicist [ˈfɪzɪsɪst]
◀ Track 3640

n. 物理學家

▶Stephen Hawking was an English theoretical physicist.
史蒂芬·霍金是一位英國的理論物理學家。

physics [ˈfɪzɪks]
◀ Track 3641

n. 物理學

▶Newton and Einstein's major theories explained the law of physics.
牛頓和愛因斯坦的主要理論解釋了物理學的定律。

pianist [pɪˈænɪst]
◀ Track 3642

n. 鋼琴家

▶The Chinese concert pianist has performed with leading orchestras from the United States, Europe, and Canada.
這位中國鋼琴演奏家有和美國、歐洲及加拿大的知名交響樂團合作演出過。

piano [pɪˈæno] n. 鋼琴
◀ Track 3643

▶The piano lesson will start at three this afternoon.
鋼琴課今天下午三點開始。

pick [pɪk]
◀ Track 3644

v. 挑；撿；選；摘

▶The fortune teller asked me to pick a Tarot card from the desk.
算命師叫我從桌上選一張塔羅牌。

pickle [ˈpɪk!]
◀ Track 3645

n. 醃過的醬菜

▶I don't want sliced pickles in my submarine sandwich.
我的潛艇堡三明治不要加醃菜。

pickpocket
🔊Track 3646

[ˋpɪkˌpɑkɪt] **n.** 扒手

▶Beware of the pickpockets when you travel to foreign countries.
去國外旅遊時要小心扒手。

picnic [ˋpɪknɪk] **n.** 野餐
🔊Track 3647

▶It's a nice day. We can have a picnic somewhere.
今天天氣不錯。我們找個地方去野餐吧。

v. 野餐

▶We picnicked at the river bank.
我們在河邊野餐。

picture [ˋpɪktʃɚ]
🔊Track 3648

n. 圖片；照片

▶The counselor pointed out that the pictures drawn by his patients can reveal their emotional states.
諮商師指出，他的病人所畫的圖片可以顯示出他們的情緒狀態。

v. 想像；畫；拍攝

▶I can picture the scene that we have a warmly-decorated house.
我可以想像我們有一個裝飾溫暖的家。

pie [paɪ]
🔊Track 3649

n. 餡餅；派（有餡的酥餅）

▶It's better to make the crust of and the stuffing of the pie separately.
這派的皮和餡料最好要分開做。

piece [pis]
🔊Track 3650

n. 一片；一塊；一張；一件；破片

▶This is not difficult at all. It's a piece of cake.
這一點也不難。小事一樁。

補充片語 a piece of cake 小事

pig [pɪg] **n.** 豬
🔊Track 3651

▶The pig is the twelfth of all zodiac animals.
豬在生肖裡排第十二個。

pigeon [ˋpɪdʒɪn]
🔊Track 3652

n. 鴿子；鴿肉

▶A pigeon, or a dove, is usually considered a symbol of peace.
鴿子，或者白鴿，常被認為是和平的象徵。

pile [paɪl] **v.** 堆積；堆放
🔊Track 3653

▶Evidence has been piling up against you. Why don't you just confess?
現在有越來越多對你不利的證據了。你要不要直接認罪呢？

n. 堆；一堆；大量

▶When a person sits on piles of money, he tends to use it unwisely.
一個人坐擁大量財富時，往往容易揮霍。

pilgrim [ˋpɪlgrɪm]
🔊Track 3654

n. 香客，朝聖者

▶Thousands of Indian pilgrims walked toward the River Ganges.
數千名印度朝聖者往恆河走去。

pill [pɪl] **n.** 藥丸，藥片
🔊Track 3655

▶The actress suffered from insomnia, and she had to take sleeping pills every night.
這名女演員有失眠的問題，每晚都要吃安眠藥。

中級

補充片語 sleeping pill 安眠藥

相關片語 bitter pill to swallow
不得不忍受的事

▶They lost the game to Korea. It was a bitter pill to swallow.
他們比賽輸給韓國。他們只得吞下這口氣。

pillow [`pɪlo] **n.** 枕頭　　◀Track 3656

▶Helen purchased a down pillow on this website.
海倫在這個網站上面買了一個羽絨枕頭。

pilot [`paɪlət]　　◀Track 3657

n. （船的）領航員，（飛機的）駕駛員

▶The narrator of the story, The Little Prince, is a pilot who was once trapped in the dessert.
《小王子》這個故事的敘事者是一位曾被困在沙漠裡的飛行員。

v. 駕駛，領航；試用，引導

▶He will pilot the new design that the organization wants to implement.
他會試用這個組織當中會採用的新機制。

pimple [`pɪmp!]　　◀Track 3658

n. 丘疹；面皰；青春痘

▶In this article, the doctor listed ten effective medicines for pimples.
在這篇文章中，醫生列出了十個有效治療青春痘的藥物。

pin [pɪn]　　◀Track 3659

n. 大頭針；別針；胸針

▶This stunning gold-leaf pin makes an elegant addition to any coat, top, or scarf.
這個亮麗的金色葉子別針可以搭配任何外套、上衣，或圍巾，都非常高雅動人。

v. （用別針）別住；（用大頭針）釘住

▶It took them a long time to pin down the subject.
他們花了很多時間才弄清楚問題所在。

pine [paɪn] **n.** 松樹，松木　　◀Track 3660

▶Pine trees are evergreen conifers which are common in the temperate zone.
松樹是在溫帶常見的針葉樹。

v. 渴望

▶He pined for a house of his own.
他渴望有一間自己的房子。

pineapple [`paɪnˌæp!]　　◀Track 3661

n. 鳳梨

▶The chef added some pineapple to the fried rice to enhance the flavor. 廚師加入了一些鳳梨到炒飯當中以增加風味。

ping-pong [`pɪŋˌpɑŋ] =table tennis **n.** 乒乓球；桌球　　◀Track 3662

▶Ted used to play ping-pong with his father in his teens.
在十幾歲的時候，泰德都會和他的父親一起打桌球。

pink [pɪŋk]　　◀Track 3663

adj. 粉紅的；桃紅的

▶Pink Lady is a classic gin-based cocktail. 粉紅佳人是一種常見的以琴酒為基底的調酒。

n. 粉紅色

▶Pink used to be considered a color for girls, but things have changed now.
粉紅色以前被認為是女孩子的顏色，但是現在不一樣了。

pint [paɪnt] **n.** 品脱 ◀Track 3664

▶I drank two pints of beer.
我喝了兩品脱的啤酒。

相關片語 put a quart into a pint pot
做不可能做到的事

▶It's unlikely that you can put all your stuff into that suitcase. Don't try to put a quart into a pint pot.
不太可能把你所有的東西都放進那個行李箱。不要去做不可能做到的事情吧。

---

pioneer [ˌpaɪə`nɪr] ◀Track 3665
n. 拓荒者，開拓者；先軀者

▶The farmer was a pioneer who cultivated and plowed the earth in the untrodden area.
這位農夫是為開拓者，開墾了農田，耕作沒有人踏上過的土地。

v. 開創，開闢

▶The nurse pioneered an aid program to assist the kids in the rural area.
這位護士開創了一個援助計畫幫助偏遠地區的小朋友。

---

pipe [paɪp] ◀Track 3666
n. 管；煙斗；管樂器

▶The old man used a pipe cleaner to remove the moisture and residue from his smoking pipe.
老先生用一個煙管清潔器去除菸斗裡的濕氣和殘餘物。

---

pirate [`paɪrət] ◀Track 3667
n. 海盜；掠劫者；海盜船；剽竊者；侵犯版權者

▶Pirates off the coast of Somalia have been a threat to international ships.
索馬利亞外海的海盜對國際船隻來說一直是個很大的威脅。

v. 掠奪；從事掠劫；剽竊；非法翻印；做海盜

▶It's illegal to download and spread pirated movies on the Internet.
在網路上下載與傳播盜版電影是違法的。

adj. 海盜的；未經許可的

▶The industry of pirate discs has long served as a circulation channel for Chinese independent films.
盜版產業一直是中國獨立製作電影流通的一個管道。

---

pit [pɪt] ◀Track 3668
n. 窪坑，凹處；地窖；陷阱；圈套

▶A fall into a pit, a gain in your wit.
不經一事不長一智。

相關片語 dig a pit for sb. 給某人設圈套，挖陷阱給某人跳，算計某人

▶They tried to dig a pit for me, but I didn't fall for their trick.
他們試圖算計我，但我沒有上他們的當。

v. 挖坑；放入坑中；使掉入陷阱；留下凹痕

▶They tried to pit John against Paul.
他們想要使約翰反對保羅。

---

pitch [pɪtʃ] ◀Track 3669
n. 投球；音樂聲調

▶She is tone-deaf and unable to sing on pitch at all.
她是音癡，唱歌完全走音。

v. 投球

▶Now it's your turn to pitch.
現在該你投球了。

---

pity [`pɪtɪ] ◀Track 3670
n. 憐憫，同情；可惜的事

▶It's a pity that you can't go on the trip with us.
很可惜你無法和我們一起去旅行。

中級

v. 同情，憐憫

▶The cleric pitied the impoverished residents in this town and donated a large amount of necessities to them.
牧師同情這個小鎮的貧窮居民，捐贈了大量的物資給他們。

相關片語 **take pity on** 憐憫，同情

▶We took pity on the homeless man, so we offered him some daily necessities.
我們同情這位街友，所以給了他一些物資。

pizza [`pitsə] ◀Track 3671
n. 比薩；義大利肉餡餅

▶It is commonly believed that Italian invented pizza, but baked bread with toppings has actually appeared in other regions.
一般相信義大利人發明了披薩，但是有餡料的烤麵包其實在很多其他地區出現過。

place [ples] ◀Track 3672
n. 地方；居住的地方

▶Smoking in public places has been banned in this country.
在本國禁止於公開空間抽菸。

v. 放置

▶We have to consider about the quotations before we place an order.
我們在下訂單之前必須先考慮過所有的報價。

plain [plen] **n.** 平原；曠野 ◀Track 3673

▶The plains in the western region began to prospoer due to its agricultural skills.
西部地區的平原因為其農業技術而繁榮起來。

adj. 簡樸的；不攙雜的；清楚的；坦白的

▶The plain design of the dress makes it elegant.
這件洋裝的簡樸設計讓它變得很高雅。

adv. 清楚地；平易地；完全地

▶She is just plain nasty.
她簡直壞透了。

plan [plæn] **n.** 計劃 ◀Track 3674

▶We had to change to original plan because of the unexpected situation.
因為意料之外的狀況，我們必須改變原本的計畫。

v. 做計劃；規劃

▶We plan to launch a new product this season.
我們本季打算推出新產品。

plane [plen] **n.** 飛機 ◀Track 3675

▶The plane was shaking because of the turbulence.
飛機因為亂流而搖晃。

planet [`plænɪt] **n.** 行星 ◀Track 3676

▶Lonely Planet is a guide for travelers, which contains information about destinations and cuisines.
《寂寞星球》是一個給旅行者關於觀光景點與美食資訊的指南。

plant [plænt] **v.** 種植 ◀Track 3677

▶The company planted one tree for every tree that they logged.
公司每砍一棵樹，就會種一棵回去。

n. 植物；植栽

▶We had some perennial plants in the balcony. 我們在陽台種了一些多年生植物。

plastic [`plæstɪk] ◀Track 3678
n. 塑料，塑膠，塑膠製品

▶The toy is made of plastic, so it may not be broke easily. 這個玩具是用塑膠做的，所以不會很容易弄壞。

adj. 塑膠的，可塑的，易變的，易受影響的

▶The government advocated that people should reduce the use of disposable plastic bags.
政府向人民宣導要減少一次性的塑膠袋。

plate [plet] **n.** 盤子
◀⑤Track 3679

▶Mom told me to set the table, so I placed the plates and the bowls on the table.
媽叫我把餐具擺好，所以我把盤子和碗放到餐桌上。

platform [`plæt͵fɔrm]
◀⑤Track 3680
n. 講台；月台

▶The staff at the station reminded the passengers to step away from the edge of the platform. 車站的工作人員提醒乘客要遠離月台的邊緣。

play [ple]
◀⑤Track 3681
v. 玩；遊戲；彈奏（樂器）；打（球類運動）；扮演（角色）；

▶Jerry used to play hockey when he was in high school.
傑瑞高中的時候都會打曲棍球。

n. 遊戲；戲劇；活動

▶The actress will make her debut in this stage play.
這名女演員會在這次舞台劇中首度登場。

player [`pleɚ]
◀⑤Track 3682
n. 選手；玩家

▶The professional video game player practiced up to 17 hours a day.
這名專業電競選手每天練習17個小時。

playful [`plefəl]
◀⑤Track 3683
adj. 愛玩耍的；開玩笑的

▶It's improper for you to make the speech with a playful attitude.
你用嬉鬧的態度來進行這場演說是不恰當的。

playground [`ple͵graʊnd] **n.** 遊樂場
◀⑤Track 3684

▶There are some arcade playgrounds around the junior high school.
這間國中附近有好幾間遊樂場。

plead [plid]
◀⑤Track 3685
v. 辯護，抗辯；承認；以……為理

▶The victim's mother appeared on TV to plead with the abductors.
受害者的母親出現在電視上面向綁匪求情。

pleasant [`plɛzənt]
◀⑤Track 3686
adj. 愉快的；欣喜的

▶This trip to Tokyo was a pleasant one.
這次的東京之旅很愉快。

please [pliz] **v.** 使滿意
◀⑤Track 3687

▶I'd like another cup of tea, if you please.
可以的話，請再給我一杯茶。

adv. 請

▶Take the stairs, please.
請走樓梯。

pleased [plizd]
◀⑤Track 3688
adj. 高興的；滿意的

▶The committee members were quite pleased with your proposal.
委員會對你的提案感到很滿意。

pleasure [`plɛʒɚ]
◀⑤Track 3689
n. 愉快；高興；樂事

中級

▶It's my pleasure to make contribution to the community.
能為社區貢獻是我的榮幸。

plentiful [`plɛntɪfəl] 🔊Track 3690
adj. 豐富的，充足的；富裕的

▶There are plentiful mineral resources in this country.
這個國家有豐富的礦產資源。

plenty [`plɛntɪ] 🔊Track 3691
pron. 很多，大量

▶We have plenty of time to prepare for the party.
我們有很充足的時間可以準備派對。

adv. 很多，綽綽有餘地；足夠地，充分地

▶The report is plenty informative.
這個報告的資訊極為豐富。

plot [plɑt] 🔊Track 3692
n. 劇情，情節；陰謀，秘密計劃

▶The plot of the drama was actually a cliché; it's totally predictable. 這個戲劇的劇情很陳腔濫調，完全可以預測。

v. 密謀，策劃；設計情節

▶We had to plot our path out before we started the hike.
我們去登山之前，得先計畫好路線。

plug [plʌg] 🔊Track 3693
n. 插頭；塞子，栓；消防栓

▶Pull the plug after you finish using the hair dryer. 用完吹風機之後要記得拔插頭。

v. 接通電源

▶He plugged the vacuum into a wall-socket.
他把吸塵器的電源插進牆上的插座。

plum [plʌm] 🔊Track 3694
n. 洋李，梅子；紫紅色

▶I bought a bottle of plum wine, or Japanese Umeshu, at the department store.
我在百貨公司買了一瓶梅酒，或稱日本梅酒。

plumber [`plʌmɚ] 🔊Track 3695
n. 水電工

▶There is a leak in the pipe; we should ask a plumber to repair it.
水管有漏水；我們應該請水電工來修。

plural [`plʊrəl] 🔊Track 3696
adj. 複數的；多元的

▶The plural form of tooth is teeth.
"tooth" 的複數形式是 "teeth"。

n. 複數；複數形

▶The plural of "ox" is "oxen."
"ox" 的複數是 "oxen"。

plus [plʌs] **prep.** 加上 🔊Track 3697
▶Ten plus nine is nineteen.
十加九等於十九。

adj. 正的，好處，高一點

▶He has got the grade of A plus.
他得到A加的成績。

n. 好處，附加物

▶His new apartment has a plus; it is near to his office.
他的新公寓有一個好處，就是離他上班的地方很近。

pocket [`pɑkɪt] 🔊Track 3698
n. 口袋；財力

▶There is a hole in his pocket.
他的口袋破洞了。

adj. 袖珍的；小型的；零星花用的

▶Peter bought a pocket dictionary for his son.
彼得買了一本袖珍字典給他兒子。

v. 把……裝入口袋內

▶The businessman was accused of pocketing the funds of the company.
這位商人被指控盜取公司資金。

poem [ˋpoɪm] **n.** 詩
◀ Track 3699

▶The kids recited several poems composed by the Chinese poet.
這些小朋友背了幾首由中國詩人作的詩。

poet [ˋpoɪt] **n.** 詩人
◀ Track 3700

▶Emily Dickinson is one of the most well-known poets in the U.S. history.
艾蜜莉·狄更斯是美國歷史上最有名的女性詩人之一。

poetry [ˋpoɪtrɪ]
◀ Track 3701

n. （總稱）詩；詩歌；詩意

▶The student is interested in modern English poetry.
這名學生對現代英文詩很有興趣。

point [poɪnt] **v.** 指；指出
◀ Track 3702

▶The scientist pointed out that drinking coffee can reduce the risk of cardiovascular diseases.
科學家指出喝咖啡可減少心臟疾病的風險。

n. 尖端；要點；中心思想；得分

▶From my point of view, she is a good candidate for this position.
就我的觀點來看，她是很適合這個職務的人選。

poison [ˋpoɪzn]
◀ Track 3703

n. 毒；毒藥；有害之物

▶It is said that the tyrant died from the poisons given by the mysterious visitor.
據說這名暴君是因這名神秘訪客給的毒物而死。

v. 毒害

▶Some stray dogs in this neighborhood were poisoned by a villain who hates animals.
這個社區裡有些流浪狗被一個討厭動物的壞人給毒死了。

poisonous [ˋpoɪznəs]
◀ Track 3704

adj. 有毒的

▶It is said that the formula may be contaminated with viruses and is thus poisonous.
據說這個奶粉可能有病毒汙染，因此是有毒的。

poke [pok]
◀ Track 3705

v. 戳，捅；撥弄，攪動；向前突出，向前擠；激發；用拳打

▶She poked the robber in the ribs with her elbow.
她用胳膊捅歹徒的肋部。

相關片語 poke into 探聽，干涉

▶It's quite rude to poke into other people's personal affairs.
探聽別人的隱私是很不禮貌的事情。

pole [pol]
◀ Track 3706

n. （地球的）極；極地區域；極地

▶The explorer reached the Terrestrial South Pole and took a selfie there.
這個探險家到達南極，並在那裡拍了自拍照。

police [pəˋlis]
◀ Track 3707

n. 警察；警方

中級

▶The police questioned the suspicious-looking men.
警察上前盤問形跡可疑的男子。

policeman

◀Track 3708

[pə`lismən]=cop n. 警員；警察

▶The policemen dispersed the protesters who illegally gathered in front of the congress building.
警察驅離非法聚集在國會大樓外面的抗議者。

policy [`paləsı]

◀Track 3709

n. 政策；方針

▶Honesty is the best policy.
誠實為上策。

polish [`palıʃ]

◀Track 3710

n. 磨光；擦亮

▶The cosmetologist taught me how to use the nail polish.
這名美容師教我如何使用指甲油。

v. 磨光；擦亮；磨光劑

▶I tried to polish my English proficiency by watching English news everyday.
我試圖藉由每天看英語新聞來磨練英語能力。

相關片語 polish the apple 拍馬屁

▶The man said something flattering, trying to polish the apple.
這男人說了奉承的話，想要拍馬屁。

polite [pə`laıt]

◀Track 3711

adj. 禮貌的；有理的

▶It is better for you to use polite phrases in your letter to the customer.
你最好在寫給客戶的信件裡使用禮貌的措詞。

political [pə`lıtık!]

◀Track 3712

adj. 政治上的

▶The entrepreneur never reveals his political stance in public.
這位企業家從來不會公開透漏他的政治立場。

politician [‚palə`tıʃən]

◀Track 3713

n. 政治家

▶The politician holds a conservative view towards the issue of immigration.
這位政治人物對於移民議題抱持保守的態度。

politics [`palətıks]

◀Track 3714

n. 政治；政治學；政治手腕

▶Workplace politics is the interpersonal interaction that involves power and authority. 辦公室政治是涉及權力和權威的人際互動關係。

poll [pol]

◀Track 3715

n. 民意測驗；投票；投票結果

▶According to the results of the poll, the candidate from the conservative party is likely to win the campaign.
根據民意調查的結果，保守政黨的候選人可能會贏得競選。

v. 對……進行民意測驗；使投票；
獲得（票數）

▶She polled 55 percent of the vote and became the prime minister.
她獲得百分之五十五的票數，當選首相。

pollute [pə`lut] v. 污染

◀Track 3716

▶The waste water discharged from the factory may pollute the river.
由工廠排放出的廢水可能會汙染河流。

pollution [pə`luʃən] 🔊 Track 3717

n. 污染

▶The sulfer dioxide from the burning of fossil fuels may be the major cause of air pollution.
燃燒石油產生的二氧化硫可能是空氣污染的主因。

pond [pand] **n.** 池塘 🔊 Track 3718

▶Some rhinos are drinking at the pond.
有一些犀牛在池旁邊喝水。

pony [`ponɪ] 🔊 Track 3719

n. 矮種馬，小馬；小型馬

▶The wealthy man is thinking of buying his daughter a pony.
這名富翁在考慮要不要買一匹小馬給他的女兒。

pool [pul] **n.** 池；水池 🔊 Track 3720

▶The girl used a swim ring in the swimming pool.
小女孩在游泳池裡使用游泳圈。

poor [pʊr] 🔊 Track 3721

adj. 可憐的；不幸的；貧窮的

▶Jerry felt fatigued and had a poor appetite; he might have caught a cold.
傑瑞感覺疲勞且胃口不好，他可能是感冒了。

pop [pap] 🔊 Track 3722

n. 砰的一聲，啪的一聲

▶The pop sound in the microwave oven scared me.
微波爐中發出砰的一聲，嚇我一跳。

v. 發出砰（或啪）的響聲；突然出現；迅速行動；開槍

▶He hasn't popped the question yet.
他還沒有求婚。

補充片語 pop the question 求婚

popcorn [`pap͵kɔrn] 🔊 Track 3723

n. 爆米花

▶They had some popcorns and churros when they watched the movie.
他們看電影時吃了一些爆米花和吉拿棒。

popular [`papjələ] 🔊 Track 3724

adj. 流行的；普遍的；受歡迎的

▶The Billboard Music Awards are considered to be a great honor for popular music artists.
告示牌音樂獎被認為是對流行音樂工作者的一項殊榮。

population 🔊 Track 3725

[͵papjə`leʃən] **n.** 人口

▶Japan is facing the problem of aging population.
日本正面臨人口老化的危險。

pork [pɔrk] **n.** 豬肉 🔊 Track 3726

▶The lunch box comes with bone-on pork chops.
這個便當裡面有帶骨的豬排。

port [port] 🔊 Track 3727

n. 港；港市；口岸

▶Many vessels entered the country through the port in the east coast.
許多船隻是通過東海岸上的港口入境這個國家。

portable [`portəb!] 🔊 Track 3728

adj. 便於攜帶的，手提式的

中級

▶Turn off your portable computer before you go through the customs.
過海關的時候要把手提電腦關掉。

n. 手提式製品

▶My brother's radio is a portable.
我哥哥的收音機是可手提的裝置。

---

porter [`portə] ◀Track 3729
n. （機場、車站的）搬運工人，腳夫；雜務工

▶They hired a porter at the Bangkok International Airport.
他們在曼谷國際機場雇用了一位搬運工人。

---

portion [`porʃən] ◀Track 3730
n. （一）部分；（食物等的）一份，一客；一份遺產

▶The student can memorize large portions of the Lyrical Ballads from William Wordsworth.
這名學生可以背誦威廉・華滋華斯的《抒情歌謠集》裡大部分的詩詞。

---

portrait [`portret] ◀Track 3731
n. 畫像

▶In the hall hung a portrait of a general.
在大廳裡面掛著一幅將軍的畫像。

---

portray [por`tre] ◀Track 3732
v. 畫，描繪；扮演，表現

▶In this movie, the protagonist was portrayed as a mysterious man. 在這部電影中，主角被描繪成一個神秘的人物。

---

pose [poz] ◀Track 3733
v. 擺姿勢；裝腔作勢；使擺好姿勢

▶The Lin family posed for a picture on their annual gathering.
林家人在年度聚會上擺好姿勢準備拍全家福。

---

n. 姿勢；姿態

▶The video introduces some basic model poses for female models.
這部影片了介紹一些女性模特兒的基本拍照姿勢。

---

position [pə`zıʃən] ◀Track 3734
n. 位置；姿勢；地位；身份；立場；職務

▶We listed the requirement for applicants to this vacant position. 我們列出了這個職缺應徵者應該要符合的條件。

v. 把……放在適當位置

▶A well-positioned outlet may increase the sales of the products.
銷貨中心位置好的話，產品銷量就會增加。

---

positive [`pazətıv] ◀Track 3735
adj. 確定的；確信的；積極的；肯定的

▶Frank told his son to stay positive and keep trying. 法蘭克告訴他兒子要保持積極、並且持續嘗試。

---

possess [pə`zɛs] **v.** 擁有 ◀Track 3736

▶The retired civil servant possesses several real estate properties.
這位退休的公務員擁有好幾棟房產。

---

possession ◀Track 3737
[pə`zɛʃən] **n.** 擁有；所有物

▶The police found several smuggled guns in his possession.
警方發現他擁有好幾隻走私的槍。

---

possibility ◀Track 3738
[,pasə`bılətı] **n.** 可能性；可能的事；發展前途

▶There is a good possibility that he will cancel the deal.
他很有可能會取消這筆交易。

possible [`pɑsəb!] ◀≣ Track 3739

adj. 可能的；有可能的

▶They will make every possible effort to rescue the Indian girl.
他們會盡一切努力去救出那個印度女孩。

possibly [`pɑsəblɪ] ◀≣ Track 3740

adv. 也許，可能；盡全力地

▶They will possibly take a direct flight to San Francisco.
他們可能會搭直飛班機去舊金山。

post [post] **n.** 柱子；樁；杆 ◀≣ Track 3741

▶Everyone rushed to his post as soon as the fire alarm went off.
火災警鈴一響，所有人就衝向自己的崗位。

postage [`postɪdʒ] ◀≣ Track 3742

n. 郵資

▶The postage shall be paid by the addressee.
郵資是由收件人付的。

postal [`post!] ◀≣ Track 3743

adj. 郵政的，郵局的，郵遞的

▶Tina has been working as a clerk in the postal system for fifteen years.
緹娜在郵政體系中擔任公務員已經十五年了。

postcard [`post͵kɑrd] ◀≣ Track 3744

n. 明信片

▶Participants of the "post-crossing" campaign exchange postcards with pen pals from all over the world.
參加『交換明信片』活動的人和來自世界各地的筆友交換明信片。

poster [`postɚ] ◀≣ Track 3745

n. 海報，廣告，招貼，佈告

▶Sean collected the posters of Marvel movies. 西恩收集漫威電影的海報。

postman [`postmən] ◀≣ Track 3746

n. 郵差

▶The postman sorted the mails and parcels according to the route in preparation for delivery. 郵差根據路線將郵件和包裹分類，準備要送出。

postpone [post`pon] ◀≣ Track 3747

v. 使延期，延遲；延緩

▶The award ceremony was postponed, for the hosting organization did not make the trophies ready in time.
頒獎典禮被延後了，因為主辦單位沒有及時準備好獎盃。

pot [pat] **n.** 鍋子；一鍋 ◀≣ Track 3748

▶The pot would be very hot; be careful when you hold it.
這個鍋子可能會很熱，拿的時候要小心。

potato [pə`teto] **n.** 馬鈴薯 ◀≣ Track 3749

▶Potato chips can serves as a good side dish. 馬鈴薯片可以是一種很好的配菜。

potential [pə`tɛnʃəl] ◀≣ Track 3750

adj. 潛在的，可能的

▶This article talks about the potential harm of air pollution.
這篇文章談到空氣污染的潛在危險。

n. 可能性，潛力；潛能

▶I think the talented girl has limitless potentials.
我認為這個女孩有無限的潛能。

中級

pottery [`pɑtərɪ] ◀ Track 3751

n. 陶器；陶器製造；陶器廠；製陶手藝；製陶行業

▶ The theme of the exhibition is ancestral pottery.
這個展覽的主題是古代的陶藝。

poultry [`poltrɪ] ◀ Track 3752

n. 家禽，家禽肉

▶ The government is trying to keep the contagious disease of poultry from spreading.
政府試圖阻止鳥禽類的疾病擴散。

pound [paʊnd] ◀ Track 3753

v. （連續）猛烈敲擊；（心臟）劇跳；搗碎；腳步沉重地行走；隆隆地行駛

▶ My heart kept pounding as I walked onto the stage to address to my peer schoolmates.
要走上台對同學們致詞的時候，我的心跳得很快。

pour [por] ◀ Track 3754

v. 倒，灌；傾注，大量投入；傾瀉

▶ It never rains but it pours.
屋漏偏逢連夜雨。

poverty [`pɑvətɪ] ◀ Track 3755

n. 貧困，貧窮

▶ While people in the big city lead a luxurious life, people in the rural area still suffer from poverty.
住在大城市的人們過著奢華的生活，而住在鄉村的人們還是飽受貧窮之苦。

powder [`paʊdə] ◀ Track 3756

n. 粉；粉狀物；化妝用粉

▶ Add a teaspoon of baking powder to the paste.
加一茶匙的烘焙粉到麵團中。

v. 擦粉；把粉撒在……上

▶ She powdered the baby's bottom to stop it chafing.
她在嬰兒的屁股上擦一些粉以防磨痛。

power [`paʊə] ◀ Track 3757

n. 力量；能力；職權

▶ The man claimed that he has the supernatural power.
這名男子宣稱他有超自然的力量。

pow·erful [`paʊəfəl] ◀ Track 3758

adj. 強而有力的；有權威的

▶ His powerful words had a great influence on the people.
他強而有力的話語對人們很有影響力。

powerless [`paʊələs] ◀ Track 3759

adj. 無力量的；無能力的；無影響力的；無權力的

▶ The powerless laborers ended up losing the legal case. 結果這些沒有影響力的勞工輸掉了這次官司。

practical [`præktɪk!] ◀ Track 3760

adj. 實際的；實用的，有實用價值的；有實際經驗的

▶ Stop building castles on the cloud; your suggestions are not practical at all.
不要再畫大餅了；你的建議一點都不實際。

相關片語 **practical joke** 惡作劇，捉弄

▶ The kids played a practical joke on their teacher. 小朋友對老師惡作劇。

practice [`præktɪs]　◀Track 3761

n. 練習

▶Practice makes perfect.
熟能生巧。

v. 練習

▶The performer practices acrobatic skills every day.
這位表演者每天都練習雜耍的技術。

praise [prez]　◀Track 3762

v. 讚美；表揚

▶She was praised as the best female pianist in the twenty-first century.
她被譽為是二十一世紀最佳女性鋼琴演奏家。

n. 讚揚；稱頌

▶The Youtuber has received both praises and critiques.
這位Youtube工作者得到過讚美也接受過批評。

pray [pre] **v.** 祈禱；祈求　◀Track 3763

▶The mayor prayed for peace and prosperity of the city.
市長祈求本市和平繁榮。

prayer [prɛr]　◀Track 3764

n. 祈禱，禱告；祈禱文

▶People attending the church said their prayers at a low voice.
去教堂做禮拜的人們低聲說著禱告。

precious [`prɛʃəs]　◀Track 3765

adj. 貴重的；珍貴的

▶These photo albums contain my precious memories.
這些相本中有我珍貴的回憶。

pre·cise [prɪ`saɪs]　◀Track 3766

adj. 精確的

▶His estimation was very precise.
他的估計很精準。

predict [prɪ`dɪkt]　◀Track 3767

v. 預測，預言，預料，預報

▶The old lady predicted the tsunami in India.
這位老婦人預測到了印度會有海嘯。

prediction [prɪ`dɪkʃən]　◀Track 3768

n. 預測，預料，預報；預言的事

▶The fortune teller used Tarot reading to make predictions for my future.
這位算命師用塔羅牌預測我的未來。

prefer [prɪ`fɚ]　◀Track 3769

v. 寧願；更喜歡

▶I prefer living in the country to living in the city.
我喜歡住在鄉下勝過住在城市。

preferable [`prɛfərəb!]　◀Track 3770

adj. 更好的，更合適的；更可取的

▶Accommodation at a location near the subway station is preferable.
住宿在靠近地鐵的地方比較好。

pregnancy　◀Track 3771

[`prɛgnənsɪ] **n.** 懷孕；孕期

▶You should avoid taking in any caffeine during the pregnancy.
你在懷孕期間最好不要攝取咖啡因。

pregnant [`prɛgnənt]　◀Track 3772

adj. 懷孕的，懷胎的；充滿的，富有的；意味深長的

中級

369

▶Usually, pregnant women would take the prenatal examinationa.
懷孕的女性通常都會接受產前檢查。

preparation　◀Track 3773
[,prɛpə`reʃən] n. 準備；準備工作
▶The preparation for the gala has completed.
這場慶祝會的準備工作已經完成了。

prepare [prɪ`pɛr] v 準備　◀Track 3774
▶He spent six months preparing for the national examination.
他花了六個月準備國考。

prepared [prɪ`pɛrd]　◀Track 3775
adj. 有準備的
▶She was fully-prepared for the oral presentation. 對於這次演講她已準備充分。

presence [`prɛzns]　◀Track 3776
n. 出席；在場；面前
▶Don't curse at the presence of our honorable guest.
不要在貴賓面前罵髒話。

present [`prɛznt]　◀Track 3777
adj. 出席的；在場的；現在的；當前的
▶All the stakeholders will be present at the meeting.
所有股東都會出席這次的會議。

n. 禮物；現在
▶I bought a bike for my daughter as her birthday present.
我買了一輛腳踏車給女兒當生日禮物。

presentation　◀Track 3778
[,prizɛn`teʃən] n. 報告，介紹；呈現，提出

▶The scholar made a presentation about his findings in his research.
這位學者報告了他的研究結果。

presently [`prɛzntlɪ]　◀Track 3779
adv. 現在，目前；不久，一會兒
▶She is presently working on her doctoral thesis.
她目前正在撰寫博士論文。

preserve [prɪ`zɝv]　◀Track 3780
v 保存，防腐；保護，維持；醃肉，
把……製成果醬或蜜餞
▶The ancient people preserve food in the cellar.
古時候的人把食物保存在地窖裡。

n. 蜜餞，果醬；保護區；防護用品
▶The homemade fruit preserve is quite delicious.
這個自製的水果蜜餞很好吃。

president [`prɛzədənt]　◀Track 3781
n. 總統
▶The president planned to end the government shutdown by making a deal with the opposite party.
總統計畫要和反對黨合作，以結束政府關門的狀態。

presidential　◀Track 3782
[`prɛzədɛnʃəl] adj. 總統的，總統制的，總統選舉的；總裁的，會長的
▶The presidential election will be held at the end of the year.
總統大選將在年底舉行。

press [prɛs]　◀Track 3783
n. 新聞界；新聞輿論；壓、按；熨平、燙平

▶The entrepreneur will hold a press conference to apologize for the scandal. 這名企業家將會舉辦記者會，為了醜聞向大眾致歉。

v 按；擠；壓；催促

▶Just press one button, and the machine will produce the vegetable juice for you. 只要按一個鈕，這個機器就會為你做出蔬果汁。

pressure [`prɛʃɚ]
◀ Track 3784

n 壓力，艱難；壓，按，擠

▶The laborers were under great pressure, for the government imposes heavy taxes on them. 勞工的壓力很大，因為政府對他們課以重稅。

v 對……施加壓力；迫使

▶The people in the town were pressured to submit part of their crops to the landlord. 小鎮的人們被迫將一部分的作物繳交給地主。

pretend [prɪ`tɛnd]
◀ Track 3785

v 假裝，佯裝；假扮，裝作

▶The thief pretended to be tourists, looking for chances to steal money. 這個小偷假裝成觀光客，等待機會去偷錢。

pretty [`prɪtɪ] **adj** 漂亮的
◀ Track 3786

▶The twin sisters were very pretty, and they are adored by the elders in the family. 這對雙胞胎姊妹很漂亮，備受家裡長輩的疼愛。

adv 非常；蠻；頗

▶The procedure is actually pretty easy. You can just follow the steps on the manual.
這個過程其實相當簡單。你只要按照手冊上的步驟做就可以了。

prevent [prɪ`vɛnt]
◀ Track 3787

v 阻止；防止，預防

▶It's everyone's duty to prevent the global warming effect from getting worse.
防止全球暖化現象惡化是每個人的責任。

prevention
◀ Track 3788

[prɪ`vɛnʃən] **n** 預防

▶The government puts emphasis on the prevention of youth crime.
政府很重視青年犯罪的防範。

preview [`pri͵vju]
◀ Track 3789

n 預習，預看，預先審查；試映；預展；預告片

▶We had a preview of the new Korean drama on the Internet.
我們在網路上預先收看新的韓劇。

v 預習，預看，預先審查；試映；預告

▶I used to preview the lessons before attending class.
我以前會在上課之前預習課程的內容。

previous [`priviəs]
◀ Track 3790

adj 先前的，以前的

▶To Tom, the present job is much more challenging than the previous one.
對湯姆來說，現在的工作比之前的工作更具有挑戰性。

price [praɪs] **n** 價錢；價格
◀ Track 3791

▶The price of gold has been rising nonstop over the past decade.
黃金的價格在過去十年內不停的攀升。

v 給……定價；為……標價

▶The handbag was priced at $5,000 dollars. 這個手提包的訂價五千元。

中級

priceless [`praɪslɪs】 ◄€Track 3792
adj. 貴重的，無價的

▶Good memories with family and friends are priceless.
和家人朋友之間的美好回憶是無價的。

pride [praɪd] ◄€Track 3793
n. 自豪；得意；引以為傲的人或事物；自尊心

▶He takes pride in his talent in composing.
他對於自己作曲的才華感到自豪。

v. 使得意，使自豪

▶She prides herself in her filial piety.
她對自己克盡孝道感到自豪。

priest [prist] **n.** 牧師 ◄€Track 3794

▶The priest performed a wedding for a young couple at this church.
牧師在這間教堂為一對年輕夫妻證婚。

primary [`praɪ͵mɛrɪ] ◄€Track 3795
adj. 主要的；基本的

▶The primary cause of his failure lies in his habit of procrastination.
他失敗的主因是他拖延的習慣。

prime [praɪm] ◄€Track 3796
adj. 最初的，基本的；主要的，首位的；最好的

▶The prime minister addressed to the people on New Year's Day.
首相在新年向人民致詞。

補充片語 prime minister 首相

相關片語 die in the prime of one's life 英年早逝

▶The creator of Sponge Bob died in the prime of his life.
《海綿寶寶》的創作者英年早逝。

v. 灌注，填裝；使準備好

▶The gun was primed and ready.
槍已經裝好火藥了。

primitive [`prɪmətɪv] ◄€Track 3797
adj. 原始的，遠古的；粗糙的，未開化的；淳樸的，自然的

▶People in the isolated island led a primitive life.
在這與世隔絕島上，人們過著原始的生活。

prince [prɪns] **n.** 王子 ◄€Track 3798

▶Mike used to be the prince charming for many girls in his school.
麥可以前是學校女孩子眼中的白馬王子。

princess [`prɪnsɪs] ◄€Track 3799
n. 公主

▶In fairy tales, princesses usually would expect themselves to be rescued by a hero. 童話故事中的公主通常都會期待可以被英雄救援。

principle [`prɪnsəp!] ◄€Track 3800
n. 原則；原理；主義；信條

▶He followed the prudence principle and avoided unnecessary expenses.
他遵守謹慎的原則，避免不必要的花費。

print [prɪnt] ◄€Track 3801
v. 印；印刷；發行；出版

▶He printed out the second chapter of the book from the computer.
他從電腦上將這本書的第二章列印下來。

n. 印刷字體；印記；拷貝；印刷業

▶The author was very impressed when he saw his work in print.
作者看到自己作品付印的時候很感動。

printer [`prɪntɚ] ◄€Track 3802
n. 印表機

▶Do you know how to change the printer cartridge?
你知道怎麼換印表機墨水夾嗎？

priority [praɪ`ɔrətɪ] ◄€Track 3803
n. 優先，重點；優先考慮的事

▶Her top priority is to finish her education.
她目前優先考量的事情是完成學業。

prison [`prɪzn] ◄€Track 3804
n. 監獄；拘留所

▶The officials are considering spending 50 million dollars on building a new state prison.
這些官員們考慮要花五千萬元建造新的州立監獄。

prisoner [`prɪznɚ] ◄€Track 3805
n. 犯人；囚犯

▶The prisoners were asked to wear fetters. 犯人被要求戴著腳鐐。

privacy [`praɪvəsɪ] ◄€Track 3806
n. 隱私

▶The paparazzi were sued for invading the celebrity's privacy.
這些狗仔隊因為侵犯名人的隱私而遭控告。

private [`praɪvɪt] ◄€Track 3807
adj. 個人的；私下的

▶Fiona studied in a private school.
費歐娜念的是私立學校。

privilege [`prɪv!ɪdʒ] ◄€Track 3808
n. 特權；（個人的）殊榮；議會特權；基本權利

▶The actor was granted the privilege to meet Her Majesty.
這名演員獲得接受女王觀見的殊榮。

v. 給予……特權

▶I was privileged to work with such a competent professional like you.
能和像你一樣有能力的專業人士一起工作，我感到很榮幸。

prize [praɪz] ◄€Track 3809
n. 獎；獎品；獎金

▶He hit the jackpot and became a millionaire; however, he wasted all the prize money on gambling.
他贏得頭獎，成為百萬富翁；但是，他把所有的獎金都浪費在賭博上面了。

probable [`prɑbəb!] ◄€Track 3810
adj. 很可能發生的；很可能成為事實的；很有希望的；可信的

▶It is probable that the hikers who got lost in the mountain will be rescued.
在山裡迷路的登山客很可能會獲救。

probably [`prɑbəblɪ] ◄€Track 3811
adv. 可能；有可能地

▶This is probably your last chance to turn over a new leaf.
這可能是你最一次改過自新的機會了。

problem [`prɑbləm] ◄€Track 3812
n. 問題；難題

▶The teacher adopted problem-based learning method on the Social Studies class. 老師將問題導向的學習法應用在社會科的課堂上。

procedure [prə`sidʒɚ] ◄€Track 3813
n. 手續；程序；步驟

中級

▶The procedure of applying for a visa may take a few weeks.
申請簽證的程序可能要花幾個星期。

proceed [prə`sid]
🔊 Track 3814

v. 繼續進行；著手，開始；進行

▶You cannot proceed unless you have the permission from the supervisor.
除非有主管的批准，否則你不能繼續進行。

process [`prasɛs]
🔊 Track 3815

n. 過程，進程；步驟，程序

▶The process of negotiation was so long that the salesperson got impatient.
協商的過程如此冗長，以至於銷售員都開始不耐煩了。

v. 加工；處理；辦理

▶It is said that the processed food may contain a variety of chemical additives. 據說這個加工食品可能含有很多種化學添加物。

produce [prə`djus]
🔊 Track 3816

v. 生產；出產

▶It may take a German worker 600 hours to produce a car.
一位德國工人可能要花六百個小時才能製造出一輛車。

producer [prə`djusɚ]
🔊 Track 3817

n. 生產者；製作人

▶The film producer attended a talk show to share the anecdotes behind the scenes.
電影製作人上談話節目分享拍攝電影過程中的趣事。

product [`pradəkt]
🔊 Track 3818

n. 產品

▶We should replace the disposable products with reusable ones.
我們應該要將一次性產品取代成可重複利用的產品。

production
🔊 Track 3819

[prə`dʌkʃən] **n.** 生產；製作；產量；產物

▶Thousands of workers were involved in the production of an aircraft.
數千名工人參與飛機製作過程。

productive
🔊 Track 3820

[prə`dʌktɪv]

adj. 生產的；多產的；富有成效的

▶The writer said that he was most productive in the morning.
這名作家說在早晨他的寫作效率最高。

profession [prə`fɛʃən]
🔊 Track 3821

n. （透過教育或訓練的）職業

▶She wants to be a nurse by profession.
她想要以醫護人員作為她的職業。

professional
🔊 Track 3822

[prə`fɛʃən!] **adj.** 職業上的，職業性的；內行的，稱職的；擅長⋯⋯的

▶The professional cyclist would wear protective gears when they hit the road.
這名專業的腳踏車選手會在上路時穿戴好保護裝置。

n. 職業選手，專家，行家

▶Dozens of professionals attended this conference.
有數十名專家參與這次的研討會。

professor [prə`fɛsɚ]
🔊 Track 3823

n. 教授

▶You can find the list of the professor's publications on his personal webpage.
妳可以在教授的個人網頁上看到他著作的列表。

profit [`prɑfɪt]
◀ Track 3824

n. 利潤，盈利；收益；利益

▶All he cares about is making profits.
他只在乎賺錢而已。

| 相關片語 profit-making institution |
| 營利機構 |

▶This is not a profit-making institution; the purpose of it is to assist people in need. 這不是一個營利的機構；它的宗旨是要幫助有需要的人。

v. 有益於，有利於；得益，獲益

▶He profited greatly from a year of internship in the foreign company.
他在外資公司實習的一年，令他感到獲益匪淺。

profitable [`prɑfɪtəb!]
◀ Track 3825

adj. 有利的，有營利的；獲利的

▶It is said that selling cars is a profitable business.
據說賣車是一個有利可圖的生意。

pro·gram [`progræm]
◀ Track 3826
=programme （英式英文）

n. 節目；節目單；計劃；方案

▶You can find the schedule of the programs on the website. 妳可以在這個網站上面查到此頻道的時間表。

v. 為…… 安排節目；為（電腦）設計程式；為……制定計劃

▶The robot is programmed to take care of the elderly people.
這個機器人是設計來照顧老年人的。

progress [prə`grɛs]
◀ Track 3827

n. 前進；進步；進展

▶He made progress in his Spanish proficiency.
他的西班牙文進步了。

v. 前進

▶The country has progressed in terms of democracy.
這個國家在民主方面進步了。

progressive
◀ Track 3828

[prə`grɛsɪv] **adj.** 進步的，先進的；逐步的，發展中的；（醫）進行性的，越來越嚴重的

▶There has been a progressive decline in the salary standard in recent years.
近年來，薪資的水準逐漸降低。

n. 進步分子；革新主義者；改革派

▶The progressives of the political party promoted innovative policies.
此政黨的革新主義者推動創新的政策。

prohibit [prə`hɪbɪt]
◀ Track 3829

v. （以法令）禁止；妨礙，阻止

▶Smoking in public places is prohibited in the city.
在這個城市裡是禁止在公共場所中吸菸的。

project [prə`dʒɛkt]
◀ Track 3830

n. 計劃；企劃

▶The project will involve staffs from the Public Relation Department and the Marketing Department.
這個計畫會牽涉到公關部門和行銷部門的員工們。

prominent
◀ Track 3831

[`prɑmənənt] **adj.** 傑出的

中級

▶She was granted an honorable degree from the university for her prominent contribution in physics.
她因為對物理學有傑出的貢獻，獲頒這所大學的榮譽學位。

promise [`pramɪs]   ◀Track 3832
v. 承諾；答應；保證

▶He promised that he would never be late again. 他答應不會再遲到。

n. 承諾

▶He is a man of his words; I am sure he will keep his promise. 他是一個有誠信的人；我相信他會實踐承諾。

promising [`pramɪsɪŋ]   ◀Track 3833
adj. 有前途的，有希望的

▶The talented young man would have a promising future.
這個有才華的年輕人前途無量。

promote [prə`mot]   ◀Track 3834
v. 擢昇，晉升

▶He was promoted to be the head of the Ministry of Education.
他被拔擢為教育部長。

promotion   ◀Track 3835
[prə`moʃən] **n.** 升遷；促銷

▶The social media promotion was very effective.
這個社群媒體的促銷活動相當有效。

prompt [prampt]   ◀Track 3836
v. 促使；激勵；慫恿

▶His curiosity prompted him to dig into more details about this theory.
受好奇心驅使，他更深入研究這個理論的細節。

n. 催促；提醒；提詞

▶The prompt on the screen shows that the computer has received the order.
螢幕上的提示顯示電腦已經接受到指令了。

adj. 敏捷的，及時的，迅速的

▶The lifeguard took prompt action to rescue the drowning child.
救生員採取及時行動，救了溺水的小孩。

pronounce   ◀Track 3837
[prə`naʊns] **v.** 發音

▶There are some pictures showing how to pronounce the words in the dictionary. 字典裡有圖片，顯示出該如何進行單字發音。

pronunciation   ◀Track 3838
[prə͵nʌnsɪ`eʃən] **n.** 發音，發音法

▶The same word may have different pronunciations in British English and American English. 同一個字在英式英文和美式英文裡會有不同的發音。

proof [pruf]   ◀Track 3839
n. 證據，物證；證明

▶I need the proof of presence at the conference.
我需要這個研討會的出席證明。

adj. 不能穿透的，能抵擋的

▶The jacket is said to be bullet proof.
據說這件外套是防彈的。

proper [`prapɚ]   ◀Track 3840
adj. 適合的，適當的；合乎體統的

▶Proper phrasing is important when you write a letter to your business partner. 寫信給商業夥伴的時候，適當的措辭很重要。

properly [`prɑpɚlɪ] ◀ Track 3841
adv. 恰當地，正確地；理所當然地

▶ The video shows you how to properly fry tofu.
這個影片教你要如何適當地煎豆腐。

property [`prɑpɚtɪ] ◀ Track 3842
n. 財產，資產，所有物

▶ The real estate property in the center of the city has become more valuable.
市中心的房地產變得更有價值了。

proportion ◀ Track 3843
[prə`porʃən] **n.** 比例，比率；部分

▶ The chart shows the proportion of students taking part time jobs in different workplaces.
這個表格呈現學生在不同地方打工的比例。

proposal [prə`poz!] ◀ Track 3844
n. 計畫；建議；求婚

▶ His proposal was rejected by the committee.
他的計畫被委員會拒絕了。

propose [prə`poz] ◀ Track 3845
v. 提議；建議；求婚

▶ He proposed that we should reduce the consumption of electricity.
他建議我們減少電力的消耗。

prospect [`prɑspɛkt] ◀ Track 3846
n. （成功的）可能性；前景，前途

▶ The tourism industry has a good prospect for development.
旅遊業有很好的發展前景。

prosper [`prɑspɚ] ◀ Track 3847
v. 使繁榮，繁榮

▶ The construction of the shopping center is expected to make this community prosper.
這個購物中心的建造預期可以讓個社區變得更繁榮。

prosperity ◀ Track 3848
[prɑs`pɛrətɪ] **n.** 繁榮

▶ The future prosperity of the country lies in the quality of education of its people.
這個國家未來的繁榮取決於國民教育的品質。

prosperous ◀ Track 3849
[`prɑspərəs] **adj.** 富有的，繁榮的，昌盛的

▶ The little coastal town has developed into a prosperous city.
這個海邊的小鎮已經發展成為一個繁榮的城市了。

protect [prə`tɛkt] **v.** 保護 ◀ Track 3850

▶ The sunscreen can protect you from the harmful UV light from the sun.
這個防曬乳可以保護你不受陽光中的紫外線傷害。

protection ◀ Track 3851
[prə`tɛkʃən] **n.** 保護；防護

▶ The activists listed the measures for environmental protection, hoping the government would put more emphasis on this issue.
行動份子列出了環境保護的措施，希望政府可以更加注意這個議題。

protective [prə`tɛktɪv] ◀ Track 3852
adj. 保護的

中級

▶The protective gears cost the motorcyclist three thousand dollars.
這些摩托車的保護裝備花了這名摩托車騎士三千元。

protein [`protin] ◀≈Track 3853
n. 蛋白質

▶It is said that the fish contains high-quality protein.
據說這種魚含有高品質的蛋白質。

protest [prə`tɛst] ◀≈Track 3854
n. 抗議，異議，反對

▶There was a protest against high fuel taxes.
有人在抗議高燃料稅。

v. 抗議，反對；斷言，對……提出異議；聲明

▶The laborers protested against the long working hours.
這些勞工抗議高工時。

proud [praʊd] ◀≈Track 3855
adj. 驕傲的；得意的

▶You should be proud for such a great accomplishment.
你應該為這麼好的成就感到驕傲。

prove [pruv] v. 證明 ◀≈Track 3856
▶He took an oath to prove his loyalty for the country.
他發誓表示對國家忠心。

proverb [`pravɚb] ◀≈Track 3857
n. 諺語，俗語；眾所皆知的事

▶A proverb goes that the early bird catches the worm.
俗話說早起的鳥兒有蟲吃。

provide [prə`vaɪd] ◀≈Track 3858
v. 提供

▶He provided some useful advices for us.
他提供了一些有用的意見給我們。

province [`pravɪns] ◀≈Track 3859
n. 省，州；（相較於大都市的）地方，鄉間；（學術）領域，（工作）部門，（職務）範圍

▶The capital of the province is in the southeast part of it.
這個省的省府在該省的東南方。

psychological ◀≈Track 3860
[ˌsaɪkə`ladʒɪk!] adj. 心理的

▶The article introduces some psychological strategies that can help you strengthen your love relationship.
這篇文章介紹一些可以幫助你增進戀愛關係的心理策略。

psychologist ◀≈Track 3861
[saɪ`kalədʒɪst] n. 心理學家

▶Sigmund Freud is an influential psychologist in the twentieth century.
佛洛伊德是一位在20世紀很有影響力的心理學家。

psychology ◀≈Track 3862
[saɪ`kalədʒɪ] n. 心理學

▶Ryan aspires to major in psychology in college.
雷恩想要在大學時主修心理學。

pub [pʌb] n. 酒吧 ◀≈Track 3863
▶Some students hung out at the local pub on New Year's Eve.
有些學生在新年前夕聚在當地的酒吧裡。

public [`pʌblɪk]
adj. 大眾的；公共的；民眾的

🔊 Track 3864

▶ The public media organizations have great power in influencing people's thoughts on controversial issues.
大眾媒體組織對於人們在爭議議題的看法上，很有影響力。

n. 公眾；民眾

▶ The journalist revealed the scandal to the public.
這名記者將這樁醜聞公開給大眾知道。

publication [ˌpʌblɪ`keʃən]
n. 出版，發行；出版物，刊物；發表

🔊 Track 3865

▶ The digital publication, including e-books and digital magazines, has become more common in recent years.
數位出版，包括電子書和數位雜誌，在最近幾年變得更加普遍了。

publicity [pʌb`lɪsətɪ]
n. 公眾的注意，名聲；宣傳

🔊 Track 3866

▶ Social media, such as Twitter and Instagram, have become a common form of publicity. 像是推特、IG這類社群媒體，已經成為普遍的宣傳方式。

publish [`pʌblɪʃ] **v.** 出版
🔊 Track 3867

▶ The latest novel of J. K. Rowling has been published.
J.K. 羅琳的最新小說已經發行了。

publisher [`pʌblɪʃɚ]
n. 出版社，出版商；出版或發行者

🔊 Track 3868

▶ Can the writers retain the right to their novels if the publisher closes the business? 如果出版社結束營業，作者可以拿回小說的使用權嗎？

pudding [`pʊdɪŋ]
n. 布丁

🔊 Track 3869

▶ Mrs. Simpson made some rice puddings for her kids.
辛普森太太為她的小孩做了一些米布丁。

puff [pʌf]
v. 一陣陣地吹；噴著煙移動；喘著氣走；腫脹；使氣急；使充氣

🔊 Track 3870

▶ The old man was puffing away at a cigarette on the rock chair.
老人坐在搖椅上抽菸。

n. （一）吹，噴；一陣，一股；（抽）一口煙；呼吸；膨脹；粉撲；泡芙

▶ She blew out all the caldles on the cake with a single puff.
她一口氣吹熄蛋糕上面的所有蠟燭。

pull [pʊl]
v. 拉；拖；牽；拽；拔

🔊 Track 3871

▶ The train was pulling out when we arrived at the platform.
我們到達月台的時候，火車正要出站。

n. 拉

▶ He explains how the moon's pull affects the tides on earth.
他解釋月亮的引力是如何影響地球上的潮汐。

pump [pʌmp]
n. 泵，唧筒；抽吸

🔊 Track 3872

▶ We used a pump to draw water from the well.
我們用幫浦來汲取井裡的水。

v. 用唧筒抽

▶ They pumped air into the tire.
他們打氣到輪胎裡。

中級

pumpkin [`pʌmpkɪn]   ◀ミ Track 3873
n. 南瓜

▶We had a pumpkin pie and a roast turkey for Thanksgiving dinner.
我們吃南瓜派和烤火雞當感恩節晚餐。

punch [pʌntʃ] **n.** 拳打   ◀ミ Track 3874

▶If he say something offensive again, I will give him a punch in the face.
如果他再說冒犯的話，我就會對著他的臉揍下去。

v. 用拳猛擊；用力按

▶When you punch the green button, the machine will start operating.
當你按下綠色按鈕，機器就會開始運作。

punctual [`pʌŋktʃʊəl]   ◀ミ Track 3875
adj. 嚴守時刻的，準時的；正確的

▶Being punctual when meeting the client is the basic business manner.
和顧客見面要準時，這是基本的商場禮節。

punish [`pʌnɪʃ] **v.** 處罰   ◀ミ Track 3876

▶You can't get away with the mistake; you will be punished. 你無法逃避面對這個錯誤；你會受到懲罰的。

punishment   ◀ミ Track 3877
[`pʌnɪʃmənt] **n.** 懲罰

▶People who smuggle agricultural product will receive severe punishment.
偷渡農產品的人會受到嚴厲的懲罰。

pupil [`pjup!]   ◀ミ Track 3878
n. 小學生，學生；未成年人

▶More than half of the pupils in the school are from underprivileged background.
這所學校都有超過一半的學生都出身貧寒。

puppet [`pʌpɪt]   ◀ミ Track 3879
n. 木偶，玩偶；傀儡

▶Children like those delicate hand puppets very much.
小朋友很喜歡那些精巧的手偶。

puppy [`pʌpɪ] **n.** 小狗   ◀ミ Track 3880

▶The puppy was abandoned on the street.
這隻小狗被遺棄在路邊。

purchase [`pɝtʃəs]   ◀ミ Track 3881
n. 購買；購買之物

▶Think twice before you make a purchase on the Internet.
在網路購物之前要三思。

v. 購買

▶I purchased a piece of furniture from the second-hand goods dealer.
我在二手商品店買了一件家具。

purple [`pɝp!]   ◀ミ Track 3882
adj. 紫色的；紫的

▶The actress attended the banquet in a purple gown.
這名女演員穿著紫色的禮服出席這場晚宴。

n. 紫色

▶Purple is the lucky color for me today.
紫色是我今天的幸運色。

purpose [`pɝpəs]   ◀ミ Track 3883
n. 目的；意圖；用途

▶The multi-purpose tool can be used in several different ways.
這個多功能的工具可以用在不同的地方。

purse [pɝs]   ◀ミ Track 3884
n. 錢包；女用手提包

▶The boutique is having a sale for hand-held purse.
這家精品店的手提包正在特價中。

push [pʊʃ] **v** 推；催促

◀ Track 3885

▶She pushed her son to practice playing piano.
她督促兒子練習鋼琴。

n. 推進；努力；衝進

▶They must make a push to complete the task.
他們必須加把勁把這個任務完成。

put [pʊt]

◀ Track 3886

v 放；擺；使處於……狀態

▶It is not a good habit to put things off.
拖延事情是不好的習慣。

puzzle [ˋpʌz!]

◀ Track 3887

n. 謎；難題

▶David likes to play jigsaw puzzles.
大衛喜歡玩拼圖。

v 迷惑；為難

▶The students were puzzled by the professor's words.
學生們對教授說的話感到困惑。

中級

Qq

　　以下表格是全民英檢官方公告中級「聽、說、讀、寫」所須具備的能力，本書例句皆依此範疇特別設計，只要掃描右方QR code，就能搭配相對應的音軌實現「眼耳並用」方式，刺激左腦的語言學習功能；同時也可使用本書附贈的紅膠片，將其置於單字上，一面記憶一面自我挑戰，達到雙倍的學習成果！

聽 ▶	在日常生活中，能聽懂一般的會話；能大致聽懂公共場所廣播、氣象報告及廣告等。在工作時，能聽懂簡易的產品介紹與操作說明。能大致聽懂外籍人士的談話及詢問。
說 ▶	可在日常生活中，能以簡易英語交談或描述一般事物，能介紹自己的生活作息、工作、家庭、經歷等，並可對一般話題陳述看法。在工作時，能進行簡單的答詢，並與外籍人士交談溝通。
讀 ▶	在日常生活中，能閱讀短文、故事、私人信件、廣告、傳單、簡介及使用說明等。在工作時，能閱讀工作須知、公告、操作手冊、例行的文件、傳真、電報等。
寫 ▶	能寫簡單的書信、故事及心得等。對於熟悉且與個人經歷相關的主題，能以簡易的文字表達。

quack [kwæk]　◀Track 3888

adj. 庸醫的；冒充內行醫病的；冒牌的；吹牛的；騙人的

▶Don't be fooled by the quack doctor.
別被假冒的醫生騙了。

n. 庸醫，江湖醫生；冒充內行的人；騙子

▶The doctor was a quack; he is not a medical professional. 這個醫生是個騙子；他並不是專業的醫療人員。

qualification　◀Track 3889
[͵kwɑləfə`keʃən]

n. 資格，條件；限定性條件

▶A bachelor's degree is the first qualification to become a lawyer.
成為律師第一個條件是要有學士學位。

qualified [`kwɑlə͵faɪd]　◀Track 3890
adj. 符合資格的；具備必要條件的

▶He made a lot of efforts to become a qualified teacher.
他很努力成為一個合格的教師。

qualify [`kwɑlə͵faɪ]　◀Track 3891
v. 使具有資格；使合格；取得資格；具備合格條件

▶To qualify yourself to be a professional chef, you need to pass the certificate test.
要成為一位合格的廚師，你必須通過證照考試。

quality [`kwɑlətɪ] **n.** 品質　◀Track 3892

▶The quality of the product is guaranteed
這個產品是有品質保證的。

quantity [`kwɑntətɪ] ◀€Track 3893

n. 量；數量；分量；大量；音量

▶Goods in this mall are sold in larger quantities than usual during holidays.
這家購物中心在假期間賣的商品，份量都比平常大。

quarrel [`kwɔrəl] ◀€Track 3894

n. 爭吵，不和，吵鬧

▶It took them three days to get over the quarrel. 他們這次吵架吵了三天。

v. 爭吵，不和；埋怨，責備

▶The couple often quarreled over financial problems.
這對夫妻以前常常因為財務問題吵架。

quarter [`kwɔrtɚ] ◀€Track 3895

n. 四分之一；一刻鐘

▶It is a quarter to six now.
現在是五點四十五分。

queen [`kwin] **n.** 皇后 ◀€Track 3896

▶The queen of the country does not have actual authority, but she is still respected by the people. 這個國家的皇后沒有實際權力，但是仍受到人們的尊敬。

queer [`kwɪr] ◀€Track 3897

adj. 古怪的，可疑的；不舒服的

▶The queer actions of the man made the people around him feel uncomfortable.
這名男子的奇怪行徑讓周圍的人覺得不舒服。

相關片語 **queer fish**
　　　　古怪的人，難以理解的人

▶My neighbor is such a queer fish that my parents ask me not to get too close to him.
我的鄰居是個非常古怪的人，以至於我的爸媽叫我不要和他走得太近。

quest [kwɛst] ◀€Track 3898

v. 尋找，追求，探索；請求，要求

▶The king set off for a journey in quest of a way to be immortal.
國王開啟一趟旅程，尋找長生不老的方法。

補充片語 **in quest of** 尋找，探尋

question [`kwɛstʃən] ◀€Track 3899

n. 問題，詢問

▶Our math teacher asked us many questions in today's class to see if we preview the lessons.
我們的數學老師在今天的課堂上問了我們很多問題，以辨別我們是否有做預習。

v. 質疑；詢問

▶Nobody likes to be questioned. Please try to communicate first.
沒有人喜歡被質問，請試著先溝通。

queue [kju] ◀€Track 3900

n. （人或車輛的）隊伍，行列

▶I was surprised at the long queue in front of the deli.
我被熟食店前面的排隊人潮嚇到了。

v. 排隊，排隊等候

▶We queued up and waited for the shuttle bus.
我們排隊等待接駁車。

相關片語 **jump the queue** 插隊

中級

▶This woman was unbelievable. She jumped the queue when everyone else was quietly waiting for their turn to order the food.
當大家正在安靜地等候點餐時，這位婦女竟然插隊，讓人不可置信。

quick [kwɪk] adj. 快的
◀ Track 3901

▶The service of photographic processing is rather quick in this store.
這間店沖洗相片的服務相當快速。

quiet [`kwaɪət] adj. 安靜的
◀ Track 3902

▶I need a quiet place to finish my report.
我需要一個安靜地方來完成報告。

quilt [kwɪlt] n. 被子，被褥
◀ Track 3903

▶My grandmother knitted the quilt for me. 這個被子是阿嬤織給我的。

quit [kwɪt]
◀ Track 3904

v. 戒除；離開；退出；停止

▶It took him three months to quit smoking.
他花了三個月才戒菸。

quite [kwaɪt] adv. 相當
◀ Track 3905

▶At that time, it was quite common for teenagers to have tattoos.
當時，刺青在青少年之間相當普遍。

quiz [kwɪz]
◀ Track 3906

n. 測驗；隨堂小考

▶Mrs. Hanson had a quiz for us in class.
韓森老師給我們一個隨堂小考。

quote [kwot]
◀ Track 3907

v. 引用，引述

▶I quoted the words of Dr. Martin Luther King in my essay.
我在作文中引用了馬丁路德的話。

n. 引文；引號；經典名言

▶The webpage listed famous quotes regarding friendship.
這個網頁上列出了和友誼相關的名言。

▶ Rr

　　以下表格是全民英檢官方公告中級「聽、說、讀、寫」所須具備的能力，本書例句皆依此範疇特別設計，只要掃描右方QR code，就能搭配相對應的音軌實現「眼耳並用」方式，刺激左腦的語言學習功能；同時也可使用本書附贈的紅膠片，將其置於單字上，一面記憶一面自我挑戰，達到雙倍的學習成果！

聽 ▶ 在日常生活中，能聽懂一般的會話；能大致聽懂公共場所廣播、氣象報告及廣告等。在工作時，能聽懂簡易的產品介紹與操作說明。能大致聽懂外籍人士的談話及詢問。

說 ▶ 可在日常生活中，能以簡易英語交談或描述一般事物，能介紹自己的生活作息、工作、家庭、經歷等，並可對一般話題陳述看法。在工作時，能進行簡單的答詢，並與外籍人士交談溝通。

讀 ▶ 在日常生活中，能閱讀短文、故事、私人信件、廣告、傳單、簡介及使用說明等。在工作時，能閱讀工作須知、公告、操作手冊、例行的文件、傳真、電報等。

寫 ▶ 能寫簡單的書信、故事及心得等。對於熟悉且與個人經歷相關的主題，能以簡易的文字表達。

中級

---

rabbit [`ræbɪt] n 兔子　◀ Track 3908

▶The magician pulled out a rabbit from his hat.
這名魔術師從帽子裡抓出一隻兔子。

---

race [res]　◀ Track 3909
v 比速度；參加競賽；使全速行進；使疾走

▶Some youngsters raced on their motorbikes through the street.
有些年輕人騎摩托車競速穿越街道。

n 賽跑；競賽；人種；民族

▶There should be no discrimination against any color, race, or religion in the workplace.
職場上應該不能有任何因為膚色、種族、或宗教而產生的歧視。

---

racial [`reʃəl]　◀ Track 3910
adj 人種的；種族的

▶Racial discrimination was common in the early twentieth century in the U.S.
二十世紀初，種族歧視在美國相當普遍。

---

radar [`redɑr] n 雷達　◀ Track 3911

▶The radar can detect any vehicle approaching this building. 雷達可以偵測到任何接近這棟建築物的車輛。

---

radiation [ˌredɪˋeʃən]　◀ Track 3912
n 發光；輻射，輻射線

▶This harmful radiation may cause harm to people's health.
這種有害的輻射線對人體健康有害。

---

radical [`rædɪkl]　◀ Track 3913
adj 根本的，基本的；與生俱來的

▶The radical politician promoted innovative policies.
這名激進的政治人物推廣創新的政策。

n. 根部，基礎；（數）根號；激進分子

▶The radical was deprived of the right to serve as a civil servant.
這名激進分子被褫奪公權。

radio [ˋredɪ͵o]　Track 3914
n. 收音機；無線電廣播
▶The radio signals were interfered because of the tall building.
收音機的訊號被大樓阻擋了。

rage [redʒ]　Track 3915
n. （一陣）狂怒，盛怒；（風雨、火勢等）狂暴，肆虐；狂熱
▶He flew into a rage when he realized that his best friend betrayed him.
他知道最好的朋友背判他時，勃然大怒。

補充片語 fly into a rage 勃然大怒，暴怒

v. 發怒，怒斥；猖獗；肆虐
▶A powerful typhoon raged through the island. 強烈颱風肆虐本島。

railroad [ˋrel͵rod]
=rail·way （英式英文）n. 鐵路　Track 3916
▶There are several private railroad companies in this country.
這個國家有好幾間私人鐵路公司。

railway [ˋrel͵we] n. 鐵路　Track 3917
▶We will meet each other at the entrance of the Main Railway Station.
我們會在火車總站的入口處碰面。

rain [ren] n. 雨　Track 3918
▶According to the weather forecast, the rain wont's stop until next Monday.
根據氣象預報，雨會持續到下個星期一。

v. 下雨
▶It rained heavily yesterday evening.
昨天傍晚下了大雨。

rainbow [ˋren͵bo]　Track 3919
n. 彩虹
▶The rainbow vanished in a few minutes.
彩虹在幾分鐘之內消失了。

raincoat [ˋren͵kot]　Track 3920
n. 雨衣
▶Brian had a raincoat in his motorcycle trunk.
布萊恩在摩托車的車廂裡面放了一件雨衣。

rainfall [ˋren͵fɔl]　Track 3921
n. 降雨，下雨；降雨量
▶The annual rainfall has been decreasing in the past decade.
過去十年的年度降雨量在持續減少中。

rainy [ˋrenɪ]　Track 3922
adj. 下雨的；多雨的
▶Jessy tends to get gloomy on rainy days.
潔西一到下雨天就容易憂鬱。

raise [rez]　Track 3923
v. 舉起；提高；養育；豎起；
▶We raised our glasses and made a toast.
我們舉杯祝賀。

n. 加薪
▶They were exhilarated about the pay raise.
他們為了加薪的事情很開心。

raisin [`rezn] n. 葡萄乾
🔊 Track 3924

▶ The chef added some raisins, bread crumbles, and dried almonds to the salad.
廚師在沙拉裡面放了一些葡萄乾、麵包丁，以及杏仁果乾。

random [`rændəm]
🔊 Track 3925

n. 任意行動，隨機過程

▶ The toddler dialed the phone number at random and started to talk gibberish.
這位小朋友亂撥電話，胡言亂語一通。

補充片語 at random 隨便地，任意地

adj. 胡亂的，任意的

▶ The research took random samples as subjects.
這個研究隨機抽樣，當作研究主體。

range [rendʒ]
🔊 Track 3926

n. 範圍；區域

▶ That topic is beyond my range of interest, so I know very little about it.
那個主題超出我感興趣的範圍，所以我對它所知甚少。

v. 排列；使並列；把……分類；範圍涉及……

▶ The sizes of the shirt range from small to extra large.
這件襯衫的尺寸從小的到特大的都有。

rank [ræŋk]
🔊 Track 3927

n. 等級；身份，地位；社會階層；行列，隊伍

▶ His sales skill is of the first rank.
他的銷售技巧是第一流的

補充片語 of the first rank 第一流的

v. 排列；分等級；把……評等；列隊

▶ He was ranked second among all the professional tennis players in the world.
他在全球職業網球選手中排名第二。

rapid [`ræpɪd]
🔊 Track 3928

adj. 快的；快速的

▶ The rapid improvement of technology has brought great convenience to people's life.
快速的科技進步為人們的生活帶來很多便利。

rare [rɛr]
🔊 Track 3929

adj. 很少的；罕見的

▶ This kind of mineral is rare to see in this area.
這種礦物質在這個地區很罕見。

rarely [`rɛrlɪ]
🔊 Track 3930

adv. 很少，難得；異乎尋常地

▶ He rarely talks about his personal affairs; we know little about his background.
他很少談論個人的事情；我們不太知道他的背景。

rat [ræt] n. 老鼠
🔊 Track 3931

▶ Rats and mice actually look different.
大老鼠和小老鼠其實長得不一樣。

rate [ret]
🔊 Track 3932

n. 比例，比率；費用，價格；等級

▶ The usage rate of this medicine is relatively low.
這種藥物的使用率相對較低。

v. 對……估價；認為；列為；定……的速率；定……的費率

中級

▶The performance of the student can be rated as average.
這名學生的表現可以被認為是在平均水準。

rather [`ræðɚ] ◀Track 3933
adv. 相當；頗；寧可；倒不如

▶He was rather confident that he would win the race. 他相當有信心贏得比賽。

raw [rɔ] **adj.** 生的 ◀Track 3934
▶The raw ingredient should be preserved in the fridge.
生的食材應該要保存在冰箱裡。

ray [re] ◀Track 3935
n. 光線；熱線；射線，輻射線

▶X-ray is used for medical imaging.
X光被應用在醫療顯影上。

razor [`rezɚ] **n.** 剃刀 ◀Track 3936
▶Be careful; the razor blade may hurt you. 小心一點，刮鬍刀片可能會讓你受傷。

reach [ritʃ] ◀Track 3937
v. 抵達；到達；伸手及到；與……取得聯繫

▶It took us three hours to reach the destination. 我們花了三個小時才到達目的地。

n. 可及的範圍

▶The book on the top of the shelf is beyond her reach.
她拿不到在書櫃頂層的書。

react [rɪ`ækt] ◀Track 3938
v. 反應；影響；反抗；起作用

▶I patted the boy on the shoulder, but he didn't react.
我拍了小男孩的肩膀，但是他沒有回應。

reaction [rɪ`ækʃən] ◀Track 3939
n. 反應，感應；【化】反作用

▶The doctor observed the patient's reaction to the medication.
這名醫生觀察病人對藥物治療的反應。

read [rid] **v.** 閱讀 ◀Track 3940
▶Can you read the sign over there?
你看得到那邊的標誌嗎？

reader [`ridɚ] ◀Track 3941
n. 讀者，愛好閱讀者；讀物，讀本

▶The readers sent some feedbacks to the author of the article.
讀者寄了一些回覆給這篇文章的作者。

相關片語 **mind reader** 能讀人心思者

▶Helen is such a mind reader! I can't hide anything from her. 海倫真是有讀心術！我什麼事情都瞞不過她。

readily [`rɛdɪlɪ] ◀Track 3942
adv. 樂意地，欣然；立即；無困難地

▶These pieces of article are readily available on the Internet.
這些文章在網路上已經都可以找到了。

ready [`rɛdɪ] ◀Track 3943
adj. 準備好的

▶You should have your Declaration Form and personal ID ready before going through the customs. 通過海關之前要將申報表和個人身分證件準備好。

real [`riəl] ◀Track 3944
adj. 真的；真實的

▶The journalist is making a real-time report from the spot of the accident.
這名記者正在意外現場做即時報導。

realistic [rɪə`lɪstɪk]
◀ Track 3945

adj. 現實的，注重實際的，實際可行的

▶The boss is very realistic about the prospect of the product.
老闆對商品的展望態度相當實際。

reality [ri`æləti]
◀ Track 3946

n. 真實；現實

▶Virtual Reality technology has been used for military training.
虛擬實境的科技已經被應用在軍事訓練上。

realize [`rɪə,laɪz]
=rea·lise （英式英文）
◀ Track 3947

v. 領悟；理解

▶I didn't realize the theory behind the plan until he explained it for me.
直到他解釋，我才了解這個計畫背後的理論。

really [`rɪəlɪ]
◀ Track 3948

adv. 很；確實地；真的

▶I really appreciate your help.
我真的很感謝你的幫助。

rear [rɪr] **adj.** 後面的
◀ Track 3949

▶She looked at the rear mirror when she parked the vehicle on the roadside.
停車在路邊時，她看了看後照鏡。

n. 後部，後面

▶There are some recreational facilities in the rear of the ship.
在船的後方有一些娛樂的設施。

v. 撫養；栽培；栽種，飼養；建立

▶It takes a lot of efforts to rear a child.
養育一個小孩需要花很多的努力。

reason [`rizn]
◀ Track 3950

n. 理由；原因

▶She wants to know the real reason, not the excuses.
她想要知道真正的原因，不是藉口。

reasonable [`riznəbl]
◀ Track 3951

adj. 通情達理的，有理智的；合乎情理的；適當的；公道的

▶The real estate property was sold at a reasonable price.
這件房地產物件以合理的價格售出。

rebel [`rɛbl]
◀ Track 3952

n. 造反者，反叛者

▶Several rebels were arrested when they tried to cross the border.
數名叛軍在試圖穿越邊境時遭到逮捕。

v. 造反，反叛，反抗

▶Some teenagers tend to rebel against their parents.
有些青少年容易反抗他們的父母親。

rebuild [ri`bɪld]
◀ Track 3953

v. 重建，改建；使恢復原貌

▶We donated money to help the victims of the tsunami to rebuild their homes.
我們捐款給海嘯受災戶，幫助他們重建家園。

recall [rɪ`kɔl]
◀ Track 3954

v. 回想，回憶起；召回；收回，撤銷

▶Thousands of cars of this model were recalled for flaws in the security system.
因為車輛的安全系統有瑕疵，數千輛此種款式的車被召回。

n. 回想，回憶；召回；撤銷

中級

▶The recall of the sad memories made him feel sorrowful.
想起悲傷的回憶時，他感到悲傷。

receipt [rɪ`sit] **n.** 收據
◀Track 3955

▶If you want to have a refund, you need to show the receipt.
想要退款的話，你需要出示收據。

receive [rɪ`siv]
◀Track 3956
v. 收到；獲得

▶We will deliver the goods as soon as we receive the payment.
收到貨款後，我們會立即出貨。

receiver [rɪ`sivɚ]
◀Track 3957
n. 受領人，收件人；接待者；聽筒，受話器

▶Put the address of the receiver on the top of the envelope.
將收件人地址寫在信封上方。

recent [`risnt]
◀Track 3958
adj. 最近的；不久前的

▶A recent study shows that a keto diet can help people lose weight. 最近的研究指出，生酮飲食可以幫助人減肥。

recently [`risntlɪ]
◀Track 3959
adv. 最近；近來；不久前

▶I have been bombarded with ads of household appliances recently.
最近我一直被家電的廣告轟炸。

reception [rɪ`sɛpʃən]
◀Track 3960
n. 接待，接見；接待會，宴會

▶More than one hundred guests attended their wedding reception party.
超過一百位賓客去參加他們的婚宴。

相關片語 **reception room** 會客室

▶I will meet my client at the reception room at 10:00 A.M.
我今天早上十點會在會客室見客戶。

recession [rɪ`sɛʃən]
◀Track 3961
n. 衰退，衰退期；後退，退回；退場

▶The economic recession caused thousands of people to lose their jobs.
經濟衰退造成數千人失業。

recipe [`rɛsəpɪ]
◀Track 3962
n. 食譜；烹飪法；訣竅

▶I bought a recipe for vegetarian dishes. 我買了一本做素食的食譜。

recite [rɪ`saɪt] **v.** 背誦
◀Track 3963

▶Mr. Trump's granddaughter can recite traditional Chinese poems.
川普先生的孫女會背誦中國古詩。

reckless [`rɛklɪs]
◀Track 3964
adj. 不在乎的，魯莽的

▶The reckless drive who ran through a red light almost caused an accident.
這名闖紅燈的魯莽駕駛差點造成車禍。

recognition
◀Track 3965
[͵rɛkəg`nɪʃən] **n.** 認出，辨識；承認，認可

▶I haven't seen my cousin for a decade; she has changed beyond recognition.
我已經十年沒見到我的表妹，她已變得我都認不出來了。

補充片語 **beyond recognition**
無法認出

recognize
🔊 Track 3966

[`rɛkəgˌnaɪz] **v** 認出，識別，認識；
正式承認

▶I can recognize some of the Korean characters, but I am not a proficient Korean reader.
我認得出一些韓文字，但是我沒辦法很流利地閱讀韓文。

recommend
🔊 Track 3967

[ˌrɛkə`mɛnd] **v** 推薦，介紹，建議

▶The travel agency recommended the itinerary that covers five Scandinavian countries. 這間旅行社推薦了這個涵蓋北歐五國的行程。

record [`rɛkəd][rɪ`kɔrd]
🔊 Track 3968

n 記載；紀錄；前科紀錄；成績；
最高紀錄；

▶They keep a record of the students' test scores to see if they make any improvement. 他們紀錄這些學生的分數來看他們是否有進步。

v 記錄；錄音

▶The mobile gadget can record your heartrate and the steps you walk in a day.
這個行動裝置可以記錄你的心跳速率和你在一天之中所走的步數。

recorder [rɪ`kɔrdə]
🔊 Track 3969

n 記錄器，錄音機；記錄者，書記員；
錄音師

▶Few people use an audio tape recorder nowadays.
現在很少人會使用錄音機。

recover [rɪ`kʌvə]
🔊 Track 3970

v 重新獲得；恢復（原狀）；挽回；彌補

▶It took her three months to recover from the injury.
她受傷後三個月才復原。

recovery [rɪ`kʌvərɪ]
🔊 Track 3971

n 恢復，康復，復原

▶He made a full recovery from the illness and returned to work this week.
他完全康復，並且在這星期回來上班了。

recreation
🔊 Track 3972

[ˌrɛkrɪ`eʃən] **n** 消遣，娛樂

▶He regards reading as a form of recreation.
他把讀書當作是消遣。

rectangle [rɛk`tæŋgl̩]
🔊 Track 3973

n 矩形；長方形

▶The tofu was cut into the shape of a rectangle.
這個豆腐被切成一個長方形。

recycle [ri`saɪkl̩]
🔊 Track 3974

v 使再循環；使再利用；回收

▶The plastic bottles were recycled and reused.
這些塑膠瓶被回收再使用。

red [rɛd] **adj** 紅的；紅色的
🔊 Track 3975

▶The actresses posed for photos when they walked on the red carpet.
女演員們走過紅地毯的時候擺姿勢讓人拍照。

n 紅；紅色；紅色的衣服

▶This dress comes in red and purple.
這件洋裝有紅色和紫色的款式。

中級

reduce [rɪ`djus] ◀Track 3976

v. 減少，縮小，降低

▶ They tried to reduce the consumption of electricity.
他們試圖減少耗電量。

reduction [rɪ`dʌkʃən] ◀Track 3977

n. 減少，降低，削減，縮小

▶ The company conducted a cost reduction in order to increase their profits.
這間公司為了增加收益而進行成本縮減。

reef [rif] ◀Track 3978

n. 礁，礁脈；沙洲；暗礁；礦脈

▶ Many tourists go snorkeling to appreciate the coral reef.
許多觀光客會去浮潛欣賞珊瑚礁。

refer [rɪ`fɚ] ◀Track 3979

v. 把……歸因於；論及，談到

▶ The author briefly referred to the early history of China in his article.
作者在文章中簡短地提到了中國早期的歷史。

reference [`rɛfərəns] ◀Track 3980

n. 參考；參考文獻，出處；提及

▶ The student made reference to professor Hawking's theory in his final report. 這名學生在期末報告中提到霍金教授的理論。

reflect [rɪ`flɛkt] ◀Track 3981

v. 反射，照映出；表現，反映

▶ The surface of the lake reflected the image of the mountain.
湖面上反射出山影。

reflection [rɪ`flɛkʃən] ◀Track 3982

n. 反射，回響；映像，倒影；深思，反省；想法，意見

▶ I learned how to make water reflection with Photoshop.
我學習使用Photoshop軟體來製作水中倒影的圖像。

reform [ˌrɪ`fɔrm] ◀Track 3983

n. 改革，革新，改良；革除弊端

▶ The president made a reform as soon as he took the office.
這名總統就任後，立即開始改革。

v. 改革，革新；改過，改邪歸正

▶ He reformed himself after the failure.
失敗過後，他痛改前非。

refresh [rɪ`frɛʃ] ◀Track 3984

v. 使清新；使重新提振精神；使得到補充；吃點心，喝飲料；補給

▶ He refreshed himself from weariness with a glass of iced tea.
他喝了一杯冰茶，讓自己從疲憊的狀態中恢復元氣。

refrigerator ◀Track 3985
[rɪ`frɪdʒəˌretɚ] =fridge=ice·box

n. 冰箱

▶ The digital refrigerator can adjust the temperature automatically.
這種數位冰箱可以自動調節溫度。

refugee [ˌrɛfjʊ`dʒi] ◀Track 3986

n. 難民

▶ Thousands of refugees flooded across the border between Mexico and the U.S.
數千名難民越過美墨邊境。

refusal [rɪ`fjuzl] n. 拒絕 ◀ Track 3987

▶Her proposal was met with a refusal.
她的提案遭到拒絕。

refuse [rɪ`fjuz] ◀ Track 3988
n. 廢物，垃圾，渣滓

▶The video shows you how to use organic kitchen refuse effectively.
這個影片教你如何有效利用有機廚餘。

v. 拒絕

▶I invited her to join the party, but she refused.
我邀請她參加派對，但是她拒絕了。

regard [rɪ`gɑrd] ◀ Track 3989
v. 把……看作；看待；注重

▶She regarded economic development as the most important issue.
她認為經濟發展是最重要的議題。

n. 注意；關心；問候；致意

▶Please send them my best regards.
請代我問候他們。

regarding [rɪ`gɑrdɪŋ] ◀ Track 3990
prep. 關於；就……而論

▶The news reports regarding the constitutional amendment can be seen repeatedly on TV.
有關憲法修正的新聞一直在電視上重播。

regardless ◀ Track 3991
[rɪ`gɑrdlɪs] adv. 不顧一切地，不管怎樣地

▶We tried to dissuade him from running the risk, but he crossed the river regardless.
我們試圖勸他不要冒險，但是他還是涉水渡過溪流了。

region [`ridʒən] ◀ Track 3992
n. 地區；行政區域；部位；領域

▶The local government made every effort to stop the epidemic outbreak in this region. 當地政府盡一切努力阻止傳染病在這個區域擴散。

regional [`ridʒənl] ◀ Track 3993
adj. 地區的，局部的

▶He was promoted to be the regional manager. 他晉升為區域經理。

register [`rɛdʒɪstɚ] ◀ Track 3994
v. 登記，註冊

▶They registered for the event and paid the admission fee.
他們登記報名這活動，也繳了報名費。

n. 登記，註冊；自動登錄機，收銀機

▶Their names are not on the register of voters.
他們的名字沒有在選民名冊上。

registration ◀ Track 3995
[ˌrɛdʒɪ`streʃən] n. 登記，註冊，掛號

▶Keep your personal registration number in mind.
請記得自己的個人註冊號碼。

regret [rɪ`grɛt] ◀ Track 3996
v. 後悔；懊悔；感到遺憾

▶She regretted about not being able to attend the Korean pop star's concert.
沒能參加這位韓星的演唱會，她覺得很遺憾。

n. 遺憾；悔恨；哀悼

▶Do your best and leave no regrets.
盡力而為，不要留下遺憾。

中級

regular [ˈrɛgjələ]
◀≣Track 3997

adj. 固定的；規律的

▶She works out at the gym on a regular basis.
她固定會去健身房運動。

regulate [ˈrɛgjə͵let]
◀≣Track 3998

v. 管理，規範，控制

▶The authorities tried to regulate the emission of waste gas from the local factories.
有關當局試圖規範當地工廠的廢氣排放。

regulation
◀≣Track 3999

[͵rɛgjəˈleʃən] **n.** 規章，規定；條例；管理

▶According to the regulations of the institution, employees should not reveal the internal information to unrelated parties.
根據機構的規定，員工不可以將公司內部資訊透露給不相關的單位知道。

rehearsal [rɪˈhɝsl]
◀≣Track 4000

n. 排練，試演，練習

▶The actress hurt her ankle in the rehearsal.
這名女演員在排演的時候傷了膝蓋。

rehearse [rɪˈhɝs]
◀≣Track 4001

v. 排練

▶They rehearsed for the performance.
他們為了表演排練。

reject [rɪˈdʒɛkt]
◀≣Track 4002

v. 拒絕；抵制；駁回；排斥

▶The board rejected the marketing strategies we proposed.
董事會拒絕了我們提出的行銷策略。

relate [rɪˈlet]
◀≣Track 4003

v. 有關，涉及；使有聯繫；相處

▶The institution promised to protect the benefit of any entity that is a related party of the group.
此機構承諾會保護所有與此集團有關之單位的利益。

related [rɪˈletɪd]
◀≣Track 4004

adj. 有關的

▶It is said that the official is related to a local business magnate.
據説這名官員和本地的商業大亨有關係。

relation [rɪˈleʃən]
◀≣Track 4005

n. 關係；關聯；血親關係；親屬

▶The actress did not reveal the relation between she and her daughter to the public. 這名女演員沒有對外公開她和她女兒的關係。

re·lationship
◀≣Track 4006

[rɪˈleʃənˌʃɪp] **n.** 關係；人際關係；親屬關係；婚姻關係；戀愛關係

▶Interpersonal relationship has been the source of trouble for many teenagers. 人際關係對很多青少年來説是一個煩惱的來源。

相關片語 **parent-child relationship**
親子關係

▶This book talks about how to mend parent-child relationships.
這本書在討論如何修補親子關係。

relative [ˈrɛlətɪv]
◀≣Track 4007

adj. 相對的；比較的；與……有關的

▶ Your scores for this course is relative to your attendence.
你在這堂課的成績會與出席率相關。

n. 親戚；親屬

▶Some of her relatives have immigrated to foreign countries.

她的一些親戚已經移民到國外了。

relatively [`rɛlətɪvlɪ]
◀Track 4008

adv. 相當，相對地，比較而言

▶Relatively speaking, this is a well-developed country.

相對來說，這是一個發展很好的國家。

relax [rɪ`læks]
◀Track 4009

v. 鬆弛；緩和；放鬆，休息

▶The soothing music can help me relax.

這個舒緩的音樂可以幫助我放鬆。

relaxation
◀Track 4010

[ˌrilæks`eʃən]

n. 鬆弛；放鬆；休息，消遣，娛樂

▶Our supervisor would allow no relaxation in the standard of inspection on our products.

我們主管不會容許放寬產品檢查的標準。

release [rɪ`lis]
◀Track 4011

v. 釋放，放開；豁免；發行，發表

▶Her latest album will be released in three weeks.

她的最新專輯再過三週就會發行。

n. 釋放，解放；豁免；發行，發表

▶The release of the latest model of the smartphone is a great event for our company.

新智慧手機型號的發行，是我們公司的大事。

reliable [rɪ`laɪəb!]
◀Track 4012

adj. 可信賴的；可靠的；確實的

▶This website is a reliable source of information.

這個網站是一個可靠的消息來源。

relief [rɪ`lif]
◀Track 4013

n. （痛苦，負擔的）緩和，減輕；解除；寬心，慰藉；調劑

▶To her relief, her son who served in the army came back safe and sound.

令她寬心的是，她服兵役的兒子平安無事地回來了。

relieve [rɪ`liv]
◀Track 4014

v. 減輕，緩和；解除

▶This painkiller can help you relieve the discomfort.

這個止痛藥可以幫助你舒緩不舒服的感覺。

religion [rɪ`lɪdʒən]
◀Track 4015

n. 宗教，宗教信仰；宗教團體

▶Hinduism is the major religion in India.

印度教是印度的主要宗教。

religious [rɪ`lɪdʒəs]
◀Track 4016

adj. 宗教的；篤信宗教的

▶My parents were very religious; they are devoted Buddhists.

我父母篤信宗教；他們是虔誠的佛教徒。

reluctant [rɪ`lʌktənt]
◀Track 4017

adj. 不情願的；勉強的

▶The boy was reluctant to share his toy with his classmates.

這個小男孩不願意和同學分享他的玩具。

rely [rɪ`laɪ]
◀Track 4018

v. 依靠，依賴；信賴，指望

中級

▶Helen relied on her parents for finance when she went to college.
海倫上大學的時候，靠父母的金錢援助過生活。

remain [rɪ`men]　◀Track 4019

v 剩下；繼續存在；留下；保持

▶Four players remained until the final round; they are qualified for the tournament. 四位選手留到最後一回合，他們可以參加總決賽。

remark [rɪ`mɑrk]　◀Track 4020

n 談論，評論，批評；注意，

▶The teenagers made rude remarks about the old man.
這些青少年說了對老年人不尊敬的話。

v 談到，評論；言辭；注意，察覺

▶The scholar remarked on the latest report about the effects of bulletproof coffee.
這名學者評論了最近一篇有關防彈咖啡之效果的報導。

remarkable　◀Track 4021

[rɪ`mɑrkəbl] **adj** 值得注意的，傑出的

▶Her remarkable contribution made her win the respect from the peer colleagues.
她傑出的貢獻使她獲得同事的尊敬。

remedy [`rɛmədɪ]　◀Track 4022

n 治療法；藥物；補救方法

▶The folklore remedy may be actually harmful to your health.
民俗療法實際上可能會對你的健康有害。

v 醫療，治療；補救，糾正

▶We will remedy the mistake immediately.
我們會立刻補救這個錯誤。

remember　◀Track 4023

[rɪ`mɛmbɚ] **v** 記得；記住

▶The old lady did not remember the address of her house.
這位老太太不記得她家的地址。

remind [rɪ`maɪnd]　◀Track 4024

v 提醒；使記起

▶She reminded me to hand in the Personal Leave Application.
她提醒我要繳交事假申請表。

reminder [rɪ`maɪndɚ]　◀Track 4025

n 提醒者，提醒物；令人回憶的東西；（幫助記憶的）提示；催函

▶I received a payment reminder from the bank. 我收到銀行寄來的繳款通知。

remote [rɪ`mot]　◀Track 4026

adj 遙遠的；偏僻的；關係疏遠的；（年代）久遠的；冷淡的，孤傲的；遙控的

▶The hermit lives in a remote mountian to practice meditation.
這名隱士居住在遙遠的山裡，練習冥想。

相關片語 **remote control** 遙控器

▶Did you see the remote control for the air conditioner?
你有看到冷氣的遙控器嗎？

remove [rɪ`muv]　◀Track 4027

v 移動，搬開；去除；

▶Here are some tips to remove dirt from tiles. 這裡有一些除去磁磚髒汙的秘訣。

renew [rɪ`nju]　◀Track 4028

v 更新，恢復；換新；重新開始；重申；續訂、續借

▶Gina didn't renew her gym membership, for she has been busy with work lately.
吉娜沒有去更新健身房會員資格，因為她最近工作比較忙。

rent [rɛnt]　◀Track 4029
n. 租；租借；租金；

▶The landlord wanted to raise the rent.
房東想要增加房租。

v. 租；租用

▶They rented a car when they traveled to the south.
他們租車去南方旅遊。

repair [rɪ`pɛr]　◀Track 4030
n. 修理；修補；修理工作；維修狀況；修理部位

▶The mechanic does repairs on vehicles.
這位師傅專門修理車輛。

v. 修理；修補；補救

▶Do you know how to repair a broken bike?
你知道怎麼修理一台壞掉的腳踏車嗎？

repeat [rɪ`pit]　◀Track 4031
v. 重複；重做；重讀

▶The laborer on the assembly line repeated the same movement throughout the day.
生產線上的員工一整天重複同樣的動作。

repeatedly [rɪ`pitɪdlɪ]　◀Track 4032
adv. 一再，再三，多次

▶She repeatedly reminded her son to finish the house chores.
她一再地提醒兒子要做完家務事。

repetition [ˌrɛpɪ`tɪʃən]　◀Track 4033
n. 重複；反覆；重複的事物

▶The repetition of the same phrases in your composition may make the reader feel bored.
你的作文裡出現的重複用詞可能會讓讀者感到無趣。

replace [rɪ`ples]　◀Track 4034
v. 把⋯⋯放回原處；取代，代替

▶We replaced the old bulb with a fluorescent one.
我們用日光燈泡取代舊的那個。

reply [rɪ`plaɪ]　◀Track 4035
v. 回答；答覆；回應；

▶I called the clerk, but she didn't reply.
我叫了那位店員，但她沒有回應。

n. 回覆

▶I am waiting for the reply from the client. 我在等待客戶的回覆。

report [rɪ`port]　◀Track 4036
n. 報告；報導；成績單

▶Yvonne was afraid that her parents would go nuts when they see her report card.
伊芳怕她的父母看到成績單的時候會生氣。

v. 報告

▶Ted reported to the regional manager directly. 泰德的直屬主管是區經理。

reporter [rɪ`portɚ]　◀Track 4037
n. 記者

▶The reporter had a slip of the tongue, and the clip soon spread on the Internet. 這位記者一不小心口誤，結果影片馬上在網路上被傳開。

中級

reporting [rɪ`pɔrtɪŋ] ◀€Track 4038
n. 報導

▶The reporting of your personal data won't be conducted without your consensus. 沒有經過你的同意，你的資料不會被報導出來。

represent [ˌrɛprɪ`zɛnt] ◀€Track 4039
v. 象徵，表示；作為……的代表

▶She was chosen to represent her school to join the regional speech contest.
她被選出來代表學校參加區域的演講比賽。

representation ◀€Track 4040
[ˌrɛprɪzɛn`teʃən] **n.** 代表，代理；表示；陳述

▶Our company has representations in both Europe and North America.
我們公司在歐洲和北美都設有代表。

representative ◀€Track 4041
[rɛprɪ`zɛntətɪv] **n.** 代表物，典型；代表，代理人

▶The representative of the presidential office made an official statement.
總統府的代表做了一項正式的聲明。

adj. 代表的，代表性的；代理的

▶The plea sent by the students is representativ of their opinions toward cyberbullying.
這封由學生送給校方的請願書代表了他們對於網路霸凌的心聲。

republic [rɪ`pʌblɪk] ◀€Track 4042
n. 共和國，共和政體

▶This republic was established in 1911. 這個共和國是在1911年建立的。

republican ◀€Track 4043
[rɪ`pʌblɪkən] **n.** 共和黨人士；擁護共和政體者；共和主義者

▶The republican made a public statement to show his support for the candidate.
這名共和黨人士公開聲明支持這位候選人。

adj. 共和國的；擁護共和政體的；共和主義的；共和黨的

▶The Democratic Party and the Republican Party are the major political entities in the U.S.
民主黨和共和黨是美國最大的兩個政體。

reputation ◀€Track 4044
[ˌrɛpjə`teʃən] **n.** 名譽，信譽；好名聲；聲望

▶The celebrity sued the tabloid for damaging his reputation.
這位名人指控小報破壞他的聲望。

request [rɪ`kwɛst] ◀€Track 4045
n. 要求

▶We amended the regulations at the students' request.
我們應學生的要求修改了規定。

v. 要求，請求；請求給予

▶The client requested that we should provide a two-year warranty for the product.
客戶要求我們要提供兩年的產品保固。

require [rɪ`kwaɪr] ◀€Track 4046
v. 需要；要求；命令

▶This position requires two years of work experience.
這個職缺要有兩年的工作經驗。

requirement
◀Track 4047

[rɪ`kwaɪrmənt]

n. 需要；必需品；必要條件；要求

▶The hardware requirement for the software is illustrated in the manual.
說明書上有載明這個軟體的硬體需求。

---

rescue [`rɛskju]
◀Track 4048

n. 援救，營救

▶Call this number whenever you have trouble, and we will come to your rescue.
遇到麻煩時就打這支電話，我們會去救你。

v. 營救，救援

▶The firefighter rescued the baby from the burning house.
消防隊員從火場中救出小嬰兒。

---

research [rɪ`sɝtʃ]
◀Track 4049

n. 研究，調查，探究

▶Watch the format when you prepare a research proposal.
做研究提案的時候要注意格式。

v. 研究，探究；做學術研究；調查

▶The doctor researched on the cause of cancer.
這名醫生研究癌症的起因。

---

researcher [ri`sɝtʃɚ]
◀Track 4050

n. 研究人員，調查者

▶The researchers will interview the subject after the experiment.
實驗之後，研究人員會訪問受試者。

---

resemble [rɪ`zɛmbl]
◀Track 4051

v. 類似，像

▶Ted resembles his father.
泰德長得像他的爸爸。

---

reservation
◀Track 4052

[ˌrɛzɚ`veʃən] **n.** 保留；自然保護區；預訂，預訂的房間（或座位）

▶We have made a reservation at the luxurious hotel.
我們已經預訂高級飯店的房間了。

---

reserve [rɪ`zɝv]
◀Track 4053

n. 儲備物，儲備金；儲藏，保留；儲備；預備軍

▶She taught all the craft skills to her apprentice without reserve.
她將工藝知識毫無保留地傳給學徒。

補充片語 without reserve 毫無保留地

v. 保存，保留；預訂，預約

▶These seats are reserved for the VIPs.
這些座位是預留給貴賓的。

---

residence [`rɛzədəns]
◀Track 4054

n. 居住，合法居住資格；住所

▶Some paparazzi stayed outside the residence of the celebrity who was involved in a scandal. 有些狗仔記者守在這個涉及醜聞的名人住所外面。

相關片語 permanent residence permit 永久居留許可

▶It took the immigrant ten years to obtain the permanent residence permit.
這位移民花了十年才得到永久居留許可。

---

resident [`rɛzədənt]
◀Track 4055

n. 居民；定居者

▶Residents in this town would be imposed with a penalty if they litter at random.
這個小鎮的居民如果亂丟垃圾會被罰錢。

中級

adj. 居住的，定居的；固有的，內在的；常住的；住在任所的

▶Ted is a resident student in this school.
泰德是這所學校的寄宿學生。

resign [rɪ`zaɪn]
◀Track 4056

v. 放棄，辭去

▶May resigned from the position of prime minister after she was impeached by the congress.
梅伊遭到國會彈劾之後就辭去總理的職務。

resignation
◀Track 4057

[ˌrɛzɪg`neʃən] **n.** 辭職

▶The politician did not mention his plan after the resignation.
這名政治人物並未提到辭職之後的計畫。

resist [rɪ`zɪst]
◀Track 4058

v. 抵抗，反抗，抗拒；忍耐，忍住

▶She couldn't resist the temptation of sweets even though she is on a diet.
雖然她正在節食，還是抵擋不了甜食的誘惑。

resistance [rɪ`zɪstəns]
◀Track 4059

n. 抵抗；反抗；抵抗力

▶Her resistance against stress and frustration has become stronger after working for several years.
工作幾年之後，她對壓力和挫折的抵抗力變強了。

resistant [rɪ`zɪstənt]
◀Track 4060

adj. 抵抗的，抗……的

▶The watch is water-resistant.
這只手錶是防水的。

resolution
◀Track 4061

[ˌrɛzə`luʃən] **n.** 決心，決定；解答，解決

▶They had a meeting to figure out a resolution to the problem.
他們舉行了一個會議來想出解決方案。

resolve [rɪ`zɑlv]
◀Track 4062

v. 解決，解答；決心，決定；決議，作出正式決定；分解

▶The students resolved to abandon the unreasonable rule.
學生們決心要廢除這條不合理的規定。

resource [rɪ`sors]
◀Track 4063

n. 資源；物力；財力

▶The country is known for its rich natural resource.
該國以自然資源豐富著名。

respect [rɪ`spɛkt]
◀Track 4064

n. 尊敬；尊重；注重；

▶We showed our respect to the veteran soldier. 我們對老兵表示尊敬。

v. 尊敬；

▶It's a social norm to respect the elderly people in this country.
在這個國家，尊敬老人是社會禮俗。

respond [rɪ`spɑnd]
◀Track 4065

v. 作答，回應

▶We are waiting for the supplier to respond to our request.
我們在等供應商回覆我們的要求。

response [rɪ`spɑns]
◀Track 4066

n. 回應，回覆，回答

▶She rang the doorbell, but there was no response. 她按了門鈴，但沒人回應。

responsible
🔊 Track 4067

[rɪˋspɑnsəbl] **adj.** 有責任的；負責任的

▶They were responsible to make a layout for the new office.
他們負責畫新辦公室的平面圖。

responsibility
🔊 Track 4068

[rɪˏspɑnsəˋbɪlətɪ] **n.** 責任；職責；責任感

▶The responsibility of taking care of the children falls on me.
照顧小孩的責任在我的身上。

相關片語 **take responsibility for**
為……負責

▶Everyone should take responsibility for environmental protection.
每個人都該負責保護環境。

相關片語 **sense of responsibility**
責任感

▶He has a strong sense of responsibility, so he will surely accomplish the task.
他責任感很強，所以一定會完成任務的。

rest [rɛst] **n.** 休息
🔊 Track 4069

▶Let's take a rest in the porch.
我們在門廊邊休息一下吧。

v. 休息

▶The doctor told him that he should rest for a few days after the operation.
醫生告訴他說手術後要休息幾天。

restaurant
🔊 Track 4070

[ˋrɛstərənt] **n.** 餐廳

▶There are some restaurants serving exotic foods in this street.
這條街上有些賣異國食物的餐廳。

restless [ˋrɛstlɪs]
🔊 Track 4071

adj. 靜不下來的；永無安寧的；受打擾的；焦燥不安的；躁動的

▶The coyote was restless; it kept pacing in the cage.
這匹土狼靜不下來；牠一直在籠子裡來回踱步。

restore [rɪˋstor]
🔊 Track 4072

v. 恢復，使復原；使恢復健康；修復；使復職

▶He restored energy after a good night's sleep.
經過一夜好眠，他恢復了精神。

restrict [rɪˋstrɪkt]
🔊 Track 4073

v. 限制，限定；約束

▶The number of visitors to this museum was restricted.
博物館的參觀人數是受限制的。

restriction
🔊 Track 4074

[rɪˋstrɪkʃən] **n.** 限制；約束；限定；限制規定

▶There are some restrictions for the carry-on luggage.
針對隨身行李有一些限制規定。

restroom [ˋrestrum]
🔊 Track 4075

n. 洗手間；廁所；盥洗室

▶The restroom is under the stairs.
洗手間在樓梯下方。

result [rɪˋzʌlt]
🔊 Track 4076

n. 結果；後果；

▶She overslept; as a result, she was late for work.
她睡過頭；結果，她上班遲到了。

中級

v 產生；發生；導致……結果

▶It is said that the emission of carbon dioxide resulted in greenhouse effect. 據說二氧化碳的排放導致了溫室效應。

retain [rɪ`ten]　　◀€Track 4077

v 保留，保持；留住；攔住；記住

▶The employee wants to retain his place in the office, so he works very hard. 這名員工想要保住飯碗，所以工作特別努力。

retire [rɪ`taɪr] **v** 退休　◀€Track 4078

▶Rita will retire next month, so we will have a farewell party for her. 瑞塔下個月要退休，所以我們會為她辦一個歡送派對。

retreat [rɪ`trit]　　◀€Track 4079

n 撤退；撤退信號；隱退

▶It is said that the country's global power is in retreat. 據說這個國家的國際性權威正在衰退中。

v 撤退；退避；退出

▶The captain ordered that all sailor should work together so they could retreat from the storm. 船長下令所有水手要合作，他們才能脫離暴風雨。

return [rɪ`tɜ-n]　　◀€Track 4080

v 返回；歸；回復；歸還；

▶People in the small town worked together to help the stranded dolphin return to the sea. 這個小鎮的居民團結起來，幫助擱淺的海豚返回大海。

n 返回；歸；回報；報答

▶He bought a house for his parents as a return to their love and care. 他買了一棟房子給父母，作為對他們的愛跟關懷的報答。

reunite [ˌrijuˋnaɪt]　◀€Track 4081

v 使再結合；使重聚

▶Ryan reunited with his teammates from the college basketball team after twenty years. 時隔二十年，雷恩和他大學時籃球校隊的隊友重聚。

reveal [rɪˋvil]　　◀€Track 4082

v 顯露出；揭示，揭露；暴露，洩露

▶The secret agent was cautious for fear of revealing his identity. 這名密探很謹慎，深怕會洩漏自己的真實身分。

revenge [rɪˋvɛndʒ]　◀€Track 4083

n 報復，復仇

▶She vowed to take revenge on those who bullied her. 她發誓要對霸凌她的人復仇。

v 報復，替……報仇

▶The man revenged against his opponent in the final game. 這名男子在決賽的時候向對手復仇了。

review [rɪˋvju]　　◀€Track 4084

n 複習；溫習；再檢查；複審；評論；

▶The critique made a review of the movie on his own blog. 這位評論家在自己的部落格發表對這部電影的評論。

v 複習

▶I reviewed the lesson for the exam. 為了準備考試，我複習了課程內容。

revise [rɪˋvaɪz]　　◀€Track 4085

v 修訂；校訂；修改

▶My supervisor asked me to revise the marketing plan. 我的主管要我修改行銷計畫。

中級

revision [rɪ`vɪʒən]
🔊 Track 4086

n. 修訂，校訂；修訂版

▶ The revision of the report should be more logical and organized. 這個報告的修訂版應該要更有邏輯、更有組織。

revolution
🔊 Track 4087

[ˌrɛvə`luʃən] **n.** 革命

▶ The Industrial Revolution brought a great impact on the manufacturing industry.
工業革命對製造業帶來很大的影響。

revo·lutionary
🔊 Track 4088

[ˌrɛvə`luʃənˌɛrɪ] **adj.** 革命的

▶ The Internet has brought revolutionary changes in the way people gain information. 網路對人們獲取資訊方式造成革命性的改變。

reward [rɪ`wɔrd]
🔊 Track 4089

n. 報答，報償，賞金，酬金

▶ The kid got a reward for returning the lost bag to its original owner. 小朋友因為將遺失的手提袋歸還原物主而獲得獎賞。

v. 報答，酬謝；報應，懲罰（壞人）

▶ After finishing the report, I rewarded myself by watching two episodes of my favorite Korean drama. 寫完報告之後，我看了兩集喜愛的韓劇來獎賞自己。

rewrite [ri`raɪt]
🔊 Track 4090

v. 重寫，改寫，加工編寫

▶ The author rewrote the script to make the story more dramatic.
作者改寫了劇本讓故事更加戲劇化。

n. 重寫，改寫（的文稿）；
加工編寫的新聞稿

▶ The rewrite of the manuscript was more organized.
手稿重寫之後變得更有組織了。

rhyme [raɪm]
🔊 Track 4091

v. 押韻；做押韻詩；把……寫成詩；
用詩敘述

▶ The word "fate" rhymes with "mate."
"fate" 和 "mate" 這兩個字有押韻。

n. 韻腳；押韻文，押韻詩

▶ The professor had the students highlight the rhymes of the poem.
這名教授要求學生把詩的韻腳做註記。

rhythm [`rɪðəm]
🔊 Track 4092

n. 節奏，韻律

▶ The dancers danced to the rhythm of the beat. 舞者們跟著節拍的韻律跳舞。

ribbon [`rɪbən]
🔊 Track 4093

n. 緞帶，飾帶，帶狀物；鋼捲尺

▶ The lady tied yellow ribbons on the old oak tree in front of her house. 這位女士在家門前的老橡樹上掛了黃色的緞帶。

rice [raɪs] **n.** 米；米飯
🔊 Track 4094

▶ Put rice and a proper amount of water in the inner bowl of the electric cooker.
把米和適量的水放進電鍋的內鍋裡。

rich [rɪtʃ]
🔊 Track 4095

adj. 富裕的；豐富的；有錢的；

▶ It's a healthy habit to eat foods rich in vitamin C.
多吃富含維他命C的食物是健康的習慣。

n. 有錢人

▶ The gap between the rich and the poor had widened in the past deceade. 過去十年來，貧富差距增加了。

riches [`rɪtʃɪz]　🔊 Track 4096

n. 財富，財產；富有，豐饒

▶His riches did not make him feel content and happy.
他的財富並沒有使他感到滿足和開心。

相關片語 **from rags to riches**
由窮致富，白手起家

▶His parents worked from tags to riches, and now they own two companies.
他的父母白手起家，現在有兩間公司。

rid [rɪd]　🔊 Track 4097

v. 使免除，使擺脫，清除

▶There are some tips to rid your house of the termite.
這裡有些秘訣可以幫你擺脫家中的白蟻。

riddle [`rɪdl]　🔊 Track 4098

n. 謎，謎語；謎一般的人；莫名其妙的事情；難題

▶On Lantern Festival, Chinese people would solve lantern riddles for fun.
元宵節時，中國人會猜燈謎來娛樂自己。

v. 出謎，解謎；使困惑；打謎地說；佈滿，充滿

▶The program is riddled with unpleasant facts and rude languages.
這個節目充滿令人不愉快的事實和粗魯的語句。

ride [raɪd]　🔊 Track 4099

v. 騎馬；乘車；乘車旅行；乘坐；搭乘

▶You should have the basic manners when you ride the bus.
搭乘公車時，你需要有基本的禮節。

n. 騎；乘坐；搭乘；乘車旅行；

▶She can give us a ride this evening.
她今天傍晚可以載我們一程。

rider [`raɪdɚ]　🔊 Track 4100

n. 騎乘（馬或機車等）的人，搭乘（馬或車）的人

▶All riders of the scooters should wear helmets. 騎機車的人都該戴安全帽。

ridiculous [rɪ`dɪkjələs]　🔊 Track 4101

adj. 可笑的

▶It is ridiculous to spend so much time on the trivial details and ignore the core theme of the issue. 注重微小的細節卻忽略這個議題的中心主旨是很可笑的。

rifle [`raɪfl]　🔊 Track 4102

n. 步槍，來福槍

▶The hunter had a rifle in his possession.
這名獵人擁有一把來福槍。

v. 用步槍射擊；洗劫，劫掠；快速翻找

▶He rifled through the dresser drawers to look for his watch.
他翻遍衣櫃找他的手錶。

right [raɪt]　🔊 Track 4103

adj. 對的；正確的；右邊的

▶There is nothing right in his right brain, and there is nothing left in his left brain.
他的右腦裡面沒有一樣事情是正確的，而他的左腦裡面什麼也不剩。

adv. 對；正確地；向右

▶Turn right at the next intersection, and you can see your destination.
在下個路口右轉，你就可以看到目的地了。

n. 右邊；右側；權利

▶The book you are looking for is on the shelf to your right.
你尋找的書就在你右邊的書櫃上。

ring [rɪŋ]

◀ Track 4104

v. 按鈴；敲鐘；打電話；（鐘或鈴）響

▶ The doorbell rang, but nobody wanted to answer it.
門鈴響了，但沒人想去應門。

n. 戒指

▶ Gina lost her wedding ring in the swimming pool.
吉娜在游泳池裡弄丟了她的婚戒。

---

ripe [raɪp] **adj.** 成熟的

◀ Track 4105

▶ The farmer taught us the tips to pick the ripe peaches.
農夫教我們採摘成熟水蜜桃的秘訣。

---

rise [raɪz]

◀ Track 4106

v. 上升；升起；上漲；增加；

▶ We were impressed when we saw the sun rising from the horizon.
我們看到太陽從地平面升起時都相當感動。

n. 增加；上漲；上升；提升；發跡

▶ It is said that there will be a rise in the prices of daily necessities.
據說民生用品要漲價了。

---

risk [rɪsk] **n.** 風險，危險

◀ Track 4107

▶ People who love greasy foods have higher risks of getting cardiovascular diseases. 喜歡吃油膩食物的人具有較高罹患心血管疾病的風險。

v. 使遭受危險，以……做賭注

▶ The firefighter risked his life to rescue the terminally ill old man in the house.
消防隊員冒生命危險去救在屋子裡患有末期疾病的老人。

---

rival [`raɪvl̩]

◀ Track 4108

n. 競爭者，對手

▶ The two companies used to be business rivals, but this year, they worked together on a new product.
這兩家公司以前是商場上競爭的對手，但是今年他們合作推出一項新產品。

adj. 競爭的

▶ The U.S. and Russia used to be rival countries. 美國和俄國以前是競爭的國家。

v. 與……競爭，與……匹敵，比得上

▶ He is very competitive; I'm afraid that I cannot rival with him.
他很有競爭力，我恐怕不是他的對手。

---

river [`rɪvɚ] **n.** 河；河流

◀ Track 4109

▶ The factory discharged contaminated waste water into the river.
這家工廠排放汙染的廢水到河流裡。

---

roach [rotʃ] **n.** 蟑螂

◀ Track 4110

▶ The roaches are covering the burger. It is gross!
蟑螂爬滿了這個漢堡。太噁心了！

---

road [rod] **n.** 馬路

◀ Track 4111

▶ The demonstrators occupied the road to protest against the new policy.
抗爭者佔據馬路，抗議新政策。

---

roar [ror]

◀ Track 4112

v. 吼叫，呼嘯；大聲狂笑，叫喊

▶ The wind roared through the valley, making a scary sound.
風呼嘯地吹過山谷，製造出可怕的聲音。

n. 呼嘯，怒號；轟鳴聲，喧鬧聲，大笑聲

▶ We could hear the roar of the lion at the other end of the zoo. 我們在動物園另一段就可以聽到獅子咆哮聲。

相關片語 **roar oneself hoarse**
喊得喉嚨沙啞

中級

▶The angry man roared himself hoarse, but no one could help him.
這名生氣的男人喊到喉嚨沙啞，但沒有人能夠幫助他。

roast [rost] v 烤；炙；烘　◀Track 4113

▶We roasted the beef and seasoned it with salt and pepper.
我們烘烤牛肉，並用鹽和胡椒調味。

adj. 烘烤的

▶The roast vegetables taste delicious.
烤蔬菜很好吃。

n. 烘烤；烤肉會

▶We dived in the roast hosted by the chef.
我們在主廚所舉辦的烤肉會上大快朵頤。

rob [rab]　◀Track 4114

v 搶劫；盜取；非法剝奪

▶The pickpocket robbed me of my wallet. 這名扒手搶了我的皮夾。

robber [ˋrabɚ]　◀Track 4115

n. 搶劫者，強盜

▶The robber was arrested before he could leave the country with the money.
搶匪在攜帶贓款離境之前就被逮捕了。

robbery [ˋrabərɪ]　◀Track 4116

n. 搶劫，盜取，搶劫案；搶劫罪

▶The local police are working hard to fight against crimes like theft and robbery.
當地警察努力打擊偷竊及強盜等犯罪行為。

robe [rob]　◀Track 4117

n. 長袍；睡袍；浴袍

▶An old man in a white robe shows up at the gate.
有一位穿著白袍的老人出現在大門。

robot [ˋrobət] n 機器人　◀Track 4118

▶The hotel is known for its robot that works as a concierge.
這個飯店因這個機器人接待員而著名。

rock [rak] n 岩石；石塊　◀Track 4119

▶The hikers sat on the rock and took a rest. 登山客坐在大石頭上面休息。

v 搖動；使搖晃

▶Don't rock the suspension bridge when you cross it.
通過吊橋的時候不要搖晃它。

rocket [ˋrakɪt]　◀Track 4120

n. 飛彈，火箭，火箭彈

▶Mr. Trump refers to the leader of North Korea as a "little rocket man" in his tweet. 川普先生在推特貼文中說北韓領導人是「小火箭人」。

v 用火箭運載；向前急衝；飛快進行；迅速上升

▶House prices in the downtown are rocketing up.
市中心的房價在飆漲。

rocky [ˋrakɪ]　◀Track 4121

adj. 岩石的，多岩石的，岩石

▶The rocky landscape in the national park is very impressive to the tourists.
這個國家公園內的岩石地景令許多觀光客印象深刻。

rod [rad]　◀Track 4122

n. 棒，竿，桿；枝條，藤條

▶Spare the rod, spoil the kid.
不打不成才。

role [rol] n 角色；作用　◀Track 4123

▶He played the role of the broker between the two parties.
他在兩黨間扮演説客的角色。

---

roll [rol]　◀̇Track 4124

v 滾動；轉動；搖擺；搖晃

▶Roll the scroll so you can see the content below.
滾動卷軸就可以看到底下的內容。

n 滾動；一捲；捲餅

▶Tina bought a roll of toilet paper.
緹娜買了一卷廁所用的衛生紙。

---

romance [roˋmæns]　◀̇Track 4125

n 戀愛，風流韻事；愛情故事；羅曼蒂克氣氛，浪漫情調；羅曼語（拉丁系）

▶The movie was adapted from the true story of the famous physicist's romance. 這部是根據一位知名物理學家的真實愛情故事改編而成的。

v 寫傳奇，虛構故事；和……談戀愛，向……求愛，追求

▶The newly weds were romancing under the stary night. 這對新婚夫妻在繁星點點的夜空下談情説愛。

adj 羅曼語的

▶The Romance languages are a language family in the Indo-European languages.
羅曼語是印歐語系的一個分支。

---

romantic [rəˋmæntɪk]　◀̇Track 4126

adj 浪漫的，羅曼蒂克的；傳奇性的，富浪漫色彩的；虛構的；不切實際的

▶She has romantic illusions about becoming a famous pianist. 她對於成為一位有名的鋼琴演奏家有很多浪漫的幻想。

---

roof [ruf] **n** 屋頂　◀̇Track 4127

▶The tiles of the roof fell off after the typhoon.
颱風過後，屋頂上的磚瓦掉落了下來。

---

room [rum]　◀̇Track 4128

n 房間；室；空間；場所

▶Will there be enough room to store the goods? 會有足夠的空間存放貨物嗎？

---

rooster [ˋrustɚ]　◀̇Track 4129
=cock **n** 公雞；狂妄自大的人

▶He is an arrogant rooster, and he always looks for fights.
他是個狂妄自大的人，總是在找人吵架。

---

root [rut]　◀̇Track 4130

n 根；根部；根基；根源；

▶We have to find the root of the problem and eradicate the trouble.
我們要找到問題的根源，徹底解決煩惱。

v 使紮根；使固定；生根；根源於

▶The instinct of fear is rooted in human nature. 害怕的本能根植在人性之中。

---

rope [rop]　◀̇Track 4131

n 繩子；繩索

▶We learned how to tie a rope to another rope at the camp. 在營隊中，我們學習如何將兩條繩子綁在一起。

---

rose [roz]　◀̇Track 4132

n 玫瑰

▶The pedals of roses can be used to make tea. 玫瑰花的花瓣可以用來泡茶。

---

rot [rɑt]　◀̇Track 4133

v 腐爛，腐朽；腐壞，衰敗

中級

▶The meat would rot and attract flies if you don't put it in the refrigerator.
如果不把肉放在冰箱哩，它會腐敗並且引來蒼蠅。

n. 腐爛，腐壞；腐敗，墮落；蠢話；蠢事

▶Stop talking rot and focus on the real business.
不要說廢話了，專注在正事上。

rotten [`rɑtn]
🔊 Track 4134

adj. 腐爛的

▶The rotten fish gave off a bad smell.
這條腐敗的魚發出惡臭。

rough [rʌf]
🔊 Track 4135

adj. 粗糙的；粗製的；幹粗活的；粗俗的；狂暴的；艱難的

▶The rough surface of the road made it difficult to drive through it.
路表面不平坦，開車經過不容易。

adv. 粗糙地；粗略地；粗暴地

▶The basketball team of the school had a bad reputation for playing rough.
這個學校的籃球隊打法粗野，名聲很差。

round [raʊnd]
🔊 Track 4136

adv. 環繞地；在周圍；在附近；到各處

▶The superintendent showed the students round in the dorm.
舍監帶學生繞一圈看宿舍環境。

prep. 環繞；在……周圍；去……四處

▶The moon goes round the earth.
月亮繞地球運行。

n. 一輪；一回合；循環；**adj.** 圓的

▶The tennis player of our school took the lead in the second round.
我們學校的網球選手在第二回合領先。

route [rut]
🔊 Track 4137

n. 路線，路程；航線

▶The route of the flight is showed on the screen in front of you.
這班機的路線已經顯示在你前面的螢幕上。

v. 按規定路線走；安排……的路線或程序

▶The travel agent routed us through Spain. 這間旅行社安排我們經過西班牙。

routine [ru`tin]
🔊 Track 4138

n. 例行公事，日常工作，慣常程序

▶It is her daily routine to make a work journal.
寫工作日誌，是她的每日慣常程序。

adj. 日行的，例行的，一般的

▶She spend some time to deal with the routine work and saved more time to deal with impromptu tasks.
她花一些時間處理例行公事，留下更多時間處理臨時的事務。

row [raʊ] **n.** 一列；一排
🔊 Track 4139

▶The soldiers stood in rows in the morning assembly. 朝會時，士兵成排站好。

v. 划船

▶The girl did not know how to row a boat. 這位小女孩不知道怎麼划船。

royal [`rɔɪəl]
🔊 Track 4140

adj. 王室的；皇家的

▶People in the country were very excited about the royal wedding.
這個國家的人們對於皇室婚禮感到很興奮。

rub [rʌb] **v.** 擦；摩擦
🔊 Track 4141

▶Don't rub your eyes with dirty hands.
不要用髒手揉眼睛。

rubber [`rʌbɚ] ◀Track 4142

adj. 橡膠製成的；

▶She tied her hair with a rubber band.
她用橡皮筋綁頭髮。

n. 橡膠

▶The Malaysian farmers make a living by producing rubber.
馬來西亞的農夫靠生產橡膠維生。

rubbish [`rʌbɪʃ] ◀Track 4143

n. 垃圾，廢物

▶Don't talk rubbish! Make some constructive suggestions.
不要說廢話！做些有建設性的建議吧。

adj. 垃圾的；糟透的

▶The performer was a rubbish magician; the audience was regretting paying for the tickets.
這個表演者是一位很糟糕的魔術師，觀眾都後悔買票進場。

rude [rud] ◀Track 4144

adj. 魯莽的；無禮的

▶The rude boy cursed in front of the school administrator. 這位無禮的男孩在學校行政人員面前罵髒話。

rug [rʌg] ◀Track 4145

n. （鋪於室內的）小地毯

▶The rug was stained with red wine.
地毯上有紅酒留下的污漬。

ruin [`rʊɪn] ◀Track 4146

n. 毀滅；毀壞；廢墟、遺跡

▶We visited the ruins of the ancient church.
我們參觀了古代教堂的遺跡。

v. 毀

▶Our plan to prank the teacher was ruined.
我們捉弄老師的計畫被破壞了。

rule [rul] ◀Track 4147

n. 規則；規定；慣例

▶Follow the rules when you play the game.
玩遊戲要遵守規則。

v. 統治；管轄

▶The ethic group that once ruled the country was eliminated in the war.
這個曾經統治此區域的民族在戰爭中被消滅了。

ruler [`rulɚ] ◀Track 4148

n. 尺；統治者

▶The ruler of the country has been in reign for four decades.
這個國家的統治者已經在位四十年了。

rumour [`rumɚ] ◀Track 4149

=ru·mor **n.** 謠言，謠傳

▶Rumor has it that the superstar will visit the local pub this evening.
有謠傳說這位超級巨星今晚會來到這家本地的酒吧。

run [rʌn] ◀Track 4150

v. 跑；奔馳；經營

▶It's not easy to run a family business.
經營家族事業並不容易。

n. 跑；奔馳

▶The dogs has a good run in the meadow. 狗兒在草地上盡情奔跑。

runner [`rʌnɚ] ◀Track 4151

n. 跑步者；賽跑者

中級

▶The organizers of the marathon race offered refreshment for the runners.
這個馬拉松比賽的主辦單位為跑者準備了點心。

running [`rʌnɪŋ] ◀Track 4152
n. 跑步，賽跑；流出；（機器）運轉；（機構）管理

▶The running of the machine was quite smooth.
這台機器的運作很順暢。

adj. 奔跑的；（水）流動的，流出的；（機器）運轉的；流鼻水的，出膿的

▶It is said that the rover detected running water on Mars.
據說探測器在火星上發現流動的水。

rural [`rʊrəl] ◀Track 4153
adj. 農村的，有鄉村風味的，田園的；生活於農村的；農業的

▶People in the rural area tend to live in a slow pace.
住在農村地區的人們，生活步調比較慢。

rush [rʌʃ] ◀Track 4154
v. 衝；闖；趕緊；急速行動

▶He rushed to the hospital to see his wife.
他趕到醫院去看他的太太。

n. 衝；奔；急速行動；匆忙；緊急

▶Take your time. There is no rush.
慢慢來。不急。

Russia [`rʌʃə] **n.** 俄羅斯 ◀Track 4155
▶Russia has postponed manned rocket launches this year.
俄國延後今年發射載人太空船的計畫。

Russian [`rʌʃən] ◀Track 4156
adj. 俄羅斯的；俄語的

▶No one in our office could read the Russian message.
我們辦公室沒有人能讀懂這篇俄文的訊息。

n. 俄國人；

▶I know that Russian; he has been a diplomat for many years.
我知道那位俄國人；他當外交官很多年了。

rust [rʌst] ◀Track 4157
n. 鏽，鐵鏽；（腦子）遲鈍；（能力）荒廢；鐵鏽色

▶There are patches of rust on the surface of the iron door.
這扇鐵門的表面有斑斑鏽跡。

v. 生鏽；（腦子）變遲鈍；（能力）荒廢；成鐵鏽色

▶The retired engineer's programming skill has rusted, for he stopped coding two years ago.
這位退休工程師的程式設計能力變鈍了，因為他兩年前就沒在用電腦編碼了。

rusty [`rʌstɪ] ◀Track 4158
adj. 生鏽的；鐵鏽色的；褪色的，破舊的，過時的；荒廢的

▶My Spanish is a bit rusty, for I haven't practiced it for several months.
因為好幾個月沒練習，我的西班牙文變生疏了。

▶ Ss

　　以下表格是全民英檢官方公告中級「聽、說、讀、寫」所須具備的能力，本書例句皆依此範疇特別設計，只要掃描右方QR code，就能搭配相對應的音軌實現「眼耳並用」方式，刺激左腦的語言學習功能；同時也可使用本書附贈的紅膠片，將其置於單字上，一面記憶一面自我挑戰，達到雙倍的學習成果！

聽 ▶	在日常生活中，能聽懂一般的會話；能大致聽懂公共場所廣播、氣象報告及廣告等。在工作時，能聽懂簡易的產品介紹與操作說明。能大致聽懂外籍人士的談話及詢問。
說 ▶	可在日常生活中，能以簡易英語交談或描述一般事物，能介紹自己的生活作息、工作、家庭、經歷等，並可對一般話題陳述看法。在工作時，能進行簡單的答詢，並與外籍人士交談溝通。
讀 ▶	在日常生活中，能閱讀短文、故事、私人信件、廣告、傳單、簡介及使用說明等。在工作時，能閱讀工作須知、公告、操作手冊、例行的文件、傳真、電報等。
寫 ▶	能寫簡單的書信、故事及心得等。對於熟悉且與個人經歷相關的主題，能以簡易的文字表達。

中級

sack [sæk]　◀Track 4159

v 裝、入袋；（口）開除，解僱；洗劫

▶The rebel troop sacked the village and killed hundreds of people.
這些叛軍洗劫了城市並屠殺了上百人。

n 粗布袋；睡袋

▶The kid put the dolls into the sacks and stored them in the attic.
這位小朋友用麻布袋把娃娃裝好，收在閣樓裡面。

相關片語 **hit the sack** 上床睡覺，就寢

▶After an exhausting work day, she hit the sack early.
在疲累的一天工作之後，她早早就寢。

sacrifice [`sækrə͵faɪs]　◀Track 4160

v 犧牲；虧本出售

▶My parents have sacrified a lot for me. 我父母為我犧牲很多。

n 牲禮，祭品；犧牲；犧牲的行為

▶They bring the sacrifices to the temple.
他們把獻祭品帶到廟宇裡。

sad [sæd]　◀Track 4161

adj. 悲傷的；悲哀的

▶The movie was so sad the many of the audience shed tears while watching it.
這部電影太哀傷了，很多觀眾邊看邊掉淚。

sadden [`sædn]　◀Track 4162

v 使悲傷，使難過；悲哀，哀痛

▶I am deeply saddened by the loss that you and your family have.
我對您家人的損失感到難過。

safe [sef]　◀Track 4163

adj. 安全的；平安的

▶Jenny was relieved that her son came back from the battle field safe and sound.
珍妮因為她的兒子平安從戰場歸來而感到鬆一口氣。

n. 保險箱

▶I stored the jewelries that my grandparents gave me in the safe.
我將祖父母傳給我的珠寶保存在保險箱裡。

safely [ˋseflɪ]
◀ Track 4164

adv. 安全地；可靠地，有把握的；穩固地

▶The kids are safely fastened into their car seats. Let's hit the road. 小朋友已經安全地繫好安全帶了。我們出發吧！

safety [ˋseftɪ]
◀ Track 4165

n. 安全；平安

▶The instructor are illustrating the regulations of road safety to the kids.
講師正在對小朋友解釋道路安全的規則。

sail [sel]
◀ Track 4166

v. 航行；開船；駕駛（船）

▶The sailors wrer both nervous and excited when they sailed to the new continent.
水手們航向新大陸的時候，既緊張又興奮。

n. 乘船航行；船隻；船帆

▶They could not spread the sail because of some minor problems.
因為一些小錯誤，他們無法揚帆。

sailing [ˋselɪŋ]
◀ Track 4167

n. 航海，航行；航班；帆船運動

▶The sailing begins at 4 o'clock in the morning.
早晨四點起航。

sailor [ˋselɚ]
◀ Track 4168

n. 船員；水手

▶The sailor initiated a fight at the local bar.
這名水手在本地的酒吧引發一場爭執。

sake [sek] n. 目的；緣故
◀ Track 4169

▶For the sake of efficiency, the workers created a system to share the workd load for the project.
為了達到好的效率，員工們創造出一個好的系統，分攤計畫的工作量。

salad [ˋsæləd] n. 沙拉
◀ Track 4170

▶Jessie only had salad and fruits for meals in order to lose weight.
為了減重，潔西只吃沙拉和水果。

salary [ˋsælərɪ] n. 薪資
◀ Track 4171

▶The salary of the job was not specified in the recruitment ad.
這個徵人廣告上面沒有註明工作的薪資。

sale [sel]
◀ Track 4172

n. 出售；銷售額；拍賣

▶Accodding to the real estate agent, the house for sale originally belongs to a movie star.
房地產仲介員説，這棟要出售的房子原本為一位電影明星所有。

salesman [ˋselzmən]
◀ Track 4173

n. 推銷員；男店員

▶The salesman was very persuasive; I bought the product he was promoting.
這位推銷員很有説服力；我買了他推薦的產品。

salesperson
◀Track 4174

[`selz͵pɝsn] **n.** 店員；售貨員

▶ "You look stunning in that white dress," said the salesperson.
「您穿這件白色禮服太美了，」銷售員說。

---

salt [sɔlt] **n.** 鹽
◀Track 4175

▶ Add some salt and pepper to increase the flavor of the steak.
加一些鹽和胡椒來增加牛排的風味吧。

---

salty [`sɔltɪ] **adj.** 鹹的
◀Track 4176

▶ Have you tried salty ice cream?
你有嚐過鹹的冰淇淋嗎？

---

same [sem]
◀Track 4177

pron. 相同的事物

▶ Her bought a stylish backpack, and I wanted to have the same.
她買了一個很時尚的後背包，我也想買個一樣的。。

adj. 一樣的

▶ I shall never make the same mistake.
我不會再犯同樣的錯誤了。

---

sample [`sæmpl]
◀Track 4178

n. 樣品；試用品；例子

▶ We sent some samples along with the catalogue to our potential client.
我們寄了一些樣品和商品型錄給潛在的顧客。

v. 抽樣檢查；品嘗；體驗

▶ They sampled some local cuisines at the night market.
他們在夜市吃了一些本地的美食。

---

sanction [`sæŋkʃən]
◀Track 4179

n. 認可，批准；贊許，支持

▶ Without his sanction, I can't access to the data base.
沒有他的許可，我無法使用資料庫。

v. 認可，批准；支持，鼓勵；對……實施制裁

▶ We can not proceed before the proposal is sanctioned.
計畫沒有獲得許可之前，我們不能繼續進行。

---

sand [sænd] **n.** 沙
◀Track 4180

▶ The kids built a sand castle in the beach.
小朋友在沙灘上面建造一個沙堡。

---

sandwich [`sændwɪtʃ]
◀Track 4181

n. 三明治

▶ We made some sandwiches for the picnic.
我們做了一些三明治去野餐。

---

satellite [`sætl͵aɪt]
◀Track 4182

n. 衛星，人造衛星

▶ There are numerous artificial sateliete orbiting the earth.
外頭有許多人造衛星繞著地球運行。

adj. 衛星的

▶ Many residents in the satellite cities work in the metropolitan area.
許多衛星都市的居民在大都會區工作。

---

satisfaction
◀Track 4183

[͵sætɪs`fækʃən] **n.** 滿足，滿意，稱心，樂事

▶ To his satisfaction, his son won the law school scholarship.
令他開心的是，他兒子拿到法律學院的獎學金。

中級

satisfactory

Track 4184

[ˌsætɪsˋfæktərɪ] **adj.** 令人滿意的，良好的，符合要求的

▶His performance was satisfactory, so he got a pay raise this year.
他的表現很令人滿意，所以他獲得加薪的機會。

satisfy [ˋsætɪsˌfaɪ]

Track 4185

v. 使滿意；使滿足；滿足

▶The functions of the machine satisfied their needs.
這個機器的功能使他們滿意。

Saturday [ˋsætɚde] =Sat. **n.** 星期六

Track 4186

▶Tom works out at the gym every Saturday.
湯姆每周六都會去健身房運動。

sauce [sɔs] **n.** 醬；醬汁

Track 4187

▶Soy sauce is a flavorful seasoning ingredient in Chinese cuisines.
醬油是中國菜餚中很受歡迎的調味料。

saucer [ˋsɔsɚ]

Track 4188

n. 茶托；淺碟

▶She offered tea to the guests in her best cup and saucer.
她用最好的杯子和茶托請客人用茶。

sausage [ˋsɔsɪdʒ]

Track 4189

n. 香腸，臘腸

▶Eating processed meats such as sausages and bacons may increase the risk of cancer.
吃香腸、培根這類加工肉品可能會增加罹癌的風險。

save [sev]

Track 4190

v. 救；挽救；節省；儲蓄；保留

▶They had to tighten the belt and save money at the end of the month.
到了月底，他們必須要省吃儉用。

saving [ˋsevɪŋ]

Track 4191

n. 節約，節儉；救助；儲金，存款

▶He spent all his savings on this sports car.
他把所有的存款花在這輛跑車上。

saw [sɔ] **v.** 鋸；鋸開

Track 4192

▶The worker sawed the wood into two pieces.
工人把木頭鋸成兩段。

n. 鋸子

▶The metal-cutting saw cost me two hundred dollars.
我花兩百元買了這把鐵鋸子。

say [se] **v.** 說；講述

Track 4193

▶What does the doctor say about his illness?
醫生針對他的病情是怎麼說的？

say·ing [ˋseɪŋ]

Track 4194

n. 說話，發表言論

▶As an old saying goes, "Honesty is the best policy."
俗話說的好：「誠實為上策。」

相關片語 **go without saying** 不言而喻，不用說，毫無疑問地

▶This was a good deal. It goes without saying that we should make the purchase.
這筆交易很划算。毫無疑問地，我們應該買。

中級

scale [skel]
◀̈ Track 4195

n. 刻度；比例；規模；磅秤

▶ The scale is not accurate; it overestimates the weight of the parcel.
這個秤不準；它把包裹顯示地太重了。

scan [skæn]
◀̈ Track 4196

v. 細看，審視；粗略地看，瀏覽

▶ I scanned through the article, trying to find out the key words in it.
我瀏覽這篇文章，想要找當中的關鍵字。

n. 細看；瀏覽；掃描

▶ The scan of his brain revealed a tumor.
他的腦部掃描顯示了一顆腫瘤。

scarce [skɛrs]
◀̈ Track 4197

adj. 缺乏的，不足的；稀有的，

▶ Clean water was scarce in the town which was just struck by tsunami.
剛被海嘯襲擊過的小鎮裡，缺乏乾淨的用水。

| 相關片語 | **make oneself scarce** |
離開，溜走

▶ I made myself scare from the spot of the accident to avoid troubles.
我從意外現場溜走以免惹上麻煩。

scarcely [`skɛrslɪ]
◀̈ Track 4198

adv. 幾乎不，幾乎沒有；絕不

▶ The celebrities scarcely attended classes, yet they graduated and got the diploma.
這些名人很少出席課程，但他們畢業了也拿到學位。

scare [skɛr]
◀̈ Track 4199

v. 驚嚇，使恐懼；把……嚇跑

▶ The sudden noise scared me.
這個突然發出的聲響嚇到我了。

n. 驚嚇，驚恐；恐慌

▶ There was a scare of the epidemic of pigs in the country.
豬的傳染病在這個國家引發了一陣恐慌。

scared [skɛrd]
◀̈ Track 4200

adj. 害怕的；不敢的

▶ She was too scared to walk into that deseted house.
她太害怕了，不敢走進荒廢的房子裡。

scarf [skɑrf] **n.** 圍巾
◀̈ Track 4201

▶ The girl put on a scarf, for it was freezing outside.
外面很冷，所以女孩戴上圍巾。

scary [`skɛrɪ]
◀̈ Track 4202

adj. 引起驚慌的，可怕的

▶ The facial expression of the actor was so scary that some kids in the audience cried.
這位演員的表情太可怕，所以觀眾當中有小朋友嚇哭了。

scatter [`skætɚ]
◀̈ Track 4203

v. 使消散，使潰散；撒，散布；（砲火）散射

▶ The mist scattered at dawn.
清晨時，霧散去。

n. 消散，分散，潰散；散播；零星散布

▶ A scatter of critiques on ths article were posted on the bulletin board system.
在這個留言板系統中有一些對這篇文章的零星批評。

scene [sin]
◀Track 4204

n. 場面；景色；（事件發生的）地點；（戲劇的）場景

▶Some people walked through the scene of the crime without being aware of it. 有些人經過這個犯罪場景卻毫不自知。

scenery [`sinərɪ]
◀Track 4205

n. 風景，景色；舞台布景

▶The scenery of the national park was breathtaking.
這個國家公園的風景美得令人屏息。

schedule [`skɛdʒʊl]
◀Track 4206

n. 時間表，日程表；時刻表；行程

▶We were behind the schedule due to some technical problems.
我們因為技術的問題，進度落後。

v. 將……排入行程；將……列入計劃；安排，預定

▶The conference is scheduled on January 19th.
這個研討會將於一月十九日舉行。

scheme [skim]
◀Track 4207

n. 計劃，方案；詭計，陰謀

▶He had a hare-brained scheme for starting his own business.
他有一個瘋狂的計畫，要創立自己的生意。

v. 計劃，設計；密謀，策劃

▶Some of the assistants were scheming against the minister.
有些助理在密謀對這位部長不利。

scholar [`skɑlɚ] **n.** 學者
◀Track 4208

▶The scholar has published dozens of research papers.
這位學者發表過好幾十篇研究文章。

scholarship
◀Track 4209

[`skɑlɚˌʃɪp] **n.** 獎學金

▶He won the scholarship, so he can have the subsidies for the exchange program. 他獲得獎學金，所以他可以獲得交換學生的補助。

school [skul] **n.** 學校
◀Track 4210

▶He studied at the culinary school for three years.
他在廚藝學校就讀三年。

schoolboy [`skulˌbɔɪ]
◀Track 4211

n. 男學生

▶The schoolboys queued to get on the school bus.
這群男學生們排隊上校車。

schoolmate
◀Track 4212

[`skulˌmet] **n.** 同學

▶We were schoolmates when we studied in the language institute.
我們在語言學校是同學。

science [`saɪəns] **n.** 科學
◀Track 4213

▶He teaches social science in the middle school.
他在中學教社會科學。

scientific [ˌsaɪənˈtɪfɪk]
◀Track 4214

adj. 科學的；符合科學規律的；用於科學的；嚴謹的，有條理的

▶This theory is not verified with scientific evidence.
這個理論沒有科學根據。

scientist [`saɪəntɪst]
◀Track 4215

n. 科學家

▶Several scientists support the theory that there would be life on Mars.
有幾位科學家支持火星上有生命的理論。

scissors [`sɪzɚz] ◀Track 4216
n. 剪刀

▶Put the scissors back to the cabinet after using it.
剪刀使用完畢要放回櫃子裡。

scold [skold] **v** 責罵 ◀Track 4217

▶She didn't scold her son for breaking the antique vase.
她沒有因為兒子打破古董花瓶就責備他。

scoop [skup] ◀Track 4218
v 用勺舀，用鏟子鏟；舀空；挖空

▶I scooped some mashed potato from the bowl.
我從碗裡挖了一些馬鈴薯泥。

n. 勺子；戽斗；匙，勺；凹處；【口】最新獨家報導，最新內幕消息

▶The journalist got a bonus for obtaining a scoop.
這名記者因為拿到獨家報導的消息而獲得獎金。

scooter [`skutɚ] ◀Track 4219
n. 踏板車；小輪摩托車

▶Remember to wear a helmet when you ride a scooter.
騎摩托車要戴安全帽。

score [skor] **v** 得分 ◀Track 4220

▶The player had a chance to score, but he missed it.
這位球員原本有機會得分，但錯失了機會。

n. 分數；比數

▶He got a high score in the exam and was admitted to the prestigious school.
他在考試中得高分，被名校錄取。

scout [skaʊt] ◀Track 4221
n. 偵察兵，偵察艦；偵查，搜查；球探、星探等發掘新人者

▶The basketball player was discovered by a talent scout in the regional games.
這位籃球選手在區域比賽中被球探發掘。

補充片語 talent scout 星探

v 偵查，搜查；（經過尋找）發現

▶The soldier used a binocular to scout the actions of the enemy.
士兵用望遠鏡偵查敵人的行動。

scratch [skrætʃ] ◀Track 4222
v 搔，抓；抓破；劃傷；潦草地塗寫

▶The mosquito bite was itching, so I couldn't help to scratch it.
蚊子咬的傷口很癢，我忍不住去抓它。

n. 抓痕，擦傷；刮擦聲；亂塗

▶The cat left some scratches on the couch.
貓咪在沙發上留下一些刮痕。

scream [skrim] ◀Track 4223
v 尖叫；發出尖銳刺耳的聲音；大聲叫嚷地抗議

▶The drowning woman screamed for help.
這名溺水的女人大聲呼救。

n. 尖叫聲；尖銳刺耳的聲音

▶I heard a cream from upstairs.
我聽到樓上有尖叫聲。

中級

screen [skrin]

🔊 Track 4224

n. 屏；幕；簾；螢幕；紗窗、門

▶ The resolution of the screen is rather high. 這個螢幕的解析度相當高。

v. 遮蔽；掩護；放映（電影）

▶ Where will they screen the movie? 他們會在哪裡放映這部電影呢？

screw [skru]

🔊 Track 4225

v. 旋，擰；用螺絲固定，擰緊；扭歪（臉）；強迫，壓榨

▶ She screwed her eyes with a sense of disguset when she heard the offensive remarks. 聽見了這番冒犯性的言論之後，她瞇緊了眼，露出一股嫌惡感。

n. 螺絲，螺絲釘

▶ Turn the screw clockwise to tighten it. 順時針將螺絲轉緊。

adj. 螺絲的，螺旋的

▶ The design of the indoor spiral staircase is special. 這個室內螺旋梯的設計很特別。

相關片語 **have a screw loose**（有根螺絲鬆了）有點不正常，有毛病

▶ That man keeps talking to himself. I think he has a screw loose. 那個男人一直自言自語。我想他可能有點不正常。

scrub [skrʌb]

🔊 Track 4226

v. 用力擦洗，刷洗；揉；擦掉

▶ I scrubed the bathtub and the toilet last Saturday. 我上週六刷了浴缸和馬桶。

n. 擦洗，擦淨；刷洗

▶ She gave her hands a scrub after cleaning the gardon. 清理花園之後，她把雙手刷洗乾淨。

sculpture [`skʌlptʃɚ]

🔊 Track 4227

n. 雕刻品，雕塑品，雕像

▶ There is a sculpture of Venus at the entrance of the museum. 博物館入口有一個維納斯的雕像。

sea [si] **n.** 海

🔊 Track 4228

▶ The old man went fishing on the sea and witnessed a whale. 這名老人到海上捕魚，看到一頭鯨魚。

seafood [`si‚fud]

🔊 Track 4229

n. 海鮮

▶ I am allergic to seafood. 我對海鮮過敏。

seagull [`sigʌl] =gull **n.** 海鷗

🔊 Track 4230

▶ The seagulls hovered over the yacht. 這群海鷗在遊艇上方盤旋。

seal [sil]

🔊 Track 4231

v. 密封；蓋章於，（以蓋章的方式）批准；確定

▶ We had a long negotiation before we sealed the deal. 我們在確認合約之前協商了很久。

n. 印章；封印；封條

▶ I haven't tear up the seal because I am not sure what was in the box. 我還沒打開封條，因為我不知道箱子裡面是什麼。

search [sɝtʃ]

🔊 Track 4232

n. 搜查；搜尋；調查

▶ The search of the missing hiker lasted for three days. 搜尋走失登山客的行動持續了三天。

v. 搜查;細看

▶We searched on the Internet for information about the asteroid.
我們在網路上搜尋有關這個小行星的資訊。

seaside [`si͵saɪd]
🔊 Track 4233

n. 海邊,海濱

▶They dined at a restaurant by the seaside.
他們在海邊的餐廳用餐。

adj. 海邊的,海濱的

▶The seside scrubs can protect the soil from erosion.
海邊的小樹叢可以防止土壤侵蝕。

season [`sizn]
🔊 Track 4234

v. 為……調味

▶The chef used some herbs to season the risotto.
這位主廚用一些香草來為這個燉飯調味。

seat [sit] n. 座位
🔊 Track 4235

▶Please yield the priority seat to those in need.
請將博愛座讓給需要的人。

v. 就座

▶The kids are securely seated in the back of the car.
小朋友安全地坐在車子後方。

second [`sɛkənd]
🔊 Track 4236

n. 秒;瞬間;片刻;第二名

▶The calculation was completed within two seconds.
計算在兩秒之內就完成了。

adj. 第二的;次要的

▶He won the second place in the race.
他在比賽中得第二名。

adv. 其次;居次地

▶He came second in the job interview, but he was recruited in the end.
他在面試中位居第二,但他最後還是有被錄取。

secondary
🔊 Track 4237

[`sɛkən͵dɛrɪ] **adj. 第二的;中等的;次要的**

▶He completed his secondary education in the U.S.
他在美國受中等教育。

second-hand
🔊 Track 4238

[`sɛkəndhænd] **adj. 二手的,中古的**

▶Second-hand smoke is harmful to our health.
二手煙對我們的健康有害。

adv. 間接地;做為舊貨

▶I got the information second-hand.
我是間接得到這項資訊的。

secret [`sikrɪt]
🔊 Track 4239

adj. 秘密的;私下的;神秘的

▶The secret agent was cautious for fear of revealing his identity.
這名密探很謹慎,怕洩漏了身分。

n. 秘密

▶The paparazzi threatened the celebrity to publicize his secret.
狗仔隊威脅名人要將他的秘密公開。

secretary [`sɛkrə͵tɛrɪ]
🔊 Track 4240

n. 秘書

▶As a private secretary to the company chairman, Mary sometimes has to deal with his personal affairs.
作為公司董事長的私人秘書,瑪莉有時候要替他處理個人的事宜。

中級

section [`sɛkʃən]
🔊 Track 4241

n. 部分；地段；切下的部分

▶The second section of the thesis is a review of previous studies regarding this topic.
這篇論文的第二部分是針對這個主題的文獻回顧。

sector [`sɛktɚ]
🔊 Track 4242

n. 地區，部門；區段；行業

▶The electronics sector was said to be rather profitable in the last quarter.
據説電子部門在上一季賺很多錢。

secure [sɪ`kjʊr]
🔊 Track 4243

v. 關緊；使安全；弄到

▶Remember to secure the windows before the typhoon hits.
颱風來襲之前，記得關緊窗戶。

adj. 安全的；安心的；確定無疑的；穩固的

▶His words made me feel secure.
他説的話讓我覺得安心。

security [sɪ`kjʊrətɪ]
🔊 Track 4244

n. 安全

▶The guards were responsible for the security of the invaluable jewelry.
這些保全人員負責保護無價珠寶的安全。

see [si]
🔊 Track 4245

v. 看到；看見；理解；將……看作

▶The veretan workers have seen the ups and downs of the company.
資深員工看過公司的起起落落。

seed [sid]
🔊 Track 4246

n. 種子；籽；根源

▶He was blamed for sowing seeds of disputes among his siblings.
他因為在手足之間種下紛爭的根源而受到責備。

seek [sik]
🔊 Track 4247

v. 尋找；探索；追求

▶They were seeking recognition from their parents.
他們想尋求父母的認同。

seem [sim]
🔊 Track 4248

v. 看起來好像；似乎

▶They seem to be quite familiar with the system.
他們似乎對這套系統很熟悉。

seesaw [`si,sɔ]
🔊 Track 4249

n. 翹翹板

▶Kids are not allowed to use the seesaw in the park for the time being due to safety concerns.
因為安全的疑慮，小朋友暫時不准使用公園裡的翹翹板。

seize [siz]
🔊 Track 4250

v. 抓住；奪取；逮捕；沒收

▶The singer seized the opportunity to promote the songs she composed.
歌手抓住機會宣傳她作的歌曲。

相關片語 **be seized with panic**
驚慌失措

▶She was seized with panic when she was confronted with a robber.
她遇到搶匪時驚慌失措。

seldom [`sɛldəm]
🔊 Track 4251

adv. 很少

▶I seldom use online messengers to contact with my friends.
我很少使用線上通訊軟體和朋友聯絡。

select [sə`lɛkt] v 挑選
◀ Track 4252

▶The manager selected a team to carry out the special plan.
經理挑選一組人馬來進行這項計畫。

selection [sə`lɛkʃən]
◀ Track 4253

n 選擇；選拔；挑選

▶The selection of the representative for the school underwent some problems.
挑選學校代表的過程出現了一些問題。

self [sɛlf]
◀ Track 4254

n 自身；自己；自我

▶Reflecting on her former self, Mary thought it was time to make changes.
反省過去的自己，瑪莉覺得是時候要改變了。

selfish [`sɛlfɪʃ]
◀ Track 4255

adj 自私的

▶Being selfish is human nature, but being altruistic is a virtue.
自私是人類的天性，但是利他是種美德。

sell [sɛl] v 賣；出售
◀ Track 4256

▶They sold the house at the price of one billions dollars.
他們以十億元的價格出售這棟房子。

semester [sə`mɛstɚ]
◀ Track 4257

n 學期

▶The term paper is due on the last day of the semester.
期末報告的期限是這學期最後一天。

send [sɛnd]
◀ Track 4258

v 發送；派遣；寄

▶Those Jewish people were sent to the concentration camp.
那些猶太人被送進集中營。

senior [`sinjɚ]
◀ Track 4259

adj 年長的，年紀較大的；地位較高的，較資深的；高級的；（大學）四年級的

▶The senior students gave their textbooks to the juniors.
大四的學生們把他們的教科書送給學弟妹。

n 較年長者；前輩，上司，學長；（大學）四年級生

▶The seniors in the company gave an orientation to the novice workers.
公司裡的資深員工為新進員工做了簡介。

sense [sɛns]
◀ Track 4260

n 感覺；感官；意識；意義

▶The kids had a sense of achievement when they completed the report. 小朋友們在完成報告的時候覺得很有成就感。

v 感覺到；意識到；了解

▶They didn't sense the danger when the villan approached them.
壞人接近他們的時候，他們並沒有意識到危險。

sensible [`sɛnsəbl]
◀ Track 4261

adj 明智的；察覺到的

▶She remains calm and sensible under all kinds of circumstances.
她在所有狀況下都是保持冷靜且明智。

sensitive [`sɛnsətɪv]
◀ Track 4262

adj 敏感的，易怒的，易受傷害的，神經過敏的

中級

▶The patient became sensitive to light.
這名病人變得對光線很敏感。

sentence [`sɛntəns] ◀Track 4263
n. 句子

▶Long sentences in the composision are not always a plus.
文章中出現長句子不一定是好的。

n. 審判，宣判，判決

▶The offence carries a five-year sentence.
此違法行為可判五年監禁。

v. 審判，判決

▶The Canadian citizen was sentenced to death for smuggling drugs to China.
這名加拿大人因為走私毒品到中國而被判死刑。

separate [`sɛpə͵ret] ◀Track 4264
adj. 分開的；單獨的；個別的

▶These are two separate consepts; don't mix them together.
這兩個是不同的概念；別混淆了。

v. 分割；分離

▶The twins were separated due to the civil war.
這對雙胞胎因為內戰而被分隔兩地。

separation ◀Track 4265
[͵sɛpə`reʃən] **n.** 分開；分離

▶The separation of powers is common in democratic countries.
權力分立在民主國家中是常見的。

Sep·tem·ber ◀Track 4266
[sɛp`tɛmbə] =Sept. **n.** 九月

▶In this country, there are three national holidays in September.
在這個國家，九月裡有三個國定假日。

series [`siriz] ◀Track 4267
n. 系列；連續

▶A series of plane crash accidents raised concerns about aviation security.
一連串的墜機意外，讓人們擔心飛航安全。

serious [`sɪrɪəs] ◀Track 4268
adj. 嚴重的；嚴肅的；認真的

▶She is serious about opening a bakery of her own.
她很認真要開一家自己的烘焙坊。

servant [`sɝvənt] ◀Track 4269
n. 僕人

▶The servant finished the house chores efficiently before the master came home.
主人回家之前，僕人很有效率地把家事都完成了。

serve [sɝv] ◀Track 4270
v. 為……服務；供應（飯菜）；端上；任職；服刑

▶The waiter served the dishes and introduced the ingredients to the diners.
這位服務生端上菜餚，並且為用餐者介紹食材。

service [`sɝvɪs] **n.** 服務 ◀Track 4271
▶Good customer servise is the key element of a business.
做生意，好的客戶服務是關鍵。

session [`sɛʃən] ◀Track 4272
n. 會議；（法院）開庭；會期，開庭期間；學期；講習班；授課時間

▶The legal amendment was completed in this legislative session.
法律修正案在這次的立法院會期完成了。

set [sɛt]　◀Track 4273

n. 一套；一組；一部

▶She has a set of tools for manicure.
她有一整套的美甲工具。

v 放；置；設置；調整

▶May helped her mother set the table.
梅伊幫她的媽媽擺好桌子。

adj. 固定的；下定決心的；準備好的

▶We just need to make some minor changes in the paper, and we'll be all set.
我們只要把報告中一些地方稍微修改就準備好了。

settle [`sɛtl]　◀Track 4274

v 安頓；安排；安放；確定；使安下心來；解決

▶The immigants settled down in the coastal town.
這些移民人士在海邊的小鎮居住了下來。

settlement　◀Track 4275

[`sɛtlmənt] **n.** 解決；協議；安頓；安身

▶They finally reached the settlement after a law suit that lasted for three years.
訴訟三年之後，他們終於達成和解了。

settler [`sɛtlə]　◀Track 4276

n. 移居者，開拓者；（糾紛的）解決者；（問題的）決定者

▶The early settlers of the area cultivated the land.
早期的開發者開墾了這裡的土地。

set-up [`sɛt,ʌp]　◀Track 4277

n. 【口】組織，機構；計劃，方案；（事情的）安排

▶The set-up of the project is detailed in this brochure.
這個計畫的細節詳載於這本小冊子中。

seven [`sɛvn] **n.** 七；七歲　◀Track 4278

▶Seven is a lucky number for Michael.
對麥可來說，七是一個幸運的數字。

adj. 七的

▶Seven cats were found in this pit.
在這個小洞裡發現了七隻貓。

seventeen [,sɛvn`tin]　◀Track 4279

n. 十七

▶Nine plus eight is seventeen.
九加八等於十七。

adj. 十七的；十七個的

▶There are seventeen booths in the venue of the exhibition.
這個展覽的會場有十七個攤位。

seventy [`sɛvntɪ] **n.** 七十　◀Track 4280

▶He got seventy in the test.
他在考試中得到七十分。

adj. 七十的；七十個的

▶They ordered seventy lunch boxes for the attendees of the conference.
他們訂了七十個餐盒給研討會的參加者。

several [`sɛvərəl]　◀Track 4281

adj. 幾個的

▶There are several important events in June.
六月有幾個重大的活動。

pron. 幾個

中級

▶Several of the employees in the company studied EMBA in NTU.
這家公司有幾位員工曾在台大修商業管理學程。

se·vere [sə`vɪr] ◀ Track 4282
adj. 嚴重的；嚴厲的；劇烈的

▶She suffered from a severe headache after hearing the noise.
她聽到噪音之後就感到劇烈的頭痛。

sew [so] ◀ Track 4283
v. 縫補，縫合；縫製

▶She sewed the button to the shirt.
她把扣子縫到襯衫上面。

sex [sɛks] ◀ Track 4284
n. 性別，性；性行為

▶After the examination today, we will learn about the sex of the baby.
在今天的檢查之後，我們就會知道寶寶的性別了。

sexual [`sɛkʃʊəl] ◀ Track 4285
adj. 性的，性別的；關於性關係的

▶The ad was banned because it was considered to carry sexual innuendo.
這個廣告被禁播，因為其被認為帶有性暗示。

補充片語 sexual innuendo 性暗示

sexy [`sɛksɪ] **adj.** 性感的 ◀ Track 4286
▶The sexy dress of the actress is very eye-catching.
這名女星的性感洋裝很吸引目光。

shade [ʃed] ◀ Track 4287
n. 蔭；陰涼處；陰暗

▶The hikers took a rest in the shade of the tree.
登山者在樹蔭下休息。

v. 遮蔽，遮蔭

▶She shaded herself from the sun with an umbrella.
她用傘遮陽光。

shadow [`ʃædo] ◀ Track 4288
n. 影子，陰影，陰暗處；尾隨者

▶The man who stood in the shadow looked strange.
那名站在陰影中的男人看起來很詭異。

v. 遮蔽，投陰影於；使變暗；尾隨，盯梢

▶The detective was shadowing the suspect of the criminal case.
這名偵探在跟蹤這項犯罪案件的嫌犯。

adj. 非官方的，非正式的；影子內閣的

▶He is the Shadow Minister of Defense.
他是影子內閣的國防部長。

shady [`ʃedɪ] ◀ Track 4289
adj. 成蔭的，陰暗的；可疑的

▶Tina was concerned about the shady character who was following her, so she pretended to call the police.
緹娜有點擔心一直跟在她後面的可疑人物，所以她假裝打電話給警察。

shake [ʃek] ◀ Track 4290
v. 震動；搖動；動搖

▶The earth shaked when the volcano erupted.
火山爆發的時候，地在震動。

n. 搖動；震動；握手；地震

▶The shake of his hand caused the photo to be blurry.
他手晃動，造成相片模糊。

shall [ʃæl] ◀⟨ Track 4291

aux. 將；會（用於第一人稱，亦可用於問句第一、三人稱）

▶Shall we call it a day?
我們要不要下班了？

shallow [`ʃælo] ◀⟨ Track 4292

adj. 淺的；淺薄的；膚淺的

▶His shallow opinion was not taken seriously by his teachers.
他粗淺的意見沒有被老師們認真看待。

shame [ʃem] ◀⟨ Track 4293

n. 羞恥（感）；羞辱；帶來恥辱的人或事；憾事

▶It was a shame that he should lose the game to a novice player.
他比賽輸給新手，真是可恥。

相關片語 **bring shame on sb.**
使某人蒙羞

▶The knight brought shame on his family because of his shady deeds.
因為舉止不光明磊落，這名騎士使家族蒙羞。

v. 使感到羞恥，使蒙羞；使相形見絀

▶She was shamed for forgetting the lines.
她因為忘記台詞而感到羞恥。

shameful [`ʃemfəl] ◀⟨ Track 4294

adj. 可恥的，丟臉的

▶She considered failing the test as a shameful thing.
她認為考試不及格是一件可恥的事情。

shampoo [ʃæm`pu] ◀⟨ Track 4295

n. 洗髮精

▶She always used fragrant shampoos.
她總是使用有香味的洗髮精。

v. 洗（頭髮）

▶The curtain was shampooed last weekend.
這個窗簾上個週末被洗過了。

shape [ʃep] ◀⟨ Track 4296

n. 形狀；形式；（健康的）情況

▶The chocolate was cut into the shape of a heart. 巧克力被切成愛心形狀。

v. 形成；塑造；使成形

▶Early education is important for shaping the kid's character.
早期教育對於形塑小孩的性格相當重要。

share [ʃɛr] ◀⟨ Track 4297

n. 一份；（分擔的）一部份；分攤

▶She left after she finished her share of work.
她做完她份內的工作後就離開了。

v. 分擔；分享

▶They shared the joy of welcoming their baby with us.
他們與我們分享喜獲子女的喜悅。

shark [`ʃɑrk] ◀⟨ Track 4298

n. 鯊魚；貪婪狡猾的人；詐騙者

▶The swimmers rushed ashore when they found a skark in the sea.
游泳者發現鯊魚在海中，急忙趕著上岸。

sharp [ʃɑrp] ◀⟨ Track 4299

adj. 尖銳的；鋒利的；急劇的

The blade of the knife is rather sharp; be careful when you use it.
這把刀的刀鋒很利，使用時請小心。

sharpen [`ʃɑrpn] ◀⟨ Track 4300

v. 削尖，使變鋒利；加劇

中級

▶The cold weather sharpened his discomfort in my joints.
天氣冷使我的關節感到更加不舒服。

shave [ʃev]   ◀Track 4301
v. 刮（鬍子等）

▶He hasn't shaved for a week.
他一個禮拜沒刮鬍子了。

shaver ['ʃevɚ]   ◀Track 4302
n. 理髮師；剃鬍刀；小伙子

▶I bought a shaver for my father as his birthday gift.
我買了刮鬍刀給我爸爸做他的生日禮物。

she [ʃi] pron. 她   ◀Track 4303

▶She deserves better treatment than this.
她值得比這個更好的對待。

she'd [ʃid]   ◀Track 4304
abbr. 她會、她已（she had或she would的縮寫）

▶She'd be rather satisfied when she learns about your achievement.
當她知道你的成就時，一定會很滿意的。

sheep [ʃip] n. 羊；綿羊   ◀Track 4305

▶The farmer showed us how to shave sheep.
農夫示範如何幫羊剃毛。

sheet [ʃit]   ◀Track 4306
n. 床單；（一張）紙

▶She jotted down the key points of the lecture on a sheet of paper.
她在一張紙上記下演講的重點。

shelf [ʃɛlf] n. 架子；擱板   ◀Track 4307

▶The album she wants to buy is on the top of the shelf.
她想要買的那張專輯在架子的頂端。

shell [ʃɛl]   ◀Track 4308
n. 殼；外殼；甲殼

▶Ellen picked a shell from the seashore and brought it home.
艾倫從沙灘上撿了一個貝殼並且把它帶回家。

she'll [ʃil]   ◀Track 4309
abbr. 她會（she will的縮寫）

▶Tell her the truth. She'll understand.
告訴她實話吧。她會理解的。

shelter ['ʃɛltɚ]   ◀Track 4310
n. 避難所；遮蔽物；庇護，掩蔽

▶They took shelter in the cave during the storm.
暴風雨時，他們在山洞裡避難。

v. 掩蔽，遮蔽；庇護；避難

▶He was guilty for sheltering the criminal.
他犯下藏匿犯人的罪行。

shepherd ['ʃɛpɚd]   ◀Track 4311
n. 牧羊人

▶The shepherd whistled and the sheep gathered in front of him.
牧羊人一吹口哨，羊群就聚集到他面前。

v. 牧（羊）；指導，帶領；護送

▶The zookeeper shepherded the penguins into the cave.
動物園管理員將企鵝趕入洞穴中。

she's [ʃiz]   ◀Track 4312
abbr. 她是（she is的縮寫）

▶ She's the most devoted worker in our company.
她是我們公司最奉獻心力的員工。

shift [ʃɪft]　◀Track 4313

v. 轉移，替換；變換

▶ Why do you keep shifting channel?
你為什麼一直轉台呢？

n. 轉換，轉移；輪班

▶ Daved worked night shifts for three consecutive days.
大衛已經連續三天值夜班。

shine [ʃaɪn] **v.** 發光；照耀　◀Track 4314

▶ The joy of winning the prize shone on her face.
得獎的喜悅顯露在她的臉上。

shiny [`ʃaɪnɪ] **adj.** 發光的　◀Track 4315

▶ The shiny neon lights are a symbol of prosperity of the city.
閃亮的霓虹燈是這座城市繁榮的象徵。

ship [ʃɪp] **n.** 船　◀Track 4316

▶ The wrecks of the ship were finally found after three decades.
船隻的殘骸在三十年後終於被發現了。

v. 船運；運送

▶ The goods will be shipped after the payment is made.
付款之後就會出貨。

shirt [ʃɝt]　◀Track 4317

n. 襯衫；男式襯衫

▶ The yellow tie doesn't match the blue shirt.
這條黃色的領帶和藍色的襯衫不搭。

shock [ʃak]　◀Track 4318

n. 衝擊；震驚；打擊；中風

▶ The new that his daughter got pregnant was a shock to Ted.
女兒懷孕的消息對泰德來說是個衝擊。

shocked [ʃakt]　◀Track 4319

v. 使震動；使震驚；使人感到震驚

▶ We were all shocked by the news that the sports meeting was cancelled.
我們聽說運動會取消的消息都感到很震驚。

shoe [ʃu] **n.** 鞋子　◀Track 4320

▶ The dance shoes of the ballerina were worn out.
這位芭蕾舞女演員的舞鞋都穿壞了。

shoot [ʃut]　◀Track 4321

v. 放射；開槍；射中；幼芽

▶ The hunter shot the cheetah but missed.
獵人開槍射擊印度豹結果沒打中。

n. 射擊；拍攝；狩獵會；幼芽

▶ Bamboo shoots are commonly used in Chinese cuisines.
竹筍是中國菜裡常見的食材。

shop [ʃap]　◀Track 4322
=store **n.** 商店

▶ The antique shop is having a sale.
這間古董店正在辦特賣會。

v. 購物；逛商店

▶ Some foreign tourists like to shop for local handcrafts when they visit this town.
有些外國遊客來到這個小鎮時喜歡購買當地的手工藝品。

中級

shopkeeper
🔊 Track 4323

[ˋʃɑpˏkipɚ] **n** 店主，店經理

▶The shopkeeper is out of town today.
老闆今天不在城裡。

shopping [ˋʃɑpɪŋ]
🔊 Track 4324

n 買東西，購物

▶People in the downtown area enjoy the convenience of online shopping.
城裡的人們享受網路購物的便利。

shore [ʃɔr] **n** 岸；濱
🔊 Track 4325

▶Some dolphins were stranded on the shore. 有些海豚擱淺在岸上。

short [ʃɔrt]
🔊 Track 4326

adj 矮的；短的

▶The short clips on Tik Tok are quite popular these days.
最近抖音上面的短視頻相當受歡迎。

shortage [ˋʃɔrtɪdʒ]
🔊 Track 4327

n 缺少，不足，匱乏

▶People in the remote village suffer from the shortage of clean water and daily necessities.
住在這個偏遠村莊的居民因乾淨用水和日常用品的短缺而受苦。

shortcoming
🔊 Track 4328

[ˋʃɔrtˏkʌmɪŋ] **n** 缺點，短處

▶Even the most achieved man in the company has some shortcomings.
即使是公司裡最有成就的人也會有一些缺點。

shortcut [ˋʃɔrtˏkʌt]
🔊 Track 4329

n 捷徑；近路；快捷辦法

▶The taxi driver claimed that he took the shortcut, but it took me longer to reach my destination.
計程車司機說他是抄截徑，但是我花了更長的時間才到達目的地。

補充片語 take a shortcut 抄近路

shorten [ˋʃɔrtn]
🔊 Track 4330

v 使變短，縮短，減少

▶The High Speed Rail has shortened the travel time between Taipei and Kaphsiung.
高鐵已經縮短了台北到高雄的交通時間。

shortly [ˋʃɔrtlɪ]
🔊 Track 4331

adv 立刻，馬上，不久；簡短地

▶We will deal with the problem shortly.
我們會很快地處理這個問題。

shorts [ʃɔrts]
🔊 Track 4332

n 短褲；寬鬆運動短褲

▶It's considered improper to wear shorts and slippers to the office.
一般認為穿短褲和拖鞋去上班是不適當的。

short-sighted
🔊 Track 4333

[ˋʃɔrtˋsaɪtɪd] **adj** 近視的；目光短淺的

▶Don't be short-sighted; think about the long-term effect of your deeds.
目光別太短淺，要考慮你的作為會造成什麼長遠的影響。

shot [ʃɑt]
🔊 Track 4334

n 射擊；射門；嘗試

▶The audience cheered after the player made a good shot.
這名選手漂亮地射擊之後，觀眾歡呼。

should [ʃʊd] **aux.** 應該 ◀Track 4335

▶You should watch your diet to remain slim.
你要注意飲食才能保持苗條。

shoulder [ˋʃoldɚ] ◀Track 4336

n. 肩膀

▶The worker carried two sacks of wheat on his shoulders.
工人扛了兩袋小麥在肩膀上。

shouldn't [ˋʃʊdnt] ◀Track 4337

abbr 不該（**should not**的縮寫）

▶They shouldn't keep the money as their own.
他們不應該把這筆錢據為己有。

shout [ʃaʊt] ◀Track 4338

v. 呼喊；喊叫

▶The robber shouted at the bank clerks, demanding that they hand over the money.
搶匪對銀行行員大喊，要求他們把錢交出來。

n. 呼喊；喊

▶The children's shouts could be heard from outside of the school gate.
小朋友的叫喊聲從校門外面就聽得見了。

shovel [ˋʃʌvl̩] ◀Track 4339

n. 鏟子；鐵鍬

▶The gardener needs a new shovel.
這名園丁需要一個新的鏟子。

v. 用鏟子剷；用鐵鍬挖；用剷工作

▶He shoveled the snow off the roof.
他用鏟子把雪從屋頂上面鏟下來。

show [ʃo] ◀Track 4340

v. 顯示；顯露；展示；演出；出示；帶領

▶The director of the personnel department showed us around in the company.
人事部門的主任帶我們參觀公司。

n. 展覽；表現；表演；演出節目

▶The show was postponed due to some glitches in the sound system.
這場表演因為音響系統有些問題而延後了。

shower [ˋʃaʊɚ] ◀Track 4341

n. 陣雨；淋浴

▶She took a shower after working out in the gym.
去健身房運動之後，她沖了一個澡。

v. 下陣雨；沖澡

▶Hardly had we arrived home did it start to shower.
我們一回到家，就開始下雨了。

shrimp [ʃrɪmp] **n.** 蝦 ◀Track 4342

▶The shrimp cocktail is a great appetite.
雞尾酒蝦是一個很好的開胃菜。

shrink [ʃrɪŋk] ◀Track 4343

v. 縮，縮小；退縮；變小；退

▶He shrank when he realized how demanding the job was.
他知道這個工作有多麼嚴苛之後，就退縮了。

n. 收縮；畏縮；【俚】精神科醫生

▶The young lady was encouraged to visit a shrink after the traumatic experience.
在歷經創傷之後，這名年輕女士被鼓勵去看精神科醫生。

shrug [ʃrʌg] ◀Track 4344

v. 聳（肩）

中級

429

▶He just shrugged when I asked him why he failed the test.
我問他為什麼考試不及格的時候，他只是聳聳肩膀。

n. 聳肩

▶The guest skipped the question of the host with a shrug.
來賓聳肩，不回答主持人的問題。

相關片語 **shrug off** 不理

▶He could shrug off the troubles and focus on things that really matter.
他可以不理這些煩惱，專注在真正重要的事情上面。

shut [ʃʌt] v 關閉
◀Track 4345

▶The machine suddenly shut down because of the power outage.
因為停電的關係，機器突然關閉了。

shuttle [ˈʃʌtl̩]
◀Track 4346

n. 梭子；短程穿梭運行的車輛

▶The shuttle bus was scheduled to set off at 10:00 A.M.
接駁車預計在早上十點出發。

v 短程穿梭般運送；短程穿梭般往返

▶We shuttled the students between the two campuses of the university.
我們將學生來回載往兩個大學校區之間。

shy [ʃaɪ]
◀Track 4347

adj. 害羞的；靦腆的

▶He was too shy to speak to the girl he had a crush on.
他太害羞不敢跟喜歡的女生說話。

sick [sɪk]
◀Track 4348

adj. 病的；想吐的；對……厭煩的

▶He was sick of the words of the hypocratic politician.
他對於那個虛偽政治人物的話感到厭煩。

sickness [ˈsɪknɪs]
◀Track 4349

n. 病，疾病；噁心，嘔吐

▶The passenger suffered from motion sickness.
乘客暈車了。

相關片語 **sickness leave** 病假

▶Rita took a sickness leave, so I took over her tasks.
瑞塔請病假，所以我代為處理她負責的事情。

side [saɪd] n 邊；面；一方
◀Track 4350

▶Bullying and being bullied are often two sides of the same coin.
霸凌和被霸凌常常是一體兩面。

sidewalk [ˈsaɪdˌwɔk]
◀Track 4351
=pave·ment （英式英文）

n. 人行道

▶The water hydrant on the sidewalk was broken.
人行道上的消防栓被弄壞了。

sigh [saɪ] v 嘆息
◀Track 4352

▶She sighed with relief when she knew that she passed the certificate test.
她通過證照考試的時候，放鬆地嘆了一口氣。

n. 嘆息，嘆氣

▶He let out a sigh of relief when he finished the model ship inside the bottle.
他完成瓶中船模型時，鬆了一口氣。

sight [saɪt]
🔊 Track 4353

n. 視覺；看見；視界

▶ At the sight of the cockroach, the girl started to scream.
一看見蟑螂，女孩就開始尖叫。

相關片語 **lost sight of** 忽略

▶ He didn't lose sight of discretion even in the moment of joviality.
即使在歡樂的氣氛中，他也不會忘記行事要謹慎。

sightseeing [`saɪtˌsiɪŋ]
🔊 Track 4354

n. 觀光；遊覽

▶ The tourists enjoyed sightseeing in this ancient city.
這群觀光客很喜歡在這座古城中的觀光活動。

sign [saɪn] **v.** 簽名
🔊 Track 4355

▶ The author signed on the books for the readers.
這名作家為讀者簽書。

n. 記號；標牌；手勢

▶ There is a direction sign by the road.
路旁有一個指引方向的標牌。

signal [`sɪgnl]
🔊 Track 4356

n. 信號

▶ The signal was interfered because of the skyscrapers.
信號被摩天大樓所阻擋。

v. 用信號發出；打信號；以動作示意

▶ The manager signaled me to bring the document into the meeting room.
經理用動作示意要我拿資料去會議室。

signature [`sɪgnətʃɚ]
🔊 Track 4357

n. 簽名

▶ The mitt with the signature of the famous baseball player was sold at a high price on the auction. 知名棒球選手簽名的手套在拍賣會上以高價賣出。

significance
🔊 Track 4358

[sɪg`nɪfəkəns] **n.** 重要性；意義，含義

▶ Their opinion were of little significance.
他們的意見無關緊要。

significant
🔊 Track 4359

[sɪg`nɪfəkənt] **adj.** 有意義的；重要的

▶ This project is a significant breakthrough in our business.
這項計畫是我們事業的重大突破。

相關片語 **significant other** 另一半

▶ You should be honest with your significant other.
你應該要對另一半誠實。

silence [`saɪləns]
🔊 Track 4360

n. 沉默；無聲

▶ Silence is gold.
沉默是金。

silent [`saɪlənt]
🔊 Track 4361

adj. 沉默的；默不作聲的

▶ The suspect remained silent when the prosecutor questioned him.
檢察官訊問嫌犯的時候，他沉默不語。

silk [sɪlk] **n.** 絲
🔊 Track 4362

▶ The scarf is made of silk.
這條圍巾是絲做成的。

adj. 絲的；絲織的

▶ The silk fabric was sold at a high price.
這個絲綢質料以高價售出。

中級

silly [`sɪlɪ]

◀Track 4363

adj. 糊塗的;愚蠢的

▶He said some silly words to the girl he had a crush on.
他對喜歡的女孩子説了一些愚蠢的話。

silver [`sɪlvɚ]

◀Track 4364

n. 銀;銀色;銀牌

▶Silver and gold are the colors representive of prosperity and wealth.
銀色和金色是象徵繁榮和財富的顏色。

adj. 銀的

▶The silver bullet was used to kill the monster.
銀色子彈被用來殺死怪物。

similar [`sɪmələ]

◀Track 4365

adj. 相似的;相像的

▶His opinion is similar to ours.
他的看法和我們相似。

similarity

◀Track 4366

[ˌsɪmə`lærətɪ] **n.** 類似;相似

▶We were accused of plagiarizing becaue our report had a lot of similarities with a previous research.
我們被指控抄襲,因為我們的報告和一個先前的研究有很多相似處。

simple [`sɪmpl]

◀Track 4367

adj. 簡單的;簡樸的;單純的

▶He leads a simple and thrift life.
他過著簡樸節儉的生活。

simplify [`sɪmplə͵faɪ]

◀Track 4368

v. 簡化,使單純

▶This version of the Shakesperean play, which had been simplified, was the required material for the students.
這個簡化版的莎士比亞劇本是這些學生的必讀教材。

simply [`sɪmplɪ]

◀Track 4369

adv. 簡單地;樸素地;僅僅;簡直

▶This is simply beyond my competence.
這簡直超出我能力範圍了。

sin [sɪn]

◀Track 4370

n. (道德上的)罪孽,罪惡;(違反禮俗的)過錯

▶To the Christians, gluttony is a sin.
對基督教徒而言,暴食是種罪。

v. 犯罪,違命;犯過失

▶Everyone must have sinned to some extent.
每個人一定都在某些程度上犯過錯誤。

相關片語 **as ugly as sin**
非常醜陋,非常難看

▶Finding esxcuses was as ugly as a sin.
找藉口這件事很難看。

since [sɪns]

◀Track 4371

conj. 自從;既然;因為

▶The players went back to their home country since their team were eliminated from the tournament.
因為沒進入總決賽,這些選手就返回自己國家了。

prep. 自……以來

▶I have been working on my thesis since last January.
我從去年一月開始就在寫論文了。

adv. 此後;之前

▶He immigrated to Canada, and I haven't heard from him ever since.
他移民到加拿大之後，我就沒再聽到他的消息了。

sincere [sɪn`sɪr]
◀Track 4372

adj. 誠摯的；衷心的

▶I expressed my sincere gratitude with a hand-written card.
我用手寫的卡片表達誠摯的感謝。

sincerely [sɪn`sɪrlɪ]
◀Track 4373

adv. 衷心地，誠摯地

▶We sincerely hope that the Democratic Party could win the election campaign.
我們衷心希望民主黨可以贏得這次選舉。

sing [sɪŋ] v 唱；唱歌
◀Track 4374

▶She has a beautiful voice; she must be good at singing.
她有美妙的嗓音，她一定很會唱歌。

Singapore
◀Track 4375

[`sɪŋgə,por] **n.** 新加坡

▶We will catch our transit flight in Singapore.
我們會在新加坡轉機。

Singaporean
◀Track 4376

[,sɪŋgə`pɔrɪən] **adj.** 新加坡的，新加坡人的

▶In Singaporian English, some sentences are simplified.
在新加坡英文裡，有些句子會被簡化。

n. 新加坡人

▶The Singaporean will study EMBA with us is the following months.
這位新加坡人接下來幾個月會和我們一起學習商業管理學程。

singer [`sɪŋɚ]
◀Track 4377

n. 歌手；歌唱家

▶The singer who wins the competition will have a chance to release a personal album.
贏得這場比賽的歌手，將有出個人專輯的機會。

singing [`sɪŋɪŋ] **n.** 唱歌
◀Track 4378

▶Singing and watching movies are her favorite pastimes.
唱歌和看電影是她最喜歡的休閒活動。

single [`sɪŋgl̩]
◀Track 4379

adj. 單一的；單身的

▶The single mother stuggled to raise up her two children.
這名單親媽媽努力扶養她的兩個孩子。

n. 單個；單身者；單打比賽

▶She won the women's singles in the badminton competition in London.
她在倫敦贏得女子羽球單打的比賽。

singular [`sɪŋgjələ]
◀Track 4380

adj. 單數的，單一的；非凡的，卓越的；異常的，奇異的

▶People say that Dr. Hawking has some singular characteristics.
人們説霍金博士有一些奇異的特質。

sink [sɪŋk]
◀Track 4381

n. 流理台；水槽

▶Mike replaced a rusty sink with a new one.
麥克把生鏽的水槽換成了新的。

v. 下沉；沒落

▶The boat sank after it hit the rock.
船撞到礁岩後就沉了。

中級

sip [sɪp] v 小口喝
Track 4382

▶The barista sipped the coffee to tell its quality.
咖啡師啜飲咖啡，判斷它的品質。

n. 啜飲

▶We had a sip of the tea and enjoyed its fragrance.
我們小口飲茶，享受它的香氣。

sir [sɝ]
Track 4383

n. 先生；老師；長官

▶Good evening, sir. How may I help you?
先生晚安。請問需要什麼協助嗎？

sister [`sɪstɚ] n 姐妹
Track 4384

▶My younger sister dreamt to be a fashion model.
我妹妹過去想要當時尚模特兒。

sit [sɪt] v 坐
Track 4385

▶The cat sat on the toilet lid and wouldn't leave.
貓坐在馬桶蓋上不肯離開。

site [saɪt]
Track 4386

n. 地點，場所；舊址；部位

▶The architect went to the construction site and gave instructions to the workers.
這名建築師到工地去給工人指示。

相關片語 camping site（露營）營地

▶A wild bear sneaked into the camping site to steal food.
一隻野熊潛入了營地偷吃食物。

situation [ˌsɪtʃʊ`eʃən]
Track 4387

n. 處境，境遇；情況，情形

▶We could not take any further actions before the situation is clear.
在狀況明確之前，我們不能做任何進一步的動作。

six [sɪks] pron. 六個；n 六
Track 4388

▶Six plus three equals nine.
六加三等於九。

adj. 六的

▶The parcel contains six books.
這個小包裹中裝有六本書。

sixteen [`sɪks`tin]
Track 4389

n. 十六

▶Nine pluse seven equals sixteen.
九加七等於十六。

adj. 十六的；十六個的

▶Sixteen students in the class are near-sighted.
班上有十六個學生近視。

sixty [`sɪkstɪ]
Track 4390

n. 六十；六十年代

▶These car were produced in the sixties.
這些車是在六十年代製造的。

adj. 六十的；六十個的

▶There are around sixty people gathering in front of the police station.
大約有六十個人現正聚集在警察局前面。

size [saɪz] n 尺寸；大小
Track 4391

▶The model wearing the size of six was once criticized for being "out of shape."
這名穿六號尺寸的的模特兒曾經被批評「身材走樣」。

skate [sket]
◀≣Track 4392

n. 冰鞋；四輪溜冰鞋

▶My birthday wish is to get a pair of skates.
我的生日願望就是要得到一雙溜冰鞋。

v. 溜冰

▶Some kids skated on the iced river.
有些小孩在結冰的河上溜冰。

skating [`sketɪŋ]
◀≣Track 4393

n. 溜冰，滑冰

▶We went skating in the ice palace in the downtown area.
我們去市中心的冰宮溜冰。

sketch [skɛtʃ]
◀≣Track 4394

n. 速寫，素描；略圖，草稿

▶She made a lively sketch of her cat.
她為貓咪畫了栩栩如生的素描。

v. 寫生，速寫；為……畫草圖

▶He sketched the aboriginal woman in ten minutes.
他在十分鐘內畫了一幅原住民婦女的素描。

ski [ski] **n.** 滑雪板
◀≣Track 4395

▶The tourists rent skis at the ski resort.
這群觀光客在滑雪度假村裡租借滑雪板。

v. 滑雪

▶The local residents sometimes ski on this trail.
當地居民有時候會在這條小路上滑雪。

skiing [`skiɪŋ] **n.** 滑雪
◀≣Track 4396

▶The map will show you the spots that fit your skiing ability.
這張地圖會顯示符合你滑雪能力的滑雪地點。

skill [`skɪl]
◀≣Track 4397

n. （專門）技術；技巧；技能

▶Translation requires good skills in comprehending source language and great proficiency in target language.
翻譯需要對原言很好的理解能力，以及對目標語言很好的流利度。

skilled [skɪld]
◀≣Track 4398

adj. 熟練的；有技能的

▶The skilled labors can get a higher salary.
技術純熟的勞工可以得到較高的薪水。

skillful [`skɪlfəl]
◀≣Track 4399

=skilful （英式英文）

adj. 有技術的；熟練的

▶My father is a skillful carpenter; he made a shelf and a rocking chair for my grandfather.
我爸爸是個技術很好的木工；他幫我的祖父做了一個書架和一張搖椅。

skim [skɪm]
◀≣Track 4400

v. 撇去，去除；飛快地掠過；瀏覽

▶She skimmed the greasy layer of the soup to remove the fat.
她撇過湯上面那油膩的一層，把油去掉。

n. 撇；撇去的東西；略過；表面層；脫脂牛奶

▶The skim of the ice on the car melt as the sun rose.
太陽出來時，車上這層薄冰就融化了。

skin [skɪn] **n.** 皮；皮膚
◀≣Track 4401

▶Allergies to seefood cause him to have rashes on the skin.
對海鮮過敏導致他皮膚上出現疹子。

中級

skinny [ˈskɪnɪ] ◀€ Track 4402

adj. 皮的；皮包骨的、極瘦的

▶The skinny boy was bullied at school.
這名削瘦的男孩在學校遭到霸凌。

skip [skɪp] ◀€ Track 4403

v. 跳來跳去，跳躍；略過

▶The lecturer skipped a PPT slide and moved on to the next section.
這名演講者跳過一張投影片，繼續講下一個段落。

n. 跳，蹦；省略

▶She gave a skip of joy when she learned that she was admitted to her dream university.
聽到自己考上夢想的大學，她高興地跳了起來。

skirt [skɝt] ◀€ Track 4404

n. 裙；裙子

▶She bought a lace skirt on Amazon.
她在亞馬遜網站上買了一件蕾絲的裙子。

v. 位於……邊緣；繞過……的邊緣

▶We drove along the road which skirted the town.
我們沿著繞行村莊的道路開。

sky [skaɪ] **n.** 天空 ◀€ Track 4405

▶The view of the azure sky and ocean was stunning.
藍天碧海的景色很美。

skyscraper ◀€ Track 4406

[ˈskaɪˌskrepɚ] **n.** 摩天大樓，參天高樓

▶Dozens of skyscrapers were established in the city in the last decade.
在過去十年間，城市裡建了好幾十棟的摩天大樓。

slang [slæŋ] **n.** 俚語 ◀€ Track 4407

▶I had trouble understanding the slangs in the teenagers' conversation.
我聽不太懂這群青少年對話中的俚語。

slave [slev] **n.** 奴隸 ◀€ Track 4408

▶The slaves were emancipated after the Civil War.
南北戰爭之後，奴隸就被解放了。

v. 奴隸般工作；苦幹

▶We slaved over the project, but everything turned out to be in vain.
我們埋頭苦幹進行計畫，但最後所有事情都是白費工夫。

slavery [ˈslevərɪ] ◀€ Track 4409

n. 奴役，奴隸制度；奴隸身分

▶Slavery still remains in some of the underdeveloped countries.
奴隸制度在一些落後國家中仍然存在。

sleep [slip] **v.** 睡覺 ◀€ Track 4410

▶The panda sleeps for more than ten hours a day.
熊貓每天睡十個小時以上。

n. 睡眠

▶Depravation of sleep may cause poor work efficiency.
睡眠不足會造成工作效率低。

sleepy [ˈslipɪ] ◀€ Track 4411

adj. 昏昏欲睡的；想睡的

▶The students became sleepy in the first session in the afternoon.
學生在下午第一節課感到昏昏欲睡。

sleeve [sliv] ◀€ Track 4412

n. 袖子；袖套

▶There are some patches on the sleeves of this shirt.
這件襯衫袖子上面有一些補丁。

相關片語 **roll up one's sleeves** （捲起袖子）準備行動，準備幹活

▶He rolled up his sleeves and started to work on his album.
他準備要開始籌備自己的專輯。

slender [`slɛndɚ] ◀╡Track 4413
adj. 修長的；苗條的；纖細的；微薄的

▶She watches over her diet and exercises regularly to remain slender.
她很注意飲食，並且規律運動，以保持苗條。

slice [slaɪs] ◀╡Track 4414
n. （一）薄片，片；部分，份

▶I had a slice of the cheese cake for afternoon tea.
我下午茶吃一塊起司蛋糕。

v. 把……切成薄片；切下，切開；把……分成部分

▶The chef demonstrated how to slice the onion without shedding tears.
廚師示範如何切洋蔥不會流淚。

slide [slaɪd] ◀╡Track 4415
v. 滑；滑落；悄悄地走

▶He slid into the bad habit of phubbing on the smart phone.
他養成低頭滑手機的壞習慣。

n. 溜滑

▶There is an inflated escape slide beside the stairs.
樓梯旁邊有一個充氣的逃生滑梯。

slight [slaɪt] ◀╡Track 4416
adj. 輕微的；少量的；極不重要的

▶There is a slight difference between the two academic programs.
這兩個學術課程之間有些微的差異。

v. 輕視；藐視；怠慢

▶The professor never slighted his peers; he respected the professional suggestions from his colleagues.
教授從來不會輕視同輩，他尊重同事給的專業建議。

n. 輕蔑，怠慢

▶Despite the words of slight from his colleagues, Mina strived to accomplish the task.
儘管同事說了些怠慢言語，米娜還是努力把任務完成了。

相關片語 **in the slightest** 絲毫

▶He could not comprehend the complex issue in the slightest.
他一點也無法理解那個複雜的問題。

slightly [`slaɪtlɪ] ◀╡Track 4417
adv. 輕微地，稍微地；嬌弱地

▶The price of the smartphone is slightly higher than that one.
這個手機的價格比那一台稍高。

slim [slɪm] ◀╡Track 4418
adj. 苗條的；微薄的；少的

▶The slim salary was not enough to support his family.
這份微薄的薪水是不夠扶養家庭的。

slip [slɪp] ◀╡Track 4419
v. 滑動；滑跤；滑落；溜

中級

▶She slipped out of the classroom when the teacher was not paying attention. 她趁老師不注意時溜出教室。

n. 滑動；下降；失足；意外事故

▶The slip of the pen had him criticized by many readers.
這次筆誤令他受到很多讀者批評。

slippers [`slɪpɚz]　◀Track 4420
n. 室內便鞋；淺口拖鞋

▶She attached a mop to the slippers so that she could clean the floor as she walked in the house.
她將抹布黏在拖鞋底下，這樣就可以在室內走路時清理地板。

slippery [`slɪpərɪ]　◀Track 4421
adj. 滑的，容易滑的；油滑的，靠不住的；須小心對待的；不穩定的

▶The wet and slippery road caused a car accident. 濕滑的道路造成車禍。

相關片語 **as slippery as an eel**
滑如泥鰍；如泥鰍般狡猾

▶That guy is as slippry as an eel; don't trust him.
那個人狡猾如泥鰍，別相信他。

slogan [`slogən]　◀Track 4422
n. 口號；標語

▶The slogan of McDonald's is known to many people.
麥當勞的標語很有名。

slope [slop]　◀Track 4423
n. 傾斜，坡度，斜面

▶The huge stone rolled down the slope and hit the cars parked by the roadside.
這個巨石滾下斜坡，撞到停在路邊的車。

v. 傾斜；使有坡度；【口】溜走

▶The trail sloped down to the community park. 這個小徑歪斜著往下到社區公園。

slow [slo]　◀Track 4424
adj. 慢的；緩緩的；耗時的；慢了的

▶I was not used to the slow pace in the small town.
我不習慣小鎮的緩慢步調。

v. 放慢；使慢；變慢

▶The runner slowed down in the last keilmeter of the race.
在最後一公里時，這名跑者放慢了速度。

adv. 慢了地；慢慢地

▶The clock runs slow, for it's out of battery. 因為電池沒電，時鐘越走越慢。

small [smɔl]　◀Track 4425
adj. 小的；少量的；瘦小的

▶Jerry rent a small apartment near his university.
傑瑞在他的大學附近租了一間小公寓。

smart [smart] **adj.** 聰明的　◀Track 4426

▶The smart kid knows how to flatter his parents to get what he wants.
這位聰明的小朋友知道怎麼迎合父母來得到他想要的東西。

smell [smɛl]　◀Track 4427
n. 氣味；嗅覺

▶The bad smell of the rotten meat made me feel like vomiting.
腐肉的壞氣味讓我覺得想吐。

v. 聞；嗅；聞出；發出氣味；有氣味

▶The burning incense smells gross.
燃燒中的線香聞起來臭臭的。

smile [smaɪl] **v.** 微笑　🔊Track 4428

▶We smiled at each other when we realized the connotations of the professors' words.
了解教授言外之意之後，我們對彼此微笑一下。

n. 微笑

▶The smile on her face showed that she was off guard.
她臉上的笑容顯示她卸下心防了。

smog [smɑg] **n.** 煙霧　🔊Track 4429

▶Breathing in smog may be harmful to the respiratory system.
吸入煙霧可能對呼吸系統有害。

smoke [smok]　🔊Track 4430
n. 煙；煙霧；一口煙

▶The kid in the burning house was chocked by the smoke.
火場中的小孩被濃煙嗆到。

v. 抽菸

▶He is a chain smoker; he has been smoking for more than a decade.
他是個老菸槍，他已經抽菸十年以上了。

smoking [`smokɪŋ]　🔊Track 4431
n. 抽菸

▶Smoking may cause lung cancer.
吸菸可能導致肺癌。

adj. 可抽菸的，冒煙的

▶The smoking chimneys of the factory was an iconic sight of the small town.
工廠冒煙的煙囪是這個小鎮常見的景象。

smoky [`smokɪ]　🔊Track 4432
adj. 冒煙的，煙霧彌漫的，冒氣的，有煙味的

▶We could not see anything in the smoky room.
在充滿煙霧的房間裡，什麼也看不見。

smooth [smuð]　🔊Track 4433
adj. 平滑的；平穩的；平坦的；流暢的，悅耳的；平和的，圓滑的；溫和的

▶She uses some moisturizer to keep her skin smooth.
她使用一些護膚霜使皮膚保持光滑。

v. 使平滑；使平坦；使優雅；變緩和；消除（皺紋、障礙、分歧等）

▶The activists devoted a lot of efforts to smooth the country's path to democratic reform.
這些激進份子投入很多努力讓國家民主改革之路更順利。

snack [snæk]　🔊Track 4434
n. 小吃；點心

▶The kindergarten kids had some snacks at three o'clock in the afternoon.
幼稚園小朋友在下午三點吃了一些點心。

v. 吃快餐；吃點

▶They snacked on some nuggets.
他們吃了一些雞塊當點心。

snail [snel] **n.** 蝸牛　🔊Track 4435

▶The aborigines considered fried snails a delicacy.
原住民認為炸的蝸牛是一個美味佳餚。

snake [snek] **n.** 蛇　🔊Track 4436

▶The snake got stuck on the railway and was run over by the train.
這條蛇卡在鐵軌上，被火車輾過。

中級

snap [snæp]

v. 猛咬；突然折斷；啪地關上

▶The angry boy snapped the pencil into two in anger.
他這位生氣的男孩將鉛筆折成兩半。

adj. 突然的，冷不防的

▶He made a snap decision on purchasing the apartment.
他匆忙下決定，買下這棟公寓。

n. 猛撲；攫奪；突然折斷；劈啪聲；快照；輕鬆的工作；脆餅

▶The door closed with a strang sound of snap.
門以一種奇怪的聲響啪地一聲關上了。

sneak [snik]
◄Track 4438

v. 偷偷地走；偷偷地逃避

▶The student sneaked out, trying to skip the class. 學生偷跑出教室，想要翹課。

sneakers [`snikɚz]
◄Track 4439

n. 運動鞋

▶The athlete keeps his first pair of sneakers that his mother bought for him. 這名運動員保留著他的第一雙球鞋。那是他母親買給他的。

sneaky [`sniki]
◄Track 4440

adj. 鬼鬼祟祟的

▶The sneaky actions of the shady character caught our attention.
這位形跡可疑的人所做的鬼祟行動引起了我們的注意。

sneeze [sniz] **v.** 打噴嚏
◄Track 4441

▶I sneezed as soon as I entered the dusty room.
我一到這個佈滿灰塵的房間就打噴嚏。

n. 噴嚏，噴嚏聲

▶His loud sneezes interrupted the lecturer.
他極大的噴嚏聲打斷了演講者。

相關片語 **not to be sneezed at**
不可輕視，不容小覷

▶We should take this match seriously. Our opponent is nothing to sneeze at.
我們要認真看待這場比賽。我們的對手不容小覷。

snow [sno] **n.** 雪
◄Track 4442

▶Some seals got lost in the snow; they couldn't find their way back to the seashore.
有些海豹在雪中迷路，牠們找不到回去海岸邊的路。

v. 下雪

▶It has snowed for three consecutive days.
已經連續下雪三天了。

snowman [`sno,mæn]
◄Track 4443

n. 雪人

▶The kids covered the snowman with their old clothes.
小朋友拿他們的舊衣服穿在雪人身上。

snowy [snoɪ] **adj.** 下雪的
◄Track 4444

▶On snowy days, drivers would be expecially careful on the road.
下雪的時候，駕駛們在路上會特別小心。

so [so]
◄Track 4445

adv. 這麼；多麼；如此地；因此

▶The coffee was so delicious that I asked for a refill.
這個咖啡太好喝了，所以我要求續杯。

conj. 所以；因此

▶He was under the weather, so he called in for a sick leave.
他不太舒服，所以打電話來請病假。

soap [sop] **n.** 肥皂
🔊 Track 4446

▶She used a lot of water to wash off the bubbles of the soap.
她用很多水把肥皂的泡泡沖掉。

v. 用肥皂洗

▶She soaped herslf all over.
她把自己全身上下塗滿肥皂。

sob [sɑb]
🔊 Track 4447

v. 嗚咽，嗚泣，哭訴

▶The lost boy stood by the street, sobbing.
走失的男孩站在街上哭。

| 相關片語 **sob oneself to sleep**
哭著入睡 |

▶She sobbed herself to sleep after she broke up with her boyfriend.
她和男朋友分手之後哭到睡著。

n. 嗚咽聲，嗚泣聲

▶The sobs from upstairs in the middle of the night were really creepy.
半夜樓上傳來的嗚泣聲讓人覺得很害怕。

soccer [`sokɚ]
🔊 Track 4448

n. 足球；足球運動

▶Conan plays soccer with his friends after school.
柯南放學後和同學一起踢足球。

sociable [`soʃəbl]
🔊 Track 4449

adj. 好交際的，社交性的，友善

▶The sociable personality made Randy a popular figure on campus. 好交際的個性讓藍迪在校園中成為受歡迎的人物。

social [`soʃəl]
🔊 Track 4450

adj. 社會的；社交的

▶The young ladies learned about social etiquette at school.
年輕女士們在學校學習社交禮儀。

society [sə`saɪətɪ]
🔊 Track 4451

n. 社會；社團；交際；交往

▶Members of the film society gathered every Saturday evening.
電影社團的成員每周六晚間聚會。

socket [`sɑkɪt]
🔊 Track 4452

n. 托座；插座；插口；（人體的）窩，槽，臼

▶The electric socket is beside the cabinet. 電源插座在櫃子旁邊。

socks [sɑks] **n.** 襪子
🔊 Track 4453

▶I was shocked when I learned that Peter never wore socks.
當我知道彼得從來不穿襪子的時候，我感到很震驚。

soda [`sodə]
🔊 Track 4454

n. 蘇打；蘇打水；汽水

▶The bartender added some soda to the cocktail.
調酒師在雞尾酒中加了一些汽水。

sofa [`sofə] **n.** 沙發
🔊 Track 4455

▶The Corgi snuggled with its owner on the sofa.
柯基犬在沙發上與主人依偎在一起。

中級

soft [sɔft]
🔊 Track 4456

adj. 柔軟的；輕柔的；柔和的

▶The soft music is soothing and relaxing.
這個柔和的音樂讓人覺得放鬆。

softball [`sɔft͵bɔl]
🔊 Track 4457

n. 壘球，壘球運動

▶The girls played softball in PE class.
女孩們在體育課時打壘球。

software [`sɔft͵wɛr]
🔊 Track 4458

n. （電腦）軟體

▶Click on the button of "help" to find instructions of installing the software.
點擊「取得協助」的按鈕，找到安裝軟體的指引。

soil [sɔɪl]
🔊 Track 4459

n. 泥土，土壤；土地，領土；溫床；污物；糞便，肥料；墮落

▶The exchange student was excited to step on the foreign soil .
這位交換學生在踏上異國土地時感到很興奮。

v. 弄髒，玷污；變髒

▶She soiled her hands when working in the orchard.
她在果園中工作的時候弄髒了雙手。

solar [`solɚ]
🔊 Track 4460

adj. 太陽的，日光的；利用太陽

▶They installed a solar power panel on their roof.
他們在屋頂上裝太陽能板。

soldier [`soldʒɚ]
🔊 Track 4461

n. 軍人；士兵

▶The soldier would never surrender to the enemy.
這名軍人永遠不會向敵人投降。

solid [`salɪd]
🔊 Track 4462

adj. 固體的，實心的；純的；牢靠的

▶He didn't have solid evidence to prove his innocence.
他沒有足夠的證據證明自己的清白。

n. 固體；立方體；固態物；固體食物

▶Heat may casue the mineral to turn from the solid state into liquid state.
熱能可以讓礦物質從固體變成液體。

solution [sə`luʃən]
🔊 Track 4463

n. 解答；解決辦法

▶The solution to the puzzle will be shown in the next section of the program.
謎題的解答會在節目的下個段落中呈現。

solve [salv] **v.** 解決
🔊 Track 4464

▶They tried every possible way, but still failed to solve the problem.
他們嘗試過各種方法，但還是無法解決這個問題。

some [sʌm] **pron.** 一些
🔊 Track 4465

▶Some of the staff may be recruited to the project team.
職員當中有一些人可能會被招募到計畫團隊中。

det. 一些的

▶Some sudents will go further their studies after graduation, while some might be looking for jobs.
有些學生畢業後會繼續念書，而其他人則會去找工作。

somebody
◀ Track 4466

[`sʌm͵badɪ]=some·one pron. 某人

▶Somebody called and said that he has something urgent to tell Mr. Watson, but he didn't leave any message.
有人打來說有急事要和華生先生說，但他沒有留言。

somebody's
◀ Track 4467

[`sʌm͵badɪz] abbr. 某人的；某人是
（**somebody is**的縮寫）

▶Somebody's purse was left on the MRT train.
有人把錢包遺留在捷運車廂中了。

somehow [`sʌm͵haʊ]
◀ Track 4468

adv. 由於某種未知的原因

▶Somehow I feel that he is not trustworthy.
不知為何，我覺得不能信任他。

someone [`sʌm͵wʌn]
◀ Track 4469

=somebody pron. 某人；有人

▶Don't be a hater on the Internet; someone would be hurt because of your nasty messages.
不要當網路酸民，有人會因為你惡意的留言而受傷。

something [`sʌmθɪŋ]
◀ Track 4470

pron. 某事；某件

▶It seems that something is bothering you.
你似乎正在煩惱某事。

sometimes
◀ Track 4471

[`sʌm͵taɪmz] adv. 有時候

▶They sometimes take actions without any plan.
他們有時候會完全沒有計畫就行動。

somewhat
◀ Track 4472

[`sʌm͵hwɑt] adv. 有點；稍微

▶The streets in my hometown has somewhat changed during the past few years.
我家鄉的街道在過去幾年有些改變。

somewhere
◀ Track 4473

[`sʌm͵hwɛr] adv. 某處；某個地方

▶After a long negotiation with the client, we are finally getting somewhere.
和顧客協商很久之後，終於有些進展了。

son [sʌn] n. 兒子
◀ Track 4474

▶She was really proud of her son.
她為兒子感到很驕傲。

song [sɔŋ] n. 歌曲；曲子
◀ Track 4475

▶The Shark Baby Song went viral on the Internet.
鯊魚寶寶歌在網路上被很多人分享。

soon [sun]
◀ Track 4476

adv. 馬上；立刻

▶After the Youtuber attend the TV show, she soon became very popular.
網路頻道經營者上過電視節目之後，立刻變得很受歡迎。

sore [sor] adj. 疼痛的
◀ Track 4477

▶He suffered from sore throat and runny nose.
他喉嚨痛又流鼻水。

n. （身體或精神的）痛處；瘡；潰瘍

中級

▶She brought up those old sores when we quarreled with each other.
我們吵架時，她又提起那些陳年舊帳。

sorrow [`sɑro]
n. 悲痛；悲哀

◀Track 4478

▶She was overwhelmed with sorrow when her pet cat died. 她的寵物貓死掉的時候，她悲傷得不能自己。

sorry [`sɑrɪ]
adj. 抱歉的；難過的

◀Track 4479

▶I feel sorry for your loss.
我為您的損失感到遺憾。

sort [sɔrt] **n.** 種類；類型

◀Track 4480

▶This shop offers all sorts of antique furniture.
這家店提供各種類型的古董家具。

v. 將……分類；區分

▶She sorted the documents by the years. 她依年份將文件分類。

soul [sol] **n.** 靈魂；心靈

◀Track 4481

▶He is the soul of the party.
他是這場派對的靈魂人物。

sound [saʊnd]
adj. 健康的，健全的，狀況良好的

◀Track 4482

▶After serving in the military for two years, he was still sound in body and mind.
在服兵役兩年之後，他還是身心健康。

soup [sup] **n.** 湯

◀Track 4483

▶The chef tasted the soup before he served it to the diners.
主廚在將湯端給客人之前，先試吃了一下。

sour [`saʊr]
adj. 酸的；酸臭的

◀Track 4484

▶The milk would go sour if you leave it under room temperatrure for too long.
如果把牛奶放在室溫下太久，它會酸掉。

source [sors]
n. 源頭；根源；來源

◀Track 4485

▶Check if the source of the news is reliable before you share it with your friends. 和朋友分享消息之前，要先確認消息來源是否可靠。

south [saʊθ] **n.** 南；南方

◀Track 4486

▶I will go to the university in the south.
我會去南方上大學。

adv. 朝南；往南；向南

▶The witness told the police that the criminal headed south.
目擊者告訴警方，罪犯往南方逃了。

adj. 南方的；南部的

▶The south part of the island has not been cultivated.
這個島嶼的南部還未開發過。

southeast [ˌsaʊθ`ist]
n. 東南，東南方；東南部

◀Track 4487

▶They build a fire power plant in the southeast of the island. 他們在這座島嶼的東南方建造一座火力發電廠。

adv. 在東南，向東南，來自東南

▶The migrant birds headed southeast.
這群候鳥往東南方飛。

adj. 東南的；向東南的；東南部的

▶There are some famous wineries in the southeast part of the country.
這個國家的東南部有一些知名的酒莊。

southern [`sʌðən]
◀Track 4488

adj. 在南方的；來自南方的

▶There is a slum in the southern part of the city.
這個城市的南方有個貧民窟。

---

south-west
◀Track 4489

[ˌsaʊθ`wɛst] **n.** 西南，西南方；西南部

▶He is from the southwest of the country.
他來自這個國家的西南部。

adv. 在西南，向西南，來自西南

▶They drove southwest to the mining community.
他們開車往西南方，去那個採礦的小鎮。

adj. 西南的；向西南的；西南部的

▶There are some aboriginal tribes in the southwest part of the county.
這個縣的西南方有一些原住民部落。

---

souve·nir [`suvəˌnɪr]
◀Track 4490

n. 紀念品；紀念物；伴手禮

▶I brought some souvenirs from Rome for my family.
我從羅馬帶了一些紀念品回來給我的家人。

---

sow [so]
◀Track 4491

v. 播種；散布，傳播

▶His preaches may sow seeds of hatred in the extremists.
他佈道的內容可能會在極端分子心中種下仇恨的種子。

---

soy sauce [`sɔɪ-sɔs]
◀Track 4492

n. 醬油

▶He added some soy sauce to add flavor to the braised pork.
他加了一些醬油調味燉豬肉。

---

soybean [`sɔɪbin]
=soy·a bean/soy **n.** 大豆
◀Track 4493

▶Miso is made from fermented soybeasns.
味增是發酵的大豆做成的。

---

space [spes]
◀Track 4494

n. 空間；場所；空地；宇宙、太空

▶The parking spaces in the office building are all occupied.
這棟辦公大樓裡的停車位都已經被佔滿了。

---

spacecraft
◀Track 4495

[`spesˌkræft] **n.** 太空船

▶The spacecraft is scheduled to lauch next month.
這艘太空船預計下個月發射。

---

spade [sped]
◀Track 4496

n. （撲克牌中的）黑桃；鏟子

▶He has the Ace of Spades.
他手上有黑桃的王牌。

---

spaghetti [spə`gɛtɪ]
◀Track 4497

n. 義大利麵

▶He had a Bolognese spaghetti for lunch.
他午餐吃義大利肉醬麵。

---

spare [spɛr]
◀Track 4498

adj. 多餘的，剩下的；備用的；節約的；少量的

▶They made use of the spare time to finishe the jigsaw puzzle.
他們用剩下的時間來完成這個拼圖。

▶They spared no effort to complete the task.
他們為了完成這個任務不遺餘力。

中級

補充片語 spare no effort 不遺餘力

n. 備用品；備用輪胎；備用零件

▶Excuse me. I forgot to bring my pen with me. Do you have a spare?
不好意思。我忘記帶筆了。你有備用的嗎？

spark [spɑrk] Track 4499

n. 火花，火星；生氣，活力；跡象，痕跡

▶There are some sparks in the electric cord.
這個電線裡面有些火花。

v. 發出火花；發動，點燃；激勵，鼓舞

▶This incident sparked his interet in stage play.
這個事件引起他對舞台劇的興趣。

sparkle [`spɑrkl] Track 4500

v. 發火光，閃耀；（才氣）煥發

▶Her eyes sparkled when she talked about her creation.
她談論創作時，眼中閃爍著光芒。

n. 火花，閃光；（才氣）煥發；活力，生氣

▶The interesting topics added sparkles to the conversation.
這些有趣的話題讓對話更有活力。

sparrow [`spæro] Track 4501

n. 麻雀

▶I heard the chirps of the sparrows in the early morning.
一大清早我就聽到麻雀的叫聲。

speak [spik] v. 說；說話 Track 4502

▶They have never spoken with each other since they broke up.
他們分手之後就沒再跟彼此說話過了。

speaker [`spikɚ] Track 4503

n. 說話者；說某種語言的人；演說家；擴音機

▶The eloquent speaker has a special charisma.
這位口才很好的演說者有種特別的魅力。

spear [spɪr] n. 矛；魚叉 Track 4504

▶The spear is made of bamboo.
這個魚叉是用竹子做成的。

v. 用矛或魚叉刺、戳

▶They speared the fish for dinner.
他們用叉子捕魚當晚餐。

special [`spɛʃəl] Track 4505

adj. 特別的

▶The TV stations would produce some special programs for Chinese New Year.
電視台會製作農曆新年的特別節目。

n. 特別的東西；特刊；特餐

▶The special on Friday is the risotto.
周五的特別菜是義大利燉飯。

specialized Track 4506

[`spɛʃəlˌaɪzd] adj. 專門的；專科的；專業的

▶He is specialized in data analysis.
他的專長是資料分析。

species [`spiʃiz] Track 4507

n. 種類；（生）種

▶The giant panda is an endangered species.
大熊貓是一種瀕危動物。

specific [spɪ`sɪfɪk] Track 4508

adj. 特殊的，特定的；明確的，具體的

▶The prfessor expected your report to be specific and to the point.
教授期望你的報告是明確而且切中要點的。

spectator [spɛk`tetɚ] ◀ Track 4509

n.（比賽等的）觀眾；旁觀者

▶The spectators booed the player when he used foul language against the umpire.
當球員以粗話辱罵裁判時，觀眾對他發出噓聲。

speech [spitʃ] ◀ Track 4510

n. 演說；說話；致辭

▶The president's inauguration speech was broadcast live on the Internet.
這位總統的就職致詞在網路上直播。

speed [spid] **n.** 速度 ◀ Track 4511

▶The train was running at a high speed.
火車高速行進中。

v. 迅速前進；加速

▶The sports car can speed up to 120 kilometers with 20 seconds.
這台跑車可以在20秒內加速到時速120公里。

spell [spɛl] ◀ Track 4512

n. 咒語；符咒；著魔

▶The witch cast a spell on the princess.
巫婆對公主下咒語。

spelling [`spɛlɪŋ] ◀ Track 4513

n. 拼字；拼寫；拼法

▶The software can help you find out the mistakes of spelling in your report.
這個軟體可以幫你找出報告中的拼字錯誤。

spend [spɛnd] ◀ Track 4514

v. 花費（時間、金錢、精力）

▶They spet a lot of time solving the jigsaw puzzle.
他們花很多時間拚好這個拼圖。

spice [spaɪs] **n.** 香料 ◀ Track 4515

▶The vendor in the bizaar sells some special spices.
這個市集的小販賣一些特別的香料。

v. 加香料於

▶The chef spiced the soup with come herbs.
廚師用一些香草調味這道湯品。

spicy [`spaɪsɪ] ◀ Track 4516

adj. 加有香料的；辛辣的

▶The foreign visitor loved the spicy taste of the beef soup.
這位外國的觀光客很喜歡牛肉湯的辣味。

spider [`spaɪdɚ] **n.** 蜘蛛 ◀ Track 4517

▶The deserted house was covered with spider webs.
廢棄的小屋充滿蜘蛛網。

spill [spɪl] ◀ Track 4518

v. 使溢出，使濺出；洩漏（秘密）

▶The boiliong water spilt over the pot.
滾水溢出鍋子外面。

n. 溢出；濺出；散落

▶The waiter cleaned the spill with a paper napkin.
服務生用紙餐巾清理溢出的東西。

spin [spɪn] ◀ Track 4519

v. 紡；吐（絲），結（網）；旋轉；編造，虛構

中級

▶The acrobat performer show the audience how to spin a top.
這名雜耍表演者向觀眾展示如何抽陀螺。

n. 旋轉；（車）疾馳；（飛機）盤旋下降；情緒低落；驚慌失措

▶She was in a spin over the applications to her ideal university.
她被申請理想大學的手續搞得昏頭轉向。

spinach [ˋspɪnɪtʃ] ◀Track 4520
n. 菠菜

▶The kids were afraid of the taste of the spinach.
小朋友害怕波菜的味道。

spirit [ˋspɪrɪt] ◀Track 4521
n. 精神；心靈；本意

▶It doesn't matter how much the present cost. It is the spirit that counts.
禮物多少錢不重要。重要的是心意。

spiritual [ˋspɪrɪtʃʊəl] ◀Track 4522
adj. 精神上的

▶He is my spiritual mentor; his encouragement means a lot to me.
他是我的心靈導師；他的鼓勵對我意義重大。

spit [spɪt] ◀Track 4523
v. 吐（口水、痰等）

▶Do not spit in public.
不要在大庭廣眾之下吐口水。

n. 唾液，口水；微雨，小雪

▶Hank's spit flew as he spoke on the stage.
漢克在台上說話的時候口沫橫飛。

spite [spaɪt] **n.** 惡意 ◀Track 4524

▶The villains broke his car windows out of spite.
這群惡棍們出於惡意打破了他的車窗。

splash [splæʃ] ◀Track 4525
v. 濺污；潑濕；使液體飛濺；【口】揮霍錢財

▶The waiter splashed the wine on the guest by accident.
服務生不小心把酒潑濺到客人身上。

n. 潑，灑，濺潑聲；濺上的污漬

▶The dog jumped into the pond with a splash. 狗撲通一聲跳進河裡。

相關片語 **make/create a splash**
引起轟動

▶He created a splash with his astonishing remarks.
他驚人的言論造成轟動。

splendid [ˋsplɛndɪd] ◀Track 4526
adj. 燦爛的；極令人滿意的

▶The splendid sunshine and the beautiful scene made me feel delighted.
燦爛的陽光和美麗的景色讓我覺得很開心。

split [splɪt] ◀Track 4527
v. 劈開，切開，撕裂；分裂

▶We splited the watermelon in half with a knife.
我們用刀子把西瓜切成兩半。

n. 裂縫，裂痕；分裂；（舞蹈中的）劈腿

▶There was a split in the class before the singing contest.
歌唱比賽之前，班上出現分裂。

adj. 裂開的，劈開的；分裂的，分離的

▶The mushrooms grew from the split log. 香菇從劈開的圓木中長出來。

spoil [spɔɪl] v 寵壞；毀壞 ◀ Track 4528

▶The rich man spoiled his daughter by offering her anything she asked for.
富翁只要女兒要什麼都會給她，把她給寵壞了。

n 戰略物，戰利品；競選勝利獲得的好處；獵物，贓物

▶The thieves divided up the spoils and separated from each other.
小偷們把贓物分了之後就分道揚鑣了。

spokesman [`spoksmən] n 發言人 ◀ Track 4529

▶The spokesman of the company had a press conference to make a formal statement.
公司的發言人開記者會發表正式的聲明。

sponsor [`spansɚ] ◀ Track 4530
v 資助，支持，倡議

▶They sponsored the charity campaign.
他們贊助這個慈善活動。

n 發起人，主辦者；贊助者；保人

▶The name of the sponsor was printed on the brochures of the activity.
贊助人的名字印在活動手冊上面。

spoon [spun] ◀ Track 4531
n 湯匙；一匙

▶The kid had a spoon of the soup and spitted it out.
小朋友喝了一湯匙的湯，就把它吐出來。

sport [sport] n 運動 ◀ Track 4532

▶She is not into sports; she prefers static activities.
她對運動不感興趣；她比較喜歡靜態的活動。

sportsman ◀ Track 4533
[`sportsmən] n 喜好運動的人、運動家

▶Respecting the game is what a good sportsman should do.
尊重比賽是一個運動家應該做的事情。

sportsmanship ◀ Track 4534
[`sportsmən ʃɪp] n 運動員精神

▶The athlets shaked hands with each other before and aftet the match to show the sportsmanship. 比賽前後，運動員互相握手，表現出運動家精神。

spot [spɑt] ◀ Track 4535
n 斑點；污點；場所；職位

▶Use the detergent to remove the spots of ink on the white shirt.
用這個洗潔劑清除白襯衫上面的墨水汙點。

v 玷污；弄髒；認出、發現

▶I spotted the suspect of the murder case near the crime scene.
我在犯案現場附近看到謀殺案的嫌疑犯。

spray [spre] ◀ Track 4536
n 浪花，飛沫；噴霧，噴霧器

▶A spray of chilli water made the robber struggle with pain.
辣椒水噴霧讓搶匪痛苦掙扎。

v 噴灑，噴

▶She sprays water on the strawberry plant every morning.
她每天早上給草莓灑水。

spread [sprɛd] ◀ Track 4537
v 使伸展；張開；塗、敷；散佈

▶She spread the paper on the table before she practices calligraphy.
她在練習書法之前，將紙攤開在桌上。

中級

n. 伸展；擴張；蔓

▶The authorities concerned are taking measures to stop the spread of the disease.
有關當局正採取措施阻止疾病蔓延。

---

sprinkle [`sprɪŋkl]　◀Track 4538

v. 灑，噴淋；使成點狀分布；點綴；下毛毛雨

▶According to the weather report, it will sprinkle this afternoon.
氣象報告說今天下午會下毛毛雨。

n. 毛毛雨；少量散步的東西；撒在表面的屑狀物

▶We put a sprinkle of salt on the surface of the steak.
我們在牛排的表面撒上一些鹽。

---

spy [spaɪ] **n.** 間諜，密探　◀Track 4539

▶The identity of the spy was revealed.
這名間諜的身分被揭穿了。

v. 當間諜；暗中監視；偵查；看見

▶He disguised as a businessman to spy the enemy.
他偽裝成商人，暗中監視敵人。

相關片語 **spy out the land** 摸清情形

▶The journalist made some inquiries about the sandal, trying to spy out the land.
記者詢問關於弊案的問題，想要摸清情形。

---

square [skwɛr]　◀Track 4540

n. 正方形；方型廣場

▶An outdoor concert will be held at the square in front of the municipal government office.
有一場室外音樂會將會在市政府辦公室前的廣場舉行。

adj. 正方形的；正直的；平方的；令人滿意的

▶There is an socket in each corner of the square room.
這個正方形房間的每個角落都有一個插座。

---

squeeze [skwiz]　◀Track 4541

v. 榨，擠，壓；緊握；強取；壓縮；勉強得到

▶I squeezed some lemon juice on the fish.
我擠了一些檸檬汁到這個魚肉上。

n. 壓榨；緊握；少量的榨汁；擁擠的一群；拮据

▶The manager gave my hand a squeeze.
經理緊握了我的手一下。

相關片語 **put the squeeze on sb.**
對……施加壓力

▶They put the squeeze on me, trying to force me into signing the contract.
他們對我施加壓力，想要逼我簽合約。

---

squirrel [`skwɝəl]　◀Track 4542

n. 松鼠

▶Don't feed the squirrel in the park.
不要餵食公園裡的松鼠。

---

stab [stæb]　◀Track 4543

v. 刺，戳；刺入，刺傷

▶The assassin stabbed the politician's abdomen with a knife.
刺客將刀刺進政客的腹部。

n. 刺，戳；刺破的傷口；突發的一陣（驚奇或疼痛）；【口】嘗試

▶He felt a stab of pain in the back.
他感到背部一陣疼痛。

stable [`stebl] adj. 穩定的 ◀ Track 4544

▶The operation system of the computer is not very stable.
這台電腦的運作系統不太穩定。

n. 馬房，馬棚，馬槽

▶He worked in a riding stable.
他在養馬場工作。

stadium [`stedɪəm] ◀ Track 4545

n. 體育場

▶The stadium can accommodate more than one thousand spectators.
這個體育場可以容納超過一千名觀眾。

staff [stæf] ◀ Track 4546

n. （全體）職員，（全體）工

▶The boss treated the whole staff of the company to a feast.
老闆請全體員工吃大餐。

v. 給……配備職員

▶The company was staffed with more than fifty workers.
這家公司有超過五十名員工。

stage [stedʒ] n. 舞台 ◀ Track 4547

▶The stage was decorated with neon lights. 舞台上裝飾著霓虹燈。

staircase [`stɛrˌkes] ◀ Track 4548

n. 樓梯

▶It's not allowed to place your personal stuff in the staircase.
不可以放置個人物品在樓梯間中。

相關片語 moving staircase 電梯

▶The moving staircase was not functioning normally this morning.
今天早上電梯沒有正常運作。

stairs [stɛrz] n. 樓梯 ◀ Track 4549

▶We took the stairs because the elevator was under repair.
因為電梯在整修，我們就爬樓梯。

stake [stek] ◀ Track 4550

n. 樁，棍子；股本，利害關係；賭注，賭金；危險，風險

▶We started our own business at the stake of losing our savings.
我們冒著失去積蓄的風險，建立自己的生意。

相關片語 pull up stakes 拔樁撤帳篷；跳槽（離開工作很久的工作或住很久的房子）

▶He pulled up stakes and transfered to another company.
他跳槽到其他的公司去。

stamp [stæmp] n. 郵票 ◀ Track 4551

▶The portrait of the monarch was printed on the stamps.
這名君主的頭像被印在郵票上。

v. 貼郵票於

▶The envelope was stamped, which means the postage was already paid.
郵票已經貼在信封上，代表郵資已付。

stand [stænd] v. 站；站立 ◀ Track 4552

▶He stood on the ladder to change the bulb.
他站在梯子上面換燈泡。

n. 站立；立場；攤子

▶There are dozens of stands in the bazaar.
這個市集當中有很多攤位。

中級

standard [`stændəd] ◀Track 4553
n. 標準；水準；規格

▶They had a high standard for the quality of their products.
他們對自己產品的要求很高。

adj. 標準的

▶They held a standard test to screen the qualified students for the program.
他們舉行一個標準考試來篩選和有資格就讀於此學程的學生。

star [star] **n.** 星星；明星 ◀Track 4554

▶They observed the stars in the night sky.
他們觀察夜空中的星星。

v. 當明星；主演

▶Brad Pett had starred in many well-known movies.
布萊德彼特主演過許多知名的電影。

stare [stɛr] **v.** 盯，凝視 ◀Track 4555

▶They stared at the screen during the game.
比賽進行中，他們緊盯著螢幕看。

n. 凝視，注視，瞪眼

▶He gave her an angry stare.
他怒視著她。

相關片語 **be staring sb. in the face**
就在某人眼前；十分明顯

▶The fact is staring you in the face; why aren't you aware of it?
事實就在你眼前；你怎麼沒發現呢？

start [start] **v.** 開始 ◀Track 4556

▶They started a campaign to raise fund for the underprivileged kids.
他們開始一個計劃進行募資，幫助貧困的小孩。

n. 開始；開端

▶He was very supportive to us from the start.
他從一開始就對很支持我們。

starvation ◀Track 4557
[star`veʃən] **n.** 飢餓；挨餓；餓死

▶Some kids in the area struck died of starvation.
在這個區域中有些小孩死於飢餓。

starve [starv] ◀Track 4558

v. 餓死；挨餓；餓得慌；渴望

▶Some animals starved to death during the drought.
有些動物在乾旱期間餓死。

state [stet] ◀Track 4559
n. 狀況，狀態；形態；情勢；國家，政府；身份，地位

▶There are currently fifty states in the U.S.
目前在美國有五十個州。

adj. 正式的，官方的；國家的，政府的

▶The state law forbits desserting pets.
州立法律禁止丟棄寵物。

相關片語 **state banquet** 國宴

▶The report is about the dishes of the state banquet.
這篇報導是有關於國宴的菜餚。

v. 陳述；聲明；說明

▶He stated his political position in the commentary on the news.
他在對這個新聞的評論中表明了自己的政治立場。

statement [`stetmənt] ◀Track 4560
n. 陳述；說明；正式聲明

▶The formal statement was released as soon as the scandal was publicized.
這項正式聲明在醜聞爆發之後就被公布了。

station [ˈsteʃən] ◀Track 4561

n. 車站；站、局、所

▶I work in the office building next to the train station.
我在火車站旁邊的辦公大樓上班。

stationery ◀Track 4562

[ˈsteʃənˌɛrɪ] **n.** 文具

▶Some students like to hang out at the stationery store near the school.
有些學生喜歡一起去學校旁邊的文具店。

statue [ˈstætʃʊ] ◀Track 4563

n. 雕像，塑像

▶The statue of martyr was damaged by some protesters.
烈士的雕像遭到抗議份子的破壞。

status [ˈstetəs] ◀Track 4564

n. 地位；身分

▶The status of women has been elevated in this country.
在這個國家中，婦女的地位有提升。

stay [ste] ◀Track 4565

v. 停留；暫住；保持；止住

▶We stayed in a hostal when we visited Denmark.
去丹麥旅遊時，我們住在青年旅館。

n. 停留

▶We had a good time during our stay in the Scandinavia region.
我們在斯堪地那維亞地區的停留期間玩得很開心。

steady [ˈstɛdɪ] ◀Track 4566

adj. 穩定的，平穩的；鎮靜的，沉穩

▶There is a steady growth in the economy of the country.
這個國家的經濟有穩定的成長。

v. 使穩固；使鎮定；變穩，穩固

▶He steadied his nerves before he contacted his ex-girlfriend.
他在連絡前女友之前，先穩定自己的心情。

steak [stek] ◀Track 4567

n. 牛排；肉排；魚排

▶I'd like my steak to be medium.
我想要五分熟的牛排。

steal [stil] **v.** 偷；偷竊 ◀Track 4568

▶He stole confidential information from the opponent company.
他從敵對的公司那裏偷取機密資訊。

steam [stim] ◀Track 4569

n. 蒸汽；水蒸汽；精力；氣力

▶The train used to be powered by steam. 火車以前是用蒸氣發動的。

v. 蒸煮；蒸發；用蒸汽開動

▶My mother is steaming the rice dumplings.
我媽媽正在蒸粽子。

steel [stil] **n.** 鋼；鋼鐵 ◀Track 4570

▶We offer a two-year warranty for the stainless steel door.
我們為這個不鏽鋼門提供兩年保固。

v. 鋼化；使像鋼，使堅強，使下決心

▶She has steeled herself to study abroad.
她下定決心要出國留學。

中級

steep [stip]
🔊 Track 4571

adj. 陡峭的;急劇升降的;(價格)過高的,不合理的

▶The hikers struggled to walk up the steep hill.
登山者掙扎地爬上陡峭的山丘。

steer [stɪr]
🔊 Track 4572

v. 掌舵,駕駛;指導,帶領,

▶She steered the discussion back to the theme.
她將討論帶回主題。

stem [stɛm]
🔊 Track 4573

v. 起源於;抽去……梗或莖

▶The word "tsunami" stems from Japanese.
「tsunami」這個單字是源自於日文。

n. 莖,幹,柄;船頭;詞幹

▶The stem and the petals of the rose were separated.
玫瑰花的莖和花瓣被分開了。

相關片語 **from stem to stern**
從(船)頭到(船)尾,完全

▶We inspected the manufacturing machine from stem to stern.
我們從頭到尾把生產機器檢查了一遍。

step [stɛp]
🔊 Track 4574

n. 腳步;一步的距離;步驟

▶Watch you steps when you board the train. 上車的時候注意腳步。

v. 踏、跨步;踏(進);踩

▶He wanted to step out of his comfort zone, so he moved out of his parents' house. 他想要跨出舒適圈,所以從父母的房子搬出去了。

stepfather
🔊 Track 4575

[`stɛp‚faðɚ] **n.** 繼父;後父

▶She accused her stepfather of abusing her.
她控訴她的繼父虐待她。

stepmother
🔊 Track 4576

[stɛp‚mʌðɚ] **n.** 繼母;後母

▶Cinderella's stepmother binded her feet to fit in the glass shoes.
仙杜瑞拉的繼母把腳纏小以穿進玻璃鞋。

stereo [`stɛrɪo]
🔊 Track 4577

adj. 立體聲的,立體音響的

▶There are some glitches in the stereo system, so the concert was postponed.
因為音響系統有點問題,所以演唱會延後了。

n. 立體音響裝置;體視系統;立體電影

▶Tom spent thirty thousand dollars on the stereos.
湯姆花了三萬元買這台立體音響裝置。

stick [stɪk]
🔊 Track 4578

n. 枝條;棍棒;手杖;棒狀物

▶The bird perched on the tree stick.
有一隻鳥兒棲息在枝條上。

v. 釘住;黏貼;伸出

▶We stick a coat hanger on the wall.
我們在牆上黏了一個外套的掛勾。

sticky [`stɪkɪ]
🔊 Track 4579

adj. 黏的;泥濘的;濕熱的

▶The sticky and stuffy air in the hot summer day makes me feel drowsy.
夏天濕黏的空氣讓我覺得昏昏欲睡。

stiff [stɪf]
◀ Track 4580

adj. 硬挺的；僵硬的；不靈活的

▶His neck seemed to be stiff after a long working day.
工作一天之後，他脖子似乎很僵硬。

adv. 僵硬地，堅硬地；完全地，極其

▶She was scared stiff when seeing a zombie approaching her.
看到殭屍接近她，她嚇得不敢動。

still [stɪl] **adv.** 仍然；還是
◀ Track 4581

▶My high school teacher still looks very young after teaching for thirty years.
我的高中老師教書三十年之後看起來還是很年輕。

adj. 靜止的

▶The time seemed to be still when she told a unfunny joke.
她講了一個不好笑的笑話，時間彷彿靜止了。

stimulate [`stɪmjə‚let]
◀ Track 4582

v. 刺激，促使；起刺激作用

▶Don't say something mean to stimulate her.
不要說惡意的話去刺激她。

sting [stɪŋ]
◀ Track 4583

v. 刺，螫，叮；刺痛；傷害

▶She felt dizzy after being stung by an unknown insect.
被一隻不明昆蟲叮咬過之後，她感覺到頭暈。

n. 螫針；（植物的）刺；刺痛；諷刺，挖苦

▶The school basketball team felt the sting of defeat.
學校籃球隊嘗到輸掉比賽的痛苦。

stingy [`stɪndʒɪ]
◀ Track 4584

adj. 吝嗇的；小氣的

▶The stingy old man would not offer any help to those in need.
這名吝嗇的老人不肯對需要幫助的人伸出援手。

stir [stɝ] **v.** 攪拌；攪動
◀ Track 4585

▶Don't stir the soup before it boils.
湯煮滾之前不要去攪動它。

n. 微動；騷動

▶The protesters caused a stir, for they blocked the road and interrupted the traffic.
抗爭者造成了騷動，因為他們擋住道路，還阻礙交通。

stitch [stɪtʃ]
◀ Track 4586

n. 一針，針線；針法；一件衣服

▶The stitches on the seam of the sleeves could be clearly seen.
袖子接縫上的針線痕跡清楚可見。

v. 縫，繡；縫合

▶The doctor stitched the wound on his leg.
醫生縫合他腳上的傷口。

stock [stɑk]
◀ Track 4587

n. 貯存，蓄積；庫存品，存貨

▶Let's order some tissues. We are running out of stock.
我們訂購一些衛生紙吧。快要沒有存貨了。

補充片語 out of stock 沒有庫存

v. 辦貨，進貨；貯存，庫存

▶Piles of books were stocked in the garage.
有成堆的書貯存在車庫裡。

中級

adj. 庫存的，現有的；平凡的，慣用的

▶Instead of taking our request seriously, she gave her stock reply and sent us away.
她沒有認真看待我們要求，而是用慣用的回答把我們打發走。

stocking [`stɑkɪŋ] ◀€Track 4588
n. 長襪

▶The kids believed that Santa will place gifts in the stockings as long as they behave themselves.
小朋友相信只要他們乖乖的，聖誕老人就會放禮物在他們的長襪裡。

stomach [`stʌmək] ◀€Track 4589
=tum·my **n.** 胃；肚子；胃口

▶Ted called in sick because he suddenly felt an acute pain in his stomach.
泰德突然覺得肚子劇烈疼痛，所以打電話來請病假。

stomachache ◀€Track 4590
[`stʌmək͵ek] **n.** 胃痛

▶She bought some over-the-counter medicine to relieve the stomachache.
她買了一些成藥來緩解胃痛。

stone [ston] **n.** 石頭 ◀€Track 4591

▶She never shows compassion for the needy people. She has a heart of stone.
她從來不會同情有需要的人。她的心真是石頭做的。

stool [stul] ◀€Track 4592
n. 凳子；馬桶；糞便

▶The kid sat on a stool and had his snacks.
小朋友坐在凳子上面吃點心。

相關片語 **fall between two stools**
兩頭落空

▶The books falls between two stools—it's too easy for the professionals, and it has too many jargons for general readers.
這本書兩頭落空，對專業人士來說太簡單，對一般讀者來說又太多專業用語。

stop [stɑp] **v.** 停；阻止 ◀€Track 4593

▶They tried to stop her from jumping off the cliff.
他們企圖阻止她跳下懸崖。

n. （車）站

▶There are ten more stops before we reach our destination.
到達目的地之前還有十站。

store [stor] **n.** 店；商店 ◀€Track 4594

▶There is a stationery store near my school. 我的學校旁邊有一間文具店。

v. 儲存；存放

▶We stored the furniture in the garage.
我們將家具存放在車庫裡。

storey [`storɪ] ◀€Track 4595
=sto·ry （美式英文） **n.** 樓層

▶Frank purchased a house with four storeys.
法蘭克買了一棟四層樓的房子。

storm [stɔrm] **n.** 暴風雨 ◀€Track 4596

▶The hikers took shelter in the cave during the storm.
這群登山者在暴風雨期間於山洞中避難。

stormy [`stɔrmɪ] ◀€Track 4597
adj. 暴風雨的

▶The noises on the stormy night gave me the creeps.
暴風雨夜晚的噪音令我感到毛骨悚然。

story [`storɪ] n. 故事　　◀Track 4598

▶The writer collected the folklore stories and compiled them into a book.
作家收集傳奇故事，寫成一本書。

storyteller　　◀Track 4599

[`storɪ͵tɛlɚ] n. 講故事的人；說書人；短篇小說作家；【口】說謊者

▶The toddlers were enchanted by the storyteller.
小朋友著迷於那名說書人的故事。

stove [stov] n. 火爐；爐灶　◀Track 4600

▶Remember to turn off the gas stove when you leave the kitchen.
離開廚房的時候要記得關瓦斯爐。

straight [stret]　　◀Track 4601

adv. 直地；直接地；正直坦率地

▶We went straight to our destination.
我們直接前往目的地。

adj. 筆直的；平直的；正直坦率的

▶The drunk man could not walk on a straight line.
這名醉漢無法直線行走。

strange [strendʒ]　　◀Track 4602

adj. 奇怪的；奇妙的；陌生的

▶Everything was strange to the uptown boy when he first visited the downtown area.
住在郊區的男孩第一次到市中心的時候覺得每樣事物都很奇妙。

stranger [`strendʒɚ]　　◀Track 4603

n. 陌生人

▶Mom told me not to talk to strangers on the way to school.
媽媽叫我去在上學途中不要跟陌生人說話。

strategy [`strætədʒɪ]　　◀Track 4604

n. 戰略，策略，計謀，對策

▶The professor researches on foreign-language learning strategies.
這名教授研究外語學習策略。

straw [strɔ] n. 吸管　　◀Track 4605

▶The platic straw will be forbidden next year.
明年將會禁用塑膠吸管。

strawberry　　◀Track 4606

[`strɔbɛrɪ] n. 草莓

▶The sweet and sour taste of strawberries is very favorable.
草莓酸酸甜甜的味道很令人喜愛。

stream [strim]　　◀Track 4607

n. 溪；溪流

▶The factory discharged waste water into the stream in front of it.
工廠將廢水排入它前面的河流中。

street [strit]　　◀Track 4608

n. 街道；馬路

▶The street was in sheer darkness when the street lamps suddenly went off.
路燈突然熄滅時，街道一片漆黑。

strength [strɛŋθ]　　◀Track 4609

n. 力；力量

中級

▶She didn't have enough strength to carry the box.
她沒有足夠的力氣去搬那個紙箱。

strengthen ◀ Track 4610

[`strɛŋθən] **v** 加強，增強，鞏固

▶She worked on her professional skills to strengthen her competitiveness.
她增強專業知識，以加強競爭力。

stress [strɛs] ◀ Track 4611

v 強調；著重

▶The boss stresses on social etiquette when interacting with the client.
老闆強調和客戶互動時的社會禮節。

n 壓力；著重

▶She was overwhelmed by the stress of taking care of her mother.
她被照顧母親的壓力逼得喘不過氣。

stretch [strɛtʃ] ◀ Track 4612

v 伸直；伸展；延伸

▶Stretch your limbs and warm up your body before you get into the swimming pool.
進到游泳池前要伸展四肢並且暖身。

n 伸長，伸展；過度使用

▶The great stretch of the open field belongs to the landlord.
這一大片土地都是屬於這個地主的。

相關片語 **stretch one's legs**
散步，走動，遛遛腿

▶He likes to stretch his legs after dinner in a summer evening.
在夏天傍晚，他喜歡吃飽晚餐後去散步。

strict [strɪkt] ◀ Track 4613

adj 嚴格的；嚴厲的

▶She was very strict with her daughter.
她對女兒很嚴格。

strike [straɪk] **v** 打；擊 ◀ Track 4614

▶The tree stuck by lightning miraculously survived.
被雷劈到的樹木奇蹟似地存活下來了。

n 打擊；攻擊；空襲

▶The general commended to launch an air strike on the enemy's camp.
將軍下令空襲敵軍的營地。

string [strɪŋ] ◀ Track 4615

n 細繩；線；一串

▶The string of beads were passed down from my great grand mother.
這串念珠是我的曾祖母傳下來的。

v （用線）串，綁，束，串起；上弦；伸展，拉直；使振奮；戲弄

▶They strung the rope from one pole to the other.
他們把繩子拉在兩根桿子之間。

strip [strɪp] ◀ Track 4616

n 條，帶，細長片；一行，一列

▶A strip of fabric was found at the crime scene. It was probably ripped off from the suspect's coat.
犯罪現場找到一塊布。可能是從嫌疑犯身上的外套扯下來的。

v 剝去，剝奪；刪除；使成細條

▶They can not strip the public of the right to know the truth.
他們不能剝奪大眾知道真相的權利。

strive [straɪv] ◀ Track 4617

v 努力；苦幹

▶They strived to accomplish the task assigned by the general manager.
他們努力完成總經理交辦的事務。

stroke [strok]
◀ᴇ Track 4618

n. 打，擊，敲；（划船或游泳的）一划；（網球等）一抽；（病）突發；中風；突然的一擊，一下子

▶He passed away after suffering from a stroke last weekend.
他在上周末中風之後就過世了。

v. （用手）撫，摸，捻；踢，擊；輕拂

▶She stroked out your name on the guest list.
她從賓客名單中將你的名字劃掉了。

相關片語 **not do a stroke of work**
什麼工作都不做

▶Gary just sat at the desk, not doing a stroke of work.
蓋瑞只坐在椅子上，什麼工作也不做。

strong [strɔŋ]
◀ᴇ Track 4619

adj. 強壯的；強健的；堅強的

▶The strong words of the candidate were very convincing to the voters.
這名候選人有力的致詞對選民來說很有說服力。

structure [`strʌktʃɚ]
◀ᴇ Track 4620

n. 結構，構造；組織；構造體

▶The structure of the building was designed to be earthquake-resistant.
這棟大樓的結構是防震的設計。

v. 構造，組織；安排；建造，使成體系

▶You have to structure your essay to meet the requirement of the publisher.
你需要將文章的組織修改成符合出版者需要的樣子。

struggle [`strʌgl]
◀ᴇ Track 4621

n. 奮鬥；鬥爭；難事；奮鬥；掙扎；艱難地行徑；對抗

▶The struggle of the single mother aroused the compassion of the public.
這位單親媽媽的奮鬥引起大眾的同情。

v. 奮鬥；掙扎；艱難地行徑；對抗

▶The woman was striving to carry the baby trolley on to the bus.
這位女士掙扎著把娃娃車搬上公車。

stubborn [`stʌbɚn]
◀ᴇ Track 4622

adj. 倔強的；頑固的

▶She was as stubborn as a mule.
她像驢子一樣固執。

student [`stjudnt]
◀ᴇ Track 4623

n. 學生

▶The students who failed the test will be asked to take the remedy course.
考試不及格的學生被要求去上補救教學課。

studio [`stjudɪ͵o]
◀ᴇ Track 4624

n. （畫家等的）工作室；畫室

▶The artist worked in his studio for ten consecutive hours.
這名藝術家連續十個小時在畫室裡面工作。

study [`stʌdɪ]
◀ᴇ Track 4625

n. 學習；研究；課題

▶She went abroad for further studies.
她去國外深造。

v. 學習

▶The scientist studies the habitat and lifestyle of the endangered species.
這位科學家研究瀕危物種的棲息地和生活習慣。

中級

stuff [stʌf] **n.** 東西，物品 ◀Track 4626

▶Rita spent a whole night packing her stuff before moving to the new apartment.
搬到新公寓之前，瑞塔花了一整晚打包東西。

v. 裝，填，塞；把……裝滿；使……吃得過飽

▶She stuffed the wardrobe with dresses and shirts.
她把衣櫃塞滿洋裝和襯衫。

stupid [ˋstjupɪd] ◀Track 4627
adj. 笨的；愚蠢的

▶We won't make the stupid mistake again.
我們不會再犯這個愚蠢的錯誤了。

style [staɪl] ◀Track 4628
n. 風格；文體；流行款式；式樣

▶This album collects songs of different music styles.
這張專輯收錄不同音樂類型的歌曲。

subject [ˋsʌbdʒɪkt] ◀Track 4629
adj. 易受……的；以……為條件的

▶Innocent-looking girls were subject to frauds.
看起來很無辜的女孩容易受騙。

v. 使隸屬，使服從；使蒙受

▶They are subjected to follow the supervisor's advice.
他們必須服從主管的建議。

n. 主題

▶The subject of the program is not well-received by the public.
這個節目的主題不太受到大眾的歡迎。

submarine [ˋsʌbməˏrin] **n.** 潛艇；海底生物；水下裝置 ◀Track 4630

▶The sailors in the submarine belong to the Australian Navies.
這艘潛艇上的水手是隸屬於澳洲海軍管轄。

adj. 海底的；水下的

▶The submarine cables across the Atlantic was said to be damaged.
據說橫越大西洋的海底電纜被破壞了。

相關片語 **submarine sandwich**
潛艇型三明治

▶I don't want pickles in my submarine sandwich.
我的潛艇堡三明治不要加酸菜。

substance [ˋsʌbstəns] ◀Track 4631
n. 物質，實質；本旨，要義；財產，財物

▶The chemical substance was safely stored in the warehouse.
這個化學物質被安全的存放於倉庫裡。

substitute ◀Track 4632
[ˋsʌbstəˏtjut] **n.** 代替人；代替物；代用品

▶The substitute actor was asked to dress up like the protagonist.
替身演員被要求要穿著像主角一樣。

v. 用……代替；代替

▶We substituted the electric cooker with a microwave oven.
我們用微波爐取代了電鍋。

相關片語 **substitute teacher** 代課老師

▶The substitute teacher only worked here for hald a year.
這名代課老師只在這裡工作了半年。

subtract [səbˋtrækt] ◀Track 4633
v. 減；減去

▶Ten substract three equals seven.
十減去三等於七。

suburb [`sʌbɝb]　◀Track 4634

n.（城市周圍的）近郊住宅區（或村，鎮），郊區

▶Peter sold the apartment in the downtown and bought a mansion in the suburbs.
彼得賣掉市中心的公寓，買了郊區的豪宅。

subway [`sʌb͵we]　◀Track 4635
=un·der·ground
=tube（英式英語）
=MRT=me·tro **n.** 地下鐵

▶The subway was very crowded during rush hours.
地下鐵在尖峰時刻非常擁擠。

succeed [sək`sid]　◀Track 4636

v. 成功；取得成功

▶She succeeded in obtaining the admission to the prestigious university.
她成功獲得知名大學的入學許可。

success [sək`sɛs] **n.** 成功　◀Track 4637

▶His success in business was not achieved overnight.
他在商業上的成功不是一夜之間達成的。

successful　◀Track 4638

[sək`sɛsfəl] **adj.** 成功的

▶The successful entrepreneur shared his experience with the youngsters.
這名成功的企業家和年輕人分享他的經驗。

such [sʌtʃ] **adj.** 如此的　◀Track 4639

▶It was such a boring performance that many viewers fell asleep. 那是如此無聊的表演，以至於許多觀眾睡著了。

suck [sʌk] **v.** 吸；吮；啜　◀Track 4640

Helen asked her son not to suck his fingers.
海倫叫她兒子不要吮吸手指。

相關片語 **teach one's grandmother to suck eggs** 班門弄斧

▶Showing off your knowledge in front of the expert is like teaching your grandmother to suck eggs.
在專家面前賣弄知識，就是在班門弄斧。

sudden [`sʌdn]　◀Track 4641

adj. 突然的

▶Her sudden disappearance ten years ago remained to be a mystery.
她十年前突然消失，至今仍是未解之謎。

suddenly [`sʌdnlɪ]　◀Track 4642

adv. 忽然

▶The burglar suddenly broke in, asking us to hand in our money.
盜賊突然闖進來，要求我們交出錢財。

suffer [`sʌfɚ]　◀Track 4643

v. 遭受；經歷

▶Chirlden in the war zones suffer from poverty.
戰地孩童飽受貧窮之苦。

suffering [`sʌfərɪŋ]　◀Track 4644

n.（身體或精神上的）痛苦；勞苦；苦難的經歷；令人痛苦的事

▶The suffering of child laborers was pitiful. 童工受的苦難很令人同情。

中級

sufficient [sə`fɪʃənt] ◄Track 4645
adj. 足夠的，充分的；有充分能力

▶The power plant can generate sufficient electricity for the whole island.
這座發電廠可產生足夠供應全島的電力。

sugar [`ʃʊgɚ] **n.** 糖 ◄Track 4646

▶Eliminating sugar from daily diet may be helpful for your health.
減少日常飲食中的糖分對健康有益。

suggest [sə`dʒɛst] ◄Track 4647
v. 建議

▶He suggests that we should take our client to the famous Chinese restaurant.
他建議我們帶客戶去知名的中國餐廳。

suggestion ◄Track 4648
[sə`dʒɛstʃən] **n.** 建議；提議

▶I purchased the wireless vacuum cleaner at her suggestion.
我聽她的建議，買了這個無線吸塵器。

suicide [`suə,saɪd] ◄Track 4649
n. 自殺

▶The number of suicide has increased over the past few years.
過去幾年自殺的數量增加了。

相關片語 **commit suicide** 自殺

▶The man who was accused of negligent at duty committed suicide.
這名被指控怠忽職守的男人自殺了。

suit [sut] ◄Track 4650
n. （一套）西裝；套；組

▶He wore a suit to the formal occasion.
他穿著西裝出席正式場合。

v. 適合；與……相配；使適合

▶The job suits him a lot.
這份工作很適合他。

suitable [`sutəbl] ◄Track 4651
adj. 適當的

▶I prepare a suitcase of a suitable size to pack my carry-on luggage. 我準備了適當大小的行李箱裝隨身上機的行李。

suitcase [`sut,kes] ◄Track 4652
n. 小型行李箱，手提箱

▶Some passengers abandoned their broken suitcase at the airport.
有些旅客會將壞掉的行李箱丟在機場。

sum [sʌm] ◄Track 4653
n. 總數，總和；一筆（金額）

▶We haven't calculated the sum of our monthly expenses.
我們還沒計算本月花費的總金額。

v. 計算……的總和；總結，概括

▶He summed up the conclusions we reached in the meeting.
他總結了我們在會議中達成的結論。

summarize ◄Track 4654
[`sʌmə,raɪz] **v.** 總結，概括，概述

▶The author of the book summarizes three effective ways of studying new subjects. 這本書的作者總結了三種學習新科目的有效方式。

summary [`sʌmərɪ] ◄Track 4655
n. 總結，摘要

▶He made a summary of the key points in the professor's speech.
他替教授的演講做了摘要。

summer [`sʌmɚ] ◀ Track 4656

n. 夏天

▶Last summer, the temperature in Europe reached above 40 degress Celcius.
去年夏天，歐洲的溫度達到攝氏40度以上。

summit [`sʌmɪt] ◀ Track 4657

n. 尖峰，峰頂；最高官階，

▶Leaders of twenty countries gathered in Copenhagen for the World Summit.
二十個國家的領導人聚集在哥本哈根參加世界高峰會。

sun [sʌn] **n.** 太陽；日 ◀ Track 4658

▶Several planets, including Earth, orbit around the sun.
包括地球在內的好幾個行星都繞太陽運行。

sunbathe [`sʌnˌbeð] ◀ Track 4659

v. 沐日光浴

▶Some tourists are sunbathing on the beach.
有一些觀光客在沙灘上做日光浴。

Sunday [`sʌnde] =Sun. **n.** 星期天 ◀ Track 4660

▶She is a devoted Christian. She goes to the church every Sunday.
她是一位虔誠基督徒。她每個星期天去教堂。

sunlight [`sʌnˌlaɪt] ◀ Track 4661

n. 日光，陽光

▶The UV radiation in the sunlight may be harmful to your skin.
太陽光當中的紫外線輻射可能對你的皮膚有害。

sunny [`sʌnɪ] **adj.** 晴天的 ◀ Track 4662

▶It was sunny today, so my mom dried the quilt on the balcony
今天天氣很好，所以我媽拿棉被去陽台曬。

sunrise [`sʌnˌraɪz] ◀ Track 4663

n. 日出；日出時間；日出景象

▶On New Year's Day, some people went to the summit of the mountain to watch the sunrise.
新年第一天，有些人到山頂上去看日出。

sunset [`sʌnˌsɛt] ◀ Track 4664

n. 日落；日落時分；日落景象

▶The view of sunset at the harbor is very impressive.
港邊的日落景色很令人印象深刻。

super [`supɚ] ◀ Track 4665

adj. 特級的；特佳的；極度的

▶The quality of the sugar apple produced in this town is super.
這個小鎮出產的釋迦品質特別好。

adv. 非常；極度

▶I was super lucky to see the NBA star, LeBron James, in person.
親眼見到NBA球星勒布朗·詹姆士，真是超級幸運。

superb [suˈpɝb] ◀ Track 4666

adj. 極好的，一流的

▶Her culinary skill is suberb.
她的廚藝一流。

superior [səˈpɪrɪɚ] ◀ Track 4667

adj. （在職位，地位等方面）較高的；較好的，較優秀的；高傲的，有優越感的

中級

▶Terry likes to act as if he were superior to all his colleagues, so he is the least popular person in this office.
泰瑞總喜歡表現地好像他優於所有的同事，所以他是這間辦公室裡最不受歡迎的人。

n. 上司；長輩；佔優勢者

▶When the superior asked me to take full responsibility for the mistake, I could only accept it.
當上司要我承擔錯誤的所有責任時，我也只能接受。

supermarket
◀ Track 4668

[`supɚˌmɑrkɪt] **n.** 超級市場

▶The supermarket will have a sale of frozen seafoods this evening.
超市今晚的冷凍海鮮會有特價。

supervisor
◀ Track 4669

[ˌsupɚˋvaɪzɚ] **n.** 監督人；管理人；指導者

▶Your supervisor will be the final decision maker, not you.
你的主管是最後下決定的人，不是你。

supper [`sʌpɚ]
◀ Track 4670

=din·ner **n.** 晚餐

▶No matter how busy he is, he would have supper with his family.
不管他有多忙，都會和家人一起吃晚餐。

supply [səˋplaɪ]
◀ Track 4671

n. 供應；供給；生活用品；補給品

▶The supply of daily necessity is sufficient. 日用品的供給很充足。

v. 供應；提供

▶We supplied the school kids with lunch boxes.
我們提供學童午餐餐盒。

support [səˋport]
◀ Track 4672

n. 支持

▶Words can express our gratitude toward your support.
言語無法表達我們對你們的支持的感謝。

v. 支持；資助；撫養

▶Rita had to take part time jobs, for her parents couldn't support her through college.
瑞塔必須要打工，因為她的父母無法支持她念完大學。

supporter [səˋportɚ]
◀ Track 4673

n. 支持者；擁護者；支援者；扶養者，贍養者

▶The senator is a supporter of women's right.
這位參議員是婦權運動的支持者。

suppose [səˋpoz]
◀ Track 4674

v. 猜想

▶I suppose the stock prices will rise in the following days.
我猜想接下來幾天股價可能會上漲。

supposed [səˋpozd]
◀ Track 4675

aux. 期望，認為必須

▶He is supposed to submit a report today.
他今天應該要交一份報告的。

adj. 假定的，假設的，想像的，被信以為真的

▶This is just a supposed case. Don't take it as true.
這是一個假定的狀況。不要當真。

supreme [səˋprim]
◀ Track 4676

adj. 最高的，至上的；最大的

▶The president is the supreme leader of the enterprise.
總裁是公司的最高領導人。

sure [ʃʊr] ◀⣿Track 4677
adj. 確信的;一定的

▶We are sure of his competence to finish the job.
我們確定他有能力完成這項工作。

adv. 的確

▶This phenomenon is sure rare in this region.
這個現象在此區域的確很少看見。

surely [`ʃʊrlɪ] ◀⣿Track 4678
adv. 確實,無疑,一定;想

▶He will surely be elected as the president of our country.
他一定會當選本國的總統。

surf [sɜ·f] **n.** 拍岸浪花 ◀⣿Track 4679

▶The Golden Retriever was excited to see the surf on the beach.
那隻黃金獵犬因為看到岸上的浪花而顯得興奮。

v. 衝浪;在網路上或電視上搜索資料或快速地看

▶We surfed the Internet to see the result of the latest election poll.
我們上網看最新的選舉民調結果。

surface [`sɜ·fɪs] ◀⣿Track 4680
n. 表面;外表

▶On the surface, she is cold and indifferent. In private, she is enthusiastic and easygoing.
表面上,她很冷漠。私底下,她很熱情又好相處。

surfing [`sɜ·fɪŋ] ◀⣿Track 4681
n. 作衝浪運動

▶Gary likes to go surging on the weekend. 蓋瑞喜歡在週末去衝浪。

surgeon [`sɜ·dʒən] ◀⣿Track 4682
n. 外科醫生

▶The surgion performed an operation on the boy to remove the brain tumor.
這名外科醫生為小男孩動手術移除腦瘤。

surgery [`sɜ·dʒərɪ] ◀⣿Track 4683
n. 外科;外科醫學

▶The surgery lasted for eight hours.
這場手術持續了八小時。

surprise [sə·`praɪz] ◀⣿Track 4684
n. 驚喜;驚訝

▶The party for my parents was supposed to be a surprise, but they knew about it in advance.
這場派對原本是要給父母的驚喜,但他們提前知道了。

v. 使驚喜

▶We surprised our guests with a homemade dinner.
我們自己煮晚餐,給客人一個驚喜。

surprised [sə·`praɪzd] ◀⣿Track 4685
adj. 感到驚喜的;感到驚訝的

▶I was surprised to run into my roommate in college at the airport the other day.
前幾天我因為在機場巧遇以前大學的室友而感到驚訝。

surrender [sə·`rɛndə·] ◀⣿Track 4686
v. 使投降,使自首;交出,放棄

中級

▶He surrendered his dream of being a diplomat and became a consecutive interpreter.
他放棄成為外交官的夢想，變成一個逐步口譯師。

| 相關片語 | **surrender oneself to**
自首，向……投降 |

▶The soldier suffered from brutal tortures because he refused to surrender himself to the enemy.
士兵因為拒絕向敵人投降而遭到酷刑對待。

n. 投降，屈服，自首

▶They were forced to make an unconditional surrender.
他們被迫要無條件投降。

surround [sə`raʊnd]
◀ Track 4687

v. 圍繞，圍住；包圍；大量供給

▶The town was surrounded by the river. 小鎮被這條河流圍繞。

n. 圍繞物

▶The surround of the fireplace is covered by ashes.
壁爐周圍被灰燼覆蓋。

surroundings
◀ Track 4688

[sə`raʊndɪŋz] **n.** 環境；周圍的事物，周圍的情況

▶The chameleon took camouflage and blended into the surroundings.
這隻變色龍進行偽裝，融入周圍的景色裡。

survey [sə`ve]
◀ Track 4689

n. 調查，調查報告；民意調查

▶They made a survey to investigate what part-time jobs college students would take.
他們做調查，想了解大學生會做什麼兼職工作。

v. 俯視，眺望，環視；全面考察；審視，檢驗；調查

▶We surveyed on the potential customers to see their preference on the products.
我們調查潛在顧客對產品的偏好。

survival [sə`vaɪvl]
◀ Track 4690

n. 倖存，殘存；倖存者

▶The kid's survival after being lost in the woods for one week was considered a miracle. 這個小孩在森林裡迷路一個星期還能生還被視為是個奇蹟。

survive [sə`vaɪv]
◀ Track 4691

v. 活下來；倖存

▶The sailors considered it a blessing to survive the storm on the sea.
水手們認為能在海上的暴風雨中存活下來是上天保佑。

suspect [sə`spɛkt]
◀ Track 4692

v. 察覺；懷疑

▶We suspected that the one of the employees revealed the confidential information to our opponent.
我們懷疑其中一位員工將機密資訊洩漏給敵對的公司。

n. 嫌疑犯，可疑分子

▶The suspect was kept in custody for two weeks.
這名嫌疑犯被羈押兩個星期。

adj. 可疑的，受到懷疑的，不可信的

▶His motives were suspect.
他的動機相當可疑。

suspend [sə`spɛnd]
◀ Track 4693

v. 懸掛；使懸浮；中止；使暫停（職務、活動、學業等）；暫時取消

▶His driver's license was suspended for the drunk driving case.
他的駕照因為酒駕而被暫時吊銷。

suspension
🔊 Track 4694

[sə`spɛnʃən] **n.** 懸掛；暫停，中止；停職，停學；暫緩執行，暫停支付

▶The basketball player was punished with a suspension from the team.
這位籃球選手被懲罰停賽。

suspicion [sə`spɪʃən]
🔊 Track 4695

n. 懷疑，疑心，猜疑

▶Mutual suspicion may lead to an unmendable relationship.
互相猜忌可能會導致關係無法修復。

suspicious [sə`spɪʃəs]
🔊 Track 4696

adj. 猜疑的，疑心的，多疑的

▶The old lady was suspicious of everything that his housekeeper told her. 老太太對管家告訴她的所有事情都抱著懷疑態度。

swallow [`swɑlo]
🔊 Track 4697

n. 吞；嚥

▶The kid could not take the medicine in one swallow.
這個小孩無法一口吞下這些藥。

v. 吞嚥；吞下；忍受

▶She couldn't swallow her displeasure and was determined to revenge.
她無法吞下不愉快的感覺，決定要報復。

swan [swɑn] **n.** 天鵝
🔊 Track 4698

▶Some Asian tourists were surprised to see the black swans. 有些亞洲的觀光客在看到黑色天鵝時感到驚訝。

swear [swɛr]
🔊 Track 4699

v. 發誓，宣誓；詛咒，罵髒話

▶The witness swore to tell the truth on the court.
目擊者在法庭上發誓會據實以告。

sweat [swɛt]
🔊 Track 4700

v. 出汗；使幹苦活；焦慮

▶She went for a run along the river bank and sweated a lot.
她去邊跑步，流了很多汗。

n. 汗，汗水；焦急不安；苦差事

▶She ran errands for her boss with beads of sweat on her forehead.
她替老闆跑腿，額頭上都是汗水。

sweater [`swɛtɚ]
🔊 Track 4701

n. 毛衣

▶It has been a trend to wear ugly sweaters on Chirstmas party.
在聖誕派對上穿醜毛衣已經是個流行趨勢。

sweep [swip] **v.** 掃
🔊 Track 4702

▶She sweeps the room every day.
她每天都會掃這個房間。

sweet [swit] **adj.** 甜的
🔊 Track 4703

▶The tangerines were sweet.
這些橘子很甜。

n. 糖果

▶She had a decayed tooth because she ate too much sweets.
她因為吃太多糖果而蛀牙。

swell [swɛl]
🔊 Track 4704

v. 腫脹；（地）隆起；（水）上漲；增大，增強；情緒高漲；驕傲自大

中級

467

▶She sprained her ankle, and it began to swell.
她扭傷腳踝,且腳踝開始腫了起來。

n. 鼓起,腫脹;增大,增強;隆起,洶湧

▶The swell of population has caused a shortage in the supplies of daily necessities.
人口擴張造成資源供應不足。

swift [swɪft]　◀Track 4705

adj. 快速的,立即的,(行動)快的

▶They took swift actions to deal with the problem.
他們採取立即的行動處理這個問題。

n. 雨燕

▶The swifts nested by the eaves.
雨燕在屋簷下築巢。

swim [swɪm] **v.** 游泳　◀Track 4706

▶The athlete swam across the straits and broke his personal record.
運動員游泳穿越海峽,打破個人的紀錄。

swimming [`swɪmɪŋ]　◀Track 4707

n. 游泳

▶To our surprise, tigers are good at swimming.
令我們驚訝的是,老虎很擅長游泳。

swimsuit [`swɪmsut]　◀Track 4708

n. 泳衣

▶The Australian people had a party in swimsuit at the beach to celebrate Christmas.
澳洲人在海灘上辦泳衣派對來慶祝聖誕節。

swing [swɪŋ]　◀Track 4709

v. 搖擺;擺動

▶The soldiers swing their arms as they stride across the road.
軍人大步走過道路,擺動著手臂。

n. 搖擺;擺動

▶The swing of the ship made some passengers suffer from motion sickness.
船隻搖擺,導致有些乘客暈船了。

switch [swɪtʃ]　◀Track 4710

v. 打開或關掉(開關);為……轉接(電話);改變;調換,交換

▶If you switch off the computer now, you might lose some of the data you are working on.
如果你現在將電腦關機,可能會遺失一些正在處理的資料。

n. 開關;轉轍器;變更,更改;調換,交換

▶He pressed the wrong switch, so there is no reaction in the machine.
他按錯開關了,所以機器沒有反應。

sword [sord] **n.** 刀,劍　◀Track 4711

▶The knight slayed the evil dragon with his sword.
這名騎士用劍砍殺了惡龍。

syllable [`sɪləbl]　◀Track 4712

n. 音節

▶The word "expensive" had three syllables.
「expensive」這個單字有三個音節。

symbol [`sɪmbl]　◀Track 4713

n. 象徵;標誌;記號

▶We used the symbol of "x" to represent an unknown number.
我們用「x」這個記號來表示不明的數字。

symbolize

◄€ Track 4714

[`sɪmbḷˌaɪz] **v** 象徵，標誌；用符號表示

▶Yello roses may symbolize friendship and caring.
黃色玫瑰可能代表友情和關懷。

sympathetic

◄€ Track 4715

[ˌsɪmpəˋθɛtɪk] **adj.** 同情的，有同情心的；贊同的

▶We are sympathetic about your problem, but there is not much we can do for you.
我們對您的問題深感同情，但我們能為您做的事並不多。

sympathize

◄€ Track 4716

[`sɪmpəˌθaɪz] **v** 同情，憐憫；體諒，支持

▶We sympathize with our classmate whose parents died in the plane crash.
我們同情那位父母在空難中喪生的同學。

sympathy [`sɪmpəθɪ]

◄€ Track 4717

n. 同情，同情心；同感；慰問，弔唁

▶We showed sympathy for the homeless man.
我們對那名無家可歸的男子表示同情。

symphony [`sɪmfənɪ]

◄€ Track 4718

n. 交響樂，交響曲

▶The musician spent three years on composing the symphony. 這位音樂家花了三年的時間創作這首交響曲。

symptom [`sɪmptəm]

◄€ Track 4719

n. 症狀；徵兆

▶A fevor, a sore throat, and a runny nose are common symptoms of a cold.
發燒，喉嚨痛，流鼻水是常見的感冒症狀。

syrup [`sɪrəp]

◄€ Track 4720

n. 糖漿；果汁

▶The maple syrup made the vanilla ice cream taste wonderful.
楓糖漿讓香草冰淇淋變的很好吃。

system [`sɪstəm]

◄€ Track 4721

n. 系統；制度

▶The education system in Germany is different from that in Taiwan.
德國的教育體系和台灣的不同。

systematic

◄€ Track 4722

[ˌsɪstəˋmætɪk]

adj. 有系統的；徹底的，有條理的

▶The secretary is systematic in dealing with cleric work.
這位秘書在處理文書工作上很有條理。

中級

▶ Tt

　　以下表格是全民英檢官方公告中級「聽、説、讀、寫」所須具備的能力，本書例句皆依此範疇特別設計，只要掃描右方QR code，就能搭配相對應的音軌實現「眼耳並用」方式，刺激左腦的語言學習功能；同時也可使用本書附贈的紅膠片，將其置於單字上，一面記憶一面自我挑戰，達到雙倍的學習成果！

聽 ▶	在日常生活中，能聽懂一般的會話；能大致聽懂公共場所廣播、氣象報告及廣告等。在工作時，能聽懂簡易的產品介紹與操作説明。能大致聽懂外籍人士的談話及詢問。
說 ▶	可在日常生活中，能以簡易英語交談或描述一般事物，能介紹自己的生活作息、工作、家庭、經歷等，並可對一般話題陳述看法。在工作時，能進行簡單的答詢，並與外籍人士交談溝通。
讀 ▶	在日常生活中，能閱讀短文、故事、私人信件、廣告、傳單、簡介及使用説明等。在工作時，能閱讀工作須知、公告、操作手冊、例行的文件、傳真、電報等。
寫 ▶	能寫簡單的書信、故事及心得等。對於熟悉且與個人經歷相關的主題，能以簡易的文字表達。

table [ˋtebl̩] **n.** 桌子；餐桌　◀ Track 4723

▶ I helped my mom set the table before the guest arrived.
在客人來之前，我幫媽媽把桌子佈置好。

tablecloth [ˋtebl̩͵klɔθ] ◀ Track 4724

n. 桌巾，桌布

▶ My mom bought a red plaid tablecloth.
我媽買了一條紅色方格圖樣的桌巾。

tablet [ˋtæblɪt] **n.** 藥片　◀ Track 4725

▶ I bought a pill grinder to make the tablet into powders.
我買了磨藥器來把藥片磨成粉狀。

相關片語 **tablet computer** 平板電腦

▶ With this wireless gadget, you can project the images on the tablet computer to the big screen.
以這個無線工具，你可以將平板電腦上的影像投射到大螢幕上。

tack [tæk] ◀ Track 4726

n. 大頭釘，圖釘；行動步驟，方針

▶ My brother hammered a tack in to the wooden pillar to hang a picture.
我哥用槌子把大頭釘敲進木頭柱子，用來掛一幅畫。

v. 用平頭釘釘

▶ I tacked the hanger to the wooden cabinet.
我用平頭釘把掛勾固定到櫃子上面。

tag [tæg] **n.** 牌子，標簽　◀ Track 4727

▶ Check the price tag before you purchase the coat. Are you sure you can afford it?
買外套之前先看標價。你確定你錢夠嗎？

v. 給……加標籤；添加，附加；給……加罪名

▶ He was tagged as a corruptor.
他被貼上了貪污者的標籤。

Taichung [`taɪ`tʃɔŋ] ◀Track 4728

n. 台中

▶Jenny bought some Sun Cakes when she visited Taichung.
珍妮去台中玩的時候買了一些太陽餅。

---

tail [tel] ◀Track 4729

n. 尾巴；尾部；尾狀物

▶The puppy was chasing its tail.
小狗在追自己的尾巴玩。

---

tailor [`telɚ] ◀Track 4730

n. （男）裁縫師；服裝店

▶The tailor took measurement for him to make the suit.
裁縫師為他量尺寸來做西裝。

v. 裁縫；做裁縫；修改

▶The dress is finely-tailored; it can make you look slimmer. 這件洋裝剪裁得很好；它可以讓你看起來更苗條。

Tainan [`taɪ`nɑn] **n.** 台南 ◀Track 4731

▶Teddy rent a bike to move around in Tainan City.
泰迪租了一台腳踏車在台南市區間穿梭。

Taiwan [`taɪ`wɑn] ◀Track 4732

n. 台灣

▶Taipei 101 is one of the most famous tourist spots in Taiwan.
台北101是台灣最有名的觀光景點之一。

Taiwanese ◀Track 4733

[ˌtaɪwəˈniz] **adj.** 台灣的；台灣人的；

▶Many foreign tourists are impressed with the hospitality of Taiwanese people. 許多外國觀光客對台灣人的好客態度印象深刻。

n. 台灣人；台灣話

▶The Russian model is learning to speak Taiwanese.
這位俄國模特兒正在學習説台灣話。

---

take [tek] ◀Track 4734

v. 拿；取；帶去；接受；承擔

▶Take Mr. Thompson for example; he always treats his wife gently.
以湯姆先生為例；他總是對太太很溫柔。

---

tale [tel] ◀Track 4735

n. 故事，傳説；謊話，捏造的話

▶The man likes to talk about tall tales.
這個人喜歡説誇大的話。

相關片語 **fairy tale** 童話故事

▶Pearl read some fairy tales as bedtime stories for her daughter.
寶兒在女兒睡前會讀一些童話故事給他聽。

---

talent [`tælənt] ◀Track 4736

n. 天賦；能力

▶The prodigy has a great talent for music.
這位神童有極佳的音樂天賦。

---

talented [`tæləntɪd] ◀Track 4737

adj. 有天分的，有天才的；有才能

▶She is talented in culinary arts.
她很有烹飪的天分。

---

talk [tɔk] **v.** 説話 ◀Track 4738

▶We haven't talked to each other since we had a fight last week.
自從上周吵架之後，我們就沒有再跟彼此説話了。

n. 談話；交談

▶I had a decent talk with Mr. Kim, and we have now reached an agreement on this issue.
我跟金先生好好談過了，我們現在對這個議題達成了共識。

talkative [`tɔkətɪv]
Track 4739
adj. 喜歡說話的；多嘴的；健談的

▶They were too talkative, so I never mention any personal affairs to them.
他們太多嘴了，所以我從來不會向他們提到我個人的事。

tall [tɔl] adj. 高的
Track 4740

▶Most of the models in the fashion show are about six feet tall.
這場時裝秀多數的模特兒身高都一百八十公分左右。

tame [tem]
Track 4741
adj. 經過馴養的，馴服的；溫順的；聽使喚的

▶The ranger of the national park warned us that the raccoons are not tame.
國家公園的管理員警告我們說這些浣熊並不是溫馴的。

v. 馴化，馴服；制服，使順從

▶The owner of the circus tamed the animals and made them perform in front of the audience. It's actually cruel.
馬戲團老闆馴服這些動物，讓牠們在觀眾面前表演。這其實蠻殘忍的。

tangerine
Track 4742
[`tændʒəˌrin] **n.** 橘子

▶The tangerine peel could be used as a seasoning in Chinese cooking.
橘子皮可以在中國菜裡當作佐料。

tank [tæŋk]
Track 4743
n. （貯水、油、氣的）箱、櫃、槽

▶They used the water tank in front of the house to store rainwater.
他們使用房子前面的水箱貯存雨水。

tap [tæp]
Track 4744
v. 裝上塞子；裝竊聽器；接通

▶They were tapped by the enemy.
他們遭到敵人竊聽。

n. 龍頭，閥門；（酒桶的）塞子；竊聽器

▶It's better to boil the waster from the tap before you drink it.
水龍頭的水最好還是煮滾過再喝。

tape [tep]
Track 4745
n. （錄音或錄影）磁帶；膠布；膠帶

▶I tied the parcel with tape before mailing it.
郵寄之前，我將包裹用膠帶包好。

v. 用膠布貼牢；將……錄音；將……錄影

▶They taped the price label on the package of the product.
他們將標價貼在產品包裝上。

target [`tɑrgɪt]
Track 4746
n. （欲達到的）目標；（攻擊、批評、嘲笑的）對象

▶Her target is to save one million dollars before she is thirty.
她的目標是三十歲之前存到一百萬。

v. 以……為目標；以……為對象

▶The ad put out by the school was targeted at students who wish to study overseas.
這間學校貼出來的廣告是以想要出國留學的學生做目標的。

task [tæsk]
◀ Track 4747

n. 任務；差事；作業

▶ Our team was assigned to accomplish the difficult task.
我們的團隊被指派要完成這項困難的任務。

taste [test]
◀ Track 4748

n. 味覺；味道；滋味；一口

▶ The taste of the dish reminds me of the braised pork rice made by my mother.
這道菜的味道讓我想到我媽媽做的滷肉飯。

v. 嚐；嚐到；嚐起來；吃起來

▶ The soup tastes sour.
這道湯嘗起來是酸的。

tasty [`testɪ]
◀ Track 4749

adj. 美味的，可口的；高雅的，大方的；性感的，誘人的

▶ Her homemade quiche looks tasty.
她自製的鹹派看起來很美味。

tax [tæks] **n.** 稅，稅金
◀ Track 4750

▶ The laborers were protesting against the high fuel tax.
勞工在抗爭高燃料稅。

v. 向……課稅；收費；使負

▶ The rich people were taxed for the profits they gained on exporting products.
富人因為出口商品而獲得的利益被扣稅。

taxi [`tæksɪ]
◀ Track 4751

=tax·i·cab=cab **n.** 計程車

▶ They took a taxi to the destination to save time.
他們為了節省時間，搭計程車到目的地。

tea [ti] **n.** 茶
◀ Track 4752

▶ The tea tasted so good that I felt really relaxed.
這茶太好喝了，我感到非常放鬆。

teach [titʃ] **v.** 教學；教導
◀ Track 4753

▶ The old master taught his apprentice the unique crafty skill.
老師傅教徒弟這個獨特的工藝技術。

teacher [`titʃɚ] **n.** 老師
◀ Track 4754

▶ She worked as a substitute teacher in the middle school last year.
她去年在這所中學當代課老師。

中級

Teacher's Day
◀ Track 4755

[`titʃɚz-de] **n.** 教師節

▶ On Teacher's Day, the students are always trying to play pranks on their teachers. 教師節的時候，學生總是想辦法對老師惡作劇。

team [tim] **n.** 隊；隊伍
◀ Track 4756

▶ The baseball team was dismissed after the scandal of the company that sponsored it.
這支棒球隊伍在贊助公司的醜聞曝光之後就被解散了。

teapot [`ti͵pɑt] **n.** 茶壺
◀ Track 4757

▶ The teapot is made of porcelain.
這個茶壺是用瓷做成的。

tear [tɛr] **n.** 眼淚
◀ Track 4758

▶ Tears rolled down her cheeks, but she would not let anyone know she was crying.
眼淚從臉頰流下，但她不願意讓任何人知道她在哭。

v. 撕開；拔掉；扯破

▶The boy tore a page off the picture book.
小男孩把圖畫書的一頁給撕了下來。

tease [tiz]
■€Track 4759

v. 戲弄，逗弄；取笑

▶Stop teasing her! You have better things to do.
不要嘲笑她了！你們還有別的事可做吧。

n. 戲弄，取笑；愛戲弄人的人；
賣弄風騷的女孩

▶That naughty girl is such a big tease; she often gets into trouble for this personality.
那個調皮的女孩很喜歡捉弄人，她常常因為這個個性惹上麻煩。

technical [`tɛknɪkl]
■€Track 4760

adj. 技術的，科技的；專門的，技術性的

▶She is our technical advisor. We consult her when there are glitches in the machine.
她是我們的技術顧問。我們如果機器有問題就會請教她。

technician [tɛk`nɪʃən]
■€Track 4761

n. 技術人員，技師，技術精湛者

▶She aspires to be an electrical technician after graduation.
她畢業之後想要當一位電工技師。

technological
■€Track 4762

[tɛknə`ladʒɪkl] **adj.** 技術（學）的，
工藝（學）的；因新技術而造成的

▶The issue of technological unemployment has aroused the attention of the officials.
技術失業的問題已經引起官員的注意。

相關片語 **highly technological crime** 高科技犯罪

▶Highly technological crime, such as hacking, would cause great losses to the public. 高科技犯罪，像是入侵電腦，可能會造成大眾的損失。

technology
■€Track 4763

[tɛk`nalədʒɪ] **n.** 工藝，技術，科技

▶The development of technology has brought convenience to modern people.
科技的發展已為現代人的生活帶來便利。

teen [tin]
■€Track 4764

n. 十幾歲；青少年

▶She was quite interested in hip hop dance in her teens.
她十幾歲時很喜歡嘻哈舞蹈。

adj. 十幾歲的，十幾的；青少年的

▶Many teenagers nowadays are groupies; they follow the updates of their teen idols.
許多青年人是追星族；他們會關注青少年偶像的一舉一動。

teenage [`tin‚edʒ]
■€Track 4765

adj. 十幾歲的；青春期的

▶Most people are not sure about their career path in their teenage years.
大多數人十幾歲的時候都不清楚自己的職業志向。

teenager [`tin‚edʒɚ]
■€Track 4766

n. 青少年

▶Some teenagers in the neighborhood joined a local gang, which worries me a lot. 這附近有些青少年加入了本地的幫派，讓我很擔心。

telegram [ˋtɛləˌgræm] ◀Track 4767

n. 電報

▶Her father dispatched a telegram to her.

她的父親發了一封電報給她。

---

telephone [ˋtɛləˌfon] ◀Track 4768
=phone **n.** 電話

▶They shared interesting things in their life with each other on the telephone.

她們在電話中與彼此分享生活的趣事。

v. 打電話給；打電話告知

▶I telephoned her to inform her that she has a registered mail.

我打電話告訴她說她有一封掛號信。

---

telescope [ˋtɛləˌskop] ◀Track 4769

n. （單筒）望遠鏡

▶The pervert peeped into his neighbor's house with a telescope.

這名變態用望遠鏡偷看鄰居家。

---

televise [ˋtɛləˌvaɪz] ◀Track 4770

v. 電視播送；播送電視節目

▶The World Cup Football Game was televised throughout the world.

世界盃足球賽在全球電視轉播。

---

television [ˋtɛləˌvɪʒən] ◀Track 4771
=TV **n.** 電視；電視機

▶With the development of Internet, television is not the main resource of information anymore.

因為網路的發展，電視已經不再是主要的資訊來源。

---

tell [tɛl] ◀Track 4772

v. 告訴；講述；吩咐

▶She was hiding something from us. She didn't tell us the truth.

她對我們隱瞞一些事情。她沒有對我們說實話。

---

temper [ˋtɛmpɚ] ◀Track 4773

n. 情緒；性情，脾氣

▶He doesn't know how to control his temper.

他不知道如何控制自己的脾氣。

相關片語 **lose one's temper** 發脾氣

▶Mr. Hawking lost his temper when he realized that he was cheated by his wife.

霍金先生知道他的太太對他不忠，便大發脾氣。

v. 鍛鍊；調和，捏和（黏土）；使溫和，使緩和

▶The difficulties in the process of negotiation with his client tempered his mind.

和客戶溝通時遇到的困難磨練了他的心智。

---

temperature ◀Track 4774

[ˋtɛmprətʃɚ] **n.** 溫度；氣溫；體溫

▶The temperature outdoor has dropped to minus ten degrees Celsius.

室外的溫度已經降到攝氏零下十度了。

---

temple [ˋtɛmpl] ◀Track 4775

n. 廟宇；寺廟；神殿；教堂

▶The artist researched the frescos in the ancient temple.

這名藝術家研究古代神殿的壁畫。

---

temporary ◀Track 4776

[ˋtɛmpəˌrɛrɪ] **adj.** 臨時的；暫時的

中級

▶He wanted to find a decent job instead of working as a temporary labor all the time.
他想要找穩定的工作，而非總是做臨時工。

ten [tɛn] n. 十；十歲
◀ Track 4777

▶I was at the age of ten when I learned that there is no Santa. 我是十歲的時候知道世界上沒有聖誕老公公的。

adj. 十的；十個的

▶The sign says we only had ten seconds to cross the street.
標示說我們只有十秒鐘可以穿越馬路。

tenant [`tɛnənt]
◀ Track 4778
n. 房客；承租人；住戶

▶The tenant has failed to pay the rent on time for two consecutive months.
房客已經連續兩個月沒有按時繳房租了。

tend [tɛnd]
◀ Track 4779
v. 走向，去向；傾向，易於

▶She tends to think that everyone who approaches her has a malicious attempt.
她傾向於覺得每個接近她的人都不懷好意。

tendency [`tɛndənsɪ]
◀ Track 4780
n. 傾向；性向，僻性；趨勢，潮流

▶The tendency of carrying reusable utensils has become more and more popular.
帶可重複使用餐具的潮流越來越普遍了。

相關片語 **violent tendency** 暴力傾向

▶The man shows a violent tendency. We had better stay away from him.
那個男人有暴力傾向。我們最好離他遠一點。

tender [`tɛndɚ]
◀ Track 4781
adj. 嫩的；敏感的；溫柔的；幼弱的

▶The nanny at the nursing home is tender to the toddlers.
托嬰之家的保母對小朋友很溫柔。

tennis [`tɛnɪs] n. 網球
◀ Track 4782

▶I wish there were a tennis court on our campus.
我真希望學校裡面有網球場。

tense [tɛns]
◀ Track 4783
adj. 拉緊的，繃緊的

▶The tense and oppressive working environment has caused great pressure on the employees. 緊繃又壓抑的工作環境對員工造成很大的壓力。

v. 拉緊，繃緊，變得緊張

▶All his muscles were tensed as the game was about to begin.
比賽即將開始，他全身肌肉緊繃。

tension [`tɛnʃən]
◀ Track 4784
n. 拉緊，繃緊；緊張，緊張局勢

▶She suffered from nervous tensions as the deadline of the report was around the corner. 報告截止日快到的時候，她受神經緊張之苦。

tent [tɛnt] n. 帳篷
◀ Track 4785

▶We set up the tent and built the camp fire. 我們搭好帳篷並升起營火。

term [tɝm]
◀ Track 4786
n. 學期；任期；期限；條款；關係

▶The president fulfilled his promise to the voters during his term of office.
總統在任職期間實現了對選民的承諾。

terminal [`tɝ-mənl̩] ◀Track 4787

n. 末端，終點，極限；總站；航空站，航廈

▶The shuttle bus sends passengers to and forth between the terminals.
接駁車在航廈之間來回載運旅客。

adj. 末端的，終點的；末期的，晚期的；每期的

▶There are three more stops before we reach the terminal station.
還有三站就到達終點站了。

terrible [`tɛrəbl̩] ◀Track 4788

adj. 可怕的；嚇人的；令人不快的

▶Losing the game was a terrible blow to her.
輸掉這場比賽對她來說是可怕的打擊。

terrific [tə`rɪfɪk] ◀Track 4789

adj. 可怕的；嚇人的；非常好的

▶This novel is considered a terrific literary work by the contemporary critiques.
這本小說被當代的評論家認為是文學佳作。

terrify [`tɛrə,faɪ] ◀Track 4790

v. 使害怕

▶I was terrified by the bloody scenes in the horror movie.
我被恐怖電影中的血腥場面嚇到。

territory [`tɛrə,torɪ] ◀Track 4791

n. 領土，版圖；（知識的）領域，（行動的）範圍

▶The soldiers fought to protect the territory of their nation.
士兵們為了保護國家領土而戰。

相關片語 **not one's territory**
不是某人的內行領域

▶Electromagnetics is not my territory.
電磁學不是我擅長的領域。

terror [`tɛrə] ◀Track 4792

n. 恐怖，驚駭；引起恐怖的人或事物；恐怖行動，恐怖統治；極討厭的人

▶Residents in the war-torn area lived in terror; they were afraid that air strikes may occur anytime.
戰爭地區的居民活在恐懼中，他們害怕空襲隨時會發生。

test [tɛst] ◀Track 4793

n. 試驗；測驗；小考

▶They made a simple test to see if this is genuinely gold.
他們做了簡單的測試來看這是否為真金。

v. 測試；檢驗

▶The monarch tested the loyalty of his knights.
這名君王測試其騎士的忠誠度。

text [tɛkst] ◀Track 4794

n. 正文；課文，課本；版本；文字

▶The full text of the announcement takes more than ten pages.
這項聲明全文常超過十頁。

textbook [`tɛkst,bʊk] ◀Track 4795

n. 課本；教科書

▶The government has a guideline to regulate the content and structure of the textbooks for middle schools.
政府有一套綱要來規範中學教科書的內容和架構。

than [ðæn] ◀Track 4796

conj. 比；比較；與其；除了……之外

▶I would rather go for a run than staying at home being a couch potato.
我寧願去跑步，也不要在家裡躺在沙發上不動。

prep. 比起……；超過

▶In my opinion, she is much smarter than her brother.
就我的意見來看，她比她的哥哥還要聰明很多。

thank [θæŋk] **v.** 感謝　◀ Track 4797

▶I thanked the hostess for her hospitality.
我謝謝女主人的熱情款待。

n. 感謝；謝意

▶I expressed my thanks to my teacher by sending her a hand-drawn card.
我用手繪卡片表達我對老師的謝意。

thankful [`θæŋkfəl]　◀ Track 4798

adj. 感謝的

▶She was thankful to the doctor who performed the plastic surgery for her.
她感謝替她做整型手術的醫生。

Thanks·giv·ing　◀ Track 4799
[ˏθæŋks`gɪvɪŋ]
=Thanks·giv·ing Day

n. 感恩節

▶The whole family gathered for the Thanksgiving dinner.
整個家族的人聚在一起吃感恩節晚餐。

that [ðæt]　◀ Track 4800

conj. 因為；由於；為了；引導名詞子句

▶She was so intelligent that she went to college when she was twelve.
她聰明到十二歲就去上大學了。

pron. 那個；那人

▶The production efficiency in this quarter is better than that in the last quarter.
這一季的生產效率比上一季的好。

adj. 那個

▶That car belongs to the principal.
那輛車是校長的。

adv. 那樣

▶Try again. It isn't that difficult.
再試一次吧。沒有那麼困難。

that's [ðæts]　◀ Track 4801

abbr. 那是（**that is**的縮寫）

▶That's not the truth.
那不是真的。

the [ðə]　◀ Track 4802

art. 這（些）；那（些）

▶The news reports are all against the politician.
這些新聞報導都對那位政治人物不利。

theater [`θɪətə]　◀ Track 4803
=theatre （英式英語）

n. 劇場；電影院

▶The seats in the theater are specially designed for 4D movies.
這個戲院的座位是特別設計來看4D電影的。

theft [θɛft]　◀ Track 4804

n. 偷竊，盜竊

▶The case of the unbelievable theft was solved within three days.
這起令人感到不可置信的竊盜案件在三天之內就偵破了。

their [ðɛr] **det.** 他們的
◀ Track 4805

▶Their argument was not robust.
他們的論點並不穩固。

theirs [ðɛrz]
◀ Track 4806

pron. 他們的（東西）

▶Our proposal is much more logical than theirs. 我們的提案比他們的有條理多了。

them [ðɛm] **pron.** 他們
◀ Track 4807

▶The clients will arrive soon. We are supposed to welcome them at the gate.
客戶快到了。我們應該要在大門迎接他們。

theme [θim]
◀ Track 4808

n. 論題，話題；主題

▶The program was banned on TV because its theme caused too much controversy. 這個節目因為主題製造了太多爭議而在電視上面被禁播了。

themselves
◀ Track 4809

[ðəm`sɛlvz] **pron.** 他們自己

▶The tourists in the hostel would do the laundry themselves.
住在青年旅館的旅客會自己洗衣服。

then [ðɛn] **adv.** 那時；然後
◀ Track 4810

▶Our offer was rejected. What does the client prefer, then? 我們提供的服務被拒絕了。那麼，客戶是想要什麼呢？

adj. 當時的

▶The building was constructed in 2004. The then principal hoped the new facilities could attract more students.
這棟大樓是在2004年建造的。當時的校長希望新的設施可以吸引更多學生。

theory [`θiəri]
◀ Track 4811

n. 學說，理論；意見，揣測

▶Her theory is that the kids could learn two languages at the same time.
她的理論是小孩子可以同時學習兩種語言。

相關片語 **in theory** 理論上

▶It sounds good in theory, but it is not practical.
這理論上聽起來很好，但並不實際。

therapy [`θɛrəpɪ]
◀ Track 4812

n. 治療，療法

▶The folklore therapy was developed by an amateur doctor who doesn't have a medical degree.
這種民俗療法是由一位沒有醫學學位的業餘醫生發明的。

there [ðɛr]
◀ Track 4813

adv. 在那裡；到那裡

▶Kevin immigrated to Canada and went to college there.
凱文移民到加拿大，並在那裡讀大學。

pron. 那個地方；那裡

▶There is a beautiful monument in our new campus.
我們的新校區裡有一個漂亮的紀念碑。

therefore [`ðɛr͵for]
◀ Track 4814

adv. 因此

▶I think, therefore I am.
我思故我在。

there's [ðɛrz]
◀ Track 4815

abbr. 那裡有（**there is** 的縮寫）

▶He can't play chess as well as her. There's no comparison.
他下棋沒有下得和她一樣好。根本沒得比。

中級

these [ðiz]
pron. 這些人；這些東西

▶These are the documents that you have to sort this afternoon.
這是你今天下午要分類的文件。

adj. 這些

▶These questions are much more difficult than the previous ones.
這些問題比先前的問題更加困難。

◀ Track 4816

they [ðe] **pron.** 他們

▶They are supposed to attend the meeting this afternoon.
他們應該要出席今天下午的研討會。

◀ Track 4817

they'd [ðed]
abbr. 他們會、他們已（they would、they had的縮寫）

▶Please give them a hand. They'd appreciate your help.
請幫他們一下。他們會很感謝你。

◀ Track 4818

they'll [ðel]
abbr. 他們會（they will的縮寫）

▶Don't worry. They'll come back safe and sound.
別擔心，他們會平安回來的。

◀ Track 4819

they're [ðer]
abbr. 他們是（they are的縮寫）

▶They're about to succeed.
他們快要成功了。

◀ Track 4820

they've [ðev]
abbr. 他們已（they have 的縮寫）

▶They've changed their mind.
他們改變心意了。

◀ Track 4821

thick [θɪk]
adj. 厚的；粗的；濃的

▶The thick sea ice in the Arctic has been melting in the past decade.
北極的厚冰層過去十年來一直在融化。

◀ Track 4822

thief [θif] **n.** 小偷

▶The thief sprained his ankle when he was trying to run away.
小偷想要跑走時扭傷了腳踝。

◀ Track 4823

thin [θɪn]
adj. 瘦的；薄的；稀少的

▶They were very cautious as if they were walking on the thin ice.
他們謹慎小心，如履薄冰。

◀ Track 4824

thing [θɪŋ] **n.** 事情；東西

▶The most important thing is to take good care of your family.
最重要的事情是要好好照顧你的家人。

◀ Track 4825

think [θɪŋk]
v. 想；認為；想起；打算

▶I can't think of a reason why they wouldn't stay.
我想不通為什麼他們不願意留下來。

◀ Track 4826

thinking [ˋθɪŋkɪŋ]
n. 思想，思考

▶Positive thinking is sometimes helpful to you.
正向思考有時對你會有幫助。

adj. 思想的，有理性的，好思考的

▶Any thinking person would not fall for the fraud.
只要稍微用點腦，就不會被這個騙局所害。

◀ Track 4827

third [θɝd]　◀ Track 4828

adj. 第三的；三分之一

▶The girl who suffered from a rare disease could not survive until her third birthday.
這名罹患罕見疾病的女孩活不到三歲。

adv. 第三

▶Heart disease came third on the list of common chronic diseases for modern people.
心臟病在現代人常見的慢性病中排名第三。

n. 第三名；三分之一

▶She was the third in the singing contest. 她是這場歌唱比賽中的第三名。

thirst [θɝst]　◀ Track 4829

n. 渴，口渴；渴望

▶They drank the spring water to quest their thirst. 他們喝泉水來止渴。

v. 口渴；渴望

▶He thirsted for wealth and fame.
他渴望財富和名聲。

thirsty [ˋθɝstɪ]　◀ Track 4830

adj. 渴的；口渴的；渴望的

▶I felt thirsty after eating up the whole pack of potato chips.
吃完一整包洋芋片之後，我感覺口渴。

thirteen [ˋθɝtin]　◀ Track 4831

n. 十三；十三個；十三歲

▶Six plus seven equals thirteen.
六加上七是十三。

adj. 十三的；十三個的

▶She was thirteen when she uploaded her first music video to Youtube.
她上傳第一支音樂影片到Youtube 網站時才十三歲。

thirty [ˋθɝtɪ] **n.** 三十　◀ Track 4832

▶Ten times three equals thirty.
十乘以三等於三十。

adj. 三十

▶Thirty percent of the participants in the survey showed positive attitude toward this computer software.
這個調查中有百分之三十的受訪者對這個電腦軟體有正面的態度。

this [ðɪs] **pron.** 這個　◀ Track 4833

▶I think you can do better than this.
我想你可以做得比這好。

adj. 這個

▶This campaign was initiated by a female entrepreneur.
這個活動是由一位女性創業家發起的。

adv. 這麼；像這樣地

▶I have never been this close to such a celebrity like you.
我從來沒有這麼接近像你一樣的名人過。

thorough [ˋθɝo]　◀ Track 4834

adj. 徹底的

▶We had a thorough inspection on the machine.
我們徹底地檢查了這台機器。

those [ðoz] **pron.** 那些　◀ Track 4835

▶The teenagers reached out to help those who are in need.
這群年輕人去幫助了那些需要幫助的人。

adj. 那些的

▶Those baskets are for collecting the oranges.
那些籃子是用來採集柳橙的。

中級

though [ðo]
◀Track 4836

conj. 雖然；儘管

▶Though they went through so much hardship, they did not give up easily.
雖然他們經過很多苦難，卻沒有輕易放棄。

adv. 然而

▶I didn't expect them to make any contribution, though.
但我是不期待他們為會有什麼貢獻啦。

thought [θɔt]
◀Track 4837

n. 思維；想法；考慮

▶The negative thoughts kept him from trying again. 負面想法讓他無法再試一次。

thoughtful [`θɔtfəl]
◀Track 4838

adj. 深思的，沉思的；經認真思考的；細心的，體貼周到的

▶We were in a thoughtful mood after we listened to her lecture.
聽了她的演講後，我們陷入沉思。

thousand [`θaʊznd]
◀Track 4839

n. 一千；一千個

▶The face value of the bill is one thousand. 這張鈔票的面額是一千元。

adj. 一千的；成千的；無數的

▶The car has run for more than a thousand miles after it was produced.
這台車生產之後跑了超過一千英里。

thread [θrɛd]
◀Track 4840

n. 線，線狀物；頭緒

▶We had a thread of hope when the philanthropist promised to support our campaign.
慈善家答應支持我們的活動時，我們有了一線希望。

v. 穿（針線），把……穿成一串；通過，穿透過

▶The explorers threaded the desert area which has been untrodden for decades. 這些探險家穿越幾十年沒有人走過的沙漠地區。

threat [θrɛt]
◀Track 4841

n. 威脅，恐嚇；構成威脅的人或事

▶The terrorists posed a threat to the security of the local residents.
這群恐怖分子對當地居民的安全造成威脅。

threaten [`θrɛtn]
◀Track 4842

v. 威脅，恐嚇，揚言要……

▶The hijacker threatened to explode a bomb if the captain did not follow his words.
這名劫機者威脅要引爆炸彈，如果機長不按照他指示而做的話。

three [θri] **n.** 三；三個
◀Track 4843

▶Three plus two equals five.
三加二等於五。

adj. 三的

▶The boy was three when he made his debut.
這個男孩初次登上舞台時才三歲。

throat [θrot] **n.** 喉嚨
◀Track 4844

▶He got the fish bone stuck in his throat.
魚骨頭卡在他的喉嚨裡。

through [θru]
◀Track 4845

prep. 穿過；通過

▶We went through the forest to reach the remote village.
我們穿過森林到達偏遠的村莊。

adv. 穿過;通過;從頭到尾

▶They binge-watched the Korean drama the whole night through.
他們徹夜狂看韓劇。

throughout [θru`aʊt] ◀Track 4846
prep. 遍佈;從頭到尾;貫穿

▶The convenience store has branches throughout the country.
這家便利商店在全國都有分店。

throw [θro] **v.** 丟 ◀Track 4847

▶The mischievous boy threw stones at the stray dog.
頑皮的小男孩對流浪狗丟擲石頭。

thumb [θʌm] **n.** 拇指 ◀Track 4848

▶The magician held the card between his thumb and forefinger.
魔術師用大拇指和食指夾著卡片。

thunder [`θʌndɚ] ◀Track 4849
n. 雷聲;雷

▶The kittens were frightened by the thunder.
這群小貓被雷聲嚇到。

v. 打雷;發出雷般聲響;大聲斥責

▶The trucks thundered through the street. 卡車大聲地通過街道。

thunderstorm ◀Track 4850
[`θʌndɚ‚stɔrm] **n.** 大雷雨

▶After the thunderstorm, there was a flood in the small village.
大雷雨過後,小鎮淹水了。

Thursday [`θɝzde] ◀Track 4851
=Thurs./Thur. **n.** 星期四

▶Thanksgiving is celebrated on the fourth Thursday in November.
感恩節於十一月的第四個星期四慶祝。

thus [ðʌs] **adv.** 因此 ◀Track 4852

▶She went on a business trip for three days. Thus, she asked her neighbor to look after her cat.
她要去出差三天。所以,她請鄰居照顧她的貓

ticket [`tɪkɪt] **n.** 票 ◀Track 4853

▶They ordered tickets to May Day's concert on the Internet.
他們在網路上訂五月天演唱會的門票。

tickle [`tɪkl̩] ◀Track 4854
v. 呵癢,使發癢;使發笑;觸

▶The doctor tickled the baby's belly and made him laugh.
醫生搔癢小寶寶的肚子逗他笑。

tide [taɪd] **n.** 潮汐 ◀Track 4855

▶Time and tide wait for no man.
歲月不饒人。

tidy [`taɪdɪ] ◀Track 4856
adj. 整齊的;井然有序的

▶The secretary always keeps her desk tidy.
這位秘書總是把桌子整理得很乾淨。

v. 收拾

▶The author introduces some tips of tidying things up in her new book.
這名作家在新書中介紹一些整理東西的訣竅。

tie [taɪ] ◀Track 4857
n. 領帶;聯繫;束縛

中級

▶ After negotiating for several months, we built business ties with the foreign company.
經過幾個月的協商之後，我們和這家外國公司建立商業關係。

v. 繫；綁；打結；結為夫妻

▶ The fisher tied the boat to the wooden pile by the harbor.
這名漁夫把船隻綁在港口旁邊的木樁上。

tiger [`taɪɡɚ] **n.** 虎
◀ Track 4858

▶ The claws of the tiger were pulled off. Why was anyone so brutal?
老虎的爪子被拔掉了。為什麼有人這麼殘忍？

tight [taɪt]
◀ Track 4859

adj. 緊的；緊貼的；密封的；（比賽）勢均力敵的

▶ The principal has such a tight schedule that we seldom see him on campus.
校長的日程表是如此緊湊以至於我們很少在校園中看到他。

adv. 緊緊地，牢牢地

▶ The owner of the dog tied the leash tight. 這名狗狗的主人把牽繩綁緊了。

tighten [`taɪtn]
◀ Track 4860

v. 使變緊，使繃緊

▶ The runner tightened her shoelaces before the race.
跑者在賽跑前將鞋帶繫緊。

相關片語 **tighten one's belt**
束緊腰帶過日

▶ We had to tighten our belt at the end of the month.
到了月底，我們得束緊腰帶過日子。

till [tɪl]=un·til
◀ Track 4861

prep. 直到⋯⋯才

▶ We started at the starry night sky and chatted till dawn.
我們盯著夜空，聊到天亮。

conj. 直到⋯⋯

▶ Tina waited until her husband came home. 緹娜一直等到她老公回家。

timber [`tɪmbɚ]
◀ Track 4862

n. 木材，木料

▶ The timber in the warehouse caught fire. 倉庫的木柴著火了。

time [taɪm] **n.** 時間
◀ Track 4863

▶ We had enough time to go through the details in the report.
我們有足夠的時間可以看這份報告的細節。

v. 為⋯⋯計時；預定⋯⋯的時間

▶ The train is timed to arrive in Moscow at 8 o'clock. 火車預計八點到達莫斯科。

timetable [`taɪm͵tebl]
◀ Track 4864

n. （車次的）時刻表；時間表

▶ Check the timetable of the High Speed Rail on its official website.
在官方網站上面查高鐵的時刻表。

v. 把⋯⋯排入時間表；把⋯⋯排入時刻表；把⋯⋯列入課程表

▶ We timetabled the meeting at 10 a.m.
我們將會議時間訂於早上十點。

timid [`tɪmɪd]
◀ Track 4865

adj. 膽小的，易受驚的，羞怯的

▶ The timid boy would not look people in the eyes when talking to others.
這個膽小的男孩，和人說話時不敢直視對方。

tin [tɪn]
◀ Track 4866
n. 錫；馬口鐵，鍍錫鐵皮；罐

▶I made stilts with tins and sticks.
我用錫鐵罐和棍子做了高蹺。

tiny [`taɪnɪ]
◀ Track 4867
adj. 極小的；微小的

▶The meticulous lady would not miss any tiny mistake when she is proofreading a manuscript.
校對手稿時，這位細心的女士從來不會放過任何微小的錯誤。

tip [tɪp] **n.** 小費
◀ Track 4868
▶A five percent tip was added to the bill.
帳單上有多加百分之五的小費。

v. 給……小費

▶The wealthy man tipped the maid who cleaned his room.
這位富翁給打掃他房間的房務女士小費。

tiptoe [`tɪp‚to]
◀ Track 4869
v. 踮著腳；踮起腳走；躡手躡腳

▶We tiptoed in the living room for fear of waking up our parents.
我們在客廳墊腳走路，怕吵醒爸媽。

n. 腳尖

▶The thief walked on tiptoe in the corridor.
小偷在走廊上墊腳尖走路。

tire [taɪr]
◀ Track 4870
=tyre （英式英文）**n.** 輪胎

▶Our schedule was delayed because we had a flat tire on the road.
我們行程延誤了，因為在路上車輪胎沒氣。

v. 使疲倦，使厭煩

▶The mundane work tired him.
乏味的工作令他疲倦。

tired [taɪrd]
◀ Track 4871
adj. 疲累的；厭倦的

▶He was tired of doing the repetitive work.
他厭倦一再重複工作。

tiresome [`taɪrsəm]
◀ Track 4872
adj. 令人疲勞的，使人厭倦的；討厭的，煩人的

▶It was tiresome to deal with the clerical work.
處理文書工作很累。

tiring [`taɪərɪŋ]
◀ Track 4873
adj. 累人的，令人疲倦的；麻煩的，無聊的

▶I'd like to have some refreshments after the tiring meeting.
在無聊的會議之後，我想要吃點心。

tissue [`tɪʃʊ]
◀ Track 4874
n. 面紙、衛生紙；薄織物；（動植物）組織

▶It was said that the price of tissue will rise next year.
據說明年衛生紙價會調漲。

title [`taɪtl]
◀ Track 4875
n. 標題；書名；頭銜；名稱

▶Judging from the title of the book, it should be about economics.
根據這本書的標題，它應該是關於經濟學。

to [tu] **prep.** 向；往；到
◀ Track 4876
▶The train to Pusan will depart in ten minutes.
往金山的火車，十分鐘後發車。

中級

485

inf. 不定詞
▶To see is to believe.
眼見為憑。

toast [tost]　◀Track 4877
n. 吐司；烤麵包片；**v.** 烤（麵包）；烘（手或腳）
▶The automatic toast maker costs about three thousand dollars.
這台自動吐司機大約要三千元。

tobacco [tə`bæko]　◀Track 4878
n. 菸草，菸草製品；抽菸
▶Some people use Nicotine patch to help them get rid of the addiction to tobacco.
有些人用尼古丁貼片幫助戒掉菸癮。

today [tə`de] **adv.** 今天　◀Track 4879
▶The education system today is different from that in the last century.
現在的教育系統和上個世紀的不同。

n. 今天
▶Today is not my day.
我今天運氣不好。

toe [to] **n.** 腳趾；足尖　◀Track 4880
▶Tom kept stepping on his partner's toes while dancing.
跳舞時，湯姆一直踩到舞伴的腳趾。

tofu [`tofu]　◀Track 4881
=bean curd **n.** 豆腐
▶Stinky tofu is often seasoned with pickles. 臭豆腐常常會搭配泡菜。

together [tə`gɛðɚ]　◀Track 4882
adv. 一起；合起來

▶The students had to work together to complete the project.
學生們必須要合作才能完成這個計畫。

toilet [`tɔɪlɪt]　◀Track 4883
n. 馬桶；廁所、洗手間
▶The automatic toilet seat is controlled by a microcomputer chip.
這個自動馬桶座是微電腦晶片控制的。

tolerable [`tɑlərəbl]　◀Track 4884
adj. 可忍受的
▶This level of noise was not tolerable to me.
這個噪音的程度令我無法忍受。

tolerance [`tɑlərəns]　◀Track 4885
n. 寬容
▶The teacher has no tolerance to cheating in exams.
這名老師對考試作弊毫不寬待。

tolerant [`tɑlərənt]　◀Track 4886
adj. 忍受的，容忍的，寬恕的；有耐性的；有耐藥力的
▶The rock climber trained himself to be tolerant of scorching weather.
這位攀岩者訓練自己忍受酷熱的天氣。

tolerate [`tɑlə͵ret]　◀Track 4887
v. 忍受，寬容
▶She could not tolerate any visible dirt in the house.
她不容許家裡有明顯的灰塵。

tomato [tə`meto]　◀Track 4888
n. 番茄

▶People in Bunol, a small town in Spain, celebrate the tomato festival annually.
西班牙小鎮布諾的居民，每年都會慶祝番茄節。

tomb [tum] n. 墓碑

◀Track 4889

▶Some of the tombs in the graveyard were covered with weeds.
這個墓園中有些墓碑被雜草覆蓋。

相關片語 **Tomb-sweeping Day**
清明掃墓節

▶On Tomb-sweeping Day, many people would worship their ancestors.
在清明節，許多人會去祭拜祖先。

tomorrow [tə`mɔro]

◀Track 4890

adv. 明天

▶The tournament will be held tomorrow.
決賽明天進行。

n. 明天

▶Tomorrow is a big day. We will launch our new product.
明天是個大日子。我們要發行新產品。

ton [tʌn]

◀Track 4891

n. 噸；公噸；大量，許多

▶Tons of plastic waste was produced each year.
每年都有好多噸的塑膠垃圾被製造出來。

相關片語 **weigh a ton** 非常沈重

▶Did you carry a dictionary in your backpack? It weighs a ton!
你在背包裡面裝字典嗎？它好重！

tone [ton]

◀Track 4892

n. 色調；音調；腔調；氣氛

▶He always speaks in a teasing tone to his younger sister.
他總是用嘲笑的口吻和她妹妹說話。

v. 調音；為⋯⋯定調；裝腔作勢地說；增強，提高

▶The training of weight lifting has toned up my muscles.
舉重的訓練讓我的肌肉變得更強健了。

補充片語 **tone up** 強化，提高

▶Jogging regularly is a good way to tone up your body.
規律地慢跑是一個強化體質的好方法。

tongue [tʌŋ]

◀Track 4893

n. 舌頭；說話方式；語言

▶He had a slip of tongue and apologized for his mistake later.
他不小心口誤，並在稍後為自己的錯誤道歉。

tonight [tə`naɪt]

◀Track 4894

adv. 今晚

▶We will have a house warming party tonight.
我們今晚會辦一個喬遷新居的派對。

n. 今晚

▶Tonight is the time when we can observe the lunar eclipse with our naked eyes.
今晚就是我們可以用肉眼觀察月蝕的時間。

too [tu] adv. 太；也

◀Track 4895

▶They were too stiff to learn Waltz.
他們太僵硬了，學不了華爾滋。

tool [tul]

◀Track 4896

n. 工具；方法；手段

中級

▶ Body language is an important tool for communication.
肢體語言是一個很重要的溝通工具。

tooth [tuθ] n. 牙齒
🔊 Track 4897

▶ It's a good habit to brush your teeth after each meal.
每餐飯後都刷牙是一個好習慣。

toothache [`tuθˌek]
🔊 Track 4898
n. 牙痛

▶ She is suffering from a bad toothache, but she would not go to see a dentist.
她牙齒很痛，但是她不想去看牙醫。

toothbrush
🔊 Track 4899
[`tuθˌbrʌʃ] n. 牙刷

▶ The dentist wrote a review on the newly-released electric toothbrush.
這名牙醫針對這隻剛上市的電動牙刷寫了一篇評論。

toothpaste
🔊 Track 4900
[`tuθˌpest] n. 牙膏

▶ What should I do if I swallow the toothpaste by accident?
如果我不小心把牙膏吞下去該怎麼辦？

top [tɑp]
🔊 Track 4901
n. 頂端；頂部；上方；頂點

▶ The chef sprinkled some sugar on the top of the cake.
廚師在蛋糕的上方灑糖粉。

adj. 頂上的；最高的；居首位的

▶ The project is of top importance; we should deal with it first.
這個計畫是最重要的；我們要首先處理它。

v. 給……加蓋；達到……的頂部；高於

▶ The Fuji Mountain is topped with snow all year round.
富士山頂終年積雪。

topic [`tɑpɪk]
🔊 Track 4902
n. 題目；話題；標題

▶ When the host realized that the topic embarrassed the guest, she changed the subject of the conversation immediately.
當主持人發覺來賓對這個話題感到尷尬時，她立刻就換了對話的主題。

torch [tɔrtʃ]
🔊 Track 4903
n. 火炬，火把；手電筒；（文化、知識的）光；（對某人的）愛火

▶ The runner handed the torch on to the representative of the city which will host the next Olympic Games.
跑者將火炬傳給下個奧運主辦城市的代表。

▶ The old palace was put to the torch.
那間古代宮殿已經付之一炬了。

補充片語 **put to the torch**
付之一炬；燒掉

v. 縱火

▶ They torched document to destroy the evidence of their evil deeds.
他們縱火燒了文件以毀滅他們惡行的證據。

tornado [tɔr`nedo]
🔊 Track 4904
n. 龍捲風，旋風，颶風

▶ The storm chaser recorded how the tornado struck the town and uploaded the video to the Internet.
追風者錄下龍捲風襲擊小鎮的情況，並將影片上傳到網路上。

tortoise [`tɔrtəs]
🔊 Track 4905
n. 烏龜，陸龜；行動遲緩的人

▶The hare sat on the tortoise and had a free ride.
野兔坐在烏龜身上搭便車。

toss [tɔs] ◀≣Track 4906

v. 拋，扔，投；突然抬起；擲幣打賭；甩頭離去

▶Some tourists tossed coins into the wishing well.
有些遊客丟擲硬幣到許願池裡。

n. 拋，扔，投；投擲的距離；擲幣決定

▶We decided who played first with a toss of a coin.
我們用擲錢幣來決定誰先開球。

相關片語 **not give a toss** 毫不在乎

▶I don't give a toss about their critiques.
我毫不在乎他們的批評。

total [`totl] ◀≣Track 4907

adj. 總記的；全體的

▶The total number of the students in the school has been gradually decreasing in the past few years.
學校學生總數在過去幾年來逐漸減少。

n. 總數

▶The total of the vacuum cleaners we sold last year remain unknown.
去年吸塵器的總銷售量還不清楚。

v. 合計為；總計

▶The number of foreigners applying for political asylum in Canada totaled two hundred. 總共有兩百名外國人申請加拿大的政治庇護。

touch [tʌtʃ] **v.** 摸；觸碰 ◀≣Track 4908

▶Don't touch the bake pan with your hand; you'll get burned.
不要用手碰烤盤，你會燙傷的。

n. 觸覺；觸感；接觸；聯繫

▶Let's stay in touch.
我們保持聯繫吧。

tough [tʌf] ◀≣Track 4909

adj. 堅韌的；強硬的；不屈不撓的；不幸的；棘手的；嚴格的

▶This is a tough problem. We may have to spend a lot of time on it.
這個問題很難處理。我們可能會花很多時間在那上面。

n. 粗暴的人；暴徒；惡棍

▶ A gang of toughs robbed the car from the man.
一幫惡棍搶奪了那名男子的車。

v. 堅毅地抵抗

▶In face of all the difficulties, she tought them out and finally started her own business.
面對所有困難，她堅強地撐過去，最後成功創業。

tour [tʊr] ◀≣Track 4910

n. 旅行；旅遊；巡迴演出

▶The tour included the art museum and the aquarium.
這次的旅行包括了美術館和水族館。

v. 旅行；在……旅遊

▶We toured around the old city and visited the Parthenon Temple.
我們在舊城裡旅遊並參觀了帕德嫩神廟。

tourism [`tʊrɪzəm] ◀≣Track 4911

n. 旅遊，觀光；旅遊業，觀光業

▶Tourism is important for the economic development in this African country.
觀光業對這個非洲國家的經濟發展很重要。

中級

tourist [`tʊrɪst]
◀ᵉ Track 4912

n. 旅遊者；旅客，觀光客

▶The wall of the ancient temple was covered with graffiti from tourists.
這座古廟的牆上滿是觀光客的塗鴉。

相關片語 **tourist attraction**
觀光勝地，旅遊勝地

▶Taroko Gorge is one of the most popular tourist attractions in Taiwan.
太魯閣是台灣一個很受歡迎的觀光勝地。

tow [to] **v.** 拉，拖，牽引
◀ᵉ Track 4913

▶Her car was towed away because she occupied the parking space reserved for the handicapped.
她的車被拖走了，因為她占用殘障車位。

n. 拉，拖，牽引

▶I called for a road rescue service. My car broke down and I need someone to give it a tow.
我打電話請求道路救援。我車子拋錨了，需要有人拖車。

to·ard [tə`wɔrd]
◀ᵉ Track 4914
=to·ards **prep.** 朝；向

▶The valedictorian walked toward the stage confidently.
這名畢業生代表自信滿滿地走向舞台。

towel [`taʊəl] **n.** 毛巾
◀ᵉ Track 4915

▶I never use the towel in the hotel room because I am not sure whether it is sanitized.
我從來不用飯店的毛巾，因為我不確定它是否有消毒過。

tower [`taʊɚ]
◀ᵉ Track 4916

n. 塔；高樓

▶The soldier scouted the actions of the enemy on the tower.
這名士兵從高塔上面偵測敵軍的活動。

town [taʊn] **n.** 城鎮
◀ᵉ Track 4917

▶The town in the boarder was occupied by the rebel army.
這座邊境的小鎮被反叛軍佔領了。

toy [tɔɪ] **n.** 玩具
◀ᵉ Track 4918

▶The plastic toy was not worthy of two hundred dollars.
這個塑膠玩具不值兩百元。

trace [tres] **v.** 追蹤
◀ᵉ Track 4919

▶The dog could trace the whereabouts of the suspect by his smell.
這隻狗可以透過嫌犯的味道追蹤他的下落。

n. 蹤跡

▶There is no trace of the endangered species in the wild.
在野外已經看不到這個瀕危物種的蹤跡了。

track [træk]
◀ᵉ Track 4920

n. 行蹤；軌道；小徑

▶We took a stroll down the track in the woods.
我們沿著森林的小路散步。

v. 跟蹤；追蹤

▶The police tracked down the illegal drug dealers.
警方追蹤到了非法走私毒品的罪犯。

trade [tred] **n.** 交易；貿易
◀ᵉ Track 4921

▶The trade between China and the U.S. remained prosperous in the past few years.
過去幾年中美之間的貿易維持繁榮。

v. 進行交易；交換；做買賣

▶The government traded with terrorist group to make sure the hostage was safe. 政府和恐怖份子團體進行交易，確保人質安全。

trademark
◀Track 4922

[`tred͵mɑrk] **n.** 商標；（人或物的）標記，特徵

▶The company has modified its trademark to illustrate the inner renovation of it.
公司修改了商標，象徵內部的革新。

trader [`tredɚ]
◀Track 4923

n. 商人，商船；交易人

▶The trader was accused of selling counterfeit products.
這名商人被指控販賣偽造的商品。

tradition [trə`dɪʃən]
◀Track 4924

n. 傳統；慣例

▶It is a tradition that the elders give kids in the family red envelopes with lucky money inside during Chinese New Year.
過年時，長輩給家中小孩壓歲錢紅包是一項傳統。

traditional [trə`dɪʃənl]
◀Track 4925

adj. 傳統的；慣例的

▶Gina was born in a traditional family; her parents are very conservative.
吉娜出生在傳統的家庭；她的父母很保守。

traffic [`træfɪk] **n.** 交通
◀Track 4926

▶The traffic was horrible during rush hours.
尖峰時間的交通非常糟糕。

tragedy [`trædʒədɪ]
◀Track 4927

n. 悲劇；悲劇性事件，慘案，災難

▶Two car racers were killed in the accident. What a tragedy!
兩名賽車手在意外中喪生。真是個悲劇！

tragic [`trædʒɪk]
◀Track 4928

adj. 悲劇的；悲慘的，不幸的；悲痛的

▶The plane crash was a tragic accident.
這次空難真是不幸的意外。

trail [trel] **n.** 痕跡
◀Track 4929

▶The hikers found trials of wild deer in the forest.
這群登山者在森林裡面發現野生鹿的足跡。

v. 拖曳；跟蹤；追獵；蔓生

▶The police trailed the source of the goods and found the manufacturer of the counterfeit products.
警方追蹤商品的來源，發現了偽造品的製造商。

train [tren] **n.** 火車
◀Track 4930

▶My brother displays his various models of trains in the showcase.
我哥用櫥櫃展示他的多種火車模型。

v. 訓練；培養；接受訓練；鍛鍊

▶The service dog was trained to assist visually-impaired people.
這隻導盲犬受過訓練，協助眼盲的人。

training [`trenɪŋ]
◀Track 4931

n. 訓練，培養

▶The academic training from the institution has made her a qualified instructor.
這個機構的學術訓練使她成為一位合格的講師。

中級

相關片語 **on-the-job training** 在職訓練

▶Our company offers on-the-job training for novice workers.
我們公司有為新進員工提供在職訓練。

transfer [træns`fɝ] ◀ Track 4932

n. 遷移，移交，轉讓

▶The transfer of our office site was announced on the website.
我們辦公室的搬遷消息已公布在官方網站上。

v. 搬，轉換，調動；換車，轉學；轉讓，讓渡

▶Mary's mother has transferred her to a school in our neighboring county.
瑪莉的媽媽已經幫她轉學到隔壁縣的學校了。

transform ◀ Track 4933

[træns`fɔrm] **v.** 使改變；轉換；改造

▶Steve transformed the garage in his father's house into his studio.
史提夫將父親家的車庫改造成自己的工作室。

transit [`trænsɪt] ◀ Track 4934

n. 運輸；公共交通運輸系統

▶The rapid transit system reaches most of the metropolitan area.
捷運系統可達大部分的都會地區。

translate [træns`let] ◀ Track 4935

v. 翻譯，轉譯；（以不同的說法）解釋，說明

▶The volunteers translated English documents into Mandarin for the sponsors.
志工們替贊助者將英文文件翻譯成中文。

translation ◀ Track 4936

[træns`leʃən] **n.** 翻譯；譯文，譯本

▶The translation made from the robot was unreadable.
這個機器人做的翻譯令人無法理解。

translator ◀ Track 4937

[træns`letɚ] **n.** 譯者，譯員，翻譯；翻譯家；翻譯機

▶The portable translator machine may be of great help when you travel to a foreign country.
這個可攜式翻譯機可能是你去國外旅遊時的好幫手。

相關片語 **automatic language translator** 自動語言翻譯機

▶The design of the automatic language translator is not sophisticated enough.
這個自動語言翻譯機的設計還不夠精密。

transplant ◀ Track 4938

[træns`plænt] **n.** 移植；移植器官

▶The transplant has caused rejection in the patient.
病人對移植器官有排斥反應。

v. 移植；移種；移居

▶The old oak tree was transplanted to the park due to the road-widening work.
老榆樹被移植到公園中，以便進行道路拓寬。

transport [`træns,port] ◀ Track 4939

n. 運輸；交通工具；交通運輸系統

▶The municipal government has increased budget for improving the public transport in the new fiscal year.
新的一年，市政府有增加預算要改善大眾運輸系統。

v. 運送，運輸；搬運

▶ The goods will be transported to Shanghai by boat.
這些貨物會透過船運送到上海。

transportation
🔊 Track 4940

[ˌtrænspəˈteʃən] **n.** 運輸，輸送；運輸工具，交通工具；旅費，交通費

▶ Public transportation system is a very important infrastructure of a city.
運輸系統對一個城市來說是很重要的建設。

trap [træp]
🔊 Track 4941

v. 設陷阱捕捉；使落入圈套；堵塞

▶ The con artist trapped the old lady to transmit money to a hacked account.
詐騙者設陷阱讓老婦人匯錢到一個遭盜用的帳戶裡。

n. 陷阱；圈套

▶ The old man set a trap to catch the hare.
老人設陷阱要抓野兔。

trash [træʃ]
🔊 Track 4942

n. 垃圾；廢物；無用的人

▶ The man has been hoarding trash in his house for years.
這個人多年來一直在家中累積垃圾。

travel [ˈtrævl̩]
🔊 Track 4943

v. 旅行；移動

▶ Rita traveled to Europe and Africa during her gap year.
瑞塔上大學前，到歐洲和非洲旅行了一年。

n. 旅行；遊歷；旅遊業；移動

▶ The ten day's travel by train through Europe was unforgettable.
搭火車遊歐洲十天的這趟旅程令人難忘。

traveler [ˈtrævlɚ]
=traveller （英式英文）
🔊 Track 4944

n. 旅行者，旅客

▶ Nowadays, some travelers would look for choices of accommodation on Airbnb. 現在有些旅行者會去Airbnb網站尋找住宿的選擇。

traveling [ˈtrævl̩ɪŋ]
=travelling （英式英文）
🔊 Track 4945

adj. 流動的；旅行用的；旅行的

▶ I looked for a traveling companion by posting a piece of article on the online bulletin board system.
我在線上公告系統張貼文章來找旅行夥伴。

tray [tre]
🔊 Track 4946

n. 盤子、托盤，文件盒

▶ The clerk signaled me to put the changes in the tray on the counter.
這名公務員示意我將零錢放在櫃台上的托盤裡。

treasure [ˈtrɛʒɚ]
🔊 Track 4947

n. 金銀財寶；貴重物品

▶ Legend has it that the pirates hid the treasures on the deserted island.
傳說海盜將金銀財寶藏在這座無人島上。

v. 珍惜；珍視

▶ I treasure the kinship with my brother and sister.
我很重視我和哥哥姊姊之間的關係。

treat [trit]
🔊 Track 4948

v. 對待；處理；治療；款待、請客

▶ I treated the task my boss assigned to me seriously.
我很認真看待我老闆交代給我的任務。

中級

n. 請客

▶ Order whatever you like on the menu. It's the boss's treat today!
點菜單上任何你喜歡的菜吧。今天是老闆請客！

treatment [`tritmənt]　◀Track 4949
n. 對待；處理；治療；療法

▶ She couldn't afford the medical treatment, so she turned to her parents for help.
她負擔不起醫療費用，所以請求父母的協助。

treaty [`tritɪ]　◀Track 4950
n. 條約，協定，契約，協議

▶ The government has signed a treaty to regulate the CO2 emission of domestic factories.
政府簽訂條約要規範國內工廠的二氧化碳排放。

tree [tri] **n.** 樹　◀Track 4951

▶ The industrialization of the area caused deforestation; there are few trees in the hills now.
這地區的工業化造成森林消失；山上已經很少樹了。

tremble [`trɛmbl]　◀Track 4952
v. 發抖，顫震；搖晃；擔憂

▶ The bank clerk trembled when the robber shouted threatening words at her.
搶匪對銀行行員大聲威脅，她嚇得發抖。

n. 震顫，發抖；震動

▶ I could tell from the tremble in her voice that she was really angry.
從她顫抖的聲音裡，我可以感覺到她很生氣。

tremendous　◀Track 4953
[trɪ`mɛndəs] **adj.** 巨大的，極大的；極度的，驚人的；很棒的

▶ The 2014 tsunami caused tremendous damage to India.
2014年的海嘯對印度造成極大的損失。

trend [trɛnd]　◀Track 4954
n. 走向，趨勢；傾向，時尚

▶ Subscribe our magazine, and you can keep up with the latest fashion trend.
訂閱我們的雜誌，你就能跟上最新的流行趨勢。

相關片語 **buck the trend** 逆勢而行

▶ Though many people said that the market was shrinking, we bucked the trend and made our product a hit.
雖然很多人說市場正在萎縮，我們還是逆勢而行讓商品大賣。

trial [`traɪəl]　◀Track 4955
n. 試用；試驗；棘手的事；審問、審判

▶ You don't have to make a full payment during the trial period.
試用期間不用付清全額款項。

triangle [`traɪˏæŋgl]　◀Track 4956
n. 三角形

▶ The kid was measuring the length of the three sides of the triangle.
這名小朋友在量三角形三邊的長度。

tribe [traɪb]　◀Track 4957
n. 部落，種族；一幫，一夥；緊密聯繫的群體

▶ People living in the aboriginal tribe are known for being heavy drinkers.
這個原住民部落的人以愛喝酒聞名。

trick [trɪk]　🔊 Track 4958

n. 詭計；花招；竅門；手法；戲法；特技

▶Don't fall for his trick again. Didn't you learn the lesson last time? 不要再被他的花招騙了。你上次沒有學到教訓嗎？

v. 哄騙；戲弄

▶They tried to trick me into swallowing the plastic candy.
他們想要騙我吞下這個塑膠做的糖果。

tricky [`trɪkɪ]　🔊 Track 4959

adj. 狡猾的；機警的，足智多謀的；困難的，棘手的

▶The tricky student hid his cheat sheet in his sleeves.
這位狡猾的學生把小抄放在袖子裡。

trip [trɪp] **n.** 旅行；行程　🔊 Track 4960

▶Ms. Dunkin is out of town; she has gone on a family trip.
鄧肯女士不在城裡；她去參加家族旅遊了。

triumph [`traɪəmf]　🔊 Track 4961

n. 勝利；成功；因為勝利而帶來的喜悅

▶The concession of the government was considered a triumph for the protestors.
政府的讓步被視為是抗爭者的勝利。

v. 獲得勝利；歡慶勝利

▶The man triumphed his inner weakness and faced the challenges.
那個男人戰勝內心懦弱並且面對挑戰。

相關片語 **triumph over** 打敗，戰勝

▶The tennis player triumphed over his opponent and won the championship in the tournament. 那名網球選手戰勝對手，贏得錦標賽的冠軍。

trouble [`trʌbḷ]　🔊 Track 4962

n. 麻煩；困境；費事；騷亂

▶You might get into trouble if you don't pay the personal income tax on time.
如果不按時繳個人所得稅，你可能會惹上麻煩。

v. 麻煩；使憂慮；使疼痛；費心

▶I don't mean to trouble you, but can you show me how to operate the system again?
我不想麻煩你，但可以再教我一次如何操作這個系統嗎？

trousers [`traʊzɚz]　🔊 Track 4963
=pants（美式英文）**n.** 褲子

▶She bought a new pair of work trousers. 她買了一件新的工作褲。

truck [trʌk] **n.** 卡車　🔊 Track 4964

▶Jenny learned how to drive a truck when she was sixteen.
珍妮十六歲的時候學習如何駕駛卡車。

true [tru] **adj.** 真的　🔊 Track 4965

▶The movie was based on a true story.
這部電影是以真實故事為基礎的。

trumpet [`trʌmpɪt]　🔊 Track 4966

n. 喇叭；小號

▶The old man played trumpet in the restaurant and made a living on tips.
這名老人在餐廳吹奏喇叭，靠著打賞的錢維生。

trust [trʌst] **n.** 信任；信賴　🔊 Track 4967

▶How can you maintain the relationship if there is no trust between you?
如果你們之間沒有信任，關係要如何維繫下去呢？

中級

v 相信；信賴；依靠

▶Mr. Chang trusted his financial advisor.
張先生信任他的理財顧問。

truth [truθ] **n.** 真相；實情　◀Track 4968

▶The journalist was trying to conceal the truth and spread fake news.
這名記者想要掩蓋事實，散播假新聞。

try [traɪ]　◀Track 4969

v. 嘗試；試圖；努力

▶Why don't you try again?
你為什麼不再試一次呢？

n. 嘗試；努力

▶It's worth a try.
再試一次也無妨。

T-shirt [`ti.ʃɝt]　◀Track 4970
=tee-shirt **n.** T恤；短袖圓領汗衫

▶There is a blood stain on the T-shirt of the war correspondent.
這位戰地記者的T恤上面有血漬。

tub [tʌb]　◀Track 4971
n. 盆；桶；浴缸；（放冰淇淋的）杯

▶Mandy's dream is to have a big tub in her bathroom so she can relax after a long day.
曼蒂的夢想就是浴室裡有大浴缸，這樣她就可以在疲倦的一天後放鬆。

tube [tjub]　◀Track 4972
=underground railway
n.（英）地下鐵

▶We moved around by the tube when we traveled to London.
我們去倫敦旅行時，搭地鐵四處遊走。

Tuesday [`tjuzde]　◀Track 4973
=Tues./Tue. **n.** 星期二

▶Fiona takes night shifts on Tuesday and Wednesday.
費歐娜週二和週三值晚班。

tummy [`tʌmɪ]　◀Track 4974
=stomach **n.** 胃；肚子；啤酒肚

▶Mom applied an ointment on my tummy to sooth the pain.
媽媽在我的肚子上塗了藥膏來緩解疼痛。

tunnel [`tʌnl̩]　◀Track 4975
n. 隧道；地道

▶The Snow Mountain Tunnel is currently the longest tunnel in Taiwan.
雪山隧道是目前台灣最長的隧道。

turkey [`tɝkɪ]　◀Track 4976
n. 火雞；火雞肉

▶We had turkey for Thanksgiving dinner. 我們感恩節晚餐吃火雞。

turn [tɝn]　◀Track 4977
v. 轉；翻轉；轉向；轉身；變化

▶She turned around to show us the exquisite design of her dress.
她轉身向我們展示她身上洋裝的精緻設計。

n. 轉向；依次輪流的機會

▶It was my turn to take out the garbage.
該我去倒垃圾了。

turtle [`tɝtl̩]　◀Track 4978
n. 海龜；龜肉

▶The turtles laid eggs in the not-too-far-away sand beach.
海龜在不遠的沙岸產卵。

TV [ti-vi] **n.** 電視　　◀ᴇ Track 4979

▶Helen recorded her favorite TV show so that she could watch it later.
海倫錄下她最喜歡的電視節目以便稍後觀看。

---

twelve [twɛlv] **n.** 十二　◀ᴇ Track 4980

▶Divide thirty-six by three and you will get twelve.
三十六除以三等於十二。

adj. 十二的

▶There are twelve animals in the Chinese zodiac.
中國生肖裡面有十二種動物。

---

twenty [ˋtwɛntɪ] **n.** 二十　◀ᴇ Track 4981

▶Ten times two equals twenty.
十乘以二等於二十。

adj. 二十的

▶Twenty percent of the students in the class are taking part-time jobs.
這班上有百分之二十的學生在打工。

---

twice [twaɪs] **adv.** 兩次　◀ᴇ Track 4982

▶I go to the gym to swim with my friends twice a week.
我每週和朋友去健身房游泳兩次。

---

two [tu] **n.** 二；兩歲；兩點　◀ᴇ Track 4983

▶I rolled the dice and got a two.
我擲骰子得到兩點。

adj. 二的；兩個的

▶The two cars were parked too close to each other.
這兩台車停得靠太近了。

---

type [taɪp]　◀ᴇ Track 4984
v. 打字；用打字機打

▶The secretary typed out the report, and the manager found some typos in it.
這名秘書將報告打了出來，而經理則是找到了一些打字錯誤。

n. 類型；型式；樣式

▶The hotel offers different types of rooms, such as single rooms, double rooms, and suites.
這間旅館提供不同類型的房間，包括單人房、雙人房、以及套房。

---

typhoon [taɪˋfun]　◀ᴇ Track 4985
n. 颱風

▶There was a blackout and water outage when the typhoon passed through our city.
當颱風經過我們的城市時，停電又停水。

中級

▶ Uu

以下表格是全民英檢官方公告中級「聽、說、讀、寫」所須具備的能力，本書例句皆依此範疇特別設計，只要掃描右方QR code，就能搭配相對應的音軌實現「眼耳並用」方式，刺激左腦的語言學習功能；同時也可使用本書附贈的紅膠片，將其置於單字上，一面記憶一面自我挑戰，達到的雙倍的學習成果！

聽 ▶	在日常生活中，能聽懂一般的會話；能大致聽懂公共場所廣播、氣象報告及廣告等。在工作時，能聽懂簡易的產品介紹與操作說明。能大致聽懂外籍人士的談話及詢問。
說 ▶	可在日常生活中，能以簡易英語交談或描述一般事物，能介紹自己的生活作息、工作、家庭、經歷等，並可對一般話題陳述看法。在工作時，能進行簡單的答詢，並與外籍人士交談溝通。
讀 ▶	在日常生活中，能閱讀短文、故事、私人信件、廣告、傳單、簡介及使用說明等。在工作時，能閱讀工作須知、公告、操作手冊、例行的文件、傳真、電報等。
寫 ▶	能寫簡單的書信、故事及心得等。對於熟悉且與個人經歷相關的主題，能以簡易的文字表達。

ugly [`ʌglɪ]
◀ Track 4986

adj. 醜的；難看的；可怕的

▶It turned ugly when the two brothers fought over the heritage of their late father.
兩兩兄弟爭奪父親的遺產時，場面變得難看。

umbrella [ʌm`brɛlə]
◀ Track 4987

n. 雨傘

▶It looks like it's going to rain. Bring an umbrella with you.
好像要下雨了，帶把傘吧。

unable [ʌn`ebl̩]
◀ Track 4988

adj. 不能的，不會的；無能力的，無法勝任的

▶The British man has a strong accent. I was unable to understand him.
英國男人口音很重。我聽不懂他的話。

unaware [ˌʌnə`wɛr]
◀ Track 4989

adj. 不知道的，未察覺的

▶The woman was unaware that her son followed a stranger and went out of the shopping mall.
女士不知道自己的兒子跟著陌生人走出了購物中心。

unbelievable
◀ Track 4990

[ˌʌnbɪ`livəbl̩] **adj.** 難以相信的；不可相信的；非常驚人的

▶It was unbelievable that the amateur car racer triumphed the professional F1 car racer.
業餘賽車手贏過專業的F1賽車手，很令人不敢相信。

uncle [`ʌŋkl̩]
◀ Track 4991

n. 叔叔；舅舅；伯伯；姑丈；姨父等對年長男子的稱呼

▶I was an intern in my uncle's company last summer.
我去年在叔叔開的公司實習。

unconscious

◀€Track 4992

[ʌn`kɑnʃəs] **adj.** 不省人事的，失去知覺的；未發覺的；無意識的

▶The driver was unconscious when the police pulled him out of the crushed car.
警察從撞壞的車裡將駕駛救出來的時候，他是沒有意識的。

under [`ʌndɚ]

◀€Track 4993

prep. 在……下；

▶Some homeless men took shelter under the bridge.
有些街友在橋下避難。

adv. 在下方；在下面

▶I went under the water and saw the beautiful coral reefs.
我潛到水底下，看到一些美麗的珊瑚礁。

underground

◀€Track 4994

[`ʌndɚ͵graʊnd]

adj. 地面下的；秘密的，不公開的

▶The villagers drilled a well to access the underground water.
村民挖井取用地下水。

adv. 在地下

▶The extremist group was driven underground to stay away from governmental intervention.
這個激進團體往地下發展以遠離政府干涉。

n. 地面下層；（英）地下鐵；地下組織

▶The easiest way to move around London is to take the underground.
在倫敦最容易四處移動的方式就是搭乘地鐵。

underline [͵ʌndɚ`laɪn]

◀€Track 4995

v. 在下面劃線

▶The professor underlined the illogical part of the report and asked the student to revise it.
教授將不合邏輯地方畫線，要求學生重寫。

underpass

◀€Track 4996

[`ʌndɚ͵pæs] **n.** 地下道

▶There is an underpass that connects the two campuses of the university.
有一個地下道連接大學的兩個校區。

understand

◀€Track 4997

[͵ʌndɚ`stænd] **v.** 理解；明白

▶They could understand our situation and postponed the payment due day.
他們能理解我們的狀況，延後了繳款期限。

understanding

◀€Track 4998

[͵ʌndɚ`stændɪŋ]

n. 了解，領會；理解力；諒解，同感；共識

▶Though they didn't speak the same language, they managed to reach mutual understanding. 雖然他們說的語言不同，他們還是能夠互相理解。

adj. 了解的，能諒解的，寬容的；有理解力的，聰明的

▶She is an understanding girl. She wouldn't be angry over trivial things.
她是很通情達理的女生。她不會因為小事生氣的。

undertake

◀€Track 4999

[͵ʌndɚ`tek] **v.** 著手做，進行；從事；承擔，接受；答應，保證

▶They will undertake the renovation of the studio.
他們會著手進行工作室的整修工作。

中級

underwater ◀€ Track 5000

[ˋʌndɚˏwɔtɚ] **adv.** 在水中，在水下

▶The magician managed to the break the lock and escape from the cage underwater.
魔術師能夠在水面下解開索並且逃出籠子。

adj. 水中的，水面下的

▶The ancient underwater construction was considered a wonder by the archeologist. 這個古代的水下建築被考古學家認為是一個奇蹟。

underwear ◀€ Track 5001

[ˋʌndɚˏwɛr] **n.** 內衣

▶Diana only wears underwears made of high-quality textile.
黛安娜只穿材質高級的內衣。

underweight ◀€ Track 5002

[ˋʌndɚˏwet] **adj.** 重量不足的，體重不足的

▶The children who suffered from malnutrition were obviously underweight.
營養不良的小孩明顯體重不足。

unexpected ◀€ Track 5003

[ˏʌnɪkˋspɛktɪd]
adj. 想不到的，突如其來的，意外的

▶It was unexpected that the NBA star would show up at our commencement ceremony. 這名美國職籃球星現身我們的畢業典禮，真令人意想不到。

unfortunate ◀€ Track 5004

[ʌnˋfɔrtʃənɪt] **adj.** 不幸的，倒霉的；可惜的，令人遺憾的

▶We pitied the lady for her unfortunate experience.
我們同情這位女士的不幸遭遇。

unfortunately ◀€ Track 5005

[ʌnˋfɔrtʃənɪtlɪ]
adv. 不幸地；遺憾地，可惜地

▶Unfortunately, the rescue team did not find the missing hiker.
不幸地，搜救隊伍沒能找到失蹤的登山者。

unfriendly ◀€ Track 5006

[ʌnˋfrɛndlɪ] **adj.** 不友善的，有敵意的

▶The nuns in the temple were unfriendly to foreign visitors.
這間廟宇的尼姑對於外國觀光客不友善。

unhappy [ʌnˋhæpɪ] ◀€ Track 5007

adj. 不高興的；不幸的；對……不滿意的

▶The boss was unhappy about the sales figure of the last quarter.
老闆對上一季的銷售數字不太滿意。

uniform [ˋjunəˏfɔrm] ◀€ Track 5008

n. 制服

▶The real estate agent would wear their uniform when they show the potential client the properties for sale.
房屋仲介帶潛在顧客看房屋物件時，都會穿著制服。

adj. 相同的；一致的

▶The showcase of the old painting was kept at a uniform temperature to protect the antique. 古畫的展示箱都會保持一致的溫度來保護骨董。

union [ˋjunjən] ◀€ Track 5009

n. 結合；合而為一；聯盟；工會，聯合會；結婚；（大學）社團

▶The union of the two schools will allow students more choices in subjects and classes. 這兩所學校結合，會使學生有更多的科目和課程可以選擇。

相關片語 **labor union** 工會

▶The labor union will initiate a demonstration against the increase of minimum monthly working hours.
工會將會發起抗爭，抗議每月基本工時增加。

unique [juˋnik]   ◀Track 5010
adj. 獨一無二的；唯一的

▶Her unique music style made the audience very impressive with her songs.
她獨特的音樂風格，使觀眾對她的歌曲印象深刻。

unit [ˋjunɪt]   ◀Track 5011
n. 單位；單元；一組；一個；一套

▶The enterpriser planned his schedule with a basic unit of half an hour.
企業家以半小時為單位計畫他的日程表。

unite [juˋnaɪt]   ◀Track 5012
v. 使聯合，統一，使團結；使結婚；混合

▶The two magnate united in the project and they almost monopolized the market.
兩大巨擘在這個計畫中聯手，幾乎壟斷了市場。

united [juˋnaɪtɪd]   ◀Track 5013
adj. 聯合的，統一的；團結的，一致的

▶The country has diplomatic ties with many countries in the United Nation, but it could not be recognized as a member of the U.N.
這個國家和許多聯合國的國家有邦交，但是它卻無法成為聯合國的成員。

unity [ˋjunətɪ]   ◀Track 5014
n. 單一性，一致性；團結，聯合，統一；和諧，融洽

▶The presidential candidate called for the unity in the party so that she could win the election campaign.
這名總統候選人呼籲黨內團結，如此她才能夠贏得選舉。

universal [͵junəˋvɝsḷ]   ◀Track 5015
adj. 全體的，普遍的；宇宙的，全世界的；萬能的，通用的

▶Smile is a universal language.
微笑是全世界通用的語言。

n. 普通性，普遍現象，通用原則

▶Helping the needy people is one of the universals of all human society.
幫助需要幫助的人是所有人類社會共通的原則。

universe [ˋjunə͵vɝs]   ◀Track 5016
n. 宇宙；全人類；全世界

▶Dr. Hawking has his own theory about the origin of the universe.
霍金博士對宇宙緣起有一套自己的理論。

university [͵junəˋvɝsətɪ]   ◀Track 5017
n. 大學

▶He supported himself through university by taking part-time jobs at the supermarket and the movie theater.
他在超市和電影院打工，支持自己讀完大學。

unknown [ʌnˋnon]   ◀Track 5018
adj. 未知的；默默無聞的；不知道的

中級

▶It was surprising that the unknown actress was nominated for the Best Supporting Actress in the Academy Award.

令人驚訝的是，這名默默無名的女演員被提名為奧斯卡最佳女配角候選人。

unless [ʌnˋlɛs] conj. 除非　◀Track 5019

▶She will not sign on the divorce agreement unless you promise her the compensation she wants.

除非你承諾給她補償金，否則她不會簽下離婚同意書。

unlike [ʌnˋlaɪk]　◀Track 5020

prep. 不像，和……不同，與……相反

▶Unlike her brother, Vicky is a very athletic person. 和她哥哥不同，薇琪是一個很愛好運動的人。

unlikely [ʌnˋlaɪklɪ]　◀Track 5021

adj. 不太可能的，不可能發生的，不像是真的

▶It is unlikely that she could finish her master's thesis within a week.

她不太可能在一週之內完成她的碩士論文。

until [ənˋtɪl]　◀Track 5022

conj. 直到……時；在……之前

▶I didn't go to bed until I felt really exhasuted last night.

我昨晚一直到很疲倦時才去睡覺。

prep. 直到……時，直到；在……之前

▶We will wait until tomorrow morning.
我們會等到明天早上。

untouched [ʌnˋtʌtʃt]　◀Track 5023

adj. 未觸動過的；原樣的；未受損傷的；無動於衷的

▶The dish remained untouched when the diners left.

食客離開的時候，菜餚原封不動。

unusual [ʌnˋjuʒʊəl]　◀Track 5024

adj. 不尋常的；稀有的；獨特的

▶The leaves of the bamboos turned red, and the unusual scene was reported on the local TV news .

竹子的葉子變紅，這個不尋常的景象在本地電視新聞上面報導出來。

up [ʌp]　◀Track 5025

adv. 向上；增加；上揚

▶The prices of daily necessities kept going up.

民生物品的價格持續上漲。

prep. 向……上；在……上

▶The exit is up those stairs.
出口在那邊樓梯上面。

adj. 向上的；上行的；起床的

▶There is an up trend in the number of applicants for subsidies for single families.

單親家庭補助的申請人數量在增加中。

upon [əˋpɑn]　◀Track 5026

prep. 在……之上；在……之後立即

▶She placed a slice of cheese upon the dough before sending it into the oven.

她把一片起司放在麵糰上面再將它送進烤箱。

upper [ˋʌpɚ]　◀Track 5027

adj. 較高的；上層的；上游的

▶He bit his upper lip, trying not to show his agony.

他咬著上唇，隱藏自己的痛苦。

n. 鞋幫；上舖；安非他命；上排假牙

▶He polished his shoe upper before the important event began.
在重要會議開始之前，他擦亮自己的鞋幫。

upset [ʌpˋsɛt]　◀Track 5028

adj. 翻倒的，翻覆的；心煩的，苦惱的

▶She was upset when she realized how hard it could be to make ends meet. 她理解到收支平衡有多困難的時候感到心煩意亂。

n. 翻倒，混亂；心煩意亂；（腸胃）不舒服；吵架

▶The huge waves caused the upset of the boat, and three crew members were still missing.
大浪造成船隻翻覆，有三位船員失蹤。

v. 弄翻，打亂；意外擊敗；使心煩意亂，使生氣；使（腸胃）不適

▶The mean words of her opponents upset her a lot.
對手的惡意中傷讓她很不開心。

upstairs [ˋʌpˋstɛrz]　◀Track 5029

adv. 在樓上；往樓上

▶She went upstairs just a few minutes ago.
她幾分鐘之前上樓了。

adj. 樓上的

▶My upstairs neighbor likes to play rock music with his stereo at midnight.
我樓上的鄰居喜歡在半夜用音響放搖滾樂。

n. 樓上

▶They renovated the upstairs and rented it out to make extra income.
他們整修樓上並將它出租，以賺取額外的收入。

upward [ˋʌpwɚd]　◀Track 5030

adj. 往上的，向上的，升高的，趨好的

▶She made upward glances at the billboard on the buildings.
她往上看建築物上的廣告看板。

urban [ˋɝbən]　◀Track 5031

adj. 城市的；居住在城市的

▶Many skyscrapers were built in the urban area over the past few years.
在過去幾年市區內建造了許多摩天大樓。

urge [ɝdʒ]　◀Track 5032

v. 催促；激勵，力勸；慫恿；極力主張

▶His parents urged him to complete his college education and get the bachelor's degree. 他的父母催促他完成大學教育並取得學士學位。

n. 衝動，迫切要求；強烈慾望

▶After working hard for the whole year, I have an urge to go on a vacation abroad. 辛苦工作一整年之後，我有一股衝動要去國外旅行。

urgent [ˋɝdʒənt]　◀Track 5033

adj. 緊急的，急迫的

▶Zoe made an urgent call to her colleague when she realized that she forgot to bring an important document with her.
柔伊發現自己忘記帶重要文件時，緊急打了一通電話給同事求救。

us [ʌs] **pron.** 我們　◀Track 5034

▶We left the contact information to the salesperson so he could send the catalogue to us later.
我們留連絡資訊給銷售業務員，以便他寄送產品型錄給我們。

中級

USA [ju-ɛs-e] 🔊 Track 5035
n. 美利堅合眾國；美國

▶The bond of USA was considered a solid investment.
美國的債券被視為是一個很好的投資。

usage [`jusɪdʒ] 🔊 Track 5036
n. 使用，用法；習慣，習俗；慣用法

▶The websites listed some common usages of English idioms with Chinese explanations.
這個網站上面有一些常見的英文片語用法以及中文的解釋。

use [juz] **v.** 使用；利用 🔊 Track 5037

▶She used the baby powder to absorb the excess moisture on the baby's skin.
她使用嬰兒爽身粉來吸收寶寶身上過多的濕氣。

n. 使用；利用

▶We recorded the use of money with a bookkeeping App.
我們用一個記帳應用程式來記錄錢的使用。

used [juzd] 🔊 Track 5038
adj. 舊了的；用舊了的

▶The secondhand goods store sells used furniture and household electric appliances.
這家二手商品販賣店販賣二手的家具和家電。

v. 曾經

▶I used to play table tennis with my colleagues after work, but now we are all too busy to exercise.
以前下班後我會和同事一起打桌球，但是我們現在都忙到沒時間運動。

useful [`jusfəl] 🔊 Track 5039
adj. 有用的；有幫助的；有助益的

▶There are some useful tips of cleaning the kitchen in the book.
這本書中有些實用的清理廚房秘訣。

useless [`juslɪs] 🔊 Track 5040
adj. 無用的，無效的，無價值的；（人）無能的

▶The veteran worker thinks that some of the knowledge students learned at school is useless.
資深員工認為有些學生在學校學的知識是沒用的。

user [`juzɚ] 🔊 Track 5041
n. 使用者；用戶

▶Facebook was accused of stealing users' personal information.
Facebook被指控竊取用戶的個人資訊。

usual [`juʒʊəl] 🔊 Track 5042
adj. 平常的；慣常的

▶Sarah didn't take the usual path home; she made a detour to explore the district.
莎拉沒有走平常的路回家；她繞路探索一下這一區。

usually [`juʒʊəlɪ] 🔊 Track 5043
adv. 慣常地；通常地

▶She usually brings a lunch box to the office to save money.
她為了省錢，通常會帶便當到辦公室。

▶ Vv

以下表格是全民英檢官方公告初級「聽、說、讀、寫」所須具備的能力，本書例句皆依此範疇特別設計，只要掃描右方QR code，就能搭配相對應的音軌實現「眼耳並用」方式，刺激左腦的語言學習功能；同時也可使用本書附贈的紅膠片，將其置於單字上，一面記憶一面自我挑戰，達到的雙倍的學習成果！

聽 ▶	能聽懂與日常生活相關的淺易談話，包含價格、時間及地點等。
說 ▶	能朗讀簡易文章、簡單地自我介紹，對熟悉的話題能以簡易英語對答，如問候、購物、問路等。
讀 ▶	可看懂與日常生活相關的淺易英文，並能閱讀路標、交通號誌、招牌、簡單菜單、時刻表及賀卡等。
寫 ▶	能寫簡單的句子及段落，如寫明信片、便條、賀卡及填表格等。對一般日常生活相關事物，能以簡短的文字敘述或說明。

中級

vacant [`vekənt]
◀Track 5044

adj. 空的；未被佔用的；空缺的；空閒的；（心靈）空虛的

▶There is no vacant room in the hotel tonight.
今晚旅館沒有空房了。

vacation [ve`keʃən]
◀Track 5045

n. 假期；休假

▶They went on a long vacation in Australia. 他們去澳洲度長假。

vague [veg]
◀Track 5046

adj. 模糊不清的，朦朧的；不明確的，曖昧含糊的

▶I don't know the address of the restaurant. I only have a vague impression of its location.
我不曉得餐廳的地址，我只對位置有模糊的印象。

vain [ven]
◀Track 5047

adj. 無益的；徒然的；虛榮的

▶She tried to convince her parents to buy an iPhone for her, but in vain.
她想叫她的父母買一隻iPhone手機給她，但沒用。

補充片語 in vain 徒勞，無結果

Valentine's Day
◀Track 5048

[`væləntaɪnz-de] **n.** 情人節

▶The businessman had special promotions for the Valentine's Day.
這名商人舉辦情人節促銷活動。

valley [`vælɪ]
◀Track 5049

n. 山谷；溪谷

▶We drove through the valley and reached the city on the other side of the mountain.
我們開車穿過山谷，到達山另一邊的城市。

valuable [`væljʊəbl] ◀⁞Track 5050
adj. 值錢的，貴重的；有價值的，有用的

▶The wealthy man kept all his valuable things in the safe.
這名富翁將所有值錢的東西放在保險箱裡。

value [`vælju] ◀⁞Track 5051
n. 價值；重要性；價值觀

▶The value of the painting was overestimated. 這幅畫的價值被高估了。

v. 估價；重視；珍視

▶I value our friendship very much.
我很珍惜我們之間的友情。

van [væn] ◀⁞Track 5052
n. 有蓋小貨車；廂型車

▶We delivered goods to the customers with a van.
我們用小貨車送貨去給客戶。

相關片語 **moving van** 傢俱搬運車

▶We hired a moving van to carry our stuff to the new apartment.
我們租了一台家俱搬運車將我們的東西載到新公寓。

vanish [`vænɪʃ] ◀⁞Track 5053
v. 消失，突然不見

▶The model suddenly vanished from the stage in the middle of the performance.
這名模特兒在表演中途突然從舞台上消失。

vapor [`vepɚ] ◀⁞Track 5054
=vapour （英式英文）

n. 水汽，蒸汽；煙霧；無實質之物，幻想

▶The vapor in the air formed the cloud.
天空中的水氣形成雲。

variety [və`raɪətɪ] ◀⁞Track 5055
n. 多樣化，變化；種種

▶The bakery offers a variety of pastry.
這家烘焙坊有賣很多種糕點。

various [`vɛrɪəs] ◀⁞Track 5056
adj. 不同的，各種各樣的，形形色色的

▶The counselor's clients came to her for various reasons.
這名諮商師的個案病人因為各種不同的原因來找她。

vary [`vɛrɪ] ◀⁞Track 5057
v. 使不同；改變；使多樣化；偏離，違反

▶ My morning schedule varies from time to time.
我早上的行程時不時會有變化。

相關片語 **vary from person to person** 因人而異

▶The needs for accommodation vary from person to person.
住宿的需求因人而異。

vase [ves] **n.** 花瓶 ◀⁞Track 5058

▶Linda visited the clay studio and created a unique hand-made vase
琳達參觀了一間陶藝工作坊，並做了一個獨一無二的手工花瓶。

vast [væst] ◀⁞Track 5059
adj. 廣闊的，浩瀚的；龐大的，巨額的；【口】莫大的

▶The vast majority of Taiwanese high school graduates would go to college.
絕大多數的台灣高中畢業生會去念大學。

VCR [vi-si-ɑr]　◀≋Track 5060
=video cassette recorder n. 卡式錄放影機
▶After Vincent bought the home theater system, he put the VCR aside.
買了家庭劇院系統之後，文生就將卡式錄放影機放到一邊。

vegetable [`vɛdʒətəbl]　◀≋Track 5061
n. 蔬菜；青菜
▶Taking in enough green vegetables is important for your health.
吃足夠的綠色青菜對健康很重要。

adj. 蔬菜的；植物的
▶The vegetable products were recalled for high level of chemical residues
蔬菜產品被召回，因為有過高的化學物質殘留。

vegetari·an　◀≋Track 5062
[͵vɛdʒə`tɛrɪən] adj. 素食的；吃素的
▶Anna decided to become a vegetarian for environmental protection.
安娜為了環保決定成為一名素食者。

n. 素食者
▶In the club for vegetarians, members would share information of good vegan restaurants with each other.
在這個素食社團中，成員會互相介紹好吃的素食餐廳。

vehicle [`viɪkl]　◀≋Track 5063
n. 運載工具；車輛；飛行器；傳播媒介，工具，手段
▶The vehicle is powered by electricity instead of burning fossil fuels.
這輛車是電動的，不是燃燒石化燃料。

vendor [`vɛndɚ]　◀≋Track 5064
n. 攤販；小販；叫賣者
▶The vendors in the bazaar were peddling for their handcrafts.
市場的手工藝品小販們正在進行叫賣。

venture [`vɛntʃɚ]　◀≋Track 5065
n. 冒險；冒險事業，投機活動
▶No venture, no success.
不入虎穴，焉得虎子。（不敢冒險，何以成功。）

v. 使冒險；以……作賭注；大膽提出（或說出）；敢於
▶The adventurer ventured into the untrodden area in the Antarctic.
這名探險家冒險進入南極洲無人區。

verb [vɝb] n. 動詞　◀≋Track 5066
▶The second chapter of the grammar book introduces the model verbs in English.
這本文法書的第二章介紹英文中的情態動詞。

verse [vɝs]　◀≋Track 5067
n. 詩，韻文，詩句，詩作；（聖經的）節
▶The lyricist composed a verse in memory of the martyr.
這位作詞家寫了篇韻文紀念烈士。

相關片語 **chapter and verse** 確切依據，準確依據
▶She explained the news at our request, chapter and verse.
她在我們的要求之下說明了新聞的確切依據。

version [`vɝʒən]　◀≋Track 5068
n. 譯文，譯本；描述，說法；變化形式；改編形式，改寫本；版本

中級

▶The illustrated version of The Little Prince was very popular.
這本有插畫版本的《小王子》很受歡迎。

very [`vɛrɪ] adv 非常
◀Track 5069

▶The online streaming platform is very popular in Asia.
這個線上串流平台在亞洲很受歡迎。

adj. 正是；恰好是

▶He is the very first man who applied for the patent of the technique.
他正是第一個為這項技術申請專利的人。

vessel [`vɛsl] n 船；艦
◀Track 5070

▶The vessel made it maiden voyage in the 1960s.
這艘船在1960年代進行首航。

相關片語 blood vessel 血管

▶When the weather is cold, the blood vessels in your arm may be more visible.
天氣冷的時候，手上的血管可能會看得更清楚。

vest [vɛst]
◀Track 5071

n 背心；汗衫；內衣

▶The bodyguard of the politician wore bulletproof vests when they are on duty.
這名政治人物的保鑣在值勤時會穿著防彈背心。

victim [`vɪktɪm]
◀Track 5072

n 犧牲者；受害者

▶Families of the victims who died in the plane crash could receive a compensation.
這場空難的罹難者家屬可以獲得賠償金。

victory [`vɪktərɪ] n 勝利
◀Track 5073

▶The gala was to celebrate the victory of the school basketball team.
這場派對是要慶祝學校籃球隊的勝利。

video [`vɪdɪ‚o]
◀Track 5074

n 錄影節目；電視；影片

▶The video is a documentary of the wild life in Amazon Forest. 這個影片是一部亞馬遜森林野生動物的紀錄片。

v 錄像；錄製

▶We used the webcam to video the award ceremony.
我們用錄影機錄下頒獎典禮的狀況。

videotape [`vɪdɪo`tep]
◀Track 5075

n 錄影帶，錄像帶

▶There are some footages of the family reunions in this videotape.
這個錄影帶中有以前家庭聚會錄下的影像。

v 錄影

▶The entrepreneur's speech on our commencement was videotaped and uploaded to YouTube.
這位企業家在我們畢業典禮的演講被錄了下來並上傳到YouTube網站。

view [vju] n 景色；看法
◀Track 5076

▶The suite of the seaside hotel has a great view of the ocean.
濱海飯店的套房有很棒的海景。

v 觀看；看待；將……視為

▶I viewed him as my mentor.
我將他視為我的心靈導師。

vigor [`vɪgɚ]
◀Track 5077

=vigour （英式英文） n 體力，
精力，活力；強健，茁壯；氣勢，魄力

▶ This debate competition was so full of vigor!
這場演講比賽真是充滿活力！

vigorous [`vɪgərəs]　◀Track 5078
adj. 精力充沛的，強健的；強而有力的

▶The vigorous cheerleaders created a lively atmosphere in the sports meeting.
這群活力充沛的啦啦隊員使運動會的氣氛變得很有活力。

village [`vɪlɪdʒ]　◀Track 5079
n. 村；村落；村莊

▶The people in the remote village are in lack of medical resources.
這個偏遠小鎮的人們缺乏醫療資源。

vinegar [`vɪnɪgɚ] **n.** 醋　◀Track 5080

▶Nina added a little vinegar on the rice to make the texture fluffy.
妮娜在飯裡加一點醋讓口感變的蓬鬆。

violate [`vaɪəˌlet]　◀Track 5081
v. 違背，違反；侵犯，妨礙；褻瀆；（對婦女）施暴

▶The autocratic government was accused of violating human right.
此專制政府被指控侵犯人權。

violation [ˌvaɪə`leʃən]　◀Track 5082
n. 違背，違反；違反行為

▶They were fined for the violation of intellectual property.
他們因為侵犯智慧財產權而被罰款。

violence [`vaɪələns]　◀Track 5083
n. 暴力

▶Verbal violence may cause trauma in children's mind.
語言暴力可能會導致小孩心靈受創。

相關片語 **domestic violence** 家庭暴力

▶Dial 133 to report a case of domestic violence.
請撥133回報家暴案件。

violent [`vaɪələnt]　◀Track 5084
adj. 猛烈的；暴力的

▶The violent vibration of the plane in the turbulence cause several passengers to get hurt.
飛機遇到亂流，猛烈搖晃，造成數名乘客受傷。

violet [`vaɪəlɪt]　◀Track 5085
n. 紫羅蘭，紫羅蘭花，紫羅蘭色；羞怯的人

▶Cindy looked after the violets in the garden with patience.
辛蒂耐心地照顧花園中的紫羅蘭。

adj. 紫蘿蘭的；紫蘿蘭色的，紫色的

▶You look elegant in that violet dress.
你穿那件紫羅蘭色的洋裝看起來很高雅。

相關片語 **shrinking violet** 非常害羞的人；會怯場的人

▶She is a shrinking violet. She might not dare to speak in front of all the guests at the year-end party.
她是很害羞的人，可能會不敢在尾牙派對上向賓客致詞。

violin [ˌvaɪə`lɪn] **n.** 小提琴　◀Track 5086

▶The craft master has produced several hand-made violins for world-renowned musicians.
這位名家已經為許多世界知名的音樂家手工製作過好幾架小提琴了。

中級

violinist [ˌvaɪə`lɪnɪst] 🔊 Track 5087

n. 小提琴家，小提琴手

▶ The young violinist studied in The Juilliard School. 這位年輕的小提琴家在茱麗亞音樂學院學習。

virgin [`vɝdʒɪn] 🔊 Track 5088

n. 處女，未婚女子；童男

▶ Nutured by years of social street protests, the man is not a political virgin as many claim him to be at tall.
這名男子多年參與社會街頭抗議，其滋養早讓他熟悉政治生態，不像許多人說的一樣。

adj. 處女的；貞潔的；未玷污的；未開發的；未加工的，初榨的

▶ The virgin forest was considered the final resort for the endangered species.
這片未開發的森林被視為是瀕危物種的最後棲息地。

相關片語 **extra virgin olive oil**
特級初榨橄欖油

▶ The extra virgin olive oil is said to be high in monounsaturated fats.
據說這個特級初榨橄欖油富含單不飽和脂肪。

virtue [`vɝtʃu] **n.** 美德 🔊 Track 5089

▶ My mother keeps telling me that honesty is a virtue.
我的媽媽一直告訴我，誠實是種美德。

virus [`vaɪrəs] **n.** 病毒 🔊 Track 5090

▶ The viruses of measles may spread through air.
麻疹的病毒可能會透過空氣傳染。

visible [`vɪzəbl̩] 🔊 Track 5091

adj. 可看見的

▶ The spores of fungi are not visible to human eyes.
菌類孢子是人類眼睛看不見的。

vision [`vɪʒən] 🔊 Track 5092

n. 視力；所見事物；洞察力，眼光

▶ The lady had a blurred vision after she contracted cataract.
這位女士因為罹患白內障而視力模糊。

補充片語 **twenty-twenty vision**
正常視力

▶ The fighter pilot had a twenty-twenty vision. 這位飛官視力正常。

visit [`vɪzɪt] **v.** 參觀；拜訪 🔊 Track 5093

▶ The students visited several prestigious universities in the U.S., including Harvard, Stanford, and UCLA.
這群學生去參訪了幾間美國知名大學，包括哈佛大學、史丹佛大學，以及加州大學洛杉磯分校。

n. 參觀；拜訪；暫住；逗留

▶ We had a good time during our visit in Europe.
我們去歐洲旅遊的時候很開心。

visitor [`vɪzɪtɚ] 🔊 Track 5094

n. 訪客；遊客.

▶ Visitors to the shrine were asked to be solemn.
神社的參觀者被要求要保持肅穆。

visual [`vɪʒuəl] 🔊 Track 5095

adj. 視力的，視覺的；光學的；靠目視的

▶ Visual aids such as posters or PowerPoint slides are considered important for an effective presentation.
對一個有效的報告來說，像是海報和投影片這類視覺輔助被認為是很重要的。

vital [`vaɪtl]　◀ Track 5096

adj. 生命的；維持生命所必需的；充滿活力的；極其重要的，必不可少的

▶Water and Oxygen are vital for human beings. 水和氧氣對人類來說是必不可少的。

相關片語 **vital signs** 生命徵象（呼吸、心跳、血壓、體溫等）

▶The machine was used to detect the vital signs in the wrecks to see if there were any survivors in the collapsed building.
這台機器用來偵測殘骸中的生命徵象，找出倒塌大樓是否有生還者。

vitamin [`vaɪtəmɪn]　◀ Track 5097

n. 維他命

▶The patient shows signs of vitamin B deficiency. 病人有缺乏維他命B的徵象。

vivid [`vɪvɪd]　◀ Track 5098

adj. 強烈的，（色彩）鮮艷的；有生氣的，活潑的；生動的，逼真的

▶Her vivid personality traits made her a desired employee in our public relation department. 她活潑的個性，令她成為我們公關部門會需要的員工。

vocabulary　◀ Track 5099

[və`kæbjə͵lɛrɪ] **n.** 字彙；詞彙

▶The series of books were ranked according to the level of the chosen vocabulary. 這一系列的書依照所選字彙的程度來分級的。

voice [vɔɪs] **n.** 聲音　◀ Track 5100

▶The sailor claimed that he heard the voice of a mermaid.
這名水手宣稱他聽見了美人魚的聲音。

volcano [vɑl`keno]　◀ Track 5101

n. 火山

▶Yangmingshan is said to be a dormant volcano.
據說陽明山是一座休火山。

volleyball [`vɑlɪ͵bɔl]　◀ Track 5102

n. 排球；排球運動

▶Volleyball is a popular team sport among girls in our school.
排球在我們學校的女孩子當中是很受歡迎的團隊運動。

volume [`vɑljəm]　◀ Track 5103

n. 冊；卷；音量

▶The collection of folklores in the country came in two volumes.
這本民俗故事集分成兩冊。

voluntary [`vɑlən͵tɛrɪ]　◀ Track 5104

adj. 自願的，志願的；故意的；自發的，自覺的

▶She is a voluntary worker in the refugee shelter.
她是難民避難所的志工。

volunteer [͵vɑlən`tɪr]　◀ Track 5105

n. 自願者，義工，志願兵

▶The volunteer in the nursing home cared about the mental health of the elderly residents.
療養院的志工關心住院長者的心理健康。

v. 自願做，自願提供，自願服務

▶She volunteered to paint the school fence to win the commendation.
她為了記嘉獎，自願粉刷學校的圍牆。

中級

vote [vot] ◀€Track 5106

n. 選舉；投票；選票

▶She won the most votes and was elected as the leader of the student association.
她贏得最多票數，當選學生會長。

v. 投票；表決；投票決定

▶The students voted to decide on the destination of the graduation trip.
學生們投票決定畢業旅行的目的地。

voter [`votɚ] ◀€Track 5107

n. 選舉人；投票人

▶Many of the registered voters in this district work overseas.
這個行政區中有許多登記投票者是在海外工作的。

vowel [`vauəl] **n.** 母音 ◀€Track 5108

▶A vowel can form a syllable by itself.
母音可以自成一個音節。

voyage [`vɔɪdʒ] ◀€Track 5109

n. 航海，航行；乘船旅遊

▶The hot air balloon voyage may take two hours.
這趟熱氣球航行大約兩小時。

v. 航空，航海，航行，旅行；飛過，渡過

▶The spaceship voyaged across the galaxy in search of planets that may have signs of life.
這艘太空船航行過整個星系尋找可能的生物。

Ww

以下表格是全民英檢官方公告中級「聽、說、讀、寫」所須具備的能力，本書例句皆依此範疇特別設計，只要掃描右方QR code，就能搭配相對應的音軌實現「眼耳並用」方式，刺激左腦的語言學習功能；同時也可使用本書附贈的紅膠片，將其置於單字上，一面記憶一面自我挑戰，達到雙倍的學習成果！

聽 ▶	在日常生活中，能聽懂一般的會話；能大致聽懂公共場所廣播、氣象報告及廣告等。在工作時，能聽懂簡易的產品介紹與操作說明。能大致聽懂外籍人士的談話及詢問。
說 ▶	可在日常生活中，能以簡易英語交談或描述一般事物，能介紹自己的生活作息、工作、家庭、經歷等，並可對一般話題陳述看法。在工作時，能進行簡單的答詢，並與外籍人士交談溝通。
讀 ▶	在日常生活中，能閱讀短文、故事、私人信件、廣告、傳單、簡介及使用說明等。在工作時，能閱讀工作須知、公告、操作手冊、例行的文件、傳真、電報等。
寫 ▶	能寫簡單的書信、故事及心得等。對於熟悉且與個人經歷相關的主題，能以簡易的文字表達。

中級

wage [wedʒ] ◀Track 5110

n. 工資，薪水，報酬

▶ The average hourly wage of the beverage shop is about 150 NT dollars.
平均來說飲料店的時薪大約是150元台幣。

相關片語 **minimum wage** 最低工資

▶ The national minimum wages were increased after the new law was implemented. 執行新法後，國家法定最低薪資已經增加了。

v. 進行，從事，發動

▶ Syria and Iran waged war for many years.
敘利亞和伊朗打過多年的戰爭。

相關片語 **wage slave** 薪水奴隸

▶ The laborers called themselves wage slaves.
這些勞工自稱為是薪水的奴隸。

wagon [`wægən] ◀Track 5111

n. 運貨馬車

▶ The merchant traveled through the dessert with his wagon loaded with goods.
商人帶著載滿貨物的馬車穿越沙漠。

waist [west] n. 腰；腰部 ◀Track 5112

▶ After the accident, the man was paralyzed from the waist down.
意外之後，這名男子自腰部以下癱瘓了。

wait [wet] ◀Track 5113

v. 等；等候；等待

▶ I waited in line for two hours to buy the limited edition of NBA player figurine.
我排隊等兩個小時，為了要買限量NBA球星公仔。

waiter [`wetɚ]
🔊 Track 5114

n. 侍者；服務生

▶ The waiter of the restaurant was asked to memorize the ingredients of all dishes on the menu.
這家餐廳的服務生被要求要背下菜單上所有菜餚的材料。

waitress [`wetrɪs]
🔊 Track 5115

n. 女侍者；女服務生

▶ The waitress cut the steak for the diners.
女服務生為用餐者切開牛排。

wake [wek]
🔊 Track 5116

v. 醒來；覺醒；喚醒；弄醒

▶ The Sleeping Beauty was woken by the pygmies.
睡美人被小精靈喚醒了。

waken [`wekn]
🔊 Track 5117

v. 醒來；喚醒，弄醒；覺醒；激發

▶ The noises of the passing vehicles on the road wakened me up in the middle of the night.
半夜我被路上的車聲吵醒。

walk [wɔk]
🔊 Track 5118

v. 走；散步；陪……走

▶ It took us half an hour to walk to the train station.
走路到火車站花了我們半小時。

n. 走；步行；散步

▶ It's a ten minutes' walk from my house to my school.
從我的家裡走到學校十分鐘左右。

Walkman [`wɔkmən]
🔊 Track 5119

n. 隨身聽

▶ I left my Walkman on the bus.
我把隨身聽忘記在公車上了。

wall [wɔl] n. 牆；牆壁
🔊 Track 5120

▶ The old man built a brick wall to separate his yard from his neighbor's garden.
老人築牆將自己的前院和鄰居的花園隔開。

wallet [`wɑlɪt]
🔊 Track 5121

n. 皮夾；錢包

▶ There is no cash in the wallet.
這個錢包裡面沒有現金。

waltz [wɔlts]
🔊 Track 5122

n. 華爾滋舞，華爾滋舞曲

▶ Learning to dance Waltz was considered a social etiquette by the European people.
學習跳華爾滋舞曾被歐洲人視為是一種社會禮儀。

v. 跳華爾滋舞；輕快地走動；旋轉；輕鬆順利地前進

▶ When Mandy waltzed into the classroom, the professor had been lecturing for half an hour.
曼蒂慢吞吞地走進教室的時候，教授已經講課半個小時了。

相關片語 **waltz off with sth.**
偷走某物；輕易贏得某事物

▶ Betty waltzed off with the championship in the national tournament.
貝蒂在這次全國錦標賽中輕而易舉地贏得冠軍。

wander [`wɑndɚ]
🔊 Track 5123

v. 閒逛，漫遊，徘徊於……；偏離正道；迷路；失神

▶I saw a kangaroo wandering in the street when I drove home.
我開車回家時看到袋鼠在路上閒晃。

want [wɑnt] v 想要
◀Track 5124

▶The toddler wanted to buy the toy, but his parents wouldn't let him.
這位小朋友想要買玩具，但是他的父母不讓他買。

war [wɔr]
◀Track 5125

n 戰爭；競賽；對抗

▶I will never give in. Let there be war!
我不會退讓的。開戰吧！

ward [wɔrd]
◀Track 5126

n 病房；牢房；行政區；受監護的人；看護，監禁，拘留

▶The war felon was kept in the ward in the basement.
這位戰犯被關在地下室的牢房裡。

v 避開，擋開，避免

▶The soldiers were ordered to ward over the fortress.
士兵們受命令要守住這個堡壘。

warfare [`wɔr͵fɛr]
◀Track 5127

n 戰爭，衝突，交戰狀態

▶The technique was applied in the science of warfare.
這種技術被應用在軍事科學中。

warm [wɔrm]
◀Track 5128

adj 溫暖的；暖和的

▶The warm and dry weather in the area is suitable to grow tea trees.
這個地區溫暖乾燥的天氣很適合茶種植茶樹。

v 使溫暖；使暖和

▶We had hot pot to warm ourselves up on the cold day.
在很冷的日子裡，我們火鍋來暖和自己。

warming [`wɔrmɪŋ]
◀Track 5129

adj 讓人感到暖和的

▶Her warming words were a great comfort for me.
她溫暖人心的話讓我覺得很受到安慰。

warmth [wɔrmθ]
◀Track 5130

n 溫暖，親切；熱情

▶The owner of the hostel welcomed us with warmth.
青年旅館的老闆親切地歡迎我們。

warn [wɔrn]
◀Track 5131

v 警告，告誡，提醒

▶The official warned that travelers to the war-struck countries should take extra caution. 官員警告要到戰爭國家的旅行者要特別謹慎。

warning [`wɔrnɪŋ]
◀Track 5132

n 警告，告誡，先兆，徵候

▶Red is usually thought of as a sign of warning.
紅色常常被視為是一種警告。

adj 警告的，告誡的，引以為戒的

▶The police fired a warning shot to disperse the mob.
警察鳴槍警告暴民退散。

warship [`wɔr͵ʃɪp]
◀Track 5133

n 軍艦

▶The U.S., China, and Russia are said to have invincible warships.
據說美國、中國和俄國擁有無敵的戰艦。

中級

wash [waʃ] **v** 洗；沖洗 ◄€Track 5134

▶They washed off the graffiti on the wall.
他們把牆上的塗鴉洗掉。

washing [`waʃɪŋ] ◄€Track 5135

n 洗滌，洗漱；洗好或待洗的衣物；洗滌劑

▶They dried the washing by hanging them at outside.
他們將洗好的衣物掛在外面晾乾。

相關片語 **washing powder** 洗衣粉

▶The washing powder contains a special chemical to produce more foam.
這種洗衣粉有一種可以製造更多泡沫的化學物質。

was·n't [`wazɪt] ◄€Track 5136

abbr. （過去式）不是、還沒（**was not**的縮寫）

▶He wasn't aware that his Facebook account was hacked.
他沒察覺到自己的臉書帳號被盜了。

waste [west] **n** 浪費 ◄€Track 5137

▶He considers binge watching Korean dramas is a waste of time.
他覺得連續看韓劇是浪費時間。

v 浪費

▶Don't waste your money on it. Its cost-performance ratio is very low.
不要浪費錢。它的價格效益很低。

watch [watʃ] ◄€Track 5138

n 手錶；看守；監視；警戒

▶The prisoners were kept under close watch.
犯人被嚴密看守。

v 看

▶We watched the movie on the big screen. 我們用大螢幕看這部電影。

watchman [`watʃmən] ◄€Track 5139

n 夜間看守人，巡夜者；警備員

▶The watchman found a suspicious man in the neighborhood.
夜間看守員發現附近地區有個可疑的男子。

water [`wɔtɚ] **n** 水 ◄€Track 5140

▶Residents in the remote town suffered from water scarcity.
偏遠小鎮的居民受缺水之苦。

v 澆水；給水

▶Don't water the cactus every day.
不用每天給仙人掌澆水。

waterfall [`wɔtɚ‚fɔl] ◄€Track 5141

n 瀑布

▶The waterfall was frozen due to the sudden drop in the temperature.
因為溫度驟降，瀑布結冰了。

watermelon ◄€Track 5142

[`wɔtɚ‚mɛlən] **n** 西瓜

▶Watermelon juice is my favorite beverage in summer.
西瓜汁是我夏天最喜歡的飲料。

waterproof ◄€Track 5143

[`wɔtɚ‚pruf] **adj** 防水的

▶The wrist watch is waterproof.
這款腕錶是防水的。

n 防水材料，防水布；【英】雨衣

▶The scooter rider put on the waterproof before he hit the road.
摩托車騎士上路前先穿上了雨衣。

v. 使防水

▶They covered the roof with a special material to waterproof it.
他們在屋頂上覆蓋特殊的材質使它變得防水。

---

wave [wev]
🔊 Track 5144

n. 波浪；浪潮；揮手；捲髮

▶The storm on the sea caused huge waves.
海上的暴風雨引起大浪。

v. 對……揮手；揮動；使形成波浪

▶The servant waved at his master as she drove her car away.
僕人在主人開車出門時對她揮手。

---

wax [wæks] **n.** 蠟
🔊 Track 5145

▶They sealed the carton with wax.
他們用蠟封起紙箱。

adj. 蠟製的

▶Many wax sculptures of celebrities are displayed in this museum.
有很多名人的蠟像在這個博物館展出。

v. 打蠟

▶They waxed the floor before the ceremony began.
在典禮開始之前，他們將地板打蠟。

---

way [we]
🔊 Track 5146

adv. 非常，大大地（加強語氣）

▶Algebra is way too difficult for kindergarten kids.
代數對於幼稚園小朋友來說太難了。

---

we [wi] **pron.** 我們
🔊 Track 5147

▶We often share jokes in the family line group.
我們常常在家族的Line群組中分享笑話。

---

weak [wik]
🔊 Track 5148

adj. 虛弱的；柔弱的；衰弱的

▶His vision gets weak because he spent too much time phubbing on the smart phone.
他因為太常滑手機結果視力變弱了。

---

weaken [`wikən]
🔊 Track 5149

v. 削弱，減弱，減少；變虛弱

▶His stamina weakened because of the oppressive atmosphere in his workplace.
他的鬥志因為工作場所的壓抑氣氛而減弱。

---

wealth [wɛlθ] **n.** 財富
🔊 Track 5150

▶He accumulated wealth over the decades and became a billionaire.
他數十年來累積財富，成為一個億萬富翁。

---

wealthy [`wɛlθɪ]
🔊 Track 5151

adj. 富裕的

▶The luxurious hotel room was reserved by a wealthy woman.
這個豪華的旅館房間被一位有錢的女士預訂了。

---

weapon [`wɛpən]
🔊 Track 5152

n. 武器；兇器

▶The president of the company claimed that the country has the most advanced weapon in the world.
這個國家的總統宣稱該國有世界最先進的武器。

---

wear [wɛr] **v.** 穿；戴
🔊 Track 5153

▶I wore the necklace Grandma gave to me to my niece's coming-of-age ceremony. 我帶著祖母送我的項鍊去參加我姪子的成年禮。

中級

n. 穿；配戴；服裝

▶ The casual wear was not appropriate for the formal occasion.
休閒的穿著在這個正式的場合不太合適。

weather [ˋwɛðɚ] ◀Track 5154
n. 天氣

▶ According to the weather forecast, it will sprinkle tomorrow morning.
根據氣象報導，明天早上會有零星降雨。

weave [wiv] ◀Track 5155
v. 編織，編製；編造；結網；迂迴行進

▶ The spider waved a web to catch its prey. 蜘蛛織網捕捉獵物。

n. 織法，編法；編織式樣；織物

▶ The traditional weaves are one of the most popular handcrafts in the souvenir shop. 這些傳統編織品是紀念品商店最受歡迎的手工藝品之一。

web [wɛb] ◀Track 5156
n. 網；網路；蜘蛛網

▶ The gangsters built up a complex web to block out any police intervention.
這群幫派份子建立了一個複雜的網絡來阻絕任何警方的介入。

相關片語 **a web of lies**
編織成網的謊言，一套謊言

▶ What he said was a web of lies. Don't trust him.
他說的是全是謊言。不要相信他。

wed [wɛd] ◀Track 5157
v. 嫁；娶；與……結婚

▶ The princess wedded a man with a humble background.
公主和一位出身平凡的男子結婚。

we'd [wid] ◀Track 5158
abbr. 我們已、我們會（ we had、we would 的縮寫）

▶ We'd avoid any mistakes in the procedure.
我們會避免過程中有任何錯誤。

wedding [ˋwɛdɪŋ] ◀Track 5159
n. 婚禮

▶ Their wedding is so full of love and we all had a good time. 他們的婚禮真是充滿著愛，我們都度過了很棒的時光。

Wednesday [ˋwɛnzde] ◀Track 5160
=Wed., Weds. **n.** 星期三

▶ She asks for a personal leave this Wednesday. 她這個星期三要請事假。

weed [wid] ◀Track 5161
n. 雜草，野草；香菸，煙草；軟弱無用的人，廢物

▶ We mowed the weeds in the backyard.
我們清除了後院的雜草。

v. 除掉（雜草）；清除廢物，淘汰

▶ The weak teams were weeded out in the regional tournament.
這個較弱的隊伍在區域錦標賽中被淘汰了。

week [wik] **n.** 星期；週 ◀Track 5162

▶ It has been a busy week.
這週真的很忙。

weekday [ˋwikˌde] ◀Track 5163
n. 平日；工作日

▶ Fiona sometimes goes to the gym in the evening of the weekdays.
費歐娜有時會在平日的傍晚去健身房。

weekend [ˋwikˋɛnd]　◀ Track 5164

n. 週末

▶The community college offers free culinary courses on weekends.
這個社區大學在週末提供免費的烹飪課程。

weekly [ˋwiklɪ]　◀ Track 5165

adj. 每週的；一週一次的；週刊的

▶You can find relevant information about activities on campus on the weekly post of the university.
你可以在大學的週報看到校園活動的相資訊。

adv. 每週地；每週一次

▶I volunteer at the local orphanage weekly.
我每星期到本地的孤兒院做義工。

n. 週刊；週報

▶The latest issue of Business Weekly was sold out.
最新一期的商業周刊賣完了。

weep [wip]　◀ Track 5166

v. 哭泣，流淚；悲歎，哀悼

▶The girl wept for the death of her pet hamster.
女孩為了她死掉的寵物黃金鼠哀悼。

n. 哭泣；眼淚

▶We didn't see any weep on the late president's funeral.
我們沒看到任何人在已故總統的喪禮上哭泣。

weigh [we]　◀ Track 5167

v. 秤重；有……重量；考慮；權衡

▶We weighed the pros and cons of investing in that venture company.
我們權衡投資那家創投公司的好處和壞處。

weight [wet] **n.** 體重　◀ Track 5168

▶She cut down on the intake of calories, trying to lose weight.
她減少攝取熱量，想要減重。

welcome [ˋwɛlkəm]　◀ Track 5169

v. 歡迎

▶The owner of the castle welcomed us at the gate.
城堡的主人在大門迎接我們。

adj. 受歡迎的；被允許的；可隨意使用的

▶A nasty soul is not welcome in heaven.
天堂不歡迎邪惡的靈魂。

n. 歡迎；款待

▶We received a hospitable welcome in the small Peruvian town.
我們在這個祕魯小鎮受到熱情歡迎。

welfare [ˋwɛlˌfɛr]　◀ Track 5170

n. 福利；福祉；福利事業，救濟事業

▶The municipal government will put more emphasis on social welfare in the new year.
新的一年，市政府會更加重視社會福利。

adj. 福利的；福利事業的；接受社會救濟的

▶The students are raising funds for the welfare institution.
學生正在為了這個福利機構募款。

well [wɛl]　◀ Track 5171

n. 井；水井；油井；來源，源泉

▶The kid who accidentally fell into the well was rescued.
意外掉進水井裡的小孩獲救了。

we'll [wil]　◀ Track 5172

abbr. 我們會（**we will**的縮寫）

中級

▶We'll keep you informed about the updates of international news.
我們會通知您最新的國際新聞。

well-known ◀Track 5173
[`wɛl`non] **adj.** 眾所周知的，出名

▶The town is well-known for its porcelain crafts.
這個小鎮以瓷器工藝著名。

we're [wɪr] ◀Track 5174
abbr. 我們是（**we are**的縮寫）

▶We're looking forward to your visit.
我們期待您來參訪。

weren't [wɜnt] ◀Track 5175
abbr. （過去式）不是（**were not**的縮寫）

▶You weren't paying attention, were you?
你沒在注意聽，對吧？

west [wɛst] **n.** 西邊；西方 ◀Track 5176

▶My apartment is to the west of the municipal office building.
我的公寓在市政大樓的西邊。

adv. 向西；往西；自西

▶According to the witness, the abductors headed west after they took the ransom.
目擊者表示，綁匪拿走贖金後就往西邊逃了。

adj. 西部的；向西的；由西邊來的

▶The west part of India was struck by torrential rain.
印度的西部遭到暴雨侵襲。

western [`wɛstən] ◀Track 5177
adj. 西部的；朝西的；西方的；歐美的

▶Now, many blockbusters are western movies with big budgets.
現在很多賣座片都是大手筆的西方電影。

n. 西方人；歐美國家的人；西部片

▶Some critics wonder why Westerns are seldom nominated for Oscar awards. 有些評論家納悶為何西部片很少獲得奧斯卡提名。

westerner [`wɛstənə] ◀Track 5178
n. 西方人，歐美人

▶Some westerners appraised the metro system in Taipei.
有些西方人讚美台北的捷運系統。

wet [wɛt] **adj.** 濕的 ◀Track 5179

▶It must have rained last night; the surface of the road is still wet.
昨晚一定下雨了；路面還是濕的。

v. 弄濕

▶Wet the floor and then clean it with the mop.
把地面弄濕，然後用拖把清理乾淨。

we've [wiv] ◀Track 5180
abbr. 我們已（**we have**的縮寫）

▶We've received your application and will reply as soon as possible.
我們已收到您的申請並且會儘快回覆。

whale [hwel] **n.** 鯨魚 ◀Track 5181

▶It is said that whales communicate with each other by echolocation.
據說鯨魚透過回聲定位法和彼此溝通。

what [hwɑt] **pron.** 什麼 ◀Track 5182

▶What do you usually do in your leisure time?
你閒暇時通常做什麼呢？

adj. 什麼；何等

▶What kind of excuse is that?
那是哪門子的藉口啊？

---

whatever [hwɑt`ɛvɚ]　◀Track 5183

pron. 無論什麼

▶Gina was born in a wealthy family; she could have whatever she wants.
吉娜出生在富有家庭；她要什麼就有什麼。

adj. 無論什麼的；不管什麼樣的

▶Whatever reason you have, show up for the meeting on time.
不管你有什麼理由，都要準時參加會議。

---

what's [hwats]　◀Track 5184

abbr. 是什麼（**what is**的縮寫）

▶What's keeping you from pursuing your goal?
是什麼阻止你去追求目標呢？

---

wheat [hwit] **n.** 小麥　◀Track 5185

▶The brewer produces wine with wheat. 釀酒者用小麥製酒。

> 相關片語 **separate the wheat from the chaff** 鑑別優劣，分辨好壞，去蕪存菁

▶The university held an entrance exam to separate the wheat from the chaff.
大學辦了入學考試來挑選好的學生。

---

wheel [hwil]　◀Track 5186

n. 輪子；車輪；方向盤

▶It was the first time that Rita held the steering wheel.
瑞塔是第一次握方向盤。

---

when [hwɛn]　◀Track 5187

conj. 在……的時候

▶I was doing the laundry when the postman rang the doorbell.
郵差按門鈴時我正在洗衣服。

adv. 何時

▶When will we set off? I can't wait.
我們什麼時候會出發？我等不及了。

pron. 何時

▶Since when did the big sale for sports gear begin? I must have missed so many good deals!
運動用品特賣會是什麼時候開始的？我肯定錯過了很多好東西！

---

whenever [hwɛn`ɛvɚ]　◀Track 5188

adv. 無論何時；究竟何時

▶Whenever will he quit the bad habit of smoking?
他究竟何時才會改掉抽菸的壞習慣？

conj. 每當；無論何時

▶I have to reply right away whenever my boss texts me.
無論老闆什麼時候傳訊息給我，我都得要立刻回覆。

---

when's [hwɛnz]　◀Track 5189

abbr. 是什麼時候（**when is**的縮寫）

▶When's she coming back?
她什麼時候會回來？

---

where [hwɛr] **adv.** 哪裡　◀Track 5190

▶Where will you go for the honeymoon trip?
你們蜜月旅行要去哪？

conj. 在……的地方

▶This is the place where I will open my store.
這就是我要開店的地點。

中級

where's [hwɛrz] ◀≋Track 5191

abbr. 在哪裡（**where is** 的縮寫）

▶ Where's the coffee shop you brought up the other day?
你前幾天提到的咖啡店在哪裡呢？

wherever [hwɛrˋɛvɚ] ◀≋Track 5192

adv. 無論在何地；究竟在何處

▶ Wherever did you go last night?
你昨晚到底去哪裡了？

conj. 無論在哪裡；無論到哪裡；無論在什麼情況下

▶ Wherever we go in the city, we can see surveillance cameras. 在城市裡不管到哪裡都可以看到監視錄影機。

whether [ˋhwɛðɚ] ◀≋Track 5193

conj. 是否

▶ We are not sure whether the leader of the Senate will reconcile with the president.
我們不確定參議院院長是否會與總統和解。

which [hwɪtʃ] ◀≋Track 5194

pron. 哪一個；哪一些

▶ Which of the singers got the highest score in the contest?
哪一個歌手在比賽中得到最高分？

adj. 哪一個；哪一些

▶ Support which political party you identify with the most.
支持你最能認同的那一個政黨。

whichever ◀≋Track 5195

[hwɪtʃˋɛvɚ] **det.** 無論哪個，無論哪些

▶ Whichever job you take, you have to do your best.
無論做什麼工作，都應該盡力而為。

pron. 無論哪一個；究竟哪個

▶ Whichever he takes is fine with me.
他拿哪一個，我都沒意見。

while [hwaɪl] ◀≋Track 5196

conj. 當……的時候；

▶ The owner of the house went in while the thief was rummaging for valuables.
當小偷翻箱倒櫃找值錢東西的時候，屋主就進門了。

n. 一會兒；一段時間

▶ We stayed at the café for a while.
我們在咖啡廳待了一會。

whip [hwɪp] ◀≋Track 5197

n. 鞭子；抽打；攪拌器

▶ We reported the annoying old man who constantly lashed his dogs with long whips.
我們投訴了那個討人厭的老人，因為他不斷用長鞭打他的狗。

v. 鞭笞，抽打；攪打；煽動；急走；徹底擊敗

▶ I whipped the cream before mixing it with the flour.
我將奶油攪拌過再和麵粉混和。

whisper [ˋhwɪspɚ] ◀≋Track 5198

n. 耳語；私語；傳聞、流言

▶ The refugees talked in whispers for fear that they would be found by the patrols.
難民低聲說話，深怕會被巡邏隊發現。

v. 低語；私下說；低聲說

▶ The manager whispered something to the secretary, and she seemed to be surprised.
經理低聲對祕書說了一些話，她似乎很驚訝。

whistle [ˈhwɪsl̩]　◀ミTrack 5199

v. 吹口哨，吹哨子；呼嘯；吹口哨示意

▶ Superman seemed to feel nothing when the bullet whistled past him.
子彈嗖嗖飛過他時，超人似乎一點感覺都沒有。

n. 口哨，警笛；哨音

▶ The whistle of the referee signified that No. 4 played foul.
裁判的哨音表示四號選手犯規了。

相關片語 blow the whistle on
告密，阻止，使……停下

▶ He blew the whistle on the case that the manager was embezzling the funds of the company.
他告密指出經理正在盜用公司的資金。

white [hwaɪt]　◀ミTrack 5200

adj. 白的；白色的

▶ She wore a white gown at the reception party.
她在接待會上穿著白色禮服。

n. 白色

▶ White is often considered to represent innocence and purity.
白色常被認為代表著純潔與無辜。

who [hu] **pron.** 誰；什麼人　◀ミTrack 5201

▶ Who told you the secret?
誰告訴你這個祕密的？

who'd [hud]　◀ミTrack 5202

abbr. 誰會、誰已（who would、who had 的縮寫）

▶ Who'd believe in his words?
誰會相信他的話？

whoever [huˈɛvɚ] =whomever　◀ミTrack 5203

pron. 無論誰；到底是誰

▶ Whoever breaks into the system will be caught immediately.
不管是誰侵入這個系統都會立刻被逮捕。

whole [hol]　◀ミTrack 5204

adj. 全部的；整個的；所有的

▶ The whole class was against the proposal.
整個班級都不贊成這個提案。

n. 全部；全體

▶ The whole of France was upset with the legal pack.
法國全國都對這個法案不滿。

whom [hum]　◀ミTrack 5205

pron. 誰；任何人

▶ Whom should we ask about this project? 關於這個計畫，我們應該請教誰？

who's [huz]　◀ミTrack 5206

abbr. 是誰（who is的縮寫）

▶ Who's joining the trip?
誰要參加這趟旅行呢？

whose [huz] **det.** 誰的　◀ミTrack 5207

▶ Whose luggage is this? 這是誰的行李？

why [hwaɪ] **adv.** 為什麼　◀ミTrack 5208

▶ Why did he lie to us?
他為什麼對我們說謊呢？

conj. ……的原因；為何

▶ The reason why she canceled the trip was unclear.
她取消旅行的原因並不清楚。

中級

wicked [`wɪkɪd]
Track 5209

adj. 邪惡的，缺德的；頑皮的；惡劣的，有害的；過分的；很棒的

▶ The wicked wizard was expelled by the villagers.
這名邪惡的巫師被村民趕走了。

wide [waɪd]
Track 5210

adj. 寬的；寬鬆的；廣泛的

▶ The road was wide enough for two cars to pass at the same time.
這條路夠寬，兩台車可以同時通過。

widen [`waɪdn]
Track 5211

v. 放寬；加大；擴大

▶ To widen the road, the city government had to tear down some of the old houses along the street.
為了拓寬道路，市政府必須要拆除街道兩邊的舊房子。

widespread
Track 5212

[`waɪd͵sprɛd]

adj. 普遍的，廣泛的；分布廣的

▶ There is a widespread belief that organic produces are fertilized with human excreta. 有機農作物被廣泛相信是用人類的排泄物做肥料。

width [wɪdθ] **n.** 寬度
Track 5213

▶ We measure the length and width of the house with a laser ruler.
我們用雷射尺測量房子的長度和寬度。

wife [waɪf]
Track 5214

n. 妻子；太太；夫人

▶ Mr. Bush missed his late wife very much. 布希先生很想念他已故的妻子。

wild [waɪld]
Track 5215

adj. 野生的；未被馴養的；粗野的；瘋狂的；猛烈的

▶ It is said that wild coffee trees will be extinct in a few decades.
據說野生咖啡樹再過幾十年就會滅絕。

n. 荒野；未被開發之地

▶ The panda was sent back to the wild.
這隻熊貓被放回野外。

wilderness
Track 5216

[`wɪldə͵nɪs]

n. 荒漠，無人煙處；不受控制的狀態

▶ No one knows why the castle was built in the wilderness. 沒人知道為什麼這座城堡會被建造在荒野裡。

| 相關片語 **in the wilderness**（政治上）不再處於重要地位或具影響力 |

▶ The politician was in the wilderness after he lost in the election campaign.
這名政治人物在輸掉選舉之後就不再有影響力了。

wildlife [`waɪld͵laɪf]
Track 5217

n. 野生生物，野生動物

▶ She worked as a rancher in a wildlife sanctuary.
她在野生動物保護區當管理員。

wildly [`waɪldlɪ]
Track 5218

adv. 野生地；失控地；粗暴地；瘋狂地

▶ The Husky ran wildly in the park after his owner loosened the leash.
主人鬆開鍊條之後，這隻哈士奇就在公園裡暴衝。

will [wɪl]
Track 5219

n. 意志，毅力；心願，目的；遺囑

▶The patient survived cancer with his iron will.
這名病人透過堅強的意志戰勝了癌症。

相關片語 **will to live** 求生意志

▶The rescue team encouraged the victim trapped in the wrecks, and hoped that she could keep her will to live.
救難隊鼓勵被困在瓦礫隊中的受害者，希望她保持求生的意志。

willing [ˋwɪlɪŋ] 　🔊 Track 5220
adj. 願意的

▶She was not willing to share the resources with us.
她不願意和我們分享資源。

willow [ˋwɪlo] 　🔊 Track 5221
n. 柳，柳樹

▶We took pictures of the willows beside the lake.
我們拍了湖邊柳樹的照片。

win [wɪn] v. 贏；獲勝 　🔊 Track 5222

▶We won the game and got a great amount of prize money.
我們贏得比賽，得到大筆獎金。

n. 獲勝；成功

▶The team got seven consecutive wins in this season.
這支隊伍這一季連續獲得七勝。

wind [wɪnd] n. 風 　🔊 Track 5223

▶The whistling wind in the middle of the night was frightening to me.
半夜呼嘯的風聲對我來說很嚇人。

window [ˋwɪndo] 　🔊 Track 5224

n. 窗戶

▶The burglar broke into the house through the window.
小偷從窗戶潛進屋內。

windy [ˋwɪndɪ] 　🔊 Track 5225
adj. 颳風的；多風的

▶It's not a good choice to play badminton outdoors on such a windy day.
在風那麼大的日子於戶外打羽毛球不是個好選擇。

wine [waɪn] 　🔊 Track 5226
n. 酒；葡萄酒；水果酒

▶We had some red wine while having the steak.
我們吃牛排配紅酒。

wing [wɪŋ] n. 翅膀 　🔊 Track 5227

▶The eaglet was trying to spread its wings and learn how to fly.
這隻幼兒老鷹試著振翅學會飛翔。

wink [wɪŋk] 　🔊 Track 5228

v. 眨眼；使眼色，眨眼示意；假裝無視；閃爍

▶She winked to signal me that there was a mistake on my PPT slide.
她對我眨眼表示我的簡報投影片上有錯誤。

n. 眨眼，眼色；閃爍，閃耀；瞬間，霎時

▶She caught my attention with a wink and a smile.
她對我眨眼又微笑，引起我的注意。

相關片語 **in the wink of an eye**
一瞬間，一眨眼的時間

▶The wonderful trip ended in the wink of an eye.
美好的旅行一眨眼就結束了。

中級

相關片語 **sleep a wink**
打個盹，闔一下眼

▶I slept a wink during the recess between classes.
我在課程休息時間闔眼休息了一下。

winner [ˋwɪnɚ]　◀Track 5229
n. 贏家；獲勝者；優勝者

▶The winner of the jeopardy game can have a free trip to Europe.
贏得闖關挑戰遊戲的人可以獲得免費歐洲旅行。

winter [ˋwɪntɚ] **n.** 冬天　◀Track 5230

▶They need an indoor heater to fight the cold weather in winter. 他們需要室內的暖氣來對抗冬天寒冷的天氣。

wipe [waɪp]　◀Track 5231
v. 擦，擦乾，擦去，抹

▶His words wiped away my fear.
他的話抹去了我恐懼。

相關片語 **wipe the smile off one's face** 讓人笑不出來；掃某人的興

▶Her sarcastic words wiped the smile off my face.
她諷刺的話使我笑不出來。

n. 擦，揩

▶The statue needs a good wipe. It's all covered with dust.
這個雕像要好好擦一擦。它整個被灰塵覆蓋。

相關片語 **wipe the floor with**
完全打敗，使潰敗

▶The tennis player wiped the floor with all her opponents.
這位女網選手擊敗了所有的對手。

wire [waɪr]　◀Track 5232
n. 金屬線；電纜；電話線

▶There is a fence of steel wire around the power generator.
發電機四周有鋼絲製成的圍籬。

相關片語 **on the wire**
使用電話中；正在講電話

▶Ms. Sandburg is on the wire now.
桑柏格女士正在電話中。

v. 用金屬線綁、連接、加固；給……裝電線；用電報發送，拍電報

▶Every room in the apartment is wired for internet connection.
這個公寓每個房間都加裝網路線。

wisdom [ˋwɪzdəm]　◀Track 5233
n. 智慧，才智；知識，學問；古人名訓

▶I was inspired by the words of wisdom of the old lady.
我受到這位老婦人的智慧話語啟發。

相關片語 **wisdom tooth** 智齒

▶I finally decided to have my wisdom tooth pulled off. 我最後決定要拔掉智齒。

wise [waɪz]　◀Track 5234
adj. 有智慧的；明智的

▶He looked wise, but he always talked nonsense.
他看起來很聰明，但是他總是在胡扯。

wish [wɪʃ] **v.** 希望；但願　◀Track 5235

▶I wish there will not be wars anymore.
我希望再也不會有戰爭。

n. 願望；心願；祝福

▶Send my best wishes to your parents.
向你的父母表達我的祝福吧。

wit [wɪt] ◀€Track 5236
n. 智力；機智；智慧；富有智慧的人

▶Our client was impressed with his wits.
我們的顧客對他的機智印象深刻。

相關片語 **have one's wits about one** 保持警覺，時刻警覺

▶He had his wits about him while negotiating with the robber.
他和搶匪溝通時保持警覺。

witch [wɪtʃ] **n.** 女巫 ◀€Track 5237

▶Macbeth listened to the witch and believed that he should be the next king.
馬克白聽了女巫的話，深信他是下一任國王。

with [wɪð] ◀€Track 5238
prep. 和……一起

▶I had the chocolate with mocha.
我吃巧克力配抹茶。

withdraw [wɪðˋdrɔ] ◀€Track 5239
v. 抽回，收回；提領；撤銷；離開；退出

▶I withdrew part of my monthly salary to pay the utility bills.
我領取月薪的一部分來付水電費。

within [wɪˋðɪn] ◀€Track 5240
prep. 在……範圍內；不超過；在……內部

▶I have to finish the report within tow hours.
我必須在兩個小時內完成這份報告。

adv. 在裡面；在內部

▶I believe that she is pure within.
我相信她內心純潔。

without [wɪˋðaʊt] ◀€Track 5241
prep. 沒有

▶Without his parents' financial support, he would not have started his own business. 沒有父母的經濟支援，他是不可能有辦法創業的。

witness [ˋwɪtnɪs] ◀€Track 5242
n. 目擊者，見證人；證詞；證據

▶The witness of the murder case was threatened by the suspect.
這名謀殺案的目擊者受到嫌疑犯的威脅。

v. 目擊；證明；為……作證

▶I witnessed the process of the creation of this masterpiece.
我見證了這幅傑作的創作過程。

wizard [ˋwɪzɚd] **n.** 巫師 ◀€Track 5243

▶He passed the test of Hogwarts and became a qualified wizard. 他通過霍格華茲的考試，成為了合格的巫師。

wok [wak] ◀€Track 5244
n. 鑊；中式炒菜鍋

▶The Chinese-made cast iron wok cost me nine hundred dollars.
這個中國製的鑄鐵炒鍋花了我九百元。

wolf [wʊlf] **n.** 狼 ◀€Track 5245

▶The wolf fell into the trap and got badly hurt. 這匹狼落入陷阱受了重傷。

woman [ˋwʊmən] ◀€Track 5246
n. 女人；婦女

▶She was one of the activists who fought for women's suffrage in the United States.
她是爭取美國婦女投票權的行動份子之一。

中級

wonder [`wʌndɚ]
🔊 Track 5247

v. 納悶；想知道

▶I wonder how he came to this conclusion.
我納悶他是怎麼做出這個結論的。

n. 驚奇；驚歎；奇觀、奇事

▶The Great Wall in China is considered a wonder by many foreign tourists.
中國的長城被許多外國觀光客視為奇觀。

wonderful
🔊 Track 5248

[`wʌndɚ-fəl] **adj.** 美好的；神奇的；極好的

▶What a wonderful day! Let's go out for a hike.
天氣多好啊！我們去健行吧！

won't [wont]
🔊 Track 5249

abbr. 不會（will not的縮寫）

▶We won't dine in that restaurant again.
我們再也不會去那家餐廳用餐了。

wood [wʊd]
🔊 Track 5250

n. 木頭、木材；森林、樹林

▶We collected some wood to build a campfire.
我們撿拾了一些木頭來升營火。

wooden [`wʊdn]
🔊 Track 5251

adj. 木製的；僵硬的

▶The wooden cabinet cost thirty thousand dollars.
這個木製的櫥櫃要價三萬元。

wool [wʊl]
🔊 Track 5252

n. 羊毛；毛線；毛織品

▶This type of wool is pretty expensive.
這種羊毛種類相當昂貴。

相關片語 lose one's wool 發怒；發火

▶He lost his wool when he realized that his colleague stole his idea.
他知道同事盜用他的想法時，就發怒了。

word [wɝd]
🔊 Track 5253

n. 字；一句話；言辭；談話

▶His friends' words mean more to him than his parents' advices.
對他來說朋友的話比父母的忠告更重要。

work [wɝk]
🔊 Track 5254

n. 工作；事；職務

▶The construction work will last for about three months.
這個建造工作將會持續三個月左右。

v. 工作；幹活；（機器）運轉

▶The computer stopped working after I pressed the wrong button.
我按錯按鈕，電腦就停止工作了。

workbook [`wɝk‚bʊk]
🔊 Track 5255

n. 習題簿，練習簿；業務手冊，工作筆記本

▶The teacher wrote down some comments on the students' workbook.
老師在學生的習題簿上寫了一些評語。

worker [`wɝkɚ]
🔊 Track 5256

n. 工人；勞工；勞動者；工作者

▶The workers in the country have been living on a low income for several years.
這個國家的勞工已經好幾年靠著微薄收入過活了。

working [`wɝkɪŋ]
🔊 Track 5257

adj. 工作的；有效的；操作的；有工作的

▶The social worker offered some useful piece of advices to the working parents.
社工為要上班的父母提供有用的建議。

n. **工作，勞動；運轉；經營，操縱**

▶The instructor explained the working of the machine with a poster. 這名講師拿一張海報解釋這台機器的運作方式。

相關片語 **working holiday** 打工度假

▶Tina plans to take a working holiday in Australia after she graduates from high school.
緹娜計畫高中畢業之後要去澳洲打工度假。

workshop [ˋwɝkˏʃɑp]

Track 5258

n. **工作坊，小工廠；研討會，專題討論會**

▶The teachers attended a workshop to discuss how to incorporate picture books into English teaching.
老師們參加工作坊學習要如何將繪本融入英語教學中。

world [wɝld] n. 世界

Track 5259

▶The wealth of the top-ranking rich people could support a lot of poor people in the world. 頂尖富人的財富可以養活世界上的許多窮人。

adj. **世界的**

▶Overuse of natural resources may have a negative effect on world economy.
過度使用自然資源可能會對世界經濟有負面影響。

worldwide

Track 5260

[ˋwɝldˏwaɪd] **adv.** **在世界各地；在全世界**

▶The effect of social media has reached worldwide.
社群網站的影響力已經遍佈全球。

adj. **遍及全球的，全球性的**

▶The company offers the service of worldwide delivery.
這間公司提供全球貨運服務。

worm [wɝm]

Track 5261

n. **蟲，蠕蟲，蛀蟲；可憐蟲，懦夫**

▶The girl screamed when she saw the worm in her tea.
這名女孩看到茶裡的蟲子嚇得尖叫。

v. **使蠕動；使緩慢前進；潛行，潛入；擺脫困境**

▶They wormed their way through the forest.
他們緩慢地穿過了森林。

相關片語 **worm out** 擺脫；刺探出

▶He wormed out of the difficulties despite the lack of support.
儘管缺少資源，他還是擺脫了問題。

相關片語 **a can of worms** 複雜的問題

▶She was bothered by a can of worms the first year she got promoted as the manager. 她升上經理的第一年，就遇到多複雜的問題。

worn [worn]

Track 5262

adj. **用舊的，磨壞的；精疲力盡的，憔悴的**

▶Her jeans were worn, but she would not abandon it.
她的牛仔褲都破了，但是她捨不得丟。

相關片語 **worn out** 疲累不堪

▶After the lengthy meeting, the employees were all worn out.
經過冗長的會議，員工都精疲力盡了。

worried [ˋwɝɪd]

Track 5263

adj. **擔憂的，擔心的**

▶She was worried that she would lose money in the stock market.
她擔心股票會賠錢。

worry [`wɝɪ] ◀ Track 5264
v. 擔心；擔憂

▶He doesn't worry about his qualification for the job.
他不擔心自己擔任這份工作的資格。

n. 擔心；憂慮；令人擔憂的事

▶He mentioned his worry about his mother's illness to me.
他對我提到他對母親病情的擔心。

worse [wɝs] ◀ Track 5265
adj. 更差的；更壞的；更糟糕的；（並）更重的

▶Nothing is worse than being forced to swallow the green pepper.
沒有什麼事比被迫吃下青椒更糟的了。

adv. 更糟；更壞；更惡化

▶She sang worse than anyone in her class.
她唱歌唱得比班上任何人都糟。

n. 更糟的狀況

▶The worse is we might be punished for the mistake.
更糟的是我們可能會因為這個錯誤受罰。

相關片語 **go from bad to worse**
越來越糟

▶His illness has gone from bad to worse.
他的病情每況愈下。

worst [wɝst] ◀ Track 5266
adj. 最差的；最壞的

▶She is the worst skater.
她溜冰溜得最差。

adv. 最壞地；最惡劣地；最不利地

▶He did the worst in the exam in the class. 他是班上考最差的。

n. 最壞的狀況

▶Plan for the worst and wish for the best.
為最壞狀況做打算，並且祈禱最好的狀況。

worth [wɝθ] ◀ Track 5267
adj. 有……的價值；值……

▶The genuine leather purse is worth three thousand NT dollars.
這個真皮皮包價值台幣三千元。

n. 價值；值一定金額的數量

▶The worth of the diamond ring has not been estimated.
這個鑽戒的價值還沒有被估計。

worthless [`wɝθlɪs] ◀ Track 5268
adj. 無價值的，無用的；不中用的

▶He was dismissed as a worthless fool. 他被貶低成一個不中用的笨蛋。

worthwhile ◀ Track 5269
[`wɝθ`hwaɪl] **adj.** 值得花費時間（或金錢）的，值得做的；有真實價值的

▶He thought it's worthwhile to spend a year being an apprentice of the master.
他認為花一年當這位大師的學徒是值得的。

worthy [`wɝðɪ] ◀ Track 5270
adj. 有價值的；值得的，配得上的；足以……的

▶The National Palace Museum is worthy of a visit.
故宮博物院值得去參觀。

n. 知名人士，傑出人士

▶Many worthies in the electronics industry attended the conference.
許多電子業的知名人士出席這場研討會。

would [wʊd] ◀Track 5271
aux. 會；將；要；願意

▶Would you please lower you voice?
你可以降低音量嗎？

wouldn't [ˋwʊdnt] ◀Track 5272
abbr. （過去式）不會（**would not**的縮寫）

▶They wouldn't accept your suggestion.
他們不會接受你的建議。

wound [wund] ◀Track 5273
n. 傷口；創傷；

▶Miraculously, the knife wound in his arm healed within two hours. 他手臂上的刀傷奇蹟似地在兩個小時內癒合了。

v. 使受傷；傷害

▶Your harsh words may wound the child' pride.
你的嚴厲話語可能會傷害小孩的自尊。

wow [waʊ] ◀Track 5274
interj. （表示驚訝，欣喜或痛苦的叫聲）哇，噢

▶Wow! What a fantastic show!
哇！真是精采的表演！

v. 使驚訝，使驚豔

▶The amateur singer's performance wowed the judges of the talent show.
這位業餘歌手的表演令選秀節目的評審驚艷。

wrap [ræp] ◀Track 5275
v. 包，裹；穿外衣，披圍巾；偽裝；使全神貫注

▶She wrapped the souvenir with a pink paper.
她用一張粉紅色的紙把紀念禮品包起來。

n. 包裹物，覆蓋物；外衣，圍巾，披肩；墨西哥捲

▶My mom made the wrap of the steamed spring roll by herself.
我媽自己做潤餅捲的外皮。

wrapping [ˋræpɪŋ] ◀Track 5276
n. 包裝紙，包裝材料

▶She tore off the wrapping of the gifts.
她把禮物的包裝紙撕掉。

wreck [rɛk] ◀Track 5277
n. 失事，遇難；（失事的）殘骸；破壞

▶The wreck of the ship was found in the sea ten years after the accident.
這艘沉沒船隻的殘骸在意外發生十年後才在海裡被發現。

v. 使失事，遇難；損害

▶The typhoon wreaked havoc on the southern part of the island.
颱風肆虐這個島的南部。

wrinkle [ˋrɪŋkl̩] ◀Track 5278
n. 皺紋；難題

▶She believes that Botox injection can smooth the wrinkles on her face.
她相信注射肉毒桿菌可以幫她撫平臉上的皺紋。

v. 使起皺紋；皺起來

▶The silk shirt wouldn't wrinkle.
這件絲綢襯衫不會起皺紋。

wrist [rɪst] ◀Track 5279
n. 腕；腕部；腕關節

中級

▶He wore a wrist brace when he played tennis.
他打網球時會戴護腕。

write [raɪt] v 寫
🔊 Track 5280

▶If you want to be a writer, you can write down random ideas on a notebook.
如果你想要當一名作家的話，你可以在筆記本上寫下隨性的點子。

writer [`raɪtɚ]
🔊 Track 5281
n. 作家；作者；撰稿人

▶The writer would not comment on the adapted movie of his novel.
這位作家不願對由他小說改編的電影發表評論。

writing [`raɪtɪŋ]
🔊 Track 5282
n. 書寫，寫作；筆跡；文學作品；文件

▶I can recognize my father's writing. I'm sure this letter is not written by him.
我認得出我爸爸的筆跡。我確定這封信不是他寫的。

相關片語 the writing on the wall
凶兆，不祥之兆

▶The rising of the profit-seeking enterprise income tax was the writing on the wall to our company.
營利事業所得稅上漲對我們公司來說是不祥之兆。

wrong [rɔŋ]
🔊 Track 5283
adj. 錯誤的；不對的；出毛病的

▶Your working attitdue is just wrong. Please be responsible.
你的工作態度真是完全錯誤。請負起責任。

adv. 錯誤地；不正當地

▶I didn't mean to hurt them. They got me wrong.
我沒有要傷害他們。他們誤會我了。

n. 錯誤

▶It's important to teach your child how to tell right from wrong.
教導你的小孩如何分辨是非很重要。

▶ Xx

　　以下表格是全民英檢官方公告中級「聽、說、讀、寫」所須具備的能力，本書例句皆依此範疇特別設計，只要掃描右方QR code，就能搭配相對應的音軌實現「眼耳並用」方式，刺激左腦的語言學習功能；同時也可使用本書附贈的紅膠片，將其置於單字上，一面記憶一面自我挑戰，達到雙倍的學習成果！

聽 ▶	在日常生活中，能聽懂一般的會話；能大致聽懂公共場所廣播、氣象報告及廣告等。在工作時，能聽懂簡易的產品介紹與操作說明。能大致聽懂外籍人士的談話及詢問。
說 ▶	可在日常生活中，能以簡易英語交談或描述一般事物，能介紹自己的生活作息、工作、家庭、經歷等，並可對一般話題陳述看法。在工作時，能進行簡單的答詢，並與外籍人士交談溝通。
讀 ▶	在日常生活中，能閱讀短文、故事、私人信件、廣告、傳單、簡介及使用說明等。在工作時，能閱讀工作須知、公告、操作手冊、例行的文件、傳真、電報等。
寫 ▶	能寫簡單的書信、故事及心得等。對於熟悉且與個人經歷相關的主題，能以簡易的文字表達。

中級

X-ray [`ɛks`re]　　◀ Track 5284

n. X光；X光檢查；X光照片

▶Excessive exposure to X-ray is said to be harmful to human health.
過度接觸X光據說對人體有害。

v. 用X光檢查

▶The dentist X-rayed his gum and tooth to locate the cavity.
牙醫用X光檢查他的牙齦和牙齒來找到蛀牙的位置。

xerox [`zɪrɑks]　　◀ Track 5285

n. 靜電複印機；影印機

▶We rented a Xerox machine from their company.
我們向他們公司租一台影印機。

▶ Yy

　　以下表格是全民英檢官方公告中級「聽、説、讀、寫」所須具備的能力，本書例句皆依此範疇特別設計，只要掃描右方QR code，就能搭配相對應的音軌實現「眼耳並用」方式，刺激左腦的語言學習功能；同時也可使用本書附贈的紅膠片，將其置於單字上，一面記憶一面自我挑戰，達到雙倍的學習成果！

聽 ▶	在日常生活中，能聽懂一般的會話；能大致聽懂公共場所廣播、氣象報告及廣告等。在工作時，能聽懂簡易的產品介紹與操作説明。能大致聽懂外籍人士的談話及詢問。
説 ▶	可在日常生活中，能以簡易英語交談或描述一般事物，能介紹自己的生活作息、工作、家庭、經歷等，並可對一般話題陳述看法。在工作時，能進行簡單的答詢，並與外籍人士交談溝通。
讀 ▶	在日常生活中，能閱讀短文、故事、私人信件、廣告、傳單、簡介及使用説明等。在工作時，能閱讀工作須知、公告、操作手冊、例行的文件、傳真、電報等。
寫 ▶	能寫簡單的書信、故事及心得等。對於熟悉且與個人經歷相關的主題，能以簡易的文字表達。

yam [jæm] ◀ Track 5286
=sweet po·ta·to
n. 山芋類植物（如山藥、甘藷、馬鈴薯等）
▶The hand-made traditional Chinese yam cake tastes delicious.
這個傳統中式芋頭糕很好吃。

yard [jɑrd] **n.** 院子；庭院 ◀ Track 5287
▶She grows some herbs in the front yard. 她在前院種了一些藥草。

yawn [jɔn] **v.** 打呵欠 ◀ Track 5288
▶Mr. Hanson yawned over the talk show.
韓森先生看著談話節目打哈欠。

n. 呵欠；乏味的人或事物
▶The cartoon was a big yawn for the teenage students.
這部卡通對這些十幾歲的學生來説很無聊。

yeah [jɛə] ◀ Track 5289
interj. 對啊！好耶！
▶"I'm starting my own business." "Oh, yeah! Congratulations."
「我要創業了。」「噢，好耶！恭喜。」

year [jɪr] **n.** 年 ◀ Track 5290
▶I calculated the sum of my possession at the end of the year.
我在年底計算了我的總資產金額。

yearly [ˋjɪrlɪ] ◀ Track 5291
adv. 每年；一年一度
▶I made the yearly visit to my mentor. He taught me how to truly meditate.
我每年去拜訪我的心靈導師，他教導我如何真正地進行冥想。

yell [jɛl] **v.** 叫喊；吼叫著説 ◀ Track 5292

▶The instructor yelled at the trainees.
這名教練對著受訓者大喊。

n. 叫喊聲；吼叫聲

▶I heard a yell from the manager's office.
我聽到總經理辦公室傳來吼叫聲。

yellow [ˋjɛlo]
Track 5293

adj. 黃的；黃色的

▶Look for yellow cars first when you want to hail a cab.
如果你要招計程車，先搜尋黃色的汽車。

n. 黃；黃色；黃色的衣服

▶In ancient China, yellow is a color used by the emperor.
古代中國，黃色是帝王用的顏色。

yes [jɛs]
Track 5294

=yeah **interj.** 好極了；真的

▶"Our proposal was accepted by the board." "Yes! We did it."
「我們的提案被董事會接受了。」「太棒了！我們做到了。」

adv. 是；是的

▶"Off with his head!" "Yes, your majesty."
「把他拖下去砍頭！」「是的，陛下。」

yesterday [ˋjɛstɚde]
Track 5295

n. 昨天

▶Yesterday was my mother's birthday, and we had a fun time together.
昨天是我媽生日，我們聚在一起玩得很開心。

adv. 在昨天

▶The moon was strangly beautiful with orange halos around it yesterday.
月亮昨天帶有橘色光暈，詭異地很美麗。

yet [jɛt]
Track 5296

adv. （用於否定句）還沒；已經

▶She hasn't decided what to order yet.
她還沒有決定要點什麼。

conj. 然而；卻

▶He was running out of money, yet he reserved a luxurious suite.
他快沒錢，卻訂了一間豪華飯店套房。

yogurt [ˋjogɚt]
Track 5297

=yoghurt **n.** 酸奶；酸乳酪；優格

▶She only has yogurt or oatmeal for breakfast.
她早餐只會吃優格或者燕麥。

yolk [jok] **n.** 蛋黃
Track 5298

▶She separated the yolk and the egg white with a spoon.
她用湯匙將蛋黃和蛋清分開。

you [ju] **pron.** 你
Track 5299

▶Are you sure you want to quit?
你確定你要放棄嗎？

you'd [jud]
Track 5300

abbr. 你會、你已（**you had**、**you would** 的縮寫）

▶You'd regret your decision after ten years. 你十年後會後悔自己的選擇。

you'll [jul]
Track 5301

abbr. 你會（**you will**的縮寫）

▶You'll face a lot of difficulties; just remember to stick with your principles.
你會遇到很多困難，就是謹記著堅守原則就好。

中級

young [jʌŋ] 🔊 Track 5302

adj. 年輕的；年幼的

▶ Young people nowadays have no patience to spend years to master a professional skill. 現在的年輕人沒有耐心花數年熟練一門專業技術

n. 年輕人們；青年們

▶ The sports attracts the young as well as the old.
這項運動老少咸宜。

youngster [ˈjʌŋstɚ] 🔊 Track 5303

n. 小孩、兒童；年輕人

▶ The bay is a popular surfing area for youngsters.
這個海灣是受年輕人歡迎的衝浪地點。

your [jʊɚ] 🔊 Track 5304

det. 你的；你們的

▶ Your mail was sent to a wrong address.
你的信件被寄到錯的地址了。

you're [juɚ] 🔊 Track 5305

abbr. 你是（**you are**的縮寫）

▶ You're are destined for greatness
你注定要成為偉人的。

yours [jʊrz] 🔊 Track 5306

pron. 你的（事物）；你們的（事物）

▶ Take the car. It's yours.
收下這輛車吧。它是你的了。

yourself [jʊɚˈsɛlf] 🔊 Track 5307

pron. 你自己；你們自己

▶ Take good care of yourself.
好好照顧你自己。

youth [juθ] 🔊 Track 5308

n. 青春時代；青年；年輕；青春

▶ She used to be passionate about Ancient Roman Architecture in her youth.
她年輕的時候很喜歡古羅馬建築。

youthful [ˈjuθfəl] 🔊 Track 5309

adj. 年輕的；富青春活力的；朝氣蓬勃的

▶ Though she is in her sixties, she remains youthful because she exercises regularly.
雖然她六十幾歲了，她還是靠著規律運動保持青春活力。

you've [juv] 🔊 Track 5310

abbr. 你已（**you have**的縮寫）

▶ You've missed the deadline. Try again next year.
你已經錯過了期限。明年再試試吧。

yucky [ˈjʌkɪ] 🔊 Track 5311

adj. 討人厭的；難以下嚥的；難聞的

▶ The yucky smell of the leftover made me feel nauseous.
廚餘那種討人厭的氣味讓我覺得噁心

yummy [ˈjʌmɪ] 🔊 Track 5312

adj. 好吃的；美味的

▶ The fried chicken is really yummy.
炸雞真好吃。

▶ Zz

以下表格是全民英檢官方公告中級「聽、說、讀、寫」所須具備的能力，本書例句皆依此範疇特別設計，只要掃描右方QR code，就能搭配相對應的音軌實現「眼耳並用」方式，刺激左腦的語言學習功能；同時也可使用本書附贈的紅膠片，將其置於單字上，一面記憶一面自我挑戰，達到雙倍的學習成果！

聽 ▶	在日常生活中，能聽懂一般的會話；能大致聽懂公共場所廣播、氣象報告及廣告等。在工作時，能聽懂簡易的產品介紹與操作說明。能大致聽懂外籍人士的談話及詢問。
說 ▶	可在日常生活中，能以簡易英語交談或描述一般事物，能介紹自己的生活作息、工作、家庭、經歷等，並可對一般話題陳述看法。在工作時，能進行簡單的答詢，並與外籍人士交談溝通。
讀 ▶	在日常生活中，能閱讀短文、故事、私人信件、廣告、傳單、簡介及使用說明等。在工作時，能閱讀工作須知、公告、操作手冊、例行的文件、傳真、電報等。
寫 ▶	能寫簡單的書信、故事及心得等。對於熟悉且與個人經歷相關的主題，能以簡易的文字表達。

中級

zebra [ˋzibrə] n. 斑馬 🔊 Track 5313

▶ The zebra stripe pattern is used as a mark for pedestrian crossing.
斑馬線條紋被用來標記行人穿越道。

zero [ˋzɪro] 🔊 Track 5314

n. 零；零號；零度；無；烏有

▶ It's okay that you achieved zero today. We've all been there.
今天一無所獲沒有關係的，我們都這樣過。

adj. 零的；全無的

▶ I have zero experience in marketing.
我一點行銷經驗也沒有。

zone [zon] n. 地帶；地區 🔊 Track 5315

▶ Pine leave trees are common in the temperate zone.
針葉樹在溫帶地區很常見。

相關片語 time zone 時區

▶ Taiwan and Japan belong to different time zones.
台灣和日本在不同時區。

v. 劃區；使分成區或地帶

▶ This area has been zoned as a conservation park.
這個區域被劃為保育公園。

zoo [zu] n. 動物園 🔊 Track 5316

▶ The koalas in the petting zoo got sick.
寵物動物園裡的無尾熊生病了。

NOTE

中級

英語學習 系列 *008*

GEPT全民英檢中級單字100%攻略
：左腦式聽力學習╳紅膠片高效練習！

徹底激發你的潛力，發揮你的實力，英檢中級高分過關！

作　　　者	張慈庭英語教學團隊◎著
顧　　　問	曾文旭
總 編 輯	王毓芳
編 輯 統 籌	耿文國、黃璽宇
主　　　編	吳靜宜
執 行 主 編	姜怡安
執 行 編 輯	李念茨
特 約 編 輯	陳其玲、妍君
美 術 編 輯	王桂芳、張嘉容
文 字 校 對	江宗翰
封 面 設 計	阿作
法 律 顧 問	北辰著作權事務所　蕭雄淋律師、幸秋妙律師

初　　版	2019年03月
出　　版	捷徑文化出版事業有限公司──資料夾文化出版
電　　話	（02）2752-5618
傳　　真	（02）2752-5619
地　　址	106 台北市大安區忠孝東路四段250號11樓-1

定　　價	新台幣499元／港幣166元
產品內容	1書＋1紅膠片＋1mp3 QR code

總 經 銷	知遠文化事業有限公司
地　　址	222新北市深坑區北深路3段155巷25號5樓
電　　話	（02）2664-8800
傳　　真	（02）2664-8801

港澳地區總經銷　和平圖書有限公司	
地　　址	香港柴灣嘉業街12號百樂門大廈17樓
電　　話	（852）2804-6687
傳　　真	（852）2804-6409

▲本書圖片由 Shutterstock、123RF提供。

捷徑 Book站

現在就上臉書（FACEBOOK）「捷徑BOOK站」並按讚加入粉絲團，
就可享每月不定期新書資訊和粉絲專享小禮物喔！

http://www.facebook.com/royalroadbooks
讀者來函：royalroadbooks@gmail.com

國家圖書館出版品預行編目資料

GEPT全民英檢中級單字100%攻略：左腦式
聽力學習╳紅膠片高效練習！/張慈庭英語教
學團隊著. -- 初版. -- 臺北市：
資料夾文化, 2019.03
　面；　公分（英語學習：008）

ISBN 978-957-8904-60-6(平裝)

1. 英語　2. 詞彙

805.1892　　　　　　　　　　107019525